1) pawn broker

{ meeting in
(description of his family
innocent drunk girl
letter from mother — sister
beating of horse
marrying
chance meeting — overheard
about pawn shop

CRIME AND PUNISHMENT

MURDERS

2) Note from police

FYODOR DOSTOEVSKY

CRIME AND PUNISHMENT

A New Translation by Michael R. Katz

LIVERIGHT PUBLISHING CORPORATION

A Division of W. W. Norton and Company

Independent Publishers Since 1923

NEW YORK | LONDON

For information about permission to reproduce selections from this book,
write to Permissions, Liveright Publishing Corporation,
a division of W. W. Norton & Company, Inc.,
500 Fifth Avenue, New York, NY 10110

For information about special discounts for bulk purchases, please contact
W. W. Norton Special Sales at specialsales@wwnorton.com or 800-233-4830

Manufacturing by LSC Harrisonburg
Book design by Ellen Cipriano
Production manager: Anna Oler

Library of Congress Cataloging-in-Publication Data

Names: Dostoyevsky, Fyodor, 1821–1881, author. | Katz, Michael R., translator.
Title: Crime and punishment / Fyodor Dostoevsky ; a new translation by
Michael R. Katz.
Other titles: Prestuplenie i nakazanie. English (Katz)
Description: First edition. | New York ; London : Liveright Publishing
Corporation, 2018.
Identifiers: LCCN 2017027422 | ISBN 9781631490330 (hardcover)
Classification: LCC PG3326.P7 2018 | DDC 891.73/3—dc23
LC record available at https://lccn.loc.gov/2017027422

ISBN 978-1-63149-531-1 pbk.

Liveright Publishing Corporation
500 Fifth Avenue, New York, N.Y. 10110
www.wwnorton.com

W. W. Norton & Company Ltd.
15 Carlisle Street, London W1D 3BS

6 7 8 9 0

INTRODUCTION

The decade of the 1860s was one of the most turbulent in Russian history. Russia's ignominious defeat in the Crimean War had exposed the deficiencies of the autocracy; the accession of Alexander II to the throne in 1855 promised significant changes. His reign is known as "the era of great reforms." Organs for local self-government (*zemstvos*) were established to deal with local economic needs; judicial reforms were instituted to promote the speedy and equitable administration of justice; and military reforms were enacted to modernize the Russian army. The greatest and best known of Alexander's "great reforms" was, of course, the long-awaited emancipation of the serfs in 1861 (two years before Lincoln's Emancipation Proclamation freeing the slaves).

Fyodor Dostoevsky's *Crime and Punishment* was first published in the literary journal the *Russian Messenger* in twelve monthly installments during 1866, in the middle of this turbulent decade. The novel reflects the social upheaval and the major changes in Russian society after centuries of serfdom. With growing migration to the cities, poverty became a constant hardship for new urban dwellers. There was an increase in violence as a result of difficult economic conditions. The murder rate rose, and the Russian press reported on horrendous crimes in graphic detail. Drunkenness, prostitution, disease, unemployment, family breakups, and abandoned children all came to typify the nature of Russian reality in the 1860s.

A new generation of young people advanced a variety of radical new ideas. The liberal "men of the '40s" were gradually replaced by the radical "men of the '60s." Ivan Turgenev's novel *Fathers and Children* (1862) popularized the figure of the "nihilist" (a person who rejects all established religious and moral principles) in his hero Bazarov. Nikolai Chernyshevsky, in his controversial work *What Is to Be Done?* (1863), developed a theory of rational egoism based on the ideas of English utilitarians and French utopian socialists. Active polemics between the older generation and the "new people" were carried on in the press. Dostoevsky was strongly opposed to these radical new ideas and challenged them in considerable depth in his journalistic writings and in his fiction.

■   ■   ■

Fyodor Mikhailovich Dostoevsky was born in 1821 at St. Mary's Hospital for the Moscow poor, where his father served on the staff after a career in the Russian army medical service. His grandfather had been a Uniate priest, and the family claimed to have descended from seventeenth-century nobility. Dostoevsky's mother was the daughter of Moscow merchants.

From 1837 to 1843, the young man attended the Military Engineering School in St. Petersburg, followed by a brief period of government service. In 1839, while still at school, Dostoevsky learned that his father had been murdered by peasants on the small estate he had recently purchased just south of Moscow. The exact circumstances were unclear, but the event made an enormous impression on the young man and was reflected in his later writing.

During this time, Dostoevsky read widely in Russian and Western literatures. Among Russian writers, he read the works of Karamzin, Pushkin, and Lermontov. He especially admired Gogol, whose intensely imaginative writings emphasized the plight of the downtrodden "little people" of the capital. Among European authors, Dostoevsky read Homer, Shakespeare, the French dramatists, Diderot, Voltaire, Hugo, Zola, Balzac, Goethe, Schiller, and Dickens. In 1844, Dostoevsky resigned his position in the service and decided to try his luck in the literary world of St. Petersburg. His first endeavor was a translation of

Balzac's *Eugénie Grandet*, a novel focused on greed, money, love, obsession, and self-sacrifice.

Dostoevsky's first original work was an epistolary novel entitled *Poor Folk* (1846) about an impoverished copy clerk who is hopelessly in love with a young woman he can never possess. The preeminent Russian critic Vissarion Belinsky was delighted with the work and proclaimed that a "new Gogol" had arrived on the literary scene. Unfortunately, his second work, published the same year, was much less well received. *The Double*, a psychological tale of fantasy, obsession, and madness, was dismissed by the critics because the author appeared to have abandoned the social and political themes that characterized *Poor Folk*.

Some years earlier, Dostoevsky had begun attending meetings of the Petrashevsky Circle, a literary discussion group in St. Petersburg organized by Mikhail Petrashevsky, a follower of the French utopian socialist Charles Fourier. The members of the circle included writers, teachers, students, minor government officials, and army officers. While differing in their political views, most of them were opponents of the tsarist autocracy and Russian serfdom. At one meeting in 1847, Dostoevsky read aloud Belinsky's forbidden "Letter to Gogol," in which Gogol was pilloried for giving up progressive social themes in favor of religious conservatism. The meeting was interrupted by the police and the participants arrested. Dostoevsky was interrogated, jailed, and condemned to death. He was led out to a parade ground to be shot, but at the last minute a reprieve arrived and he was spared execution in a gesture epitomizing Tsar Nicholas I's cruel flair for melodrama.

Dostoevsky's sentence was commuted to hard labor and he spent the 1850s first in a prison labor camp and then in exile as an army private. He was permitted to return to St. Petersburg some ten years later under the more enlightened reign of Alexander II.

Upon his return, he wrote and published a prison memoir entitled *Notes from the House of the Dead* (1860–62), in which he described his own experience as well as the lives of the variety of prisoners he'd encountered in Siberia. One year after that, he published his *Notes from Underground* (1864), the first part of which was a spirited polemic against Chernyshevsky's rational egoism and utilitarianism as

expressed in *What Is to Be Done?* The second part of this deeply prob-
ing work, an effort to explain how and why the hero has taken refuge
in the underground, reveals the underground man's character in three
distinct novelistic episodes. This strange work has been described as a
"prologue" to the author's "five-act tragedy"—that is, as an introduction to Dostoevsky's five major novels written between 1866 and 1880:
Crime and Punishment (1866), *The Idiot* (1868–69), *Devils* (or *Demons*
or *The Possessed,* 1871–72), *The Raw Youth* (or *The Adolescent,* 1875),
and *The Brothers Karamazov* (1880).

■ ■ ■

Crime and Punishment (1866) has long been considered the quintes-
sential Russian novel. When it was translated into English in 1886, the
critical reaction to it was mixed: on the one hand, it was greeted as a
"work of extraordinary excellence, as a novel of a hitherto unknown
stirring realism"; on the other hand, the book was condemned as "incoherent and inartistic."*

There is no doubt that *Crime and Punishment* remains the single
most widely known Russian novel. In addition to capturing the attention of a large general readership since the time of its appearance, it
continues to be included every year in numerous college and university
courses, not only on Russian literature, but also on Russian history and
culture, and in surveys of the European novel and world literature. The
book has also been widely adopted for use in secondary schools. Students of all ages and backgrounds respond with passionate attentive-
ness to this classic text; its literary, historical, cultural, and spiritual
values still speak to them and provoke vigorous, wide-ranging discus-
sions. The novel is also a popular choice of book clubs, reading groups,
and study circles.

In a curious twist of fate for the novel's reputation, when the young
"hacker/whistleblower" Edward Snowden was restricted to the transit
area of the Moscow airport, his lawyer thoughtfully provided him with

---

* Helen Muchnic, *Dostoevsky's English Reputation,* 1881–1936 (New York: Octagon Books,
1969), 10.

appropriate reading material to occupy his time and prepare him for what might turn out to be a longer stay in Russia. To that end, he presented Snowden with works by three Russian writers, including only one novel: Dostoevsky's *Crime and Punishment*.

■ ■ ■

A translator of Dostoevsky faces many challenges and choices. Modern literary Russian consists of a splendid amalgamation of the spoken dialect of the Eastern Slavs (the so-called Old Russian) and the ancient written language of the Russian Orthodox Church (known as Old Church Slavonic). This linguistic blend has, since the time of Pushkin, provided an exceptionally rich source of images and diction for Russian writers. For example, early in Dostoevsky's novel (part I, chapter 2), his hero, Raskolnikov, stumbles into a tavern and encounters the extravagantly morose figure of Marmeladov, who immediately senses a sympathetic listener and promptly launches into his long, pathetic life story. Taunted by rude remarks from the tavern keeper and some inebriated patrons, Marmeladov concludes with what can only be called a "sermon," in a proclamatory biblical style that weaves quotations from the Gospel into his own speech, and that before our very eyes improbably but effectively transforms him into his own literary version of Christ. Marmeladov goes so far as to impersonate Christ and to speak in what he takes to be His voice. This combination of solemn rhetorical eloquence and grotesque comedy is unparalleled in literature. It introduces the principal religious theme of the work, one that will appear in Raskolnikov's first dream, in all of his epiphanic moments (usually as he wanders around St. Petersburg), and reach its final form in the frequently misunderstood, much maligned, but clearly indispensable Epilogue to the novel. In this translation, I attempt to express the richness of registers or tones— and thus the extraordinary poignancy—of such decisive moments.

Dostoevsky's characters must be seen as unmistakably distinct individuals—not only the main figures (Raskolnikov, Sonya, Svidrigaylov, and Porfiry Petrovich), but also the secondary ones (Marmeladov, Razumikhin, Dunya, Luzhin, etc.). Each character speaks in his or her own Russian idiolect. It is the translator's task to capture the distinct characteristics of their individual speech. Even the least important figures prove to be altogether unique and engaging; for example, the drunken peasants in Raskolnikov's first dream, though totally illiterate, are made vividly and hilariously present by virtue of the quirkiness of their speech, which is rude, abusive, and riotous.

In addition, this version attempts to convey Dostoevsky's fine and subtle sense of humor. His descriptions and dialogues brim over with wit, irony, and sarcasm. The playful repartee between the hero Raskolnikov and the examining magistrate Porfiry Petrovich provides numerous opportunities for the author to display, and the translator to convey, that cunning humor. However, in order to do so, the translator needs to develop a genuine feel for the subtle tone and a sense of the delicate timing, and also be able to express the author's quick and unexpected shifts in diction.

■   ■   ■

There are numerous ways to read *Crime and Punishment* and endless riches to be discovered when rereading the book. I would like to call the reader's attention to just a few of these. During the course of the novel, Raskolnikov has a series of disturbing dreams. These episodes are of crucial importance in characterizing the hero, exploring his motives, revealing his conscience, and developing the book's defining themes. From the first dream of the beaten mare in part I to the final dream of the Asian plague in the Epilogue, Raskolnikov's "subconscious" is sending the hero and the reader important communications, reports from hidden dimensions of his experience that must not be ignored.*

I would also like to draw the reader's attention to what I would refer to as the many "-cides" of Dostoevsky. The critic Mikhail Bakhtin reminds us that while Tolstoy writes at length in his fiction about the subject of death, Dostoevsky writes novels about murders. *Crime and Punishment* begins with a double homicide; it contains allegori-

---

* For a detailed discussion, see my *Dreams and the Unconscious in Nineteenth-Century Russian Fiction* (Hanover, NH: University Press of New England, 1984), 95–105.

cal suicides ("I killed myself," says Raskolnikov to Sonya, "not the old woman"), as well as an actual suicide and an attempted suicide; one critic even develops the theme of Raskolnikov's displaced, allegorical "matricide" in killing the pawnbroker, as well as his culpability in his own mother's death as described in the Epilogue.[*]

That Epilogue continues to puzzle many readers. Does it represent a significant departure from the text? Is it merely an artificial way to end the novel and the hero's suffering? Or is it justified by the hero's striving for some ultimate illumination, moving beyond the partial illumination provided by the numerous epiphanic moments he experiences during the course of the action? In the author's *Notebooks* containing plans and drafts of the novel, we find the fascinating hint of an alternative conclusion: "The End of the Novel: Raskolnikov goes to shoot himself."[†] In view of this darker possibility, the reader is free to make up his or her own mind about the meaning of the Epilogue and its appropriateness as the last word in this extraordinary novel.

A work preoccupied with murder and its implications, *Crime and Punishment* is first and foremost a fascinating detective novel—but one in which we know from the very beginning who committed the heinous crime. As one critic wittily observed, the novel is not a "who dunnit?" but rather a "why he dunnit?" On this, the 150th anniversary of the work's publication, it is altogether fitting to present a new translation as an act of celebration. I offer this version to the reader in the hopes of helping extend the life of this irreplaceable book as far into the future as can be imagined.

Michael R. Katz
Middlebury College
December 2016

---

[*] Edward Wasiolek, "Raskolnikov's Motives: Love and Murder," *American Imago* 31 (Fall 1974): 252–69.

[†] *The Notebooks for "Crime and Punishment,"* edited and translated by Edward Wasiolek (Chicago: University of Chicago Press, 1967), 243.

NOTE ON THE TRANSLATION

The edition used for this translation is volume 6 of Dostoevsky's *Polnoe sobranie sochinenii v tridtsati tomakh* (Complete Collected Works in Thirty Volumes) published in Leningrad by Nauka in 1973.

I am indebted to my predecessors and to their versions of *Crime and Punishment*: we all learn from each other, and translation becomes a collaborative enterprise.

I wish to express my sincere gratitude to my colleagues and students at Middlebury College: in particular, Professor Stephen Donadio for his unflagging encouragement and wise advice, lecturer emerita Alya Baker for her invaluable help with the original text, Christopher Ross for his excellent editing and proofreading, and Matthew Blake for his numerous questions and suggestions; and to my wife, Mary Dodge, and our daughter, Rebecca Esko, for their continued love and support.

I am also grateful to Carol Bemis, my editor at Norton, and her staff for guiding this work through to completion.

NAMES OF PRINCIPAL CHARACTERS

Raskólnikov, Rodión Románovich or Romа́nych
    (Ródya, Ródenka, Ródka)

       Pulkhériya Aleksа́ndrovna—his mother

       Avdótya Románovna (Dúnya, Dúnechka)—his sister

Razumíkhin or Vrazumíkhin, Dmítry Prokófich—his friend

Alyóna Ivánovna—the pawnbroker

Lizavéta Ivánovna—her sister

Marmeládov, Semyón Zakhárovich or Zakhárych—former civil servant

       Katerína Ivánovna—his wife

       Sófiya Semyónovna (Sónya, Sónechka)—his daughter

       Three other children: Polína (Pólya, Pólenka, Pólechka)

              Lénya (Lída, Lídochka)

              Kólya (Kólka)

Svidrigáylov, Arkády Ivánovich—landlord; Dunya's former employer

       Márfa Petróvna—his wife

Lúzhin, Pétr Petróvich—Dunya's fiancé

Lebezyátnikov, Andréy Semyónovich or Semyónych—his friend

Porfíry Petróvich—examining magistrate; distant relative of
    Razumikhin's

Lippevékhsel, Amáliya Ivánovna—Marmeladov's landlady

Zosímov—a doctor

Zamétov, Aleksándr Grigórevich—chief police clerk

Ilyá Petróvich—nicknamed "Pórokh" (gunpowder)—police lieutenant

NOTE ON THE CHARACTERS' NAMES

Raskolnikov   *raskól* = schism; *raskólnik* = schismatic or dissenter

Razumikhin   *rázum* = reason, good sense

Marmeladov   *marmelád* = jam, jelly

Sofiya   "wisdom" (Greek)

Luzhin   *lúzha* = puddle, pool

Lebezyatnikov   *lebezít'* = to fawn, cringe

CRIME AND PUNISHMENT

PART I

I

In the beginning of July, during an extremely hot spell, toward evening, a young man left his tiny room, which he sublet from some tenants who lived in Stolyarnyi Lane, stepped out onto the street, and slowly, as if indecisively, set off towards the Kokushkin Bridge.

He had successfully managed to avoid meeting his landlady on the staircase. His small room, more like a closet than an apartment, was tucked under the roof of a tall five-story building. The landlady of the apartment, who rented him this room and provided both dinner and a servant, lived below in a separate apartment on the same staircase; every time he left to go out, he had to pass the landlady's kitchen door, which was almost always left open onto the landing. Every time the young man passed, he felt a painful and fearful sensation, one that he was ashamed of and that made him wince. He was deeply in debt to the landlady and was afraid to face her.

It wasn't that he was so fearful and cowed; in fact, it was just the opposite; but for some time he had been in an irritable and anxious state, similar to hypochondria. He had become so absorbed in himself and so isolated from others that he was afraid of meeting anyone, not only his landlady. He was crushed by poverty, but even his constrained circumstances had ceased to burden him of late. He had completely stopped handling his own everyday affairs and didn't wish to deal with them. He was not actually afraid of his landlady, no matter what she intended to do to him. But to stop on the staircase, put up with all sorts of nonsense about ordinary rubbish that didn't concern him at all, her constant pestering about payment, her threats and complaints, and, in the face of it all, to have to dodge her, make excuses, tell lies— no thank you; it was better to slip past somehow, like a cat on a staircase, and steal away unnoticed.

However, this time the fear of meeting his creditor surprised even him as he made his way out to the street.

"What sort of feat am I about to attempt, yet at the same time I'm afraid of such nonsense!" he thought with a strange smile. "Hmm . . . yes . . . everything lies in a man's hands, and still he lets it slip by, solely out of cowardice . . . that's an axiom. . . . It would be interesting to know what people fear the most. Most of all they fear taking a new step, uttering a new word of their own. . . . But I'm babbling too much. It's because I'm not doing anything that I'm babbling. That may be the case: I'm babbling because I'm not doing anything. And it's in the last month I've learned to prattle, lying for days and nights in my corner, thinking about . . . 'once upon a time. . . .' Well, why am I going out now? Can I really be capable of doing *that*? Is *that* really serious? No, it's not serious at all. So, I'm amusing myself for the sake of fantasy: games! Yes, that's it, games!"

It was stiflingly hot outside; moreover, the stuffiness, the crush of people, lime plaster everywhere, scaffolding, bricks, dust, and that particular summer stench, so familiar to every Petersburg resident lacking the means to rent a summer dacha—all this suddenly and offensively struck the young man's already distraught nerves. The unbearable stench of cheap taverns, which were particularly numerous in this part of the city, and the drunkards encountered constantly, despite its being a weekday, completed the repulsive and grim scene. For a moment, a feeling of the deepest loathing flashed across the young man's delicate features. Incidentally, he was remarkably handsome, with splendid dark eyes and dark brown hair; he was taller than average, slender, and well built. But soon he seemed to slip into profound pensiveness, even, it would be more accurate to say, into a state of oblivion. He walked along not noticing his surroundings, not even wanting to take notice of them. From time to time he merely muttered something to himself, from his penchant for monologues, which he immediately acknowledged to himself. At that moment he himself was aware that at times his thoughts were confused and that he was feeling very weak: it was the second day he'd eaten hardly anything at all.

He was so poorly dressed that someone else, even someone used to seeing such, would be ashamed to appear on the street during the day wearing such ragged clothes. However, the district was one where it was difficult to shock anyone with one's apparel. The proximity of the Haymarket, the abundance of certain establishments, and, primarily, the population of tradesmen and craftsmen, all crowded into these streets and lanes of central Petersburg, sometimes filled the general panorama with such subjects that it would be strange to be surprised at all on meeting another such figure. But so much malicious contempt had already accumulated in the young man's soul that, in spite of all his own sometimes very immature squeamishness, when he was out on the street he was not in the least embarrassed by his tattered clothes. It was another matter altogether when he met some of his acquaintances or former comrades, whom, in general, he didn't much like seeing. . . . However, when one drunkard, who for some unknown reason was being transported somewhere along the street in an enormous cart harnessed to a huge dray horse, suddenly shouted to him, in passing, "Hey, you, you German hatmaker!" and roared as loud as he could, pointing his finger at him—the young man suddenly stopped and violently grabbed his own hat. It was a tall, round top hat bought at Zimmerman's shop, but already worn out, and now of a completely faded reddish-brown color, with many holes and stains, lacking a brim, and leaning to one side at a most unattractive angle. However, it was not shame that seized him but a completely different feeling, more resembling fear.

"I knew it!" he muttered in confusion. "That's exactly what I thought! This is the most disgraceful part! It's just this kind of foolish thing, a really trivial detail that can spoil the whole plan! Yes, a hat that's too noticeable. . . . It's funny-looking, and therefore noticeable. . . . With my tattered clothes I really need a peaked cap, even an old one, flat as a pancake, not this monstrosity. No one wears hats like this; it can be recognized a mile away and remembered . . . that's the main thing, remembered afterward, and there's your evidence. One has to be as inconspicuous as possible. . . . Details, details are the main thing! It's the details that always ruin everything . . ."

He had only a little way to go; he even knew exactly how many paces it was from the gate of his own building: seven hundred and thirty. Once, when entirely lost in his daydreams, he'd happened to count them. At the time he himself still didn't believe in his dreams and was merely irritating himself with their repugnant, though seductive audacity. Now, however, a month later, he'd begun to regard them in a different light, and in spite of all his mocking monologues about his own powerlessness and indecisiveness, he'd grown accustomed, even against his will, to considering this "repulsive" dream something of a feat, although he still didn't believe in it himself. Now he was even on his way to carry out a trial run of his endeavor; with every step his agitation grew stronger and stronger.

With a sinking heart and nervous trembling, he approached an immense building, one wall of which opened onto a narrow canal, the other onto Sadovaya Street. This building consisted of small apartments inhabited by all sorts of tradesmen—tailors, locksmiths, cooks, various Germans, streetwalkers, low-ranking civil servants, and others. People entering and leaving the building kept darting under both gates and across both courtyards. Three or four doormen worked there. The young man was very pleased when he didn't encounter any of them and managed to slip unnoticed right through the gates and directly onto the staircase. The staircase was dark and narrow, "a back entrance," but he knew that already, having studied it, and he liked this whole setting: in such darkness even casting a curious glance wouldn't be dangerous. "If I'm so afraid now, what would happen if I somehow managed to commit the actual *deed*?" he thought inadvertently as he climbed up to the fourth floor. Some ex-military porters blocked his way as they carried some furniture out of one apartment. He already knew that a German, a civil servant, had been living there with his family: "It must be that the German's moving out now and, consequently, on the fourth floor, on this staircase, on this landing only the old woman's apartment will be occupied for a certain time. That's good . . . just in case," he thought again and rang the old woman's bell. The bell jingled feebly, as if it were made of tin and not copper. Such bells could be found in almost all similar small buildings. He'd already forgotten the ring of this bell, and now this particular sound suddenly seemed to remind him of something and summon it clearly into mind. . . . He even shuddered, since his nerves had been so frayed of late. A few moments later, the door opened a tiny crack: the inhabitant peered out at the caller with visible distrust, and all that could be seen in the darkness were her flashing beady eyes. But, seeing so many people on the landing, she felt emboldened and opened the door wide. The young man stepped across the threshold into a dark vestibule divided by a partition from a tiny kitchen. The old woman stood before him silently, regarding him inquisitively. She was a small, dried-up miserable old woman, about sixty years old, with piercing, malicious little eyes, a small sharp nose, and her bare head. Her light blond, slightly grayed hair was thickly smeared with grease. Around her long, thin neck, resembling a chicken leg, was draped some sort of flannel rag, and over her shoulders, in spite of the heat, a worn-out, faded fur-trimmed jacket hung loosely. The old woman kept coughing and wheezing. It must have been that the young man glanced at her with some special sort of look, because her former distrust suddenly flashed in her eyes again.

"Raskolnikov, a student. I was here about a month ago," the young man hastened to mumble with a slight bow, recalling that he should be more courteous.

"I remember, dearie, I remember very well that you were here," the old woman replied distinctly, as before not taking her inquisitive eyes from his face.

"So, ma'am, here I am again about the same sort of thing," Raskolnikov continued, a little flustered and surprised by the old woman's distrust.

"But maybe she's always like this, and I just didn't notice it last time," he thought with an unpleasant feeling.

The old woman was silent, as if lost in thought; then she stepped to one side and, pointing at the door into her room, she said, allowing him to pass:

"Go in, dearie."

The small room, into which the young man stepped, with its yellow wallpaper, geraniums, and muslin curtains on the windows, was at that moment brightly illuminated by the setting sun. "*Then*, of course, the sun will be shining the same way!" flashed through Raskolnikov's mind, and he cast a swift glance at everything in the room to take it all in and remember its arrangement. But there was nothing special in there. The furniture, all very old and made of yellow wood, consisted of a sofa with an enormous carved wooden back, an oval table in front of it, a dressing table with a pier mirror standing between the windows, chairs along the walls, and two or three cheap pictures in yellow frames depicting young German ladies with birds in their hands—that's all the furniture there was. A lamp was burning in the corner in front of a small icon. Everything in the room was very clean: the furniture and floors had been polished to a high gloss; everything gleamed. "Lizaveta's work," thought the young man. It was impossible to find even one speck of dust in the whole place. "This is the kind of cleanliness that can be found in the apartments of wicked old widows," Raskolnikov thought to himself, and with curiosity he cast a sidelong glance at the cotton curtain hanging in front of the door into a second little room, which contained the old woman's bed and dresser, and into which he'd never looked. The whole apartment consisted of these two rooms.

"What do you want?" the old woman asked sternly as she entered the room; as before, she stopped in front of him so she could peer directly into his face.

"I've brought something to pawn—here, ma'am!" He took from his pocket an old flat silver watch. There was a globe depicted on the back of the case. The chain was made of steel.

"Time's up for the last pledge you brought. The month ended two days ago."

"I'll pay you the interest for another month; have patience."

"It's up to me, dearie, whether I have patience or decide to sell your item now."

"How much for this watch, Alyona Ivanovna?"

"You come here with rubbish, dearie; it's worth almost nothing. Last time I gave you two rubles for that ring, but you can buy a new one at the jeweler's for a ruble and a half."

"Give me four rubles. I'll redeem it; it was my father's. I'll be getting some money soon."

"One ruble and a half, sir, with interest in advance, if you want it."

"A ruble and a half!" cried the young man.

"As you wish." And the old woman handed him back the watch. The young man took it and was so angry that he was just about to leave; but then he reconsidered, remembering that he had nowhere else to go, and that he'd come for a different reason.

"All right!" he said rudely.

The old woman dug into her pocket for her keys and went into the other room behind the curtain. The young man, left alone in the middle of the room, listened carefully and tried to imagine what she was doing. He could hear her unlocking the dresser. "It must be the topmost drawer," he thought. "She must carry her keys in her right pocket. . . . All of them as one bunch, on a steel ring. . . . And there's one key that's bigger than all the others, three times bigger, with a notched tip; it's not for the dresser, of course. . . . Therefore, there must be some kind of box or chest. . . . That's odd. All chests have that kind of key. . . . But this is all so vulgar . . ."

The old woman came back.

"Here you are, dearie: if I take ten kopecks per ruble* per month, that comes to fifteen kopecks for one and half rubles for the month ahead. So, at the same rate for the last two rubles, you still owe me twenty kopecks in advance. In all, then, it comes to thirty-five kopecks. So now, in exchange for the watch, you get one ruble, fifteen kopecks. Here, take it."

"What? Only one ruble and fifteen kopecks now?"

"Exactly."

The young man didn't argue and took the money. He looked at the old woman and was in no rush to leave, just as if he wanted to say or do something else, but it seemed as if he himself didn't know precisely what . . .

---

* One ruble was equivalent to 100 kopecks.

"In a few days, Alyona Ivanovna, perhaps I'll bring you something else . . . a fine . . . little . . . silver . . . cigarette case. . . . As soon as I get it back from a friend . . ." He became flustered and fell silent.

"Well, dearie, we'll talk about it then."

"Good-bye. . . . Are you always home alone? Your sister's never here?" he inquired as casually as possible, passing though the hall.

"What business do you have with her, dearie?"

"Nothing special. I merely asked. And now you're. . . . Good-bye, Alyona Ivanovna."

Raskolnikov left in an absolute confusion that kept growing more and more intense. As he went down the staircase, he even paused several times, as if suddenly struck by something. Finally, now out on the street, he exclaimed:

"Oh, God! How repulsive this all is! Can I really, really . . . no, it's rubbish, absurdity!" he added conclusively. "How could such a horrible thing enter my mind? Yet my heart seems capable of such filth! The main thing is: it's filthy, foul, vile, vile! Yet for the last month I've been . . ."

But he couldn't express his agitation, either in words or exclamations. The feeling of infinite revulsion that had begun to oppress and torment his heart as he'd been coming to see the old woman had now reached such proportions and was so palpable that he didn't know where to hide from his anguish. He walked along the sidewalk like a drunk, without noticing the passersby, and bumping into them; he came to his senses only at the next street. After looking around, he saw that he was standing next to a tavern, the entrance to which was down a staircase leading from the street level, into the cellar. Just at that moment, two drunks emerged from the door, supporting each other and cursing, and climbed up to the street. Without much thought, Raskolnikov went right down the stairs. He'd never frequented taverns before, but now his head was spinning; besides, he was suffering from a burning thirst. He felt like drinking a cold beer, all the more so since he attributed his sudden weakness to the fact that he was hungry. He sat down at a sticky table in a dark, dirty corner, ordered a beer, and gulped down the first glass. Everything receded immediately, and his thoughts became clear. "It's all rubbish," he said hopefully. "There's no reason to get so distraught! It was merely physical upset! One glass of beer, a piece of rusk,* and then, in a minute, my mind grows strong, my thoughts grow clear, and my intentions are reinforced! Ugh, what nonsense it all is!" In spite of this contemptuous disdain, he seemed cheerful already, as if suddenly liberated from some terrible burden, and he cast his eyes amicably over those present. But even at that moment he had a distant premonition that all his assurance of better times was also morbid.

Not many people were left in the tavern at that time. Besides those two drunks he met on the staircase, a whole group left right after them, about five men with an accordion and a young girl. Afterward it became quiet and spacious. There sat: one fellow who looked like a tradesman, drunk, but not too, nursing his beer; his large, fat pal, wearing a short jacket, sporting a gray beard, very intoxicated, dozing on the bench; from time to time this fellow would suddenly, as if half asleep, start snapping his fingers, fling his arms out wide, and jerk the top half of his body around without getting up from the bench, meanwhile warbling some nonsense as he tried to recall a few lines, something like:

> I loved my wife for one whole year,
> For one who-ole year I lov-ved my wi-fe . . .

Or, suddenly rousing himself, he would begin again:

> As I walked along Podyachesky Lane,
> I found my former wife . . .

But no one shared his merriment; his taciturn companion even regarded all these outbursts with hostility and distrust. There was one other man there; from his looks he might have been a former civil servant. He sat apart with his glass of vodka, occasionally taking a drink and glancing around. He was also in a state of some agitation.

---

* A hard, dry biscuit.

II

Raskolnikov was not accustomed to the crowd, and as has already been said, he'd been avoiding any social contact, especially of late. But now, for some reason, he was suddenly drawn to people. Something was happening within him, something new, and at the same time he felt a kind of yearning for people. He was so exhausted from his whole month of concentrated melancholy and gloomy agitation that he felt like taking a breath in another world, wherever it was, and in spite of the filth of his surroundings, he now remained in the tavern with pleasure.

The owner of the establishment was in another room but frequently entered the main room, coming down the stairs from somewhere above, indicated first by the appearance of his fashionable shiny boots, with their large red tops. He was wearing a light coat and a terribly stained black satin vest without a tie, and his entire face seemed smeared with oil as if it were an iron lock. Behind the bar stood a lad about fourteen years old, and there was another, younger boy who served food if anyone ordered something. There were sliced pickles, black rusks, and pieces of fish; it all smelled very bad. It was so stuffy that it was even unbearable to sit there; everything was so saturated by the smell of alcohol that it seemed a person could become drunk in about five minutes just inhaling the air.

Sometimes meetings occur, even with completely unfamiliar people in whom we begin to take an interest right from the first glance, somehow suddenly, unexpectedly, before one word is spoken. That was precisely the impression made on Raskolnikov by the patron who was sitting alone and who looked like a former civil servant. Several times afterward the young man recalled this first impression and even ascribed it to a premonition. Raskolnikov kept glancing over at the man, particularly, of course, because the man was staring persistently at him; it was obvious that the man very much wanted to strike up a conversation. The civil servant regarded the others in the tavern, even the owner, as somehow ordinary; he was even bored by them; at the same time, he felt a trace of haughty scorn, as if they were people of a lower order or a lower cultural level, to whom there was nothing to say. He was a man already past fifty, of average height and solid build, with graying hair and a large bald spot, a yellow, even greenish face swollen by constant drunkenness, puffy eyelids under which shone, like little slits, tiny but animated small reddish eyes. But there was something about him that was very strange, even some kind of enthusiasm glowing in his eyes—perhaps also meaning and intelligence—and at the same time there also seemed to be a trace of madness. He was dressed in an old, completely worn-out tailcoat, missing most of its buttons. Only one was still holding on somehow, but that was how he fastened it, apparently hoping to maintain some shred of dignity. His shirtfront protruded from under his heavy cotton vest, all wrinkled, soiled, and stained. His face had been shaved, like a civil servant's, but a long time ago, and his gray whiskers had already begun to grow back densely. There was indeed in his bearing something to suggest a solid civil servant. But he was anxious, raked his fingers through his hair, and sometimes supported his head with both hands, resting his elbows, in their frayed sleeves, on the soiled, sticky table. At last he looked directly at Raskolnikov and said, in a loud, firm voice:

"Do I dare, my kind sir, address you with a decent question? Even though you don't appear to be a person of consequence, my experience tells me that you're an educated man and not accustomed to drink. I myself have always respected education combined with heartfelt feelings, and in addition, I'm a titular counselor.* Marmeladov—that's my name; a titular counselor. Dare I ask if you're also a civil servant?"

"No, I'm a student," the young man replied, in part surprised by the man's particularly ornate speech, and by the fact that he'd been addressed so directly, so point-blank. In spite of his recent momentary desire to seek some connection with other people, at these first words directed at him he suddenly sensed his usually unpleasant and irritating feeling of revulsion toward any unknown person who intruded upon or merely wanted to impose upon his person.

"A student, naturally, or former student!" the civil servant cried. "Just as I thought! Experience, my dear sir, repeated experience!" And, as a sign of boasting, he pointed a finger at his own forehead. "You were a student or you've studied at the university! Allow me . . ." He stood, nodded, grabbed his carafe, his glass, and sat down next to the young man, at a slight angle away. He was drunk, but spoke volubly and boldly, losing track only occasionally and dragging out his words. He fell upon Raskolnikov even with some voraciousness, as if he also hadn't spoken with anyone for a whole month.

"Kind sir," he began almost solemnly, "poverty is no vice; that's a known truth. I know even more so that drunkenness is not a virtue. But destitution, dear sir, destitution—that is a vice. In poverty you can still preserve the nobility of your innate feelings, while in destitution you never do and no one does. For destitution you're not even driven away with a stick—you're swept out of human company with a broom so that it will be even more humiliating; and that's fair, for in my destitution I'm the first one prepared to humiliate myself. Hence, the tavern! Dear sir, a month ago a certain Mr. Lebezyatnikov gave my wife a beating; but my wife is not like me! You understand, sir? Allow me to inquire further, just so, even out of mere curiosity: have you ever spent a night sleeping on a hay barge on the Neva?"

"No, I haven't," replied Raskolnikov. "Why do you ask?"

"Well, sir, that's where I'm coming from; it's already my fifth night . . ."

---

* A fairly low rank in the Russian civil service, corresponding to that of a captain in the army.

He filled his glass, drank it down, and fell to musing. And it was true that here and there some small strands of hay were sticking to his clothes and even to his hair. It was very likely that he hadn't washed or changed his clothes in those five days. His hands were especially grimy, greasy, and reddish, and his fingernails were black.

His conversation seemed to arouse general, though listless attention. The boys behind the counter started giggling. The tavern keeper, it seemed, purposely came down from the upper room to hear this "amusing fellow," and sat a ways off, yawning lazily but ostentatiously. Obviously, Marmeladov had been known here for a long time. He had probably acquired this proclivity for ornate speech as a result of frequent conversations in taverns with various strangers. In some drunkards this habit becomes a necessity, primarily among those who receive harsh treatment at home and who are ordered about. That's why in drunken company they always seem to crave justification, and if possible, even respect.

"What an amusing fellow!" the tavern keeper said loudly. "How come you don't work, huh, if you're a civil servant? Why don't you serve?"

"Why don't I serve, my dear sir?" Marmeladov seized on the question, turning exclusively to Raskolnikov as if he'd posed it. "Why don't I serve? Don't you think my heart aches over the fact that I grovel to no avail? When, one month ago, Mr. Lebezyatnikov beat my wife with his own hands, as I lay there drunk, don't you think I suffered? Allow me to ask you, young man, has it ever happened that you had to . . . hmm . . . beg for a loan of money without hope?"

"It has . . . but what do you mean without hope?"

"I mean completely hopelessly, knowing in advance that nothing will come of it. For example, you know beforehand, absolutely, that this most well-intentioned and most useful citizen won't give you money under any circumstances because why, I ask, why should he? After all, he knows I won't pay it back. Out of compassion? But Mr. Lebezyatnikov, who's a follower of the latest ideas, was explaining to me just the other day that in our era compassion has even been prohibited by science and that this is already being done in England, where they've developed political economy. Why then, I ask, should he give me anything? Yet, knowing beforehand that he won't, you still set off on your way and . . ."

"Why do you set off?" added Raskolnikov.

"What if there's no one else to see, nowhere else to go? Everyone has to have somewhere to go. Because there comes a time when it's absolutely essential to go somewhere. When my only daughter went out for the first time with a streetwalker's yellow ticket,* then I went out, too. (My daughter makes her living by streetwalking, sir . . .)," he added in parentheses, regarding the young man with some anxiety. "Never mind, my dear sir, never mind!" he hastened to declare immediately, even with apparent calm, when the two lads standing at the bar chuckled and the tavern keeper smiled. "Never mind, sir! I don't take offense at their heads nodding, because everyone knows everything already; nothing's secret, that shall not be made manifest; I regard all this not with contempt, but with humility. Let it go! Let it! 'Behold the man!'† Allow me, young man, can you. . . . But no, it should be explained more powerfully and imaginatively: looking at me at this very moment, it's not a matter of *can* you, rather it's *dare* you state positively that I am not a swine?"

The young man uttered not one word in reply.

"Well, sir," the speaker continued steadfastly, even with a reinforced sense of self-respect, having paused to let another outburst of laughter in the room die down. "Well, sir, I may be a swine, but she is a lady! I am made in the image of a beast, but my wife, Katerina Ivanovna, is an educated person, born the daughter of a field officer. I may be a scoundrel, but she's been raised with a noble heart and brought up with magnanimous feelings. Meanwhile . . . oh, if only she pitied me! My dear, dear sir, every man needs to have at least one place where he's pitied! And while Katerina Ivanovna is a generous woman, she's unjust. . . . While I myself understand that when she pulls tufts of my hair, she's doing so from a feeling of pity in her heart (for, I repeat without embarrassment, she does pull tufts of my hair, young man)," he

---

* Prostitutes in Russia were registered with the police and required to carry yellow identity cards.

† Pontius Pilate's words in John 19:5 when presenting Jesus to the crowd.

confirmed in a dignified tone after hearing laughter once again, "but, my God, what if even once she. . . . But no! No! It's all in vain, and there's nothing more to be said! Nothing at all! For more than once have I got what I wanted, more than once have I been pitied, but . . . but such is my nature, I'm a born beast!"

"That's for sure!" observed the tavern keeper, with a yawn.

Marmeladov resolutely banged his fist on the table.

"Such is my nature! Do you know, sir, do you know, that I even pawned her stockings? Not her shoes, sir, since that would have resembled the normal course of events, but her stockings, I pawned her stockings, sir! I also hocked her mohair shawl, a gift, an earlier one, her own, not from me. We live in a chilly corner, and this past winter she caught a cold and began coughing, even spitting up blood. We have three small children, and Katerina Ivanovna works from morning to night, scrubbing and washing and bathing the children, since she's used to cleanliness from early childhood, but she has a weak chest and is predisposed to consumption—that I feel. How can I not feel it? And the more I drink, the more I feel it. That's why I drink, because I'm seeking compassion and feeling in this drinking. . . . It's not joy I seek, only sorrow. . . . I drink because I genuinely want to suffer!" And then, as if in despair, he rested his head on the table.

"Young man," he continued, raising his head again, "I can read some sorrow in your face. I saw it when you entered, and that's why I turned to you right away. In telling you the story of my life, I don't wish to parade my disgrace before these idlers here, who know it all already; I'm seeking a sensitive, educated man. Do you know that my wife was educated in a provincial school for children of the nobility, and at the award ceremony she was chosen to perform the shawl dance* in the presence of the governor and other distinguished guests, for which she received a gold medal and a certificate of merit? A medal . . . well, we sold that medal . . . a long time ago . . . hmm . . . the certificate's still in her trunk, and she recently showed it to our landlady. Even though she has endless quarrels with the landlady, she

---

* A dance associated with upper-class young ladies, especially those educated in socially desirable finishing schools.

wanted to show off to someone and tell her about those happy days in the past. I don't condemn her, I don't, because these things are preserved in her memory, and all the rest has turned to dust! Yes, yes; she's a hot-tempered woman, proud and obstinate. She washes the floor herself and has only black bread to eat, but she won't tolerate any disrespect. That's why she wouldn't tolerate Mr. Lebezyatnikov's rudeness, and when he gave her a beating, she took to her bed more as a result of her feeling than from the actual blows. She was already a widow when I married her, with three children, each smaller than the other. Her first husband was a cavalry officer, and she married him for love and ran away from her parents' house with him. She loved her husband dearly, but he took to gambling, ended up in court, and soon died. He'd begun beating her toward the end; although she didn't let him get away with it, about which I have detailed documentary evidence; she weeps to this day when she remembers him and reproaches me. I'm glad, very glad that even in her imagination she can see herself as being happy for a while. . . . After his death she was left with three young children in a distant and dreadful provincial town, where I was also staying at the time; she was living in such hopeless poverty—even though I've had many different experiences, I can't even begin to describe her situation. Her family refused to help her. Besides, she was proud, extremely proud. . . . And then, my dear sir, then, being a widower myself, and having a fourteen-year-old daughter, I proposed to her because I couldn't bear to see such suffering. You can judge for yourself the degree of her misfortune, that she, an educated and well-brought-up woman from an eminent family, agreed to marry the likes of me! But she did! Weeping and wailing, wringing her hands, she did! Because she had nowhere else to go. Do you understand, do you really understand, dear sir, what it means when a person has nowhere else to go? No! You don't understand it yet. . . . For one whole year I fulfilled my obligation devotedly and devoutly and never touched the bottle"—he pointed to the bottle—"because I do have feelings. But even then I couldn't please her, even with that; it was afterward, when I lost my job, which wasn't my fault, but it happened because of changes in the department that I turned to drink! It's already been about half a year, after our wanderings and numerous misfortunes, since we finally turned up in this splendid capital with all of its many monuments. And I found a job here. . . . I found one and then I lost it. Do you understand, sir? This time it was my own fault, because I had reached the end of my rope. . . . Now we live in a little corner, at our landlady's, Amaliya Fedorovna Lippevekhsel, but I don't know how we manage to live and pay her. Many others live there besides us. . . . It's Sodom, sir, of the most hideous kind . . . hmm . . . yes. . . . Meanwhile my daughter from my first marriage has grown up; I won't describe what she had to suffer while growing up, my daughter, from her stepmother. Because although Katerina Ivanovna is filled with kindly feelings, she's a hot-tempered and irritable lady, and she can snap. . . . Yes, sir! There's no reason to recall it! As you can well imagine, Sonya received no education. About four years ago, I tried to read some geography and world history with her; but since I myself was weak in those areas and we had no suitable textbooks, and the books we did have . . . hmm . . . well, we don't even have those books now, all our reading ended then and there. We stopped at the Persian king Cyrus the Great.* Then, once she was older, she read some books of romantic content as well as several others, given to her by Mr. Lebezyatnikov. One was Lewes's *Physiology.*† Do you happen to know it, sir? She read it with great interest and even read some passages aloud to us: and that was her entire education. Now I'm turning to you, my dear sir, on my own behalf, with a confidential question of my own: in your opinion, can a poor but honest girl earn a living by honest work? She can't earn even fifteen kopecks a day, sir, if she's honest, since she possesses no special skills, and that's even if she works all the time! Besides, the state councillor Ivan Ivanovich Klopshtok—have you ever heard of him? Not only hasn't he paid her yet for the half dozen fine cotton shirts she made him, but he even drove her out with insults, stamping his feet and calling her names, claiming that the collars were the wrong size and had been sewn in crooked. Meanwhile the children go hungry. . . . And then Katerina Ivanovna, wringing her hands, paces

---

* Cyrus was a Persian ruler in the sixth century B.C.E.

† George Lewes (1817–1878) wrote *The Physiology of Everyday Life* (1859); it was translated into Russian in 1861 and became very popular among Russian progressives.

the room, her face flushed with the red blotches that always accompany that illness: 'You live here with us,' she says, 'like a sponger; you eat and drink and enjoy the warmth, but what's there to eat and drink when these little ones haven't seen a crust of bread for three days?' I was lying there at the time . . . why not say it? I was a little drunk, sir, and I heard my Sonya (she's very meek and has such a soft voice . . . she's fair-haired and her face is always so pale and thin), say: 'Oh, Katerina Ivanovna, must I really go out and do that?' Meanwhile, Darya Frantsevna, a malevolent woman well known to the police, had reported her to the landlady several times. 'So what?' replied Katerina Ivanovna, with a mocking laugh, 'What are you saving yourself for? What a treasure!' But don't blame her, don't, dear sir, don't blame her! She wasn't in her right mind when she said it; she was agitated, sick, and the children were crying because they hadn't eaten, and she said it more as an insult than as what she really meant. . . . Because Katerina Ivanovna is the sort of person who, as soon as the children begin crying, even when they're hungry, begins to beat them right away. And then I saw how Sonechka, around six o'clock, got up, put on a kerchief, her hooded cloak, and left the apartment; she came back at nine. She walked in and went straight up to Katerina Ivanovna and silently put thirty silver rubles down on the table in front of her. She didn't utter one word as she did, didn't even look at her, but merely picked up our large green shawl (we have one that we use), covered her head and face completely, and lay down on the bed, facing the wall, but her whole body and her little shoulders were trembling. . . . Meanwhile, sir, I lay there, in the same condition as before. . . . And then I saw, young man, I saw how Katerina Ivanovna, also without saying a word, went up to Sonechka's bed and knelt there all evening, kissing her feet; she was unable to stand, and then, embracing, they both fell asleep together . . . both of them . . . both of them . . . yes, sir . . . while I . . . I lay there drunk, sir."

Marmeladov fell silent, as if his voice had broken off. Then he suddenly filled his glass, drank it down quickly, and grunted.

"Since then, sir," he continued after a brief pause, "since then, as a result of one unfortunate incident and the fact that some ill-intentioned people informed the authorities, which Darya Frantsevna had encouraged because she felt as if she hadn't been treated with appropriate respect, since then my daughter, Sofiya Semyonovna, was compelled to obtain the yellow card of a prostitute, and as a result has no longer been able to reside with us. It was the landlady, Amaliya Fedorovna, who wouldn't allow it (Darya Frantsevna had previously encouraged her in this), as well as Mr. Lebezyatnikov . . . hmm. . . . That entire episode with Katerina Ivanovna occurred because of Sonya. At first he himself tried to have his way with her, and then he suddenly became very touchy: 'How can I, such a cultured person,' he says, 'continue to live in the same apartment with a person like her?' Katerina Ivanovna wouldn't tolerate it and got involved . . . and thus the incident occurred. . . . And now Sonechka stops by mostly after dark, comforts Katerina Ivanovna, and leaves whatever money she can. . . . She lives in the apartment of the tailor Kapernaumov, renting a room from them; he's lame and afflicted with a speech defect and his entire large family has the same defect. His wife has it, too. . . . They all live together in one room; Sonya has her own room, with a partition. . . . Hmm, yes. . . . These people are very poor and all afflicted with this speech defect . . . yes. . . . One morning I'd just woken up, sir, put on my ragged clothes, raised my hands to heaven, and set off to see His Excellency, Ivan Afanasevich. Do you happen to know His Excellency, Ivan Afanasevich? No? Then you don't know such a virtuous man! He's like wax . . . wax before the face of the Lord; he melts like wax! After hearing me out, he even grew tearful. 'Well, Marmeladov,' he says, 'you've disappointed my expectations once before. . . . I'll take you on again as my own responsibility,' that's what he said. 'Remember this,' he said, 'and now go away!' I kissed the dust at his feet, mentally, because he wouldn't have allowed it, being a person of such high rank and modern ideas about public service; I returned home, and when I announced that I'd been reinstated in my job and would be receiving a salary, Lord, what a commotion it caused!"

Marmeladov paused again, overcome with strong emotion. Just then a whole group of men entered from outside, already quite drunk, with the sound of a rented accordion and the soft, cracked voice of a seven-year-old child singing "The Little Farm." It grew loud. The tavern keeper and the waiters attended to the new arrivals. Marmeladov, who didn't pay any attention to these people, continued his story. He already seemed very weak, but the more intoxicated he grew, the more talkative he became. His recollections of his recent successes at work seemed to invigorate him, and some were even reflected in his face by a sort of radiance. Raskolnikov listened attentively.

"This took place, good sir, about five weeks ago. Yes. . . . They'd both just found out, Katerina Ivanovna and Sonechka, good Lord, and it was as if I'd been admitted to the heavenly kingdom. It used to be that I'd lie around like a beast, and receive only abuse! But that day: they walked around on tiptoe and kept the children quiet: 'Semyon Zakharych is tired from his work; he's resting: shh!' They'd serve me coffee before I went off to work, and they'd even heat up some cream! They began to buy real cream, do you hear? I have no idea how they scraped the money together to provide me with a decent uniform, eleven rubles and fifty kopecks. Boots, the finest calico shirtfronts, and a uniform: they threw it all together splendidly for eleven and a half rubles. The first day, I arrived home from work in the morning and saw that Katerina Ivanovna had prepared two courses, soup and salted beef with horseradish, something we'd never even dreamt of before. She doesn't own a dress . . . that is, none at all, sir, and now she looked as if she were going out visiting; she was all dressed up; it wasn't as if she had anything to use, she did it all from nothing; her hair was done up, she had a clean white collar and sleeve covers; she looked like a completely different person, much younger and prettier. Sonechka, my little sweetheart, had merely provided the money, while for the time being, she said, she thought it wouldn't be proper for her to visit us too often, except after dark, so no one would see her. You hear, do you hear? I came home after dinner to have a little rest, and what do you think? Katerina Ivanovna simply couldn't resist: a week before she'd had a really terrible quarrel with the landlady, Amaliya Fedorovna, and now she'd invited her to come for a cup of coffee. They sat there for two hours whispering all the time: 'Now,' Katerina says, 'since Semyon Zakharych is back at work and receiving a salary, and he's even been to see His Excellency; His Excellency came out himself, told everyone else to wait, while he took Semyon Zakharych by the arm and escorted him into his office. You hear, do you hear? "Of course," he says to him, "I remember your service, Semyon Zakharych, and although you displayed a fondness for that trivial frailty, now, since you've made a promise, and besides, without you things had started to go badly." (You hear, do you hear?) "I hope," he says, "now on your word of honor,"— that is, all of it, I tell you, she made up the whole story, not as a result of thoughtlessness, sir, but so she could boast a bit! No, sir, she herself believed the whole thing; she was consoling herself using her own imagination, so help me God! I don't condemn her; no, I don't condemn her for this at all! When, six days later, I brought my first wages home—twenty-three rubles and forty kopecks—when I brought it all home, she called me a sweetie: 'You're such a sweetie,' she said! We were all alone, sir, do you understand? Well, it's not for my looks, and besides, what sort of husband am I? No, she pinched my cheek: 'You're such a sweetie!' she said."

Marmeladov paused, was about to smile, but suddenly his chin began to quiver, though he restrained himself. This tavern, his debauched appearance, his five nights on a hay barge, his bottle, and, at the same time, this painful love for his wife and family disconcerted his listener. Raskolnikov attended intensely, but with painful emotion. He was annoyed with himself that he'd dropped into the tavern.

"Dear sir, dear sir!" Marmeladov exclaimed after recovering. "Oh, sir, you may find all this amusing, as do the others, since I'm only upsetting you with the foolishness of all these petty details of my domestic life, but I don't find it amusing in the least! That's because I can feel it all. . . . I spent the rest of that entire heavenly day of my life and all that evening in fleeting dreams: that is, how I'd arrange everything, outfit the children, provide peace of mind to my wife, and return my only begotten daughter to the bosom of the family from her disgrace. . . . And more, much more. . . . It's permitted, sir. Well, sir, my good sir"— Marmeladov suddenly seemed to shudder, raise his head, and stare at his listener—"well, sir, the next day, after all these daydreams, that is, exactly five days ago, toward evening, by clever stealth, like a thief in the night, I stole the key from Katerina Ivanovna's box, took out what was left of the money I'd brought home, I don't recall how much it was, and now, look at me, all of you! I've been away from home five days; they're looking for me, it's the end of my job, and my uniform is left in some tavern near the Egyptian Bridge; I traded it for these clothes . . . and it's the end of everything!"

Marmeladov struck his fist on his forehead, clenched his teeth, closed his eyes, and placed his elbow firmly on the table. But in a moment his face suddenly changed; he glanced at Raskolnikov with some sort of assumed cunning and feigned insolence, started laughing, and said:

"I visited Sonya today. I went to ask her for some money to buy a drink so I could get rid of my hangover! Tee-hee!"

"Did she really give you any?" someone who'd just come in cried, then burst out laughing.

"This bottle was bought with her money, sir," Marmeladov uttered, addressing Raskolnikov exclusively. "She gave me thirty kopecks, with her own hands, her last coins, all there was, I could see for myself. . . . She didn't say a word, merely looked at me in silence. . . . That doesn't happen here on earth, but up there . . . they grieve over people, they weep, but they do not reproach them, they don't! But that hurts more, sir, much more, sir, when they don't reproach them! Thirty kopecks, yes, sir. But she needs them herself now, doesn't she? What do you think, my dear sir? Now she has to keep herself clean. This extra cleanliness costs money, do you understand? Do you? Well, she also has to buy makeup, doesn't she? Starched petticoats, the kind of stylish shoes that display her little feet when she has to step over a puddle. Do you understand, do you, sir, what this cleanliness means? Well, sir, I, her own father, took those thirty kopecks to ease my hangover! And I'm drinking, sir! I've already spent it all on drink, sir! Well, who would feel sorry for the likes of me? Eh? Do you feel sorry for me now, sir, or not? Tell me, sir, do you feel sorry or not? Ha, ha, ha!"

He wanted to refill his glass, but there was nothing left. The bottle was empty.

"Why should anyone feel sorry for you?" demanded the tavern keeper, who'd turned up next to them once again.

There was a burst of laughter and even some cursing. The listeners laughed and cursed, and even those who weren't listening joined in, simply looking at the sorry sight of the former civil servant.

"Sorry? Why feel sorry for me?" Marmeladov cried suddenly,

standing up, his arm outstretched, now genuinely inspired, as if he'd been waiting for those words. "Why feel sorry? you ask. No, there's no reason to feel sorry for me! I should be crucified, nailed to a cross, not pitied. But crucify me, oh Judge, crucify me, and after having crucified me, then feel sorry for me! I myself will come and ask to be crucified, for it's not joy I seek, but sorrow and tears! Do you think, oh, shop-keeper, that your bottle has afforded me any pleasure? Sorrow, sorrow is what I sought in its depths, sorrow and tears, and I found them and tasted of them; but He who has pitied all men and who has understood everyone and everything, He will take pity on us; He and no one else; He is the judge. He will come on that day and He will ask: 'Where is thy daughter who sacrificed herself for her wicked and consumptive stepmother and for a stranger's little children? Where is thy daughter who pitied her earthly father, a useless drunkard, and who was not dismayed by his beastliness?' And He will say: 'Come forth! I have already forgiven thee. . . . I have forgiven thee once. . . . Thy many sins are now also forgiven, for thou hast loved much. . . .' And He will forgive my Sonya, He will; I know that He will forgive her. . . . Just a little while ago when I was with her, I felt this in my heart! And He will judge and forgive everyone, both the good and the evil, the wise men and the humble. . . . And when He has finished with everyone, then He will summon us, too: 'Come forth,' He will say, 'even ye! Come forth, ye drunkards, come forth, ye weaklings, come forth, ye shame-less ones!' And we will all come forth, without shame, and we will stand before Him. And He will say, 'Ye are swine! Ye are made in the image of the beast and ye bear his mark; but ye also shall come forth!' And the wise men and the learned men will exclaim, 'Lord! Wherefore do You receive these people?' And He will say, 'I receive them, oh, ye wise men, I receive them, oh, ye learned men, because not one of them hath ever considered himself worthy. . . .' And He will stretch forth His arms to us, and we will kiss His hands . . . and we will weep . . . and we will understand all things! Then will we understand all things! And everyone will understand . . . even Katerina Ivanovna . . . she, too, will understand. . . . Oh, Lord, Thy kingdom come!"

Deep in thought, he sank down on the bench, weak and exhausted, looking at no one, oblivious of his surroundings. His words made quite an impression; silence reigned for a moment, but soon the previous laughter and curses resumed.

"Know-it-all!"

"Damned liar!"

"Bureaucrat!"

And so on and so forth.

"Let's go, sir," Marmeladov said suddenly, raising his head and turning to Raskolnikov. "Take me home . . . to Kozel's house, in the courtyard. It's time . . . to Katerina Ivanovna . . ."

Raskolnikov had been wanting to leave for some time; he himself had even thought about helping the other man get home. Marmeladov's legs were much weaker than his words, and he leaned heavily on the young man. They had only about two or three hundred paces to walk. The closer they got to his house, the more and more the drunken man was overcome by embarrassment and fear.

"I'm not afraid of Katerina Ivanovna now," he muttered in agitation. "It's not that she'll begin tearing out my hair. What do I care about my hair? It's nothing! That's what I say! It'll even be better if she begins tearing it out! That's not what I'm afraid of. . . . I'm . . . afraid of her eyes . . . yes . . . her eyes. . . . I'm also afraid of the red blotches on her cheeks . . . and then—I'm afraid of her breathing. . . . Have you ever heard how people with this illness breathe . . . when they're distraught? I'm also afraid of the children's crying. . . . Because if Sonya hasn't fed them, then . . . I don't know what! I just don't! But I'm not afraid of a beating. You should know, sir, not only are such beatings not painful, I even enjoy them. . . . For I myself couldn't do without them. It's better that way. Let her beat me; it relieves her soul. . . . It's better that way. . . . Here's the house. Kozel's house. He's a locksmith, a German, he's rich . . . lead on."

They entered from the courtyard and went up to the fourth floor. The farther they climbed, the darker the stairs became. It was almost eleven o'clock, and even though at that time of year there's no real night in Petersburg, it was very dark at the top of the stairs.

The small sooty door at the end of the stairway, at the very top, was open. A candle stub lit the poorest of rooms, only ten paces long; it was entirely visible from the hallway. Everything was thrown about and in disarray, especially the children's clothing. A bedsheet with holes in it had been hung across the back corner. Behind it, most likely, stood a bed. There were only two chairs in the room itself and a very tattered oilcloth sofa, in front of which stood an old kitchen table made of pine, unpainted and uncovered. At the edge of the table was a partially burned tallow candle stub in an iron candlestick. It turned out that Marmeladov lived in a separate room, not in that corner; his room was one through which people had to pass. The door to the farthest rooms or cells, into which Amaliya Lippevekhsel's apartment had been divided, stood slightly ajar. There was a great deal of noise and shouting. There was loud laughter. It seemed that people were playing cards and having tea. Sometimes the most indecorous words emerged.

Raskolnikov recognized Katerina Ivanovna immediately. She was a terribly emaciated woman, thin, rather tall and elegant, with lovely dark brown hair still, and real red blotches on her cheeks. She paced back and forth in her little room, arms folded across her chest, lips parched, gasping unevenly for breath. Her eyes were shining as if she had a fever, but her glance was sharp and steady, and her consumptive and agitated face made a morbid impression in the last light of the flickering candle end quivering on her face. She seemed to Raskolnikov to be about thirty years old and was certainly no match for Marmeladov. . . . She didn't hear and didn't see the men entering; she seemed to be in some sort of stupor in which she neither saw nor heard anything. It was stuffy in the room, but she hadn't opened the window; there was a stench emanating from the staircase, but the door stood open; waves of tobacco smoke wafted in from the inner rooms through the open door; she was coughing but hadn't closed the door. The youngest girl, around six years old, was asleep on the floor, sitting up somehow, hunched over, her head resting on the sofa. The little boy, a year older than her, was trembling in the corner and crying. He'd probably just been beaten. The eldest daughter, around nine years old, was as tall and slim as a matchstick, wearing only a wretched, very tattered blouse, and draped over her bare shoulders a decrepit cotton shawl that had probably been made for her about two years ago, because now it didn't even reach her knees; she stood in the corner next to her younger brother, embracing his neck with one long arm, desiccated as a matchstick. She seemed to be comforting him, whispering something to him, doing all she could so he wouldn't start whimpering again, while at the same time she followed her mother with her very, very large dark eyes, which seemed even larger on her emaciated and frightened little face. Marmeladov, before entering the room, sank to his knees in the doorway, while he pushed Raskolnikov forward. The woman, noticing a stranger, paused distractedly in front of him; having returned to her senses momentarily, she seemed to be wondering why he'd come in. But most likely she imagined that he was heading into the other rooms, since theirs served as the passageway. Realizing this and not paying any more attention, she went to the hall door to close it; then, catching sight of her husband kneeling on the threshold, she suddenly screamed.

"Ah!" she cried in a rage. "So you've come back! You crook! You monster! Where's the money? What's left in your pocket? Show me! And your clothes? Where are your clothes? Where's the money? Tell me . . ."

She rushed at him to begin searching. Marmeladov obediently and calmly raised both his arms to the sides to make it easier to search his pockets. There wasn't a kopeck left.

"Where's the money?" she screamed. "Oh, Lord, did he really spend it all on drink? There were twelve silver rubles left in the box!" Suddenly, in a rage, she grabbed hold of his hair and dragged him into the room. Marmeladov himself made it easier for her, crawling on his knees meekly behind her.

"Even this gives me enjoyment! Even this isn't painful, but en-joy-ab-le, my dear-est kind sir," he cried, being shaken by his hair and even bumping his forehead once on the floor. The child who was asleep on the floor woke up and began crying. The little boy in the corner couldn't restrain himself, began shaking, burst into tears, and, in a terrible fright, almost a fit, rushed to his sister. The older girl, half awake, trembled like a leaf.

"Drank it up! All of it, he drank it all up!" the poor woman shouted in despair. "And those aren't his clothes! They're hungry, hungry!" (Wringing her hands, she pointed to the children.) "Oh, what a cursed life! And you, aren't you ashamed?" she said, turning suddenly on

Raskolnikov. "From the tavern! Were you drinking with him? Were you drinking with him, too? Get out!"

The young man hastened to leave without saying a word. Besides, the interior door swung open, and several curious onlookers peeked in. Impudent people in skullcaps were stretching their heads forward, laughing and smoking cigarettes or pipes. There were people wearing bathrobes, some left completely unfastened, or wearing almost indecent summer clothes; others held cards in their hands. They laughed especially heartily when Marmeladov, being dragged by his hair, cried that he found it enjoyable. They even began coming into the room; at last one could hear a sinister screech: it was Amaliya Lippevekhsel forcing her way through to impose a sort of order and to frighten the poor woman for the hundredth time with her insulting command to vacate the apartment by the following day. As he left, Raskolnikov managed to shove his hand into his pocket, grab the change left from the ruble he'd cashed at the tavern, and place it on the windowsill unobserved. Then, once on the staircase, he reconsidered and wanted to return.

"What a foolish thing I just did," he thought. "They have Sonya, and I need the money myself." But after some thought, he realized that it was already impossible to take it back and he wouldn't do it, anyway; he gave up and returned to his own apartment. "Sonya also has to buy makeup," he went on, grinning sarcastically as he walked along the street. "This cleanliness costs money. . . . Hmm. But maybe Sonechka won't make any money today, because there's always risk involved, hunting for valuable game, prospecting for gold. . . . Without my money, they might still have nothing at all tomorrow. . . . Ah, that Sonya! What a gold mine they've discovered! And they mine it! I'll say they do! And they've gotten used to it. They shed a few tears and then they got used to it. Man's a scoundrel: he can get used to anything!"

He started musing.

"But what if I'm wrong?" he suddenly cried inadvertently. "What if man's really not a *scoundrel*, in general—that is, the whole human race; that would mean that all the rest is prejudice, merely imagined fears, and there are no boundaries, and that's how it should be!"

III

It was already late in the day when he awoke after a disturbed sleep, but the sleep hadn't fortified him. He woke up feeling aggravated, irritable, and spiteful and looked around his small space with contempt. It was a tiny closet of a room, some six paces long, and it had the most pitiful appearance, with dusty yellowish wallpaper peeling away in many places. The ceiling was so low that even a slightly tall man would find it unnerving, and it always seemed to him that at any moment he might bump his head against it. The furniture suited the room: there were three old chairs, not in good condition, and a painted table in the corner holding a few books and notebooks. A glance at even one volume, all covered in dust, would make it clear that it had been a while since anyone's hand had touched these books. Finally, a large, ungainly sofa took up almost the entire wall and about half the width of the whole room; at one time it had been covered in chintz, but now it was in tatters and served as Raskolnikov's bed. He often slept on it just as he was, without undressing, without a sheet, covering himself with his old shabby student's overcoat, with one small pillow at the head of the bed, under which he would place all the linen he owned, both clean and dirty, so that his head was raised a bit. A small table stood in front of the sofa.

It was hard to sink lower or become more slovenly, but Raskolnikov found this aspect even pleasant in his current frame of mind. He had definitely withdrawn from everyone, like a turtle into its shell, and even the face of the servant, who was obliged to wait on him and who would sometimes enter his room, aroused his bile and occasioned tremors. That sometimes happens with those monomaniacs who are too focused on something. The landlady had stopped providing him with food about two weeks ago, and up to the present he hadn't taken it upon himself to have it out with her, even though he went without his dinner. The cook Nastasya, the landlady's only servant, welcomed the lodger's mood and had completely stopped sweeping and straightening his room, except that about once a week she would sometimes take a broom to it, as if by accident. It was she who had just awakened him.

"Get up! Why are you sleeping?" she yelled at him. "It's past nine o'clock. I brought you some tea. Do you want it? You're wasting away!"

The lodger opened his eyes, shuddered, and recognized Nastasya.

"Is that tea from the landlady or what?" he asked, slowly and painfully raising himself up a bit on the sofa.

"The landlady! Ha!"

She placed her own cracked teapot in front of him, with its diluted tea and two yellow lumps of sugar.

"Here, Nastasya, take this, please," he said, fumbling in his pocket (he'd been sleeping in his clothes), and he pulled out a handful of copper coins. "Go buy me a roll. And get me a little sausage from the sausage maker, the cheapest sort."

"I'll bring you a roll in a moment, but wouldn't you like some cabbage soup instead of sausage? It's from yesterday and it's good. I saved you some, but you came home late. It's good cabbage soup."

When she'd brought in the soup and he'd set about eating it, Nastasya sat down on the sofa next to him and started chatting. She was a peasant woman and very talkative.

"Praskovya Pavlovna wants to complain to the police about you," she said.

He winced deeply.

"To the police? What does she want?"

"You don't pay her any money and you won't vacate the room. It's clear what she wants."

"Oh, hell, that's all I needed," he muttered, grinding his teeth. "No, that's not . . . a good thing right now. . . . She's a fool," he said aloud. "I'll go see her today. I'll talk to her."

"She may be a fool, just like I am, but what about you? Are you clever, lying here like a sack, with nothing to show for it? Before, you said, you used to teach children; why don't you do anything now?"

"I do . . ." Raskolnikov said reluctantly and harshly.

"What do you do?"

"I work . . ."

"What kind of work?"

"I think," he replied seriously after a little pause.

Nastasya simply collapsed in laughter. She was easily amused, and when she found something funny, she laughed inaudibly, her whole body rocking and shaking until she felt sick.

"Have you thought up a lot of money?" she was finally able to utter.

"Without boots, you can't go teach. Besides, I spit on them."

"Don't spit into the well you drink from."

"They pay me almost nothing to teach children. What can you do with kopecks?" he continued reluctantly, as if replying to his own thoughts.

"You want all your capital at once?"

He regarded her with a strange look.

"Yes, all my capital," he replied firmly, after a slight pause.

"Well, better to go slowly, or you'll scare me; I'm already very frightened. Should I get you a roll, or not?"

"As you like."

"Oh, I forgot! A letter came for you yesterday while you were out."

"A letter! For me? From whom?"

"I don't know from whom. I paid the mailman three kopecks. Will you pay me back?"

"Bring it to me, for heaven's sake, bring it!" Raskolnikov cried in great excitement.

A minute later, the letter appeared. Just as he thought: it was from his mother, in Ryazan Province. He even turned pale as he took it. He hadn't received any letters in some time; but now something else suddenly took hold of his heart.

"Nastasya, go away, for heaven's sake; here's your three kopecks, only go away right now, for heaven's sake!"

The letter trembled in his hands: he didn't want to open it in her presence: he wanted to be *alone* with the letter. After Nastasya left, he quickly raised the letter to his lips and kissed it; then for a long time he gazed at the handwriting of the address, at his mother's familiar, beloved, tiny slanted writing, she who'd once taught him how to read and write. He took his time; he even seemed afraid of something. He finally opened it: the letter was long, thick, and weighed almost a full ounce; two large pieces of writing paper were covered with tiny script.

"My dear Rodya," his mother wrote. "It's been more than two months since I've written you a letter, as a result of which I've suffered, at times even lost sleep, wondering about you. But most likely you won't blame me for my unintended silence. You know how I love you; you're all we have, Dunya and I, you mean everything to us, all our hope, all our aspiration. I was so upset when I learned that you'd left the university several months ago because you were unable to support yourself, and that your lessons and other sources had ended! How could I help you with my pension of only one hundred and twenty rubles a year? As you well know, I'd borrowed those fifteen rubles I sent you four months ago from our local merchant Afanasy Ivanovich Vakhrushin, on the promise of my pension. He's a good man and was your father's acquaintance. But in giving him the right to receive my pension for me, I was obliged to wait until I repaid my debt, and that's only just happened, so all this time I haven't been able to send you anything. But now, thank God, it seems I can send you some more; in general, we can even boast of good fortune now about which I hasten to inform you. In the first place, could you guess, dear Rodya, that your dear sister has been living with me for the last month and a half, and we'll no longer be separated in the future. Praise the Lord, her torments have ended, but I'll tell you everything in order, so you'll know what's happened and what we've been keeping from you up to now. When you wrote to me about two months ago that you'd heard from someone or other that Dunya had to endure much rudeness in Mr. Svidrigaylov's house and you asked me for a more detailed explanation— what could I write to you at that time? If I'd told you the whole truth, you'd probably have dropped everything and rushed to see us, even come on foot, because I know your character and your feelings, and you wouldn't have allowed your sister to be insulted. I myself was in despair, but what could I do? Even I didn't know the whole truth then. The main difficulty was that Dunya, who'd entered their household last year as a governess, had received an advance of one hundred rubles, on the condition that a certain amount would be deducted from her salary each month; therefore, she couldn't leave her position until she'd repaid her debt. This amount (I can now explain it all to you, precious Rodya) she'd accepted mostly so she could send you sixty rubles, which you needed then and which you received from us last year. At the time we deceived you, writing that it had come from Dunya's savings, but that wasn't so. Now I'm telling you the whole truth because everything's suddenly changed, by the will of God, for the better, and so you'll know how much Dunya loves you and what a precious heart she has. As a matter of fact, right from the start Mr. Svidrigaylov treated her very rudely and made various impolite remarks and insults to her at the table. . . . But I don't want to dwell on these agonizing difficulties and upset you for no reason, since all of that's stopped. In brief, in spite of the kind and generous treatment by Marfa Petrovna, Mr. Svidrigaylov's wife, and all the servants, Dunechka had a very difficult time, especially when Mr. Svidrigaylov, following old regimental custom, was under the influence of Bacchus. But what happened afterward? Just imagine that this madman had conceived a passion for Dunya sometime earlier, but had been concealing it under the guise of rudeness and contempt for her. Perhaps he himself was ashamed and horrified to see that he himself, at his age and as the father of a family, harbored such frivolous hopes; therefore, he inadvertently took his anger out on Dunya. Perhaps by his rude treatment and mockery he wanted to hide the whole truth from other people. But, in the end, he couldn't restrain himself and dared make an open and vile proposition to Dunya, promising her various rewards; moreover, he said he would forsake everything and go to another village with her or, perhaps, even abroad. You can imagine her suffering! It was impossible for her to leave her position at that time, not only because of her financial obligation, but because she wanted to spare Marfa Petrovna, who might suddenly conceive a hatred for her, and consequently arouse discord in the household. It would create a huge scandal for Dunechka; she'd never be able to escape it. There were many other reasons why Dunya couldn't consider removing herself from this horrible house earlier than six weeks. Of course, you know Dunya, you know how clever she is and what a strong character she has. She can tolerate many things and find so much generosity within herself even in the most extreme circumstances, so as not to lose her strength. She didn't even write to me about all this so as not to upset me, though we often exchanged news. The finale was unexpected. Marfa Petrovna accidentally overheard her husband imploring Dunechka in the garden. Misinterpreting the whole affair, she blamed Dunya for everything, thinking that she was the cause of it all. It occasioned a terrible scene right there in the garden: Marfa Petrovna even struck her, and didn't want to listen to reason. She shouted for a whole hour and finally ordered that Dunya be sent back to me in town on a simple peasant's cart, onto which they tossed all her things, linens, dresses, in any which way, untied and unpacked. Then it began to pour down rain; Dunya, insulted and disgraced, had to make the trip, all eleven miles, with a peasant in an open cart. Now just imagine, how and what could I write in reply to your letter that I'd received two months ago? I myself was in despair. I dared not tell you the truth because you'd be so unhappy, bitter, and angry. And what could you do? You might have gotten yourself into trouble; besides, Dunya wouldn't allow it. I couldn't just fill my letter with nonsense about this and that, when I felt such sorrow in my soul. Rumors about this episode circulated through the whole town for an entire month, and it reached the point where Dunya and I couldn't even go to church because of all the contemptuous looks and whispers. Remarks were even uttered aloud in our presence. All of our acquaintances shunned us, and everyone stopped greeting us. I learned for certain that some merchants' shop assistants and some office clerks wanted to insult us in the worst possible way by tarring the gates of our house so that the landlord would demand that we vacate our apartment. The cause of all this was Marfa Petrovna, who'd managed to denounce and slander Dunya in every household. She was acquainted with everyone in town, and during that month she visited town continually. She's somewhat talkative and loves to go on about family matters, especially complaining about her husband to each and every person, which is not a good thing; so she spread the whole story in a very short time, not only in town, but throughout the district. I fell ill, but Dunya was stronger than I was; if you'd only seen how she endured it all and how she consoled and reassured me! She's an angel! But, by God's grace, our torments ended. Mr. Svidrigaylov thought better of it, repented, probably taking pity on Dunya, and presented to Marfa Petrovna clear and complete evidence of Dunya's innocence, namely this: a letter that Dunya had felt compelled to write and convey to him, even before Marfa Petrovna came upon them in the garden, one that remained in his possession after Dunya's departure. The note asked him to cease these personal declarations and secret meetings that he'd insisted on. In this letter she reproached him in the most impassioned way and with total indignation for his dishonorable treatment of Marfa Petrovna. She reminded him that he was a father and the head of a household, and, finally, she said how vile it was for him to torment and distress a young woman who was already in distress and defenseless. In a word, dear Rodya, this letter was so nobly and poignantly written that I sobbed while reading it and to this day can't do so without shedding tears. Contributing to Dunya's exoneration came the testimony of those servants who saw and knew much more than Mr. Svidrigaylov supposed, as always happens. Marfa Petrovna was completely astounded and 'once again crushed,' as she herself acknowledged; on the other hand, she was fully convinced of Dunechka's innocence. The very next day, Sunday, heading directly to church, she tearfully implored Our Lady to give her the strength to bear this new ordeal and carry out her duty. Then, right after church, without making any stops, she came to us and told us everything. She wept bitterly and, with full repentance, embraced Dunya and begged her forgiveness. That same morning, without tarrying, she set off right from our house to all the households in town, and in each one, shedding tears, she restored Dunya's innocence and the nobility of her feelings and behavior in the most flattering terms. She showed everyone Dunechka's handwritten letter to Mr. Svidrigaylov, read it aloud, and even allowed people to make copies of it (which, it seems to me, was going too far). In this way it took her several days to visit everyone in town, so that some people felt offended that she was partial to others. Lines were formed since she was expected in advance at every household and everyone knew that on such and such a day Marfa Petrovna would read the letter there. At each reading, people would line up who'd already heard the letter read several times in their own homes and in those of their other acquaintances. In my opinion, much of this, very much, was unnecessary; but such was Marfa Petrovna's character. At least she fully restored Dunechka's honor. All the vileness of this affair left an indelible disgrace on her husband as the main culprit, so that I even began to feel sorry for him. People dealt too severely with that madman. Soon Dunya was invited to give lessons in several households, but she refused. In general, people suddenly began treating her with special respect. All of this served principally to further the unexpected circumstance by which, one can say, our entire fate is now being altered. You should know, dear Rodya, that a suitor has proposed to Dunya and she's already given her consent, which I'm writing to inform you about immediately. Even though this matter was conducted without your advice, you probably won't bear any grudge either against me or your sister, since you yourself will see, from the facts, that it was impossible to delay or wait for your answer to arrive. Besides, you yourself couldn't have judged it accurately without being here. This is how it happened. He's already a court councillor, this Petr Petrovich Luzhin, a distant relative of Marfa Petrovna's, who herself helped a great deal in this affair. It all began with his expressing a desire through her that he wished to make our acquaintance; he was received properly, had some coffee, and the next day sent a letter in which he very politely stated his proposal and asked for a swift and definitive answer. He's a practical, busy man, just about to leave for Petersburg, so he values every minute. Of course, at first we were very surprised, since all this took place so swiftly and unexpectedly. All that day we pondered and considered it together. He's a reliable, well-to-do person, works in two places, and has already amassed some capital. It's true that he's forty-five, but he has a rather pleasant appearance and can still be attractive to women; he's also an extremely solid and decent man, only a little gloomy and a bit arrogant. But perhaps it only seems that way, at first glance. I advise you, dear Rodya, when you meet him in Petersburg, which will happen quite soon, not to judge him too quickly and heatedly, as you sometimes do, if at first glance you think something about him is not quite right. I say this just in case, although I'm sure that he'll make a pleasant impression on you. Besides, in order to determine what sort of person he is, one must deal with him gradually and carefully, so as not to fall into error or prejudice, which is difficult to correct or smooth over afterward. And Petr Petrovich, at least from many indications, is an extremely respectable man. On his first visit, he stated that he was a positive person; he shares to a large extent, as he himself explained it, 'the convictions of our younger generation,' and he is an enemy of all prejudices. He said a great many other things because he seems a bit vain and very much likes to be listened to, but that's almost not a fault. Of course, I understood very little, but Dunya explained to me that although he is not a well-educated man, he is clever and, it seems, kind. You know your sister's character, Rodya. She's a strong young woman, sensible, patient, and generous, although she has an impassioned heart, as I've come to know well. Of course, there's no particular love involved, either on her side or on his, but Dunya, in addition to being a clever young woman, is also a lofty creature—an angel. She'll consider it her duty to make her husband happy, and he, in turn, will concern himself with his wife's happiness, which, for the time being, we have no major reason to doubt, even though, I must admit, this whole affair was concluded rather quickly. Besides, he's a very prudent man and of course will realize that his own conjugal happiness will be more assured the happier Dunechka is with him. As for the fact that there are some irregularities in his character, some old habits, even some disagreement in their views (which can't be avoided even in the happiest of marriages), on that count Dunechka told me that she's relying on herself and there's no reason to be concerned, that she can tolerate a great deal on the condition that their future relations will be fair and honest. For example, he seemed a bit harsh to me at first; but that could be precisely because he's such a straightforward man, and it's absolutely so. For example, during his second visit, after he'd already received her consent, he expressed in our conversation that previously, even before he knew Dunya, he'd intended to marry an honest young woman, but one without a dowry, and certainly one who'd already experienced poverty; because, as he explained, a husband should in no way be obligated to his wife, and that it's much better if the wife considers her husband to be her bene-factor. I'll add that he expressed himself a little more gently and affectionately than I described, but I've forgotten his exact words, and recall only the idea; besides, he said it without any premeditation. Obviously it just slipped out in the heat of conversation, so that afterward he even tried to correct himself and soften it. But it still seemed somewhat harsh to me, and I conveyed this to Dunya later. But she replied, even somewhat annoyed, that 'words are not the same as deeds,' and of course that's fair. Before deciding, Dunechka didn't sleep the whole night; supposing that I was already asleep, she got out of bed and spent the whole night pacing back and forth in the room. Finally she knelt down and prayed fervently in front of the icon for a long time; in the morning, she announced to me that she'd made a decision.

"I've already mentioned that Petr Petrovich is now heading to Petersburg. He has important business there, since he wants to open a public lawyer's office in the capital. He's been engaged for a while in various legal actions and lawsuits, and a few days ago he won an important case. He has to go to Petersburg because he has an important matter pending in the Senate. Thus, dear Rodya, he might prove extremely useful for you in all sorts of ways; Dunya and I have already supposed that you, even from this day forward, might definitely launch your future career and consider your fate now clearly determined. Oh, if only this were to come to pass! It would be such a benefit that one would have to regard it as nothing other than a gift to us directly from the Almighty. Dunya dreams only about this. We even dared mention a few words on this account to Petr Petrovich. He expressed himself cautiously and said that of course, since he wouldn't be able to get along without a secretary, naturally it would be better to pay a salary to a relative, rather than to a stranger, if that person turns out to be competent to carry out his duties (as if you could turn out to be incompetent!). Then he expressed his doubt that your studies at the university would allow you time to work in his office. The matter was left there for the moment, but now Dunya can think about nothing but this. For the last few days, she's simply been in a sort of excited state and has devised an entire scheme about how you could become Petr Petrovich's comrade and even his partner in his legal affairs, all the more so since you yourself are studying law. I'm in complete agreement with her, Rodya, and share all her plans and hopes, seeing their complete likelihood. In spite of Petr Petrovich's present, extremely understandable evasiveness (because he doesn't know you yet), Dunya's quite sure that she'll manage it all by means of her good influence over her future husband, and she's convinced of that. Of course, we were careful not to let anything slip out about these future dreams of ours, especially about your becoming his partner. He's a pragmatic person and might take it very coolly, since all this might seem to him to be only dreams. Similarly, neither Dunya nor I have said a word to him about our strong hope that he would help us support you financially while you're at the university. We didn't talk about it, first because it might happen later of its own accord; probably, he himself, without unnecessary words, will propose it (as if he could refuse this to Dunya), all the more so since you yourself might become his right-hand man in the office and then you would receive this assistance not in the form of charity, but as earned income. That's what Dunya wants to arrange and I agree with her completely. The second reason we didn't say anything was because I particularly wanted to put you on an equal footing with him at our impending meeting with him. When Dunya told him about you with such enthusiasm, he replied that one must first take a close look at anyone to form a judgment about him, and that he would reserve for himself the right to form his own opinion of you until he made your acquaintance. You know, my precious Rodya, it seems to me, for several reasons (however, by no means related to Petr Petrovich, but just so, for some of my very own, personal, perhaps even old-womanish whims)—it seems to me that perhaps I'd be better off if, after their wedding, I were to live on my own, as I do now, and not with them. I'm absolutely sure that he'd be so generous and considerate as to invite me and propose that I not be separated from my daughter. If he hasn't said so up to now, naturally it's because that's what he intends even without words; but I'll refuse. I've noticed more than once in life that husbands are not very fond of their mothers-in-law; not only do I not want to be the slightest burden to anyone, but I myself want to be completely free, while I still have my own crust of bread to eat and children such as you and Dunechka. If possible, I'll settle somewhere near both of you, because, Rodya, I saved the most pleasant news for the end of my letter: you should know, my dear, that very soon we may all be together again and the three of us will embrace after our separation of almost three years! It's *definitely* been decided that Dunya and I will leave for Petersburg, I don't know exactly when, but, in any case, very, very soon, perhaps even in a week. Everything depends on the instructions of Petr Petrovich, who will let us know as soon as he gets his bearings in Petersburg. For several reasons he wants to hasten the marriage ceremony and even, if possible, hold the wedding before the next church fast, and if that doesn't work, then as soon as possible after the Fast of the Assumption. Oh, I'll take you to my heart with such happiness! Dunya's excited and elated at the prospect of seeing you, and once she said, as a joke, that she'd marry Petr Petrovich for that reason alone. She's an angel! She has nothing to add for you now, but she told me to write only that she has so many things to talk over with you, so very many things, that she won't even pick up a pen now because she couldn't convey it all in just a few lines, and she'd only upset herself; she told me to send you her warmest embrace and countless kisses. But, in spite of the fact that we may very soon be meeting in person, I'll still be sending you some money in a few days, as much as I can. Now that everyone has learned that she'll be marrying Petr Petrovich, my credit has suddenly improved, and I know for sure that Afanasy Ivanovich will trust me, on account of my pension, even up to seventy-five rubles, so I may be able to send you twenty-five or thirty rubles. I'd send you more, but I'm concerned about our expenses for the trip. Although Petr Petrovich was kind enough to take upon himself a portion of the cost of our journey to the capital, namely, he offered to convey at his expense our baggage and a large trunk (somehow through his acquaintances there), we still have to consider our arrival in Petersburg, where we can't show up without a kopeck, if only for the first few days. Meanwhile, Dunechka and I have calculated everything precisely, and it turns out that the trip will cost us very little. We're only sixty miles from the railroad station, so just in case, we've made an agreement with a peasant driver here whom we know. And after that, Dunechka and I will happily travel in a third-class railway car. Thus, I may manage to send you not twenty-five rubles, but more likely thirty.

Enough: I've completely filled two entire sheets, and there's no space left; it's our whole story: so many events have accumulated! And now, my precious Rodya, I embrace you until our upcoming meeting and I give you my maternal blessing. Love Dunya, your sister, Rodya; love her as she loves you, and know that she loves you without limit, more than she loves herself. She's an angel; and you, Rodya, you mean everything to us, all our hope, all our aspiration. If only you're happy, then we'll be happy, too. Are you still saying your prayers to God, Rodya, as you did before, and do you still believe in the goodness of our Creator and Savior? I'm afraid in my heart that you may have been visited by the latest fashionable disbelief. If that's so, then I pray for you. Remember, my dear, how in your childhood, when your father was still alive, you mumbled your prayers on my lap and how happy we all were then! Good-bye, or, rather, *till we meet!* I embrace you very, very warmly and kiss you endlessly.

Yours till the grave,
Pulkheriya Raskolnikova"

Almost all the while Raskolnikov was reading, from the very beginning of the letter, his face was bathed in tears. However, after he'd finished, his face was pale, distorted by a spasm, and a painful, angry, spiteful smile curled on his lips. He lay his head down on his meager, worn-out pillow, and he thought; he thought for a long time. His heart was pounding, and his thoughts were violently agitated. At last he felt stifled and cramped in that little yellow room of his, which resembled a cupboard or a trunk. His gaze and his thoughts demanded space. He grabbed his hat and left, this time no longer afraid of meeting anyone on the staircase; he'd forgotten all about that. He took a route across Voznesensky Prospect toward Vasilievsky Island, as if hastening there on business, but, as was his custom, he walked without noticing the street, whispering and even talking aloud to himself, which fact greatly astonished the passersby. Many people thought he was drunk.

IV

His mother's letter tormented him. But as far as the basic, most important point was concerned, he had no doubts even for one moment, even while he was reading the letter. The very heart of the matter was resolved in his mind, resolved once and for all: "This marriage will never take place as long as I live, and to hell with Mr. Luzhin!"

"Because this matter is obvious," he muttered to himself, smirking and maliciously celebrating in advance the triumph of his decision. "No, Mama, no Dunya, you can't deceive me! And what makes it even worse, they apologize for not asking my advice and for deciding the matter without me! I'll say! They think it's impossible to break it off now; we'll see if it's possible or not! What a splendid excuse: 'Petr Petrovich, they say, is such a businesslike man that he can't possibly get married in any other way than in a hurry, almost en route on a train.' No, Dunya, I can see everything, and I know what those *many things* are that you want to talk over with me; I also know what you worried about all night, pacing the room, and what you prayed about before the icon of Our Lady of Kazan,* the one that Mama has in her bedroom. It's a steep climb to Golgotha.† Hmm . . . so, in other words, it's been decided once and for all: you're pleased, Avdotya Romanovna, to marry

---

* A famous Russian icon depicting the Virgin and kept in the Kazan Cathedral in Petersburg.

† According to the Gospels, a site immediately outside Jerusalem's walls where Jesus was crucified.

that practical, rational man who's amassed his capital (who's *already* amassed his capital; that's more impressive, more imposing), who's working in two places, who shares the convictions of our younger generation (as Mama writes), and who '*seems* to be a kind man,' as Dunya herself says. That word *seems* is the most splendid of all! And this same Dunechka is planning to marry that *seems*! Splendid! Splendid!

". . . However, I'm curious: why did Mama write to me about 'our younger generation'? Simply to characterize that man or with some future goal in mind: to persuade me to look kindly on Mr. Luzhin? Oh, how cunning! I'm curious to resolve one more aspect: to what extent were they both open with each other that day and night, and then during the following days? Were all the *words* spoken honestly between them, or did they both understand that each of them felt the same thing in her heart and mind, and there was no reason to utter it aloud or to talk about it. Most likely, that's part of what happened; it's clear from the letter: he seemed *a bit* harsh, and naïve Mama let her views slip out to Dunya, while she, of course, got angry and 'replied somewhat annoyed.' I'll say! Who wouldn't be enraged when the matter's so clear even without such naïve questions, when it's all been decided, and there's nothing more to say? Then she writes to me, 'Love Dunya, Rodya; she loves you more than she loves herself'; isn't that a feeling of remorse secretly tormenting her for having agreed to sacrifice her daughter for her son? 'You're our hope, you're our everything!' Oh, Mama!" Spite was seething in him more and more intensely, and if he'd encountered Mr. Luzhin at that very moment, he might just have killed him!

"Hmm, it's true," he continued, pursuing the vortex of thoughts spinning in his head. "It's true that 'one must deal with him gradually and carefully to determine what sort of person he is,' but Mr. Luzhin's character is obvious. The main thing is 'he's a businesslike man' and '*seems* to be kind': what a joke that he took the conveyance of their baggage upon himself and that he's shipping a large trunk at his own expense! How could he be unkind? Meanwhile, both of them, his fiancée and her mother, hire a peasant and will ride in his cart, covered with bast matting! (I've gone like that myself.) Never mind! It's only sixty miles and then 'we'll happily travel in a third-class railway car' another six hundred miles. That's sensible: you must cut your coat to fit your cloth; and you, Mr. Luzhin, what about it? After all, she's your fiancée. . . . How could you not know that her mother's borrowing money in advance against her pension to cover the cost of their journey? Of course, here you have a common commercial transaction, an undertaking for mutual profit with equal shares; in other words, he's splitting their expenses in half; 'bread and salt in common, but bring your own tobacco,' as the proverb says. But here that efficient man has hoodwinked them a bit: the baggage costs less than their passage and might even go for free. Why don't they both see it, or do they take no notice of it on purpose? But they're content, content! Just think, these are the flowers: the real fruit lies ahead! It's not his stinginess or miserliness that's important here, but the *tone* of it all. It'll become the tone of their future marriage, it's a prophecy. . . . And Mama, why's she splurging anyway? What'll she have left after she arrives in Petersburg? Three silver rubles or two 'little paper bills,' as that . . . that old pawnbroker says? How does she plan to live in Petersburg afterward? Why, she's already managed to guess for whatever reasons that it'll be *impossible* for her and Dunya to live together after the marriage, even at first. That nice man, most likely, somehow let it *slip*, he gave himself away, even though Mama brushes it off completely, 'I,' she says, 'I'll refuse.' Well then, what will she rely upon: on her hundred and twenty ruble pension, after she deducts the money she owes Afanasy Ivanovich? She'll knit little winter scarves or sew little sleeve covers, and ruin her aging eyes. But those little scarves will add only twenty rubles a year to her hundred and twenty, that much I know. That means they'll still have to rely on Mr. Luzhin's noble generosity: 'He himself,' she says, 'he'll propose it, he'll entreat me.' Not a chance! It's always the same with these Schilleresque beautiful souls:* up to the last moment they dress a person in peacock feathers, until the last moment they hope for the good, not the bad; and although they have a feeling about the other side of the coin, they won't utter a single word about it to themselves for any reason. The thought alone

---

* An ironic reference to the lofty idealism of the German Romantic writer Friedrich Schiller (1759–1805).

offends them; they brush away the truth until the person they've so embellished rubs their noses in it with his own hands. I'm curious as to whether Mr. Luzhin has received any official decorations; I'll bet he has the Order of Saint Anna* and that he wears it at dinners with contractors and merchants. He might even put it on for his wedding. But to hell with him!

"Well, never mind Mama, she can think what she wants—that's who she is; but what about Dunya? Dear Dunechka, I know you so well! You were almost twenty the last time we saw each other: I understood your character already. Mama writes that 'you can tolerate many things.' That much I knew. I knew that two and a half years ago and have been thinking about it since then, precisely about this, that 'Dunya can tolerate many things.' If she can bear Mr. Svidrigaylov and all the aftermath, that means she really has a high tolerance. Now she imagines, together with Mama, that she can even tolerate Mr. Luzhin, expounding his theory regarding the advantage of wives rescued from poverty and husbands who do them such a great honor and make it clear at their very first meeting. Well, then, let's suppose he did 'let it slip,' even though he's a rational man (so perhaps he didn't let it slip at all, but intended to spell it out as early as possible); but Dunya, what about Dunya? It must have been clear to her what sort of person he was and with whom she'd have to live. She would eat only black bread and drink only water rather than sell her soul or give up her moral freedom in exchange for comfort; she wouldn't trade it for all of Schleswig-Holstein,† let alone for Mr. Luzhin. No, that wasn't the Dunya I knew, and . . . and she can't have changed that much now! That's for sure! Those Svidrigaylovs are tough! It's hard to spend your whole life as a governess earning only two hundred rubles and traipsing around the provinces; but still I know my sister would sooner go work with Negroes on a plantation or with Latvian peasants for a Baltic German‡ than defile her spirit and her

---

* A decoration awarded for civilian service to the government.

† Denmark, Austria, and Prussia were engaged in a war over these duchies in 1864.

‡ The plight of Latvian peasants was much in the news in the 1850s and 1860s; they were frequently compared to black American slaves and to Russian serfs.

moral feelings by a relationship with a man she doesn't respect and with whom she has nothing in common—forever, merely for personal gain! Even if Mr. Luzhin were made of the purest gold or solid diamond, even then she wouldn't agree to become Mr. Luzhin's legal concubine! Why is she agreeing now? What's the point? What's the answer? It's clear: she wouldn't sell herself on her own, for her own comfort, even to save herself from death, but she would sell herself for someone else! She'd sell herself for a dear, beloved person! That's the crux of the matter: she's selling herself for her brother and for her mother! She'll sell everything! Oh, with such an opportunity we'll suppress moral feeling; we'll bring our freedom, serenity, even our conscience, everything, everything to the flea market. To hell with life! As long as our beloved creatures are happy. Moreover, we'll devise our own casuistry, we'll learn from the Jesuits, and perhaps we'll reassure ourselves for a while, persuade ourselves that it's necessary, really necessary for a good cause. That's just how we are and it's clear as day. It's clear there's no one else involved except Rodion Romanovich Raskolnikov, standing front and center. Yes, indeed, we can arrange for his happiness, support him at the university, make him a partner in the law office, guarantee his entire future; perhaps afterward he'll become wealthy, honored, and respected, maybe end up famous. And Mother? Why here's her Rodya, her precious Rodya, her firstborn! How could she not sacrifice a daughter for such a firstborn son? Oh, loving, unjust hearts! What of it? Perhaps we wouldn't even reject Sonechka's fate! Sonechka, Sonechka Marmeladova, eternal Sonechka, as long as the world lasts! The sacrifice, have you both measured the enormous sacrifice? Really? Are you strong enough? Will it succeed? Is it sensible? Do you realize, Dunya, that Sonechka's fate is no worse than yours would be with Mr. Luzhin? 'There's no particular love involved,' Mama writes. But what if there's disgust, contempt, loathing—then what? Then it turns out, once more, of course, that you have to '*keep yourself clean*.' Isn't that right? Do you understand, do you really understand what that cleanliness entails? Do you understand that Luzhin's idea of cleanliness is just the same as Sonechka's, perhaps even worse, nastier, filthier, because you, Dunechka, can count on a life of luxury, whereas with Sonya, it's simply a matter of life and death! 'This cleanliness is costly, Dunechka, very costly!' Well, and if you're not up to it, will you repent? So much sorrow, grief, curses, and tears hidden from everyone, so much, because you're no Marfa Petrovna, are you? And what'll happen to our mother then? Why, even now she's distraught, she's suffering; but what about then, when she sees everything as it really is? What about me? What did you really think of me? I don't want your sacrifice, Dunya; I don't want it, Mama! It won't take place as long as I live, it won't, it won't! I won't accept it!"

He suddenly came to his senses and stopped.

"It won't take place? What'll you do so that it won't? Forbid it? What right do you have? What can you promise them in return to have such a right? To devote your whole destiny to them, your future, *when you complete your course of studies and attain a position*? We've heard all that before, and it's just an attempt to frighten us, but now? You have to do something right now, do you understand? What are you doing in the meantime? You're robbing them. They get their money as credit against that hundred-ruble pension or as an advance from the Svidrigaylovs! How will you protect them from those Svidrigaylovs or from Afanasy Ivanovich Vakhrushin, you future millionaire, you, you Zeus, disposing of their fates? In ten years? But in ten years, Mother will have managed to go blind from knitting scarves and perhaps from shedding tears; she'll waste away from fasting; and my sister? Well, just think what can happen to her in ten years or during that time? Can you guess?"

That's how Raskolnikov tortured and teased himself with these questions, even deriving some enjoyment from it. Besides, all these questions weren't new or unexpected, but old ones, painful, and persistent. They'd begun tormenting him a long time ago and had rent his heart to pieces. All this current anguish had taken root in him ages ago; it had grown, accumulated, and of late matured and intensified, having assumed the form of a terrible, wild, fantastic question that tormented his heart and mind, irresistibly demanding a solution. Now the letter from his mother had suddenly struck him like a thunderbolt. Clearly it was unnecessary to be dejected now or to suffer passively, merely considering these questions insoluble; instead, it was absolutely necessary to do something right now, as soon as possible. No matter what, he had to decide to do something, or else . . .

"Or renounce life altogether!" he cried suddenly in a frenzy. "Submit to fate as it is, once and for all, and stifle everything in me, rejecting any right to act, live, or love!"

" 'Do you understand, do you really understand, dear sir, what it means when a person has nowhere else to go?' " All of a sudden he recalled Marmeladov's question from the day before. 'Because everyone has to have somewhere to go . . .' "

He suddenly shuddered: one thought, also from the day before, flashed through his mind again. But he hadn't shuddered because of that thought. He'd known, he'd had a *premonition*, that it would "flash through" his mind and he'd already been expecting it; and this thought was not from the day before at all. But the difference was that a month ago, even as recently as yesterday, it had been only a daydream, but now . . . now it suddenly appeared not as a daydream, but in some new, awe-inspiring, completely unfamiliar form, and all of a sudden he himself became aware of it. . . . His head throbbed, and things grew dark before his eyes.

He glanced around hurriedly; he was looking for something. He wanted to sit down and was searching for a bench. Just then he was making his way along Konnogvardeisky Boulevard. A bench was visible in the distance, about a hundred paces ahead. He walked as quickly as he could, but along the way he had a little adventure that attracted all his attention for a few minutes.

Looking for a bench, he noticed just in front of himself, some twenty paces ahead, a woman walking along the street. At first, he paid her no attention, just as he hadn't focused on other things appearing before him up to now. Many times it had happened that he was walking home and didn't recall the route he'd taken; he'd grown used to that. But there was something strange about this woman that caught his eye from the first glance, so that gradually his attention began to be focused on her—reluctantly at first, as if with annoyance, but then it grew stronger and stronger. Suddenly he wanted to understand precisely what was so strange about her. First of all, she must have been a very young woman; she was walking along bareheaded in the heat, without parasol or gloves, waving her arms in a ludicrous manner. She was wearing a silk dress made of some light fabric ("some kind of cloth"), but in a very odd way, scarcely fastened, and torn at the waist in the back, a large piece of material detached and hanging loose; a little scarf had been tossed over her bare neck, but it protruded crookedly to one side. To top it all off, the young woman was walking unsteadily, stumbling, even swaying from side to side. In the end, this encounter attracted all of Raskolnikov's attention. He caught up with the young woman at the bench, but, upon reaching it, she collapsed into one corner, threw her head against the back of the bench, and closed her eyes, obviously from extreme exhaustion. Examining her closely, he guessed at once that she was completely drunk. It was a strange and absurd sight to behold. He even wondered whether he might be mistaken. Before him was an extremely young face, about sixteen, perhaps even only fifteen—a little face, under fair hair, pretty, but quite flushed and seemingly swollen. The young woman seemed to understand very little; she had crossed one leg over the other and was displaying more of it than was proper, and, by all indications, she had very little awareness that she was outside on the street.

Raskolnikov didn't sit down and didn't want to walk away; he stood in front of her in a quandary. This boulevard was always deserted, and now, after one o'clock and in such heat, there was almost no one there at all. However, just to one side, about fifteen paces away, at the edge of the street, stood a gentleman, who, by all appearances, also very much wanted to approach the young woman for some purpose. He, too, had probably seen her from a distance and was trying to catch up with her, but Raskolnikov had hindered him. The gentleman cast angry glances at him, trying, however, not to make them too obvious, waiting his turn impatiently until the annoying vagabond left. The matter was clear. This gentleman was about thirty, stout, plump, hale and hearty, with pink lips, a little mustache, and very foppishly dressed. Raskolnikov got very angry; he suddenly wanted to insult this fat dandy. For a moment, he left the young woman and approached the gentleman.

"Hey you, you Svidrigaylov! What do you want here?" he cried, clenching his fists and laughing, his lips foaming with rage.

"What's the meaning of this?" the gentleman asked sternly, frowning in haughty astonishment.

"Clear off, that's what!"

"How dare you, you scum!"

He brandished his switch. Raskolnikov threw himself at the man with his fists, without even considering that the plump gentleman could easily get the better of two men his size. But just at that moment someone grabbed him forcefully from behind: a policeman now stood between them.

"Enough, gentlemen, we'll have no fighting in public places, if you please. What do you want? Who are you?" he asked Raskolnikov sternly, noticing his tattered clothes.

Raskolnikov looked at him attentively. He had a manly soldier's face, with a gray mustache, sideburns, and an intelligent expression.

"You're exactly what I want," he cried, grabbing him by the arm. "I'm a former student, Raskolnikov. . . . You should know that, too," he said, turning to the gentleman. "Please come along with me; I'll show you something . . ."

After taking the policeman by the arm, he pulled him over to the bench.

"Here, look, she's completely drunk and was just walking along the boulevard; heaven knows who she is or where she's from, but she doesn't look like that's her profession. Most likely someone got her drunk and tricked her . . . for the first time . . . you understand? Then they turned her loose onto the street. Look, her dress is torn; you can see how it was put on: someone else dressed her, she didn't do it herself, and it was by someone's clumsy hands, men's hands. That's obvious. And now look over here at this dandy, with whom I was just about to fight; I'm not acquainted with him; this is the first time I've seen him. He, too, must have noticed along his way that she was drunk and unaware of where she was and now he very much wants to go up and grab her—since she's in such a state—and take her off somewhere. . . . That's probably what's happening; believe me, I'm not mistaken. I myself saw him observing and following her, but I interfered, and now he's waiting until I leave. He's just withdrawn a little, as if to roll a cigarette. . . . How can we get her away from him? How can we get her home? Think hard!"

The policeman understood everything in an instant and thought about it. The fat gentleman's intention, of course, was easily explicable, but there was the girl. The officer bent over to get a closer look at her, his features reflecting genuine compassion.

"Ah, what a shame!" he said, shaking his head. "She's still just a child. They tricked her, that's for sure. Listen here, miss," he said to her. "Where might you live?" The young woman opened her tired, bleary eyes, regarded her interrogators dully, and waved them away with her arm.

"Listen," said Raskolnikov, "here." (He fumbled in his pocket and pulled out twenty kopecks he found there.) "Here, call a cab and have him take her home. If only we could find out her address!"

"Young lady, hey, young lady," the policeman began again, after taking the money. "I'll call you a cab and get you home myself. Where to? Huh? Where might you be living?"

"G'way! Wha' pests!" muttered the girl, waving her arm again.

"Ah, dear me, this is bad! Ah, aren't you ashamed, young lady? What a shame!" he said, shaking his head again, feeling embarrassed, compassionate, and indignant. "What a dilemma!" he said, turning to Raskolnikov, right there and then looking him over rapidly from head to toe. Raskolnikov must have appeared a bit strange to the policeman: he was in tatters, yet was giving away his own money!

"Did you come upon them far from here?" he asked.

"I tell you, she was walking ahead of me, swaying, right here along the boulevard. When she reached this bench, she collapsed."

"Ah, what shameful things occur nowadays in this world, oh Lord! Such a simple girl, and drunk already! She's been tricked, that's for sure. And her dress is torn. . . . Ah, there's such depravity in this day and age! She's probably from a good family, but without much money. . . . There are many young women just like her nowadays. She looks delicate, too, as if she might be a lady." He bent over her once more.

Perhaps he had daughters of his own like her—"as if she might be a lady and looks delicate," well mannered and already imitating all the latest fashions . . .

"The main thing is," Raskolnikov entreated, "to get her away from that scoundrel! Why is he still here, threatening to commit some outrage? It's absolutely clear what he wants. What a scoundrel, and he won't go away!"

Raskolnikov spoke loudly and pointed directly at him. The man heard him and was about to get angry again, but reconsidered and limited himself merely to a contemptuous glance. Then he slowly withdrew ten paces or so farther and stopped again.

"We may be able to get her away from him, sir," replied the police officer thoughtfully. "If only she'd tell us where to take her, otherwise. . . . Young lady, young lady!" he said, leaning over her.

All of a sudden she opened her eyes wide, looked attentively, as if she understood something or other, stood up from the bench, and walked back in the direction she'd come from.

"Phew, these shameless beasts, always pesterin' me!" she muttered, waving her arm once again. She walked quickly, swaying violently as she had before. The dandy followed her, but along the opposite side of the boulevard, and didn't take his eyes off her.

"Don't worry, I won't let him get her, sir," said the mustachioed policeman and set off after them.

"Hey, such depravity these days!" he repeated aloud with a sigh.

At that moment, it was as if something stung Raskolnikov and seemed to transform him in an instant.

"Hey, listen!" he yelled after the mustachioed policeman.

He turned around.

"Forget it! What's it to you? Let it be! Let him amuse himself." (He pointed at the dandy.) "What's it matter to you?"

The policeman didn't understand and stared at him wide-eyed. Raskolnikov burst into laughter.

"Hey!" said the officer, waving his arm, and followed the dandy and the girl, probably thinking that Raskolnikov was insane or something far worse.

"He's made off with my twenty kopecks," Raskolnikov muttered spitefully when left alone. "Well, let him get some money from that fellow, too, and then he'll let the girl go off with him, and that'll be the end of it. . . . Why am I getting involved here, trying to help? Why should I help? What right do I have to help? Let them devour each other alive—what's it to me? How did I dare part with those twenty kopecks? Were they really mine to give away?"

In spite of these strange words, he felt very wretched. He sat down on the deserted bench. His thoughts were scattered. . . . In general, it was hard for him at that moment to think about anything at all. He wanted to sink into forgetfulness, to forget everything, then wake up and start all over again.

"The poor girl!" he said, looking at the deserted corner of the bench. "She'll come to her senses, weep for a while, and then her mother will find out. . . . At first she'll beat her, then whip her, severely and shamefully, and then, perhaps, drive her away. . . . And if she doesn't drive her away, Darya Frantsevna will get wind of it, and then my little girl will start scurrying from place to place. . . . Then right to the hospital: that's always how it is with those girls who live with their virtuous mothers and who fool around on the sly; well, and then to the hospital again . . . then vodka . . . and taverns . . . back to the hospital . . . in two or three years—she'll be a cripple, and all in all she'll get to live only to eighteen or nineteen. . . . As if I haven't seen the likes of her? How have they all turned out? Just like that. . . . Phew! Let her! That's the way it has to be, they say. A certain percentage, they say, has to go away every year . . . go away somewhere . . . probably to the devil, so as to invigorate the rest and not interfere with them. A percentage!* They really have such fine words: they're so comforting and erudite. Once stated, a percentage, there's nothing more to worry about. If it had been some other word, well then . . . it might be more troubling. . . . What if Dunechka somehow winds up in that percentage? If not that one, then a different one?

"Where am I going?" he wondered to himself. "It's strange. I went out for some reason. As soon as I read the letter, I went out. . . . To Vasilievsky Island, I'm going to Razumikhin, that's where, right

---

* A reference to positivistic and utilitarian ethics.

now . . . I remember. But why on earth? Why exactly did the thought enter my mind to visit Razumikhin now? That's remarkable!"

He was surprised at himself. Razumikhin was one of his former comrades at the university. It was remarkable that Raskolnikov, who'd been at the university, had hardly any comrades, avoided everyone, visited no one, and received them only unwillingly. Soon everyone turned away from him. Somehow he took no part whatsoever in general gatherings, conversations, amusements, anything. He studied diligently, unsparingly, and for that they respected him, but no one liked him. He was very poor and somehow arrogantly proud and uncommunicative; it was as if he were concealing something inside. To some of his comrades it seemed that he regarded them, everyone, from on high, as children, as if he'd surpassed them in his development, knowledge, and convictions, and regarded their convictions and interests as beneath him.

For some reason, he'd become friends with Razumikhin—that is, not exactly friends, but he was more sociable with him, more honest. But it was impossible to be in any other relationship with Razumikhin. He was an unusually cheerful and sociable fellow, good-natured to the point of innocence. Nevertheless, beneath this innocence were concealed both depth and dignity. His best friends realized this, and everyone liked him. He was very clever, although sometimes really naïve. His appearance was expressive—tall, thin, always badly shaven, and he had black hair. Sometimes he got into brawls, and he was reputed to be a very strong man. One night, in a group, he floored all six and a half feet of an officer of the law with one blow. He could drink without limit, but could also abstain totally; at times he could be unacceptably mischievous, but he could also refrain from mischief completely. Razumikhin was also remarkable in that no failures ever troubled him and no adverse circumstances could ever seem to weigh him down. He could be lodged even on a rooftop and endure intolerable hunger and extraordinary cold. He was very poor and he alone supported himself completely, earning money by some sort of work. He knew an enormous number of sources that he could draw upon, naturally, for extra work. One year he didn't heat his room all winter and maintained that it was even more pleasant because a person can sleep better in the cold. At the present time, he had also been forced to leave the university, but not for long; with all his might he was hastening to improve his circumstances so that he could continue his studies. Raskolnikov hadn't been to see him for the last four months or so, and Razumikhin didn't even know where his friend's apartment was. Once somehow, about two months ago, they were about to meet on the street, but Raskolnikov turned away and even crossed over to the other side of the street so he wouldn't be noticed. But Razumikhin, even though he did notice him, passed him by, not wishing to disturb his *friend*.

"As a matter of fact, for some time I've been wanting to ask Razumikhin for work, to arrange some lessons or something else for me . . ." Raskolnikov thought, having hit upon this idea, "but how can he help me now? Suppose he does arrange some lessons, suppose he even shares his last kopecks with me, if he has any to share, so that I could even buy some boots, have my clothes mended, and offer some lessons . . . hmm. Well, and then what? What can I do with a few five-kopeck pieces? Do I really need that now? In truth, it's ridiculous that I've set out to see Razumikhin . . ."

The question of why he'd just set out for Razumikhin's agitated him more than he himself even realized; he searched anxiously for some sinister meaning for himself in this seemingly most ordinary action.

"So, did I really want to resolve this whole matter with Razumikhin alone and find a way out through him?" he asked himself in astonishment.

He reflected, rubbed his forehead, and then, strange to say, after considerable thought, a very curious idea somehow unexpectedly, suddenly, almost of its own accord, entered his head.

"Hmm . . . to Razumikhin," he uttered suddenly with total composure, as if a definitive solution was contained within this idea, "I'll go to Razumikhin, of course I will . . . but—but not now. . . . I'll go see him . . . on another day, I'll go after *that*, when *that's* already been done and everything will begin anew . . ."

All of a sudden, he came to his senses.

"After *that*," he cried, jumping up from the bench. "Will *that* actually happen? Will *that* really and truly occur?"

He abandoned the bench and set off walking, almost running; he wanted to turn back, head home, but suddenly felt terribly repulsed by the idea of going home: it was there, in his corner, in that awful cupboard of a room, that *that* had been ripening for more than a month; he set off wherever his legs would carry him.

His nervous trembling had become somewhat feverish; he even started shivering; he felt a chill, in spite of the great heat. He began, with a kind of effort, almost unconsciously, according to some inner necessity, to examine all the things he was encountering, as if urgently seeking diversion, but he didn't succeed very well and continually lapsed into thought. When, shuddering, he once again lifted his head and glanced around, he immediately forgot what he'd been thinking about and even where he'd been going. In that way, he walked all across Vasilievsky Island and came out to the Little Neva, crossed a bridge, and turned toward the Islands.* At first his tired eyes, accustomed to the dust of the city, the lime plaster, and the huge, crowded, oppressive buildings, took pleasure in the verdure and freshness. There was no stuffiness, no stench, no taverns. But soon these new, pleasant sensations also became painful and annoying. At times he stopped in front of some dacha adorned with greenery, looked through the fence, and in the distance, on the balconies and terraces, glimpsed fashionably dressed women and children running around in the garden. The flowers interested him particularly; he looked at them longest of all. He also encountered luxurious carriages and men and women on horseback; he followed them attentively with his eyes and forgot about them before they had vanished from sight. Once he stopped and counted his money: it turned out that he had about thirty kopecks. "I gave twenty to the policeman and three to Nastasya for the letter—so yesterday

---

* St. Petersburg is situated along the shores of the Neva Bay of the Gulf of Finland and on islands in the river delta.

I must have given the Marmeladovs forty-seven or fifty kopecks," he thought, calculating for some reason, but soon even forgot why he'd taken the money out of his pocket. He remembered why as he was passing an establishment, something like an eating house, and felt that he wanted to have a bite to eat. Upon entering the building, he downed a shot of vodka and ate a little pie with some sort of filling. He finished it along the way. He hadn't had any vodka for a long time and it had an immediate effect, although he had only one shot. His legs suddenly grew heavy, and he began to feel a strong urge to sleep. He started for home; but when he reached Petrovsky Island, he paused in complete exhaustion, turned off the road, walked over to some bushes, dropped down on the grass, and immediately fell sound asleep.

In a morbid condition, our dreams are often distinguished by their extraordinary clarity, intensity, and a heightened resemblance to reality. Sometimes an outrageous scene takes shape, yet its setting and its entire course of development are so plausible and possess such subtle, unexpected details artistically corresponding to the total picture, that the dreamer couldn't possibly conceive of them while awake, even if he were an artist like Pushkin or Turgenev. Such dreams, morbid dreams, are always remembered long afterward and produce a powerful impression on a person's distraught and already overwrought organism.

Raskolnikov had a terrible dream. He dreamt of his childhood, while they were still living in their little town. He was a boy of about seven and was walking along with his father outside town late one holiday afternoon. It was a gray day; the weather was stifling, and the place looked exactly as he remembered it: when compared, it was much more obscure even in his memory than it now appeared in his dream. He could see the town very clearly, as if he held it in the palm of his hand; there were no trees nearby; somewhere very far away, on the edge of the horizon, was a small, dark thicket. A tavern stood a few paces beyond the last garden of the town; it was a large building and always made a very unpleasant impression on him; it even frightened him whenever he happened to walk past it with his father. There was always such a large crowd of people in front of it, shouting, laughing, cursing, howling in such dreadful, hoarse voices, and often brawling; people with such drunken and dreadful mugs were always lingering outside. . . . Whenever he encountered them, he always pressed up against his father and trembled. The country road that ran past the tavern was always so dusty and black. It was a winding road; after about three hundred paces it curved to the right, toward the cemetery. A stone church with a green cupola stood in the middle of this cemetery; he used to go there once or twice a year with his father and mother when a requiem was being sung for his grand-mother who'd died a long time ago and whom he'd never known. They always brought along a special dish on a white plate under a napkin; it was made of sweetened rice with raisins arranged on top in the shape of a cross. He loved this church and its ancient icons, most of which were lacking frames, and the old priest, with his quiv-ering head. Next to his grandmother's grave, marked by a stone, was the small grave of his younger brother, who'd died at the age of six months, and whom he also hadn't known and couldn't remember; but he'd been told that he'd had a younger brother, and every time he visited the cemetery, he crossed himself devoutly and respectfully over the grave, bowing and kissing it. And this is what he dreamt: he's walking along the road with his father toward the cemetery and going past the tavern; he's holding his father's hand and glancing over at it fearfully. This time something in particular draws his attention: it seems to be some special occasion with a motley crowd of townsfolk, peasant women and their husbands, and all sorts of riffraff. They're all drunk and singing songs; next to the tavern porch stands a strange kind of cart. It's one of those large ones to which they harness big draft horses to pull wares and barrels of wine. He's always liked look-ing at these enormous horses, with their long manes, their heavy legs clomping along calmly at a steady pace, pulling mountainous loads, never straining, as if it were even easier for them to pull a load than an empty cart. But now, strange as it seems, a peasant's small, scrawny, light brown nag is harnessed to such a large cart, one of those horses—he's seen it often—that sometimes strain to pull some huge load of firewood or hay, especially if the cart has gotten stuck in the mud or a rut. The peasants always whip the horse so terribly, so very pain-fully, sometimes even across its muzzle and eyes, and he would always feel so sorry, so very sorry to witness it that he would feel like crying, and his mother would always lead him away from the window. Now things are getting extremely boisterous: some very large and extremely drunken peasants in red and blue shirts, their heavy coats slung over their shoulders, come out of the tavern shouting, singing, and playing balalaikas. "Git in, everyone git in!" shouts one peasant, a young lad with a thick neck and a fleshy face, red as a beet, "I'll take ya all. Git in!" But there is a burst of laughter and shouting:

"That ol' nag ain't good for nothin'!"

"Hey, Mikolka, you must be outta yer head to hitch that ol' mare to yer cart!"

"That poor ol' horse must be twenty if she's a day, lads!"

"Git in, I'll take ya all!" Mikolka shouts again, jumping in first, taking hold of the reins, and standing up straight in the front of the cart. "Matvei went off with the bay," he cries from the cart, "and as for this ol' mare here, lads, she's only breakin' my heart: I don't give a damn if it kills 'er; she ain't worth her salt. Git in, I tell ya! I'll make 'er gallop! She'll gallop, all right!" And he takes the whip in his hand, getting ready to thrash the horse with delight.

"What the hell, git in!" laugh several people in the crowd. "You heard 'im, she'll gallop!"

"I bet she ain't galloped in ten years."

"She will now!"

"Don't pity 'er, lads; everyone, bring yer whips, git ready!"

"That's it! Thrash 'er!"

They all clamber into Mikolka's cart with guffaws and wisecracks. There are six lads and room for more. They take along a peasant woman, fat and ruddy. She's wearing red calico, a headdress trimmed with beads, and fur slippers; she's cracking nuts and cackling. The crowd's also laughing; as a matter of fact, how could one keep from laughing at the idea of a broken-down old mare about to gallop, trying to pull such a heavy load! Two lads in the cart grab their whips to help Mikolka. The shout rings out: "Pull!" The mare strains with all her might, but not only can't she gallop, she can barely take a step forward; she merely scrapes her hooves, grunts, and cowers from the blows of the three whips raining down on her like hail. Laughter redoubles in the cart and among the crowd, but Mikolka grows angry and in his rage strikes the little mare with more blows, as if he really thinks she'll be able to gallop.

"Take me along, too, lads!" shouts someone from the crowd who's gotten a taste of the fun.

"Git in! Everyone, git in!" cries Mikolka. "She'll take everyone. I'll flog 'er!" And he whips her and whips her again; in his frenzy, he no longer knows what he's doing.

"Papa, papa," the boy cries to his father. "Papa, what are they doing? Papa, they're beating the poor horse!"

"Let's go, let's go!" his father says. "They're drunk, misbehaving, those fools: let's go. Don't look!" He tries to lead his son away, but the boy breaks from his father's arms; beside himself, he runs toward the horse. But the poor horse is on her last legs. Gasping for breath, she stops, and then tries to pull again, about to drop.

"Beat 'er to death!" cries Mikolka. "That's what it's come to. I'll flog 'er!"

"Aren't you a Christian, you devil?" shouts one old man from the crowd.

"Just imagine, asking an ol' horse like that to pull such a heavy load," adds another.

"You'll do 'er in!" shouts a third.

"Leave me alone! She's mine!* I can do what I want with 'er! Git in, all of ya! Everyone git in! I'm gonna make 'er gallop!"

Suddenly a roar of laughter rings forth and drowns out everything: the little mare couldn't bear the hail of blows and had begun kicking feebly. Even the old man can't resist, and he starts laughing. Indeed: such a broken-down old mare, still kicking!

Two lads from the crowd grab whips and run up to the little horse to start beating her flanks. One stands on each side.

"On 'er muzzle, lash 'er eyes, 'er eyes!" Mikolka screams.

"Let's have a song, lads!" someone cries from the cart, and everyone joins in. A riotous song bursts forth, tambourines jingle, and whis-

---

* The Russian word is *dobro*, which means "property or goods" as well as "good" (as opposed to evil).

tles sound in the chorus. The peasant woman's still cracking nuts and laughing.

. . . The boy runs along the horse's side, rushes ahead, and sees how they're beating her across the eyes, right across her eyes! He starts to cry. His heart rises up in his chest, and his tears begin to flow. One of the men holding a whip lashes the boy across the face; he doesn't feel it; he's wringing his hands, shouting, and then hurls himself at the gray-haired old man with the gray beard, the one who'd been shaking his head before and condemning it all. One peasant woman takes him by the hand and tries to lead him away; but he breaks free from her and runs up to the horse again. The mare's almost at her last gasp but begins kicking again.

"To hell with ya!" screams Mikolka in a fury. He throws his whip away, bends down, and pulls a long, thick wooden shaft from the bottom of his cart; he grabs hold of one end with both hands and raises it ominously above the mare.

"He'll crush 'er!" several people shout.

"He'll kill 'er!"

"She's mine!" screams Mikolka, and swings the shaft with all his might. There is the sound of a heavy thud.

"Thrash 'er, go on! Why'd ya stop?" voices cry out from the crowd.

Mikolka swings a second time, and another mighty blow lands on the unfortunate mare's back. Her hind end sinks down completely, but she jerks and tugs, pulls with her last ounce of strength in different directions, trying to get away; but six whips lash at her from all sides, and once again the shaft is swung and comes crashing down a third time, then a fourth, evenly, with all of the man's might. Mikolka's so furious that he can't finish her off with one blow.

"She's a tough one!" cry several in the crowd.

"She's about to go down, lads, this'll do 'er in!" one enthusiast shouts from the crowd.

"Take an axe to 'er, that's what! Finish 'er off now!" shouts a third.

"Mosquitoes should eat you alive! Make way!" Mikolka shouts ferociously; he tosses the shaft aside, bends over the cart again, and pulls out an iron crowbar. "Watch out!" he cries, and with all his strength he batters his poor little horse. The blow comes crashing down; the mare staggers, drops, tries to pull, but the crowbar comes crashing down again, full force across her back, and she sinks to the ground, as if all four legs had been cut out from under her with one fell swoop.

"Finish 'er off!" yells Mikolka, and now, as if beside himself, he jumps down from the cart. A few lads, also red-faced and drunk, grab whatever comes to hand—whips, sticks, the shaft—and run up to the dying mare. Mikolka stands on one side and begins to strike her back for no reason. The old nag stretches out her muzzle, gasps for breath, and dies.

"He finished 'er off!" shout several voices in the crowd.

"Still, she didn't gallop!"

"She's mine!" yells Mikolka, the crowbar still in his hands, his eyes bloodshot. He stands there as if feeling sorry that there's nothing more to strike.

"It's really true: you're not a Christian!" voices cry from the mob.

But the poor boy's now beside himself. With a shout he pushes his way through the crowd and runs to the mare, embraces her bloody, lifeless muzzle, and kisses her, kisses her eyes, her lips. . . . Then he suddenly springs up and in a rage hurls himself at Mikolka to pummel him with his little fists. At that moment his father, who'd been chasing him, finally grabs hold of him and leads him away from the crowd.

"Let's go! Let's go!" he says to the boy. "Let's go home!"

"Papa! Why did they . . . kill . . . the poor little horse?" he sobs, but his breath falters, and his words emerge as screams from his constricted chest.

"They're drunk, acting up; it's none of our business. Let's go!" says his father. The boy puts his arms around him, but his chest feels tight. He wants to catch his breath, cries out, and wakes up.

Raskolnikov awoke in a sweat, his hair drenched from perspiration; he was panting and raised himself up on his elbows in horror.

"Thank heavens, it was only a dream!" he said, sitting up under the tree and taking in a deep breath. "But what's this all about? Is it a fever beginning? Such a hideous dream!"

He felt as if his whole body had endured a beating; his soul seemed confused and wretched. He sat up and rested his elbows on his knees, supporting his head with both hands.

"Oh, God!" he exclaimed. "Will I really do it, will I really take an axe, hit her over the head with it, crush her skull? I'll slip in the warm, sticky blood, break the lock, steal, and tremble; then I'll hide, all covered in blood . . . with an axe. . . . Oh, Lord, will I really do it?"

As he said this, he trembled like a leaf.

"But what am I thinking?" he continued, exclaiming again as if in deep amazement. "I knew that I wouldn't endure it, so why am I still tormenting myself? Why just yesterday, yesterday, when I went to conduct that . . . *test*, even then I understood perfectly well that I wouldn't endure it. . . . So what am I doing now? Why am I still in doubt? Only yesterday, going down the stairs, I realized how mean, vile, base, how base it all is . . . when I lay *awake* I felt nauseous and horrified by the idea alone.

"No, I can't go through it, I can't! Even if there's no doubt whatsoever in all my calculations, even if everything I've decided this past month is clear as day, as correct as arithmetic. Oh, Lord! I still can't do it! I can't endure it, I can't! Why, why have I been tormenting myself?"

He stood up, looked around in astonishment, as if wondering why he had come here, and set off for Tuchkov Bridge. He was pale, his eyes burning, all his limbs exhausted, but he suddenly seemed able to breathe more easily. He felt that he had gotten rid of a terrible burden, one that had been oppressing him for so long a time, and his soul suddenly seemed light and peaceful. "Oh, Lord!" he prayed. "Show me the way, and I will renounce this cursed . . . scheme of mine!"

Crossing the bridge, he calmly and peacefully looked at the Neva, at the bright setting of the burning red sun. In spite of his weakness, he didn't even feel the least tiredness. It was as if an abscess on his heart that had been coming to a head all month had suddenly burst. Freedom, freedom! Now he was free from all those evil charms, sorcery, witchcraft, and delusions.

Afterward, when he recalled this moment and everything that happened to him during these days, minute by minute, point by point, piece by piece, one circumstance always struck him as a superstitious occurrence, even though in essence it wasn't all that unusual, but later it constantly seemed to be a kind of premonition of his fate.

Namely: he could never understand or explain to himself why, so tired and worn out, when it would have been most advantageous for him to go home by the shortest, most direct route, instead he headed home across Haymarket Square, which was completely unnecessary. The detour was not long, but obvious and totally unneeded. Of course he had returned home dozens of times without recalling the route he took. But why, he always asked himself, why did such an important, such a decisive meeting and, at the same time, such an extremely accidental meeting on the Haymarket (where he had no reason at all to be), why did it take place then, at that hour, at that moment of his life, precisely when he was in that mood, precisely in those circumstances, when only it, that meeting, could have had the most crucial, most decisive impact on his entire fate? It was as if it had been waiting to ambush him!

It was almost nine o'clock when he passed through the Haymarket. All the merchants at their tables, stands, shops, and stalls were locking up their establishments, removing and packing up their wares, and dispersing to their homes, just as their customers were. Around the eating houses on the filthy, stinking lower floors of the buildings on Haymarket Square, and especially in the taverns, were gathered all sorts of craftsmen and ragpickers. Raskolnikov loved these places primarily, just as he did all the nearest lanes, when he would walk the streets aimlessly. Here his tattered clothes attracted no unwarranted attention and he could make his way in any apparel without creating a scandal. At Konnyi Lane, on the corner, stood a tradesman and his wife, a peasant woman, at two tables with wares they were selling: threads, braids, calico head scarves, and so on. They were also packing to go home, but lingered as they chatted with a passing acquaintance. This acquaintance was Lizaveta Ivanovna, or simply Lizaveta, as everyone called her, the younger sister of that very same old woman, Alyona Ivanovna, the widow of a collegiate registrar and moneylender, where Raskolnikov had been the day before when he had gone to pawn his watch and conduct his *test*. . . . He had known everything about this Lizaveta for some time now and was even slightly acquainted with her. She was a tall, awkward, timid, humble unmarried woman, almost feebleminded, thirty-five years old, living as a complete slave in her sister's house, working for her day and night, trembling in her presence, even enduring beatings from her. She was standing deep in thought with a bundle in front of the tradesman and the peasant woman, listening to them attentively. They were explaining something to her with particular passion. When Raskolnikov suddenly caught sight of her, some sort of strange feeling, similar to deepest astonishment, seized him, even though there was nothing astonishing about the meeting.

"You really should decide on your own, Lizaveta Ivanovna," the tradesman was saying loudly. "Come back tomorrow, around seven o'clock. They'll be here, too."

"Tomorrow?" Lizaveta replied slowly and pensively, as if unable to make up her mind.

"That Alyona Ivanovna's really terrified you!" yammered the tradesman's wife, a brash wench. "I look at you and see that you're just like a little child. She's not even your real sister, but your half sister, and she's got you under her thumb."

"This time don't say anything to Alyona Ivanovna," her husband interrupted her. "That's my advice. Come see us without asking her. It's a good deal. Then your sister will figure it out, too."

"Should I come?"

"Seven o'clock tomorrow; they'll be here, too, and you'll decide on your own."

"We'll put up the samovar," the wife added.

"All right, I'll come," said Lizaveta Ivanovna, still pondering, and slowly started on her way.

Raskolnikov passed by just then and didn't overhear any more. He walked by quietly, unnoticed, trying not to miss a single word. His initial amazement was gradually replaced by terror, as if a chill were running up and down his spine. He had found out, he had suddenly, abruptly, and completely unexpectedly found out that tomorrow, at precisely seven o'clock in the evening, Lizaveta, the old woman's sister and the only person who lived with her, would be away from home, and, as a result, the old woman, at precisely seven o'clock in the evening, *would be at home alone.*

There were only a few paces left to his apartment. He entered like a person condemned to death. He wasn't thinking about anything, nor could he even think; he suddenly felt with his entire being that he no longer possessed any freedom of thought or willpower, and that everything had been decided once and for all.

Of course, even if he'd had to wait years for a convenient opportunity, even then, having a plan, it would most likely have been impossible to reckon on a more apparent step toward fulfilling his plan than that which had suddenly been presented now. In any case, it would be difficult to discover the day before and for certain, with greater precision and the least amount of risk, without any dangerous inquiries or investigations, that tomorrow, at such and such a time, such and such an old woman, on whose life an attempt would be made, would be at home alone, absolutely alone.

VI

Afterward Raskolnikov happened to learn somehow precisely why the tradesman and his wife had invited Lizaveta to visit. The matter was most ordinary and didn't involve anything unusual at all. An impoverished family that had recently arrived was selling some items, dresses and so on, all women's goods. Since it was unprofitable to sell them at the market, they were looking for a trader, and Lizaveta engaged in that kind of commerce. She took a commission, went about on business, and had a large clientele because she was so honest and always set the best price: whatever price she stated, she stuck to it. In general she said very little and, as already indicated, she was very humble and timid . . .

But lately Raskolnikov had become superstitious. He retained traces of it for a long time afterward, almost indelibly. And in this entire affair he was always inclined subsequently to see some strangeness, as it were, some mystery, as though particular influences or coincidences were in evidence. Last winter, Pokorev, a student he knew, had been about to leave for Kharkov and mentioned, in passing, the address of an old woman, Alyona Ivanovna, in case he needed to pawn something. He didn't look her up for a long time because he was giving lessons and managing somehow. About a month and a half ago, he remembered her address; he had two items suitable for pawning: his father's old silver watch and a small gold ring with three little red stones, given to him by his sister as a gift, a keepsake, at their parting.

He decided to take the ring; after locating the old woman, right from the first glance, without knowing anything in particular about her, he conceived an insurmountable loathing for her; he received two "small notes" from her and on his way home dropped by a shabby little tavern. He ordered tea, sat down, and lapsed into deep thought. A strange idea had emerged in his head, like a baby chick pecking its way out of its egg, and it interested him greatly.

At another table close to his sat a young officer and a student with whom he was not acquainted and whom he was unable to recall later. They had been playing billiards and were now drinking tea. All of a sudden he heard the student say something to the officer about the money-lender, Alyona Ivanovna, the widow of the collegiate registrar, and he mentioned her address to him. That alone seemed somehow strange to Raskolnikov: he'd just come from there, and here they were talking about her. Of course it was a coincidence, but he couldn't shake off the extremely extraordinary impression, and now it seemed that someone was trying to nudge him in that direction: the student suddenly began telling his comrade various details about this Alyona Ivanovna.

"She's well known," he said. "You can always get some money from her. She as rich as a Yid,* can lend you five thousand just like that, but she doesn't balk at taking a pledge worth a single ruble, either. Many of our students have been to see her. But she's an awful bitch . . ."

He started describing how nasty she was, how willful, and said that if you were even one day late in redeeming your pledge, the item would be gone. She gives you four times less than the pledge is worth, he said, deducts five or even seven percent interest a month, so on and so forth. The student got carried away blabbing and, in addition, said that the old woman has a sister, Lizaveta, whom she beats constantly and keeps totally enslaved, like a little child, even though she herself is small and vile, while Lizaveta's at least six feet tall . . .

"She's quite a phenomenon!" exclaimed the student and burst into laughter.

They began talking about Lizaveta. The student did so with some

---

* Dostoevsky uses the derogatory term for Jew (*zhid*), rather than the neutral word (*evrei*).

particular enjoyment and kept laughing, while the officer listened with great interest and asked the student to send this Lizaveta around to him to mend some linen. Raskolnikov didn't utter a word during this conversation, yet he learned everything all at once: Lizaveta was the old woman's younger half sister (they had different mothers) and was already thirty-five years old. She worked for her sister day and night and served at home in place of a cook and a laundress; she also sewed to order, washed other people's floors, and turned all the money over to her sister. She dared not accept any orders or work without the older woman's permission. The old woman had already drawn up her will, which Lizaveta herself knew, as well as the fact that she wouldn't receive even half a kopeck, except for personal property, chairs, and so forth. All the money was to be left to a monastery in the Novgorod Province, for the eternal remembrance of her soul. Lizaveta was a woman of the lower middle class, not like her sister, who had married an official; she was terribly unattractive, extremely tall, with long, large, apparently turned-out feet, always wore worn-out goatskin shoes, and kept herself neat and clean. The main thing, however, that astonished and amused the student was that Lizaveta was continually pregnant . . .

"But didn't you say she's a freak?" remarked the officer.

"Yes, so dark-skinned, as if she's a disguised soldier, but you know, she's not really a freak. She has such a kind face and eyes. Even very kind. The proof is that many men find her attractive. She's quiet, gentle, meek, and agreeable, agreeable to everything. She even has a very nice smile."

"I see that you fancy her, too, don't you?" the officer asked with a laugh.

"Because of her strangeness. No, but here's what I can tell you. I could kill and rob that cursed old woman, and can assure you, feel no pangs of conscience," the student added passionately.

The officer burst out laughing once again, but Raskolnikov shuddered. This was so strange!

"Allow me to pose a serious question to you," the student said, growing excited. "I was joking just now, of course, but look: on the one hand, here's a stupid, mindless, worthless, spiteful, sick old hag, needed by no one—on the contrary, causing harm to everyone; she herself doesn't know what she's living for, and she'll die of her own accord tomorrow. Do you understand? Do you?"

"Well, I do," replied the officer, staring attentively at his impassioned comrade.

"Listen further. On the other hand, there are young, fresh forces, going to waste for lack of support, by the thousands, all over the place. A hundred, even a thousand good deeds and undertakings could be planned and performed with the old woman's money that's being left in her will to a monastery! Hundreds, maybe thousands of beings could be set on the right path; dozens of families could be rescued from poverty, kept from dissolution, from ruin, debauchery, and venereal hospitals—all this with her wealth. Murder her and take her money and then use it to dedicate yourself to the service of all humanity and to the common good: what do you think, wouldn't thousands of good deeds make up for one little, tiny crime? Thousands of lives saved from wrack and ruin—for one life? One death and a hundred lives in exchange—it's a matter of arithmetic! What's the life of that consumptive, stupid, spiteful old woman worth on the common scale? No more than that of a louse, a cockroach—not even that much, because the old woman's harmful. She consumes other people's lives: just the other day she bit Lizaveta's finger out of spite; they almost had to amputate!"

"Of course she doesn't deserve to live," observed the officer, "but that's nature."

"Hey, friend, nature can be rectified and directed; without that, one would drown in prejudices. Without that, there wouldn't be even one great man. They say, 'duty, conscience.' I don't want to speak against duty and conscience—but how are we to understand them? Wait, I'll pose one more question to you. Listen!"

"No, you wait; I'll pose a question to you. You listen!"

"Go on!"

"Now you're ranting and raving, but tell me this: would you *yourself* kill the old woman or not?"

"Of course not! I'm talking about justice. . . . This has nothing to do with me . . ."

"In my opinion, if you won't dare to do it yourself, it's not a matter of justice! Let's play another round!"

Raskolnikov was in a state of extreme agitation. Of course, all this was the most ordinary, most common run of ideas and conversation of young people, the sort he had heard many times before in other forms and with other themes. But why precisely now did he happen to over-hear just such a conversation and such ideas when in his own mind . . . *exactly the same ideas* had recently arisen? And why precisely at this moment, just as he was carrying the germ of this idea away from the old woman's apartment, had he just happened upon this conversation about her? This coincidence always seemed strange to him. This insig-nificant conversation in the tavern had an extraordinary impact on him during the further development of this affair: it was as if it really was a premonition, a sign . . .

■   ■   ■

After returning from the Haymarket, he threw himself down on his sofa and sat there motionless for a whole hour. Meanwhile, it grew dark; he didn't have any candles, and it never even occurred to him to light one. He couldn't recall a thing: was he really thinking about anything at that time? Finally he felt the return of his recent fever and chills, and surmised with pleasure that he could also lie down on the sofa. Soon a heavy, leaden sleep settled upon him, as if oppressing him.

He slept for an unusually long time and had no dreams. Nastasya, who came in at ten o'clock the next morning, roused him with dif-ficulty. She brought him some tea and bread. The tea was weak once again and supplied in her own teapot.

"Look at him, he's asleep!" she cried with indignation. "He's con-stantly sleeping!"

He raised himself up with effort. His head ached; he tried to stand up, turned around in his little room, and fell back down on the sofa.

"Going back to sleep!" Nastasya cried. "Are you ill, or what?"

He made no reply.

"Want some tea?"

"Later," he said with effort, closing his eyes once more and turning toward the wall. Nastasya stood over him for a while.

"Maybe he really is ill," she said, turned away, and left.

She came in again at two o'clock with some soup. He was lying there just as before. The tea was untouched. Nastasya was offended and began shaking him angrily.

"Still snoozing!" she cried, regarding him with disgust. He raised himself and sat up, but said nothing to her and looked at the floor.

"Are you sick or what?" Nastasya asked and once again received no reply.

"At least you ought to go outside," she said after a brief pause, "and get some fresh air. Are you going to eat something?"

"Later," he said weakly. "Go away!" he added, waving his arm.

She stood there a little while longer, regarded him with compassion, and left the room.

A few minutes later, he raised his head and stared at the tea and soup for a long time. Then he picked up the bread, picked up a spoon, and started to eat.

He ate a little, without much appetite, three or four spoonfuls, as if automatically. His head ached less. After this, he stretched out again on the sofa, but couldn't fall asleep; he lay there without moving, facedown, buried in his pillow. He kept having daydreams, and they were very strange, indeed: most often he imagined that he was somewhere in Africa, in Egypt, on some sort of oasis. A caravan was taking a rest; camels were lying down peacefully; all around, palm trees grew in a complete circle; everyone was having dinner. He kept drinking water, right from the stream that was there beside him, flowing and murmuring. It was cool there and the water was so marvelously blue and cold, running over multicolored stones and over such pure, golden, glistening sand. . . . Suddenly he heard a clock clearly chiming. He shuddered, came to, raised his head, looked out the window, guessed the time, and jumped up, having come to his senses completely, as if someone had torn him away from the sofa. He approached the door on tiptoe, opened it very quietly, and listened for any noise on the staircase below. His heart was pounding dreadfully. But all was quiet on the staircase, as if everyone was asleep. . . . It seemed reckless and bizarre that he could have been sleeping in such oblivion since yesterday, and that he hadn't yet done anything, made any preparations. . . . Meanwhile, perhaps the clock was chiming six o'clock. . . . An unusual, feverish, bewildering burst of activity suddenly overtook him, replacing his sleep and stupor. However, there wasn't much preparation to be done. He made every effort to remember everything and forget nothing; his heart was still pounding, thumping so hard that it became hard for him to breathe. First, he had to make a loop and sew it into his coat—that would take only a minute or so. He groped under his pillow and found among the linen stuffed there an old, ragged, unwashed shirt. He tore off a strip from its tatters, about two inches wide and about fourteen inches long. He folded the strip in two, took off his loose, sturdy summer coat made out of a thick cotton material (it was his only outside coat), and began sewing both ends of the strip together under the left sleeve. His hands shook as he sewed, but he overcame that, so that nothing would be visible from the outside when he put his coat on again. He had long ago prepared a needle and thread, and they had lain wrapped in paper in the little table. As for the loop, that was his own very clever idea: it was designed to hold the axe. After all, he couldn't walk along the street carrying an axe in his hands. And if he were to hide it under his coat, he'd still have to hold it with his hand, but that would be noticeable. Now, with a loop, he merely had to insert the head of the axe and it could hang there comfortably, inside under his armpit, for the whole way there. If he put his hand into his side pocket, he could grasp the handle to make sure it didn't swing; and since the coat was very loose, a genuine sack, the fact that he was keeping hold of it with the hand in his pocket wouldn't be noticed from outside. He had conceived of this loop two weeks ago.

After finishing his sewing, he thrust his fingers into a small opening between his "Turkish" sofa and the floor, groped around inside the left corner, and pulled out the *pledge* he'd prepared long ago and hidden there. This pledge, however, wasn't really a pledge at all, but simply a smoothly fashioned wooden block, no larger than a silver cigarette case in size and thickness. He'd come upon this block by chance on one of his walks, in a certain courtyard where a workshop was located in one wing of the building. Then he'd added a smooth thin metal strip to the block, most likely broken off from something, which he'd also found on the street at the same time. After putting the two pieces together, the metal smaller than the wooden one, he'd tied them together with string, fastened tightly crosswise; then he'd wrapped them neatly and smartly in clean white paper and tied them with a thin ribbon, also crosswise, and made the knot so that it would be difficult to untie. This was done in order to divert the old woman's attention for a while, since she would begin to struggle with the knot and thus he could seize the moment. The iron plate had been added to give the pledge weight, so that at first the old woman wouldn't guess that the "object" was made of wood. All of this had been kept hidden under the sofa in his room until the right moment. Suddenly, just as he'd picked up the pledge, he heard a voice coming from somewhere in the courtyard below shouting:

"It's way past six!"

"Way past! My God!"

He rushed to the door, listened cautiously, grabbed his hat, and started down the thirteen steps, carefully, inaudibly, like a cat. The most important matter lay ahead—stealing an axe from the kitchen. He had long ago decided that he had to use an axe to do the deed. He also had a folding garden knife, but he couldn't rely on a knife or, particularly, on his own strength; therefore, he had settled definitively on an axe. Let us note, by the way, one peculiarity regarding all his definitive decisions already reached in this affair. They shared one strange trait: the more definitive they were, the more outrageous, the more absurd they immediately became in his own eyes. In spite of all his tormenting inner conflict, he never, even for one moment, could believe in the feasibility of his plans during all this time.

And even if it sometimes happened that everything was understood and definitively resolved and that no further doubts remained—in that case, it seems, he would have renounced all of it as an absurdity, a monstrosity, and an impossibility. An enormous number of unresolved points and doubts still remained. As for where he could acquire an axe, that detail didn't faze him in the least, since there was nothing easier. Especially in the evenings, Nastasya was frequently away from the house: either she ran off to the neighbors or to a shop, and the door was always left wide open. The landlady quarreled with her only about this oversight. And so, when the time came, all one had to do was enter the kitchen on the sly and grab the axe, then later, an hour later (when everything was finished), go in and put it back. But doubts still remained: let's suppose he returned an hour later to put it back, but Nastasya was also there. Of course, he'd have to pass by and wait until she left again. What if during that time the axe was needed, she began looking for it, and started yelling—that would arouse suspicion or, at least, grounds for suspicion.

But all of these were just trifles he hadn't even begun to worry about, and there was no time to do so. He thought about the main point and put off the details until such time as he himself *would be sure of everything*. But that seemed decidedly unrealizable. At least, that was how he saw it. He couldn't, for example, imagine that at some time he would stop thinking, get up, and—simply go there. . . . Even his recent test (that is, his visit with the intention of definitively scoping out the place) had been no more than an *attempt at a test*, far from the real thing, merely: "Let me go," he says, "and attempt it; why just dream about it?" And right away he couldn't stand it, spat in disgust, and ran away, furious with himself. Meanwhile, it would seem, he had already completed his entire analysis, in the sense of resolving the question morally: his casuistry had been sharpened like a razor, and he himself could no longer find any conscious objections. In the last instance, he simply no longer trusted himself and stubbornly, slavishly, looked for objections everywhere, gropingly, as if someone were forcing him to do it and dragging him there. This last day, which had dawned so unexpectedly and resolved everything all at once, acted on him almost completely mechanically: it was as if someone took him by the hand and pulled him along behind, irresistibly, blindly, with unnatural strength, without resistance. It was exactly as if a corner of his clothes had become enmeshed in the cogwheel of a machine and it had begun to pull him in.

From the beginning—or, rather, for a long time before—he'd been preoccupied by one question: why are almost all crimes so conspicuous, so easily discovered, and the traces of almost all criminals revealed so obviously? Little by little he arrived at diverse and curious conclusions; in his opinion, the main reason was contained not so much in the material impossibility of concealing the crime, but in the criminal himself: the criminal himself, almost every one of them, at the very moment of the crime, is subject to some failure of willpower and reason, which are replaced, instead, by phenomenal childish thoughtlessness, precisely at the moment when reason and caution are most needed. According to his conviction, it turned out that this eclipse of reason and failure of willpower seize a person just like an illness, develop gradually, and reach their climax not long before the execution of the crime; they continue in the same form at the very moment of the crime and still for some time afterward, depending on the individual; then they pass away, as does any illness. The question remains: does the illness give birth to the crime itself, or is the crime, somehow by its own nature, always accompanied by something like an illness? He still felt it was beyond his power to resolve this question.

After arriving at these conclusions, he decided that in his own case, in this affair, there could be no such morbid reversals, that he would retain his reason and his willpower, essentially, all during the implementation of his plan, for the sole reason that what he had planned— was "not really a crime . . ." We will omit the long process by which he arrived at this last conclusion; even without that, we have raced too far ahead. . . . We will merely add that in general the factual, purely material difficulties of this affair played a very secondary role in his mind. "One must simply exercise one's willpower and all one's reason over these difficulties, and they will all be overcome in their time, when one becomes familiar with all the details of this affair in all of its precision." But the affair hadn't begun. He continued to believe least of all in his final decisions, and when the time came, everything turned out differently, somehow unintentionally, almost unexpectedly.

One extremely insignificant circumstance landed him in an impasse, even before he went down the stairs. Having reached the landlady's kitchen, its door wide open as usual, he carefully peeked in to have a look around beforehand: by any chance was the landlady herself in there during Nastasya's absence, and if not, was the door to her room firmly closed so that she couldn't look out when he entered to take the axe? Imagine his astonishment when he suddenly saw that not only was Nastasya home this time, and in the kitchen, but that she was busy working: she was taking the laundry out of a basket and pinning it up to dry! Seeing him, she stopped hanging the linens, turned to him, and regarded him all the while he was passing. He looked away and walked by, as if not noticing anything. But that spelled the end of the whole affair: he had no axe! He felt utterly defeated.

"What on earth gave me the idea," he wondered as he approached the entranceway, "what gave me the idea that she wouldn't be home precisely at this moment? Why, why, why did I decide this with such certainty?" He was crushed, even somehow humiliated. He felt like mocking himself spitefully. . . . He seethed with blind, brutal rage.

He paused in the entryway to reflect. To set off along the street, just so, as if to take a stroll, just for appearance's sake, was repulsive; to go back home was even more repulsive. "What an opportunity has been lost forever!" he muttered, standing aimlessly in the entrance, directly opposite the door to the caretaker's small dark lodgings, also left open. All of a sudden he shuddered. From the caretaker's room, only two paces away, under a bench on the right, something gleamed before his eyes. . . . He looked around cautiously—no one was there. He approached the lodge on tiptoes, went down two steps, and in a low voice called the caretaker. "Just as I thought, he's not home! He must be close by, however, in the courtyard, because the door's wide open." He rushed at the axe (it was an axe) and pulled it out from under the bench, where it had been lying between two logs; right there, before he left, he secured the axe in the loop, thrust both hands into his pockets, and left the lodge; no one noticed him! "If not by reason, then with the devil's help," he thought, chuckling strangely. This chance occurrence bolstered him enormously.

He walked along the street quietly and *steadily*, without hurrying, so as not to arouse any suspicions. He didn't look at any passersby, even trying not to glance into their faces at all, and to be as unnoticeable as possible. Then he suddenly remembered his hat! "My God! I even had some money a few days ago and could have bought myself a cap!" A curse burst forth from his soul.

Glancing by chance with one eye into a shop, he noticed that there, on the wall clock, it was already ten minutes past seven. He needed to hurry and, at the same time, to make a detour: he wanted to approach the building in a roundabout way, from the other side . . .

Previously, when he had imagined all this, he'd sometimes thought he'd feel very afraid. But now he didn't feel very afraid; in fact, he didn't even feel afraid in the least. He was even preoccupied at the time by some extraneous thoughts, but not for very long. Passing the Yusupov Garden, he was about to consider the idea of placing tall fountains there, thinking how well they would refresh the air in all the squares. Little by little he came to the conviction that if the Summer Garden could be extended to include the entire Field of Mars and even connect it with the gardens at the Mikhailovsky Palace, that it would be a splendid and most useful thing for the city. Then suddenly something caught his interest: why exactly was it that in all large cities people were somehow inclined to live and settle, not out of necessity alone, precisely in those parts of town where there were no gardens, no fountains, and where filth and stench prevailed, as well as all sorts of vileness. Then he recalled his own strolls through the Haymarket, and a moment later he came back to his senses. "What nonsense," he thought. "No, it's better not to think at all!"

"That's probably the way men being led to their execution slide into thinking about all the things they encounter along their way," flashed through his mind, but it merely flashed, like a bolt of lightning; he himself extinguished this thought as quickly as possible. . . . Now he was getting very close; here's the house, here's the gate. Suddenly a clock struck once from somewhere. "What's that? Could it really be half past seven? It couldn't be; the clock must be fast!"

To his good fortune, once again he managed to get through the gates successfully. Moreover, as if on purpose, at that very moment just before him a huge load of hay was entering the gate, completely shielding him while he was walking through the gateway; just as the cart was passing into the courtyard, he managed to slip in to its right. There, on the other side of the cart, he could hear several voices shouting and arguing. But no one had noticed him, and he didn't happen to run into anyone. Many windows looking out onto this huge square courtyard were open at this time, but he didn't raise his head—he didn't have the strength. The staircase leading to the old woman's apartment was close by, just to the right of the gate. He was already on the first step . . .

Catching his breath and pressing his hand against his pounding heart, feeling and adjusting the axe again, he began climbing the stairs cautiously and quietly, constantly listening for any sounds. But this time the staircase was completely empty; all the doors were closed; he didn't encounter anyone at all. However, on the second floor, the door to one empty apartment stood wide open and painters were working inside it, but they didn't even notice him. He stood there a while, thought a bit, and walked on. "Of course, it would be better if no one were here at all, but . . . there are two more floors above them."

But here's the fourth floor, here's the door, and here's the apartment directly opposite; that one's also empty. On the third floor, by all indications, the apartment right under the old woman's was unoccupied as well: the nameplate, nailed to the door, had been removed—they must have moved away! He gasped for breath. For one moment, a thought flashed through his mind: "Should I leave?" But he didn't heed it and began listening at the door to the old woman's apartment: dead silence. Then he listened again for sounds on the staircase, listening attentively, for a long time. . . . Then he glanced around for the last time, crept up to the door, straightened his clothes, and adjusted the axe in its loop again. "Do I look pale . . . very pale?" he wondered. "Am I much too agitated? She's so mistrustful. . . . Shouldn't I wait a little longer . . . until my heart stops pounding?"

But his heart didn't stop. On the contrary, as if intentionally, it pounded even harder and harder and harder. . . . He couldn't stand it anymore, stretched out his hand slowly, and rang the doorbell. A moment later he rang it again, louder.

No answer. There was no reason to ring in vain, and it wasn't in his nature. The old woman, of course, was at home, but she was suspicious and alone. He knew her habits in part . . . and once again he leaned his ear right against her door. Whether his feelings were so attuned (which, in general, is hard to assume), or whether the sound really was audible, all of a sudden he detected what seemed like the cautious movement of a hand on the lock handle and what struck him as the rustle of clothes against the door. Someone stood imperceptibly next to the lock and, precisely the way he was doing outside, was listening, hiding inside, apparently, also pressing one ear to the door . . .

He shifted his position on purpose and muttered something a bit louder so as not to appear as if he were sneaking up; then he rang a third time, but softly, firmly, without any impatience. Recalling it all later, plainly and clearly—this moment was etched in his mind forever—he couldn't understand where he'd acquired so much cunning, all the more so since his mind seemed to cloud over at times, while he was hardly aware of his body. . . . A moment later he heard the bolt being thrown.

VII

Just as before, the door opened a little tiny crack; once again, two sharp, distrustful eyes stared out at him from the darkness. At this point Raskolnikov became confused and was about to make a significant mistake.

Fearing that the old woman would get frightened that they would be all alone, and doubting that his appearance would reassure her, he grabbed the door and tugged it toward him so she wouldn't feel the urge to pull it closed again. Seeing this, she neither pulled the door back nor let go of the handle, the result being that he almost yanked her out onto the landing along with the door. Seeing that she now stood blocking the doorway and wouldn't let him pass, he advanced directly on her. She jumped back in fright, tried to say something, but seemed unable to speak; she stared at him, her eyes open wide.

"Hello, Alyona Ivanovna," he began as casually as possible, but his voice didn't obey, broke off, and began trembling. "I've brought you . . . something . . . let's go over there . . . to the light . . ." And, moving away from her, he entered the room directly, without invitation. The old woman ran in after him and recovered her powers of speech.

"Good Lord! What's all this? Who are you? What do you want?"

"For pity's sake, Alyona Ivanovna . . . you know me . . . Raskolnikov. . . . Here, I've brought the pledge I promised a few days ago . . ." He handed her the packet.

The old woman was about to examine the pledge, but instead stared directly into the eyes of her uninvited guest. She regarded him carefully, spitefully, and suspiciously. A minute passed; it even seemed as if her eyes reflected something like a smirk, as if she'd already guessed his whole plan. He felt that he was becoming confused, almost frightened, so frightened that if she kept staring at him like that without saying anything for another minute or so, he'd run away from her.

"Why are you looking at me like that, as if you don't recognize me?" he asked suddenly, also with anger. "If you want it, take it; if not, I'll go elsewhere; I don't have much time."

He hadn't planned to say this, but it was uttered just so, all by itself.

The old woman came to her senses; her guest's decisive tone, apparently, reassured her.

"Why are you in such a hurry, sir? What is it?" she asked, regarding the pledge.

"A silver cigarette case. I told you last time."

She reached out her hand to take it.

"But why are you so pale? Even your hands are trembling! Have you just come from the baths?"

"It's a fever," he replied abruptly. "You grow pale, like it or not . . . if you don't eat anything," he added, barely able to utter the words. His strength was deserting him again. But his reply seemed credible; the old woman took the pledge.

"What is it?" she asked, staring at Raskolnikov once again, weighing the pledge in her hand.

"It's an item . . . a cigarette case . . . silver. . . . Have a look."

"But it doesn't seem to be silver. . . . Look at how tightly it's wrapped."

Trying to untie the knot and turning toward the light from the window (all of her windows were locked, in spite of the stuffiness), she left him alone for a few seconds and stood with her back to him. He unbuttoned his coat and freed the axe from its loop but didn't remove it yet, merely keeping hold of it with his right hand under his coat. His hands were terribly weak; he felt how with each moment they grew number and more wooden. He was afraid that he might let go of the axe and drop it . . . all of a sudden, his head seemed to be spinning.

"You certainly wrapped it tightly!" cried the old woman in annoyance, moving back in his direction.

There was not a moment to spare. He withdrew the axe completely, raised it with both his arms, hardly aware of himself, and almost with no effort, almost mechanically, brought the butt end down onto her head. It was as if he had no strength. But as soon as he let the axe fall once, he felt a new strength in himself.

The old woman was bareheaded, as always. Her light-colored hair, sparse and with gray patches, smeared generously with grease as usual, was braided into a thin pigtail tucked under a comb of horn that stuck out at the nape of her neck. As a result of her small size, the blow came down on the crown of her head. She cried out, but very weakly, and suddenly collapsed completely onto the floor, although she'd managed to raise both hands to her head. In one she kept hold of the "pledge." Then he struck her a second time and a third with all his might, still using the butt of the axe and hitting her crown. Blood gushed forth as if from an overturned glass, and her body tumbled backward. He stepped away, let her fall, and then bent down to peer into her face; she was already dead. Her eyes were wide open as if they wanted to jump out, and her forehead and entire face were wrinkled and distorted by a spasm.

He placed the axe on the floor next to the dead woman and immediately reached into her pocket, trying not to get covered with her spurting blood—into that same right pocket from which she'd taken her keys the last time. He was in full possession of his faculties; there was no dizziness or blackout, but his hands were still shaking. He remembered afterward that he was very focused, careful, trying hard not to get smeared. . . . He pulled out the keys right away; as before, they were all in one bunch, on one steel ring. He ran into the bedroom at once. It was a very small room with an enormous glass case filled with icons. A large bed stood against the opposite wall, extremely tidy, covered by a silk patchwork quilt. There was a dresser against the third wall. It was odd: as soon as he tried to select a key to the dresser, as soon as he heard the jingling, a shudder seemed to pass through him. He suddenly wanted to abandon the whole thing again and escape. But this feeling lasted for only a moment; it was too late to leave. He even chuckled to himself, as another distressing idea suddenly rushed into his head. All of a sudden it seemed to him that the old woman might still be alive and might revive. Tossing away the keys and leaving the dresser, he ran back to the body, grabbed the axe, and brandished it once again over the old woman, but he didn't lower it. There was no doubt that she was dead. Bending down and peering at her once more, he saw clearly that her skull was broken and even dislodged slightly to one side. He wanted to insert his fingers to feel it, but pulled his hand back; it was obvious even without that. Meanwhile, a large pool of blood had formed. Suddenly he noticed a cord around her neck; he pulled it, but the cord was strong and didn't break; besides, it was soaked in blood. He tried to yank it from her chest, but something got in the way, and it wouldn't budge. In his impatience, he was about to swing the axe again to break the cord right there, on her body, from above, but he didn't dare; with difficulty, soiling both his hands and the axe, after a struggle lasting a few moments, he used the axe to break the cord without touching the body and removed it; he wasn't mistaken—it held a purse. There were two crosses hanging from the cord, one made of cypress and the other of copper and, in addition, a small enameled icon; there, together with them, hung a small greasy suede purse with a steel frame and clasp. The purse was crammed full; Raskolnikov stuffed it into his pocket without examining it and tossed the crosses back onto the old woman's chest; this time he also grabbed the axe and rushed back into the bedroom.

He seized the keys in a terrible hurry and once more began fiddling with them. But somehow he failed to open the dresser: none of the keys fit the locks. It wasn't that his hands were trembling so much, but he kept making mistakes: he would see, for example, that a key wasn't the right one, it didn't work, but he kept on trying it. Suddenly he recalled and realized that there was one large key with a big tooth, together with the other smaller keys, and that it certainly wouldn't fit the dresser (this thought had occurred to him last time), but, rather, would belong to some small trunk or chest in which everything might be hidden. He abandoned the dresser and immediately crawled under the bed, knowing that old women usually store chests under their beds. It was just as he thought: there was a good-sized chest, more than two feet long, with a rounded top, covered in red leather, decorated with small steel tacks. The key with the big tooth was exactly the right one and opened the chest. On top, under a white cloth, lay a rabbit-fur coat, trimmed with red silk; underneath was a silk dress, then a shawl; deeper inside, there appeared to be only clothes. First of all, he began to wipe his bloodstained hands on the red trim. "Red blood will be less noticeable on red silk," he thought and suddenly came to his senses: "Lord! Am I losing my mind, or something?" he thought in fright.

But as soon as he'd touched the clothes, a gold watch slipped out from under the fur coat. He set about rifling through everything inside. In fact, among all the clothes were various gold items—probably all pledges, redeemed and unredeemed: bracelets, chains, earrings, pins, and so forth. Some were in cases, others simply wrapped in newspaper, neatly and carefully, in double sheets, bound with ribbons. Without the least delay, he began stuffing them into the pockets of his trousers and coat without sorting them or opening the wrapping or the cases; but he didn't manage to get very far . . .

Suddenly he heard someone moving in the room where the old woman's body lay. He paused and fell silent as a corpse. But everything was quiet; of course, he must have only imagined it. All of a sudden he heard a feeble cry, as if someone was emitting quiet and intermittent moans, which then subsided. Deadly silence prevailed again for a minute or two. He was squatting down next to the chest and waiting, hardly drawing a breath; but suddenly he jumped up, grabbed the axe, and ran out of the bedroom.

In the middle of the room stood Lizaveta, holding a large bundle; she was staring in a stupor at her murdered sister, looking white as a sheet, as if lacking the strength to scream. Seeing him come running out of the bedroom, she began trembling like a leaf, a gentle trembling, and shudders ran across her entire face; she raised one arm, was about to open her mouth, but still didn't cry out; she began slowly backing away from him into the corner, eyes fixed on him, but still not screaming, as if she didn't have enough breath to scream. He rushed at her with the axe; her lips became so desperately distorted, just like those of little children when they begin to feel frightened of someone, staring at the thing that frightens them, getting ready to cry. This unfortunate Lizaveta was so simple, so helpless, and so terrified once and for all, that she didn't even raise her arms to protect her face, although that would have been the most necessary and natural gesture at that moment, because the axe was raised right above her face. She merely lifted her free left arm ever so slightly, nowhere near her face, and slowly extended it toward him, as if pushing him away. The blow struck her right on the skull, with the blade of the axe, and immediately hacked through the entire upper part of her forehead, almost to her crown. She collapsed onto the floor at once. Raskolnikov was about to panic; he grabbed her bundle, threw it down again, and ran into the entranceway.

Fear was overcoming him more and more, especially after this second, completely unanticipated murder. He wanted to run away as quickly as possible. If, at that moment, he had been in a condition to see and reason more clearly, if he could only have realized the difficulties of his position, all the desperation, all the hideousness, all the absurdity of it, and have understood how many complications, perhaps even outrages, he would still have to commit and surmount in order to escape and reach his home, it's very possible that he'd have given it all up and proceeded immediately to turn himself in, not because he feared for himself, but just as a result of his horror and disgust at what he'd done. His feeling of disgust, especially, grew with every passing moment. Not for anything in the world would he have gone back now to the chest or even entered that room.

But some sort of absentmindedness, as it were, even pensiveness, gradually began to overwhelm him; for a few moments he seemed even to fall into oblivion, or, more accurately, he kept forgetting the main point of the affair and focusing on details. But then, glancing into the kitchen and catching sight of a bucket half full of water sitting on a bench, he decided to rinse off his hands and the axe. His hands were covered with blood and sticky. He lowered the axe blade into the water, grabbed a piece of soap from a chipped saucer sitting on the windowsill, and began washing his hands right in the bucket. After doing so, he pulled out the axe, wiped off the iron blade, and for a long time, almost three minutes, scrubbed the wooden handle where it was covered in blood, even using soap to wash it away. Then he wiped everything with some laundry that was drying on a rope stretched across the kitchen; then, for a long time, he stood next to the window and with great attention examined the axe. There were no traces of blood left on it, but the wood was still damp. He carefully replaced the axe in its loop under his coat. Then, making use of the limited light in the dark kitchen, he inspected his coat, trousers, and boots. At first glance, there appeared to be nothing wrong: only a few spots of blood on his boots. He soaked a rag and wiped them off. He knew, however, that he was unable to see very well; perhaps there was something he hadn't noticed that might strike someone. He stood in the middle of the room, deep in thought. A tormenting, dark idea arose in him—the idea that he was behaving like a madman and that at this moment he was no longer able to reason or defend himself, and that perhaps it was totally unnecessary to do what he was doing now. . . . "My God! I must get away, run away!" he muttered and rushed into the entrance hall. But there such a terror awaited him—one, of course, that he'd never experienced before.

He stood there, stared, and didn't believe his eyes: the door, the outer door from the entrance hall onto the landing, the one he'd rung and entered not that long ago, stood open, open as wide as his hand: no lock, no bolt, all the time, during all this time! The old woman hadn't locked it after him, perhaps out of caution. But, by God! Then he'd seen Lizaveta! How, how on earth could he have failed to guess that she'd come from somewhere! She hadn't come through the wall.

He rushed to the door and threw the bolt.

"But no, that's not right either! I must leave, leave . . ."

He undid the bolt, opened the door, and listened on the staircase.

He stood there, listening, for a long time. Somewhere far off, down below, probably near the gates, two voices could be heard shouting loudly and shrilly, arguing and quarreling. "What are they doing?" He waited patiently. At last everything quieted down all at once, as if cut off; the men departed. He was about to leave, but all of a sudden a door one floor below opened noisily onto the landing, and someone started down the stairs, humming a tune. "They're making so much noise!" flashed through his head. He closed the door behind himself again and waited a little while. At last everything became still; there wasn't a soul. He was about to start down the stairs when suddenly he heard footsteps again.

The steps were very far off, at the bottom of the stairs, but he later recalled very clearly and distinctly that from the first sound, for some reason or other, he began to suspect that the footsteps were definitely coming *here*, that is, up to the fourth floor, to the old woman. Why? Were the sounds so special, so noteworthy, or what? The steps were heavy, even, unhurried. Now *he* had passed the first floor and kept on climbing; the steps were becoming more and more audible! He could hear a man's serious shortness of breath. He was approaching the third floor. . . . He was coming here! All of a sudden Raskolnikov felt paralyzed, as if he were asleep, dreaming that he was being chased; they were getting closer, wanting to kill him, while he was rooted to the spot and unable even to move his arms.

At last, when the visitor began climbing up to the fourth floor, only then did Raskolnikov suddenly shudder and manage to slip swiftly and nimbly back from the landing into the apartment and close the door behind himself. Then he grabbed the bolt and quietly, inaudibly slid it into place. Instinct helped him. After he did all this, he stood still without breathing, on the other side of the door. The unwelcome guest was already standing at the door, too. Now they stood on opposite sides, just as he had before with the old woman when the door had separated them, and he listened very carefully.

The visitor drew several deep breaths. "He must be large and heavy," thought Raskolnikov, squeezing the axe in his hand. As a matter of fact, it was all happening just like in a dream. The guest reached for the bell and pulled it firmly.

As soon as the tinny sound of the bell jingled, it suddenly seemed to him that there was some movement inside the room. For a few seconds he even listened in earnest. The stranger rang again, waited a while, and then suddenly, in his impatience, began tugging at the door handle with all his might. Raskolnikov stared in horror as the bolt jiggled in its latch, and he waited with dull fear for the bolt to pop out. In fact, that seemed very possible, the tugging was so violent. He quickly thought about holding the bolt with his hand, but then *he* would guess what was happening. His head was beginning to spin again. "I'm going to fall!" flashed into his mind, but the stranger began speaking, and Raskolnikov came to his senses immediately.

"What the hell are they doing in there? Are they dead to the world or did someone strangle them? Goddamn them!" he bellowed as if from a barrel. "Hey, Alyona Ivanovna, you old witch! Lizaveta Ivanovna, you indescribable beauty! Open up! Hey, goddammit, are you asleep or what?"

Once again, in a rage, he pulled the bell with all his might a dozen or more times. He was, clearly, a commanding presence and very familiar with this place.

Suddenly, at that very moment, some light, hurried footsteps could be heard not far away on the stairs. Someone else was approaching. Raskolnikov hadn't managed to discern that at first.

"Isn't anyone there?" cried the man distinctly and cheerfully, directly addressing the first visitor, who was still continuing to pull the doorbell. "Hello, Kokh!"

"Judging by his voice, he must be very young," Raskolnikov reflected suddenly.

"The devil only knows. I've almost broken the lock," replied Kokh. "And how does it happen that you know my name?"

"What do you mean? We met three days ago at the Gambrinus tavern; I beat you in three rounds of billiards!"

"Ahhh . . ."

"So they aren't in there? That's strange. Rather, it's terribly stupid. Where could the old woman go? I've got business to do."

"So do I, my friend."

"Well, what's to be done? That's it, I guess. Damn! I hoped to get some cash!" cried the young man.

"That's it, of course. Why agree on a meeting? That witch, she set the time herself. I even made a detour. Where in hell could she go gallivanting, I don't understand. The old witch stays at home all year, mopes around, her feet ache, and now, all of a sudden, she picks up and goes out for a stroll!"

"Maybe we should ask the caretaker?"

"What?"

"Where they went and when they'll be back?"

"Hmm . . . what the hell . . . we'll ask. But she doesn't go anywhere . . ." He tried the door handle again. "Damn, there's nothing to
be done—let's go!"

"Wait!" the young man cried suddenly. "Look: you see how the
door gives a bit when you pull at it?"

"So?"

"That means it's not locked, only fastened, I mean bolted! Do you
hear how the bolt rattles?"

"So?"

"Why don't you understand? That means someone's at home. If
they'd both left, the door would have been locked with a key from the
outside, and not with the bolt from inside. Listen—do you hear how
the bolt rattles? To fasten it from inside, someone has to be at home,
do you understand? In other words, they're home, just not opening
the door."

"Ah! Indeed!" cried the astonished Kokh. "So they're really in
there!" He began rattling the door violently.

"Wait!" cried the young man again. "Don't yank it! Something's
not right about it. You rang the bell, pulled it, but they didn't open;
that means they've either both fainted, or else . . ."

"What?"

"Here's what: let's go find the caretaker; let him rouse them."

"Right!" They both started downstairs.

"Wait! You stay here while I run down for the caretaker."

"Why should I stay?"

"Who knows what might happen?"

"All right . . ."

"I'm preparing to become an examining magistrate!* It's obvious,
ob-vi-ous that something's not right here," cried the young man, and
he set off down the stairs at a run.

Kokh remained there, gently rang the bell again, which jingled
only once; then, as if reflecting and examining, he tried the door handle again, moving it up and down, to convince himself once more that

---

* A new position in the Russian civil service created by the legal reforms of 1864, to carry out
investigations into allegations of criminality.

it was latched by only the bolt. Then, puffing, he bent over and began peering into the keyhole; but the key had been inserted from inside, and therefore nothing was visible.

Raskolnikov stood there clutching his axe. He seemed to be in a stupor. He was even ready to fight with them if they entered the room. While they were knocking and talking, the idea occurred to him several times of ending it all and calling out to them from his side of the door. At times he wanted to begin swearing at them, taunting them, until they managed to force the door open. "Hurry up!" flashed through his mind.

"What's happened to him, damn it . . ."

Time was passing, one minute, then another—no one came. Kokh began to stir.

"Damn it all!" he cried suddenly and impatiently; abandoning his lookout; he, too, headed down, hastening, his boots pounding on the stairs. His footsteps receded.

"Lord, what should I do?"

Raskolnikov slid the bolt and opened the door—he heard nothing; all of a sudden, completely without thinking, he went out, closed the door behind himself as tightly as he could, and headed downstairs.

He had already descended three floors when he suddenly heard a loud noise below—where could he go? There was nowhere to hide. He started to run back upstairs, toward the apartment.

"Hey, damn it, you devil! Wait!"

Someone shouted from one of the apartments below and didn't exactly run but seemed, rather, to catapult down the stairs, shouting as loudly as he could:

"Mitka! Mitka! Mitka! Mitka! Mitka! The devil take you!"

The shout ended with a shriek; the last sounds could be heard from outside in the courtyard; then everything fell silent. But just at that same moment several people, talking loudly and quickly, began climbing the stairs noisily. There were three or four of them. He heard the clear voice of the young man: "It's them!"

In complete despair, he headed back downstairs to confront them: come what may! If they stop him, all's lost; if they let him pass, all's still lost: they'll remember him. They were about to meet; only one floor separated them—then, all of sudden, deliverance! On the right, just a few steps away from him, was the empty apartment, its door wide open, the one on the second floor in which the painters had been working, and now, as if intentionally, they had left. They must be the men who'd just run out with so much shouting. The floors had just been painted; in the middle of the room stood a small tub, a crock of paint, and a brush. In a flash, he ducked through the open doorway and concealed himself behind a door, just in time: they were now standing on the same landing. Then they turned and went up to the fourth floor, conversing loudly. He waited, tiptoed out, and ran downstairs.

There was no one on the staircase! Nor in the gateway. He passed through it and turned left, onto the street.

He knew very well, he knew extremely well, that at this very moment, they were already in the apartment; they were astonished at seeing it unlocked, when it had been locked just before; they were already staring at the bodies; no more than a minute would pass before they would begin to conjecture and realize that the murderer had just been there and had managed to hide somewhere, slip past them, and escape; perhaps they would guess that he had stopped in the open apartment while they were making their way upstairs. Meanwhile, under no pretext did he dare increase his pace significantly, although there remained about a hundred steps to the first turn. "Shouldn't I slip into some gateway and wait there in an unfamiliar staircase? No, bad idea! Should I get rid of the axe? Should I take a cab? Bad idea, very bad!"

Finally he reached a narrow street; half dead, he turned into it; here he was somewhat safe and understood this: there would be less suspicion, a crowd of people scurrying about, and he would blend into it like a grain of sand. But all of these torments had rendered him so weak that he could scarcely move. Drops of sweat poured off him; his neck was entirely soaked. "Drunk as a skunk!" someone shouted at him when he came out to the canal.

He was now beside himself; the farther he went, the worse he felt. He remembered, however, that as soon as he'd emerged along the canal, he'd grown afraid that there were so few people that he'd be more noticeable, so he wanted to turn back into the narrow street. In spite of the fact that he was almost collapsing, he managed to make a detour and approach his house from the opposite side.

He was not in complete control of his faculties when he turned into the gate of his own building; at any rate, only when he'd already reached the staircase did he remember about the axe. For the moment, there remained a very important problem: to return the axe to its place, attracting as little attention as possible. Of course, he was no longer able to realize that it might be much better not to put it back at all in its former place, but to toss it away, though somewhat later, into some other courtyard.

Everything, however, turned out all right. The door to the caretaker's lodge was closed but not locked; therefore, he was probably at home. Though even before that he'd already lost the ability to conceive of something else, so he went straight up to the door of the lodge and opened it. If the caretaker had asked, "What do you want?," perhaps he would have handed over the axe straight away. But once again the caretaker wasn't there, and he managed to return it to its previous place under the bench; he even covered it with a log as before. After that he met no one, not a single soul, on his way up to his room; the landlady's door was closed and locked. Entering his own room, he threw himself down on his sofa just as he was. He didn't sleep, but lay there in a trance. If someone had come into his room then, he would have jumped up and started shouting. Shreds and fragments of thoughts swarmed in his head; but he couldn't seize on any of them, couldn't focus on any of them, in spite of all his efforts . . .

PART

II

I

He lay there for a long time. Periodically he would seem to awaken and notice that it was already dark, but it never occurred to him to get up. At last he noticed that it had grown as light as day. He lay there on his sofa facedown, still dazed from his recent stupor. Terrible, desperate, shrill shrieks reached him from the street, sounds he heard every night under his window sometime after two in the morning. That was what woke him now as well. "Ah! Drunks are leaving the taverns," he thought. "It's after two o'clock." Suddenly he jumped as if someone had torn him from the sofa. "What! Already after two!" He sat up on the sofa—and then remembered everything. All at once he recalled it all in one moment.

At first he thought he would lose his mind. A terrible feeling of coldness seized him; but that was also a result of the fever that had begun long before, while he was still asleep. Now he suddenly felt such a chill that his teeth began chattering violently; he started shaking all over. He opened the door and listened: everything was absolutely still in the house. He looked himself over in astonishment and then surveyed everything else in his room and couldn't understand how he could have come in yesterday and failed to secure his own door with the bolt and how he had thrown himself down on his sofa not only without undressing, but even without removing his hat: it had fallen off and lay there on the floor next to his pillow. "If someone had come in, what would he have thought? That I was drunk, but . . ." He rushed

to the little window. There was sufficient light, and he began examining himself hastily, all over, from head to toe, all of his clothes: were
there perhaps any traces? But it was impossible; still trembling from
his chill, he began taking everything off and examining it again. He
turned everything over, to the last thread and shred; not trusting himself, he repeated the inspection several times. But there was nothing to
see; it seemed that there were no traces. Only where his trousers were
frayed and the fringe hung down did there remain some thick spots of
dried blood. He grabbed his large pocketknife and cut off the fringe.
There seemed to be nothing else. He suddenly recalled that the purse
and the items he'd taken from the old woman's chest were still in his
pockets! Up to this point, he hadn't even thought about taking them
out and hiding them! He hadn't even thought about them just now
as he was inspecting his clothes! Why not? In an instant, he rushed
to take the items out and toss them onto the table. After removing
everything, even turning his pockets inside out to make sure nothing was left, he carried the whole pile over to the corner of his room.
There, down below, was a spot where the wallpaper had been torn
away from the wall. He immediately began stuffing everything into
this hole underneath the torn wallpaper. "It fits! Everything's out of
sight—the purse, too!" he thought elatedly, standing up and regarding the corner foolishly, looking at the hole where the wallpaper now
bulged even more than before. Suddenly he shuddered all over in horror. "My God," he whispered in despair, "what's the matter with me? Is
it really concealed? Is this how one hides things?"

True, he hadn't counted on having any items; he'd thought there
would be only cash, and therefore he hadn't prepared a hiding place.
"But now, am I happy now?" he wondered. "Is this how one hides
things? I'm really losing my mind!" He sat down on his sofa in exhaustion, and right away an unbearable chill took hold of him again. He
automatically grabbed his winter coat, the one he'd worn as a student;
it was lying next to him on a chair and was warm, but already almost in
tatters. He covered himself with it; sleep and delirium overcame him
at once. He sank into semiconsciousness.

Not more than five minutes later he jumped up again and, all at
once, in a frenzy, flung himself at his clothes again. "How could I fall

back to sleep when nothing's been done? So it is, so it is: I haven't even removed the loop under my arm! I forgot, I forgot all about it! What a piece of evidence!" He ripped out the loop and quickly began tearing it to pieces, stuffing them under his pillow with his linen. "Shreds of torn canvas won't arouse any suspicion; so it seems, so it seems!" he repeated, standing in the middle of the room, and with painfully strained attention he began glancing around again, at the floor and everywhere else, to see if he might have forgotten something. The certainty that everything, even his memory, even his basic understanding, was deserting him was starting to torment him unbearably. "What, is it really starting, is this the punishment beginning? So that's it, that's what it is!" In fact, shreds of the fringe he had cut off his trousers were lying there on the floor in the middle of the room, so that the first person who came in would notice them! "What's happening to me?" he cried out once again, like a lost soul.

Then a strange thought occurred to him: perhaps all of his clothes were bloodstained, perhaps there were many spots, and he merely didn't see them, didn't notice them because his reason had been weakened, shattered . . . his mind darkened. . . . Suddenly he recalled that there was also blood on the purse. "Bah! So there must also be blood in my pocket, because I shoved the damp purse into it!" He turned his pocket inside out in an instant and—so it was—there were spots, traces of blood on the pocket lining! "My reason must not have deserted me entirely; I must still have my ability to reason and my memory, if I remembered and figured that out myself!" he thought elatedly, taking a deep, joyful breath of air. "It's simply feverish weakness, momentary delirium," he decided and he tore out the whole lining of his left trouser pocket. At that moment, a ray of sunlight lit up his left boot: on his sock, which stuck out, there seemed to be more spots. He shook his boot off his foot. "It's really true! The whole end of my sock is soaked through with blood." He must have stepped carelessly into that puddle then . . . "What can I do with it now? Where could I stash the sock, the fringe, the lining?"

He gathered everything up in his hands and stood in the middle of the room. "Into the stove? But they'll begin looking there first. Burn it? With what? I don't even have any matches. No, it's better to go throw it all away somewhere. Yes! Better to throw it all away!" he repeated, sitting back down on the sofa. "And right now, this very minute, without delay!" But instead of that, his head slid down onto the pillow again; an unbearable chill rendered him numb once more; he pulled his coat over himself again. For several long hours he kept imagining in fits that "right now, without putting it off, he must go somewhere and throw it all away, get rid of it, at once, as soon as possible!" Several times he wanted to tear himself away from the sofa, tried to stand up, but couldn't. At long last, a firm knock on the door roused him.

"Open up. Are you alive or not? Still dead asleep!" cried Nastasya, banging on the door with her fist. "He sleeps for days at a time, just like a mutt! What a mutt you are! Open up, will you? It's past ten."

"Maybe he's not home," said a male voice.

"Bah! It's the caretaker. . . . What does he want?" Raskolnikov wondered.

He jumped up and sat on the sofa. His heart was pounding so hard that it was aching.

"Then who fastened the hook?" Nastasya retorted, "See, he's started locking the door! You think they'll come and steal you away? Open up, you thinker, you, wake up!"

"What do they want? Why's the caretaker here? It's all clear. Resist or open the door? To hell with it!"

He stretched forward, leaned over, and raised the hook.

His room was so small that he could undo the hook without even getting out of bed.

Just as he thought: the caretaker and Nastasya were standing there.

Nastasya looked him over somewhat strangely. He cast a challenging and desperate glance at the caretaker, who silently handed him a gray piece of paper folded in two, sealed with bottle wax.

"It's a notice, from the office," he said, handing him the paper.

"From what office?"

"The police. You're being summoned to their office. It's clear what office it is."

"The police? What for?"

"How should I know? They demand it, so you go." He looked at him carefully, glanced all around, and turned to go.

"Are you really ill?" Nastasya asked, without taking her eyes off him. The caretaker also turned his head to look for a minute. "He's had a fever since yesterday," she added.

Raskolnikov made no reply and held the paper in his hands without opening it.

"You'd better not get up," Nastasya continued, feeling sorry for him and seeing that he was lowering his legs from the sofa. "If you're sick, then don't go; it'll wait. What's that in your hands?"

He looked down: in his right hand he held the torn scraps of lining, the sock, and the tatters of his torn-out pocket. He had slept with them in his hand. Later on, thinking about it, he remembered that and, half-awakening with his fever, clasped it all tightly in his hand and dozed off once again.

"Just look, he's gathered some rags and is sleeping with them, as if they were a treasure," Nastasya said, then went off into fits of painfully nervous laughter. In an instant, he shoved everything under his coat and fixed his eyes on her. Even though at that moment he could understand very little, he still felt that if the police were coming to arrest him, they wouldn't be treating him like this. "But . . . the police?"

"Would you like some tea? Yes or no? I'll bring you some; there's some left . . ."

"No . . . I'll go; I'll go right now," he muttered, getting up.

"You'll go, will you, but will you make it down the stairs?"

"I'll go . . ."

"Do as you like."

She left, following the caretaker. He rushed toward the light to examine his sock and the fringe: "There are some spots, but they're not too conspicuous; everything's so dirty, worn out, and faded. If someone didn't know about it beforehand—he wouldn't notice a thing. Nastasya couldn't see anything from a distance, thank God!" Then he opened the notice with trepidation and began reading; he read for a long time and finally understood. It was an ordinary summons from the local police to appear that very day at half past nine at the district superintendent's office.

"When has this ever happened before? I have no dealings with the police at all! And why exactly today?" he wondered in painful confusion. "Oh, Lord, let it end soon!" He was about to throw himself onto his knees to pray, but then he started laughing, not at the idea of prayer, but at himself. He began dressing hurriedly. A thought suddenly occurred to him: "If I'm done for, then so be it, it doesn't matter! I'll put on my sock! It'll get dirty in the dust, and the traces will vanish." But as soon as he put it on, he tore it off in disgust and horror. When he realized that he had no other sock, he put it back on again— and started laughing once more. "All this is so ordinary, it's all relative, all purely form." That thought occurred to him just in passing, merely at the far edge of his mind, while his entire body was trembling. "But I did put it on! All the same, I put it on!" His laughter, however, was immediately replaced by despair. "No, this is more than I can bear," he thought. His legs were shaky—"Out of fear," he muttered to himself. His head was spinning and aching from the fever. "It's a trick! They want to entrap me with their guile and then, all of a sudden, throw me off guard," he continued muttering to himself as he headed out onto the stairs. "The bad thing is that I'm almost delirious. . . . I might utter some stupid lie . . ."

On the stairs, he remembered that he was leaving all those things just as they were in the hole behind the wallpaper. "What if they come on purpose to search the place while I'm out," he wondered, hesitating. But such despair and such a cynical view of his demise, if one could call it that, suddenly overcame him, and he waved his arm with indifference and carried on.

"If only it would end soon!"

Once again it was unbearably hot outside: if only there'd been a drop or two of rain these last few days. Again dust, bricks, and plaster, again the stench of shops and taverns, again the constant drunks, the Finnish peddlers, and the run-down cabs. The sun shone so brightly in his eyes that it was painful for him to see and he felt very dizzy—the usual sensation of a feverish person who suddenly comes outside into the blinding sunshine.

Reaching the turn into *yesterday's* street, he glanced with tormenting agitation, at *that* house . . . and immediately turned away.

"If they ask, perhaps I'll even tell them," he thought as he approached the police station.

The office was about three hundred yards from his house. They had just moved into a new place, a new building, on the fourth floor. He had been to the former location once briefly, but a long time ago. Entering the gates, he saw a staircase on the right, where a peasant was coming down with a registration book in hand: "He must be a caretaker, so the office must be in here." He started up the stairs on this hunch. He didn't want to ask anyone about anything.

"I'll go in, fall on my knees, and tell them everything," he thought as he reached the fourth floor.

The staircase was narrow, steep, and covered in dirty dishwater. The kitchens of all the apartments on all four floors opened onto this staircase and remained open almost all day long. As a result, it was terribly stuffy. Caretakers with registration books under their arms filed up and down the stairs, as well as police messengers and various people of both sexes—visitors. The door to the office itself was also wide open. He entered and stood in the vestibule. Some peasants were waiting inside. The stuffiness there was also extreme; in addition, there was a nauseating smell of fresh paint, not yet dry, that had been mixed with rancid oil and used to repaint the walls. After waiting a little while, he decided to advance into the next room. The rooms were all tiny and had low ceilings. Terrible impatience pulled him farther and farther in. No one took any notice of him. Some clerks were sitting and writing in the second room, dressed only a little bit better than he was, and they were all strange-looking. He turned to one of them.

"What do you want here?"

He showed the summons he'd received from the office.

"Are you a student?" asked the man who'd glanced at the paper.

"A former student, yes."

The clerk looked him over, but without any curiosity. He was a particularly disheveled fellow with a steadfast look in his eyes.

"I won't learn anything from this fellow because he doesn't care in the least," thought Raskolnikov.

"Go over there, to the head clerk," he said and directed him to the last room.

He entered that room (the fourth in the row); it was cramped and crowded with people—they were dressed a little more neatly than those in the other rooms. There were two ladies among the callers. One was in mourning attire, poorly dressed, sitting at the table opposite the head clerk and writing down something he was dictating. The other lady, very plump, had a dark red complexion with spots; a distinguished woman, very elegantly attired, with a brooch the size of a saucer on her bosom, she stood off to one side, waiting. Raskolnikov thrust his summons at the head clerk. He looked at it fleetingly and said, "Wait," and continued to deal with the lady in mourning.

Raskolnikov breathed more easily. "It can't be that!" Little by little he began to feel calmer; he used all his strength to urge himself to cheer up and gather his thoughts.

"Some stupid thing, some very insignificant oversight, and I might have given myself away! Hmm . . . it's a pity there's no air in here," he added. "It's so stuffy. . . . My head's spinning even more . . . and my mind, too . . ."

He felt a terrible, sweeping sense of disorder. He was afraid of losing his self-control. He tried to grab hold of something and focus on it, something completely marginal, but he was unable to do so. The head clerk, however, interested him greatly: he tried to guess something about him from his face, to penetrate to his core. He was a very young man, about twenty-two, with a dark complexion and a lively countenance, seemingly older than his years, dressed fashionably like a dandy, his hair parted to the back of his head, well combed and well greased, with a large number of different rings on his white fingers scrubbed clean with a brush, and wearing gold chains on his vest. He even spoke a few words of decent French with a foreigner who was waiting there.

"Luiza Ivanovna, why don't you take a seat?" he said in passing to the well-dressed lady with the dark red complexion, who was still standing there, as if she dared not sit down, although a chair was nearby.

"Ich danke," she said softly, and lowered herself onto the chair with a sound of rustling silk. Her light blue dress trimmed with white lace spread out around her chair like a balloon and filled almost half the room. There was a strong odor of perfume. The lady was obviously embarrassed that she was occupying so much space and giving off the scent of her perfume, although she smiled in a way that combined both cowardice and impudence, but with evident discomfort.

The lady in mourning finished at last and was about to stand up. All of a sudden, an officer entered, raucously strutting and swaggering in an extremely sprightly way, threw his cockaded cap on the table, and sat down in an armchair. Upon seeing him, the elegant lady immediately jumped up and curtsied to him with great gusto. While the officer didn't pay her the least bit of attention, she dared not remain seated in his presence any longer. He was a lieutenant, the police superintendent's assistant, and had a reddish mustache protruding horizontally in both directions and extremely fine facial features, expressing nothing whatsoever, however, except a certain insolence. He regarded Raskolnikov out of the corner of his eye, in part with indignation: his apparel was too disgraceful and, in spite of all his wretchedness, his behavior didn't fit his dress; Raskolnikov, with a lack of care, stared at him so directly and for so long that the officer felt offended.

"What are you doing here?" he shouted, probably astonished that such a ragged fellow hadn't considered effacing himself when confronted with his scorching gaze.

"I was sent for . . . by this summons," Raskolnikov managed to explain.

"It concerns the recovery of some money from him, from that *student*," the head clerk hastened to reply, tearing himself away from his papers. "Here you are, sir!" he said, pointing to a place in a notebook and then tossing it at Raskolnikov. "Read it!"

"Money? What money?" wondered Raskolnikov. "But . . . this means it's certainly not about *that*!" He shuddered with delight. Suddenly he felt terribly, inexpressibly carefree. A burden had been lifted from his shoulders.

"What time were you told to appear, kind sir?" cried the lieutenant, feeling more and more offended for some reason. "You were told to come at nine o'clock and it's now already past eleven!"

"It was delivered only a quarter of an hour ago," Raskolnikov replied loudly and over his shoulder, also suddenly and unexpectedly growing angry, even taking a certain pleasure in this feeling. "Isn't it enough that I'm ill with a fever, yet I came all the same?"

"No shouting, if you please!"

"I'm not shouting; I'm speaking very calmly; it's you who is shouting; I'm a student, and I won't allow you to shout at me."

The lieutenant was so incensed that at first he was unable to utter a word; only some spit came flying out of his mouth. He jumped up from his place.

"Shut your mouth! You're in a government office. No r-r-r-udeness, sir!"

"You're in a government office, too," Raskolnikov cried, "and not only are you shouting, but you're also smoking a cigarette and being impolite to all of us." After he said this, Raskolnikov felt inexpressible pleasure.

The head clerk regarded them with a smile. The hotheaded lieutenant was obviously bewildered.

"That's none of your business, sir!" he shouted at last in an unnaturally loud voice. "Be so good as to provide the required response. Show him, Aleksandr Grigorevich.* There are complaints against you. You don't pay your debts. What an upstanding citizen you are!"

But Raskolnikov was no longer listening; he greedily snatched the document, searching for a solution to the riddle. He read it once, then again, but still didn't understand.

"What's this?" he asked the head clerk.

"Money is being demanded from you according to this promissory note. You must either pay up with all costs, fines, and so forth, or else provide a written statement indicating when you will be able to pay and, at the same time, agree that you will not leave the capital before settling the debt, and that you will not sell or conceal your property. The lender is free to sell your property and to pursue all legal steps against you."

"But I don't owe anyone any money!"

"That's none of our business. We received a legitimate claim for overdue payment on a promissory note for one hundred and fifty

---

* Zametov, the chief police clerk.

rubles, given by you to the collegiate assessor's widow, Zarnitsyna, approximately nine months ago; it was transferred by the widow Zarnitsyna as payment to the court councillor Chebarov, and it is for this reason that we're summoning you to provide a statement."

"But she's my landlady."

"What if she is?"

The head clerk regarded him with a condescending smile of pity, together with a certain exultation, as if looking at a new recruit coming under fire for the first time, as though saying, "Well, how do you feel now?" How could he possibly care about a promissory note at this time, or about some overdue payment? Was it worth even the slightest concern in its turn, even the least bit of attention? He stood there, read, listened, replied, and even asked, but he did it all automatically. The triumph of self-preservation, deliverance from threatening danger—that was what filled his entire being at this moment, without apprehension, without analysis, without future problems and solutions, without doubts and questions. It was a moment of complete, spontaneous, pure animal delight. But at this very moment there occurred something in the office akin to a thunderbolt. The lieutenant, still entirely shaken by his lack of respect, still irritated, and apparently wishing to soothe his offended vanity, began fulminating at the unfortunate "elegant lady," who'd been staring at him with a very foolish smile since he had entered the office.

"And you, madam, you old so-and-so," he shouted suddenly at the top of his lungs (the lady in mourning had already left). "What on earth was going on at your place last night? Huh? Once again you're bringing disgrace and debauchery to the whole street. Once more, fighting and drunkenness. You want to wind up in jail? I've already told you, I've warned you a dozen times, and I won't let you get away with it anymore! But you did it again, you old so-and-so!"

The paper actually dropped from Raskolnikov's hands, and he looked intensely at the elegant lady, who was being rebuked so unceremoniously. He soon realized what it was all about and even found this episode immediately to his liking. He listened with pleasure and even felt very much like laughing, and laughing, and laughing. . . . All his nerves were on edge.

"Ilya Petrovich!" the head clerk was about to say solicitously, but he paused because he knew from his own experience that it was impossible to restrain the lieutenant except by force once he was so incensed.

At first the elegant lady trembled as a result of this thunder and lightning. But it was strange: the more numerous and the harsher his words of abuse, the more civil her demeanor became, the more charming her smile directed at the fearsome lieutenant. She shifted restlessly from foot to foot and kept curtsying incessantly, biding her time impatiently until she could at last get a word in edgewise.

"Zer vas no noise und no fighting at mine haus, *Herr Kapitän*," she rattled out all of a sudden, as if scattering peas, with a heavy German accent even though she spoke Russian fluently. "Und no shkandal, none vatever, und zey came trunken, und I vill tell all, *Herr Kapitän*, und I'm not guilty. . . . I haf respectable haus, *Herr Kapitän*, und respectable vay of life, *Herr Kapitän*, and I never, never vanted no shkandal in mine haus. Und dey came completely trunken, and den dey asked for *drei* bottles more, and zen one puts hiz foots up und begins playing der piano mit hiz foots, und he breaks mine *ganz* piano, und he has no manners, none, und I say zat. And he takes ein bottle und he pokes everyone from behind mit dis bottle. Und zen I am soon calling ze caretaker und Karl comes, und he iz hitting Karl in hiz eyes, und he iz also Henrietta hitting in hiz eyes, und he is hitting me on der cheek *fünf* times. Und zat iz not proper in ein respectable haus, *Herr Kapitän*, und I'm shouting. Und he iz opening der vindow on der canal und begins squealing in der vindow like ze leetle pig; und zis iz disgrace. Foo, foo, foo! Karl pulls him from der vindow by zhaket, zis iz true, *Herr Kapitän*, he teared his zhaket. Und zen he shouts zat *man muss* pay fine *fünfzehn* rubles. Und I mineself, *Herr Kapitän*, am paying him *fünf* rubles on ze coat. Und zis nein respectable guest, *Herr Kapitän*, makes ze big shkandal! He sez, he vil make big satire on me und vil in all ze papers write on me."

"Is he a writer, then?"

"Ja, *Herr Kapitän*, and he vas a nein respectable guest, *Herr Kapitän*, in mein respectable haus . . ."

"Well, well, well! Enough! I've told you already, I did, I told you . . ."

"Ilya Petrovich!" the head clerk said again imposingly. The lieutenant shot him a swift look; the head clerk nodded his head slightly.

"Well this, my esteemed Laviza Ivanovna, is my last word, and I won't tell you again," continued the lieutenant. "If even one more scandal takes place in your respectable house, then I'll have you hauled off to the slammer, as they say in the highest circles. You hear me? So a literary man, a writer, received five rubles in your 'respectable house' for his coattail? There's another one of them, those writers!" He cast a contemptuous glance at Raskolnikov. "Three days ago there was another scandal in the tavern: a fellow ate his dinner and didn't want to pay for it; 'I'll put you,' he says, 'into my satire.' There was another one on a steamer last week: someone abused the family of a state councillor, his wife and daughter, with the foulest language. One fellow was thrown out of a pastry shop a few days ago. That's what they're like these writers, literary men, students, loudmouths. . . . Damn them! Off with you! I'll call in at your place one of these days . . . then, you watch out! You hear me?"

Luiza Ivanovna hastened to curtsy in all directions with hurried politeness, and as she did, she made her way backward toward the door. But in the doorway, her rear end collided with a stately officer who had a fresh, open face and who sported a splendid, thick blond mustache. It was none other than Nikodim Fomich himself, the district police superintendent. Luiza Ivanovna hastened to curtsy very deeply to him; hopping up and down with her rapid little steps, she flew out of the office.

"Once again an uproar, once more thunder and lightning, tornadoes and hurricanes!" Nikodim Fomich addressed Ilya Petrovich politely and amicably. "Once again they upset you and you lost your temper! I could hear it outside on the stairs."

"Whatuvit?" Ilya Petrovich said with magnanimous nonchalance (he didn't even say "What of it?" but somehow "Whatuvit?"), moving to another desk with some documents, strutting picturesquely with each step as he did so, swaying his shoulders in time with his steps. "Here you are, sir, if you'd care to see: Mr. Writer, that is, a student, that is, a former student, doesn't pay his debt. His promissory note's overdue, he won't leave his apartment, there are constant complaints against him, and he has the nerve to object to the fact that I lit a cigarette in front of him! He's behaving like a scoundrel; here, sir, just have a look at him: he's a most attractive sight!"

"Poverty's no crime, my friend, and that's that. You're known to be like gunpowder: you can't tolerate any insults. You took offense at something he said and were unable to restrain yourself," Nikodim Fomich continued, turning courteously to Raskolnikov, "but that was to no avail: he's one of our best men, our ver-r-r-ry best men, I tell you, but he's like gunpowder, pure gunpowder! He flared up, lost his temper, exploded—and that's that! All's lost! And, as a result, all that's left is his heart of gold! In his regiment he was nicknamed 'Lieutenant Porokh' . . ."*

"And what a regiment it was!" cried Ilya Petrovich, extremely pleased to be teased in that manner, but still sulking.

Raskolnikov suddenly felt like saying something particularly pleasant to all assembled.

"Pardon me, Captain," he began very casually, suddenly addressing Nikodim Fomich, "put yourself in my place. . . . I'm even prepared to beg his pardon, if I've been impolite. I'm a poor, sick student, disheartened"—he actually used the word "disheartened"—"by poverty. I'm a former student because I can no longer support myself, but I'll be receiving some money soon. . . . I have a mother and a sister in a certain province. They'll send me some money, and then I'll . . . I'll pay up. My landlady's a good woman, but she's so angry because I've lost my teaching and haven't paid my rent for the last three months that she won't even send me any dinner. . . . I don't understand what promissory note you're talking about! Now she's demanding payment according to this acknowledgment of debt: judge for yourself!"

"This doesn't concern us . . ." the head clerk began to observe again . . .

"Please, allow me, I'm in complete agreement with you, but permit me to explain," Raskolnikov began again, addressing not the head

---

* *Porokh* = gunpowder, hence the lieutenant's nickname.

clerk, but Nikodim Fomich, though making a valiant effort also to include Ilya Petrovich, who was pretending to riffle through some papers and refusing contemptuously to pay any attention to him. "Permit me to explain on my part that I've been living there for almost three years, from the time I first arrived from the provinces, and previously . . . previously . . . why not acknowledge, in turn, that from the very beginning I made a promise to marry the landlady's daughter, a verbal promise, of my own free will. . . . She was a young woman . . . in fact, I even took a liking to her . . . although I wasn't in love with her . . . in a word, it was youth, that is, I want to state that the landlady afforded me a great deal of credit and, in part, I led a life of . . . I was very frivolous . . ."

"We're not demanding such intimacies from you, my dear sir, and besides we haven't the time," Ilya Petrovich said, interrupting him rudely and with smugness, but Raskolnikov cut him off excitedly, even though it was very painful for him to continue.

"But allow me, please allow me, to tell it all to some extent . . . how it was and . . . in its turn . . . although I agree with you that it's unnecessary to recount. A year ago this young woman died from typhus, while, however, I continued to be a tenant there as I had been, and the landlady, as she moved into the apartment where she now resides, said to me . . . and she said it amicably . . . that she had every confidence in me and so on . . . but wouldn't I like to provide her with an acknowledgment of debt for one hundred and fifty rubles, the amount she'd calculated as the total of what I owed. Allow me to state, sir: she said precisely that once I gave her this document, she'd extend as much credit to me as I required once again, and never, never, for her part—and these were her exact words—never would she use that letter before I myself paid my debt. . . . And now, when I've lost my teaching and have nothing to eat, she's demanding repayment. . . . What can I say now?"

"None of these sentimental details, my dear sir, concern us," Ilya Petrovich said arrogantly. "You must respond and acknowledge your obligation, while the fact that you happened to be in love and all those tragic particulars, all that is none of our business."

"You're being . . . a bit harsh," muttered Nikodim Fomich, sitting down at the table, where he started signing documents. He was feeling somewhat embarrassed.

"So now write," the head clerk said to Raskolnikov.

"What?" he asked in somewhat of a rude manner.

"What I dictate."

It seemed to Raskolnikov that the head clerk had become ruder and more contemptuous of him after his confession, but strange to say—he suddenly felt that no one else's opinion mattered to him at all, and this change seemed to take place in one single instant. If he'd wanted to consider it for a while, then of course he'd be astounded at how he was able to speak to them that way just a minute ago, and even impose his own feelings on them. Where had these feelings come from? On the contrary, now, if the room had suddenly filled up not with police officers, but with his closest true friends, even then, it seems, he wouldn't have been able to find even one kind word to say to them, because his heart was suddenly so emptied of all emotion. Gloomy feelings of tormenting, unending loneliness and alienation suddenly and consciously took possession of his soul. It wasn't the despondency of his heartfelt outpourings in Ilya Petrovich's presence, nor was it this same despondency or the lieutenant's triumph over him that affected his heart so suddenly. What did he care about his own baseness now, or all these ambitions, lieutenants, German women, procedures, offices, so on and so forth? Even if he had been sentenced to be burned alive at that very moment, even then he wouldn't have batted an eye; it's doubtful that he would've even listened attentively to his sentence. Something totally unfamiliar was happening to him, something new, unexpected, never before experienced. It wasn't so much that he understood, but that he clearly felt, with all the strength of his feeling, that not only with his previous sentimental expansiveness, but even with whatever resources he had available, he was no longer able to communicate with these people in the police office, even if instead of their being just police officers, they were all his own brothers and sisters, even then he would have had no reason to communicate with them, not for anything in his life. Never before, up to this very moment, had he experienced any feeling so strange and so terrible. What was the most tormenting of all—was that it was more of a feeling than a conscious thought or perception, a spontaneous feeling, the most tormenting of all those feelings experienced by him in his life up to this point.

The head clerk began dictating the form of an ordinary statement in such a case, that is: "I am unable to pay, I promise to do so at some future date, I will not leave town, sell my property, or give it away, etc. etc."

"But you can't even write properly; the pen's slipping out of your hand," observed the head clerk, staring at Raskolnikov with curiosity. "Are you ill?"

"Yes . . . I feel dizzy. . . . Go on!"

"That's all! Sign it."

The head clerk took the paper and turned to other matters. Raskolnikov handed the pen back to him, but instead of getting up to leave, placed both elbows on the table and took his head in his hands. It was as if a nail were being driven into his temple. A strange thought occurred to him suddenly: to get up right then, go over to Nikodim Fomich, and tell him everything that had happened yesterday, everything to the last detail, then go with him to his own apartment and show him the things in the hole in the corner. This impulse was so strong that he'd already stood up to carry it out. "Shouldn't I take at least a moment to think about it?" flashed through his mind. "No, it's better to do it without thinking, and get it off my back!" But all of a sudden he stopped like someone rooted to the ground. Nikodim Fomich was talking heatedly to Ilya Petrovich, and some of their words reached his ears:

"It can't be; they'll release both of them! In the first place, it contradicts everything. Judge for yourself: why should they call the caretaker, if they'd done the deed? To implicate themselves? Or is it a clever trick? No, that would be too clever! Moreover, both caretakers and the woman trader saw the student Pestryakov near the gates just as he was arriving: he was out there with three friends, parted from them near the gate, and asked the caretakers about residence in the building in the presence of these friends. Well, would someone ask about residence if he'd come with such an intention? And Kokh, before he went to see the old woman, had been sitting downstairs with the silversmith for half an hour and at precisely quarter to eight went upstairs to see her. Now just consider . . ."

"But permit me, look at the contradiction that's emerged: they state that they knocked and that the door was locked, but three minutes later, when they arrived with the caretaker, it turns out that the door was unlocked."

"That's precisely the point: without fail the murderer was still inside and had locked the door. Without fail they'd have discovered him there if Kokh hadn't been such a fool and gone to fetch the caretaker. And precisely in this interval, *he'd* managed to head down the stairs and somehow slip past them. Kokh should thank his lucky stars: 'If I'd have stayed there,' he said, 'he'd have jumped out and killed me with his axe.' He wants to give thanks at a special church service, ha, ha, ha . . ."

"No one saw the murderer?"

"How could they? The building's as crowded as Noah's ark," the head clerk observed, overhearing the conversation from where he sat.

"It's clear as day, clear as day," Nikodim Fomich repeated excitedly.

"No, it's not clear at all," summed up Ilya Petrovich.

Raskolnikov took his hat and headed for the door, but he never made it that far . . .

When he came to, he saw that he was sitting on a chair, that some person was supporting him on the right, that another man was standing on his left holding a yellow glass filled with yellowish water,[*] and that Nikodim Fomich was standing in front of him, staring at him intently; Raskolnikov stood up from where he was sitting.

"What's wrong? Are you ill?" Nikodim Fomich asked him rather harshly.

"When he was signing, he could scarcely hold the pen," observed the head clerk, sitting back down at his place and returning to his papers.

"Have you been ill for long?" cried Ilya Petrovich from where he was sitting, also attending to some documents. He, too, of course, had

---

[*] Residents of Petersburg took their water from rivers and canals.

scrutinized the sick man when he'd fainted, but he'd walked away as soon as Raskolnikov had come to.

"Since yesterday," Raskolnikov muttered in reply.

"Did you go out yesterday?"

"I did."

"Sick?"

"Yes."

"At what time?"

"After seven in the evening."

"Where, if I may ask?"

"Down the street."

"Well, that's short and sweet."

To all these questions Raskolnikov replied sharply, abruptly, white as a sheet, without dropping his dark, inflamed eyes when confronted with Ilya Petrovich's gaze.

"He can hardly stand, while you think . . ." remarked Nikodim Fomich.

"Ne-ver mind!" Ilya Petrovich replied strangely. Nikodim Fomich was about to add something more, but, glancing at the head clerk, who was also staring at him intently, he fell silent. Everyone was suddenly quiet. It was strange.

"Well, sir, that's fine, sir," concluded Ilya Petrovich. "We won't detain you."

Raskolnikov left. He could hear how a lively conversation resumed as soon as he'd gone out; the questioning voice of Nikodim Fomich was heard above the others. . . . He recovered completely once outside.

"A search, a search, an immediate search!" he repeated to himself, hastening home. "Those rascals! They suspect me!" His former fear overcame him again completely from head to toe.

II

"What if there's already been a search? What if I find them there right now?"

But there was his room. Nothing and no one: no one had been there. Even Nastasya hadn't touched it. But, Lord! How could he have left all those things in that hole under the wallpaper?

He rushed to the corner, thrust his hand in, began pulling things out and loading them into his pockets. There were eight items in all: two small boxes with earrings or something of that sort—he didn't look very carefully—and four small morocco leather cases. One chain was simply wrapped up in newspaper. There was something else also wrapped in newspaper, probably a medal . . .

He stashed them all in various pockets in his coat and in his right trouser pocket, trying to make it all look less noticeable. He also picked up the purse full of things. Then he left his room, this time even leaving the door wide open.

He walked rapidly and decisively; although he felt completely devastated, he still had his wits about him. He was afraid of being followed, afraid that in half an hour, perhaps even a quarter of an hour, an order would be issued to have him followed; therefore, no matter what happened, he had to hide all traces before then. He had to act while he still had some strength left and some powers of reasoning. . . . But where should he go?

It had all been decided long ago: "Throw everything into the canal:

get rid of all traces and that would be the end of it." He had made that decision at night, in his delirium, when, as he recalled, he had tried several times to stand up and leave "quickly, quickly, and get rid of it all." But it proved to be very difficult to get rid of.

He had been wandering along the embankment of the Yekaterinsky Canal for about half an hour, perhaps even longer; several times he looked at the staircases leading down to the water. But he couldn't even conceive of carrying out his intention: either there were rafts moored at the bottom of the stairs where women were washing their linens, or else boats were tied up and the stairs were teeming with people; in addition, from there along both embankments one could be observed, noticed: it would look very suspicious if a man intentionally went down the stairs, paused, and threw something into the water. What if the cases floated instead of sank? Of course, that's what would happen. Everyone would see them. Even without that, everyone he met would look up, stare at him, as if he was all they had to be concerned about. "Why is that the case? Perhaps I'm merely imagining it?" he wondered.

Finally it occurred to him that it might be better to go somewhere farther along the Neva. There would be fewer people and he'd be less noticeable; in any event, it would be more convenient; but the main thing is that it would be farther away from where he was now. He was suddenly surprised to realize that he'd been wandering around in anguish and anxiety for an entire half hour, and in dangerous places, yet he had been unable to come up with this idea until now! Consequently, he had wasted half an hour in a foolish enterprise that had already been decided in his sleep, in his delirium! He was becoming extremely absentminded and forgetful, and he knew that himself. He definitely had to hurry!

He started walking along Voznesensky Prospect toward the Neva; but on the way, another idea suddenly occurred to him: "Why the Neva? Why into the water? Wouldn't it be better to go somewhere far away, maybe even to the Islands, and somewhere, in an isolated place, in the woods, under a bush—bury it all and mark the spot?" Even though he felt that he was in no condition to consider this idea clearly and sensibly at the time, it seemed flawless.

But he wasn't destined to reach the Islands, either: something else occurred. As he emerged from Voznesensky Prospect into the square, he suddenly saw on his left an entrance to a courtyard surrounded by windowless walls. Directly to the right of the gate stretched the long, blank unwhitewashed wall of the adjacent four-story building. To the left, parallel to the blank wall and also close to the gate, a wooden fence ran about twenty paces into the courtyard, then turned to the left. It was a deserted, enclosed space where various materials lay scattered. Farther on, in the depths of the courtyard, the corner of a low, sooty stone shed peered out from behind the fence, evidently part of a workshop. There was someone here, a carriage maker or metalworker, or someone of the kind; the entire area, right from the gates, was blackened with a great deal of coal dust. "This would be a good place to hide the stuff and get away," he thought suddenly. After seeing no one in the courtyard, he strode through the gates and noticed at once, right next to the gate, a trench dug along the fence (the kind often found in buildings with many factory workers, craftsmen, cabdrivers, etc.), and above the trench, on the fence, were the witty words scribbled in chalk regularly found in such circumstances: FOR BIDDEN TO STOPP HEAR. Good: therefore he would arouse no suspicion if he went in and paused. "Stash it all together in one pile and get away!"

Glancing around once more, he had already thrust his hand into his pocket when he suddenly noticed by the outer wall, between the gate and the trench, where the distance was about a yard wide, a large unworked block, weighing perhaps as much as fifty pounds, leaning directly against the stone wall. Beyond it lay the street, the sidewalk, and the sounds of hurrying passersby, of whom there were always quite a few; but no one could notice him behind the gate, except if someone turned in from the street, which, by the way, could easily happen, and therefore he had to hurry.

He bent over, grabbed the top of the block powerfully with both hands, gathered all his strength, and turned it over. There was a small hollow underneath; he immediately began emptying everything from his pockets. The purse wound up on top of the pile, and there still remained some space in the hollow. Then he grabbed the block again and, with one turn, shoved it back into its former place, perhaps now sitting a little bit higher. But he scraped up some dirt and pressed it around the bottom of the block with his foot. Nothing was noticeable.

Then he left the courtyard and headed off to the square. Once again he was momentarily overcome by a strong feeling of joy, such as he'd experienced before in the police station. "All traces have been buried! Who, who on earth would ever think of searching under that stone? It may have been there since the house was built and will be there just as long. And if someone did find the stash: who would suspect me? It's all over! There's no evidence!" He started laughing. Later he recalled that he had started laughing with a nervous, shallow, inaudible, long-lasting laugh, and kept laughing all the while he was crossing the square. But when he reached Konnogvardeisky Boulevard, where two days ago he had encountered that young woman, his laughter suddenly vanished. Other thoughts flooded his mind. All of a sudden he felt that it would be terribly unpleasant to pass that bench where he had sat and thought after the girl's departure, and that it would also be terribly painful to encounter that policeman with the mustache to whom he had given his twenty kopecks at the time: "To hell with him!"

He walked along, looking around absentmindedly and spitefully. All his thoughts now revolved around one main point—he himself felt that it was really the main point, and that now, precisely at this moment, he was all alone, face-to-face with this main point—and that it was even happening for the very first time after these last two months.

"To hell with it all!" he thought suddenly in a fit of unlimited malice. "Well, if it's begun, then it's begun. To hell with this new life! Lord, how stupid it all is! I've told so many lies and done nasty things today! How disgustingly I fawned and flattered that despicable Ilya Petrovich! But that's all nonsense, too! I don't give a damn about any of them or the fact that I fawned and flattered him! That's not the point! That's not it at all!"

All of a sudden he stopped; a new, completely unexpected and extremely simple question dazed and astounded him.

"If this whole affair was carried out consciously, and not in some foolish manner, if I really had a definite and definitive goal, then how is it that up to this point I didn't even peek into the purse and don't know how much I've taken? Why did I consciously assume all these torments? Why did I undertake this mean, vile, base act? Just now I wanted to throw it all into the water, the purse, together with all the items that I haven't even looked at. . . . How can this be?"

Yes, that was true. That was all true. Besides, he'd known all this before and it was not a new question for him; last night when he'd decided to throw it all into the water, it had been decided without any hesitation or objection, just as if that was how it ought to be, as if it couldn't be otherwise. . . . He knew all this and recalled it all; it was all decided yesterday, when he was bending over the old woman's trunk, pulling out those leather cases. . . . That was all true!

"It's all because I'm very ill," he decided gloomily once and for all. "I've tortured and tormented myself, and I don't even know what I'm doing. . . . Yesterday, and the day before, and during all this time I've been tormenting myself. . . . I'll get better and then . . . I won't torment myself. . . . What if I don't get better? Lord! I'm so fed up with all this!" He walked without stopping. He very much wanted to distract himself, but didn't know what to do or what to try. A new, insurmountable feeling was overtaking him more and more with every passing minute: it was some constant, almost physical repulsion for everything that he was encountering and all that surrounded him, a stubborn, malicious, hateful feeling. Everyone he met seemed repulsive to him—their faces, their walk, and their gestures. If someone had begun talking to him, he felt, he might spit at them or bite them . . .

He stopped suddenly when he emerged on the embankment of the Little Neva on Vasilievsky Island, near the bridge. "Here's where he lives, in this building," he thought. "How is it that somehow I wound up at Razumikhin's place? It's the same story as before. . . . But it's very odd: did I come here intentionally or was I simply walking and ended up here? It's all the same; two days ago . . . I said . . . I'd go see him a day after *that*. Well, so I will! As if I couldn't drop in on him now . . ."

He climbed up to Razumikhin's room on the fifth floor.

He was at home in his little room; at that moment he was busy writing; he unlocked the door himself. They hadn't seen each other in about four months. Razumikhin had been sitting there in his dressing gown, which was worn to tatters, with slippers on his bare feet; he was disheveled, unshaven, and unwashed. But his face expressed surprise.

"What's the matter with you?" he cried, examining his friend from head to foot; then he fell silent and whistled shrilly.

"Are things really so bad? My friend, you've outdone people like us," he added, looking at Raskolnikov's rags. "Sit down, you must be tired!" When his friend had collapsed on the Turkish oilcloth sofa, which was in even worse condition than Raskolnikov's own, Razumikhin suddenly realized that his guest was ill.

"You're really sick, you know that?" He reached out to take his pulse; Raskolnikov pulled his arm away.

"There's no need," he said. "I've come to . . . here's what: I have no lessons. . . . I would like to . . . but I really don't need any lessons . . ."

"You know what? You're delirious!" Razumikhin remarked, observing him closely.

"No, I'm not delirious," Raskolnikov said, standing up from the sofa. On his way to see Razumikhin, he hadn't thought about having to come face-to-face with him. Now, in one moment, he surmised, based on his experience, that he was not inclined at that minute to come face-to-face with anyone at all on earth. All his bile rose up in him. He almost choked on anger at himself for having just crossed Razumikhin's threshold.

"Good-bye!" he said suddenly and headed for the door.

"Wait a minute, you madman, wait!"

"There's no need!" Raskolnikov repeated, pulling his arm away again.

"What the hell did you come here for in the first place? Are you crazy, or what? Why . . . this is almost insulting. I won't let you go."

"Well, listen: I came to see you because besides you, I don't know anyone else who could help . . . to start . . . because you're kinder than all of them, that is, you're smarter, and you can judge. . . . But now I see that I have no need, you hear, no need at all . . . for anyone's favors or concern. . . . I myself . . . all alone. . . . That's all! Leave me in peace!"

"Wait a moment, you derelict! You're completely mad! As far as I'm concerned, you can do as you like. You see, I don't have any lessons either, but I don't give a damn; there's a bookseller at the flea market by the name of Kheruvimov who's a kind of lesson in himself. I wouldn't trade him for five lessons in any merchant's house. He does a little publishing and puts out booklets on the natural sciences—and do they sell! The titles alone are worth the price! You always say that I'm a fool; well, friend, I swear there are bigger fools than me! Now he's turned toward progressive politics; he hasn't a clue about it, but I encourage him, of course. Here are some forty pages of a German text—in my opinion, it's the dumbest charlatanism: in a word, it examines the question of whether a woman can be considered a human being or not. Well, naturally, it demonstrates solemnly that a woman is indeed a human being. Kheruvimov is planning to publish it as a contribution to the woman question;* I'm translating it; he'll stretch those forty pages to a hundred, we'll come up with the most splendid title, at least half a page long, and then we'll sell it for fifty kopecks. It'll work! I get six rubles for sixteen pages, which means about fifteen rubles for the whole thing, and I got six rubles in advance. After we finish this, we'll start translating a piece on whales, and then we'll publish the most boring scandalous sections of the second part of *Confessions*;† someone told Kheruvimov that Rousseau is like our Radishchev.‡ Of course, I won't contradict him—the hell with him! Well, how would you like to translate the second part of "Are Women Human Beings?" If you do, then take the text, take some pens and paper—it's all been provided—and here are three rubles. Since I got an advance on the whole thing, for the first and the second parts, it would come to three rubles for your share. When you finish that part—you'll get another three rubles. Here's what else: don't think I'm doing you any favors. On the contrary, just when you showed up, I was already wondering about how you could help me. In the first place, my spelling is awful; in the second, my German is sometimes simply not up to it, so I make it up and console myself by thinking that

---

* The discussion of women's rights was active among progressive circles in the 1860s.

† Jean-Jacques Rousseau's *Confessions* (1782–89) was one of the most famous autobiographies. A Russian translation appeared in 1865.

‡ Aleksandr Radishchev (1749–1802) was a leading liberal writer who opposed serfdom and the Russian judicial system.

the result comes out even better. Who knows, perhaps it's not any better, but even worse. . . . Will you take it or not?"

Without saying a word, Raskolnikov took the pages of the German article, picked up the three rubles, and walked out in silence. Razumikhin followed him with his eyes in bewilderment. But, after having reached the First Line,* Raskolnikov suddenly turned around, climbed the stairs back up to Razumikhin's, and, placing both the German pages and the three rubles down on the table, left again, without saying a word.

"Are you delirious, or what?" an enraged Razumikhin roared at last. "What sort of comedy are you playing? You've confused me completely. . . . Damn it all, why did you come here?"

"I don't need any . . . translations," muttered Raskolnikov, starting down the stairs.

"So what in hell do you need?" Razumikhin shouted from above. Raskolnikov continued down the stairs.

"Hey, you! Where do you live?"

There was no reply.

"Well, then, to hell with you!"

But Raskolnikov was already on the street. On the Nikolaevsky Bridge he was forced back to his senses once again as a result of an extremely unpleasant episode. A carriage driver struck his back soundly with a whip because Raskolnikov had nearly stumbled and fallen under the horses in spite of the fact that the driver had shouted to him three or four times. The blow from the whip infuriated him so much that he jumped aside to the bridge railing (it's unclear why he was walking down the middle where vehicles go, not pedestrians); he gnashed and ground his teeth furiously. All around, of course, laughter resounded.

"Serves him right!"

"He's some kind of rogue."

"It's a well-known trick: they pretend to be drunk and fall down intentionally under the carriage wheels. Then you're responsible for them."

---

* The streets on Vasilievsky Island are numbered and referred to as "lines."

"That's how they make their money, my dear sir, that's how . . ."

But just then, as he was standing near the railing, staring foolishly and irately after the disappearing carriage, rubbing his back, he
suddenly felt that someone was thrusting money into his hand. He
glanced around: it was an elderly woman wearing a head scarf and
goatskin shoes, accompanied by a young girl wearing a hat and carrying a green parasol, probably her daughter. "Here, my friend, for the
love of Christ." He took it, and they walked on past. It was a twenty-
kopeck piece. Judging by his clothes and appearance, they could easily
have mistaken him for a beggar, someone out asking for half-kopeck
pieces in the streets; for the gift of a twenty-kopeck piece he was probably obligated to the blow from the whip, which had caused them to
take pity on him.

He squeezed the coin in his hand, walked on about ten paces, and
turned to face the Neva in the direction of the palace. The sky had
not the slightest trace of any cloud and the water looked almost blue,
which rarely happens at the Neva. The dome of the cathedral, the
outline of which could not appear more conspicuously from any other
point of view than this spot on the bridge, some twenty paces from the
chapel, was gleaming; through the clear air one could discern every
last detail of its decoration. The pain from the whip's lash had eased,
and Raskolnikov forgot all about the blow; one anxious and somewhat
hazy thought now preoccupied him exclusively. He stood there and
gazed into the distance intently and for a long time; this place was
very familiar to him. When he'd been attending classes at the university, ordinarily—most often, on his way home—perhaps as many as a
hundred times, he'd happened to pause precisely at this spot and stare
fixedly at that genuinely majestic panorama; each and every time he
would marvel at his own indistinct and inexplicable impression. An
unaccountable chill always came over him as a result of this splendid
sight; for him, this opulent picture was filled with a deaf and mute
spirit. . . . He was surprised each time by this gloomy and enigmatic
impression; not trusting himself, he would defer its solution to the
future. All of a sudden, he recalled abruptly his former questions and
perplexity, and it seemed that this was all happening now for some
good reason. It was strange and mysterious that he had paused at the

very same place as before, as if he really imagined that he could think about the same things now as he had then, that the same subjects and images could interest him as they had before . . . not so long ago. It even struck him as almost amusing, while at the same time he felt somewhat heartsick. Somewhere down below, in the depths, visible just beneath his feet, he seemed to see all of his recent past, his previous thoughts, previous problems, previous subjects, previous impressions, this entire panorama, even himself, and everything else, everything. . . . He seemed to soar somewhere upward, and then everything disappeared from sight. . . . After making an involuntary movement of his hand, he suddenly felt the twenty-kopeck piece grasped tightly in his fist. He opened his hand, stared intently at the coin, wound up his arm, and threw it into the water; then he turned around and went home. It seemed as if at that very moment he had cut himself off with a pair of scissors from everyone and everything.

It was already evening when he arrived home; he had been out walking for about six hours. He didn't recall where he had been or how he'd come back. After getting undressed, trembling all over like a horse driven to exhaustion, he lay down on the sofa, pulled his coat over himself, and immediately lost consciousness . . .

It was deep twilight when he came to, upon hearing a terrible scream. Good Lord, what a scream! He had never before heard such unnatural sounds, such howling, wailing, gnashing, weeping, beating, and cursing. He couldn't even imagine such brutality, such rage. He raised himself up and sat on his bed, rendered immobile and tormented at every moment. But the struggle, the wailing, and the cursing became louder and louder. Then, to his enormous astonishment, he suddenly recognized his landlady's voice. She wailed, squealed, and moaned, hurrying, hastening, emitting words in such a way that it was impossible to understand what she was pleading for—of course, that they would stop beating her because she was being thrashed mercilessly on the staircase. The voice of the one beating her had become so terrible from rage and fury that it was now merely rasping hoarsely, but this person was also saying something or other, also rapidly, indecipherably, hastening, and choking. All of a sudden Raskolnikov began trembling like a leaf. He recognized that voice: it was that of Ilya Petrovich. "Ilya Petrovich is here, and he's beating the landlady! He's kicking her, knocking her head against the stairs—it's apparent and it's audible from the sounds, the wails, and the blows! What's happening? Has the world turned upside down, or what?" One could hear how on every floor, up and down the staircase, a crowd was gathering; voices could be heard, exclamations, as people came out, knocked on doors, slammed them shut, and then clustered. "But why, what for, how is it possible?" he repeated, thinking in earnest that he had gone mad. Only no, he was hearing it all too distinctly! But if that were the case, of course they'd be coming for him at any moment, "because . . . most likely, all because of that . . . what happened yesterday. . . . Good Lord!" He wanted to lock his door, but his arm wouldn't move . . . and it would have been to no avail! An icy fear seized his soul, tormented him, and immobilized him. . . . But now, at last, all this uproar, which had gone on for a good ten minutes, gradually began to subside. The landlady moaned and groaned, Ilya Petrovich still threatening her and cursing. . . . But now, finally, he, too, seemed to have quieted down; his voice could no longer be heard. "Has he really gone? Oh, Lord!" Yes, the landlady was also leaving, still moaning and weeping . . . now her door slammed shut. . . . Now the crowd was dispersing from the stairway, everyone to their own apartments—exclaiming, arguing, calling to one another, first raising their voices to shout, then lowering them to whisper. There must have been a great many of them; almost the entire building had come running. "But, my God, how is it possible? Why did he come here? What for?"

Raskolnikov collapsed weakly onto the sofa, but he could no longer close his eyes; he lay there for about half an hour in a state of suffering, with an unbearable feeling of unending terror such as he had never experienced before. Suddenly bright light illuminated his room: Nastasya came in carrying a candle and a bowl of soup. After scrutinizing him carefully and seeing that he was not asleep, she placed the candle on the table and began laying out the things she'd brought: bread, salt, the bowl, and a spoon.

"You probably haven't eaten since yesterday. You were out gallivanting the whole day; besides, you had a fever."

"Nastasya . . . why did they beat the landlady?"

She stared at him intently.

"Who beat the landlady?"

"Just now . . . half an hour ago, Ilya Petrovich, the police superintendent's assistant, on the staircase. . . . Why did he give her such a beating? And . . . why did he come here?"

Nastasya frowned and stared at him in silence for a long time. He felt very uncomfortable as a result of her stare, even frightened.

"Nastasya, why don't you say something?" he finally asked timidly in a weak voice.

"It's the blood," she replied at last, softly and as if talking to herself.

"Blood! What blood?" he muttered, growing pale and moving toward the wall. Nastasya continued staring at him.

"No one beat the landlady," she said in a stern and definitive voice. He looked at her, hardly breathing.

"I heard it myself . . . I wasn't asleep . . . I was sitting here," he said even more timidly. "I listened for a long time. . . . The superintendent's assistant came. . . . Everyone came running out onto the staircase, from all the apartments . . ."

"No one came. It's the blood crying out inside you. It's when it has no way of getting out and it's trying to clog your liver; you begin seeing things. . . . Will you eat something or not?"

He made no reply. Nastasya stood over him, staring at him, and didn't leave.

"Let me have something to drink . . . Nastasyushka."

She went downstairs and returned a few minutes later with some water in a white clay mug; but he would not remember what happened next. He remembered only that he swallowed one mouthful of cold water and spilled some from the mug on his chest. Then came unconsciousness.

III

However, Raskolnikov was not completely unconscious throughout his illness; he had a feverish condition with periods of delirium and semiconsciousness. He remembered a great deal afterward. First, there seemed to be many people surrounding him, wanting to pick him up and carry him somewhere; they stood over him, arguing and quarreling. Then he was suddenly all alone in his room; everyone had left and they were all afraid of him; from time to time, they merely opened his door slightly to have a look at him, threaten him, confer about something or other among themselves, or laugh and tease him. He recalled that Nastasya was often at his side; he distinguished one other person, someone very familiar, but who that was precisely—he was unable to discern; he was sad about that and even wept. Sometimes it seemed that he'd been lying there for about a month; another time, that it was still the same day he had fallen ill. But about *that*—he had completely forgotten about *that*; on the other hand, he constantly recalled that he had forgotten about something that he should not have forgotten about—he suffered and agonized, trying to remember; he moaned, fell into a rage or into horrible, unbearable fear. Then he would try to hoist himself up, wanting to run away, but someone always restrained him forcibly, and he would sink into weakness and unconsciousness. At last he recovered consciousness completely.

This occurred at ten o'clock in the morning. At that hour, on clear days, the sun always passed over his right wall with a long stripe of light and lit up the corner next to the door. Nastasya was standing near his bed along with one other person, who was completely unfamiliar to him and who was examining him with curiosity. He was a bearded young man wearing a caftan who resembled a member of some guild. The landlady was peering in from the half-opened door. Raskolnikov raised himself up.

"Who's that, Nastasya?" he asked, pointing to the young man.

"Look at that, he's come to!" she said.

"He's come to," echoed the stranger. Realizing that he had indeed come to, the landlady, who was peeking in from the doorway, closed it at once and hid. She was always shy and suffered conversations and explanations with difficulty; she was about forty, quite plump, with black brows and dark eyes; she was kind as a result of her stoutness and slowness; and she was even very pretty. She was more bashful than she needed to be.

"Who . . . are you?" he continued to ask, addressing the stranger. But at that moment, the door opened wide once more and in walked Razumikhin, bending his head a bit because he was so tall.

"It's like a ship's cabin," he cried upon entering. "I always bang my head; and just think, it's also called an apartment! And you, my friend, have you come to? I just learned about it from Pashenka."

"He just came to," said Nastasya.

"Just came to," echoed the stranger again, with a slight smile.

"And just who might you be, sir?" Razumikhin asked, suddenly turning to him. "I am, if you please, Vrazumikhin, not Razumikhin, as they all call me,* but Vrazumikhin, a student, the son of a gentleman, and this fellow is my friend. Well, sir, and who are you?"

"I'm an agent in the office of the merchant Shelopaev, sir, and I'm here on business, sir."

"Be so good as to have a seat on this chair," said Razumikhin, taking a seat on the chair at the other end of the small table. "It's a good thing you've come to, my friend," he said, turning to Raskolnikov. "You've hardly had anything to eat or drink in the last three days. True,

---

* See Names of Principal Characters.

you were given several spoonfuls of tea. I brought Zosimov here to see you twice. Do you remember him? He examined you carefully and said immediately that it was some nonsense—it all went to your head. Some sort of nervous nonsense, spoiled food, he said, or not enough beer and horseradish, and that's why you fell ill, but it was nothing serious, it would pass, and you'd soon be back on your feet. Zosimov's a fine fellow! He did a splendid job. Well, sir, I won't keep you any longer," he said, turning to the agent. "Would you care to clarify what you need? Note, Rodya, this is the second time someone's come from that office, only the last time it wasn't this man, but another one; he and I had a little talk. Who was it who came before?"

"That would've been two days ago, sir, exactly, sir. It was Aleksey Semyonovich; he also works in our office."

"And is he a little smarter than you are, do you think?"

"Yes, sir; he's definitely more respectable, sir."

"Commendable; well, sir, continue."

"Well, through Afanasy Ivanovich Vakhrushin, about whom, I assume, you have heard more than once, and according to your mother's request, a money order has come for you through our office," the agent began, addressing Raskolnikov directly. "If you're in complete control of your faculties, sir, I have thirty-five rubles to transfer to you, sir, since Semyon Semyonovich has received instructions from Afanasy Ivanovich, as he had previously, at your mother's request. Might you be knowing him, sir?"

"Yes . . . I remember . . . Vakhrushin," Raskolnikov said pensively.

"Listen: he knows the merchant Vakhrushin!" cried Razumikhin. "Who says he's not in control of his faculties? I now see that you're also an intelligent man. Well, sir! It's pleasant to hear such clever words."

"It's the very same Vakhrushin, sir, Afanasy Ivanovich, according to your mother's request, who once sent you some money in a similar manner; he didn't refuse to do it again this time, sir, and several days ago Semyon Semyonovich was informed that he should transfer thirty-five rubles to you, in anticipation of better times, sir."

"That phrase 'in anticipation of better times' is the best thing you've said so far; and the words about 'your mother' weren't bad, either. Well then, what's your opinion: is he in complete control of his faculties or not?"

"It seems so to me, sir. Only there should be a signed receipt, sir."

"He'll scrawl it! Do you have a book for him to write in?"

"Yes, sir, I do have a book, sir."

"Hand it over. Well, Rodya, sit up. I'll support you; just scribble 'Raskolnikov' for him; take the pen, because, my friend, money's now sweeter than syrup."

"There's no need," said Raskolnikov, pushing the pen away.

"No need for what?" asked Razumikhin.

"I won't sign it."

"What the hell? How can he do it without a signature?"

"I don't need any . . . money . . ."

"You don't need any money? You're lying, my friend, I swear! Don't worry, please, he's simply that way . . . his mind's wandering again. Besides, this sometimes happens even when he's wide awake. . . . You're a reasonable man; we'll direct him—that is, we'll simply guide his hand and he'll sign. Let's do it . . ."

"I can come some other time, sir."

"No, no; why trouble yourself again? You're a reasonable man. . . . Well, Rodya, let's not detain our guest. . . . You see, he's waiting," he said, earnestly preparing to guide Raskolnikov's hand.

"Let me alone, I'll do it myself," Raskolnikov said; he took the pen and signed the book. The agent handed over the money and withdrew.

"Bravo! And now, my friend, would you like something to eat?"

"I would," replied Raskolnikov.

"Is there any soup left?"

"It's left over from yesterday," replied Nastasya, who had been standing there all the while.

"With potatoes and rice?"

"With potatoes and rice."

"I know it by heart. Bring some soup, and some tea, too."

"I will."

Raskolnikov regarded everything with profound amazement and with slow-witted irrational terror. He decided to keep silent and wait:

what would happen next? "It seems I'm not delirious," he thought, "it seems that this is really happening . . ."

Two minutes later, Nastasya returned with some soup and declared that tea would be ready shortly. There were two soup spoons, two bowls, and complete settings: a saltcellar, pepper shaker, mustard for the beef, and so on, the likes of which he hadn't seen in quite some time. There was even a clean tablecloth.

"It wouldn't be bad, Nastasyushka, if Praskovya Pavlovna were to order two bottles of beer. We'd drink it with pleasure."

"What a sly one you are!" muttered Nastasya and went out to fulfill the request.

Raskolnikov continued staring wildly and anxiously. Meanwhile, Razumikhin sat down next to him on the sofa, clumsily, like a bear, and put his left arm around Raskolnikov's head, in spite of the fact that he could have raised his head by himself; with his right hand Razumikhin carried a spoonful of soup to his mouth, first blowing on it several times beforehand to make sure he didn't burn himself. Though the soup was barely lukewarm, Raskolnikov greedily swallowed a spoonful, then another, and a third. But after feeding him a few spoons, Razumikhin suddenly stopped and announced that they would have to consult Zosimov about what to do next.

Nastasya came in carrying two bottles of beer.

"Would you like some tea?"

"I would," Raskolnikov replied.

"Bring us some quickly, Nastasya, because I think he can have tea without consulting any medical authorities. And here's the beer!" Razumikhin sat down on his chair, reached for his bowl of soup, the beef, and began eating with such appetite as if he hadn't eaten in the last three days.

"I've been having dinner here like this for the last three days, my friend Rodya," he muttered, as best he could with his mouth filled with beef, "and it's all thanks to your nice landlady, Pashenka, who does me the honor of feeding me. Of course, I don't insist, but neither do I object. Here's Nastasya with the tea. She's so quick! Nastenka, would you like some beer?"

"What a naughty boy you are!"

"Some tea?"

"Tea, yes."

"Pour it. Wait, I'll pour it for you; sit down at the table."

He took charge immediately, poured her tea, then poured another cup, forsook his own lunch, and sat down on the sofa again. As before, he put his left arm around the patient's head, raised him up, and began to feed him teaspoons of tea, once again constantly and very diligently blowing on the spoon to cool the tea, as if the primary and most salutary point of the healing process consisted in this act of cooling. Raskolnikov kept silent and didn't resist, even though he felt he had sufficient strength to raise himself up and sit on the sofa without anyone's assistance. He felt that he could also control his own hands, hold a spoon or a cup, and perhaps even walk on his own. But with some strange, almost animal cunning, it suddenly occurred to him to hide his strength for the time being, to conceal himself, if necessary, to pretend that he didn't understand everything completely. Meanwhile he would listen and try to determine what was happening. He was unable to master his revulsion, however: after swallowing down a dozen or so spoons of tea, he suddenly freed his head, stubbornly pushed the spoon away, and threw himself back on the pillow again. Under his head now were some genuine pillows—down pillows with clean pillowcases; he noticed that, too, and took it into consideration.

"Pashenka should also send us up some raspberry jam today so I can make him a special drink," said Razumikhin, sitting back down in his place and returning to his own soup and beer.

"Where will she get raspberry jam for you?" asked Nastasya, holding a saucer in her open hand and sipping her tea "through a lump of sugar."*

"Raspberry jam, my dear, she can get in a shop. You see, Rodya, a whole story has unfolded here without you. When you made off like a rascal from me and didn't say where you lived, I was so angry that I resolved to find you and punish you. I began that same day. I walked and walked, asked and asked! I couldn't recall this apartment because

---

* Russians often sweeten their tea by placing a lump of sugar between their teeth and drinking tea "through" it.

I'd never known about it. Well, as for your previous apartment, I remembered only that it was at Five Corners, in Kharlamov's house. I searched and searched for that place—it turned out to be not in Kharlamov's, but Bukh's house—sometimes sounds get all confused! I was angry. I was so furious that the next day I went to the address bureau to give it a try, and what do you know, they located you in two minutes. You were registered there."

"Registered!"

"Indeed! Yet they couldn't find General Kobelev for someone who was looking for him. Well, sir, it's too long a story. As soon as I turned up here, I immediately learned about all your affairs; I know it all, my friend, everything; Nastasya witnessed it all. I became acquainted with Nikodim Fomich, and they pointed out Ilya Petrovich to me, and the caretaker and Mr. Zametov (Aleksandr Grigorevich, the clerk in the local office), and, finally, even Pashenka—that was the crowning achievement; and even she knows . . ."

"He sweetened her up," muttered Nastasya, with a cunning smile.

"You ought to put some sugar in your teacup, Nastasya Nikiforovna."

"You dog, you!" Nastasya cried suddenly and burst out laughing. "Besides, I'm Petrovna, not Nikiforovna," she added suddenly, after she had stopped laughing.

"We'll keep that in mind, young lady. So then, my friend, so as not to go on too long, at first I wanted to unleash an electric current here throughout, in order to root out all the prejudices in this place at once; but Pashenka was victorious. I never expected, my friend, that she'd be so . . . charming . . . eh? What do you think?"

Raskolnikov kept silent, although he didn't lift his anxious gaze from his friend's face even for a moment. He continued staring at him fixedly.

"Very charming, indeed," continued Razumikhin, not in the least flustered by his friend's silence, as if assenting to the reply he received, "and even quite something, in all respects."

"You beast!" cried Nastasya again, obviously deriving indescribable delight from this conversation.

"It's a shame, my friend, that you weren't able to deal with this matter from the very beginning. You should have treated her differently. She is, so to speak, a most unexpected character! Well, we'll talk about her later. . . . But, for example, tell me how it came about that she dared to withhold your dinner? Or, for example, that promissory note? Were you out of your mind when you signed it? Or, for example, that marriage proposal, when her daughter, Natalya Yegorovna, was still alive? I know everything! However, I see that it's a delicate matter and I'm an ass; forgive me. But as far as stupidity's concerned, don't you agree, my friend, that Praskovya Pavlovna's not as foolish as one might presume at first glance, eh?"

"Yes," mumbled Raskolnikov, looking to one side, but understanding that it was more advantageous to continue this conversation.

"Isn't it true?" cried Razumikhin, apparently overjoyed that he'd received an answer. "But she's not too clever either, is she? She's an absolutely, utterly unexpected character! I'm getting a bit flustered, my friend, I assure you. . . . She must be around forty years old. She claims she's only thirty-six and has a right to say so. However, I swear that I'm judging her more intellectually, according to certain metaphysics; you see, my friend, we've established a symbolic relationship, something like your algebra! I don't understand a thing! Well, it's all nonsense, but when she realized that you were no longer a student, that you'd lost all your pupils and shed your decent apparel and, with the death of her daughter, that there was no longer any reason to keep supporting you as a member of the family, well, she suddenly got scared. Then, since you took refuge in your little room and didn't keep on as before, she decided to throw you out of the apartment. She's been harboring this intention for some time but didn't want to forfeit that promissory note. And besides, you yourself also assured her that your mother would pay up . . ."

"I said that as a mean trick. . . . My mother's almost reduced to begging alms. . . . I lied so I could keep my room and . . . my board," Raskolnikov stated loudly and distinctly.

"Yes, you did the sensible thing. But the point is that a certain Mr. Chebarov turned up, a court councillor and a very businesslike man. Pashenka couldn't conceive of any of this on her own; she's very shy. But this businesslike man was not reserved in the least. The first thing he did was to pose a question: was there any hope of payment on that promissory note? The answer was yes, because you have the sort of mother who, with her pension of one hundred and twenty-five rubles, even if she herself didn't have anything to eat, would still send it to her Rodenka. You also have the sort of sister who would sell herself into slavery for her brother. He was counting on this. . . . Why are you getting restless? Now, my friend, I've found out all there is to know about you; it was not for nothing that you confided to Pashenka when you were still on good terms with her, and now I'm speaking out of love. . . . Here's the thing: an honest, sensitive man confides in a friend, while a businesslike man listens but keeps on eating, and then devours the other person. So she hands the promissory note over to this Chebarov in payment for something, and he lodges a formal claim, and won't be put off. When I found out, I wanted to unleash a current through him, too, to clear my conscience, but at the time I had harmonious relations with Pashenka and settled the whole matter, at its very source, by guaranteeing that you'd pay. I vouched for you, friend, do you hear? We summoned Chebarov, shoved ten rubles in his mouth, got the note back, and now I have the honor of presenting it to you— they'll take your word for it now—here, take it; I've even torn it a bit like it's supposed to be."

Razumikhin placed the acknowledgment of debt on the table. When Raskolnikov looked at it without saying a word and then turned toward the wall, even Razumikhin was a little annoyed.

"I see, my friend," he said a minute later, "that I've made a fool of myself once again. I thought I could distract you and entertain you with my chatter, but it seems that I merely aroused your anger."

"Was it you I didn't recognize when I was delirious?" asked Raskolnikov, after keeping silent for a minute and not turning his head around.

"Yes, me, and you even became frantic because I brought Zametov here with me once."

"Zametov? The clerk? Why?" Raskolnikov turned around quickly and stared directly at Razumikhin.

"What's the matter? What are you so upset about? He wanted to make your acquaintance; he and I had talked a lot about you. . . . Otherwise, from whom could I have found out so much about you? He's a fine man, my friend, most wonderful . . . in his own way, of course. We're friends now; we see each other almost every day. I've moved into this part of town. Did you know that? I just moved. I've been to Laviza's place with him a few times. You remember her, Laviza Ivanovna?"

"Did I say anything when I was delirious?"

"I'll say you did! You weren't yourself, sir."

"What did I say?"

"Good Lord, what a question! What did you say? It's well known what a fellow raves about in his delirium. . . . Well, my friend, now, so as not to lose time, let's get down to business."

He stood up from the chair and grabbed his cap.

"What did I say?"

"You're harping on the same thing! Are you afraid you revealed some secret? Don't worry: nothing was divulged about the countess.* But much was said about a bulldog, earrings, some chains, Krestovsky Island, a courtyard, Nikodim Fomich, and Ilya Petrovich, the assistant to the superintendent. Besides that, you were interested in your sock, very much so! You kept whining: give it to me, you said, that's all I want. Zametov looked in all the corners of your room to find your socks and gave them to you with his own hands scented with cologne and decked out in rings. Only then did you calm down; you clutched that junk in your hands day and night; it was impossible to get them away from you. They must still be lying somewhere under your blanket. And you asked for the fringes from your trousers, in such a tearful voice! We tried to determine what sort of fringes you wanted. But it was impossible to figure that out. . . . Well, sir, let's get down to business! Here are your thirty-five rubles; I'll take ten of them and present you with an account in about two hours. At the same time, I'll let Zosimov know, although he should have been here a while ago, since it's already past eleven. And you, Nastenka, look in on him more often in my absence, to see if he wants something more to drink or anything else . . . I'll speak with Pashenka myself and tell her what's needed. Good-bye!"

---

* Probably a reference to "The Queen of Spades" (1834), the most famous short story by Aleksandr Pushkin (1799–1837).

"He calls her Pashenka! Oh, you sly dog, you!" Nastasya said as he was leaving; then she opened the door and began listening, but couldn't refrain from running downstairs. She very much wanted to find out what he was talking about with the landlady because she was completely enamored with Razumikhin.

As soon as the door closed after her, the sick man tossed off his blanket and jumped out of bed like a madman. He'd been waiting with ardent, feverish impatience for them to leave so he could get to work in private. But what should he do, what sort of work? It was as if now, intentionally, he had forgotten. "Good Lord! Tell me only one thing: do they know about everything or not? What if they know already and they're merely pretending, teasing me while I'm lying here, and then all of a sudden they'll come in and say that it's all been known for some time and that they were simply waiting. . . . What should I do now? I forgot, as if on purpose; I remembered a moment ago, but then I suddenly forgot!"

He stood in the middle of his room and looked around in tormented bewilderment. He went to the door, opened it, and listened; but that wasn't it. Suddenly, as if recalling, he rushed to the corner where there was a hole in the wallpaper and began to examine it; he thrust his hand into the hole, felt around, but that wasn't it, either. He went to the stove, opened it, and began searching in the cinders: pieces of the trouser fringes and fragments of his torn pockets were lying inside, just as they had been when he'd thrown them in there: this meant that no one had looked inside! Then he remembered his sock, which Razumikhin had just mentioned. True, it was still lying on the sofa under his blanket, but it was so worn and dirty that of course Zametov couldn't have noticed anything in particular about it.

"Bah, Zametov! The office! Why did they summon me to the office? Where's the summons? Bah! I'm all mixed up; that was then! That was when I was examining my sock, but now . . . now I've been ill. Why did Zametov drop in to see me? Why did Razumikhin bring him here?" he muttered weakly, sitting down on his bed once more. "What's all this? Is this my delirium continuing or is this real? It seems to be really happening. . . . Ah, now I remember: to run away! To run away quickly, immediately, to run away immediately! Yes . . . but where? Where are my clothes? I have no boots. They've carried them off! Hidden them! I understand! Ah, there's my coat—they overlooked it! Here's the money on the table, thank heavens! Here's the promissory note. . . . I'll take the money and go away; I'll rent another apartment, and they'll never find me! Yes, but what about the address bureau? They'll find me! Razumikhin will find me. It's better to run away completely . . . far away . . . to America, and the hell with them! And take the promissory note . . . it'll be useful there. What else should I take? They think I'm sick! They don't even know I can walk, ha, ha, ha! I guessed from their eyes that they know everything! All I have to do is go down the stairs! What if they have a policeman standing guard? What's this? Tea? And there's some beer left, half a bottle, and it's cold."

He grabbed the bottle in which there was still about a glass left and swallowed it in one large gulp with pleasure, as if he were putting out a fire in his breast. But a minute hadn't passed before the beer had gone to his head and a slight, even pleasant chill ran up and down his spine. He lay down and pulled the blanket over himself. His thoughts, already painful and incoherent, began to get more and more confused, and soon a light, pleasant sleep came over him. With delight his head located a place on the pillow and he wrapped himself up tightly in the soft cotton blanket, which was now covering him instead of his torn overcoat; he sighed softly and fell into a deep, sound, healing sleep.

He woke up when he heard that someone had come in. He opened his eyes and he saw Razumikhin, who had opened the door wide and was standing on the threshold trying to decide whether to enter or not. Raskolnikov sat up quickly on the sofa and looked at him, as if trying desperately to remember something.

"Ah, you're not asleep; well, here I am! Nastasya, bring the bundle up here!" Razumikhin yelled down the stairs. "You'll have the account right away . . ."

"What time is it?" asked Raskolnikov, glancing around anxiously.

"You had a good sleep, my friend: it's evening now, almost six o'clock. You slept for over six hours . . ."

"Good Lord! How could I?"

"What's the problem? It's good for you! What's the hurry? Do you have a rendezvous? We have all the time in the world. I've been waiting for you for about three hours; I looked in twice, but you were asleep. I went to call on Zosimov twice, but he wasn't in and that's that! Never mind: he'll come! I also attended to my own affairs. I've moved today, completely, with my uncle. I have an uncle living with me now. . . . Well, the hell with all that, let's get down to business! Give me that bundle, Nastenka. We just now. . . . Hey, friend, how do you feel?"

"Fine. I'm not sick. . . . Razumikhin, have you been here long?"

"I said I've been waiting three hours."

"No, before that."

"What do you mean?"

"When did you start coming here?"

"I told you all this before, don't you remember?"

Raskolnikov became thoughtful. What had happened before seemed like a dream to him. He couldn't remember it on his own, and he looked questioningly at Razumikhin.

"Hmm," Razumikhin said. "You forgot! Just a little while ago it occurred to me that you still weren't quite right. . . . Now you're feeling better with the sleep. . . . Really, you look much better. Splendid! Well, let's get down to business! You'll recall it soon. Look here, my dear friend."

He began to untie the bundle, which apparently interested him greatly.

"This, my friend, believe me, is something that lies very close to my heart. We must make a man out of you. Let's begin: we'll start at the top. Do you see this cap?" he began, taking from the bundle a rather nice but at the same time very ordinary and inexpensive service cap. "Will you try it on?"

"Later, afterward," said Raskolnikov, waving it away peevishly.

"No, Rodya, my dear, don't resist, because it'll be too late; I won't sleep all night, because I bought it merely guessing your size. Perfect!" he exclaimed triumphantly, after seeing it on Raskolnikov's head. "An excellent fit! Headwear, my friend, is the first item in one's apparel, a kind of introduction. My acquaintance Tolstyakov, whenever he enters some public place where others are standing around wearing their hats and caps, feels compelled to doff his hat. Everyone thinks that he's doing it out of servility, but it's simply because he's ashamed of the bird's nest he has on his head: he's easily ashamed! Well, Nastenka, here are two different hats: this Palmerston"*—he retrieved from the corner Raskolnikov's mangled round top hat, which, for some reason, he called a Palmerston—"and this splendid item. Take a guess, Rodya; how much do you think I paid for it? What about you, Nastasyushka?" he asked, turning to her, seeing that Raskolnikov remained silent.

"I think you paid twenty kopecks for it," Nastasya replied.

"Twenty kopecks! You silly girl!" he cried, offended. "I couldn't even buy you for twenty kopecks these days—eighty kopecks! And that's only because it's been worn before. True, it comes with a guarantee: if you wear this one out, they give you a new one next year at no cost, so help me God! Well, sir, now let's go to the United Slacks of America, as we used to say in school. I warn you—I'm proud of these trousers!" He laid out in front of Raskolnikov a pair of gray slacks made of a light summer wool: "With no holes, no stains, perfectly passable, though a bit worn, with a matching vest of the same color, as fashion dictates. And that it's been worn makes it even better: it's softer, nicer. . . . You see, Rodya, to make a career for oneself in society, one must always pay attention to the season; if you don't order asparagus in January, then you can hold on to a few rubles in your wallet; it's the same with regard to these purchases. It's now the summer season, and I bought some summer clothes because autumn will require warmer clothes, so you'll have to discard these . . . all the more so since these things will have fallen to pieces by then, if not from their increased splendor, then from internal defects. Well, so what do you think? How much did I pay? Two rubles and twenty-five kopecks! And remember, it's with the same guarantee: if you wear these out, next year you get others for no charge! That's the way it works in Fedyaev's shop: you pay one time only, and that's sufficient for the rest of your life, otherwise you'd never return there again. Well, sir, now let's get to the boots— what do you think? You can see that they've been worn, but they'll do you for the next two months or so, because the material and the workmanship are foreign. The secretary of the English embassy sold

---

* Henry John Temple, 3rd Viscount Palmerston (1784–1865), was a British statesman and Liberal prime minister.

them at the flea market last week; he wore them only six days, but he really needed some cash. The price was one ruble and fifty kopecks. Good, eh?"

"Maybe they won't fit!" remarked Nastasya.

"Won't fit? And what's this?" He took from his pocket Raskolnikov's old, stiff boot, covered with dried mud and riddled with holes. "I took this monstrosity along in reserve, and they were able to determine the correct size. All of this business went smoothly. But as far as his linen's concerned, I spoke with the landlady. In the first place, here are three shirts, coarse cotton, but with fashionable fronts. . . . And so, in all: eighty kopecks for the cap, two rubles and twenty-five kopecks for the rest of the clothes, for a total of three rubles and five kopecks; one ruble and fifty kopecks for the boots—because they're very fine boots—for a total of four rubles and fifty-five kopecks, plus five rubles for all the linen—I paid the wholesale price—for a grand total of nine rubles and fifty-five kopecks. I have forty-five kopecks change: here, please take these five-kopeck coins. Thus, Rodya, all your clothes have been renewed, because, in my opinion, your overcoat is not only still serviceable, but even has a kind of elegance about it: that's what happens when you order your clothes from Charmeur's tailor shop! And as for socks and the remaining items, I leave that to you; we still have twenty-five rubles, and don't you worry about paying Pashenka the rent for the apartment; I told her your credit was limitless. And now, my friend, please let me change your linen, because some illness may still be lingering in that shirt of yours."

"Leave me alone! I don't want to!" Raskolnikov said, brushing him aside, after listening with disgust to the strained playfulness of his account of the purchase of the clothes . . .

"Hey, friend, this is impossible; why have I been wearing my boots out?" Razumikhin insisted. "Nastasyushka, don't be embarrassed, help me; that's right!" And, in spite of Raskolnikov's resistance, he managed to change his linen. Raskolnikov fell back on his pillow and for about two minutes said not one word.

"Why won't they go away and leave me alone?" he thought. "What money did you use to buy all this?" he asked at last, staring at the wall.

"Money? How do you like that? Your own money. The agent was

here a while ago, from Vakhrushin's office. Your mama sent it to you; or did you forget that, too?"

"Now I remember," said Raskolnikov, after some minutes of sullen reflection. Razumikhin frowned and regarded him uneasily.

The door opened and in walked a tall, solidly built man who looked somewhat familiar to Raskolnikov.

"Zosimov! At last!" cried Razumikhin joyfully.

IV

Zosimov, a tall, plump man, with a puffy, pale, colorless, smooth-shaven face and straight blond hair, wore glasses and had a large gold ring on one of his fat, swollen fingers. He was about twenty-seven years old. He was dressed in a large, light, fashionable coat and light-colored summer trousers. In general, everything he wore was large, dandyish, and impeccable; his linen was spotless and his watch chain was massive. His manner was slow, as if both sluggish and, at the same time, intentionally easygoing; his pretentiousness, though carefully concealed, was apparent at every moment. Everyone who knew him found this man difficult to deal with but acknowledged that he knew his business.

"I came by to see you twice, my friend. . . . You see, he's come to!" Razumikhin said.

"I see, I see; well, and just how are we feeling now, eh?" Zosimov asked, addressing Raskolnikov, staring at him directly and seating himself next to him at the foot of the sofa, where he made himself as comfortable as possible.

"He's still feeling down," Razumikhin continued. "We just changed his linen, and he almost started crying."

"That makes sense; his linen could've been changed later, if he didn't want it. . . . His pulse is strong. You still have a little headache, don't you?"

"I'm fine, completely fine!" Raskolnikov replied insistently and irritably, suddenly raising himself on the sofa, his eyes flashing; then he fell back onto the pillow again and turned his face to the wall. Zosimov observed him carefully.

"Very well . . . everything's in order," he said sluggishly. "Has he had anything to eat?"

They told him and then asked what he should be fed.

"Anything. . . . Soup, tea. . . . No mushrooms or cucumbers, of course, and he shouldn't have any beef, and . . . but why sit here chatting like this?" He exchanged glances with Razumikhin. "No more medicine or anything; I'll look in again tomorrow. . . . Perhaps even later today . . . well, yes . . ."

"I'll take him out for a walk tomorrow evening!" decided Razumikhin. "To the Yusupov Garden, and then we'll drop by the Palais de Cristal."*

"I wouldn't move him at all tomorrow, but perhaps you can, a little. . . . We'll see then."

"What a pity, I'm having a housewarming today, very close to here; I wish he could come. He could lie there on the sofa among us! Will you be there?" Razumikhin suddenly turned to ask Zosimov. "Don't forget, you promised."

"Perhaps later, if I can. What have you arranged?"

"Nothing much: tea, vodka, and herring. We'll serve a savory pie— just a few friends."

"Who, exactly?"

"They're all from around here. True, they're all new acquaintances— except for my old uncle, and he's a new acquaintance, too; he just arrived in Petersburg yesterday, on some sort of business. We see each other once every five years."

"Who is he?"

"He's been vegetating his whole life as a district postmaster. . . . He receives a small pension; he's sixty-five and hardly worth talking about. . . . But I do love him. Porfiry Petrovich will also be there; he's the local examining magistrate . . . a trained lawyer. You know him . . ."

---

* A tavern named after the Crystal Palace, a structure built of cast iron and plate glass in Hyde Park, London, to house the Great Exhibition of 1851.

"Is he also a relative of yours?" Zosimov inquired.

"A very distant one; why are you making such a face? Just because you two had words once, does that mean you won't come?"

"I don't give a damn about him . . ."

"That's even better. There'll be some students, a teacher, a civil servant, a musician, an officer, Zametov . . ." Razumikhin continued.

"Tell me, please, what do you have in common or does he have"—Zosimov nodded at Raskolnikov—"with this Zametov?"

"Oh, these squeamish people! Principles! You're stuck on your principles as if on loaded springs; you don't dare turn around on your own; in my opinion, he's a good man—that's the principle, and I don't want to hear anything else. Zametov's a splendid man."

"He greases his palms."

"Well, what if he does? I don't give a damn. What of it, anyway?" Razumikhin cried suddenly, somehow unusually annoyed. "Did I praise him for greasing his palms? I merely said that in his own way he was a good man! And I ask you directly, look around at everyone—are there really that many good men left? I'm sure that no one would give even a baked onion for me, even if you threw in all my entrails, and that's only if you were included in the bargain, too!"

"That's too little; I'd give two onions for you . . ."

"Well, I'd give only one for you! Go on, be witty! Zametov's still a young lad. I'll still pull him by the hair, because he should be drawn in and not pushed away. Once you push a man away, you can't make him any better, all the more so with a young man. One has to be twice as careful with such a lad. Hey, you progressive blockheads, you don't understand a thing! If you don't respect others, you harm yourself. . . . If you want to know, it was perhaps a shared interest that brought us together."

"I would like to know."

"It all has to do with that painter, that is, the housepainter. . . . We'll drag him out! However, there's no difficulty now. The matter's completely clear! We have to turn up the steam."

"What painter are you talking about?"

"What, didn't I tell you? No? Wait a bit, I told you only the beginning . . . about the murder of the old woman, the pawnbroker, the civil servant's widow. . . . Well, now there's a painter involved in it . . ."

"I heard about that murder before you told me, and I'm very interested in it . . . in part . . . for one reason . . . and I read about it in the papers! But now . . ."

"They also killed Lizaveta!" Nastasya blurted out suddenly, turning to Raskolnikov. She had remained in the room, standing near the door, listening.

"Lizaveta?" mumbled Raskolnikov, in a barely audible voice.

"Lizaveta, the trader, or don't you know? She used to come here downstairs. Once she mended a shirt for you."

Raskolnikov turned toward the wall and the soiled yellow wallpaper with little white flowers; he chose one ungainly white flower with some little brown lines and began staring at it: how many leaves did it have, how many serrations on each leaf, how many brown lines? He felt that his arms and legs had grown numb, as if they were paralyzed, but he didn't try to move. He just stared intently at the flower.

"So what about the painter?" Zosimov interrupted Nastasya's chatter with a certain displeasure. She sighed and fell silent.

"They consider him a suspect in the murder!" Razumikhin continued heatedly.

"What sort of evidence do they have?"

"The hell with evidence! That's just it: the evidence they have isn't really evidence; that's what we have to prove! It's exactly what happened at first when they rounded up and accused those two, what are their names . . . Kokh and Pestryakov. Phew! It's all so stupid, even loathsome to a person who has nothing to do with it! That Pestryakov may come to see me today. . . . By the way, Rodya, you already know about this; this happened before you fell ill, precisely the day you fainted in the office where they were talking about it . . ."

Zosimov regarded Raskolnikov with curiosity, but he didn't stir.

"You know what, Razumikhin? I've been watching you: what a busybody you are," remarked Zosimov.

"That may be, but all the same we'll get him out of it!" cried Razumikhin, banging his fist on the table. "What's the worst part of it? It's not that they're lying. One can always forgive that kind of lie, because it always leads to the truth. No, what's so annoying is that they're lying and believe their own lies. I respect Porfiry, but. . . . What was it, for example, that led them astray from the very start? The door was locked, but when they arrived with the caretaker, the door was unlocked. Well, that means Kokh and Pestryakov murdered them! That's their logic!"

"Don't get so upset. They've simply detained them, but one shouldn't assume. . . . By the way, I've met this fellow Kokh. It turns out he'd been buying up unredeemed pledges from the old woman. Eh?"

"What a scoundrel he is! He also buys up promissory notes. He's a businessman. To hell with him! Do you understand what it is that angers me most? It's their obsolete, vulgar, callous routine. . . . Yet here, in this case, one could adopt a whole new approach. Using only psychological facts, one could show how to follow the right path. 'But,' they say, 'we have the facts.' But facts aren't everything. At least half the case is how well one treats the facts!"

"And do you know how to treat facts?" Zosimov asked.

"It's impossible to keep silent when you feel—you feel by instinct—that you could help in this case, if only. . . . Hey! Do you know the details?"

"I'm waiting to hear about the painter."

"Well, of course! Then listen to the story: exactly three days after the murder, in the morning, they were still fussing over Kokh and Pestryakov, even though those two were able to account for their every step. The evidence was unmistakable! All of a sudden, the most unexpected fact was announced. A certain peasant named Dushkin, the keeper of a tavern opposite that same building, appears in the office and brings in a jewelry case with gold earrings and tells a whole long tale: 'A fellow comes runnin' in two days ago,' he says, 'toward evenin', just after eight o'clock.' You hear? The day and the hour! 'A painter who'd come to see me before durin' the day; his name is Mikolai, and he brings in this here box of gold earrin's with little gemstones, and asks for two rubles in exchange. When I ask him where he got 'em, he says he'd found 'em in the street. I didn't ask him any more about it'—that's Dushkin speaking—'and I gave him a note, that is, a ruble, because I thought if he didn't get it from me, he'd get it from someone else, it's all the same—he'll drink it up, so it's better for it to be in my hands: "safe find, fast find," as they say, and if somethin' comes out about it, then I could always turn it in.' Well, of course, he's spinning an old wives' tale, lying like a dog, because I know this Dushkin. He's a pawnbroker himself and is hiding stolen property. He didn't filch this thirty-ruble item from Mikolai just to 'turn it in.' He simply lost his nerve. Well, to hell with it, you hear. Dushkin continues: 'I know this here peasant Mikolai Dementev from his childhood; he's from our district and province, Zaraysk, and I'm from Ryazan. And though Mikolai isn't a drunkard, he does drink, and I knew he was workin' in this here house, paintin', together with Mitrei, and they're both from the same place. After he gets the ruble, he changes it for some coins right away, downs two glasses of vodka, takes his change, leaves, but I didn't see Mitrei with him at that time. The next day we hear that Alyona Ivanovna and her sister Lizaveta Ivanovna had been killed with an axe. We knew them, sir, and I begin worryin' about them earrin's because we knew that the dead woman lent money for pledges. I went to see them in that house and began askin' questions, carefully and quietly. The very first one I asked was 'Is Mikolai here?' Mitrei told me that Mikolai'd gone off on a spree, had come home drunk at dawn, stayed for about ten minutes, and then left again. Mitrei hadn't seen him since and was finishin' up the work alone. They were workin' on the second floor of the same staircase as the deceased. After hearin' all this, I didn't say nothing to nobody at the time'—that's Dushkin speaking—'but I found out everythin' I could about the murder and went back home with the same worries. This mornin', at eight o'clock'—that is, on the third day, you understand—'I see that Mikolai's comin' to see me, not sober, but not really dead drunk, so he could still understand conversation. He sits down on the bench and keeps silent. Besides him in the tavern at that time there was only one stranger, another man was asleep on the bench whom I knew, and my two boys. "Did you," I ask, "see Mitrei?" "No," he says, "I didn't." "And he wasn't here?" "No," he says, "not in the last two days." "Where did he sleep last night?" "In the Sands,"* he says, "near Kolomna." "And where," I say, "did you get those earrings?" "I found 'em in the street," and he says this with some uncertainty, without looking at me. "Have you heard," I ask, "that such and such happened at that same time on that very evening on that staircase?" "No," he says, "I didn't." He listens to me, his eyes wide open, and suddenly grows pale as a ghost. As I'm telling him all this, I see him reach for his cap and get ready to bolt. I wanted to keep him there; "Wait, Mikolai," I say, "won't you drink up?" I winked to my lad so he'd keep the door closed, and I came out from behind the counter; but he got away from me, ran out onto the street, down the lane—and that's the last I saw of him. That settled all my doubts; he's the culprit, no doubt about it . . .'"

"I'll say!" cried Zosimov.

"Wait! Hear the end of it! Of course, they set off as fast as possible to find Mikolai. They detained Dushkin and searched his place, Mitrei's, too; they scoured the men in Kolomna as well—suddenly, two days ago, they bring in Mikolai himself: he'd been detained near the gate of an inn. He'd arrived there, removed his cross, a silver one, and asked for a glass of vodka in exchange. They gave it to him. After waiting a few minutes, the old woman went into the cowshed and peeked through the crack. In the barn next door he'd fastened his sash to a beam, made a noose, then he stood on a stump and was trying to put the noose around his neck. The old woman shrieked at the top of her lungs and they came running: 'So, that's what you are!' 'Take me,' he says, 'to such and such a police station; I'll admit to everything.' Well, they took him to the police station, the one here, that is, with all the appropriate honors. Then it was this, that, who, how, how old—'twenty-two'—so on and so forth. Question: 'When you were working with Mitrei, did you see anyone on the staircase, at such and such an hour?' Answer: 'Of course, some people may have gone by, but we didn't notice who.' 'Did you hear anything, some noise or anything else?' 'We didn't hear nothin' unusual.' 'Did you know, Mikolai, a certain widow and her sister on that day and at that time

---

* An area between Nevsky Prospect and the Smolny Institute.

were murdered and robbed?' 'I don't know nothin' and don't have no idea. The first I heard was from Afanasy Pavlych, the third day, in the tavern.' 'Where did you get the earrings?' 'I found 'em in the street.' 'Why didn't you come to work with Mitrei the next day?' 'I was on a spree.' 'Where was that?' 'Here and there.' 'Why did you run away from Dushkin?' ''Cause I was very afraid.' 'Afraid of what?' 'They'd think I done it.' 'How could you be afraid when you yourself felt you were not guilty?' Well, Zosimov, believe it or not, that question was posed, in those exact words. I know it for a fact. They told me so. How do you like that?"

"Well, no; but there are certainly clues."

"I'm not talking about clues now. I'm talking about that question, how they themselves understand things! To hell with it! Well, they pressured him and pressured him, squeezed him and squeezed him, and he finally confessed. 'I found 'em not on the street,' he says, 'but in the 'partment where Mitrei and I was paintin'.' 'How did you find them?' 'It's that Mitrei and I was paintin' there the whole day, until eight o'clock, and we was fixin' to leave, and Mitrei takes a brush and daubs some paint on my face, he does, he daubs some paint on my face, and goes runnin' out and I run after him. So I go runnin' after him, yellin' my head off. As I was comin' down the stairs and turnin' into the gateway at full speed, I run right into the caretaker with some other gentlemen, I don't remember exactly how many, and the caretaker begins shoutin' at me, and the other gentleman also begins shoutin' 'cause me and Mitka are blockin' the way. Then I grab Mitka by the hair and knock him down and start punchin' him. Mitka, too, from underneath, grabs me by the hair and starts punchin' me, and we're fightin' not out of anger, but out of love, playin'. Then Mitka breaks free and goes runnin' out into the street and I chase after him, but don't catch up with him, and go back to the 'partment alone—'cause I have to clean up. I begin to clear things away and wait for Mitrei, in case he comes. By the door in the entranceway to the room, in the corner against the wall, I step on a small box. I look down, and there's somethin' lyin' there, wrapped in paper. I pick it up, and I see some tiny hooks, and I take hold of these hooks and there's earrin's in the little box . . .'"

"Behind the door? Lying behind the door? Behind the door?" Raskolnikov cried suddenly, regarding Razumikhin with a vague, frightened look, raising himself up slowly, leaning on his arm on the sofa.

"What of it? What's wrong with you? Why do you ask?" Razumikhin also rose from his place.

"It's nothing!" Raskolnikov replied, barely audibly, lowering himself onto his pillow again and turning to face the wall. Everyone was silent for a little while.

"He must have dozed off; he's only half awake," Razumikhin said at last, looking inquisitively at Zosimov, who shook his head slightly to indicate no.

"Well, go on," said Zosimov. "Then what?"

"Then what? As soon as he saw the earrings, he forgot all about the apartment and about Mitka, grabbed his cap, ran off to Dushkin, and, as is known, received a ruble from him, lying to him, saying that he found them in the street, and then he went off on a spree. About the murder, he confirmed what he'd said before: 'I don't know nothing and don't have no idea; I heard about it only two days ago.' 'Why didn't you come in before this?' 'I was afraid.' 'Why did you try to hang yourself?' 'From thinkin'.' 'Thinking about what?' 'They'd think I done it.' That's the whole story. Now, what do you suppose they made of all that?"

"What's to think about? There's a trail, not much of one, but something. Facts. Don't tell me they should release your painter?"

"But now they attribute the murder to him without question. They already have no doubt whatsoever . . ."

"Not true. You're getting too excited. What about the earrings? You have to agree that if on that very day and at that time the earrings from the old woman's trunk wound up in Nikolai's hands—you have to agree that they had to get there some way or other. In such circumstances that must mean something."

"How did they wind up there? How?" cried Razumikhin. "Could it be that you, Doctor, you, who, first of all, are obliged to study human nature, and you, who have the opportunity, more than most, to observe human nature, could it be that with all this evidence, you don't see what sort of creature this Nikolai is? Don't you see that from the very beginning everything he said during the interrogations was the sacred truth? That's precisely how the earrings wound up in his hands, just as he said. He stepped on the box and then picked them up!"

"Sacred truth? But he himself has admitted that he lied at first?"

"Listen to me, and listen carefully: the caretaker, Kokh, Pestryakov, another gentleman, the caretaker's wife, and the woman who was sitting with her in the lodge at the time, and the court councillor Kryukov, who, at that very moment, got out of a cab and entered through the gateway, arm in arm with a woman—everyone, that is eight or ten witnesses, unanimously testify that Nikolai had pushed Dmitry down on the ground and was lying on top of him, punching him, while he had grabbed hold of Nikolai's hair and was also punching him. They were stretched across the path, blocking their way; people were swearing at them from all sides; they were on top of one another 'like little kids' (the actual expression used by the witnesses), screeching, fighting, and laughing, each trying to outdo the other with his laughter, making the funniest faces. Then, just like children, they went running out into the street, each trying to catch the other. You hear? Now, take careful note of this: the bodies upstairs were still warm, you hear, still warm, when they found them! If they had killed the two women, or if just Nikolai had done it, broken into and robbed the trunk, or merely taken part somehow in the robbery, then let me pose just one question to you: does their mental disposition—that is, with their screeches, laughter, childish fighting under the gate—correspond to axes, blood, criminal cunning, caution, and robbery? They had just murdered them, some five or ten minutes ago—because, it turns out, the bodies were still warm—and suddenly, leaving the bodies, the apartment unlocked, and knowing that some men had just gone up there, abandoning their booty, they roll around in the road like little kids, laughing, attracting considerable attention from the ten witnesses who testify to this unanimously!"

"Of course, it's odd! Naturally, it's impossible, but . . ." Zosimov remarked.

"No, my friend, no *but*. If the earrings, which turned up in Nikolai's hands on that very day and at that time, really constitute the most important factual evidence against him—though perfectly explicable according to his own testimony, consequently, still *disputable evidence*—then one must consider the exculpatory evidence, all the more so since there are *irresistible* facts. What do you think, judging by the nature of our legal system: will they accept such facts, are they even capable of accepting them—based exclusively on a psychological impossibility, on their mental disposition—as irresistible facts obliterating all accusatory and material evidence, no matter what they are? No, they won't accept them, not for anything, because they found the box and the man wanted to kill himself, 'which couldn't happen, if he hadn't felt that he was guilty!' That's the major question, that's why I'm so excited! Understand?"

"Yes, I can see you're excited. Wait, I forgot to ask: has it been proven that the box with the earrings really came from the old woman's trunk?"

"It has been," Razumikhin replied, frowning, and added, as if reluctantly, "Kokh recognized the item and positively identified the person who'd pawned it, and he verified that the item was really his."

"That's not good. Now, one more thing: did anyone see Nikolai at the time that Kokh and Pestryakov were heading upstairs? Couldn't that prove something?" Zosimov asked.

"That's just it. No one saw him," replied Razumikhin with annoyance. "That's what's bad. Even Kokh and Pestryakov didn't notice him as they were passing by, although their testimony doesn't mean very much now. 'We saw,' they said, 'that the apartment was open, and that someone must have been working there, but in passing we didn't pay any attention and don't recall precisely whether there were workers inside at the time.' "

"Hmm. Therefore, the only exculpatory evidence is that they were punching each other and laughing. Let's suppose this is serious proof, but. . . . Now, how do you account for all these facts? How do you explain his finding the earrings, if he really found them as he maintains?"

"How? What's to explain: it's perfectly clear! At least the path this investigation must follow is clear and indicated, and it's the box that's shown the way. The real murderer dropped those earrings. The murderer was upstairs when Kokh and Pestryakov knocked, standing behind the locked door. Kokh was a fool and went downstairs. Then the murderer slipped out and ran downstairs, too, because he had no other way out. On the staircase he hid from Kokh, Pestryakov, and the caretaker in the empty apartment exactly when Dmitry and Nikolai had run out. He stood behind the door while the caretaker and the others passed. He waited until the sound of their footsteps had died down, then proceeded downstairs on his own very quietly, at the same time that Dmitry and Nikolai ran out into the street and everyone dispersed, leaving no one left under the gateway. They might even have seen him, but they didn't notice him since lots of people pass by there. He'd dropped the box from his pocket when he was standing behind the door and didn't notice that he'd done so. He had more important things on his mind. The box clearly demonstrates that he stood right there. That's all there is to it!"

"Clever! No, my friend, it is clever. But it's too clever by half!" Zosimov exclaimed.

"Why do you think so, why?"

"Because it all comes together too neatly . . . and it all works out . . . as if in the theater."

"Hey!" Razumikhin started to exclaim, but just at that moment the door opened and in walked a new person, unknown to everyone in the room.

V

This was a gentleman, no longer young, but standoffish, portly, and with a cautious, grumpy face, who began by pausing in the doorway and glancing around as though offended and with undisguised astonishment, as if asking, with the look in his eyes, "Where on earth have I come?" He surveyed Raskolnikov's cramped and shabby "ship's cabin" with uncertainty, even with the pretense of a certain fright, almost as though taking offense. With that same astonishment, he transferred his glance and stared at Raskolnikov himself, undressed, disheveled, unwashed, lying on his filthy, wretched sofa, also examining him without stirring. Then, with the same deliberation, he began scrutinizing the disheveled, unshaven, uncombed figure of Razumikhin, who stared directly into his eyes with a boldly inquisitive look without stirring from his place. A tense silence lasted a minute or so, until finally, as could be expected, there occurred a slight change of mood. It must have been that after certain extremely harsh facts caused him to realize that his exaggerated severe bearing here, in this "ship's cabin," would not get him anywhere, the gentleman softened his approach and politely, though not without some severity, turned to Zosimov and, enunciating every syllable of his question, asked:

"Are you Rodion Romanovich Raskolnikov, a student or former student?"

Zosimov stirred slowly and might have replied, had not Razumikhin, whom no one had addressed, forestalled him immediately:

"There he is on the sofa! What do you want?"

That familiar "what do you want?" brought the standoffish gentleman up short; he almost turned to face Razumikhin, but managed to restrain himself in time and turned back to Zosimov.

"There's Raskolnikov," muttered Zosimov, nodding at the patient. Then he yawned and, in so doing, opened his mouth unusually wide and kept it that way for an unusually long time. Next, he slowly reached into his vest pocket, extracted an enormous bulging gold pocket watch in a case, opened it, glanced at it slowly and lethargically, and put it back in his pocket.

Raskolnikov himself lay on his back in silence and stubbornly, though without thinking, studied the gentleman who had just entered. His face, now turned away from that particular flower on the wallpaper, was extremely pale and expressed uncommon suffering, as if he had just undergone a painful operation or had suddenly been released from some torture. The gentleman gradually began arousing his attention more and more, then his bewilderment, then uncertainty, and even some fear. When Zosimov, having pointed to him, had said, "There's Raskolnikov," he'd suddenly and quickly raised himself, as if jumping up, and sat on the edge of his bed; in an almost challenging voice, but also faltering and faint, he said:

"Yes. I'm Raskolnikov. What do you want?"

The guest looked at him intently and announced imposingly:

"Petr Petrovich Luzhin. I trust that my name is not completely unfamiliar to you."

But Raskolnikov, expecting something completely different, regarded him vacantly and pensively and made no reply, as if he were definitely hearing Petr Petrovich's name for the first time.

"What? Can it possibly be that you still haven't received any news?" asked Petr Petrovich, somewhat taken aback.

In reply, Raskolnikov slowly sank onto his pillow, placed his hands behind his head, and began staring at the ceiling. Anguish was perceptible on Luzhin's face. Zosimov and Razumikhin began scrutinizing him with even greater attention, and he finally became visibly embarrassed.

"I assumed and reckoned," he muttered, "that the letter sent more than ten days ago, almost two weeks ago, would've . . ."

"Listen, why are you still standing next to the doorway?" Razumikhin asked, suddenly interrupting him. "If you have something to say, then take a seat; you and Nastasya are crowding each other there. Nastasyushka, move aside, let him pass! Go on, there's a chair, over here! Squeeze in."

He moved the chair away from the table, left a little space between it and his knees, and waited in tense anticipation as the guest "squeezed" through this opening. The moment was chosen in such a way that it was impossible to refuse, and the guest, hurrying and stumbling, slid through this narrow space. After reaching the chair, he sat down and regarded Razumikhin suspiciously.

"Don't be embarrassed," Razumikhin rattled on. "Rodya's been ill for the last five days and was delirious for three of them. Just now he's returned to his senses and has even eaten with gusto. This is his doctor, who's just examined him. I'm Rodya's friend, also a former student, and now I'm looking after him. Don't pay any attention to us and don't be shy. Go on and say what you have to say."

"Thank you. But might I be disturbing the patient by my presence and my conversation?" Petr Petrovich asked, turning to Zosimov.

"N-no," mumbled Zosimov, yawning again, "you may even distract him."

"He's been back with us for a while, since this morning!" continued Razumikhin, whose familiarity had the air of such genuine simplicity that Petr Petrovich thought for a bit and began to take heart—in part, perhaps because this ragged and impudent fellow had introduced himself as a student.

"Your mama . . ." began Luzhin.

"Hmm!" Razumikhin said loudly. Luzhin looked at him inquisitively.

"Never mind, just so; go on . . ."

Luzhin shrugged his shoulders. "Your mama began writing a letter to you before I left. After my arrival here, I intentionally waited a few days and didn't come to see you in order to be completely certain that you'd have been apprised of the whole matter; but now, to my surprise . . ."

"I know, I know!" Raskolnikov said suddenly, with an expression of the most impatient annoyance. "So it's you? The suitor? Well, I do know! And that's enough!"

Petr Petrovich was downright offended, but remained silent. He made a concerted effort to understand what all this meant. The silence continued for a minute.

Meanwhile, Raskolnikov, who had turned toward him slightly after his response, suddenly took to staring directly at him again with some special curiosity, as if he hadn't had the chance to examine him fully before, or as if something new about his appearance had struck him. He even raised himself up intentionally from his pillow to do this. As a matter of fact, something in Petr Petrovich's general appearance did strike him as peculiar, that is, something that seemed to support the term "suitor," conveyed upon him so unceremoniously just now. In the first place, it was evident, and even too noticeable, that Petr Petrovich had made hasty efforts to use his few days in the capital to get himself all decked out and fancied up in anticipation of meeting his fiancée, which fact, however, was extremely harmless and acceptable. Even his own awareness, perhaps a bit too self-satisfied, his own awareness of this pleasant change for the better could be forgiven on such an occasion, for Petr Petrovich was close to being a bridegroom. All of his apparel had just come from a tailor, and it was all very fine, except perhaps that it was all too new and revealed his purpose too evidently. Even his foppish, trendy round hat bore witness to it: Petr Petrovich treated his hat too respectfully and held it in his hands too cautiously. Even his splendid pair of lilac-colored French gloves bore witness to the same thing, if only because he wasn't wearing them, merely holding them in his hand for show. Bright and youthful colors predominated in his apparel. He was wearing a fine summer jacket of a light brown hue, bright, lightweight trousers, the same kind of vest, brand-new refined linen, and a light cotton necktie with pink stripes, and best of all, this apparel was even becoming to Petr Petrovich. His face, extremely fresh and even ruddy, seemed younger than his forty-five years, even without his new clothes. Dark muttonchop whiskers shaded his cheeks pleasantly and thickened handsomely next to his closely shaved, shining chin. Even his hair, with only a slight trace of gray, had been combed and curled by a barber, but this fact didn't make him look comical or foolish, as usually happens with curled hair, because it inevitably conveys to the face the look of a German about to get married. If there was anything really unpleasant and repulsive in his rather handsome and respectable appearance, it was caused by other factors. After unceremoniously examining Mr. Luzhin, Raskolnikov smiled maliciously, once again lowered himself onto his pillow, and began staring at the ceiling as he had done before.

But Mr. Luzhin gathered his strength and, it seems, resolved for the time being not to notice any of this strange behavior.

"I very deeply regret that I find you in this situation," he began again, ending the silence with some effort. "Had I known you were ill, I'd have come by sooner. But, business, you understand! In addition, I have extremely important work pertaining to legal matters in the Senate. I won't even mention those concerns, which you can guess. And I await your family, that is, your mama and sister, at any moment . . ."

Raskolnikov stirred and was about to say something. His face expressed a certain agitation. Petr Petrovich paused and waited, but since nothing followed, he continued:

". . . At any moment. I've found them a place to stay for the time being . . ."

"Where?" Raskolnikov inquired faintly.

"Very close to here. At Bakaleev's house."

"That's on Voznesensky Prospect," Razumikhin interrupted. "There are two floors rented out as hotel rooms by the merchant Yushin. I've been there."

"Yes, hotel rooms . . ."

"It's a terribly filthy place: dirt, stench, full of suspicious types. Things have happened there; the devil knows who actually lives there! I myself was present at some disgraceful affair. However, it is cheap."

"Of course, I was unable to gather sufficient information about it, since I just arrived," Petr Petrovich objected delicately. "However, I chose two very, very clean little rooms, and since it's for such a short stay. . . . I've also found a real apartment, that is, our future apartment," he said, turning to Raskolnikov, "and renovations are being made to it now. Meanwhile, I myself have squeezed into some rooms, not far from here, at Madame Lippevekhsel's, in the apartment of my young friend Andrey Semyonych Lebezyatnikov. He's the one who told me about Bakaleev's house . . ."

"Lebezyatnikov?" Raskolnikov said slowly, as if recalling something.

"Yes, Andrey Semyonych Lebezyatnikov, an office worker in the ministry. Do you happen to know him?"

"Yes . . . no . . ." Raskolnikov replied.

"Forgive me, it seemed you did from your question. I was his guardian at one time . . . he's a very nice young man . . . and terribly well informed. . . . I love to meet young people. You find out what's new from them." Petr Petrovich examined all those present with a hopeful look.

"In what respect?" asked Razumikhin.

"In the most serious, so to speak, the most essential way," Petr Petrovich explained, seeming to enjoy the question. "You see, I haven't been to Petersburg in the last ten years. All these new things, reforms, ideas—all of this has managed to reach us in the provinces, but to see it more clearly and to understand it all, one must be in Petersburg. Well, sir, my idea is that you notice more and learn more when observing our younger generation. I confess that I rejoiced . . ."

"In what, precisely?"

"Your question is a broad one. I might be mistaken, but it seems that I find they have a clearer view, a more critical view, so to speak; they're more effective . . ."

"That's true," muttered Zosimov.

"Not true, they're not more effective." Razumikhin seized upon his words. "It's hard to be effective; it doesn't just descend from the heavens. For almost two hundred years, we've been weaned away from any action. . . . We may have plenty of ideas," he said, turning to Petr Petrovich, "and a desire for the good, though it's childlike. One can even find integrity, in spite of all the swindlers who've turned up among us, but there's still no efficacy! Effective people are nowhere to be seen."

"I don't agree with you," Petr Petrovich objected with visible pleasure. "Of course, there are enthusiasms, inaccuracies, but one must be indulgent: enthusiasms bear witness to their fervor for action and to incorrect external circumstances in which the matter is placed. If little has been achieved, it's because there's been so little time. I'm not even referring to the means. In my personal view, if you like, one can even say that something has been achieved: new, useful ideas have been widely circulated, several new, useful works have been disseminated in place of the previous fantastic and romantic ones. Literature has acquired a more mature outlook, and many harmful prejudices have been rooted out and ridiculed. . . . In a word, we've cut ourselves off once and for all from the past, and in my opinion, that's already an achievement, sir . . ."

"He's memorized that speech! He's showing off," Raskolnikov muttered suddenly.

"What, sir?" asked Petr Petrovich, who hadn't caught what was said, but he received no reply.

"That's all fair," Zosimov hastened to insert.

"Isn't it true, sir?" continued Petr Petrovich, glancing pleasantly at Zosimov. "You'll agree yourself," he continued, turning to Razumikhin, but now with an element of triumph and superiority, and almost adding the phrase "young man" as he spoke, "that there's been notable advancement, or, as they say now, progress, at least in the name of science and economic truth . . ."

"How banal!"

"No, it is not banal, sir! If, for example, up to now I was told to 'love my neighbor,' and did so, what came of that?" continued Petr Petrovich, perhaps with excessive haste. "What came of it was that I tore my cloak in two, gave half to my neighbor, and we both wound up half naked, just like in the Russian proverb 'If you chase two hares, you'll catch neither.' Science tells us to love ourselves first of all because everything on earth is based on personal interest. If you love yourself alone, then you'll conduct your affairs appropriately, and your cloak will remain in one piece. Economic truth adds that the more private businesses we have in society and, so to speak, the more cloaks remain intact, then the firmer its foundations and the more will be accomplished for the common good. Consequently, in acquiring solely and exclusively for myself, I'm also acquiring for all, and making sure that my neighbor receives somewhat more than a torn cloak and not because of private, solitary generosity, but as the result of general advancement. The idea is simple, but unfortunately, too long in the coming, hidden by a penchant for enthusiasm and fantasy; it seems that a little cleverness is necessary to surmise that . . ."

"Excuse me, I'm not too clever, either," Razumikhin cut in abruptly. "Therefore, let's stop here. I began with a purpose, but all of this chatter for self-amusement, all these incessant, endless commonplaces, over and over again, have become so loathsome to me over the last three years, that, so help me God, I blush when other people utter them in my presence, let alone when I myself say them. You naturally hastened to show off your knowledge. That's very understandable, and I don't condemn you. I'd only like to know now who you are, because don't you see, so many opportunists have latched onto these commonplaces of late and have distorted everything they touch to such an extent, out of their own interest, that they have defiled the entire cause. Well, sir, that's enough!"

"My dear sir," Luzhin began, wincing with a sense of his own extraordinary worth, "are you implying, so unceremoniously, that I, too . . ."

"Oh, for pity's sake. . . . Would I do that? Well, sir, that's enough!" snapped Razumikhin, then turned abruptly to Zosimov to resume their previous conversation.

Petr Petrovich proved to be clever enough to accept this explanation immediately. However, he decided to leave in a few minutes.

"I trust that now our newly formed acquaintance," he said, turning to Raskolnikov, "after your recovery and in view of the circumstances you know well, will become even stronger. . . . I especially wish you good health . . ."

Raskolnikov didn't even turn his head. Petr Petrovich was about to stand up and take his leave.

"The murderer was definitely someone who pawned something!" Zosimov declared firmly.

"Absolutely!" Razumikhin agreed. "Porfiry won't reveal what he's thinking, but he's questioning those people who pawned items."

"Are they all being interrogated?" Raskolnikov asked loudly.

"Yes, what of it?"

"Nothing."

"How is he finding them?"

"Kokh named a few. Other names were written on the wrappings of the items, and other people came forward on their own, when they heard about it . . ."

"Well, the murderer must be a cunning and experienced rogue! What impudence! What resolve!"

"That's precisely what he's missing!" Razumikhin interrupted. "That's what's leading you all astray. I maintain that he was inept and inexperienced, and this was probably his first endeavor! If you assume he was a calculating and cunning rogue, then the whole thing turns out improbably. Assume an inexperienced fellow, and it turns out that it was chance alone that saved him from disaster, and what can't chance do? He might not even have foreseen the obstacles he'd encounter! How did this affair proceed? He took items worth ten or twenty rubles, stuffed them into his pocket, searched around in the old woman's trunk, among her clothes—but later, in her dresser, in a box in the top drawer, they find fifteen hundred rubles in cash, plus some notes! He didn't know how to rob; he only knew how to murder! It was his first endeavor, I tell you, his first. He lost his head! It wasn't calculation, but chance that saved him."

"You seem to be talking about the recent murder of the old woman, the civil servant's widow," Petr Petrovich intervened, addressing Zosimov, and wishing to insert a few more clever words before he left, even though he was already standing with his hat and gloves in hand. Clearly, he was concerned about making an impression and his vanity had overcome his good sense.

"Yes. You've heard about it?"

"Of course, it occurred close by . . ."

"Do you know the details?"

"I can't say that I do; but what interests me about it is another circumstance, the whole problem, so to speak. I'm not talking about the fact that in the last five years the number of crimes among the lower class has increased. I'm not talking about the constant, universal robberies and arsons. For me the strangest thing of all is that the number of crimes among the upper class is also increasing, in parallel, so to speak. In one town, we learn that a former student has robbed the mail along the main road. Elsewhere, some people of respectable social standing are engaged in forging banknotes; in Moscow, they apprehended an entire gang counterfeiting tickets for the last public lottery—among the leading participants was one lecturer in world history. The secretary in one of our embassies was murdered for some enigmatic financial dealings. . . . Now, if this old woman pawnbroker was killed by one of her clients, it must have been someone of higher social standing, since peasants don't pawn gold items—how, then, do we explain this depravity of the civilized part of our society?"

"There have been many economic changes," Zosimov observed.

"How can that be explained?" Razumikhin latched onto the question. "It can easily be explained by their too deep-rooted lack of effectiveness."

"What do you mean, sir?"

"How did that lecturer in Moscow reply to your question of why he was counterfeiting lottery tickets? 'Everyone gets rich in his own way, so I also wanted to do so quickly.' I don't recall his exact words, but the idea was that he'd become wealthy for free, as quickly as possible, without having to work for it! They're used to having everything done for them, living off the charity of others, being spoon-fed. But when the great hour struck, they showed what they're made of . . ."

"But what about morality? And, so to speak, the rules of . . . ?"

"Why are you making such a fuss?" Raskolnikov broke in unexpectedly. "It worked out according to your theory!"

"How's that?"

"If you follow the theory that you were advocating just now to its conclusion, it turns out that one can slaughter people . . ."

"Good Lord!" cried Luzhin.

"No, that's not true!" echoed Zosimov.

Raskolnikov lay there pale, his upper lip quivering, breathing heavily.

"There are limits to everything," Luzhin continued haughtily. "The economic idea is still not an invitation to murder, and if one can merely assume . . ."

"Is it true that you," Raskolnikov suddenly interrupted again, his voice trembling with rage and the pleasure of giving offense, "is it true that you told your fiancée . . . at the very moment she accepted your proposal, that you were extremely pleased that . . . she was poor . . . because it was more advantageous to take a wife out of poverty so that you could dominate her afterward . . . and reproach her for the favors you'd bestowed on her?"

"My dear sir," Luzhin cried maliciously and irritably, flushed and flustered, "my dear sir . . . you've distorted my idea! Excuse me, but I must say that the rumors that have reached you, or, better to say, those conveyed to you, haven't the least trace of solid foundation, and I . . . I suspect who . . . in a word . . . launched this arrow . . . in a word, your mama. . . . Even before this, she seemed, in spite of all her excellent qualities, to have a somewhat ecstatic and romantic cast to her views. . . . But I was still a thousand miles away from supposing that she could represent this matter in a form so distorted by her fantasy. . . . And finally . . . finally . . ."

"Do you know what?" cried Raskolnikov, raising himself on his pillow and staring at him with a piercing, flashing glance. "Do you know what?"

"What, sir?" Luzhin paused and waited with an offended and challenging look. Several seconds passed in silence.

"If you dare once again . . . utter even one word . . . about my mother . . . I will throw you down the stairs head over heels!"

"What's the matter with you?" cried Razumikhin.

"So that's how it is!" Luzhin said, turning pale and biting his lip. "Listen to me, sir," he began in measured tones, using all his strength to restrain himself, but gasping for breath nonetheless. "From the very start I surmised your hostility, but remained here on purpose to learn even more. I could forgive a sick man and a relative a great deal, but now . . . you . . . never, sir . . ."

"I'm not ill!" cried Raskolnikov.

"All the more reason, sir . . ."

"Go to hell!"

But Luzhin was already leaving without having finished his speech, squeezing between the table and the chair again. This time, Razumikhin stood up to let him pass. Without looking at anyone, and without even nodding to Zosimov, who had already indicated to him that he should leave the sick man in peace, Luzhin left, cautiously raising his hat to his shoulder as he bent slightly when he passed through the door. Even the curve of his back seemed to express how, on this occasion, he was carrying a terrible insult away with him.

"How can you, how can you act like this?" asked the perplexed Razumikhin, shaking his head.

"Leave me alone, all of you, leave me alone!" Raskolnikov cried in a frenzy. "Will you leave me alone once and for all, you tormentors? I'm not afraid of you! I'm . . . not afraid of anyone now! Go away! I want to be alone, alone, alone, alone!"

"Let's go," said Zosimov, nodding to Razumikhin.

"But can we leave him like this?"

"Let's go," repeated Zosimov insistently, and then he walked out. Razumikhin thought for a moment and ran to catch up with him.

"It could be worse if we didn't listen to him," said Zosimov, already on the stairs. "He shouldn't become aggravated . . ."

"What's wrong with him?"

"If only he could be given some sort of beneficial push, that would do it! He was fine just a little while ago. . . . You know, he has something on his mind. Something immovable, oppressive. . . . I'm absolutely afraid of that!"

"Then there's that fellow, perhaps, this Petr Petrovich! According to their conversation, it's clear that he's marrying his sister and that Rodya received a letter about this before his illness . . ."

"Yes. The devil brought him here just now. Perhaps he's ruined the whole business. Did you notice that he was indifferent to everything, made no response to anything except for one point when he lost his self-control: the murder . . ."

"Yes, yes!" Razumikhin agreed. "I did notice it! He's interested in it and he gets frightened. That's what scared him that day at the police office when he fainted."

"You'll tell me more about it this evening, and I'll tell you something later. He interests me greatly! I'll come back in half an hour to see how he is. . . . But there won't be any pneumonia . . ."

"Thank you! Meanwhile I'll wait at Pashenka's and will check on him through Nastasya . . ."

Raskolnikov, left alone, regarded Nastasya, who was slow taking her leave, with impatience and anguish.

"Would you like some tea now?" she asked.

"Later! I want to sleep! Leave me alone . . ."

He turned feverishly to face the wall. Nastasya left.

VI

But as soon as she left, Raskolnikov stood up, fastened the hook on the door, untied the bundle of clothes Razumikhin had delivered earlier, which he'd tied up again, and began to get dressed. It was strange: he suddenly seemed completely calm; there was none of his half-crazed delirium as before, none of the overwhelming fear he'd experienced previously. For the first time, he felt a sudden, strange serenity. His movements were precise and assured, his certain intentions clear. "Today, definitely today!" he muttered to himself. Yet he understood that he was still weak, but the strongest spiritual tension that had resulted in this serenity, in unwavering resolution, was also affording him strength and self-assurance; he hoped, however, that he wouldn't keel over on the street. After having changed completely into his new clothes, he looked at the money left on the table, thought for a bit, and then put it into his pocket. He had twenty-five rubles in cash. He also picked up all the five-kopeck coins, the change from the ten rubles spent on clothes by Razumikhin. Then he quietly unlocked the door, walked out of the room, descended the staircase, and peeked into the open door of the kitchen: Nastasya was standing with her back to him, stooping to fan the fire in the landlady's samovar. She didn't hear a thing. And who'd suppose that he'd go out? A minute later, he was already on the street.

It was about eight o'clock, and the sun was sinking in the sky. Although it was as stuffy as before, he greedily inhaled the stinking, dusty air contaminated by the city. His head started to spin slightly. Some sort of wild energy suddenly shone in his inflamed eyes and in his gaunt, pale yellow face. He didn't know and didn't even think about what direction he was taking. He knew only one thing: "that he had to put an end to all *this* today, once and for all, immediately; that otherwise he wouldn't go home because *he didn't want to live this way.*" But how to end it? In what way? He didn't have the slightest idea, and he didn't want to think about it. He drove those thoughts away: thinking tormented him. He merely felt and knew that everything had to change, one way or another, "no matter how," he repeated with desperate, resolute self-assurance and decisiveness.

By force of habit he headed for the Haymarket, the usual path of his previous walks. Before he reached it, on the road, in front of a small shop, there stood a young, black-haired organ grinder playing a very sentimental song. He was accompanying a young girl, about fifteen, standing in front of him on the sidewalk, decked out as a fine lady, wearing a crinoline, a mantilla, gloves, and a straw hat with a fiery red feather; all of her clothes were old and worn out. She was singing a romance in a coarse, rough, but rather strong, pleasant voice, in expectation of receiving a two-kopeck piece from the shopkeeper. Raskolnikov stood alongside two or three bystanders, listened for a while, pulled out a five-kopeck piece, and put it into the girl's hand. She suddenly ended her song on the most sentimental high note, as if she had cut it off, and shouted abruptly to the organ grinder: "That'll do!" They both moved on to the next shop.

"Do you like street singers?" Raskolnikov said, turning suddenly to a gentleman, no longer young, who was standing next to him near the organ grinder and had the look of a flâneur. The latter regarded him with curiosity and great astonishment. "I do," Raskolnikov continued, with a look that seemed to show that he was not talking about street singers at all. "I like it when they sing with an organ grinder on a cold, dark, damp autumn evening, absolutely on a damp evening, when all the passersby have pale green, sickly faces; or, even better, when wet snow is falling straight down, without any wind, you know, and gaslights are shining through it . . ."

"I don't know, sir. . . . Excuse me," muttered the gentleman, frightened by both Raskolnikov's question and his strange look, and crossed to the other side of the street.

Raskolnikov continued straight ahead and came to that corner on the Haymarket where the trader and his wife had been buying and selling, and where they'd stood chatting that time with Lizaveta; but they weren't there now. After recognizing the spot, he stopped, looked around, and turned to a young lad in a red shirt, who was standing there yawning near the entrance to a flour shop.

"There's a man who engages in trade here on this corner, with a woman, his wife, right?"

"All kinds of people trade here," replied the lad, taking Raskolnikov's measure condescendingly.

"What's his name?"

"Just as he was christened."

"You must be from Zaraysk, right? What province?"

The lad looked at Raskolnikov again.

"We don't have any provinces where I come from, Your Excellency, but districts. It was my brother who came here, while I stayed at home, so I don't know, sir. . . . Be kind and forgive me, Your Excellency."

"Is that an eating place upstairs?"

"It's a tavern, and it has billiard tables. You can even find *preencesses* there. . . . Fine folks!"

Raskolnikov walked across the square. There, on the corner, stood a large crowd of people, all peasants. He made his way into the crowd, glancing at their faces. For some reason he felt like chatting with everyone. But the peasants didn't pay him any attention and were clustered in small groups, making a racket. He stood there awhile, thought for a bit, turned to the right, and proceeded along the sidewalk, in the direction of Voznesensky Prospect. After crossing the square, he found himself in a lane.

He frequently used to pass along this short street, which made a bend and then led from the square to Sadovaya Street. Lately, when he'd been feeling queasy, he'd even felt like returning to all these places, "to make himself even queasier." Now, as he turned into the street, he wasn't thinking about anything. There was a large building filled with taverns and other eating places; women constantly came running out, dressed as if they were "going to visit their neighbors"—bareheaded, wearing only dresses, but no coats. In two or three spots they crowded in groups on the sidewalk, primarily near the entrances to the lower floor, where, a few steps down, one could descend into various extremely entertaining institutions.* In one of them, at that moment, there was a loud noise and a commotion that filled the whole street; a guitar was being strummed, songs were being sung, and it was all very cheerful. A large group of women had collected near the door; some were sitting on the steps, others were gathered on the sidewalk, and still others were standing and chatting. Nearby on the street, a drunken soldier with a cigarette was making his way, cursing loudly; he seemed to want to go in somewhere but had forgotten where. One ruffian was cursing another, and a very drunken fellow was sprawled out in the street. Raskolnikov stopped near a large group of women. Bareheaded and all wearing cotton dresses and goatskin shoes, they were chatting in hoarse voices. Some of them were over forty years old, but others were only about seventeen; almost all had black eyes.

For some reason the singing and all that noise and commotion downstairs attracted him. . . . From there he could hear, amid the laughter and squeals, underneath the thin falsetto of the lively refrain and the accompaniment of a guitar, someone dancing for all he was worth, tapping out the rhythm with his heels. He listened intently, gloomily, and broodingly, leaning forward at the entrance, glancing curiously from the sidewalk into the room.

> *Oh, you fine policeman, you,*
> *Don't you beat me up for nothing!*

The singer's thin voice warbled. Raskolnikov desperately wanted to hear the words that were being sung, as if that were the most important thing.

"Should I go in?" he wondered. "They're laughing! All drunk. Maybe I should get drunk, too?"

---

* A euphemism for brothels.

"Are you going in, kind sir?" asked one of the women in a rather resonant voice that was not yet hoarse. She was young and not unattractive—one of the group of women.

"My, you're a pretty one!" he replied, standing up straight and glancing at her.

She smiled: clearly, she really appreciated his compliment.

"You're not so bad-looking yourself," she said.

"He's so skinny!" another woman muttered in a low voice. "Did you just get out of the hospital, or what?"

"You're all trying to look like generals' daughters, yet you have snub noses!" interrupted a peasant who had just approached; he was tipsy, wearing a heavy coat left open, with a sly grin on his mug. "Hey, what merrymaking!"

"Go on in, if you're here!"

"I will! What sweethearts!"

And he tumbled down the stairs.

Raskolnikov moved on.

"Listen, sir," one girl cried after him.

"What?"

She became embarrassed.

"I'd always be glad to share some time with you, kind sir, but now my conscience is bothering me. Give me, my fine gentleman, six kopecks for a drink!"

Raskolnikov took out whatever coins he had: three five-kopeck pieces.

"Ah, what a generous gentleman!"

"What's your name?"

"Ask for Duklida."

"No, no. What's all that?" one of the women remarked, shaking her head at Duklida. "I just don't know how she can ask like that! I'd certainly die from shame . . ."

Raskolnikov looked with curiosity at the woman who was speaking. Her face was pockmarked; she was about thirty years old, covered with bruises, and had a swollen upper lip. She spoke and criticized calmly and seriously.

"Where was it," Raskolnikov wondered as he moved farther along, "where was it that I read that a person sentenced to death, during his last hour, says or thinks that if he were made to live somewhere high up, on a cliff, on such a narrow platform that he only had room for his two feet, and he was surrounded by an abyss, an ocean, eternal darkness, eternal solitude, and eternal storms—and that if he could remain there standing on his small bit of space for his entire life, a thousand years, for eternity—it would be better to live like that than to die at once!

"Only to live, to live, to live! To live, no matter how—only to live! How true! How true, oh Lord! Man's a scoundrel! And the person who calls him a scoundrel for that is also a scoundrel," he added a moment later.

He emerged onto another street: "Bah! The Crystal Palace! Razumikhin was talking about the Crystal Palace just a little while ago. But what was it I wanted to do? Yes, read. . . . Zosimov said that he read in the papers about . . ."

"Do you have any newspapers?" he asked upon entering an extremely spacious and even orderly tavern that consisted of several rooms, though they were rather deserted. Two or three customers were drinking tea, and in one distant room a group of four was sitting, sipping champagne. It seemed to Raskolnikov that Zametov was among them, but it was difficult to tell from afar.

"So what!" he thought.

"Would you like some vodka, sir?" asked the waiter.

"I'd like some tea. And bring me the newspapers, older ones, for the last five days, and I'll give you some money for a drink."

"Yes, sir. Here's today's paper, sir. And would you like some vodka, sir?"

The older papers and tea were brought. Raskolnikov sat down and began searching through them: "Izler—Izler—Aztecs—Aztecs—Izler—Bartola—Massimo—Aztecs—Izler. . . . Damn it all! Ah, here's the news: a woman fell down the stairs—a tradesman burned up as a result of drink—a fire in the Sands—a fire on the Petersburg Side—another fire on the Petersburg Side—Izler—Izler—Izler—Izler—Massimo. . . . Ah, here it is . . ."

He finally found what he was looking for and began reading; the lines jumped before his eyes; however, he read the entire "news item" and greedily searched through following issues for the latest additions. His hands were trembling from feverish impatience as he turned the pages. All of a sudden someone sat down at his table, opposite him. He glanced up—it was Zametov, the very same, looking the same, with rings and chains, his curled and pomaded black hair parted in the same way, wearing a fashionable vest, a somewhat worn jacket, and dirty linen. He was cheerful; at least he was smiling cheerfully and good-naturedly. His dark face was a little flushed from the champagne.

"So! You're here?" he began in a puzzled voice, with a tone as if they'd known each other forever. "Razumikhin told me only yesterday that you were still delirious. How strange! I came by to see you, you know . . ."

Raskolnikov knew that he had come by. He pushed the newspapers away and turned to face Zametov. There was a smile on his lips, and some sort of new, irritated impatience shone through his smile.

"I know you came by," he replied. "I did hear that, sir. You were searching for my sock. . . . You know, Razumikhin's very fond of you; he says that you and he went to see Laviza Ivanovna, the one you were trying to help that time, winking at Lieutenant Porokh, but he didn't get it, you remember? How could he not—the matter was perfectly clear, wasn't it?"

"What a rowdy fellow he is!"

"Porokh?"

"No, your friend Razumikhin . . ."

"You live pretty well, Mr. Zametov; you get free access to the best places! Who's been just filling you full of champagne?"

"We were just . . . having a drink. . . . Don't exaggerate!"

"Your reward! You make the best use of everything!" Raskolnikov started laughing. "Never mind, my good fellow, never mind!" he added, slapping Zametov on the shoulder. "I'm not being mean, but 'it's out of love, playing,' just like that workman said when he was punching Mitka, in the case of the old woman."

"How do you know?"

"Perhaps I know more than you do."

"You're such a strange fellow. . . . You must still be very ill. You shouldn't have gone out . . ."

"So, I seem strange to you?"

"Yes. So, you're reading newspapers?"

"Yes, newspapers."

"There's a lot about all the fires . . ."

"No, I'm not reading about fires." At this point he looked at Zametov mysteriously; a sarcastic smile curled on his lips again. "No, I'm not reading about fires," he continued, winking at Zametov. "Confess, my dear young man, that you'd really like to know what I've been reading about."

"I don't care at all; I merely asked. Can't I ask? Why do you keep . . ."

"Listen. You're an educated man, a literary man, right?"

"I finished the sixth class at the gymnasium," replied Zametov with a certain dignity.

"Sixth class! Ah, quite the star pupil! With a part in your hair, rings on your fingers—you're a wealthy man! Phew, what a fine young lad you are!" At this moment Raskolnikov burst into nervous laughter, right in his face. Zametov flinched, and although he did not exactly take offense, he was extremely surprised.

"Phew, you're such a strange fellow!" repeated Zametov very seriously. "It seems to me that you must still be delirious."

"Delirious? You're all wrong, my dear! So, in your opinion, I seem strange? Well, am I arousing your curiosity, huh? Am I?"

"You are."

"Well, you mean what I've been reading about, what I've been searching for? Just see how many issues I had them bring me! Suspicious, isn't it?"

"Well, tell me."

"Are you all ears?"

"What do you mean?"

"I'll explain that to you later; but now, my dear fellow, I declare . . . no, even better, 'I confess. . . .' No, that's not right either: 'I'm making a statement, and you take it down,'" that's what! So I'm making a statement that I've been reading, that I've taken an interest in . . . that I was looking for, that I was searching . . ." Raskolnikov screwed up his eyes and waited. "What I found out—and that's exactly why I came here—about the murder of the old woman, the civil servant's widow," he said at last, almost in a whisper, drawing his face extremely close to Zametov's face. Zametov stared directly at him without stirring, not moving his face away from Raskolnikov's. Later it seemed to Zametov that the strangest thing about that moment was that their silence lasted a full minute, and for that minute they stared directly at each other.

"Well, what difference does it make what you've been reading," he cried out suddenly, in perplexity and impatience. "What do I care? What about it?"

"It's about that very same old woman," Raskolnikov continued in the same whisper, without flinching after Zametov's exclamation, "the one you were talking about at the office, you recall, when I fainted. Well, now do you understand?"

"What's all this? What do you mean, 'understand'?" asked Zametov, almost alarmed.

Raskolnikov's motionless and serious face was transformed in one moment, and he suddenly burst into the same nervous laughter as before, as if he were absolutely unable to restrain himself. And at that moment, he recalled with an extraordinarily clear sensation another recent moment when he had stood behind the door, axe in hand, with the bolt bouncing up and down; they were standing outside the apartment arguing, trying to force the door open, and he had suddenly felt like shouting at them, arguing with them, sticking his tongue out at them, taunting them, mocking them, and laughing, laughing, laughing!

"You're either out of your mind, or . . ." Zametov remarked, then paused, as if suddenly struck by a thought that passed through his mind like a bolt of lightning.

"Or? What's that 'or'? Well, what? Say it!"

"Nothing!" Zametov replied irately. "It's all nonsense!"

They both fell silent. After an abrupt, fitful burst of laughter, Raskolnikov suddenly became thoughtful and glum. He placed his elbows on the table and rested his head on his hands. He seemed to have forgotten all about Zametov. The silence lasted rather a long time.

"Why don't you drink your tea? It'll be cold," Zametov said.

"Huh? What? Tea? All right . . ." Raskolnikov took a swallow from the glass and put a small piece of bread into his mouth. Looking at Zametov, he suddenly seemed to recall everything and pulled himself together. At that moment, his face assumed its original sarcastic expression. He continued drinking his tea.

"These days a large number of swindlers have turned up," said Zametov. "Just recently I read in the *Moscow News* that a gang of counterfeiters had been apprehended. There was a whole society of them. They were forging banknotes."

"Oh, that was a long time ago! I read that a month ago," Raskolnikov replied serenely. "So, you think they were really swindlers?" he added with a laugh.

"What else could they be?"

"What else? They were children, greenhorns, not swindlers! Fifty people gathered together for that purpose! Is that possible? Three would have been too many, and even then, it would work only if they trusted each other more than they trusted themselves! If only one of them got drunk and let the cat out of the bag, the whole scheme would collapse! Greenhorns! They hire unreliable people to change banknotes in offices: can you trust perfect strangers with a job like that? Well, let's suppose those greenhorns succeeded; let's suppose each one got away with a million rubles; well, then what? For the rest of their lives? Each one would depend on all the others for the rest of their lives! They'd be better off hanging themselves! And they didn't even know how to exchange the counterfeit notes: one of them walked into the bank office, exchanged five thousand rubles, and his hands were shaking. He counted out four thousand, but took the fifth without even counting, on faith, so he could stash it in his pocket and get away as soon as possible. Well, he aroused suspicion and the whole scheme came crashing down as a result of one fool! Is that the way to do it?"

"His hands were shaking?" interrupted Zametov. "No, that's possible, sir. No, I'm absolutely sure it's possible. What if you couldn't bear the strain?"

"Of what?"

"And you, could you bear it? No, I couldn't! Confront such terrible danger for a reward of one hundred rubles! To go—where? Into a bank office with counterfeit notes, where they know all the tricks of the trade—no, I'd get frazzled. Wouldn't you, too?"

Once again Raskolnikov felt the urge to "stick out his tongue." At times a shiver ran up and down his spine.

"I wouldn't have done it like that," he began in a roundabout way. "Here's how I would have changed the counterfeit banknotes: I'd have counted the first thousand very carefully, four times over, examining each note, and then moved on to the next thousand; I'd have begun counting that one, reached the middle of the pile, and then pulled out some fifty-ruble note, held it up to the light, turned it over, and held that side up to the light, too—checking to see if it was counterfeit. 'I'm afraid,' I would say. 'Several days ago, a relative of mine lost twenty-five rubles.' And I would have told him the whole story. And when I started counting the third thousand—'No, wait, I think I miscounted the seventh hundred in the second thousand.' I'd be overcome by doubt; then I'd put down the third thousand, return to the second, and so on for all five. As soon as I'd finished, I'd pull one banknote out of the fifth thousand and one out of the second, hold them up to the light again, and I would say, looking very doubtful, 'Please exchange these,' and thus I would drive the clerk to utter exasperation, so that he'd be looking for a way to get rid of me! I'd finish all my business, start to leave, open the door—but no, excuse me, I'd go back again, ask about something else, and listen to his explanation—that's how I'd do it!"

"Phew! What terrible things you say!" Zametov said with a laugh. "But that's all just talk; in fact, if you were actually doing the deed, you'd probably falter. I tell you, in my opinion, not only you and I, but even an experienced, desperate man couldn't depend on himself. Why go so far? Here's an example: an old woman was murdered in our neighborhood. It seems it was done by a real blockhead, taking all sorts of risks in broad daylight, saved only by a miracle—and still his hands were shaking: he didn't know how to rob her, couldn't take it; it's clear from the case that . . ."

Raskolnikov seemed to take offense.

"Clear? Well, then, go find him now!" he cried, urging Zametov on maliciously.

"What of it? He'll be caught."

"By whom? By you? Will you catch him? You'll wear yourself out!

Here's what you consider most important: is the man spending the money or not? He had no money before, and then he suddenly starts spending. It must be him! A child could fool you with that argument, if only he wanted to!"

"The thing is, that's exactly what they all do," replied Zametov. "They murder shrewdly, risk their lives, then go straight to a tavern and get drunk. They're caught when they start spending. They're not all as clever as you are. Of course, you wouldn't go right to a tavern, would you?"

Raskolnikov frowned and stared directly at him.

"It seems you've developed a taste for my approach and want to know how I'd behave in this case?" Raskolnikov asked with displeasure.

"I would," Zametov replied firmly and seriously; he began speaking and staring a bit too intensely.

"Very much?"

"Very much."

"All right. This is how I'd have behaved," began Raskolnikov, once again suddenly drawing his face close to Zametov's, staring intently at him again, and whispering once more, so that this time Zametov even shuddered. "Here's what I'd have done: I'd have taken the money and the items and, as soon as I'd left, immediately, without stopping anywhere, I'd have gone off somewhere to a remote spot where there were only fences, no one around—some garden or something like that. I'd have been to the yard beforehand and have looked for a large rock, weighing some forty or fifty pounds, somewhere over in a corner, near a fence, that had perhaps been there since the house had been built; I'd have lifted up this rock—there'd have to be a space under it—and I'd have placed all the items and the money into that space. I'd have replaced the rock and put it back the same way as it was before, pressed it down with my foot, and then gone away. I wouldn't have touched it for a year, or two, or three—well, just try to find that murderer! He was here, but he's vanished!"

"You're mad," Zametov muttered, also in a whisper; then, for some reason, he moved away from Raskolnikov. Raskolnikov's eyes were shining; he'd grown terribly pale; his upper lip was trembling and shaking. He leaned toward Zametov, as close as he could get, and began moving his lips, uttering nothing at all; he stayed like that for half a minute; he knew what he was doing, but was unable to stop himself. A terrible word, like the bolt on the old woman's door, trembled on his lips: any moment the bolt would give way, any moment he would let the word out, any moment he would utter it!

"What if it was me who murdered the old woman and Lizaveta?" he said suddenly and—came to his senses.

Zametov looked at him in fright and turned pale as a ghost. His face was distorted by a smile.

"Is that possible?" he asked, barely audibly.

Raskolnikov looked at him spitefully.

"Admit that you believed me. Eh? Didn't you?"

"Not at all! Now I believe it even less!" Zametov said hastily.

"You're caught at last! The star pupil's been caught. If you 'believe it less,' that means you must have believed it before."

"Not in the least!" cried Zametov, obviously flustered. "Was that why you frightened me, just to lead me to this?"

"So you don't believe me? Then what were you talking about after I left the office, then? And why did Lieutenant Porokh interrogate me after I fainted? Hey, you," he shouted to the waiter, standing and picking up his cap. "How much do I owe you?"

"Thirty kopecks in all, sir," he replied, running over.

"Here's an extra twenty kopecks to buy yourself a drink. See how much money I have!" He stretched his trembling hand toward Zametov; it was full of banknotes—ten-ruble notes and fives, twenty-five rubles in all. "Where did I get them? Where did I get my new clothes? You know that I didn't have a kopeck before. You've probably questioned my landlady already. . . . Well, enough. *Assez causé!** Good-bye. . . . All the best!"

He left, trembling from some wild hysterical feeling mixed together with unbearable pleasure—he was feeling gloomy, however, and horribly tired. His face was distorted, as if after some sort of seizure. His exhaustion was quickly increasing. His strength was aroused and now

---

* "Enough talk; that will do!" (French).

came on suddenly with the first stimulus, with the first irritating sensation, and that waned just as quickly as the sensation faded away.

Meanwhile Zametov, left alone, sat in deep thought in the same spot for some time. Raskolnikov had unexpectedly overturned all his thoughts on a certain point and forced him to reach a definitive conclusion:

"Ilya Petrovich is a blockhead!" he decided once and for all.

Just as soon as Raskolnikov had opened the door to the street, suddenly, there on the stairs, he met Razumikhin, who was coming into the tavern. Neither saw the other, even a step away, and they almost bumped heads. For some time they measured each other with their glances. Razumikhin was greatly astonished, but all of a sudden, rage, genuine rage flashed menacingly in his eyes.

"So this is where you are!" he cried at the top of his lungs. "You ran away from your bed! I even looked for you under your sofa! We even went up to the attic looking for you! I almost gave Nastasya a beating because of you. . . . And where were you? Rodka! What does this mean? Tell me the whole truth! Confess! You hear?"

"It means that I was bored to death with all of you and want to be alone," Raskolnikov replied calmly.

"Alone? When you still can't walk, when your mug's still pale as a ghost, and you're gasping for breath! You fool! What were you doing in the Crystal Palace? Confess at once!"

"Let me go!" said Raskolnikov, attempting to move past. This drove Razumikhin into a rage; he grabbed him firmly by the shoulder.

"Let you go? You dare say, 'Let me go!' Do you know what I'm going to do with you now? I'll grab hold of you, tie you up in a bundle, carry you home under my arm, and lock you up."

"Listen, Razumikhin," Raskolnikov began softly, apparently in complete calm. "Don't you see that I don't want your kindness? What's this desire of yours to do good deeds for those who . . . who spit on them? For those who ultimately find your kindness really difficult to bear? Why did you come looking for me when I first fell ill? Perhaps I would've been glad to die? Well, haven't I shown you clearly today that you're tormenting me, and that . . . I'm fed up with you! Why this desire to torment other people? I can assure you that all this seriously interferes with my recovery, because it constantly irritates me. Zosimov left the other day so he wouldn't annoy me! Would you, too, leave me alone, for heaven's sake? Besides, what right do you have to restrain me by force? Don't you see that now I'm speaking entirely in my right mind? How, how, tell me at last, how can I finally convince you not to keep pestering me and stop you from trying to be nice to me? Say I'm ungrateful, say I'm vile, but leave me alone, all of you, for heaven's sake, leave me alone! Let me be! Let me be!"

He began serenely, taking pleasure beforehand in the venom he was about to spew, but he finished in a frenzy, gasping for breath as he had previously with Luzhin.

Razumikhin stood there, thought for a while, and removed his hand.

"Go to hell!" he said softly, almost thoughtfully. "Wait!" he roared suddenly when Raskolnikov was about to stir from where he stood. "Listen to me. I declare that all of you, to the last one, are blabberers and braggarts! As soon as you come up against some pathetic bit of suffering, you fuss over it like a hen with her egg! Even then you steal from other writers. There's not a trace of independent life in you! You're made from waxy spermaceti whale oil, and you have watery whey in your veins instead of blood! I don't trust any of you! The first thing you do in any circumstance is try not to resemble a human being! Wait!" he cried with redoubled fury, having noticed that Raskolnikov was about to take his leave again. "Hear me out to the end! You know that people are coming to my housewarming today; perhaps they've gathered already. I left my uncle there to receive the guests—and stopped in here just now. So, if you were not such a fool, not such a vulgar fool, an absolute fool, a translation from the original . . . you see, Rodya, I admit, you're clever, but you're still a fool! Well, if you were not such a fool, you'd be better off coming by my place today to spend the evening there than wearing out your new boots for nothing here. Since you're out, why not? I'd borrow a nice, soft armchair for you; my landlord has one. . . . You'd have some tea, some company. . . . Or else, you could lie down on the couch—you'd still be among us. . . . And Zosimov will be there. Perhaps you'll change your mind and come?"

"No."

"You're lying!" cried Razumikhin impatiently. "How do you know? You can't answer for yourself! You don't understand a thing. . . . I've quarreled with others a thousand times like this, broken it off, and then gone running back to them again. . . . You feel ashamed—so you go back to the person! Remember, it's Pochinkov's house, the third floor . . ."

"It seems you'll let anyone beat you up, Mr. Razumikhin, just for the enjoyment of being nice to him."

"Who? Me? I'd twist his nose if he so much as dreamt of it! Pochinkov's house, number 47, the apartment of the civil servant Babushkin . . ."

"I won't come, Razumikhin!" Raskolnikov said, turning and walking away.

"I bet you will!" Razumikhin shouted after him. "Or else you . . . or else I won't have anything to do with you! Hey, wait a moment! Is Zametov in there?"

"Yes."

"Did you see him?"

"I did."

"And talk to him?"

"I did."

"About what? Well, the hell with you, then don't tell me. Pochinkov's house, number 47, Babushkin's apartment, remember!"

Raskolnikov went as far as Sadovaya and then turned the corner. Razumikhin watched thoughtfully as he went. At last, he gestured contemptuously, entered the building, but stopped in the middle of the stairs.

"Damn it all!" he continued, almost aloud. "He talks sense, but it's as if. . . . What a fool I am! Don't madmen make sense? It seems that Zosimov was afraid of something exactly like this." He tapped his forehead. "Well, what if . . . how can I let him go away alone now? He might drown himself. . . . Hey, I've slipped up! I can't!" He ran back, chasing after Raskolnikov, but he was already gone. He spat in disgust and hastened back to the Crystal Palace to interrogate Zametov as quickly as possible.

Raskolnikov went directly to the Voznesensky Bridge, stood in the middle near the railing, rested his elbows on it, and gazed off along the bank. After parting from Razumikhin, he felt so weak that he'd scarcely managed to get there. He felt like sitting or lying down somewhere in the street. Leaning out over the water, he absentmindedly regarded the last pink glow of sunset, the row of houses, which grew darker in the deepening twilight, one distant little window, somewhere up in an attic along the left bank, shining with a flame from the last ray of sunlight that struck it for a moment, and the darkening water of the canal; he seemed to be staring at the water with particular attention. In the end, some shapes like red circles began spinning before his eyes, the houses began moving, passersby, the embankments, carriages—everything began turning and dancing around. Suddenly he shuddered, perhaps saved from another fainting spell by one riotous, hideous sight. He suddenly felt that somebody was standing near him, at his right side, next to him; he glanced up and saw a tall woman wearing a kerchief, with a yellow, elongated, emaciated face and sunken reddish eyes. She stared directly at him, but obviously didn't see anything and couldn't perceive anything. Suddenly she rested her right hand on the railing, lifted her right leg and thrust it over, then her left leg, and threw herself into the canal. The dirty water parted and swallowed its victim instantly, but in a minute the drowning woman surfaced and was carried along gently, her skirt puffed up above the water like a pillow.

"She's drowning herself! Drowning!" shouted dozens of voices; people came running, and both embankments were covered with spectators. A crowd gathered on the bridge around Raskolnikov, surrounding him and pressing in on him from behind.

"Good Lord, that's our Afrosinyushka!" a tearful woman's voice called out from nearby. "Good heavens, save her! Kind sirs, pull her out!"

"A boat! A boat!" people cried out from the crowd.

But a boat was unnecessary: a policeman ran down the steps to the edge of the canal, threw off his overcoat and boots, and plunged into the water. It didn't take much effort: the drowning woman was carried by the current to within a few feet of the edge. He grabbed her clothing with his right hand, and with his left, he took hold of a pole that his comrade had extended toward him. The drowning woman was immediately fished out of the water. She was placed on the granite blocks of the stairs. She came to quickly, raised herself, sat up, and began sneezing and sniffling, senselessly wiping her hands on her wet dress. She didn't say a word.

"She drank herself silly, kind sirs, absolutely silly," howled that same woman's voice, now standing right next to Afrosinyushka. "A few days ago she tried to hang herself, but they cut her down. Just now I went into a shop and left a young girl to watch over her—and here's what happened! She's a trader, dear sirs, one of us; we live nearby, the second house from the corner, right over here . . ."

The crowd parted while the policemen were still fussing over the young woman; someone shouted something about the police station. . . . Raskolnikov regarded everything with a strange sensation of indifference and unconcern. He felt disgusted. "No, it's vile . . . water . . . it's no good," he muttered to himself. "Nothing will come of it," he added, "there's no reason to wait. What's that about the police station? Why isn't Zametov there? It's open till ten o'clock." He turned his back to the railing and looked around.

"Well, all right! Why not?" he said decisively; he moved away from the bridge and headed in the direction of the police station. His heart was empty and hollow. He didn't want to think. Even his glum mood had passed; there was no trace of the former energy he'd felt when he'd left home "to end it all." Complete apathy had taken its place.

"Well then, it's a way out!" he thought, walking slowly and limply along the canal embankment. "Still, I'll end it because I want to. . . . But is it a way out? It makes no difference! There'll be just a square yard of space—ha! But what an ending! Is it really the end? Will I tell them or not? Oh . . . hell! I'm very tired: it would be good to lie down or sit down somewhere soon! The most embarrassing thing is that I did it very stupidly. To hell with all that! Phew, such stupid thoughts occur to me . . ."

To get to the police station, he had to go straight and then turn left at the second street: it was just a few steps away. But when he reached the first street, he stopped, thought for a bit, turned into the lane, and walked around, through two streets—perhaps without any goal, just to extend the moment and gain some time. He walked along, looking down at the ground. Suddenly it was as though someone whispered something in his ear. He raised his head and noticed that he was standing next to *that same* house, near the gates. He hadn't been back here since *that same* evening and hadn't even passed by.

An irresistible, inexplicable desire drew him. He entered, crossed under the gateway, then went into the first entrance on the right, and began climbing the familiar staircase up to the fourth floor. It was very dark on the narrow, steep stairs. He paused on each landing and looked around with curiosity. On the first-floor landing, the window frame had been removed from one window. "It wasn't like that then," he thought. Next he came to the apartment on the second floor where Nikolashka and Mitka had been working: "It's locked; the door's been freshly painted; that means it's for rent." Here's the third floor . . . and the fourth . . . "Here!" He was struck with bewilderment. The door to the apartment was wide open, there were people inside, and voices could be heard: he hadn't expected that at all. After hesitating a little, he climbed the last stairs and entered the apartment.

It was being redecorated; there were workers inside; that seemed to astound him. For some reason, he'd imagined that he would find the place just as he'd left it then, perhaps even with the bodies in the same place on the floor. But now there were bare walls and no furniture; it seemed so strange! He crossed to the window and sat down on the window seat.

There were only two workmen, both young lads, one older, and the other much younger. They were hanging new paper on the walls, white with lilac flowers, instead of the previous yellow, worn-out, faded wallpaper. For some reason, Raskolnikov didn't like that at all; he regarded the new paper with hostility, as if regretting that anything had changed.

The workmen, apparently, had lingered and now were hastily rolling up the wallpaper, planning to leave for home. Raskolnikov's appearance attracted almost no attention. They were chatting about something or other. Raskolnikov folded his arms and began listening.

"So she comes to me, that one does, in the morning," says the elder to the younger, "at the crack of dawn, all dressed up. 'What's this about?' I say. 'Why are you prancin' and struttin' in front of me?' I say.

"Cause,' she says, 'from now on, Tit Vasilich, I want you to be my lord and master.' That's what she says! And she's all dressed up: just like in a journal, a real journal."

"What's a journal, uncle?" asked the younger lad. Obviously he was "uncle's" pupil.

"A journal, my friend, is full o' pictures, colored ones, and they come to the local tailor's every Saturday, in the mail, from abroad, and they show how to dress, both for men and the same for women. There's drawin's, I mean. Men are wearin' short winter coats, but as for women, my friend, such tarts, if you gave me everythin' you have, it still wouldn't be enough."

"The things you find in this Petersburg of ours!" the younger lad said enthusiastically. "Everythin' you could possibly wish for!"

"Everythin', my young friend, absolutely everythin'," the older man affirmed instructively.

Raskolnikov stood up and went into the other room, where previously the trunk, the bed, and the chest of drawers had been: the room seemed terribly small with no furniture. The wallpaper here was still the same. In the corner he could see clearly outlined the place where the icon case had stood. He looked around and returned to his little window. The elder workman was keeping an eye on him.

"What do you want, sir?" he asked suddenly, turning to him.

Instead of a reply, Raskolnikov stood up and went to the passageway, took hold of the bell chain, and yanked it. It was the same bell, the same metallic sound! He yanked it a second time and a third; he listened and remembered. The previous, horribly tormenting, hideous feeling returned to him all the more distinctly and vividly; he shuddered with every sound, yet it seemed more and more enjoyable to him.

"What do you want? Who are you?" cried one workman, coming out to meet him. Raskolnikov entered through the door again.

"I want to rent this apartment," he said. "I'm looking around."

"People don't rent apartments at night; besides, you must come to see it with the caretaker."

"They washed the floor; will they paint it?" Raskolnikov continued. "There's no blood?"

"What blood?"

"The old woman and her sister were murdered here. There was a large pool."

"What sort of a person are you?" cried the workman apprehensively.

"Me?"

"Yes."

"You want to know? Let's go to the police station. I'll tell you there."

The workmen looked at him in confusion.

"It's time for us to go, sir. We've stayed too long. Let's go, Alyoshka. We have to lock up," the elder workman said.

"Well, let's go!" replied Raskolnikov apathetically and walked out ahead, descending the stairs slowly. "Hey, caretaker!" he cried, as he went through the gate.

Several people stood at the entrance to the house, looking at passersby on the street: two caretakers, a peasant woman, a tradesman in a robe, and someone else. Raskolnikov walked right up to them.

"What do you want?" one of the caretakers asked.

"Have you been to the police station?"

"I was just there. Why do you want to know?"

"Is anyone still there?"

"Yes."

"Is the assistant there?"

"He was for a while. What's it to you?"

Raskolnikov made no reply and stood next to him, deep in thought.

"He came to see the apartment," said the elder workman, drawing near.

"Which one?"

"Where we're working. 'Why,' he says, 'did you wash away the blood? Here,' he says, 'there was a murder, and I want to rent the apartment.' He starts ringing the doorbell, almost tore it off. 'Let's go,' he says, 'to the police station, and I'll tell you everything.' He latched onto us."

The caretaker looked at Raskolnikov in confusion and scowled.

"And just who the hell are you?" he cried more threateningly.

"I am Rodion Romanych Raskolnikov, a former student. I live at Shil's house, in the lane nearby, not far from here, apartment number

14. Ask the caretaker . . . he knows me," Raskolnikov uttered all this lazily and distractedly, without turning around, staring intently at the darkened street.

"Why'd you come to this apartment?"

"To see it."

"What's there to see?"

"Should we take him to the police station?" the tradesman ventured and then fell silent.

Raskolnikov glanced at him over his shoulder, regarded him attentively, and said just as quietly and lazily:

"Let's go!"

"And take him!" cried the tradesman, feeling encouraged. "Why was he going on about *that*? Does he have something on his mind, huh?"

"Drunk or not, God knows," muttered the workman.

"What do you want?" cried the caretaker again, beginning to grow really angry. "Why are you bothering us?"

"Are you afraid to go to the police?" Raskolnikov asked with a smirk.

"Why should I be afraid? Why are you pestering us?"

"What a rascal!" cried the peasant woman.

"Why even talk to him?" cried the other caretaker, an enormous peasant dressed in a heavy tunic and carrying keys on his belt. "Clear out! You're a rascal, all right. . . . Clear out!"

Grabbing Raskolnikov by the shoulder, he shoved him out into the street. He almost went head over heels, but didn't fall; he managed to right himself, looked at all the spectators in silence, and then walked away.

"A strange bird," said the workman.

"Folks is all strange these days," said the peasant woman.

"Still, we should've taken him to the police," added the tradesman.

"There's no reason to get mixed up in it," concluded the large caretaker. "He's a rascal, he is! He's up to something, that's clear, but if we get mixed up in it, it won't be easy to get out. . . . We know that!"

"Should I go or not?" Raskolnikov wondered, pausing in the middle of the street at the crossing and looking around, as if expecting the final word to come from someone. But there was no reply from anywhere; everything was silent and dead, like the cobblestones he walked on, dead to him, to him alone. . . . Suddenly, far off, about two hundred steps away, at the end of the street, in the thickening darkness, he made out a crowd, voices, shouting. . . . Some sort of carriage stood amidst the throng. . . . A light was shining in the middle of the street. "What's that?" Raskolnikov wondered; he turned to the right and headed toward the crowd. He seemed to be grasping at anything and smiled coldly when he realized that fact, because he had definitely decided to go to the police station and knew for sure that everything would soon end.

VII

A gentleman's fashionable carriage stood in the middle of the street, harnessed to a pair of lively gray horses. There were no passengers, and the coachman himself, after climbing down from the box, stood next to them, holding the horses by their bridle. A large crowd had gathered, and some policemen were standing in front of them. One was holding a lit lantern, with which, by leaning over, he was casting light on something lying on the pavement near the carriage wheels. Everyone was talking, shouting, and exclaiming; the coachman seemed confused and kept repeating, from time to time:

"What a shame! Lord, what a terrible shame!"

Raskolnikov got as close as he could and finally saw the object of all this commotion and curiosity. On the ground lay a man who had just been run over by the horses. He was apparently unconscious, very badly dressed, but in what had once been "respectable" clothes; he was covered in blood. Blood was flowing from his face and head; his face was all beaten, battered, and mangled. It was clear that he'd been badly trampled and was in very grave condition.

"Good Lord!" wailed the coachman. "How could I have avoided it? If I'd been racing or hadn't called out to him—but I wasn't going fast, only at a moderate pace. Everyone saw: I'm just repeating what everyone else says. A drunk can't even walk a straight line—that's well known! I saw him; he was crossing the street, reeling from side to side, and almost falling over. . . . I shouted to him once, then a second time, a third, and I reined in my horses; but he stumbled right into them and fell under their hooves! Either he did it on purpose, or else he was very drunk. . . . The horses are young, easily startled; they shied and he screamed—then it got worse . . . that's how it was."

"That's what happened!" cried a witness's voice from the crowd.

"He did shout, that's true, he shouted to him three times," echoed another.

"Exactly three times, everyone heard!" cried a third.

The coachman, however, was neither very disconsolate nor frightened. It was clear that the carriage belonged to some wealthy and influential person, who was somewhere awaiting its arrival; the policemen, of course, took great pains to expedite the matter. They would have to transport the injured man first to the police station and then to the hospital. No one knew his name.

Meanwhile, Raskolnikov had crowded in closer and had bent over the victim. Suddenly the lantern brightly lit the unfortunate man's face: he recognized him.

"I know him, I do!" he shouted, pushing to the front of the crowd. "He's a civil servant, a retired titular counselor, Marmeladov! He lives near here, in Kozel's house. . . . Get a doctor immediately! I'll pay! Here!" He pulled some money out of his pocket and kept showing it to a policeman. Raskolnikov was in a state of extreme agitation.

The policemen were pleased to learn the unfortunate man's identity. Raskolnikov identified himself, provided his address, and, with all his might, as if it concerned his own father, tried to persuade them to carry the unconscious Marmeladov home as quickly as possible.

"It's right here, only three houses away," he pleaded, "Kozel's house, a German, a wealthy man. . . . He was just on his way home, probably drunk. I know him. . . . He's a drunkard. . . . He has a family, a wife, children, and one daughter. There's no need to take him to the hospital when there's probably a doctor in his building! I'll pay for it, I will! He'll be cared for by his own people; they'll help right away, or else he'll die before he gets to the hospital . . ."

He'd even managed to slip something into the policeman's hand. The matter, moreover, was clear and legal; in any case, help was closer. Helpers were found to lift and carry the injured man. Kozel's house was only about thirty steps away. Raskolnikov walked behind, carefully supporting Marmeladov's head and showing them the way.

"This way, over here! We have to climb the stairs with his head first; turn around . . . that's the way! I'll pay, I'll be grateful," he muttered.

Katerina Ivanovna, as always when she had a free moment, had just begun pacing up and down in their small room, from the window to the stove and back again, her arms tightly folded across her chest, talking to herself and coughing. Lately, she'd begun chatting more often and at greater length with her elder little girl, the ten-year-old Polyenka, who, even though she didn't understand all that much, knew very well that her mother needed her, and therefore followed her with her large clever eyes, pretending with all her might that she understood everything. This time Polyenka was undressing her younger brother, who had been sick all day; she was getting him ready for bed. While his shirt was being changed, because it was going to be washed that night, the little boy sat up on a chair silently, straight and motionless, with a serious look on his face. His little feet were stretched out in front of him, squeezed tightly, heels together and toes turned outward. He was listening to what his mother was saying to his sister, his lips pouting, his eyes bulging, sitting still, just the way all clever little boys should sit when they are being undressed and prepared for bed. His other sister, who was even younger and wearing only rags, stood next to the screen, waiting her turn. The door to the landing was open, so that some of the waves of tobacco smoke coming from the other rooms could disperse; it was making the poor consumptive woman cough long and hard. Katerina Ivanovna seemed to have grown even thinner during the last week; the red blotches on her cheeks burned even brighter than before.

"You won't believe, you can't imagine, Polyenka," she said, pacing the room, "how cheerfully and splendidly we lived at home with your papa, how that drunkard destroyed me, and how he'll destroy all of you, too! Your papa was a state councillor and almost became a governor; there was only one step left, so everyone came to him and said, 'We already think of you, Ivan Mikhailych, as our governor.' When I . . . *cough*, when I . . . *cough, cough, cough* . . . oh, damn it!" she cried, spitting up phlegm and grabbing her chest. "When I . . . ah, when at the last ball . . . at the home of the marshal of the nobility* . . . Princess Bezzemelnaya saw me, Polya, the one who later gave me her blessing when I married your papa, she asked at once, 'Isn't that the sweet girl who did the shawl dance at her graduation?'—that tear should be mended; take a needle right now and sew it up as I taught you, or else tomorrow . . . *cough*! tomorrow . . . *cough, cough, cough* . . . it will tear even more," she cried in a violent outburst. "At that time Prince Shchegolsky, a Gentleman of the Bedchamber, had just arrived from Petersburg . . . he danced the mazurka with me and wanted to propose marriage the very next day; but I thanked him in the most flattering terms and said that my heart had belonged to another man for a long time. That other man was your father, Polya; Papa was terribly angry. . . . Is the water ready? Well, give me the shirt; where are the stockings? Lida," she said, addressing her younger daughter, "you'll go to sleep tonight without your shirt; somehow . . . and put your stockings next to it. . . . They have to be washed together. . . . Why hasn't that good-for-nothing come home, that drunkard? He's worn that shirt of his too long, like some old rag, and torn it all to pieces. . . . I want to wash it at the same time, so as not to suffer for two nights in a row! Lord! *Cough, cough, cough, cough!* Again! What's that?" she cried, glancing at the crowd in the entry and at the people carrying something, pushing into her room. "What's this? What are they carrying? Good Lord!"

"Where do we put him?" asked the policeman, looking around after they'd lugged the bloody and unconscious Marmeladov into the room.

"On the sofa! Put him right on the sofa, with his head over here," Raskolnikov said.

"He was run over on the street! Drunk!" cried someone from the entryway.

Katerina Ivanovna stood there, pale, breathing with difficulty. The children were frightened. Little Lidochka cried out, rushed to Polyenka, hugged her, and started trembling all over.

---

* The highest elected official in a province.

After seeing Marmeladov laid out, Raskolnikov rushed over to Katerina Ivanovna:

"For heaven's sake, calm down, don't be afraid!" he said very quickly. "He was crossing the street and a carriage ran him over; don't be upset; he'll come to. I had him brought here. . . . I've been here before, do you remember? He'll come to. I'll pay!"

"He got what he wanted!" Katerina Ivanovna cried in desperation and threw herself on her husband.

Raskolnikov quickly noticed that this was not the sort of woman who would faint immediately. In a flash, a pillow turned up under the unfortunate man's head, something no one else had thought of. Katerina Ivanovna began to undress him, examine him, fuss over him; she didn't become flustered; she forgot all about herself, bit her trembling lips, and suppressed the cries ready to escape her chest.

Meanwhile Raskolnikov persuaded someone to fetch a doctor. It turned out that a doctor lived two houses away.

"I've sent for a doctor," he said to Katerina Ivanovna. "Don't be distressed, I'll pay. Do you have any water? And give me a napkin, a towel, something, quickly; it's still not clear where he's been hurt. . . . He's wounded, but he's not been killed, rest assured. . . . We'll see what the doctor says!"

Katerina Ivanovna rushed to the window; there, on a broken chair in the corner, stood a large clay washbasin with water, readied for washing the children's and her husband's clothes that night. Katerina Ivanovna herself, with her own hands, performed this nighttime chore at least twice a week, and sometimes more frequently, because things had reached the point that they had almost no clean clothes to change into. Each member of the family had only one item, and Katerina Ivanovna could not stand any dirt and thought it better to torment herself at night and work beyond her strength when everyone else was asleep so that the wet clothes would have time to dry on a line before morning; she preferred to provide clean clothes for everyone, rather than to see dirt in her house. She was about to grab the washbasin and hand it over to Raskolnikov, as he had requested, but she almost stumbled with the heavy load. He'd already managed to find a towel, soak it in water, and had begun wiping the blood from Marmeladov's face.

Katerina Ivanovna stood there, inhaling painfully, holding her arms across her chest. She herself needed assistance. Raskolnikov began to think that perhaps he had done the wrong thing, having persuaded them to bring the wounded man here. The policeman also stood there, confused.

"Polya!" shouted Katerina Ivanovna. "Go fetch Sonya, quickly. If she's not home, all the same, say that her father's been run over by horses and that as soon as she gets home . . . she should come at once. Hurry, Polya! Here, wrap yourself with this shawl!"

"Run fas' as you can!" shouted the little boy from the chair. After saying this, he sank once more into his previous silent posture on the chair, his eyes bulging, his heels together, toes turned outward.

Meanwhile, the room became so full that there was no space left at all. The policemen had gone, except for one who stayed a little longer and tried to push the spectators who had come in from the stairs back out again. Almost all the lodgers at Mrs. Lippevekhsel's apartment had spilled out of the inner rooms; at first they crowded only in the doorway, but later they came bursting into the room itself. Katerina Ivanovna flew into a rage.

"At least let someone die in peace!" she screamed at the entire crowd. "What sort of spectacle have you come to watch? And smoking cigarettes! *Cough, cough, cough!* Even wearing your hats! There's someone with a hat. . . . Out! Have some respect for a dying man!"

Coughs choked her, but her threat seemed to work. Apparently, they were even somewhat afraid of Katerina Ivanovna; the lodgers, one after another, crowded back to the doorway with that same strange inner feeling of satisfaction that is always present, even in one's nearest and dearest, when sudden misfortune strikes someone close; it spares no one at all, without exception, no matter how sincere our feelings of pity and sympathy.

Behind the door, however, one could hear voices murmuring about the hospital and saying that people shouldn't be bothered here for nothing.

"It's not right to die!" cried Katerina Ivanovna. She was about to yank the door open so she could let loose a storm of abuse at them, but in the doorway she bumped into Mrs. Lippevekhsel herself, who had just heard about the accident and come running in to restore order. She was an extremely quarrelsome and disorderly German woman.

"*Ach, mein Gott!*" she cried, throwing up her hands. "Your drunken husband a horse trumpled. To hospital take him! I'm here landlady!"

"Amaliya Lyudvigovna! I beg you to think about what you're saying," Katerina Ivanovna began haughtily (she always employed a haughty tone of voice when she spoke with the landlady, so that she would "remember her place," and even now she could not deny herself that pleasure). "Amaliya Lyudvigovna . . ."

"I told you once for all that you not dare say to me Amal Lyudvigovna; I'm Amal-Ivan!"

"You're not Amal-Ivan, but Amaliya Lyudvigovna, and since I don't belong to the group of your vile flatterers, like Mr. Lebezyatnikov, who's now laughing behind the door"—the sound of laughter was coming from behind the door, as well as shouts of "They're squabbling!"—"then I will always call you Amaliya Lyudvigovna, though I really can't understand why you don't like that name. You can see for yourself what's happened to Semyon Zakharovich; he's dying. I beg you to lock the door and not to admit anyone in here. Let him die peacefully! Otherwise, I can assure you, your action will be made known to the governor-general himself. The prince knew me when I was young and unmarried, and he remembers Semyon Zakharovich very well, to whom he showed his favor many times. You know that Semyon Zakharovich had many friends and protectors, whom he abandoned out of his own noble pride, sensing his own unfortunate weakness, but now"—she indicated Raskolnikov—"a generous young man is assisting us. He has the means and connections; Semyon Zakharovich knew him as a child. You can be sure, Amaliya Lyudvigovna . . ."

All of this was uttered very quickly; the more she said, the faster it went, but a fit of coughing interrupted Katerina Ivanovna's eloquence. At that moment, the dying man came to and moaned: she rushed over to him. He opened his eyes and, still not recognizing or understanding where he was, began scrutinizing Raskolnikov, who was standing over him. He was breathing heavily, deeply, and infrequently; blood had oozed from the corners of his mouth; drops of sweat stood on his forehead. Not recognizing Raskolnikov, he began looking around. Katerina

Ivanovna regarded him with a grim but stern look; tears flowed from her eyes.

"My God! His chest's completely crushed! Blood, so much blood!" she said in desperation. "We have to take all his outer clothes off! Turn over a little, Semyon Zakharovich, if you can," she cried to him.

Marmeladov recognized her.

"A priest!" he uttered in a hoarse voice.

Katerina Ivanovna went to the window, leaned her head against the frame, and cried desperately:

"Damn it all!"

"A priest!" the dying man said again, after a moment's silence.

"They've sent for one!" Katerina Ivanovna shouted to him; he heard her cry and fell silent. He searched for her with a sad, timid look in his eyes; she turned back to him and stood at his head. He calmed down a bit, but not for long. Soon his eyes came to rest on little Lidochka (his favorite). She was trembling in the corner as if she were having a seizure, staring at him with her intense, astonished, childlike gaze.

"Ah . . . ah..." he said, indicating her with unease. He wanted to say something.

"What else?" cried Katerina Ivanovna.

"She's barefoot! Barefoot!" he muttered, with his half-witted glance fixed on the little girl's bare feet.

"Be quiet!" Katerina Ivanovna shouted at him irritably. "You yourself know why she's barefoot!"

"Thank God, the doctor!" cried Raskolnikov, overjoyed.

The doctor entered, a proper old man, a German, looking around with uncertainty. He approached the patient, took his pulse, carefully felt his head, and, with Katerina Ivanovna's help, unbuttoned his blood-soaked shirt and uncovered his chest. Marmeladov's entire chest was mangled, crushed, and mutilated. Several ribs on the right side were broken. On the left side, above his heart, there was a large, ominous, yellowish-black mark, a cruel blow from the horse's hoof. The doctor frowned. The policeman told him that the unfortunate man had been caught in the wheel and dragged along the road for some thirty paces.

"It's astonishing that he's come to," the doctor whispered softly to Raskolnikov.

"What do you think?" Raskolnikov asked.

"He'll die soon."

"Is there really no hope?"

"Not in the least! He's at his last breath. . . . His head is very badly injured. . . . Hmm. Perhaps we could let some blood . . . but . . . it'll be useless. He'll certainly die within five or ten minutes."

"Then let some blood."

"Perhaps. . . . But I warn you, it'll be absolutely useless."

Just at this time, some other steps were heard; the crowd in the entrance divided, and a priest, an old man with gray hair, appeared on the threshold, carrying the sacraments. A policeman from outside followed him in. The doctor immediately yielded his place and exchanged a meaningful glance with him. Raskolnikov asked the doctor to wait a little longer. He shrugged his shoulders and remained in the room.

Everyone backed away. The confession didn't last very long. The dying man hardly understood anything; he could only utter disjointed and inarticulate sounds. Katerina Ivanovna took Lidochka, lifted the little boy from his chair, and, moving to the corner of the room near the stove, went down on her knees and placed the children on their knees in front of her. The young girl merely trembled; as for the boy, on his bare little knees, he raised his little hand slowly, crossed himself, bowed down and touched his forehead to the floor, which, apparently, afforded him particular pleasure. Katerina Ivanovna bit her lips and held back her tears; she also prayed, at times adjusting the child's small shirt, and managing to cover the little girl's bare shoulders with a scarf that she took from the wardrobe without having to get up from her knees or interrupt her prayers. Meanwhile the doors of the inner rooms were beginning to be opened again by curious onlookers. More and more spectators, lodgers from the entire staircase, were crowding into the entrance; however, they dared not cross the threshold or enter the room. The entire scene was lit by only one candle stub.

At that moment from the entrance, Polyenka, who had gone to fetch her sister, pushed hastily through the crowd. She entered, still gasping for breath from racing home, took off her shawl, searched with her eyes for her mother, went up to her and said, "She's coming! I found her on the street!" Her mother made her kneel down and placed her nearby. From the crowd, silently and timidly, a young woman forced her way in; her sudden appearance in this room was strange, amid the poverty, ragged clothes, death, and desperation. She was also wearing tattered clothes; her apparel was shoddy, but she was decked out in the manner of the streets, with the taste and style characteristic of her own particular sphere, with an obvious and shameful purpose. Sonya paused at the threshold, but didn't cross it and looked like a lost soul. She seemed to be unaware of everything, having forgotten about her fourth-hand colorful silk dress, so inappropriate here, with its long, comical train, its enormous crinoline blocking the whole door, her light-colored shoes, her little parasol, unnecessary at night, but which she carried with her, and her ridiculous round straw hat with its bright fiery-colored feather. From under this hat, which she was wearing with a boyish tilt to one side, there peeked a thin, pale, frightened little face with a gaping mouth and eyes fixed with a look of horror. Sonya was about eighteen years old and not very tall; she was thin, but rather pretty, with fair hair and remarkable blue eyes. She stared intently at the bed and at the priest; she was also panting from running so fast. At last the whispering, some words spoken by someone in the crowd, probably reached her ears. She lowered her eyes, stepped across the threshold, and entered the room, though still remaining near the doorway.

The confession and communion ended. Katerina Ivanovna went up to her husband's bed again. The priest stepped away and, as he did, turned to say a few words of parting and consolation to Katerina Ivanovna.

"What will I do with them?" she interrupted him shrilly and angrily, pointing to the little ones.

"God is merciful. Rely on the Almighty for assistance," the priest began.

"Eh! Merciful, but not to us!"

"That's a sin, madam, a sin," the priest remarked, shaking his head.

"Isn't this a sin?" cried Katerina Ivanovna, indicating the dying man.

"Perhaps those who were the involuntary cause of his death will agree to compensate you, at least for the loss of income . . ."

"You don't understand me," Katerina Ivanovna cried indignantly, waving her arm. "Why should there be any compensation? He was drunk and wound up under the horses' hooves! What sort of income? There's no income from him, only torment. That drunkard spent it all on drink. He robbed us and went off to the tavern with the money. He's wasted their lives and mine in a tavern! Thank God he's dying! We'll lose less!"

"You should forgive in the hour of death, madam, or else it's a sin; such feelings are a great sin!"

Katerina Ivanovna was fussing over the dying man, offering him something to drink, wiping the sweat and blood from his head, adjusting his pillows and chatting with the priest, addressing him from time to time at odd moments. But now she suddenly turned on him almost in a rage.

"Hey, Father! That's all just words! Forgive him? If he hadn't been run over, he would've come home drunk tonight, his one shirt worn out and tattered, and gone right to sleep, dead to the world, while I splashed around in water until dawn, washing his and the children's clothes, drying them out the window, and then, as soon as it was light, I'd have to sit down and mend them—that's how I spend the night! Why even talk about forgiveness? Even so, I have forgiven him!"

A terrible, deep cough disrupted her words. She spat into her handkerchief and thrust it at the priest to show him, clutching her chest in pain with her other hand. The handkerchief was covered in blood . . .

The priest bowed his head and said nothing.

Marmeladov was in his last agony. He didn't take his eyes off Katerina Ivanovna's face as she leaned over him once more. He kept wanting to say something; he was trying to speak, moving his tongue with effort, uttering incoherent words, but Katerina Ivanovna understood that he wanted to ask her forgiveness, and immediately shouted at him imperiously:

"Quiet! That's unnecessary! I know what you want to say!"

The dying man fell silent, but at that moment his wandering glance fell on the door and he caught sight of Sonya . . .

Up to this point he hadn't noticed her: she stood in a corner in the shadows.

"Who's that? Who is that?" he suddenly asked in a hoarse, gasping voice, full of anxiety, looking in horror at the door where his daughter was standing as he made an effort to raise himself up.

"Lie down! Lie down now!" Katerina Ivanovna started shouting.

But with unnatural strength he managed to lean on his arm. He stared at Sonya wildly and intently for some time, as if not recognizing her. He had never seen her dressed in such clothes before. All of a sudden he recognized her, humiliated, crushed, decked out, and embarrassed, humbly awaiting her turn to bid farewell to her dying father. His face expressed infinite suffering.

"Sonya! My daughter! Forgive me!" he cried, wanting to extend his hand to her. But losing his support, he fell from the sofa and crashed facedown onto the floor. They rushed to pick him up, lay him down, but he was breathing his last. Sonya cried out weakly, rushed to him, embraced him, and almost fainted in his embrace. He died in her arms.

"He got what he wanted!" Katerina Ivanovna cried, seeing her husband's dead body. "Now what do we do? How can I afford to bury him? And how, how will I feed them tomorrow?"

Raskolnikov went up to Katerina Ivanovna.

"Katerina Ivanovna," he began, "last week your late husband told me the story of his life and all the circumstances. . . . Rest assured that he spoke about you with rapturous respect. Since that evening, when I learned how devoted he was to you all, and especially how he respected and loved you, Katerina Ivanovna, in spite of his unfortunate weakness, since that evening he and I became friends. . . . Allow me now . . . to help by repaying a debt to my late friend. Here . . . twenty rubles, I think—and if this can serve as assistance, then . . . I . . . in a word, I'll come by—I'll definitely come . . . perhaps I'll even come tomorrow. . . . Good-bye!"

He left the room quickly, hurriedly pushing through the crowd on the staircase; but there in the crowd he bumped into Nikodim Fomich, who had learned about the accident and wished to deal with it personally. They hadn't seen each other since the scene at the police station, but Nikodim Fomich recognized him instantly.

"Oh, so it's you?" he said.

"He's dead," replied Raskolnikov. "A doctor was here, a priest, too, and everything's in order. Don't disturb this very unfortunate woman;

even before this, she'd been suffering from consumption. Encourage her somehow, if you can. . . . You're a good man, I know that," he added with a smile, looking him right in the eye.

"But how is it you're covered in blood?" asked Nikodim Fomich, noticing by the light of his lantern several fresh spots on Raskolnikov's vest.

"Yes, covered in blood . . . completely!" Raskolnikov said with a particular look, and then smiled, nodded his head, and went down the stairs.

He left quietly, without hurrying, unaware of his fever, full of an immense, new feeling of full, powerful life surging within him. This feeling could be compared to that of a man condemned to death who is suddenly and unexpectedly pardoned.* When he was halfway down the stairs, the priest, who was returning home, caught up with him. After they exchanged a quiet bow, Raskolnikov silently let him pass. But when he reached the bottom, he suddenly heard hurried footsteps behind him. Someone was trying to catch up with him. It was Polyenka; she was running after him and calling to him, "Wait! Listen!"

He turned to her. She came down to the last step and stopped right in front of him, one step higher. Dim light shone in from the courtyard. Raskolnikov could make out the girl's thin but pretty little face; she smiled at him, regarding him cheerfully, in a childlike manner. She had come with a commission, one that, apparently, she liked very much.

"Listen! What's your name? Where do you live?" she asked hurriedly, her voice breaking as she gasped for breath.

He placed his hands on her shoulders and looked at her with special happiness. He found it very pleasant to look at her—he didn't know why.

"Who sent you?"

"My sister Sonya," the little girl replied, smiling even more cheerfully.

"I knew that it was your sister Sonya who sent you."

---

* Dostoevsky himself endured such an experience in 1849; he was pardoned and sent into exile.

"Mama also sent me. When my sister Sonya began speaking, Mama also came up and said, 'Hurry up, Polyenka.'"

"Do you love your sister Sonya?"

"I love her more than anyone!" Polyenka replied with special insistence, and her smile suddenly became more serious.

"And will you come to love me?"

Instead of an answer, he saw the girl's face draw near his, her full lips innocently ready to kiss him. All of a sudden her arms, thin as matchsticks, embraced him very tightly, her head rested on his shoulder, and the little girl began crying softly, pressing her face more and more tightly against him.

"I feel sorry for Papa!" she said a minute later, raising her tearstained little face and wiping her tears with her hands. "Such awful things have been happening lately," she added unexpectedly, with a particularly mature look that children intentionally acquire when they suddenly want to talk like "grown-ups."

"Did your papa love you?"

"He loved Lidochka best of all of us," she continued very seriously and without a smile, now speaking just like a grown-up. "He loved her because she was little, and also because she was ill. He was always bringing her presents. He taught us to read and taught me grammar and religion," she added with dignity. "Mama didn't say anything, but we knew that she liked that, and Papa knew, and Mama wants to teach me French because it's already time for me to be educated."

"And do you know how to pray?"

"Oh, yes, of course we do! We have for a long time. Since I'm already a big girl, I pray on my own, while Kolya and Lidochka pray aloud with Mama; first they say a Hail Mary and then one more prayer: 'O, God, forgive and bless our sister Sonya.' Then another, 'O, God, forgive and bless our other papa,' because our older father died, and he's our other papa, and we also pray for the first one."

"Polechka, my name is Rodion. Pray for me sometime, too: 'and Thy servant, Rodion.' That's all you need to say."

"I will pray for you for the rest of my life," the little girl said passionately and suddenly began laughing again. She rushed to him and embraced him tightly once more.

Raskolnikov told her his name and address and promised to stop by tomorrow without fail. As a result, the girl went away in complete ecstasy. It was after ten o'clock when he emerged onto the street. Five minutes later, he stood on the bridge, at the very same spot where the woman had thrown herself into the water not long ago.

"Enough!" he pronounced decisively and triumphantly. "Away with mirages, away with presumed fears, away with apparitions! Life exists! Didn't I just now experience real life? My life didn't end together with that old woman's! May the kingdom of heaven be hers and—enough, old woman, it's time to rest! Now it's the kingdom of reason and light, and . . . and free will and strength . . . now we'll see! Now we'll match strengths!" he added haughtily, as if addressing some dark force and calling upon it. "And there I was agreeing to live on one square yard of space!"

". . . I'm feeling very weak now, but . . . my illness seems to have passed. I knew that it would when I left a little while ago. By the way, Pochinkov's house is only a few steps away. I should definitely go to Razumikhin's, even if it's farther away. . . . Let him win his bet! Let him make fun of me—never mind, let him! Strength, strength is what's needed, because without it you can't do anything. You have to gain strength by means of strength, that's what they don't know," he added proudly and self-confidently. He left the bridge, scarcely able to move his legs. His pride and self-confidence grew minute by minute; by the next moment, he was no longer the same man he'd been just a minute ago. But what had occurred that was so special that it had transformed him so? He himself didn't know; as if grasping for straws, it suddenly seemed to him that "he could live, there was still life ahead, and it hadn't died along with that old woman." Perhaps he had hastened to reach that conclusion, but he didn't think about that.

"But I asked for 'Thy servant Rodion' to be remembered," suddenly flashed through his mind. "Well, that's . . . just in case!" he added, and then began laughing at his own childish trick. He was in an excellent frame of mind.

He found Razumikhin easily, as everyone already knew the new lodger in Pochinkov's house. The doorman showed him the way immediately. Halfway up the stairs he could already hear the noise and lively conversation of the large gathering. The door to the staircase was open wide, and he could hear shouts and arguments. Razumikhin's room was rather large, and there were about fifteen people gathered in it. Raskolnikov paused in the entryway. There, behind a partition, two of the landlord's servants were attending to two large samovars next to bottles, plates, and dishes with pies and snacks brought up from the landlord's kitchen. Raskolnikov asked for Razumikhin. He came running in ecstasy. From the first glance, it was clear that he'd had more to drink than usual. Although Razumikhin could rarely drink enough to get drunk, this time something was amiss.

"Listen," Raskolnikov hastened to say. "I've come merely to say that you won the bet and that no one knows what can happen. I can't come in. I'm too weak and will topple over any minute. So, greetings and farewell. Come see me tomorrow . . ."

"You know what? I'll escort you home! If you yourself say that you're weak, then . . ."

"What about your guests? Who's that curly-haired fellow who just looked in here?"

"That one? The devil only knows! He must be one of my uncle's friends, or else he came on his own. . . . I'll leave the guests with my uncle; he's a most treasured man; it's a pity you can't meet him. But to hell with all of them! I don't care about them now: I need to get some fresh air, so, my friend, you came at a good time. Another two minutes and I'd have gotten into a fight, so help me God! They're talking such nonsense. . . . You can't imagine what sort of whopping lies a person can tell! But why can't you imagine it? Don't we all tell lies? Well, let them. Later they won't have to lie. . . . Sit here for a minute, and I'll bring Zosimov over."

Zosimov came rushing over to see Raskolnikov, with some excitement. One could sense a special kind of curiosity in him, and soon his face brightened.

"He needs to get some sleep immediately," he decided, having examined the patient as best he could, "and take one dose before he goes to bed. Will you do it? I prepared it before . . . one powder."

"Even two of them," replied Raskolnikov.

The powder was swallowed right there.

"It's a very good idea for you to escort him," Zosimov said to Razumikhin. "We'll see what tomorrow brings, but today he seems not bad at all: a significant change from yesterday. Live and learn . . ."

"Do you know what Zosimov whispered to me just now as we were leaving?" Razumikhin blurted out as soon as they had reached the street. "I'll tell you everything, because he's such a fool. Zosimov ordered me to chat with you along the way and make you talk, and then to tell him, because he has this idea . . . that you're insane or close to it. Just imagine! In the first place, you're three times smarter than he is; in the second place, if you're not mad, why should you give a damn about what sort of crazy ideas he has; and in the third place, that hunk of meat is a surgeon by specialty, and now he's meddling in mental diseases. What encouraged him in that regard was the conversation you had today with Zametov."

"Did Zametov tell you all this?"

"He did, and a good thing he did. Now I understand all there is to know, and so does Zametov. . . . Well, in a word, Rodya . . . the thing is. . . . I'm a little tipsy right now. . . . But that doesn't matter . . . the point is that this idea . . . do you understand? This idea took hold of them . . . do you understand? That is, no one ever dared utter it aloud because it's such ridiculous nonsense, especially after they arrested that painter. All of this burst like a bubble and vanished forever. But why are they such fools? At the time I pounced a bit on Zametov—this is just between us, my friend; please don't even hint that you know about it; I've noticed that he's prickly; it was at Laviza's—but today, today it's all become clear. The main thing is Ilya Petrovich! He exploited your fainting spell at the police station, and then he himself was ashamed. I know that . . ."

Raskolnikov listened fervently. Razumikhin was letting the cat out of the bag in his drunken state.

"I fainted then because it was stuffy and smelled of oil paint," said Raskolnikov.

"No need to explain! And it wasn't only the paint: your illness had been coming on for a whole month. Zosimov can swear to it! You can't possibly imagine how demolished that fellow is now! 'I'm not even worth that man's little finger,' he said. Yours, that is. Sometimes, my friend, he has good feelings. But the lesson, the lesson you gave him today at the 'Crystal Palace' was beyond perfection! At first you scared him, drove him into a fit! You almost convinced him all over again of that hideous nonsense and then, all of a sudden—you stuck out your tongue at him: 'Aha,' you said, 'so there!' Perfection! Now he's crushed, destroyed! You're a master, so help me God, and serves him right. Hey, too bad I wasn't there! He's been waiting eagerly to see you. Porfiry also wants to make your acquaintance . . ."

"Ah . . . that one, too. . . . Just why did they think I was insane?"

"Not insane exactly. It seems, my friend, I've said too much. . . . What struck him, don't you see, is that only one thing's been of any interest to you lately . . . now it's clear why that's so . . . knowing all the circumstances . . . and how much that irritated you then and became mixed up with your illness. . . . My friend, I'm a little drunk, but, damn it all, he has this idea of his own. . . . I tell you, he's been meddling in mental illness. To hell with him!"

For half a minute, both men remained silent.

"Listen, Razumikhin," began Raskolnikov. "I want to tell you honestly: just now I was with a dying man, a civil servant who passed away. . . . I gave away all my money . . . in addition, I was kissed by a creature who, if I'd killed someone, would also have. . . . In a word, there I saw another creature . . . with a fiery-colored feather . . . but I'm getting all tangled up. I'm very weak; give me your arm . . . here's the staircase . . ."

"What's the matter with you? What is it?" Razumikhin asked anxiously.

"My head's spinning a bit, but that's not the point; it's that I'm feeling so glum, so very glum. Just like a woman . . . I swear! Look, what's that? Look here, look!"

"What is it?"

"Don't you see? There's light in my room, don't you see? Through the crack . . ."

They were now standing in front of the last staircase, next to the landlady's door, and in fact there was light coming from underneath the door to Raskolnikov's little room.

"That's odd! Perhaps it's Nastasya," remarked Razumikhin.

"She never comes to my room at this hour. She must have gone to bed some time ago. But it doesn't matter! Good-bye!"

"What do you mean? I'll escort you; we'll go in together!"

"I know we'll go in together, but I want to shake your hand here and say good-bye to you. Well, give me your hand. Good-bye!"

"What's the matter with you, Rodya?"

"Nothing. Let's go: you'll be a witness."

They began climbing the stairs, and the idea flashed through Razumikhin's mind that perhaps Zosimov was right. "Hey! I've upset him with all my chatter!" he muttered to himself. Suddenly, approaching the door, they heard voices inside the room.

"What's all this about?" cried Razumikhin.

Raskolnikov, the first to reach the door, opened it wide. He stood on the threshold like someone rooted to the ground.

His mother and sister were sitting on the sofa in his room and had been waiting for him for the last hour and a half. Why had he expected them least of all and thought about them least of all, in spite of the news he'd heard that very day that they were leaving, traveling, and were soon to arrive? For the last hour and a half they had vied with each other in interrogating Nastasya, who was still standing before them and had already managed to tell them all there was to know. They were beside themselves with fear because they had heard that he had "run away today," that he was ill, and, as was apparent from the story, he was certainly delirious! "My God, what's the matter with him?" They were both weeping, and had endured great suffering during this last hour and a half of waiting.

Their joyful, ecstatic cry greeted Raskolnikov's appearance. They both rushed to him. But he stood there like a dead man. A sudden unbearable awareness struck him like a clap of thunder. He didn't even raise his arms to embrace them: he couldn't. His mother and sister took him in their embrace, kissed him, laughed, and wept. . . . He took a step, stumbled, and collapsed onto the floor in a faint.

Alarm, cries of fear, moans. . . . Razumikhin, standing on the threshold, rushed into the room, grabbed the sick man in his powerful arms, and lay him down immediately on the sofa.

"It's nothing, nothing at all!" he cried to the mother and sister. "It's only a faint. It doesn't mean a thing! The doctor just said that he was much better, that he's completely well! Some water! There now, he's already coming to. Well, now he's come around!"

Grabbing Dunechka's hand, in such a way that he almost tore it off, he forced her to see that "he'd already come around." Both mother and sister regarded Razumikhin with tender emotion and gratitude, as if he had been sent by Providence. They had already heard from Nastasya what this "capable young man" had done for Rodya all during his illness; that phrase was how Pulkheriya Aleksandrovna Raskolnikova herself had described him in her intimate conversation with Dunya that very evening.

PART III

I

Raskolnikov raised himself and sat up on the sofa.

He motioned weakly to Razumikhin to end his nonstop stream of incoherent and passionate words of consolation addressed to his mother and sister, took them both by the hand, and for a few moments stared in silence, first at one, then at the other. His mother was frightened by his gaze. A feeling akin to suffering showed through it, but at the same time there was something immobile, almost insane. Pulkheriya Aleksandrovna burst into tears.

Avdotya Romanovna was pale, and her hand trembled in her brother's hand.

"Go home . . . with him," he said in a broken voice, indicating Razumikhin. "Until tomorrow. Tomorrow everything will. . . . When did you arrive?"

"This evening, Rodya," replied Pulkheriya Aleksandrovna. "The train was terribly late. But, Rodya, I won't leave you now under any circumstances! I'll spend the night here next to . . ."

"Don't torment me!" he said, waving his hand irritably.

"I'll stay with him!" Razumikhin cried. "I won't leave him for a single moment. To hell with all my guests. Let them climb the walls! I left my uncle in charge."

"How can I ever thank you?" Pulkheriya Aleksandrovna started to say, giving Razumikhin's hands another squeeze, but Raskolnikov interrupted her again.

"I can't stand it, I can't," he repeated irritably. "Don't torment me! Enough! Go away. . . . I can't stand it!"

"Let's go, Mama, let's just leave the room for a minute," a frightened Dunya whispered. "Obviously we're upsetting him."

"Can't I have a look at him after these last three years?" Pulkheriya Aleksandrovna said through her tears.

"Wait!" he stopped them again. "You keep interrupting me. My thoughts are getting all mixed up. . . . Have you seen Luzhin?"

"No, Rodya, but he already knows about our arrival. We heard, Rodya, that Petr Petrovich was kind enough to call on you today," Pulkheriya Aleksandrovna added with some timidity.

"Yes . . . he was kind enough. . . . Dunya, I said to Luzhin that I'd throw him down the stairs and I sent him packing . . ."

"Rodya, what are you saying? Surely, you . . . you don't want to say," Pulkheriya Aleksandrovna started again in a fright, then paused, looking at Dunya.

Avdotya Romanovna stared intently at her brother and kept waiting. Both had been informed about the quarrel by Nastasya, as much as she could understand and relate, and they were worn out by suffering from incredulity and anticipation.

"Dunya," Raskolnikov continued with effort, "I don't want this marriage to take place; therefore, first thing tomorrow you must refuse Luzhin and never mention his name again."

"My God!" cried Pulkheriya Aleksandrovna.

"Brother, think about what you're saying!" Avdotya Romanovna began to reply irascibly, but immediately restrained herself. "Perhaps you're not in a good state; you're tired," she said gently.

"Delirious? No. . . . You're marrying Luzhin on my account. But I won't accept your sacrifice. Therefore, by tomorrow, write him a letter . . . with your refusal. . . . Give it to me to read in the morning. And that'll be the end of it!"

"I can't do that!" the offended young woman cried. "What right do . . ."

"Dunechka, you're also irascible. Stop it. Tomorrow we'll. . . . Can't you see," said her mother, rushing over to Dunya. "Ah, it's better if we leave."

"He's delirious," cried the tipsy Razumikhin. "How else could he dare? Tomorrow all this nonsense will be a thing of the past. . . . But he really did drive Luzhin away today. That's what happened. And, of course, the fellow got very angry. . . . He went on at length, trying to show off his erudition, and then left, tail between his legs . . ."

"So this is true?" cried Pulkheriya Aleksandrovna.

"Until tomorrow, brother," said Dunya with compassion. "Let's go, Mama. Good-bye, Rodya!"

"Do you hear, sister?" he repeated after them, gathering up his last strength. "I'm not delirious. This marriage is an abomination. I may be a scoundrel, but you mustn't be. . . . It's enough that one of us is. . . . And even if I am a scoundrel, I'll never consider such a sister as my own. It's either me or Luzhin! Now go . . ."

"You've lost your mind! You're a despot!" roared Razumikhin, but Raskolnikov made no reply. Perhaps he didn't have enough strength to answer. He lay down on the sofa and turned to face the wall in total exhaustion. Avdotya Romanovna regarded Razumikhin with curiosity, her black eyes glowing; he even shuddered at her expression. Pulkheriya Aleksandrovna stood there stunned.

"I can't leave under any circumstances!" she whispered to Razumikhin, almost in despair. "I'll stay here, somewhere. . . . Take Dunya home."

"You'll spoil everything!" Razumikhin said, also in a whisper, losing his temper. "Let's at least go out onto the landing. Nastasya, light the way! I swear to you," he continued to whisper, already on the stairs, "just a little while ago he came close to beating us up, the doctor and me! Do you understand? The doctor! The doctor complied so as not to irritate him and left. But while I remained on guard below, he got dressed and slipped out. And now, if you irritate him, he'll slip out again at night, and he might do something to himself . . ."

"Oh, what are you saying?"

"Besides, Avdotya Romanovna can't remain in the hotel alone without you! Think about where you're staying! Why couldn't that scoundrel Petr Petrovich have found you better rooms? But, you know I'm a little drunk and that's why. . . . I called him names, but don't pay any attention . . ."

"I'll go see the landlady here," insisted Pulkheriya Aleksandrovna, "and beg her to give Dunya and me a little room for the night. I can't leave him like this, I just can't."

While saying this, they stood on the landing, right in front of the landlady's door. Nastasya lit their way from a lower step. Razumikhin was in a state of extraordinary excitement. Just half an hour ago, while escorting Raskolnikov home, although he had been excessively talkative, as he himself would admit, he'd been feeling completely fearless and almost renewed, in spite of the enormous quantity of alcohol he'd consumed that evening. Now his mood resembled something like ecstasy and, at the same time, all the alcohol he'd consumed came rushing back to his head with redoubled force. He stood there with the two women, holding them both by the hand, trying to convince them, outlining his reasons with astonishing candor. Most likely for greater persuasiveness, almost at every word, he squeezed both their hands ever so tightly, as if in a vise, almost until it hurt. He also seemed to be devouring Avdotya Romanovna with his eyes and was not in the least embarrassed about it. As a result of their discomfort, the women sometimes pulled their hands away from the bony grip of his enormous hands. Not only did he fail to notice this, he drew them even closer to him. If they had commanded him to serve them by immediately casting himself headlong down the stairs, he would have done so at once, without considering or hesitating. Agitated by the thought of her Rodya, Pulkheriya Aleksandrovna still felt that this young man was somewhat eccentric and was squeezing her hand too tightly. At the same time, she felt that he had been sent by Providence, so she didn't want to comment on these unusual details. In spite of her alarm, although Avdotya Romanovna was not a particularly fearful person, she felt some astonishment and perhaps even some fear when she met the flashing, fiery look in her brother's friend's eyes, and it was only the infinite trustworthiness inspired by Nastasya's accounts of this strange man that kept her from the temptation of escaping and dragging her mother after her. She also understood that perhaps it was no longer possible to get away from him now. After about ten minutes, however, she felt significantly calmer. Razumikhin possessed the ability to say everything he had to say in an instant, no matter what sort of mood he was in, so that people realized very quickly who they were dealing with.

"You can't go to the landlady! That's the worst thing you could do!" he cried, trying to convince Pulkheriya Aleksandrovna. "Even though you're his mother, if you stay here, you'll make him furious, and then the devil only knows what might happen! Listen, here's what I'll do: Nastasya will stay here for now, and I'll escort both of you to your rooms, because you can't go out alone on the streets. In that regard, we have here in Petersburg. . . . Well, to hell with it! Then I'll rush back here and, in a quarter of an hour, my word of honor, I'll bring you news: how he's feeling, whether he's asleep, and so on. Now, listen! I'll go back to my own apartment. I have guests, and they're all drunk. I'll grab Zosimov, the doctor who's treating him. He's at my place now, but he's not drunk. He's not a drunkard; he never drinks! I'll take him to see Rodya and then bring him to you. In other words, within the hour you'll hear two reports about him, one from the doctor, do you understand, from the doctor himself. That's even better than from me! If it's bad, I swear, I'll bring you back here; if it's good, then you can go to bed. I'll spend the whole night here, in the entrance hall, and he won't hear me. I'll have Zosimov spend the night at the landlady's, so he'll be right here if needed. So what's better for him now, the doctor or you? The doctor's more useful, much more. So, you can go home! You can't go to the landlady. I can, but you can't: she won't take you in because . . . because she's a fool. She'll be jealous of Avdotya Romanovna on account of me, if you want to know, and on account of you, too. . . . But especially Avdotya Romanovna. She's an absolutely extraordinary character, absolutely! However, I'm also a fool. . . . To hell with it! Let's go! Do you believe me? Well, do you believe me or not?"

"Let's go, Mama," said Avdotya Romanovna. "He'll do as he promises. He's revived my brother. If it's true that the doctor will agree to spend the night here, then what could be better?"

"There, you . . . you . . . understand me because you're an angel!" Razumikhin cried in ecstasy. "Let's go! Nastasya! Come up here right now and stay with him. Bring a candle. I'll be back in quarter of an hour . . ."

Even though Pulkheriya Aleksandrovna wasn't completely convinced, she no longer resisted. Razumikhin took hold of both women's arms and led them down the stairs. However, she was somewhat disconcerted: "Even though he's competent and kind," she thought, "is he in any shape to do as he promises? He's in such a state!"

"Ah, I understand. You think I'm in a state!" Razumikhin said, interrupting her thoughts, having guessed them as he took his enormous strides along the sidewalk so that both women could hardly keep up, which, by the way, he didn't even notice. "Nonsense! That is, I'm dead drunk, but that's not the point. I am drunk, but not from alcohol. It's just that as soon as I saw you, the drink went to my head. . . . To hell with me! Don't pay me any attention. I'm lying and I'm not worthy of you. . . . I'm not the least bit worthy! After I've escorted you home, I'll pour two buckets of cold water over my head right here in the canal, and I'll be fine. . . . If you only knew how much I love you both! Don't laugh and don't be angry! You can be angry with everyone else, but not with me! I'm his friend; consequently, I'm your friend, too. I so want to. . . . I felt this coming . . . last year, there was one moment when. . . . However, I didn't really feel it coming since you seemed to arrive out of nowhere. Perhaps I won't sleep at all tonight. . . . Before, this Zosimov said he was afraid Rodya might lose his mind. . . . That's why one mustn't get on his nerves . . ."

"What are you saying?" cried his mother.

"Did the doctor really say that?" asked Avdotya Romanovna, growing frightened.

"He did, but that's not the point, not at all. He gave him some medicine, a powder, I saw it, and then you arrived. . . . Hey! It would have been better if you'd come tomorrow! It's a good thing we left. Zosimov himself will report everything to you an hour from now. He's not drunk at all! And I won't be drunk then. . . . Why did I get so smashed? Because I got into an argument, damn them! I swore that I wouldn't argue! They were spouting such nonsense! I almost got into a fight! I left my uncle there to preside. . . . Well, would you believe it: they demand complete impersonality and delight in that! If only one could be other than oneself, or resemble oneself as little as possible!

That's what they consider the highest form of progress. If they would at least lie, each in his own way, but . . ."

"Listen," Pulkheriya Aleksandrovna interrupted him timidly, but that merely fanned his fervor.

"What do you think?" cried Razumikhin, raising his voice even more. "Do you think I'm not in favor of their telling lies? Rubbish! I love it when they tell lies! Lying is a privilege exclusive to humans among all other beings. It's by lying that one arrives at the truth! I tell lies; therefore, I'm human. We haven't arrived at any truths without having uttered nonsense beforehand fourteen or so times, perhaps even one hundred and fourteen times, and that's honorable in its own way; well, we can't even talk nonsense by relying on our own intelligence! You talk nonsense, but if it's your own, I'll kiss you for it. To talk one's own nonsense is almost better than spouting someone else's truth. In the first case, you're a human being; but in the second, you're only a parrot! Truth doesn't vanish, but life can be beaten to a pulp; there have been examples. Well, where are we now? All of us, without exception, as regards science, development, thought, inventions, ideals, desires, liberalism, reason, experience, and everything, everything, everything, everything, everything—we're still sitting in kindergarten! We've been pleased to make do with other people's ideas—and we've gotten used to it! Isn't that so? Aren't I right?" cried Razumikhin, shaking and squeezing the two women's hands. "Isn't that true?"

"Oh, my God, I don't know," said poor Pulkheriya Aleksandrovna.

"Yes, yes . . . although I'm not entirely in agreement with you," Avdotya Romanovna added earnestly. Then she uttered a cry because he was squeezing her hand so tightly.

"Yes? You say it's so? Well, after this you . . . you . . ." he cried in ecstasy. "You're a font of goodness, purity, reason, and . . . perfection! Give me your hand, give it to me . . . give me yours, too. I want to kiss both your hands right here, right now, on my knees!"

He fell to his knees in the middle of the sidewalk, fortunately deserted this time.

"Stop it, I beg you. What are you doing?" cried Pulkheriya Aleksandrovna, agitated in the extreme.

"Get up, get up!" Dunya said with a laugh, also agitated.

"Not for anything, not until you give me your hands! There now, enough. I've stood up. Now let's go! I'm an unhappy fool; I'm unworthy of you, I'm drunk, and I'm ashamed. . . . I'm not worthy to love you, but it's everyone's duty to bow down before you—if only they're not complete beasts! And I have bowed down. . . . Here are your rooms. For this reason alone Rodion was right to drive Petr Petrovich away earlier! How dare he put you in such rooms? It's a scandal! Do you know who comes here? And you're his fiancée! You are, aren't you? Well, I can tell you now that your fiancé's a scoundrel!"

"Listen, Mr. Razumikhin, you're forgetting yourself . . ." Pulkheriya Aleksandrovna began.

"Yes, yes, you're right. I'm forgetting myself, I'm ashamed!" Razumikhin corrected himself suddenly. "But . . . but . . . you can't be angry with me for talking like this! I'm being sincere, and it's not because. . . . Hmm. That would be vile; in a word, it's not because I . . . you. . . . Hmm. Well, so be it, there's no need. I won't say it; I dare not! We understood everything from the moment he walked in; he's not a man of our circle. It wasn't because he'd just had his hair curled at the barber's, and not because he hastened to show off his intelligence, but because he's a spy and a speculator; because he's a Yid and a buffoon, and that's clear. You think he's clever? No, he's a fool, a fool! Is he a match for you? Oh, my God! You see, ladies"—he stopped suddenly, as he was now climbing the stairs to their rooms—"even though my guests are drunk, they're all honest; and even though we're talking nonsense, because I'm also talking nonsense, we'll finally lie our way to the truth, because we're on a noble path, while Petr Petrovich . . . is not on a noble path. Although I've just cursed them soundly, I still respect them all; even though I don't respect Zametov, I still love him because—because he's a puppy dog! Even that beast Zosimov, because he's honest and knows his business. . . . But enough. Everything's been said and forgiven. It has been forgiven, hasn't it? Well, let's go. I know this hallway, I've been here before. There was a scandal right here, in the third room. . . . So, where are you? What number? Eight? Well, lock the door at night and don't let anyone in. I'll be back in a quarter of an hour with news, and then Zosimov will come a half hour later. You'll see! Good-bye, I'm off!"

"My God, Dunechka, what will happen?" said Pulkheriya Aleksandrovna, looking at her daughter, full of alarm and anxiety.

"Calm down, Mama," replied Dunya, taking off her hat and cloak. "God Himself sent us that gentleman, even though he's come straight from some sort of drinking bout. I assure you that we can rely on him. Just look at all that he's already done for my brother . . ."

"Ah, Dunechka, God only knows if he'll come! How could I abandon Rodya? That's not the way I imagined we'd find him at all! He was so stern, as if he wasn't glad to see us . . ."

Tears welled up in her eyes.

"No, that's not so, Mama. You didn't look closely, since you were crying all the time. He's so distressed by his serious illness—that's the whole reason."

"Ah, the illness! Something bad will happen, I'm sure it will! And the way he talked to you, Dunya!" said her mother, looking timidly into her daughter's eyes to read her thoughts, already feeling somewhat consoled that Dunya was defending Rodya and, therefore, must have forgiven him. "I'm sure he'll reconsider tomorrow," she added, still trying to probe.

"But I'm certain he'll say the same thing tomorrow . . . on this subject," Avdotya Romanovna said, cutting her short. That, of course, was the catch, because it was the very point Pulkheriya Aleksandrovna was now too afraid to mention. Dunya went up to her mother and kissed her. The latter embraced her warmly in silence. Then Pulkheriya Aleksandrovna sat down in nervous anticipation of Razumikhin's return and timidly began to follow her daughter, who, folding her arms, also in anticipation, began pacing the room, deep in thought. Such pacing from corner to corner in deep thought was Avdotya Romanovna's usual habit, and her mother always feared interrupting her reflections at such times.

Razumikhin, it goes without saying, was preposterous with his sudden passion, fueled by drink, for Avdotya Romanovna; but, seeing her, especially now, as she was pacing the room, her arms folded, sad and pensive, perhaps many people would excuse him, without any mention of his extraordinary condition. Avdotya Romanovna was remarkably good-looking—tall, astonishingly graceful, and strong, with a self-confidence that showed in her every gesture and in no way excluded tenderness and gracefulness from her movements. Her face resembled her brother's, but she could even be called a beauty. Her hair was dark brown, a little lighter than her brother's. Her eyes were almost black, sparkling, proud, and, simultaneously, at certain moments, unusually kind. Her complexion was pale, but not sickly pale; her face shone with freshness and good health. Her mouth was a little small; her lower lip, fresh and scarlet, protruded slightly forward, together with her chin—the single imperfection in this lovely face, but granting it a special quality and, incidentally, a slight arrogance. Her expression was always more serious and thoughtful than cheerful; on the other hand, a smile suited her face so well, as did laughter, joyful, youthful, uninhibited! It is understandable how the passionate, candid, simpleminded, honest, strong as a folkloric hero, and inebriated Razumikhin, never having seen anyone like that, would lose his head at first glance. Besides, chance, as if intentionally, had revealed Dunya for the first time at a splendid moment of love and joy at the reunion with her brother. He then saw how her lower lip trembled in indignation in response to her brother's bold and ungratefully cruel commands—and he could not resist.

However, he'd been telling the truth when, in his drunken state, he'd blurted out on the stairs that Raskolnikov's eccentric landlady, Praskovya Pavlovna, was jealous of him, not only with respect to Avdotya Romanovna, but perhaps also to Pulkheriya Aleksandrovna herself. In spite of the fact that Pulkheriya Aleksandrovna was already forty-three years old, her face still preserved traces of her former beauty; besides, she seemed much younger than her years, something that happens almost always with women who maintain their clarity of spirit, freshness of impressions, and honest, pure intensity of heart as they age. Let us add in parentheses that to maintain all this is the only way to preserve one's beauty even in old age. Her hair was already starting to turn gray and grow thin; small, radiating wrinkles had appeared around her eyes some time ago; her cheeks were sunken and dry from her cares and grief; and yet her face was still beautiful. It was the image of Dunya, only twenty years later, except for the look of her lower lip, since hers did not protrude. Pulkheriya Aleksandrovna was sensitive, though not to the point of affectation. She was shy and compliant, but only to a certain extent. She could concede a great deal, agree to many things, even those that contradicted her convictions, but there was always a limit to her honesty, her rules, and her deepest convictions that no circumstances would ever force her to cross.

Exactly twenty minutes after Razumikhin's departure there came his two soft but hurried knocks at the door: he had returned.

"I won't come in. I haven't time!" he hastened to say when they opened the door. "He's fast asleep, soundly and peacefully; God willing, he'll sleep for ten hours or so. Nastasya's there; I told her not to leave until I get back. Soon I'll bring Zosimov. He'll report to you, and then you can get some sleep. I can see that you're both completely exhausted."

He set off down the corridor.

"What an efficient and . . . devoted young man!" exclaimed the extremely elated Pulkheriya Aleksandrovna.

"He seems to be a splendid person!" replied Avdotya Romanovna with a certain passion, beginning to pace the room again.

Almost an hour later, steps were heard in the corridor and there was another knock at the door. Both women were waiting, this time completely convinced by Razumikhin's promise; in fact, he had really managed to bring Zosimov. He had agreed to leave the party immediately and have a look at Raskolnikov, but had come to see the women unwillingly and with great uncertainty, failing to trust the drunken Razumikhin. His self-esteem, however, was quickly soothed and even flattered; he realized that they really had been waiting for him as an oracle. He spent exactly ten minutes there and managed to convince them completely and appease Pulkheriya Aleksandrovna. He spoke with unusual sympathy, but with restraint and great earnestness, exactly as a twenty-seven-year-old doctor would at an important consultation. He didn't stray from his subject with a single word and demonstrated no desire whatever to engage in more personal and private matters with the two women. Having observed upon entering how dazzlingly attractive Avdotya Romanovna was, he tried all during his visit not to pay her any attention, addressing Pulkheriya Aleksandrovna exclusively. All this afforded him a sense of extreme inner satisfaction. As for the patient himself, he said that at the present time he found his condition to be extremely satisfactory.

According to his observations, the patient's illness, besides the poor material circumstances of the last few months of his life, had several other moral causes: "They were, so to speak, the result of complex moral and material influences, anxieties, apprehensions, problems, certain ideas . . . and so forth." Having noticed in passing that Avdotya Romanovna had begun listening especially carefully, Zosimov developed this theme at somewhat greater length. In reply to Pulkheriya Aleksandrovna's anxious and timid question concerning "certain suspicions regarding his sanity," he replied with a calm and candid smile that his words had been exaggerated; that, of course, the patient had a certain idée fixe, something indicating monomania—he, Zosimov, was now pursuing this extremely interesting branch of medicine—but it must be recalled that almost up until today the patient had been delirious and . . . and, of course, the arrival of his family would strengthen him, dispel these ideas, and have a salutary influence on him, "if only any new upsets could be avoided," he added with emphasis. Then he stood up, bowed imposingly and cordially, and was escorted out with blessings, warm gratitude, and prayers. Avdotya Romanovna even extended her own hand to him, and he left extremely satisfied with his visit, all the more so with himself.

"We'll talk tomorrow. Now go to bed, right now, immediately!" Razumikhin insisted, leaving with Zosimov. "Tomorrow, as early as possible, I'll come with a report."

"What an entrancing girl that Avdotya Romanovna is!" remarked Zosimov, almost licking his lips as the two of them emerged onto the street.

"Entrancing? You said entrancing?" Razumikhin roared and suddenly threw himself at Zosimov, grabbing him by the throat. "If you ever dare to . . . do you understand? Do you understand?" he shouted, shaking him by the collar and pinning him against the wall. "Do you hear me?"

"Let me go, you drunken devil!" Zosimov struggled and then, after being released, looked closely at Razumikhin and suddenly burst out laughing. Razumikhin stood there in front of him, dropping his arms, in dark and serious thought.

"Of course, I'm an ass," he said, black as a storm cloud. "But then . . . so are you."

"No, my friend, not at all. I'm not the one with absurd dreams."

They walked along in silence, and only when they arrived at Raskolnikov's apartment did Razumikhin, feeling burdened by his cares, break the silence.

"Listen," he said to Zosimov. "You're a fine fellow, but in addition to all your bad qualities, you're a lecher, that I know, and one of the filthiest. You're an anxious, weak scoundrel. You're capricious and spoiled, and you can't deny yourself anything—I call that filth, because it leads directly to filth. You've pampered yourself to such an extent that, I confess, least of all do I understand how you can be a good doctor, even a selfless one, with all this. You sleep on a feather bed (a doctor, even!), yet you get up at night to visit a patient! In three years or so, you won't be getting up to treat anyone. . . . Well, hell, that's not the point, but this is: you'll spend tonight in the landlady's apartment (I managed to persuade her!), and I'll be in the kitchen: this is your chance to get to know her better! It's not what you think! There's no hint of that, my friend . . ."

"I'm not thinking anything at all."

"Here, my friend, you'll find bashfulness, reticence, shyness, strict chastity, and given all that—after a few sighs she'll melt like wax, just like that! Save me from her, for the sake of all the devils in the world! She's a most charming creature! I'll repay you with my life, I will!"

Zosimov started laughing even more than before.

"You're really smashed! What do I want with her?"

"I assure you, it doesn't take much. Talk about whatever nonsense you want, but sit next to her and talk. Besides, you're a doctor, so you can begin to treat her for some ailment. I swear, you won't regret it. She has a piano, and I strum on it a bit. I have one song, a Russian one, genuine: 'I weep bitter tears . . .' She really loves it—well, it began with a song; but you're a virtuoso on the piano, a maestro, a Ruben-stein. . . .* I assure you, you won't be sorry!"

"Did you make any sort of promises to her? Did you sign some document? Did you promise to marry her, perhaps . . ."

"Not at all, not at all, nothing of the sort! She's not that kind of woman. Chebarov approached her . . ."

"Well, then drop her!" Zosimov exclaimed.

"It's not that easy to drop her!"

"Why not?"

"Well, it's just not, that's all there is to it! There's a complicating factor involved."

"Why did you lead her on then?"

"I didn't lead her on at all. Perhaps I myself was led on in my fool-ishness, but it's absolutely all the same to her whether it's you or me, as long as someone's sitting next to her and sighing. Here, my friend. . . . I can't express it to you; here—you're good at math, and I know you're still studying now. . . . Well, start explaining integral calculus to her, I swear I'm not joking. I'm being serious. It's really all the same to her: she'll look at you and sigh, and sit there for a whole year. By the way, for two days I was telling her at length about the Prussian House of Lords (because, what else is there to talk about with her?)—and all she did was sigh and sweat! But don't start talking about love—she's incredibly shy –show her that you can't possibly leave her—well, that's all there is to it. You'll be terribly comfortable; just like home—read, sit, lie down, write. . . . You can even kiss her, but carefully . . ."

"But why should I care about her?"

"Hey, I can't explain it to you! You see, you two are so much alike! I already thought of you before. . . . You'll end up like that! So, isn't it the same, whether it's sooner or later? Here, my friend, is the begin-ning of a feather-bed life—hey, not only a feather bed! You'll be drawn in. This is the end of the world, an anchor, a quiet refuge, the hub of the universe, the three great fishes on which the earth rests, the essence of pancakes, savory pies, an evening samovar, soft sighs, warm

---

* Anton Rubenstein (1829–1894) was a virtuoso pianist and founder of the St. Petersburg Conservatory.

jackets, heated stoves—so it's just as if you were dead, but also alive, all the advantages of both at the same time! Well, my friend, hell, I've gone on and on. It's time for bed! Listen: sometimes I wake up at night. If so, I'll go have a look at him. It's nothing, nonsense, everything's all right. Don't be alarmed. And you, you can stop by, too, if you like. But if you notice anything, delirium, for example, or fever, or something else, then wake me immediately. But that won't happen . . ."

Razumikhin awoke the next day before eight o'clock in an anxious and solemn mood. Many new and unforeseen complications had suddenly arisen that morning. He had never imagined that he would awake in such a state.

He recalled everything that had occurred the day before to the last detail and realized that something very unusual had taken place. He had experienced an impression the likes of which he had never felt before. At the same time, he was clearly aware that the dream, which had flared up in his imagination, was utterly unrealizable—so much so that he was even ashamed of it and quickly moved on to other, more important worries and complications that he had inherited after that "thrice-accursed yesterday."

His most terrible recollection was how "base and vile" he had seemed, not only because he was drunk, but because he had abused Avdotya Romanovna's fiancé in the presence of the young woman, taking advantage of her situation and, as a result of his foolishly and hastily conceived jealousy, without any knowledge of their mutual relations and obligations, not even knowing the man properly. Besides, what right did he have to judge Petr Petrovich so quickly and rashly? Who had called upon him to judge? Could a creature like Avdotya Romanovna give herself up to such an unworthy man for money? Therefore, Luzhin must possess good qualities. But those rooms? Though how could he possibly have known what sort of rooms they really were? He was busy preparing their apartment. . . . Phew, how base it all was! And what sort of defense was it that he was drunk? It was a stupid excuse that degraded him even more! *In vino veritas*, and now the whole truth had emerged, "that is, all the filth of his crude, envious heart!" Was it in any way permissible for him, Razumikhin, to harbor such a dream? Who was he compared to such a young woman: just a drunken lout and yesterday's braggart? "Is such a disparaging and ridiculous comparison even possible?" Razumikhin blushed desperately at this idea; all of a sudden, as if intentionally, at that very moment, he clearly recalled how he had told them yesterday, standing on the stairs, that the land-lady was jealous of Avdotya Romanovna with regard to him. That was intolerable! He slammed his fist into the kitchen stove with all his might, hurting his hand and dislodging one brick.

"Of course," he muttered to himself a minute later with a feel-ing of self-disparagement, "of course, it's impossible to paint over or smooth out all these mean tricks. . . . Therefore, it's no use even think-ing about it; from now on, I must appear before them in silence and . . . and fulfill my obligations . . . also in silence, and . . . and not ask their forgiveness, not say anything, and . . . and, of course, now all is lost!"

Nevertheless, while dressing, he scrutinized his apparel more carefully than usual. He didn't have any other clothes; but even if he had, perhaps he wouldn't have put them on. "Just so, he deliberately wouldn't put them on." In any case, he could not continue being a cynic and a filthy slob. He had no right to offend other people's feel-ings, all the more so since they needed him and were calling upon him. He cleaned his clothes carefully with a brush. His linen was always tolerable, and on that score he was particularly fastidious.

That morning he scrubbed himself diligently, with soap provided by Nastasya; he washed his hair, his neck, and especially his hands. When the question arose as to whether to shave his stubble or not (Praskovya Pavlovna owned an excellent razor that had belonged to her late husband, Mr. Zarnitsyn), the question was answered in the negative, even with some bitterness: "Let it stay like it is! Well, they might think I shaved especially . . . that's just what they'll think! Not for anything on earth!

"And . . . and the main thing is, he's so crude, filthy, with manners of the tavern; and . . . and, let's assume he knows he's a decent fellow, at least a little. Well, what's there to be proud of in being a decent fellow? Everyone should be decent, even better than that, and . . . still"—he remembers this—"there were certain matters . . . not exactly dishonorable, nevertheless, there they were! And what sort of thoughts had he sometimes harbored? Hmm. And to put all this alongside Avdotya Romanovna! Well, damn it all! So be it! I'll be dirty, filthy, drunken, and to hell with it! I'll be even worse!"

Zosimov, who had spent the night in Praskovya Pavlovna's living room, came upon him in the middle of this monologue.

He was heading home and, before leaving, had hastened to ask about the patient. Razumikhin reported that he was sleeping like a log. Zosimov ordered that Raskolnikov not be disturbed until he awoke. He promised to call in sometime after ten.

"If only he's at home," he added. "Damn it! It's hard to treat a patient when you have no control over his movements! Do you happen to know whether *he's* going there or *they're* coming here?"

"They're coming to him, I think," replied Razumikhin, grasping the purpose of the question. "Of course, they'll be talking about family matters. I'll leave. As a doctor, of course, you have more rights than I do."

"But I'm not a priest. I'll come and go. I have many things to do besides them."

"One thing disturbs me," added Razumikhin, frowning. "Yesterday, in my drunken state, as we walked home, I blabbed about all sorts of stupid things . . . various matters. . . . I said that you were afraid that he might . . . have a tendency toward insanity . . ."

"You also said something about it to the women yesterday."

"I know it was stupid! You can beat me, if you like! But do you really have a strong opinion?"

"It's nonsense, I tell you. What sort of strong opinion? You yourself described him as a monomaniac when you called me in on the case. . . . Well, yesterday we even fed the flames—that is, you did, with those stories . . . about the painter. Fine to talk about that when it might have been the very thing that threatened his sanity in the first place! If I'd known in detail what had happened then at the police station, that

some rascal had offended him there . . . with his suspicion! Hmm . . .
I wouldn't have allowed that conversation yesterday. These monomaniacs can make mountains out of molehills; and they can believe the
most fantastic stories. . . . As far as I can recall from yesterday, from
Zametov's account, about half the matter came clear to me. So what? I
know a case where one hypochondriac, some forty years old, was in no
condition to tolerate everyday taunts at the table from an eight-year-
old lad, and so he killed him! And here we have a man in tatters, an
arrogant policeman, the beginnings of an illness, and such a suspicion!
To a frenzied hypochondriac! In the presence of extraordinary, insane
vanity! This might even be the source of his illness! Well, to hell with
it! By the way, this Zametov really is a very nice young man, only . . .
hmm . . . there was no need for him to say all that yesterday. He's a
terrible chatterbox!"

"Who did he tell? You and me?"

"And Porfiry."

"So what if he told Porfiry?"

"By the way, do you have any influence on the two of them, his
mother and sister? They should be more careful with him today . . ."

"They'll come to an agreement!" Razumikhin replied unwillingly.

"And why did he attack Luzhin like that? He's a man of means,
and she doesn't seem repulsed by him. . . . And they're broke, right?"

"Why are you interrogating me?" Razumikhin cried irritably.
"How should I know if they're broke or not? Ask them yourself. Maybe
you'll find out . . ."

"Phew! How stupid you are sometimes! You're still showing signs
of yesterday's drinking bout. . . . Good-bye. Thank Praskovya Pavlovna
for me for last night's lodging. She locked herself away and didn't answer
when I said 'Good morning' through the door. She got up at seven
o'clock, and her samovar was brought from the kitchen through the
corridor. . . . I wasn't worthy of beholding her with my own eyes . . ."

At precisely nine o'clock, Razumikhin appeared in the rooms at
Bakaleev's. Both women had been waiting for him for some time in
hysterical impatience. They had been awake since seven, or even earlier. He entered in a mood as somber as night and greeted them awkwardly, for which he grew angry at once—at himself, of course. He was

mistaken in his calculations: Pulkheriya Aleksandrovna threw herself at him, grabbed both his hands, and almost started kissing them. He looked timidly at Avdotya Romanovna; but at that moment her haughty face expressed gratitude, friendship, and such complete and unexpected respect for him (instead of mocking glances and the involuntary, badly concealed scorn he had expected!) that in truth it would have been easier for him if they had greeted him with abuse, because now it was all too confusing. Fortunately, there was an easy topic for conversation, and he seized upon it quickly.

After hearing that "he's still not awake" but that "everything is all right," Pulkheriya Aleksandrovna declared that it was for the best "since she very, very, very much needed to talk things over first." There followed a question about tea and an invitation to have some together; they still hadn't had their tea while waiting for Razumikhin. Avdotya Romanovna rang the bell, and a filthy urchin appeared; he was told to bring tea, which was finally served, but it was so dirty and crude that the ladies were ashamed. Razumikhin was about to criticize the rooms forcefully, but, recalling Luzhin, he kept silent, felt embarrassed, and then was overjoyed when Pulkheriya Aleksandrovna's questions finally rained down on him without interruption.

Replying to them, he spoke for three-quarters of an hour, constantly interrupted and cross-examined. He managed to convey all the most important and necessary facts he knew regarding the previous year of Rodion Romanovich's life, concluding with a detailed account of his illness. He omitted, however, a great deal that needed to be omitted, including the scene at the police station, with all the consequences of that meeting. They listened eagerly to his account, but when he thought he had finished and had satisfied his audience, it turned out that as far as they were concerned, he had hardly begun.

"Tell me, tell me, what do you think. . . . Ah, excuse me. I still don't know your full name," Pulkheriya Aleksandrovna hastened to add.

"Dmitry Prokofich."

"Well, then, Dmitry Prokofich, I'd very, very much like to know . . . in general . . . how he now regards things, that is, understand me . . . how shall I put it . . . that is, it's better to say: what does he like and what not? Is he always so irritable? What desires does he have, what dreams, so to speak, if it's possible to say? What has the greatest influence on him now? In a word, I'd like to . . ."

"Ah, Mama, how can he answer all these questions all of a sudden?" remarked Dunya.

"Ah, my God, I never, never expected to meet him like this, Dmitry Prokofich."

"That's only natural, ma'am," replied Dmitry Prokofich. "I have no mother, but my uncle visits me every year and almost every time doesn't recognize me, even my appearance, and he's a clever man. A great deal of water has passed under the bridge during the three years of your separation. What can I tell you? I've known Rodion for the last year and a half. He's gloomy, somber, haughty, and proud. Lately (perhaps for quite a while), he's been worrying about his health; he's a hypochondriac. He's also generous and kind. He doesn't like to talk about his feelings and would sooner seem cruel than reveal his heart. Sometimes, however, he's not a hypochondriac at all, but cold and callously insensitive. It's almost as if there were two contradictory characters alternating within him. Sometimes he's terribly uncommunicative! He has no time for anything and everything bothers him, while he just lies there doing nothing. He's not sarcastic, not because he lacks wit: it's just that he has no time for such nonsense. He doesn't wait to hear what people are saying. He never takes an interest in what interests other people at any given moment. He values himself very highly, and, it seems, has reason to do so. Well, what else? It seems to me that your arrival will have an extremely beneficial effect on him."

"Ah, God willing!" cried Pulkheriya Aleksandrovna, tormented by Razumikhin's account of her Rodya.

At last Razumikhin looked more cheerfully at Avdotya Romanovna. During this conversation, he had glanced at her frequently but fleetingly, for only a moment, and then looked away immediately. Avdotya Romanovna either sat at the table, listening carefully, or stood up again and began pacing, as was her custom, from corner to corner, arms crossed, biting her lips, seldom asking a question, without interrupting her pacing, deep in thought. She also had the habit of not listening to what other people said. She was wearing a dark dress made of thin material, with a delicate white scarf tied around her neck. From many indications Razumikhin observed that the circumstances of both women were extremely poor. If Avdotya Romanovna had been dressed like a queen, then, it seems, he would not have been the least bit afraid of her; but now, perhaps because she was so badly dressed, and he had noticed all these shabby circumstances, fear engulfed his heart. He began to fear his every word, every gesture, which, of course, would be embarrassing for anybody, especially for a person so unsure of himself.

"You've said many interesting things about my brother's character and . . . said it in an impartial way. That's good because I thought you worshipped him," remarked Avdotya Romanovna with a smile. "It also seems true that he should have a woman near him," she added in a thoughtful mood.

"I didn't say that; but perhaps you're also right about that; however . . ."

"What?"

"He doesn't love anyone. Perhaps he'll never love anyone," replied Razumikhin abruptly.

"That is, he's incapable of loving?"

"You know, Avdotya Romanovna, you're terribly like your brother in all sorts of ways!" he blurted out suddenly, surprising even himself; but at once, recalling what he had just said about her brother, he turned red as a beet and became flustered. Avdotya Romanovna couldn't keep from laughing as she looked at him.

"You both may be mistaken about Rodya," Pulkheriya Aleksandrovna declared, somewhat offended. "I'm not talking about the present, Dunechka. What Petr Petrovich writes in this letter . . . and what you and I believed may not be the truth, but you, Dmitry Prokofich, can't imagine how prone to fantasy he is, and, how shall I put it, how capricious he is. I could never trust his character, not even when he was only fifteen years old. I'm sure that even now he could do something to himself that no one else could ever conceive of doing. . . . One doesn't have to go far: do you know how, a year and a half ago, he astounded me, shocked me, and was nearly the death of me, when he decided to marry that girl, what's her name—the daughter of this Zarnitsyna woman, his landlady?"

"Do you know the details of that episode?" asked Avdotya Romanovna.

"You think," Pulkheriya Aleksandrovna continued passionately, "my tears would have stopped him then, my entreaties, my illness, my death, perhaps, from our anguish, our poverty? He would have calmly overstepped all those obstacles. But does he really, really not love us?"

"He himself never told me a thing about that episode," Razumikhin replied cautiously, "but I heard something about it from Mrs. Zarnitsyna herself, who's also not the most communicative person. What I did hear was really rather strange . . ."

"What, what did you hear?" the two women asked together.

"Well, nothing much in particular. I merely learned that this match, already settled, and which didn't take place only because of the bride's death, was not at all to Mrs. Zarnitsyna's liking. . . . Besides that, they say the young woman was not very attractive, that is, they say she was even rather plain . . . and so sickly, and . . . and strange . . . however, it seems, she did have certain good qualities, or else there'd be no way to make sense of it. . . . There was no dowry at all, but then he wouldn't even count on that possibility. . . . In general, it's difficult to judge in such a matter."

"I'm certain that she was a worthy young woman," Avdotya Romanovna observed curtly.

"God will forgive me, but at the time I rejoiced at her death, although I really don't know which of them would've ruined the other: would he destroy her, or would she destroy him?" Pulkheriya Aleksandrovna concluded. Then, cautiously, with hesitations and constant glances at Dunya, which, obviously, were not to Dunya's liking, she started to ask about the meeting yesterday between Rodya and Luzhin. That event, apparently, disturbed her more than anything, inciting fear and trembling in her. Razumikhin related everything once more in detail, but this time he added his own conclusion. He bluntly accused Raskolnikov of intentionally insulting Petr Petrovich, hardly using his illness as an excuse.

"He had decided on this before he became ill," he added.

"I think so, too," said Pulkheriya Aleksandrovna with a defeated look. She was very surprised that this time Razumikhin was speaking about Petr Petrovich so cautiously, even with what seemed to be some respect. This also surprised Avdotya Romanovna.

"What, then, is your opinion of Petr Petrovich?" Pulkheriya Aleksandrovna asked, unable to refrain from inquiring.

"I can't hold any other opinion of your daughter's future husband," Razumikhin replied with resolution and passion. "I'm not saying this out of any vulgar politeness, but because . . . because . . . well, only because Avdotya Romanovna herself, voluntarily, was the one to choose him. If I reviled him yesterday, it was because I was dead drunk and even . . . insane. Yes, insane, I lost my head, I went crazy, completely . . . and today I'm ashamed of it!" He blushed and fell silent. Avdotya Romanovna blushed deeply but didn't break her silence. She hadn't uttered a single word from the moment they had started talking about Luzhin.

Meanwhile, Pulkheriya Aleksandrovna, without her daughter's support, was apparently in a state of indecision. At last, hesitating and glancing constantly at Dunya, she declared that now one circumstance concerned her greatly.

"You see, Dmitry Prokofich," she began. "I'll be absolutely frank with Dmitry Prokofich, right, Dunya?"

"Of course, Mama," Avdotya Romanovna remarked earnestly.

"The point is," she hastened to add, as if permission to communicate her sorrow had relieved her of a great burden. "Today, very early, we received a letter from Petr Petrovich in reply to our notifying him of our arrival yesterday. You see, yesterday he was supposed to meet us at the station, as he'd promised. Instead, a lackey was sent with the address of these rooms to show us the way, while Petr Petrovich told him to say that he himself would call on us today. Instead, this letter arrived this morning. . . . It would be better if you read it yourself. There's one thing that disturbs me a great deal . . . you'll soon see what it is for yourself, and . . . give me your honest opinion, Dmitry Prokofich! You know Rodya's character best of all, and you can advise us best of all. I warn you that Dunechka's already decided the entire matter from the outset, but I, I still don't know what to do, and . . . I've been waiting for you."

Razumikhin unfolded the letter dated the day before and read the following:

Dear Madam, Pulkheriya Aleksandrovna,

"I have the honor to inform you that because of some sudden delays, I was unable to meet you on the platform, so I sent a very efficient fellow in my place. Similarly, I must deprive myself of the honor of meeting you tomorrow morning, as a result of unavoidable business at the Senate, and so as not to interfere with your intimate reunion with your son, and Avdotya Romanovna's reunion with her brother. I shall have the honor of calling on you and paying my respects in your rooms no later than tomorrow, at precisely eight o'clock in the evening. Moreover, I take the liberty of adding the earnest and, dare I say, insistent request that Rodion Romanovich not be present at our meeting, inasmuch as he insulted me unspeakably and impolitely during my visit to his sickbed yesterday. Furthermore, I want to have a necessary and thorough discussion with you regarding one particular matter, about which I wish to learn your opinion. I have the honor of informing you in advance that if, in spite of my request, I meet Rodion Romanovich, then I will be compelled to leave at once, and you will have only yourself to blame. I am writing this on the assumption that Rodion Romanovich, who seemed so ill during my visit, suddenly recovered within two hours, and that consequently, leaving his own room, he may be able to visit you. I was convinced of this by my own eyes, having seen him yesterday in the apartment of a certain drunkard, run over by horses, who died as a result, and whose daughter, a young woman of notorious conduct, he handed up to twenty-five rubles yesterday, on the pretext of funeral expenses, a fact that shocked me greatly, knowing the difficult circumstances under which you acquired that sum of money. With that, and conveying my special regards to the respected Avdotya Romanovna, I beg you to accept my feelings of respectful devotion,

Your humble servant,
P. Luzhin.

"What shall I do now, Dmitry Prokofich?" asked Pulkheriya Ale-ksandrovna, almost in tears. "How can I tell Rodya not to come? Yesterday he so insistently demanded that Petr Petrovich be refused, and now we're told that Rodya can't be received! He'll come on purpose, as soon as he finds out, and . . . then what will happen?"

"Do as Avdotya Romanovna has decided," Razumikhin replied calmly at once.

"Oh, my goodness! She says . . . God knows what she says, and she doesn't explain her purpose to me! She says that it would be better, that is, not exactly better, but for some reason it would be absolutely necessary that Rodya also deliberately come today at eight o'clock and that they meet without fail. . . . But I didn't want to show him this letter at all, just somehow devise a trick, with your help, so that he wouldn't come . . . because he's so irascible. . . . And I don't understand at all about that drunkard who died, and what sort of daughter he had, and how he could have given this daughter his last rubles . . . which . . ."

"Which cost you so dearly, Mama," added Avdotya Romanovna.

"He was not himself yesterday," Razumikhin said pensively. "If you knew all that he'd said in the tavern, though it was clever . . . hmm! He really did say something to me yesterday about some dead man and about some young woman as we were going home, but I didn't understand a word. . . . However, yesterday I, too, was . . ."

"Mama, it would be best if we went to see him, and then, I assure you, we'll know immediately what to do. Besides, it's already time. Good Lord! It's past ten o'clock!" she cried, glancing at the magnificent gold-and-enamel watch hanging around her neck on a slender Venetian chain, at odds with the rest of her apparel. "A present from her suitor," thought Razumikhin.

"Ah, it's time! It's time, Dunechka, it's time!" Pulkheriya Aleksandrovna exclaimed. "He'll think we didn't come because we're angry about yesterday. Oh, my goodness."

Saying this, she hastened to throw on her cape and put on her hat while Dunechka also got dressed. Razumikhin noticed that her gloves were not only worn but even frayed. The obvious poverty of their apparel managed to convey to both ladies a look of special distinction, which always happens with those who know how to wear humble clothes. Razumikhin regarded Dunechka with reverence and was proud to be escorting her. "That queen," he thought to himself, "who mended her own stockings in prison looked like a real queen at that moment and even more so than during the most lavish festivities and regal entrances."*

"My goodness!" cried Pulkheriya Aleksandrovna. "Did I ever think that I'd be so afraid of a meeting with my own son, with my dear, dear Rodya, as I am now? I am afraid, Dmitry Prokofich!" she added, casting a timid glance at him.

"Don't be, Mama," said Dunya, kissing her. "It's better to have faith in him. I do."

"Ah, my goodness! I have faith, too, but I didn't sleep a wink last night!" cried the poor woman.

They left.

"You know, Dunechka, as I fell asleep toward morning, I suddenly dreamt of the late Marfa Petrovna. . . . All dressed in white . . . she approached me, took my hand, and shook her head at me harshly, so harshly, as if she was censuring me. . . . Is that a good sign? Ah, my goodness, Dmitry Prokofich, you still don't know. Marfa Petrovna died!"

"No, I don't. Who's this Marfa Petrovna?"

"It was a sudden death! Just imagine . . ."

"Later, Mama," Dunya interrupted her. "He doesn't even know Marfa Petrovna."

"Ah, you don't know her? I thought you knew everything. Forgive me, Dmitry Prokofich. These days I can hardly think straight. True, I consider that you've been sent to us by Providence, and so I was convinced that you already knew everything about it. I think of you as family. . . . Don't be angry at what I say. Ah, my goodness, what happened to your right hand? Did you hurt yourself?"

"Yes, I did," the overjoyed Razumikhin mumbled.

"Sometimes I say too much speaking right from the heart, so

---

* A reference to Queen of France Marie Antoinette (1755–1793), who was imprisoned in 1792 and executed the following year.

Dunya corrects me. . . . But, my God, what a little cell he lives in! Is he awake? And that woman, his landlady, does she consider that a room? Listen, you say he doesn't like to speak his heart, so perhaps he's fed up with my . . . weaknesses? Won't you help me learn to deal with him? How should I act? You know, I feel completely at a loss."

"Don't ask him too many questions about something if you see that he's scowling. In particular, don't ask him about his health. He doesn't like it."

"Ah, Dmitry Prokofich, it's so hard being a mother! But here's his staircase. . . . What an awful staircase!"

"Mama, you're even pale. Calm down, my dear," said Dunya, caressing her mother. "He should be pleased to see you, but you're tormenting yourself," she added, her eyes flashing.

"Wait a moment. I'll look in first to see if he's awake."

The ladies quietly followed Razumikhin up the stairs. When they approached the landlady's apartment on the fourth floor, they noticed that her door was slightly ajar and that two lively black eyes were peering at them from the darkness. When their glances met, the door slammed shut with such a bang that Pulkheriya Aleksandrovna almost cried out in fright.

III

"Better, he's better!" Zosimov cried cheerfully as they entered. He had arrived about ten minutes earlier and was seated where he'd sat yesterday, in the corner of the room on the sofa. Raskolnikov was sitting in the opposite corner, fully clothed, even carefully washed and groomed, something he hadn't done for quite some time. The room filled up immediately, but Nastasya still managed to get in behind the visitors and stood there listening.

It was true, Raskolnikov had almost recovered, especially compared to how he'd felt yesterday. But he was still very pale, distracted, and gloomy. On the outside he resembled a wounded man or someone suffering from great physical pain: his brows were knit, his lips compressed, his gaze inflamed. He said very little and that only reluctantly, as if under duress or fulfilling an obligation; a kind of uneasiness appeared at times in his movements.

All that was missing was a bandage on his arm or a taffeta cover on his finger for him to look exactly like a man who, for example, had a painful abscess on his finger, or who had injured his arm, or something of that sort.

However, even this pale and gloomy face lit up for a moment when his mother and sister came in, but it merely added to his expression of what seemed to be more concentrated torment, rather than his previous dreary distraction. The light soon faded, but the torment remained, and Zosimov, observing and studying his patient with all the youthful fervor of a doctor just beginning his practice, was surprised to notice instead of joy at the arrival of his family, some painful hidden resolve to endure unavoidable torment for another hour or two. He saw later how almost every word of the ensuing conversation seemed to touch one of his patient's sore spots and irritate it; but at the same time, he was somewhat surprised by Raskolnikov's ability to control himself today and to conceal the feelings of yesterday's monomaniac, who had been goaded almost to the point of madness by the least word spoken.

"Yes, I myself can see that I'm almost well," said Raskolnikov, kissing his mother and sister affably, as a result of which Pulkheriya Aleksandrovna also beamed. "And I'm not saying that as I did *yesterday*," he added, turning to Razumikhin and shaking his hand warmly.

"I was even surprised by his looks today," Zosimov began, overjoyed by the new arrivals because he had lost the thread of his conversation with the patient some ten minutes before. "In three or four more days, if he continues to improve, he'll be as good as he was before, that is, how he was a month or two ago . . . or, perhaps even three months. All this started a while back . . . right? Now confess that you yourself might be to blame for it," he added with a cautious smile, as if still afraid of irritating him somehow.

"It's very possible," Raskolnikov replied coldly.

"I'm saying that," Zosimov continued, growing into his role, "because, for the most part, now your complete recovery depends entirely on you. Now that it's possible to converse with you, I wanted to impress on you the importance of putting aside the initial, root causes, so to speak, that influenced the onset of your morbid condition; then you'll recover. If not, you'll get even worse. I don't know what those initial causes were, but you must know. You're a clever man and, of course, you've observed yourself. It seems to me that the origin of your distress coincides in part with your leaving the university. You mustn't remain without an occupation, because, it seems to me, work and a firmly established goal could help you immensely."

"Yes, yes, you're absolutely right. . . . I'll return to the university as soon as possible, and then everything will go . . . as smooth as silk . . ."

Zosimov, who had begun dispensing his astute advice in part for its effect on the ladies, was, of course, somewhat puzzled when, having finished his speech and having glanced at his listener, he noticed the decidedly mocking smile on Raskolnikov's face. However, that lasted for only a moment. Pulkheriya Aleksandrovna immediately began thanking Zosimov, in particular for his visit to their hotel room the evening before.

"So, he came to see you last night?" asked Raskolnikov, as if alarmed. "As a result, you didn't get any sleep after your voyage?"

"Ah, Rodya, all this happened before two o'clock. At home Dunya and I never go to bed before two."

"I, too, don't know how to thank him," continued Raskolnikov, suddenly frowning and lowering his head. "Setting aside the question of money—you'll excuse me for mentioning it," he said, turning to Zosimov, "I don't know why I deserve such special attention from you. I simply don't understand it . . . and . . . and I even find it uncomfortable that I don't understand it: I'm speaking to you frankly."

"Don't be upset," Zosimov said with a forced laugh. "Let's assume that you're my first patient. Well, some of us who've just begun to practice medicine come to love our first patients as if they were our own children; some of them almost fall in love with them. I don't have very many patients yet."

"I'm not even talking about him," added Raskolnikov, indicating Razumikhin. "He, too, has had nothing from me except insults and worries."

"Oh, what lies! You're in quite a sentimental mood today, aren't you?" cried Razumikhin.

Had he been more perspicacious, he would have seen that there was no question of a sentimental mood; rather, something completely opposite was in play. Avdotya Romanovna noticed it. She was intently and anxiously observing her brother.

"As for you, Mama, I dare not speak about you," he continued, as if he had been preparing a lesson that morning. "It was only today that I was able to imagine how you must have suffered here yesterday in anticipation of my return." After saying this, suddenly and with a silent smile, he extended his hand to his sister. But this time some genuine, unfeigned feeling shone through his smile. Dunya immediately grabbed hold of his hand and squeezed it warmly, overjoyed and grateful. It was the first time he had addressed her after yesterday's disagreement. His mother's face glowed with ecstasy and happiness at the sight of this definitive, nonverbal reconciliation between brother and sister.

"That's why I love him so!" whispered Razumikhin, always inclined to exaggerate, turning forcefully in his chair. "He has these impulses."

"How well it all turns out," his mother thought to herself. "He has such noble instincts, and how simply, delicately he's resolved yesterday's misunderstanding with his sister—merely by extending his hand with such a fine look. . . . He has such splendid eyes, and his whole face is so handsome! He's even better-looking than Dunya. . . . But, my goodness, what sort of clothes is he wearing? He's so horribly dressed! The errand boy at Afanasy Ivanovich's shop is better dressed! If only, if only I could rush up to him, embrace him, and weep—but I'm afraid, afraid . . . he's such a . . . good Lord! Now he's speaking so politely, but I'm afraid! What am I afraid of?"

"Ah, Rodya, you won't believe," she began suddenly, hastening to reply to his remark, "how . . . miserable Dunechka and I were yesterday! Now all that's over and done with and we can say that we're all happy again. Imagine, we came rushing over here to embrace you, almost right from the train, and this woman—ah, here she is! Hello, Nastasya! She suddenly tells us that you're sick and delirious, that in your delirium you just slipped away from the doctor, and they'd gone out to look for you. You can't believe what that was like! All at once I recalled the tragic end of our acquaintance Lieutenant Potanchikov, a friend of your father's—you don't remember him, Rodya—he was also delirious, and he too ran away, and fell into a well; they managed to pull him out only a day later. Of course, we imagined even worse things. We wanted to rush off in search of Petr Petrovich, so that at least with his help . . . because we were alone, completely alone," she said in a plaintive voice and suddenly broke off, having recalled that mentioning Petr Petrovich was still rather dangerous, in spite of the fact that "everyone was completely happy again."

"Yes, yes . . . all that, of course, is annoying," Raskolnikov muttered in reply, but with such a distracted and almost inattentive look that Dunechka regarded him in astonishment.

"What else was it that I wanted to say," he continued, trying to recall. "Yes. Please, Mama, and you, Dunechka, don't think that I didn't want to visit you first thing today and that I was just waiting for you to come."

"What are you saying, Rodya?" cried Pulkheriya Aleksandrovna, also surprised.

"Is he responding like this from a sense of obligation?" Dunechka wondered. "He's making peace and asking for forgiveness as if he's doing a job or reciting a lesson."

"I just woke up and wanted to come, but my clothes delayed me; yesterday I forgot to tell her . . . Nastasya . . . to wash away the blood. . . . I've only managed to get dressed now."

"Blood! What blood?" Pulkheriya Aleksandrovna cried anxiously.

"It's only . . . don't worry. The blood was because yesterday, when I was wandering around in my delirium, I stumbled upon a fellow who'd been run over . . . a civil servant . . ."

"In your delirium? But you remember everything," Razumikhin said, interrupting him.

"That's true," Raskolnikov replied, somehow in a particularly thoughtful way. "I remember everything, to the last detail, but just think: I really can't explain why I did what I did, where I went, or what I said."

"That's a very well-known phenomenon," Zosimov interjected. "The performance of acts is sometimes masterful, extremely clever, but the control of the acts, their origin, is confused and depends on various morbid impressions. It resembles a dream."

"It may be a good thing that he considers me almost insane," thought Raskolnikov.

"But healthy people can experience something similar," remarked Dunechka, regarding Zosimov uneasily.

"That's a rather accurate observation," he replied. "In that sense, really all of us behave almost in a deranged manner, and extremely frequently, with only the slight difference that the 'sick' ones are somewhat more deranged than the rest of us, and therefore it's essential to draw a distinction. It's true that there's almost no such thing as a completely well-balanced person; out of dozens, perhaps many hundred thousands, you meet only one, and he's not a very good example . . ."

At the word "deranged," carelessly dropped by Zosimov, who was getting carried away by one of his favorite themes, everyone winced. Raskolnikov sat there, as if not paying any attention, in deep thought and with a strange smile on his pale lips. He continued pondering something.

"So what happened to the man who was run over? I interrupted you!" Razumikhin exclaimed hastily.

"What?" said Raskolnikov, as if awakening from a dream. "Yes . . . I was splattered in blood when I helped carry him to his apartment. . . . By the way, Mama, I committed an unforgivable act yesterday; I must have been out of my mind. Yesterday I gave away all the money you sent me . . . to his wife . . . for the funeral. She's now a widow, a consumptive, and a pitiful woman with three young orphans, hungry . . . no one at home . . . and there's one more daughter. . . . If you'd seen it, you might have given away the money, too. . . . But, I confess, I had no right to do so, especially knowing how you came by it. To help, one must first have the right, or else: 'Crevez chiens, si vous n'êtes pas contents!'* He laughed. Isn't that right, Dunya?"

"No, it's not," replied Dunya resolutely.

"Well! You, too . . . have intentions!" he muttered, regarding her almost with hatred, smiling sarcastically. "I should've realized that. . . . Well, that's praiseworthy; it's better for you . . . and you'll reach a limit that you won't overstep—and you'll be unhappy; and if you do overstep, perhaps you'll be even unhappier. . . . However, that's all nonsense!" he added irritably, annoyed at his own involuntary passion. "I merely wanted to say that I ask your forgiveness, Mama," he concluded abruptly and sharply.

"Enough, Rodya. I'm sure that everything you do is splendid!" said his mother, overjoyed.

"Don't be so sure," he replied, twisting his mouth into a smile. A moment of silence ensued. There was something strained in this entire conversation, this silence, reconciliation, forgiveness, and everyone felt it.

---

* "Die dogs, if you're not happy!" (French).

"It's as if they're afraid of me," Raskolnikov thought to himself, scowling at his mother and his sister. And it was true that the longer Pulkheriya Aleksandrovna was silent, the more timid she really became.

"It seems that when they're far away, I loved them more," flashed through his head.

"You know, Rodya, that Marfa Petrovna died?" Pulkheriya Aleksandrovna suddenly let drop.

"Who's Marfa Petrovna?"

"Ah, my goodness, Marfa Petrovna Svidrigaylova! I wrote you so much about her."

"Ah, yes, I remember. . . . So she died? Ah, really?" He suddenly roused himself, as if waking up. "So she really died? What from?"

"Just imagine: it was all very sudden!" Pulkheriya Aleksandrovna hastened to add, emboldened by his interest. "And it happened the same time I sent you that letter, that very day! Just think, it seems that horrible man was the cause of her death. They say he gave her a terrible beating!"

"Did they really live like that?" he asked, addressing his sister.

"No, even quite the contrary. He was always very patient with her, even courteous. In many instances he was even too indulgent of her character, all seven years. . . . Somehow he suddenly lost his patience."

"Of course, he was not that horrible if he held out for seven years. Dunechka, you seem to be defending him."

"No, no, he's a horrible man! I can't imagine anyone more horrible," Dunya replied, almost with a shudder, frowning. She lapsed into thought.

"It happened in the morning," Pulkheriya Aleksandrovna continued hurriedly. "Immediately afterward, she ordered the horses harnessed so she could drive into town right after dinner because in such cases she always did that; she ate her dinner, they say, with a large appetite."

"After the beating?"

". . . But she'd always had this . . . habit: as soon as she'd eaten her dinner, so as not to be late for her drive, she headed right to the bathhouse. . . . You see, she was taking some cure with her baths; they have a cold spring, and she used to bathe in it every day, As soon as she entered the water, she suddenly had a stroke!"

"I should think so!" said Zosimov.

"Was the beating severe?"

"It doesn't really matter," replied Dunya.

"Hmm! Mama, what makes you talk about such nonsense?" Raskolnikov said suddenly with irritation, and as if unintentionally.

"Oh, my dear, I just don't know what to talk about," Pulkheriya Aleksandrovna burst out.

"Are you all afraid of me or something?" he asked with a twisted grin.

"That's really true," said Dunya, looking directly and sternly at her brother. "When Mama was coming up the stairs, she even crossed herself out of fear."

His face was suddenly distorted, as if from a convulsion.

"Ah, what are you saying, Dunya? Please don't be angry, Rodya. . . . Why say that, Dunya?" Pulkheriya Aleksandrovna asked in embarrassment. "It's true that all the way here in the train I was thinking about how we'd get to see each other, how we'd talk about everything . . . and I was so happy that I didn't even notice the long journey! But what am I saying? I'm happy even now. . . . You were wrong to say that, Dunya! I'm just so happy to see you, Rodya . . ."

"Enough, Mama," he muttered in embarrassment, squeezing her hand without looking at her. "We'll have time to talk about everything!"

After saying this, he suddenly became confused and turned pale. Once again, the previous horrible sensation of deathly cold entered his soul; once again, it suddenly became completely clear and apparent that he had just told a terrible lie. Not only would the time to talk about everything never come, but there was nothing further for him to *talk* about with anyone, ever. The impact of this tormenting idea was so strong that for a moment he almost forgot himself entirely. He stood up and, without looking at anyone, was about to leave the room.

"What are you doing?" cried Razumikhin, seizing him by the arm.

He sat down again and began glancing around in silence; everyone regarded him in perplexity.

"Why are you all so tedious?" he cried suddenly, completely unexpectedly. "Say something! Why are you sitting here like this? Well, speak! Let's start a conversation. . . . We've come together and we're sitting here in silence. . . . Well, say something!"

"Thank heavens! I thought that something like what happened yesterday was beginning again," Pulkheriya Aleksandrovna said, after crossing herself.

"What is it, Rodya?" Avdotya Romanovna asked uncertainly.

"It's nothing. I just remembered something," he replied suddenly and started laughing.

"Well, if that's all it is, then it's all right! Or else, I also began to think . . ." Zosimov muttered, getting up from the sofa. "But it's time for me to go; I'll drop in again, perhaps, and hope to find you here . . ."

He bowed and left.

"What a splendid man!" remarked Pulkheriya Aleksandrovna.

"Yes, splendid, outstanding, educated, clever . . ." Raskolnikov started talking suddenly with unexpected speed and unusual animation not seen before. "I don't recall where I encountered him before my illness. . . . It seems we met somewhere. . . . And this man's also a fine fellow!" He nodded at Razumikhin. "Do you like him, Dunya?" he asked suddenly and burst into puzzling laughter.

"Very much," replied Dunya.

"Phew, what a . . . swine you are!" Razumikhin muttered, terribly embarrassed; he blushed and stood up from his chair. Pulkheriya Aleksandrovna smiled slightly, while Raskolnikov roared with loud laughter.

"Where are you going?"

"I . . . have to go, too."

"No, you don't. Stay here! Zosimov left, so you think you should as well. Don't go. . . . What time is it? Is it twelve yet? What a nice watch you have, Dunya! Why have you fallen silent again? I'm the only one talking."

"It was a gift from Marfa Petrovna," replied Dunya.

"And a very expensive one," added Pulkheriya Aleksandrovna.

"Ah! It's so big, almost too big to be a lady's watch."

"I like watches like this," said Dunya.

"So then, it's not a gift from her suitor," thought Razumikhin, and for some reason felt overjoyed.

"I thought it was a present from Luzhin," remarked Raskolnikov.

"Oh, no. He hasn't given Dunechka anything yet."

"Ah! Do you remember, Mama, I was once in love and wanted to get married," he said suddenly, looking at his mother, who was struck by the unexpected manner and tone with which he had begun talking about it.

"Ah, my dear, yes!" Pulkheriya Aleksandrovna exchanged glances with Dunechka and Razumikhin.

"Hmm! Yes! What can I tell you? I don't even recall much. She was a sickly girl," he continued, growing thoughtful again, casting his eyes down. "Very ill; she loved to give money to the poor; she kept dreaming about a convent and once burst into tears when she started telling me about it. Yes, yes . . . I remember . . . I remember it well. She was very plain. . . . I really don't know why I felt attracted to her; perhaps it was because she was always sickly. . . . If she'd been lame or a hunchback, I probably would've loved her even more. . . ." He smiled thoughtfully. "Thus . . . it was some sort of springtime delirium . . ."

"No, it wasn't merely springtime delirium," Dunechka said with animation.

He regarded his sister intently and intensely, but he hadn't even heard or understood her words. Then, in deep thought, he stood up, approached his mother, kissed her, returned to his seat, and sat down.

"You still love her!" said Pulkheriya Aleksandrovna, touched.

"Her? Now? Ah, yes . . . you're talking about that young woman! No, it's as if it happened in another world . . . and so long ago. It seems that everything around me is happening somewhere else . . ."

He regarded them closely.

"Even you . . . it's as if I'm looking at you from a thousand miles away. . . . The devil knows why we're talking about this! Why do you keep asking?" he added in annoyance and fell silent, biting his nails and growing thoughtful once more.

"You have such an awful room, Rodya. It's like a coffin," Pulkheriya Aleksandrovna said suddenly, breaking the painful silence. "I'm sure that half the reason you became so melancholy is this room."

"My room?" he replied distractedly. "Yes, my room certainly contributed to it. . . . I thought about that, too. If you only knew what sort of strange idea you just uttered, Mama," he added suddenly, smiling in a strange way.

It would have taken just a little while longer and this company, these relatives, after a three-year separation, this intimate tone of conversation and the complete impossibility of talking about anything—all this he would have found absolutely intolerable. There was, however, one pressing matter that had to be resolved today, one way or another. He had reached this decision a while ago, when he awoke. Now he rejoiced over *that matter* as an escape.

"Here's what, Dunya," he began, speaking seriously and drily. "Of course, I ask your forgiveness for what I said yesterday, but I consider it my duty to remind you once again that I'm not retreating from the main point. It's either me or Luzhin. I may be a scoundrel, but you shouldn't be. It should be only one of us. If you marry Luzhin, I'll immediately cease thinking of you as my sister."

"Rodya, Rodya! This is the same as yesterday," cried Pulkheriya Aleksandrovna bitterly. "Why do you keep calling yourself a scoundrel? I can't stand that! It was just the same yesterday . . ."

"Brother," replied Dunya firmly and also drily. "You're making a mistake here. I thought about it all night and found where you are mistaken. It lies in the fact that you assume that I'm sacrificing myself to someone and for someone. But that's not true at all. I'm getting married for myself, because I find things difficult; of course, I'll be glad if it also turns out to be of use to my family, but that isn't the main reason for my decision . . ."

"She's lying!" he thought to himself, biting his nails in anger. "She's an arrogant woman! She doesn't want to admit that she's doing it to benefit others! Oh, these vile characters! Their love is like hatred. . . . Oh, how I . . . hate them all."

"In a word, I'm marrying Petr Petrovich," Dunechka continued, "because I'm choosing the lesser of two evils. I intend to fulfill honestly all that he expects of me; consequently, I'm not deceiving him. . . . Why did you just smile like that?"

She also flared up, and anger flashed in her eyes.

"Will you fulfill everything?" he asked, smiling maliciously.

"Up to a certain point. Both the manner and the form of Petr Petrovich's proposal revealed immediately what he's looking for. Of course, he values himself highly, perhaps too highly, but I hope that he'll also come to value me. . . . Why are you laughing again?"

"And why are you blushing again? You're lying, sister. You're lying intentionally, out of feminine obstinacy alone, merely to get your own way with me. . . . You can't respect Luzhin: I've seen him and talked to him. Consequently, you're selling yourself for money; and, consequently, in any case, you're behaving in a vile manner. I'm glad that at least you can still blush!"

"It's not true! I'm not lying!" Dunechka cried, losing all her self-control. "I'm not marrying him without being convinced that he values me and appreciates me. I'm not marrying him without the firm conviction that I can respect him. Fortunately, I can probably become convinced of this even today. Such a marriage is not a vile act, as you say! And even if you were right, if I'd really decided to commit such a vile act, isn't it really heartless of you to talk to me like this? Why do you demand of me heroism that you yourself may lack? It's despotism, coercion! If I'm to ruin someone, it's only myself. . . . I haven't murdered anyone. . . . Why are you looking at me like that? Why have you turned so pale? Rodya, what's the matter with you? Rodya, my dear!"

"Good Lord! You're causing him to faint!" cried Pulkheriya Aleksandrovna.

"No, no . . . nonsense . . . it's nothing! My head started spinning a little. I'm not fainting. . . . All you ever think about is fainting! Hmm! Now, what was I saying? Yes. How will you convince yourself today that you can respect him and that he . . . values you, was that what you said? It seems you said something about today? Or did I mishear?"

"Mama, show Petr Petrovich's letter to my brother," said Dunechka.

With trembling hands, Pulkheriya Aleksandrovna handed him the letter. He took it with great interest. But even before he unfolded it, he abruptly looked at Dunechka with astonishment.

"It's strange," he mused slowly, as if suddenly struck by a new thought. "Why am I making such a big fuss? Why such a racket? Marry whomever you like!"

He said it as if to himself, but uttered it aloud and for some time looked at his sister, as if he was puzzled.

At last he unfolded the letter, still maintaining a look of strange astonishment; then he began reading it slowly and attentively; he read it through twice. Pulkheriya Aleksandrovna was feeling particularly anxious; everyone was anticipating something extraordinary.

"I find this surprising," he began after some thought, handing the letter back to his mother, but not addressing anyone in particular. "He's here on business, he's a lawyer, and even his conversation is so . . . affected, yet his letter is so illiterate."

Everyone was stunned; that was not what they had expected.

"But they all write like that," Razumikhin noted abruptly.

"Have you read it?"

"Yes."

"We showed it to him, Rodya, we . . . conferred about it before," Pulkheriya Aleksandrovna began in her confusion.

"It's in a special lawyerly style," Razumikhin said, interrupting her. "Legal documents are still written like that."

"Lawyerly? Yes, that's it precisely, businesslike. . . . It's not that it's very illiterate, and it's not that it's very literary; it's just businesslike."

"Petr Petrovich doesn't conceal the fact that he was educated on the cheap; he even boasts of having paved his own way," remarked Avdotya Romanovna, somewhat offended by her brother's new tone.

"Well, if he boasts, then he has something to boast about—I'm not contradicting him. You, sister, seem to have been offended by the fact that out of the whole letter I ventured such a frivolous remark, and you think that I mention such trivialities intentionally to make difficulties for you because I'm annoyed. On the contrary, concerning his style, an observation occurred to me that in this present case is not at all superfluous. There's one expression in the letter, 'you will have only yourself to blame,' that puts it all very pointedly and clearly. In addition, there's the threat that if I attend the meeting, he'll leave immediately. This threat to leave—it's the same as a threat to abandon you both if you disobey him, and to abandon you now, after he's brought you to Petersburg. Well, what do you think? Would one take offense at such an expression like Luzhin's, if he"—indicating Razumikhin—"had written it, or Zosimov, or one of us?"

"N-no," replied Dunechka, growing more animated. "I understood very well that it was expressed too artlessly and that perhaps he's not a very skilled writer. . . . You're absolutely right, brother. I didn't even expect that . . ."

"It's written in legalese, and it can't be written in any other way; it came out more crudely than he might have wanted. Besides, I have to disillusion you somewhat: there's another expression in this letter that's a slander against me, and a rather vile one. I gave the money yesterday to a consumptive woman, a devastated widow, not 'on the pretext of funeral expenses,' but directly for the funeral, and not to the daughter—'a young woman of notorious conduct' as he writes (and whom I saw for the first time in my life yesterday), but to the widow herself. In all of this I see his overly hasty desire to tarnish me and provoke a quarrel with you. Again, it's expressed in legalese, that is, with too obvious a display of its own aim and with extremely naïve speed. He's an intelligent man, but in order to act intelligently—intelligence alone is not enough. All this provides a picture of the man . . . and I don't think he values you very highly. I say all this solely for your own edification, because I sincerely want the best for you . . ."

Dunechka made no reply; her decision had been made some time ago, and she was merely waiting for evening to arrive.

"Well, what have you decided, Rodya?" asked Pulkheriya Aleksandrovna, even more worried than before by his sudden, new, *business-like* tone.

"What do you mean, 'decided'?"

"Petr Petrovich writes that he doesn't want you there this evening and that he'll leave . . . if you come. So then . . . will you be here?"

"That, of course, is not for me to decide, but you, in the first place, if Petr Petrovich's demand does not offend you; and Dunya, in the second place, if she's not offended, either. I shall do as you wish," he added coolly.

"Dunechka's already decided, and I'm in complete agreement with her," Pulkheriya Aleksandrovna hastened to say.

"I decided to ask you, Rodya, to request most urgently that you be present at this meeting," said Dunya. "Will you come?"

"I will."

"And I also ask you," she said, turning to Razumikhin, "to join us here at eight o'clock. Mama, I'm also inviting him."

"That's fine, Dunechka. Well, just as you've decided," added Pulkheriya Aleksandrovna, "that's how it will be. I myself feel better. I don't like to pretend or lie. It's better to speak the whole truth . . . whether it makes Petr Petrovich angry or not."

IV

At that moment, the door opened quietly and a young woman entered the room, glancing around timidly. Everyone turned to her with astonishment and curiosity. Raskolnikov didn't recognize her at first. It was Sofiya Semyonovna Marmeladova. He'd seen her yesterday for the first time, but at such a moment, in such circumstances, and in such clothes, that he remembered an entirely different face. Now she was a modestly, even poorly dressed young woman, very young indeed, almost like a girl, with modest, proper manners, and an innocent but seemingly frightened face. She was wearing a very simple everyday dress and an old, outmoded hat on her head; but she was carrying a parasol in her hands, as she had yesterday. Unexpectedly seeing a room full of people, she wasn't merely embarrassed, but overwhelmed; she felt timid as a child and even made a move to leave.

"Ah . . . is it you?" asked Raskolnikov in extreme surprise, and he suddenly felt embarrassed.

He remembered at once that his mother and sister already knew in passing, from Luzhin's letter, about a certain young woman of "notorious" conduct. He had just now been protesting against Luzhin's slander and had just acknowledged that he had seen this girl for the first time, when suddenly she herself showed up in his room. He also recalled that he hadn't objected in any way to the phrase "notorious conduct." All this flashed through his mind vaguely in one moment. But, glancing at her more intently, he quickly saw that this humbled creature was feeling so humiliated, and he suddenly felt sorry for her. When she made a move to run away out of fear, it was as if something turned over in him.

"I wasn't expecting you," he hastened to say, stopping her with his glance. "Be so good as to take a seat. You've probably come from Katerina Ivanovna. Excuse me, not here. Sit over there . . ."

At Sonya's entrance Razumikhin, who was seated on one of Raskolnikov's three chairs, at once stood up next to the door to let her pass. Raskolnikov was about to show her to the place on the corner of the sofa where Zosimov had sat but, remembering that the sofa would be too *intimate* a place and that it also served as his bed, he hastened to point her toward what had been Razumikhin's chair.

"And you sit here," he said to Razumikhin, placing him in the corner Zosimov had occupied.

Sonya sat down, almost trembling in fear, and glanced timidly at both women. It was clear that she herself didn't understand how she could sit next to them. After realizing this, she was so frightened that she suddenly stood up again and turned to Raskolnikov in total confusion.

"I . . . I . . . came by only for a minute. Forgive me for disturbing you," she began, stammering. "I've come from Katerina Ivanovna; she had no one else to send. . . . Katerina Ivanovna wants me to implore you to attend the funeral tomorrow morning . . . during the morning service . . . at the Mitrofanyevsky Cemetery, and then to come to our apartment . . . to her place . . . for some refreshment. . . . She'd be honored. . . . She had me invite you."

Sonya stuttered and fell silent.

"I'll certainly try . . . certainly," replied Raskolnikov, also standing, also stammering, and not finishing what he was saying. "Be so good as to take a seat," he said suddenly. "I have to talk to you. Please—perhaps you're in a hurry—be so kind as to give me a few moments of your time . . ."

He pulled up a chair for her. Sonya sat down again, once more glanced hurriedly, timidly, uncomfortably at the two women, and suddenly lowered her eyes.

Raskolnikov's pale face flushed; he seemed to shudder all over; his eyes flashed.

"Mama," he said firmly and insistently, "this is Sofiya Semyonovna Marmeladova, the daughter of that unfortunate Mr. Marmeladov who was run over by horses yesterday before my very eyes and about whom I told you already . . ."

Pulkheriya Aleksandrovna glanced at Sonya, squinting slightly. In spite of all her confusion when faced with Rodya's insistent and challenging gaze, there was no way she could deny herself this pleasure. Dunechka earnestly and intently stared directly at the poor young woman's face and examined her in bewilderment. Sonya, after hearing the introduction, was about to raise her eyes again, but felt even more embarrassed than before.

"I wanted to ask you," Raskolnikov said, turning to her abruptly, "how have things been today? Did anyone disturb you at all? The police, for example?"

"No, sir, it all went. . . . It was all too clear what caused his death; they didn't disturb us; it's just that the lodgers were angry."

"Why?"

"The body was there for so long . . . it's hot now and the smell. . . . So today, just before vespers, they'll take it to the cemetery and it'll be in the chapel until tomorrow. At first Katerina Ivanovna didn't want that, but now she sees that there's no other way . . ."

"So today?"

"She asks that you do us the honor of attending the funeral in the church tomorrow, and then come to a repast at our place."

"She's arranging a wake?"

"Yes, sir. Some refreshment. She asked me to thank you very much for helping us yesterday. . . . Without you, we wouldn't have had any way of burying him." Both her lips and her chin suddenly began trembling, but she regained control, refrained from crying, and quickly lowered her eyes to the floor again.

During the conversation Raskolnikov examined her closely. She had a thin, very thin, pale little face, rather irregular, somewhat angular, with a pointed little nose and chin. It was even impossible to think of her as pretty; on the other hand, her blue eyes were so clear and, when they came to life, the expression of her face so kind and sincere, that one felt involuntarily attracted to her. There was, in addition, one special trait reflected in her face and in her entire figure: in spite of her eighteen years, she still seemed like a young girl, much younger than her years, almost a total child, and that fact sometimes appeared engagingly in several of her movements.

"But how could Katerina Ivanovna, with such meager means, arrange things, even provide refreshment?" asked Raskolnikov, prolonging the conversation intentionally.

"The coffin will be a simple one, sir . . . everything will be simple and inexpensive. . . . Katerina Ivanovna and I recently calculated it all, and there's enough to provide for the funeral repast. . . . Katerina Ivanovna would very much like it this way. One can't just . . . it would console her, sir . . . as you know, she's like that . . ."

"I understand, I do . . . of course. . . . Why are you examining my room? My mother also says that it resembles a coffin."

"You gave us all your money yesterday!" Sonechka replied suddenly, in a strong and swift whisper, and then suddenly dropped her eyes again. Her lips and chin began trembling once more. She'd been struck for some time by Raskolnikov's impoverished circumstances, and just now these words had emerged all by themselves. A moment of silence ensued. Dunechka's eyes grew clear, and Pulkheriya Aleksandrovna even looked kindly at Sonya.

"Rodya," she said, standing up. "Of course, we'll have dinner together. Dunechka, let's go. . . . And you, Rodya, should go out, take a little walk, have a rest, lie down, and then come to see us soon. . . . As things are, I'm afraid we've exhausted you . . ."

"Yes, yes, I'll come," he replied, rising and hurrying. . . . "I have some matters to attend to . . ."

"Are you really planning to have dinner apart?" cried Razumikhin, looking at Raskolnikov in surprise. "Why are you doing that?"

"Yes, yes, I'll come, of course, of course, I will. . . . But you stay here for a moment longer. Do you need him right now, Mama? Or can I perhaps take him away from you?"

"Oh, no, no! Dmitry Prokofich, will you be so good as to come and have dinner with us?"

"Please come," Dunya added.

Razumikhin bowed in farewell and shone with pleasure. For a moment, everyone suddenly felt strangely embarrassed.

"Good-bye, Rodya, that is, until we meet; I don't like saying 'good-bye.' Good-bye, Nastasya . . . oh, I just said it again!"

Pulkheriya Aleksandrovna was also about to bow to Sonechka, but somehow didn't manage it; she left the room hastily.

But Avdotya Romanovna seemed to wait her turn and, following her mother past Sonya, said farewell with a thoughtful, polite, and deep bow. Sonechka was embarrassed, and bowed somewhat hastily and fearfully, even with some painful sensation reflected in her face, as if she found Avdotya Romanovna's politeness and thoughtfulness burdensome and distressing.

"Good-bye, Dunya," cried Raskolnikov from the entrance hall. "Give me your hand!"

"I already did. Have you forgotten?" replied Dunya, affectionately and awkwardly turning to him.

"So what? Give me your hand again!"

He squeezed her fingers warmly. Dunechka smiled at him, blushed, quickly withdrew her hand, and followed her mother out, also feeling happy for some reason.

"Well, this is splendid!" he said to Sonya, returning to his room and looking directly at her. "God grant eternal peace to the departed and allow the living to go on living! Isn't that so? Isn't it? Right?"

Sonya looked at his suddenly brightening countenance with absolute astonishment; he stared intently at her in silence for several moments. At that minute, the whole story of her late father suddenly flashed into his memory . . .

■   ■   ■

"Good Lord, Dunechka!" said Pulkheriya Aleksandrovna, as soon as they had gone outside. "I'm almost glad that we left him now: it's quite a relief. Did I ever think yesterday in the train that I'd feel grateful for this?"

"I tell you once more, Mama, he's still very sick. Don't you see that? Perhaps he was worrying about us and that's what distressed him. We have to be merciful and forgive him a great many things."

"You weren't very merciful with him!" Pulkheriya Aleksandrovna immediately interrupted her, passionately and jealously. "You know, Dunya, I was looking at both of you. You're the spit and image of him, not merely in your looks as much as in your souls. You're both melancholic, both moody and hot-tempered, both haughty, and both generous. . . . It couldn't be that he's an egoist, right, Dunechka? But when I think about what'll happen this evening, my heart grows cold!"

"Don't worry, Mama. What must be, will be."

"Dunechka! Just think about the predicament we're in now! What if Petr Petrovich refuses?" poor Pulkheriya Aleksandrovna suddenly said unwisely.

"Then what will he be worth afterward?" Dunechka replied abruptly and scornfully.

"It's a good thing we left now," Pulkheriya Aleksandrovna hastened to add, interrupting her. "He was rushing to attend to some matter. Let him go for a walk, get some fresh air. . . . It's so terribly stuffy in his room. . . . How can anyone breathe here? Even outside it's like being in a room without ventilation. Good Lord, what a city! Hold on, move to one side, or you'll be crushed, they're carrying something! They're moving a piano. . . . How they're struggling. . . . I'm also afraid of that girl . . ."

"What girl, Mama?"

"That one, Sofiya Semyonovna, who was just there . . ."

"Why?"

"I just have a foreboding, Dunya. Well, whether you believe it or not, as soon as she came in, at that very moment the thought occurred to me that this is where the main problem lies . . ."

"Nothing of the sort!" cried Dunya in annoyance. "You and your forebodings, Mama! He's only known her since yesterday, and he didn't even recognize her when she entered."

"Well, you'll see! She troubles me; you'll see, you will. I was so frightened: she looked at me, really looked. Her eyes are so . . . I could hardly keep to my chair. Do you recall how he started to introduce her? It seems strange: Petr Petrovich wrote about her in such a way, yet he still introduced her to us, especially to you! Therefore, she must mean something to him!"

"It doesn't matter what he wrote! People have said things about us and written things, too, or did you forget? I'm sure that she's . . . she's very nice, and all this is nonsense!"

"God willing!"

"And Petr Petrovich is a worthless gossip," Dunechka suddenly blurted out.

Pulkheriya Aleksandrovna winced. The conversation ended.

■   ■   ■

"Here's what I wanted to discuss with you," Raskolnikov said, leading Razumikhin over to the window . . .

"So I'll tell Katerina Ivanovna that you'll come," Sonya hastened to say, bowing to take her leave.

"One minute, Sofiya Semyonovna. We have no secrets; you're not interfering. . . . I'd still like to have a few words with you. . . . Here's what," he said, breaking off without finishing and turning back suddenly to Razumikhin. "Do you know that fellow . . . what's his name? Porfiry Petrovich?"

"I'll say I do! He's a relative. What of it?" he added, his curiosity suddenly aroused.

"He's now involved with . . . well, that murder case . . . just yesterday you said something . . ."

"Yes . . . and?" Razumikhin asked, his eyes suddenly open wide.

"He's been summoning people who pawned various items with her; I also had some pledges there, some trifles: my sister's ring, which she gave me as a keepsake when I came here, and my father's silver watch. All together they're worth about five or six rubles, but they're valuable to me as mementos. So what can I do now? I don't want them to be lost, especially the watch. I was afraid that my mother would ask to see it when they began talking about Dunechka's watch. It's the only thing left of my father's. She'd be very upset if it were to disappear! Women! So, what should I do, tell me! I know that I should declare it at the police station. Wouldn't it be better to tell Porfiry Petrovich himself? What do you think? It's best to deal with it as soon as possible. You'll see: Mama will ask about it before dinner!"

"By no means at the police station, but absolutely to Porfiry!" cried Razumikhin with some unusual agitation. "Well, I'm so very glad! Why wait? Let's go there right now; it's not far away, and we'll certainly find him in!"

"Fine . . . let's go . . ."

"He'll be very, very, very glad to make your acquaintance! I've told him so much about you at different times. . . . Just yesterday I was talking about you. Let's go! So, you knew that old woman? Aha! It's all turned out so mag-ni-fi-cent-ly! Ah, yes, Sofiya Ivanovna . . ."

"Sofiya Semyonovna," Raskolnikov corrected him. "Sofiya Semyonovna. This is my friend Razumikhin, a good fellow . . ."

"If you have to go now . . ." Sonya started to say, without so much as looking at Razumikhin, and, as a result, became even more embarrassed.

"Let's go," decided Raskolnikov. "I'll call on you later today, Sofiya Semyonovna. Only tell me where you live."

It wasn't that he had lost his train of thought, but he seemed to be hurrying and avoiding her gaze. Sonya gave him her address, blushing. Everyone left together.

"Don't you lock your door?" asked Razumikhin, following them down the stairs.

"Never! For the last two years I've been wanting to buy a lock," he added casually. "Happy are those who have no reason to lock their doors, right?" he said with a laugh, turning to Sonya.

When they reached the street, they paused at the gate.

"Are you turning right, Sofiya Semyonovna? By the way, how did you find me?" he asked, as if he'd intended to say something completely different. He still wanted to look into her soft, clear eyes, but somehow couldn't manage it . . .

"You gave your address to Polechka yesterday."

"Polya? Ah, yes . . . Polechka! The little girl. . . . Is she your sister? So, I gave her my address?"

"Yes. Did you forget?"

"No . . . I remember . . ."

"And I'd heard about you before, from my late father. . . . But I didn't know your full name then, and he didn't, either. . . . But when I came today, since I learned your name yesterday . . . today I asked, 'Where does Mr. Raskolnikov live?' I didn't know you also rent a room from lodgers. . . . Good-bye, sir. . . . I'll tell Katerina Ivanovna . . ."

She was terribly glad that she'd finally gotten away; she went in haste, her eyes cast down, to get out of their sight as quickly as she could, to cover the twenty paces to the right turn as soon as possible, and to be alone at last; then she could proceed, in haste, without looking at anyone, without noticing anything, to think, recall, and ponder every word that had been uttered, each and every circumstance of the visit. Never, never before had she felt anything like this. An entirely new world, mysterious and vague, had entered her soul. She suddenly recalled that Raskolnikov himself planned to call on her today, perhaps even that morning, perhaps right now!

"But not today, please not today!" she muttered with a sinking heart, as if imploring someone like a frightened child. "Good Lord! Call on me . . . in that room. . . . He'll see. . . . Oh, Lord!"

Of course, at that moment she was unable to observe an unfamiliar gentleman following closely on her heels. He had been following her from the moment she had emerged from the gate. When all three of them, Razumikhin, Raskolnikov, and Sonya, had paused to say a few words on the sidewalk, this person walking by, passing them, suddenly shuddered, accidentally overhearing her words "I asked, 'Where does Mr. Raskolnikov live?'" He swiftly but carefully surveyed the three of them, especially Raskolnikov, to whom Sonya was speaking. Then he looked at the house and took note of it. All this happened in a moment, while walking, and the passerby, trying not to let his interest show, went on farther, reducing his speed, as if waiting for someone. He was waiting for Sonya; he saw that they were saying their good-byes and that she was heading straight home.

"But where was that? I've seen that face somewhere," he thought, recalling Sonya's features. "I must find out."

Upon reaching the corner, he crossed to the opposite side of the street, turned around, and saw that Sonya was now following him, along the same street, not noticing anything. Upon reaching the corner, she also turned into that street. He followed from the opposite sidewalk without taking his eyes off her; after covering about fifty paces, he crossed again to the side Sonya was on, caught up with her, and followed her, staying about five paces back.

He was about fifty, taller than average, portly, with broad, sloping shoulders that gave him something of a stooped look. He was fashionably and comfortably dressed and looked like a stately gentleman. He was carrying a beautiful cane, which he tapped on the sidewalk at every step, and he was wearing new gloves. His broad face, with prominent cheekbones, was rather pleasant; his complexion was fresh, not typical of Petersburg. His hair, still very thick, was completely fair, showing only a little gray; his full, thick beard, in the shape of a spade, was even lighter in color than his hair. His eyes were blue and his gaze was cold, intent, and thoughtful; his lips were red. In general he was an extremely well-preserved man who seemed much younger than his years.

When Sonya reached the canal, they found themselves together on the sidewalk. Observing her, he noticed how pensive and distracted she was. Upon reaching her house, Sonya turned in at the gate; he followed her and seemed to be somewhat surprised. Entering the courtyard, she turned right, toward the corner where a staircase led up to her apartment. "Bah!" muttered the unfamiliar gentleman, and he began climbing the stairs after her. Only then did Sonya notice him. She reached the third floor, turned down the long hallway, and rang the bell at number 9: on the door, written in chalk, were the words KAPERNAUMOV. TAILOR. "Bah!" the stranger repeated, struck by the strange coincidence, and he rang the bell next door, at number 8. The two doors were only about six paces apart.

"You're staying at the Kapernaumovs'!" he said, looking at Sonya and laughing. "He mended my vest yesterday. I live here, next to you, at Madame Resslikh's, Gertruda Karlovna. How things have turned out!"

Sonya looked at him attentively.

"We're neighbors," he continued in a particularly cheerful way. "This is only my third day in town. Well, good-bye for now."

Sonya made no reply; the door opened, and she slipped into her apartment. She felt ashamed for some reason, even a bit timid . . .

■   ■   ■

Razumikhin was in a particularly excited state as they walked to Porfiry's.

"This is excellent, my friend," he repeated several times. "I'm so glad, so very glad!"

"What are you so glad about?" Raskolnikov wondered to himself.

"I didn't know that you also had some pledges with the old woman. And . . . and . . . was it a long time ago? That is, has it been a while since you were there?"

"What a naïve fool is he!"

"When was it?" Raskolnikov paused, trying to remember. "It seems I was there about three days before her death. However, I'm not going there now to redeem those items," he said with some haste and special concern for his belongings. "Once again I have only one silver ruble . . . thanks to my damned delirium yesterday!"

He placed particular emphasis on the word "delirium."

"Well, yes, yes, yes," Razumikhin said hurriedly, for some reason agreeing with everything. "So that's why you . . . were so surprised then. . . . You know, in your delirium you kept mentioning some rings and chains! Yes, yes. . . . It's clear, now it's all clear."

"So that's it! That's how far this idea has gotten! This man would agree to be crucified for me, and he's very glad that things have *all cleared up*, because I mentioned rings in my delirium! That just confirmed what they were all thinking!"

"Will we find him at home?" he asked aloud.

"We will, we will," Razumikhin hastened to say. "He's a fine fellow, my friend, you'll see! He's a bit awkward; that is, he's a worldly man, but in another sense, I say he's awkward. He's a clever fellow, clever, even very smart, only he has a special cast of mind. . . . He's mistrustful, a skeptic, a cynic. . . . He loves to dupe people, that is, not dupe them, but fool them. . . . The old-style, physical method. . . . He knows his business, he does. . . . He was investigating a case of murder last year in which all the clues had been lost! He very, very, very much wants to make your acquaintance!"

"Why do you say 'very much?'"

"That is, not to . . . you see, lately, since you fell ill, I've frequently had the occasion to talk about you a great deal. . . . Well, he listened . . . and when he learned you were studying law and that as a result of circumstances you were unable to complete the course, he said, 'What a pity!' So I concluded . . . that is, from all of it, not just one thing; yesterday Zametov. . . . You see, Rodya, I blurted out something to you yesterday when I was intoxicated, as we were going home . . . and I fear, my friend, that you exaggerated it, you see . . ."

"What was that? That they think I'm mad? Yes, maybe it's true."

He gave a forced smile.

"Yes . . . yes . . . I mean, bah! No! Well, everything I said (about other things as well), all that was nonsense and because I was drunk."

"Why are you apologizing? I'm so fed up with all of it!" cried Raskolnikov with exaggerated irritation. However, he was in part pretending.

"I know, I know, I understand. You can be sure I understand. I'm ashamed even to mention it."

"If you're ashamed, then don't talk about it!"

They were both silent. Razumikhin was more than in ecstasy, and Raskolnikov perceived this with disgust. It also disturbed him what Razumikhin had just said about Porfiry.

"I'll have to play him for sympathy,"* he thought, turning pale, his heart pounding, "and do it as naturally as I can. The most natural thing would be not to play him at all. To say nothing at all about that! No, to *refrain* would also be unnatural. . . . Well, we'll see how it turns out there . . . right away . . . am I going there for good or for ill? The moth flies right into the flame. My heart's pounding, and that's not so good!"

"In this gray house," said Razumikhin.

"The most important thing is whether or not Porfiry knows that yesterday I was in that old crone's apartment . . . and that I asked about

---

* The original says "to sing like Lazarus," a reference to Luke 16:20. It is linked with other references to Lazarus in the novel.

the blood? I have to find that out right away, from the moment I enter, to tell by his face; o-ther-wise . . . I'll find out, no matter what!"

"Do you know what?" he said, turning suddenly to Razumikhin with a cunning smile. "Today I've noticed, my friend, that since morning you've been in an unusually excited state. Is it true?"

"What sort of excitement? I'm not excited at all," Razumikhin said, wincing.

"No, my friend, it's true, I noticed it. Before you were sitting on that chair as you've never sat before, somehow on the edge of it, shuddering from a spasm. You kept jumping up for no reason at all. Either you were angry, or else your mug became sweet as sugar. You even blushed; especially when they invited you to dinner, you blushed deeply."

"Not at all! You're lying! Why are you saying that?"

"Why are you wriggling like a schoolboy? Phew, the devil take him. He's blushed again!"

"What a swine you are!"

"Why are you so embarrassed? You Romeo! Wait a moment, I'll repeat all this today, ha, ha, ha! It'll amuse my mama . . . and someone else, as well . . ."

"Listen, listen, listen, this is serious, why it's. . . . What's next, damn it?" Razumikhin said, completely flustered and growing cold in terror. "What will you tell them? My friend, I. . . . Phew! What a swine you are!"

"Like a rose in springtime! It suits you, if you only knew: a Romeo who's six feet tall! And you've washed extra carefully today, and trimmed your nails, haven't you? When did you ever do that? So help me God, you even put pomade on your hair! Bend over!"

"Swine!!!"

Raskolnikov was laughing so hard that it seemed he could scarcely restrain himself, so they entered Porfiry Petrovich's apartment with laughter. That was just what Raskolnikov wanted: from inside his rooms they could be heard laughing, still guffawing in the entrance.

"Not a word here, or I'll . . . smash your skull!" whispered Razumikhin in a fury, seizing hold of Raskolnikov's shoulder.

V

Raskolnikov was already entering the apartment. He went in looking as if he was trying with all his might to restrain himself from bursting into laughter again. Following him, with a completely disconcerted and ferocious expression, as red as a peony, lanky and clumsy, came the embarrassed Razumikhin. His face and entire figure were at that moment really ridiculous and justified Raskolnikov's laughter. Raskolnikov, who had not yet been introduced, bowed to the host, who was standing in the middle of the room, looking at them inquisitively. Raskolnikov extended his hand and shook his host's, still apparently with extreme effort to suppress his good cheer and to utter at least two or three words to introduce himself. But as soon as he had managed to assume a serious expression and mutter something—suddenly, as if against his will, he looked at Razumikhin again and couldn't restrain himself: his suppressed laughter broke out again, all the more uncontrollably the more he tried to control himself. The extraordinary ferocity with which Razumikhin reacted to this "genuine" laughter lent this scene the appearance of the most sincere merriment and, most importantly, naturalness. Razumikhin, as if on purpose, contributed to this effect.

"Damn it all!" he roared, waving his arm and crashing into a small round table holding an almost empty glass of tea. Everything went flying and splintering.

" 'Of course, Alexander the Great was a great hero, but why break

the chairs, gentlemen?* You're destroying government property!'"
cried Porfiry Petrovich cheerfully.

The scene was as follows: Raskolnikov, forgetting that the host
was shaking his hand, was still laughing heartily; but having a sense
of proportion, he was waiting for an opportunity to end his outburst
as soon as possible in the most natural way. Razumikhin, positively
embarrassed from having knocked over the table and broken the glass,
regarded the fragments grimly, spit, and turned abruptly to the window and stood with his back to the others, his face wearing a terrible
frown, looking out the window, but seeing nothing. Porfiry Petrovich
was laughing and wished to be laughing, but it was obvious that he
needed some sort of explanation. Zametov had been seated on a chair
in the corner. He'd stood up at the guests' arrival and was standing
there waiting, his mouth wide open in a smile, but regarding the whole
scene in bewilderment and even disbelief; he looked at Raskolnikov
with some confusion. Zametov's unexpected presence struck Raskolnikov unpleasantly.

"I'll have to take that into consideration," he thought.

"Excuse us, please," he began with forced embarrassment.

"For goodness' sake, it's a pleasure to meet you, and you entered so
pleasantly, too. . . . So then, doesn't he even want to say hello to me?"
Porfiry Petrovich asked, glancing at Razumikhin.

"So help me God, I don't know why he's so angry with me. All
I said to him along the way was that he resembled Romeo, and . . . I
proved it. That's all there was to it."

"Swine!" Razumikhin blurted out without turning around.

"He must have had very serious reasons for getting so angry with
you for saying that one little word," said Porfiry with a laugh.

"Oh, you! That's the detective speaking! Well, the hell with all of
you!" Razumikhin cried. All of a sudden, now with a cheerful face, he
burst into laughter himself, as if nothing had happened, and went up
to Porfiry Petrovich.

"That'll do! We're all fools. Let's get down to business. This is my

---

* A quotation from the comedy *The Government Inspector* (1836) by Nikolai Gogol (1809–1852).

friend Rodion Romanych Raskolnikov. In the first place, you've heard about him before and wished to make his acquaintance; in the second place, he has a small matter to discuss with you. Bah! Zametov! Why are you here? You know each other, don't you? Since when?"

"What's this all about?" wondered Raskolnikov apprehensively.

Zametov seemed a little confused, but not overly so.

"We met yesterday at your place," he said casually.

"That means God spared us the trouble: last week he was constantly asking me to introduce him to you, Porfiry, but I see that you've already sniffed each other out without me. . . . By the way, where's your snuff?"

Porfiry Petrovich was dressed informally, in a dressing gown, extremely clean linen, and well-worn slippers. He was about thirty-five years old, shorter than average, portly, even with a paunch; he was clean-shaven, without a mustache or side whiskers, with closely cropped hair on his large round head, which bulged somewhat prominently at the rear. His puffy, round, somewhat snub-nosed face had a sickly, dark yellow pallor, but his expression was rather brazen and even sarcastic. It could even have been friendly had it not been for the look of his eyes, with their watery, liquid gleam, almost covered by white eyelashes, twitching as if he were winking at someone. The expression of his eyes, somewhat strangely, didn't match his whole figure, which had something womanish about it, and lent it something far more serious than one might expect at first sight.

As soon as he heard that his guest had a "small matter" to discuss with him, Porfiry Petrovich immediately asked him to sit down on the sofa. He himself sat at the other end of it and looked intently at his guest with the eager anticipation of hearing an explanation of the business, with exaggerated and overly serious attention, which can be oppressive and even confusing at first, especially for strangers, especially if what you are stating, in your own opinion, is out of proportion to the amount of unusually serious attention it receives. But in short and coherent terms, Raskolnikov clearly and accurately explained his business and was satisfied that he had even managed to take a good look at Porfiry. Not once did Porfiry Petrovich take his eyes off him all during that time. Razumikhin, who had taken the opposite seat at the same table, followed the explanation of the matter eagerly and impatiently, constantly glancing from one to the other and back again, which began to seem a bit excessive.

"Fool!" Raskolnikov silently cursed him.

"You should make a statement to the police," Porfiry replied with the same businesslike expression, "to the effect that, having learned about such and such an occurrence, that is, about the murder, you request, in turn, to inform the examining magistrate who was delegated to this case that such and such items belong to you and that you wish to redeem them . . . or something of the sort—however, they'll write it for you."

"That's just the point: at the present time, I . . ." Raskolnikov tried to appear as embarrassed as he could. "I lack the funds . . . and can't even manage such a small expenditure. . . . You see, now I'd merely like to declare that these items are mine, and when I have the funds, then I'll . . ."

"That doesn't matter, sir," replied Porfiry Petrovich, receiving this explanation of Raskolnikov's finances coldly. "However, if you like, you can write directly to me in the same vein, that having learned of this occurrence, and declaring such and such items, you request that . . ."

"Do I just write it on plain paper?" Raskolnikov hastened to interrupt, once again taking an interest in the financial side of the matter.

"Oh, the most ordinary paper will do, sir!" Porfiry Petrovich said suddenly, and regarded him with apparent mockery, squinting and seeming to wink at him. However, perhaps it only seemed that way to Raskolnikov, because it lasted for only a moment. At least, something of the sort occurred. Raskolnikov could have sworn that he had winked at him, only the devil knew why.

"He knows!" flashed through his mind like a streak of lightning.

"Excuse me for bothering you with such nonsense," he continued, a bit disconcerted. "My items are worth only about five rubles, but they're especially dear to me as keepsakes of those from whom I received them, and I confess, as soon as I learned about it, I was very frightened that . . ."

"That's why you became so upset yesterday when I told Zosimov that Porfiry was questioning the people who had pledges!" Razumikhin inserted with obvious intention.

This was unbearable. Raskolnikov couldn't refrain and cast him a vicious glance of rage with his flashing dark eyes. Then he recovered immediately.

"My friend, you seem to be making fun of me," he said, turning to him with cleverly contrived irritation. "I agree that perhaps in your eyes I'm overly concerned about these trifles; but you can't consider me an egoist or a greedy man. In my own view, these two little insignificant things are not trifles at all. I just told you that the silver watch, which is worth very little, is the only object left from my father. You may laugh at me, but my mother's come to visit"—he turned to Porfiry suddenly—"and if she finds out," he said, quickly turning back to Razumikhin, trying hard to make his voice tremble, "that this watch has been lost, then I swear, she'll be in despair! Women!"

"Not at all! I didn't mean that at all! Just the opposite!" cried the offended Razumikhin.

"Was that all right? Was it natural? Too exaggerated?" Raskolnikov wondered anxiously. "Why did I say, 'Women'?"

"Has your mother come to see you?" Porfiry Petrovich inquired for some reason.

"Yes."

"When was that, sir?"

"Last evening."

Porfiry was silent, as if pondering.

"In any case, your items couldn't possibly be lost," he continued calmly and coldly. "I've been waiting for you here for some time."

As if nothing unusual had occurred, he kindly offered an ashtray to Razumikhin, who was mercilessly scattering ashes on the rug. Raskolnikov shuddered, but Porfiry seemed not to notice him, all the while concerned only about Razumikhin's cigarette.

"What? Been waiting here! So did you know that he, too, had left pledges *there*?" cried Razumikhin.

Porfiry Petrovich addressed Raskolnikov directly:

"Your two items, the ring and the watch, were *in her room* wrapped together in one piece of paper, on which your name was clearly written in pencil, as well as the day of the month when she had received them from you . . ."

"How is it you're so observant?" Raskolnikov asked clumsily, trying hard to look him in the eye; but he was unable to endure it and suddenly added, "I asked only because there were probably many people who'd pawned things . . . so it must have been difficult for you to recall them all. . . . Yet, on the contrary, you remember them all clearly and . . . and . . ."

"Stupid! Weak! Why did I add that?"

"Almost all of them have been identified, and you were the only one who'd yet to come forward," replied Porfiry with a barely noticeable shade of mockery.

"I wasn't quite well."

"I heard about that, sir. I even heard that you were very disturbed about something or other. Even now you look a bit pale."

"Not at all . . . on the contrary, I'm completely well!" Raskolnikov replied rudely and angrily, suddenly changing his tone. Malice was seething in him, and he was unable to suppress it. "If I speak in anger, I'll give myself away!" occurred to him again. "Why are they tormenting me?"

"He wasn't quite well!" Razumikhin interjected. "What nonsense he's talking. Until yesterday he was constantly delirious. . . . Well, just think, Porfiry, he could barely stand on his feet, but as soon as we, that is Zosimov and I, let him out of our sight yesterday—he got dressed, slipped out, and was up to some mischief almost until midnight, and all this in his total delirium, I tell you. Can you imagine that? A most extraordinary episode!"

"Really in *total delirium*? You don't say!" Porfiry said, shaking his head with some kind of womanish gesture.

"Hey, that's nonsense! Don't believe it! But you don't believe him anyway," Raskolnikov blurted out with too much anger. Porfiry Petrovich, however, seemed not to have heard these strange words.

"How could you have gone out unless you were delirious?" Razumikhin asked suddenly, growing heated. "Why did you go out? For what? And why in secret? Were you in your right mind then? Now that all the danger's passed, I'm saying this directly to you!"

"I was fed up with all of them yesterday," Raskolnikov replied, turning suddenly to Porfiry with an arrogantly challenging smile. "I ran away from them to rent an apartment so they wouldn't be able to find me; I grabbed a pile of money to take with me. Mr. Zametov here even saw the money. So, Mr. Zametov, was I in my right mind yesterday or delirious? Settle this quarrel."

At that moment, he would have liked to strangle Zametov. He didn't appreciate his look or his silence at all.

"In my opinion, you spoke extremely rationally and even cleverly, sir, but you were too irritable," Zametov declared drily.

"But today Nikodim Fomich told me," Porfiry Petrovich inserted, "that he met you yesterday, very late, in the apartment of a certain civil servant who'd been run over by horses . . ."

"What about that civil servant?" Razumikhin chimed in. "Well, weren't you insane at his apartment? You gave the widow your last rubles for the funeral! So, if you wanted to help—give her fifteen or twenty, but leave yourself at least three rubles. But you handed over all twenty-five!"

"Perhaps I found a treasure somewhere—how do you know? I was feeling very generous yesterday. . . . Mr. Zametov knows I found a treasure! Excuse me, please," he said, turning to Porfiry with trembling lips, "for disturbing you with such trivial nonsense for the last half hour. You must be sick of us, right?"

"Not at all, sir, quite to the contrary, to the con-tra-ry! If you only knew how you intrigue me! It's interesting to see and hear . . . and I, I must confess, I'm so glad that you finally decided to come . . ."

"Give me some tea at least! My throat's dry!" cried Razumikhin.

"A splendid idea! Perhaps everyone will join you. Would you like something . . . more substantial before we have tea?"

"Go ahead!" said Razumikhin.

Porfiry Petrovich went to order the tea.

Thoughts were spinning like a whirlwind in Raskolnikov's head. He was terribly irritated.

"The main thing is they don't want to conceal it or stand on ceremony! And if you didn't know me, how was it you talked to Nikodim Fomich about me? It must mean that they don't even want to hide the fact that they're following me like a pack of dogs. They spit in my face quite openly!" He trembled with rage. "Well, go on and beat me, but don't play with me like a cat with a mouse. It's not polite, Porfiry Petrovich; perhaps I won't allow it, sir! I'll stand up and blurt out the whole truth right in everyone's ugly mug; you'll see how I despise you!" He caught his breath with difficulty. "But what if it only seems so to me? What if it's a mirage, and I'm mistaken about everything, furious out of inexperience, unable to keep acting this vile part? Perhaps it's all unintentional. Their words are all so ordinary, but there's something to them. . . . One can always say that, but there's something to it. Why did he say 'in her room'? Why did Zametov add that I spoke 'cleverly?' Why do they use that tone of voice? Yes . . . that tone. . . . Razumikhin was sitting here, too; why didn't it occur to him? Nothing ever occurs to that innocent blockhead! It's the fever again! Did Porfiry wink at me just now or not? Do they want to irritate my nerves or tease me? Is it all a mirage, or do they *know*? Even Zametov's impertinent. . . . Is he? Zametov reconsidered overnight. I had a feeling he'd reconsider! He feels at home here, yet he's here for the first time. Porfiry doesn't treat him as a guest and is sitting with his back to him. They came to terms *because of me*! They were definitely talking about me before we arrived! Do they know I went back to the apartment? I wish they'd get on with it! When I said yesterday I'd gone off to rent an apartment, he missed it, didn't catch it. . . . But it was clever of me to bring up the idea of the apartment: it'll be useful later on! Delirious, they say! Ha, ha, ha! He knows all about last evening! But he didn't know that my mother had come! And that old crone wrote down the date in pencil! You're lying, I won't let you catch me! They still don't have any facts; it's only a mirage! No, give me facts! The apartment's no fact, but delirium; I know what to say to them. . . . Do they know I went back to the apartment? I won't leave until I find out! Why did I come here? But now I'm getting angry, and that just might be a fact! Phew, I'm so irritable! Perhaps that's all right; it's the role of a sick man. . . . He's feeling me out. He'll try to sidetrack me. Why did I come?"

All this flashed through his head like lightning.

Porfiry Petrovich returned in a moment. He suddenly seemed more cheerful.

"You know, brother, since your party yesterday, my head's . . . I've become so muddled," he said to Razumikhin in a completely different tone of voice, laughing.

"Well, was it interesting? I deserted you yesterday at the most interesting point. Who won?"

"No one, naturally. We moved on to discuss eternal questions and wound up with our heads in the sky."

"Just imagine, Rodya, what they were going on about yesterday: is there such a thing as crime or not? I told you they were telling tall tales!"

"What's so surprising? It's an ordinary social question," Raskolnikov observed distractedly.

"The question wasn't formulated that way," remarked Porfiry.

"Not quite, that's true," agreed Razumikhin at once, hastening and getting excited as usual. "You see, Rodion: listen and give us your opinion. I'd like to hear it. I did my utmost with them yesterday and was waiting for you; I even told them about you and said you'd come. . . . It all began with the views of the socialists. Their points are well known: crime is a protest against the abnormal structure of society—and that's that, nothing else; no further reasons are permitted—nothing more!"

"That's not true!" cried Porfiry Petrovich. He grew visibly more animated and kept laughing, looking at Razumikhin, which excited the latter even more.

"Nothing else is permitted!" Razumikhin interrupted with passion. "I'm telling the truth! I'll show you their books: they say it's all because 'the environment has ruined them'—and nothing else! It's their favorite phrase! From there it follows that if society were to be organized normally, then all crimes would disappear instantly, since there'd be no reason to protest and everyone would immediately become righteous. Nature isn't taken into account; nature's banished; nature's not allowed! According to them, it's not humanity, developing historically along a *living* path to the end, which in and of itself turns into a normal society, but, on the contrary, the social system, emerging from some mathematical brain, that immediately organizes all humanity and in one moment renders it righteous and sinless, before any living progress, without any historical and living path! That's why they instinctively don't like history: they see only its 'outrages and stupidity'—and everything's explained only by stupidity! That's why they don't like the *living* process of life itself: they don't need a *living soul*! The living soul demands life; the living soul doesn't heed the laws of mechanics; the living soul is suspect; the living soul is reactionary! Even if their social system can be made out of rubber and smells a bit like carrion— it's still not alive, it has no will, it's slavish, it doesn't rebel! And the result is that all their labor goes only to laying bricks and arranging the corridors and rooms in a phalanstery.* The phalanstery's built, but human nature still isn't ready for the phalanstery; it wants life; it still hasn't completed the living process; it's too early for the cemetery! It's impossible to leap over human nature by means of logic alone! Logic can anticipate three possibilities, but there are a million of them! Cut off the whole million and reduce everything to a question of comfort! That's the simplest solution to the problem! It's clearly tempting and one doesn't have to think! The main point is—there's no need to think! The entire secret of life fits on two sheets of printer's paper!"

"There's some outburst for you; he's beating his drum! He needs to be restrained," said Porfiry with a laugh. "Just imagine," he said, turning to Raskolnikov, "that's the way it was last evening. Six voices in one room and he'd plied them all with punch beforehand—can you imagine it? No, brother, you're not telling the truth: the 'environment' plays a large role in crime, I can assure you."

"I know that it does, but tell me this: a forty-year-old man disgraces a ten-year-old girl—did the environment compel him to do it?"

"Well, strictly speaking, perhaps it was the environment," Porfiry remarked with astonishing seriousness. "A crime against a young girl can very, very often be explained by the 'environment.'"

Razumikhin was absolutely furious.

"Well, if you like, I'll *prove* to you at once," he roared, "that you

---

* A community organized according to the plan of the French utopian socialist, Charles Fourier (1772–1837).

have white eyelashes only as a result of the fact that Ivan the Great's bell tower is two hundred and fifty feet tall, and I'll prove it clearly, precisely, progressively, and even with a liberal cast. I'll do it! Do you want to bet?"

"I take the bet! Please let's hear how he proves it!"

"Damn it all, he's pretending!" cried Razumikhin, jumping up and waving his arm. "Is it even worth talking with you? He's doing all this on purpose, Rodion. You still don't know him! Yesterday he took their side only to show them up as fools. What didn't he say yesterday, good Lord! And they were so pleased with him! He can hold out like this for two weeks. Last year he assured us for some reason that he was going to become a monk: for two months he insisted on it! Not long ago he tried to convince us that he was getting married and was all ready for the ceremony. He'd even acquired new clothes for the occasion. We started to congratulate him. But there was no bride, nothing ever happened—it was all a mirage!"

"You're not telling the truth! I'd acquired new clothes before that. It was because of my new clothes that I decided to fool you all."

"Are you really such a dissembler?" Raskolnikov asked casually.

"Don't you think so? Just wait and I'll deceive you, too—ha, ha, ha! No, don't you see, I'll tell you the whole truth. Regarding all these questions, crimes, environments, and young girls—I now remember—however, it's always interested me—your little article 'On Crime' . . . or whatever it's called, I forgot the title, I can't recall it. Two months ago I had the pleasure of reading it in *Periodical Discourses*."

"My article? In *Periodical Discourses*?" Raskolnikov asked in surprise. "I did write an article in connection with some book about six months ago, when I left the university, but I sent it to *Weekly Discourses*, not *Periodical Discourses*."

"It wound up in *Periodical Discourses*."

"*Weekly Discourses* ceased publication, which is why it wasn't published there . . ."

"That's true, sir; when it ceased publication, *Weekly Discourses* merged with *Periodical Discourses*, and therefore your little article appeared in *Periodical Discourses* two months ago. Didn't you know?"

Raskolnikov really didn't know a thing about it.

"Good gracious, you can request money from them for your article! But what a temperament you have! You live such an isolated life that you don't even know things that concern you directly. That's a fact, sir."

"Bravo, Rodka! I didn't know it, either!" cried Razumikhin. "I'll run to the reading room today and ask for that issue! Two months ago? What date? I'll find it somehow. That's quite something! And he didn't even tell me!"

"How did you know that it was my article? I signed it only with my initials."

"I found out accidentally and only a few days ago. From the editor; he's an acquaintance. . . . I was very interested in it."

"I was examining, if I recall, the psychological state of the criminal during the entire commission of his crime."

"Yes, sir, and you insisted that the act of committing a crime is always accompanied by illness. It's very, very original, but . . . it wasn't that part of your little piece that caught my eye; rather, it was the idea mentioned at the end of the article, which, unfortunately, you merely touch on by implication, that there exist in the world certain people, as it were, who are able . . . that is, not that they're able, but who have every right to commit any kind of outrages and crimes, and that the laws do not apply to them."

Raskolnikov smiled at the forced and intentional distortion of his idea.

"What? What's that? A right to crime? And not because 'the environment ruined them'?" Razumikhin inquired with some alarm.

"No, no, that's not exactly why," replied Porfiry. "The point is that in his article all people are divided into 'ordinary' and 'extraordinary.' Ordinary people must live in obedience and do not have the right to overstep the law, because, don't you see, they're ordinary. But extraordinary people have the right to commit all sorts of crimes and to overstep precisely because they're extraordinary. That's what you say, it seems, if I'm not mistaken?"

"How's that? It can't be like that!" Razumikhin muttered in confusion.

Raskolnikov smiled again. He understood immediately what the point was and where he was being pushed; he remembered his article. He decided to accept the challenge.

"That's not exactly what I said," he began simply and modestly. "However, I confess that you stated it almost correctly, even, if you like, completely correctly. . . ." (He found it very pleasant to agree that it was completely correct.) "The only difference is that I don't insist in any way that extraordinary people absolutely must and are always obligated to commit all sorts of outrages, as you say. It even seems to me that such an article wouldn't be accepted for publication. I merely imply that the 'extraordinary man' has the right . . . that is, not the official right, but he himself has the right to permit his conscience to overstep . . . various obstacles, and only in the case that the execution of his idea (sometimes, perhaps, one that would benefit all mankind) requires it. You say that my article was unclear; I'm prepared to explain it to you, as best I can. Perhaps I'm not mistaken in assuming that you'd like me to; if you please, sir. In my opinion, if the discoveries of Kepler and Newton could in no way have become known to people other than through the sacrifice of the lives of one, ten, a hundred, and so on, people who interfered with their discoveries or who were obstacles blocking their way, then Newton had the right, and was even obligated to . . . *eliminate* those ten or a hundred people in order to make his discoveries known to all humanity. From this it in no way follows that Newton had the right to kill anyone and everyone he pleased, or to rob people every day at the market. Furthermore, I recall, I develop the idea in my article, that all people . . . at least the lawgivers and trailblazers of humanity, beginning with the ancients, continuing with Lycurgus, the Solons, Mohammeds, Napoleons, and so forth, each and every one of them, were criminals, just by virtue of the fact that in propagating new laws, they were at the same time destroying the old laws viewed as sacred by society and handed down by their fathers. Of course, they didn't hesitate even to shed blood, if that blood (sometimes completely innocent and valiantly shed in defense of the old laws) would help them. It's even noteworthy that a majority of these benefactors and trailblazers of humanity were particularly horrible shedders of blood. In a word, I conclude that everyone, not only the great people, but even those who stand out just slightly from the everyday rut, that is, those who are even marginally capable of uttering some new word, must, by their nature, necessarily be criminals—more or less, it goes without saying. Otherwise it would be difficult for them to break out of the rut, and, of course, they can't agree to remain in the rut, again, by their very nature; but in my opinion, they're even obligated not to agree to stay there. In a word, you see that up to this point there's nothing particularly new in what I say. This has all been written and read a thousand times. Regarding my division of people into ordinary and extraordinary, I agree that it's somewhat arbitrary, but I'm not insisting on exact numbers. I merely believe in my main idea. It consists precisely in the view that by the laws of nature, people are divided *in general* into two categories: the lower category (ordinary), that is, so to speak, material serving solely for the purpose of reproducing the species, and into people proper, that is, those who possess the gift or talent of uttering some *new word* in their milieu. Subdivisions here are naturally endless, but the notable characteristics of both categories are rather distinct: the first category, that is, the material, speaking in general, consists of conservative people by nature, well-behaved, who live in obedience and like being obedient. In my opinion, they're even obligated to be obedient because that's their destiny, and there's nothing humiliating about it for them. The second category consists of people who break the law, destroyers or, judging by their abilities, those predisposed to be so. Their crimes, it goes without saying, are relative and diverse; for the most part, in extremely diverse forms they require the destruction of the present order in the name of something better. But even if it's necessary to step over a corpse, to wade through blood in order to attain his goal, then in my opinion he may, according to his conscience, give himself permission to wade through blood, depending, however, on the nature of his idea and its dimensions— note that well. Only in that sense do I speak in my article about their right to commit a crime. (You'll recall that we began with the legal question.) However, there's no cause for alarm: the mass of humanity hardly ever recognizes this right; it punishes these men or hangs them (more or less), and does so with absolute justification, fulfilling its conservative function, although in succeeding generations this same mass of humanity places those very same people who were executed on a pedestal and worships them (more or less). The first category always comprises men of the present; the second, men of the future. The former preserve the world and increase its population; the latter move the world forward and lead it to its goal. Both have an equal right to exist. In a word, all men have equally strong rights, and—*vive la guerre éter-nelle**—until the New Jerusalem, of course!"

"So, you still believe in the New Jerusalem?"

"I do," Raskolnikov replied firmly; while saying this he stared down at the ground, as he had done during the entire course of his long tirade, having selected a spot on the rug.

"An-n-n-nd do you believe in God? Forgive me for being so curious."

"I do," repeated Raskolnikov, raising his eyes to Porfiry's face.

"An-n-nd do you believe in the raising of Lazarus?"

"I-I do. Why are you asking these questions?"

"Do you believe in it literally?"

"Literally."

"I see, sir . . . I was merely curious. Forgive me, sir. But, if you please, I'll return to the previous subject. They aren't always executed. Some, on the contrary . . ."

"Triumph during their lifetime? Oh, yes, some attain their goals in their lifetime, and then . . ."

"Then they begin executing other people?"

"If necessary, you know, and even the large majority of them do it. In general, your remark is very witty."

"Thank you, sir. But tell me this: how does one distinguish the extraordinary people from the ordinary ones? Are there some special signs at birth? I have in mind that greater accuracy is needed, so to speak, more external distinctness. Excuse the natural discomfort of a practical and well-intentioned man, but might it be possible to arrange for them to wear special clothing or to bear some mark? Because, you'll agree, if some confusion results and one of the ordinary category imagines that he belongs to the other one, and begins to 'eliminate all obstacles,' as you expressed it so fortuitously, well then . . ."

---

* "Long live perpetual war" (French).

"Oh, this happens very often! This observation of yours is even wittier than your last one."

"Thank you, sir."

"Don't mention it, sir. But consider the fact that a mistake is possible only on the part of those people in the first category, that is, the 'ordinary' people (as I called them, perhaps very inauspiciously). In spite of their inborn inclination to obey, by a certain playfulness of nature, not denied even to a cow, an extremely large number of them like to imagine themselves advanced people, 'destroyers,' and they aspire to utter a 'new word.' They do this with absolute sincerity. As a matter of fact, at the same time they very often fail to notice the genuinely 'new people,'* and even despise them as backward and incapable of higher thinking. But, in my opinion, there can be no real danger here, and you have nothing to worry about, because these people never get very far. Of course, they can sometimes be beaten for their fervor, so as to remind them of their rightful place, but nothing more. You don't even need anyone to carry out the punishment: they'll beat themselves up because they're so well behaved. Some will provide this service to others, and some will do it to themselves. . . . They impose various public punishments on themselves—and it turns out beautifully and instructively. In a word, you have no need to worry. . . . This is the law."

"Well, at least on that score you've somewhat reassured me. But here's another concern, sir: tell me, please, are there many of these people, the 'extraordinary' ones, who have the right to mow down others? Of course, I'm prepared to bow down before them, but you'll agree, it would be terrible if there were very many of them, wouldn't it?"

"Oh, don't worry about that, either," Raskolnikov continued in the same tone. "In general, an unusually small number of people are born, even strangely few, with a new idea, or who are capable of even uttering something *new*. Only one thing is clear: the order that controls the human births, all these categories and subdivisions, must be extremely closely and accurately determined by some law of nature. This law, it

---

* A reference to Nikolai Chernyshevsky's (1828–1889) influential novel, *What Is to Be Done?* (1863).

goes without saying, is now unknown, but I believe that it exists and may subsequently become known. The enormous mass of people, the material, exists on earth merely, at last, through some effort, some as yet mysterious process, by means of some crossing of generations and breeds, to exert all its strength, and at last to bring into the world at least one person out of a thousand who's in any way original. Perhaps one in ten thousand (I'm speaking approximately, by way of illustration) is born with even broader originality. With even more—one out of a hundred thousand. Men of genius—out of millions, and great geniuses, the culmination of humanity—perhaps only as a result of the passing of many thousands of millions of people across the earth. In a word, I haven't looked into the glass retort in which all this happens. But there absolutely is a definite law and there must be one; it can't all be a matter of chance."

"Are you both joking, or what?" Razumikhin exclaimed at last. "You're trying to mislead each other, aren't you? You just sit there mocking one another! Can you be serious, Rodya?"

Raskolnikov turned his pale, almost sad face to him and made no reply. Porfiry's ostensible, insistent, irritating, and *impolite* sarcasm seemed strange to Razumikhin when compared to his friend's calm, sad face.

"Well, my friend, if this really is so serious, then. . . . Of course, you're right that none of it's new and it all resembles everything we've read and heard a thousand times before. But what's really *original* in all this—and belongs exclusively to you, to my chagrin—is the fact that you sanction bloodshed as a *matter of conscience* and, excuse me for saying so, even with such fanaticism. . . . That, accordingly, is the main idea of your article. The sanctioning of bloodshed *as a matter of conscience*; why, in my opinion, that's more terrible than an official or legal sanction to shed blood . . ."

"Absolutely right, it is more terrible," echoed Porfiry.

"No, you must've gotten carried away somehow! It's all a mistake. I'll read it. . . . You were carried away! You can't really think that. . . . I'll read it."

"You won't find all that in my article; it's only hinted at there," Raskolnikov said.

"Yes, indeed," said Porfiry, unable to sit still. "Now it's almost clear to me how you regard crime, but . . . you must excuse my persistence (I'm really sorry to bother you like this), but don't you see: you've managed to reassure me now about my mistake, confusing your two categories, but . . . it's the various practical cases I still find troubling! Just suppose some person or other, let's say, a young man, imagines that he's a Spartan lawgiver like Lycurgus or a prophet like Mohammed—a future one, understandably—and let's say that he decides to remove all obstacles blocking his way. . . . 'A long campaign lies ahead of me,' he thinks, 'and I need money to undertake it.' And he starts to amass what he needs for his campaign. . . . You understand?"

Zametov, from the corner where he was sitting, suddenly snorted. Raskolnikov didn't even raise his eyes to look at him.

"I must agree," Raskolnikov replied calmly, "that such cases really must exist. Stupid and vain men in particular will swallow the bait, our young people especially."

"So you do see. Well, what then?"

"What then?" Raskolnikov smiled. "I'm not to blame for it. That's the way it is and always will be. Just now he said"—nodding at Razumikhin—"that I sanction bloodshed. So what? Society is well provided for with all its exiles, prisons, examining magistrates, and hard labor—what's there to worry about? Go look for your thief!"

"Well, and if we find him?"

"Then he gets what he deserves."

"You're so logical. And what about his conscience?"

"What business is that of yours?"

"Just so, out of human kindness."

"If someone has a conscience, and if he acknowledges his mistake, then let him suffer. That's his punishment, in addition to hard labor."

"And the real geniuses," Razumikhin asked with a frown, "those granted the right to kill, shouldn't they have to suffer at all, even for the blood they shed?"

"Why use the word 'should'? This doesn't involve a question of permission or prohibition. Let him suffer, if he pities the victim. . . . Pain and suffering are always obligatory for someone with broad intellect and deep feeling. Truly great individuals, it seems to me, must experience great sorrow in this world," he added, suddenly becoming contemplative, and no longer in a conversational mode.

He raised his eyes, regarded everyone somberly, smiled, and picked up his cap. Now he was much calmer than when he'd first arrived, and he felt this. Everyone stood up.

"Well, then, scold me or not, get angry with me or not, but I can't hold back," Porfiry Petrovich declared again. "Allow me to pose one more small question (I'm still troubling you, I know); I want to introduce one tiny little idea of mine, merely so as not to forget it . . ."

"All right, what's your little idea?" Raskolnikov asked, serious and pale, standing in front of him in anticipation.

"Here it is . . . really, I don't know how best to express it . . . this little idea of mine is so very playful . . . and psychological. . . . Well then, when you were composing your little article—could it possibly be the case, heh-heh, that you might also have considered yourself, even the tiniest bit, to be an 'extraordinary' man uttering some *new word*, in the sense that you're using it. . . . Isn't that so?"

"Very possibly," Raskolnikov replied contemptuously.

Razumikhin made a movement.

"And if so, then might you yourself have decided—well, in view of some unfortunate worldly circumstances and constraints, or for the advancement of all mankind in some way—to step over those obstacles? Say, for example, to kill and rob?"

Suddenly Porfiry seemed to wink at him with his left eye again and chuckle inaudibly, just as he had before.

"If I were to step over, then, of course, I wouldn't tell you," Raskolnikov replied with arrogant, provocative contempt.

"No, indeed, it's just that I'm interested, strictly, in clarifying the meaning of your article, merely in a literary sense, of course . . ."

"Ugh! This is so obvious and insolent!" Raskolnikov thought with disgust.

"Allow me to observe," he replied drily, "that I don't consider myself a Mohammed or a Napoleon . . . or anyone of that sort; therefore, not being one of them, I can't possibly provide you with a satisfactory explanation of how I would act, if I were."

"Well, come, come now, who among us in Holy Rus doesn't consider himself a Napoleon these days?" Porfiry suddenly asked with alarming familiarity. This time there was even something unusually distinctive in his intonation.

"Wasn't it just some sort of future Napoleon who did in our Alyona Ivanovna with an axe last week?" Zametov blurted out from his corner.

Raskolnikov was silent and stared fixedly and decisively at Porfiry. Razumikhin frowned sullenly. Even before this moment he'd begun to be aware of something unusual. He looked around in anger. There was a minute of gloomy silence. Raskolnikov turned to leave.

"You're going already?" Porfiry asked politely, extending his hand with excessive courtesy. "I'm very, very glad to have made your acquaintance. As for your petition, have no worries about it. Just write what I told you. Best of all, drop by to see me there . . . sometime soon . . . why, even tomorrow. I'll probably be in around eleven or so. We'll arrange everything . . . have a nice chat. . . . As one of the last people to have been *there*, perhaps you might be able to tell us something," he added with a good-natured look.

"Do you wish to interrogate me officially, with all the formalities?" Raskolnikov asked abruptly.

"Why on earth? For the moment, that's quite unnecessary. You didn't understand me. You see, I don't let any opportunity pass me by and . . . and I've already spoken with all those who pawned some item . . . I've taken some statements . . . and you, as the last one who. . . . By the way!" he cried, suddenly delighted for some reason. "By the way, I just remembered . . . what's the matter with me?" he turned to Razumikhin. "You know how you've been bending my ear about that fellow Nikolashka . . . yes, I know, I know," he said, turning to Raskolnikov, "that fellow's in the clear, but what can I do, and I had to trouble Mitka, too. . . . Well, here's the thing, the main point: climbing the stairs that evening . . . forgive me, you were there sometime before eight o'clock?"

"Yes," replied Raskolnikov, with the unpleasant feeling at that moment that he shouldn't have admitted it.

"So, climbing those stairs sometime before eight, did you happen to notice, on the second floor, in the open apartment—do you recall—

two workmen, perhaps even one of them? They were there painting; by any chance did you see them? It's very, very important for them!"

"Painters? No, I didn't see them," Raskolnikov replied slowly, as if searching his memory, at the same time tensing his entire being, immobilized by the torment of trying to guess where the trap lay hidden, and hoping that he wouldn't miss anything. "No, I didn't see them; in fact, I didn't even notice any open apartment. . . . But on the fourth floor"—he'd now fully discovered the trap and was feeling victorious—"I recall that a civil servant was moving out of his apartment . . . opposite Alyona Ivanovna's . . . I remember . . . that I clearly remember. Soldiers were carrying out a sofa, and I had to press up against the wall. . . . But painters—no, I don't recall any painters. . . . And there wasn't any open apartment anywhere. No, there wasn't . . ."

"What are you talking about?" Razumikhin cried suddenly, as if coming to his senses and now understanding what was being said. "The painters were there working on the day of the murder, but he was there three days before. What are you asking him?"

"Ugh! I got mixed up!" Porfiry said, slapping his forehead. "Devil take it, this case is too much for my poor brain!" he added, turning to Raskolnikov as if apologizing. "It would've been important for us to know if someone had seen them that same evening before eight o'clock, in that apartment, and it just occurred to me that you might be able to tell us. . . . I got all mixed up!"

"You must be more careful," Razumikhin observed gloomily.

These last words were uttered in the entrance hall. Porfiry Petrovich escorted them to the door with utmost politeness. They both emerged onto the street feeling sullen and morose, and for a few steps didn't exchange a word. Raskolnikov took a deep breath. . . .

VI

"... I don't believe it! I can't believe it!" a perplexed Razumikhin repeated, trying with all his might to refute Raskolnikov's conclusions. They were already nearing Bakaleev's house, where, in their rented rooms, Pulkheriya Aleksandrovna and Dunya had been waiting for them for quite a while. Razumikhin frequently paused along the way, impelled by the heat of the conversation, confused and agitated solely by the fact that it was the first time they had spoken plainly about *that*.

"Then don't believe it!" replied Raskolnikov with a cold, calm grin. "As usual, you didn't notice anything, while I was weighing every word."

"You're mistrustful, that's why you weighed every word.... Hmm. Really, I agree that Porfiry's tone was rather strange, and especially that scoundrel Zametov! You're right, there was something in it—but why? Why?"

"He changed his mind overnight."

"On the contrary, the contrary! If they'd had that brainless idea, they'd have tried with all their might to conceal it and hide their cards so they could catch you afterward.... But now—it's insolent and careless!"

"If they really had any facts, that is, genuine facts, or some kind of well-founded suspicions, they'd really have tried to conceal the game, in the hope of winning even more. (But they'd have conducted a search long ago!) However, they don't have any facts, not one—it's all a mirage, it cuts two ways, merely a passing fancy—and they're trying to use insolence to confuse the matter. Perhaps Porfiry's angry that there are no facts and so he burst out with all that. Perhaps he has some intention. . . . He seems to be a clever man. . . . Maybe he wanted to frighten me by showing that he knows. . . . There's psychology for you, my friend. . . . However, it's horrid to have to explain all this. Leave it alone!"

"It's insulting, insulting! I understand you! But . . . now, since we've begun talking openly (and it's excellent that we've begun. I'm glad!)— now I can confess to you frankly, that I noticed this idea of theirs a while ago, all this time, it goes without saying, merely as a hint, a creeping suspicion. But why on earth should they have even a creeping suspicion? How dare they? Where, where are the roots hidden? If you only knew how angry I was! What: just because you're a poor student, disfigured by poverty and hypochondria, on the brink of a cruel illness and delirium, which might already have begun (make a note of that!), you're mistrustful, proud, knowing your own worth, you've spent six months all alone seeing no one, wearing tattered clothes and boots without soles—standing in front of some policemen, tolerating their abuse; and then you're confronted with an unexpected debt, an overdue promissory note to the court councillor Chebarov, stinking paint, hundred-degree heat, stifling air, a crowd of people, an account of the murder of a person where you'd been the day before, and all this—on an empty stomach! How could you keep from fainting? And to base it all on that? On that? The hell with it! I understand how annoying it is, but in your place, Rodka, I'd have burst out laughing in their faces, or better still: I'd have spat right in their ugly mugs, the thicker the better, and have landed a few dozen slaps on all of them, skillfully, as one always should, and that would be the end of it. The hell with them! Take heart! What a disgrace!"

"He did a good job laying it all out," thought Raskolnikov.

"The hell with them? But there's an interrogation tomorrow as well!" he said bitterly. "Do I really have to explain it all to them? I'm annoyed that I humiliated myself with Zametov in the tavern yesterday . . ."

"The hell with it! I'll go see Porfiry myself! We're related, so I'll squeeze it out of him, let him explain the root of the matter! And as for Zametov . . ."

"He's finally guessed!" thought Raskolnikov.

"Wait!" cried Razumikhin, suddenly seizing him by the shoulder. "Stop! You're wrong! I've just thought it through: you're wrong! What sort of a dirty trick was it? You say the question about the workers was a dirty trick? See through it: if you'd done *that*, would you let it slip that you saw the workmen . . . painting the apartment? On the contrary: you wouldn't have seen anything, even if you really had seen it! Who would testify against himself?"

"If I had done *that deed*, then I would've definitely said that I saw the painters and the apartment," Raskolnikov continued, stating his reply unwillingly and with apparent disgust.

"But why testify against yourself?"

"Because only peasants and the most inexperienced novices flatly deny everything during interrogations. A person who's somewhat intelligent and experienced tries as much as possible to admit readily to all external and inevitable facts; he merely looks for other reasons, introduces his own particular and unexpected aspect, which lends them a different significance and reveals them in a completely new light. Porfiry could count on my answering like that and saying what I saw to establish credibility; then I'd bring up something to explain . . ."

"But he would've told you immediately that the workmen couldn't have been there two days before; consequently, you were there precisely on the day of the murder, after seven o'clock. He'd have caught you with a detail!"

"That's exactly what he was counting on, the fact that I wouldn't have had time to think, that I'd hasten to reply more plausibly, and would forget that the workmen couldn't have been there two days before."

"How could you forget that?"

"Easy as pie! Clever people get tripped up most easily on just such insignificant details. The cleverer a person is, the less he suspects that he'll be tricked by something so simple. You have to trick the cleverest person with the simplest matter. Porfiry isn't as stupid as you think at all . . ."

"But after this, he's a scoundrel!"

Raskolnikov couldn't keep from laughing. But at the same moment, his own animation and the enthusiasm with which he had laid out the last explanation seemed strange to him, since he had conducted the entire previous conversation with grim disgust, apparently for his own aims and of necessity.

"I'm beginning to enjoy certain aspects of this," he thought to himself.

But at almost the same time he suddenly felt strangely upset, as if an unexpected and alarming thought had struck him. His anxiety increased. They had arrived at the entrance to Bakaleev's house.

"Go in alone," said Raskolnikov suddenly. "I'll be back shortly."

"Where are you going? We've just arrived."

"I really have to. I have to do something. . . . I'll be back in half an hour. . . . Tell them."

"As you like. I'll go with you."

"Really? Do you also want to torment me to death?" he cried with such bitter irritation, with such a despairing look, that Razumikhin gave up. He stood on the stairs for some time and watched grimly as his friend walked off quickly in the direction of his street. At last, clenching his teeth and tightening his fists, swearing that he'd squeeze Porfiry Petrovich like a lemon that very day, he climbed the stairs to try to relieve Pulkheriya Aleksandrovna, who was already feeling anxious because of their long absence.

When Raskolnikov arrived at his building, his temples were damp with sweat and he was breathing heavily. He quickly climbed the stairs, entered his unlocked room, and immediately fastened the door with the hook. Then in a fearful, frantic manner, he rushed to the corner, to the very same hole underneath the wallpaper where he had stashed the items, thrust in his hand, and for several minutes searched the opening carefully, examining every nook and cranny and all the folds of the wallpaper. Not finding anything, he stood up and took a deep breath. As he had been approaching Bakaleev's house a while ago, he'd suddenly imagined that some item, some small chain, cuff link, or even the paper in which the items were wrapped, with the old woman's marks on it, might somehow have slid down and gotten lost in a little crack, and then might suddenly emerge before him as unexpected and incontrovertible evidence.

He stood as if lost in thought, and a strange, humble, half-vacant grin crossed his lips. At last he picked up his cap and quietly left the room. His thoughts were muddled. He was still preoccupied as he emerged from the gate.

"There he is! That's him!" cried a loud voice. He raised his head.

The caretaker was standing at the door of his little room and pointing him out to a small man who looked like a tradesman, dressed in a vest and some sort of long robe, and who from a distance very much resembled a peasant woman. His head, in a soiled cap, hung down, and his entire figure seemed stooped. His flabby, wrinkled face indicated that he was over fifty; his small, swollen eyes looked grim, stern, and discontented.

"What is it?" asked Raskolnikov, approaching the caretaker.

The tradesman squinted at him sullenly and examined him fixedly and carefully, without hurrying; then he turned away slowly and, without saying a word, walked through the gate and into the street.

"What's all this?" cried Raskolnikov.

"That man was asking if a student lived here; he gave your name and asked whose room you rented. Then you came out, I pointed to you, and he went on his way. That's all."

The caretaker was also a bit perplexed, but not too; he thought a little longer, turned around, and went back into his room.

Raskolnikov rushed after the tradesman and saw him right away, walking along the other side of the street at his previous steady and unhurried pace, his eyes lowered to the ground, as if thinking about something. He soon caught up with him, and for some time walked along behind him; at last he came even with him and glanced into his face from alongside. The man noticed him right away, looked at him quickly, but lowered his eyes once more. They continued walking thus for another minute, one next to the other, without exchanging a word.

"You were asking the caretaker . . . about me?" Raskolnikov said at last, but somehow in a low voice.

The tradesman made no reply and didn't even look up. They were silent again.

"Why did you . . . come and ask for me . . . and now you're silent. . . . What's this all about?" Raskolnikov's voice broke off, as if the words were unwilling to be uttered clearly.

This time the tradesman raised his eyes and regarded Raskolnikov with a sinister, gloomy look.

"Moiderer!" he said suddenly in a low but clear, intelligible voice.

Raskolnikov walked along next to him. His legs suddenly felt weak, and a chill ran up his spine; for a moment, his heart skipped a beat, but then it started pounding, as if it had come loose. They continued that way for about a hundred paces, once again in silence.

The tradesman didn't look at him.

"What are you talking about? What? Who's the murderer?" muttered Raskolnikov, barely audibly.

"*You're* the moiderer," he insisted, even more distinctly and commandingly, with a grin of contemptuous triumph, and once more glanced directly at Raskolnikov's pale face and into his lifeless eyes. They both approached the crossing. The tradesman turned into the street on the left and kept going without looking back. Raskolnikov stood still for a long time and watched him go. He saw how the tradesman walked about fifty paces, then turned around and looked at him, remaining motionless on the same spot. It was impossible to make it out, but it seemed to Raskolnikov that this time he smiled again with a cold, contemptuous, triumphant grin.

With faint, weak steps, trembling knees, and a terrible chill, Raskolnikov turned back and climbed the stairs to his little room. He took off his cap, put it on the table, and stood still for about ten minutes. Then, feeling feeble, he lay down on the sofa and stretched out painfully with a weak groan. His eyes were closed. He lay there for half an hour.

He didn't think about anything. There were some thoughts or fragments of thoughts, some images, disordered and unconnected—faces of people he had seen way back in his childhood or encountered somewhere only once and couldn't really even remember; the bell tower of the Voznesensky Church; the billiard table in a tavern with some officer standing next to it; the smell of cigars in a basement tobacco shop; a beer hall; a back staircase, completely dark, splattered with dirty dishwater and strewn with eggshells; and the sound of Sunday church bells floating in from somewhere. . . . Objects shifted and swirled, like a whirlwind. He even found some things pleasant and tried to hold on to them, but they faded. In general, something oppressed him inside, but not too much. Sometimes he even felt good. . . . The slight chill hadn't passed, but that, too, was almost pleasant to experience.

He heard Razumikhin's hurried steps and his voice; he closed his eyes and pretended to be asleep. Razumikhin opened the door and stood on the threshold for some time, as if in thought. Then he quietly stepped into the room and cautiously approached the sofa. He could hear Nastasya's whisper:

"Don't disturb him. Let him have a good sleep; then he'll have something to eat."

"Indeed," replied Razumikhin.

They both left quietly and closed the door. Another half hour passed. Raskolnikov opened his eyes and lay back again, clasping his hands behind his head.

"Who is he? Who's that person who emerged from under the earth? Where was he, and what did he see? He saw everything, no doubt. Where was he standing then and how could he see? Why is he appearing only now from under the ground? How could he have seen—is it possible? Hmm . . ." continued Raskolnikov, growing cold and shuddering. "And the jeweler's case that Nikolai found behind the door: was that also possible? Evidence? You overlook one of a million details—and there's evidence the size of an Egyptian pyramid! A fly passed by, and it saw! Is this all possible?"

With loathing he suddenly felt how weak he had grown, physically weak.

"I should've known all this," he thought with a bitter grin. "Knowing myself, having had a *premonition* about myself, how did I dare take an axe and get stained with blood? I should have known ahead of time. . . . Eh! I really did know beforehand!" he whispered in despair.

"No, those people aren't made like this; a true *master*, to whom all things are permitted, destroys Toulon, carries out carnage in Paris, *forgets* an army in Egypt, *loses* half a million men in a Moscow campaign, and gets away with a clever pun at Vilna. And then, after his death they erect statues to him—it goes without saying that *everything* is permitted to him. No, clearly such men are not made of flesh and blood, but of bronze!"

All of a sudden, an unexpected extraneous thought almost made him laugh:

"Napoleon, the pyramids, Waterloo—and a scraggly, vile widow, an old woman, a moneylender, with a red trunk under her bed—what a mouthful even for Porfiry Petrovich to swallow! How could he do it? His sense of aesthetics would interfere: would a Napoleon stoop to crawl under an 'old woman's' bed? Hey, what nonsense!"

At times he felt that he was raving: he would sink into a mood of feverish excitement.

"That old crone is rubbish!" he thought heatedly and impetuously. "The old woman was no more than a mistake; she wasn't the point! The old woman was merely an illness. . . . I wanted to hurry up and overstep. . . . I didn't kill a person, I killed a principle! A principle is what I killed, but I didn't step over at all; I remained on this side. . . . The only thing I managed to do was to kill. And, it turns out, I didn't even do that right. . . . A principle? Why did that fool Razumikhin abuse the socialists a while ago? They're hardworking folk, businesslike people, contributing to the 'common good.' No, life's been given to me once and it'll never come again; I don't want to wait for the 'common good.' I want to live myself, or else it's better not to live at all. What of it? I merely didn't want to pass a hungry mother, clutching a ruble in my pocket, while waiting for the 'common good.' They say, 'I'll carry one small brick for universal happiness and as a result I'll feel my heart at peace.' Ha, ha! Why did you leave me out? I live only once, and I also want to. . . . Hey, I'm an aesthetic louse, nothing more," he added suddenly and burst out laughing like a madman. "Yes, I'm really a louse," he continued, clinging to his thought with malice, burrowing into it, playing with it, enjoying it. "If only because in the first place, I'm now thinking about the fact that I'm a louse; secondly, for a whole month I've been pestering most gracious Providence, summoning it as a witness that I'm undertaking this not for my own sake and whims, I said, but because I have a majestic and worthwhile goal. Ha, ha! And, in the third place, because I proposed to observe all possible fairness in the execution, weights and measures, and arithmetic: out of all the lice on earth, I picked the least useful and, after killing her, proposed to take from her exactly as much as I needed for the first step, no more, no less (and the remainder, it goes without saying, would go to a monastery, according to the terms of her will—ha, ha!). . . . Therefore, therefore, ultimately I'm a louse," he added, grinding his teeth, "because I myself, perhaps, am even viler and filthier than that murdered louse, and I had a *premonition* earlier that I'd say that to myself *after* I killed her! Can anything compare with such horror? Oh, the vulgarity! The baseness! Oh, how I understand the 'Prophet' with a scimitar on a steed. Allah commands, and 'trembling' creatures obey! The Prophet was correct, completely correct, when he placed a won-der-ful artillery battery across a street somewhere and mowed down the innocent and the guilty, without deigning to explain himself! Obey, trembling creature, and *do not desire*, because that's not your business! Oh, never, never will I forgive that old woman!"

His hair was soaked with perspiration, his trembling lips were parched, his motionless gaze directed at the ceiling.

"My mother, my sister, how I loved them! Why do I hate them now? Yes, I hate them, I physically hate them. I can't stand to have them near me. . . . A while ago I went up and kissed my mother, I remember. . . . To embrace her and think that if she knew, then . . . could I really have told her then? I'm capable of that. . . . Hmm! *She* should be the same as I am," he added, thinking with effort as if struggling with approaching delirium. "How, how I hate that old woman now! It seems I'd kill her again if she ever came back to life! Poor Lizaveta! Why did she turn up there? It's strange, however: why do I hardly think about her, as if I hadn't killed her? Lizaveta! Sonya! Poor, meek creatures with meek eyes. . . . Dear souls! Why don't they weep? Why don't they moan? They give away everything . . . they look meekly and softly. . . . Sonya, Sonya! Gentle Sonya!"

He drifted into sleep; it seemed strange to him that he didn't remember how he turned up on the street. It was already late evening. Twilight was growing deeper, the full moon was shining more and more brightly, but the air was somehow very stuffy. Crowds of people were walking along the streets; craftsmen and workers were returning home, others were out for a stroll; the air smelled of lime, dust, and stagnant water. Raskolnikov was gloomy and anxious: he remembered very well that he had left home with some intention, that he had something to do, and that he should hurry, but he had forgotten what it was. Suddenly he stopped and noticed that on the other side of the street, on the sidewalk, stood a man waving to him. He crossed the street toward him, but suddenly this man turned and walked away as if nothing had happened, his head lowered, without turning around or giving any sign that he had waved. "Enough of this—did he wave?" wondered Raskolnikov and began following him. Before going ten paces, he suddenly recognized him and became frightened; it was the former tradesman, wearing the same robe and with the same stoop. Raskolnikov walked along at a distance; his heart was pounding; they headed into an alley—the tradesman still didn't turn around. "Does he know that I'm following him?" wondered Raskolnikov. The tradesman went through the gate to a large house. Raskolnikov approached the gate and began looking: would he glance back and beckon to him? Indeed, after passing through the gateway and emerging into the courtyard, the tradesman suddenly turned around and seemed to beckon to him again. Raskolnikov passed through the gateway, too, but the tradesman was no longer in the courtyard. He must have turned at once into the first stairway. Raskolnikov rushed after him. In fact, two flights above, he heard someone's measured, unhurried footsteps. It was strange, but this staircase seemed familiar! There was a window on the first floor; moonlight was shining through the glass mournfully and mysteriously; here's the second floor. Oh! It was the same apartment in which the painters had been working. . . . How come he hadn't known that right away? The footsteps of the man ahead died away. "He must have stopped, or else he's hiding somewhere." Here's the third floor; should he go on? How quiet it was, even frightening. . . . But he walked on. The sound of his own footsteps scared and alarmed him. "Good Lord, it's so dark! The tradesman must be hiding in some corner. Ah!" The door to the apartment stood open onto the landing; he thought for a bit and then went in. It was very dark and deserted in the entryway; there was not a soul, as if everything had been removed. Quietly, on tiptoe, he went into the living room; the entire room was brightly lit by moonlight. Everything was just as it had been before: chairs, mirror, yellow sofa, and framed pictures. The huge, round copper-red moon shone directly in through the windows. "This stillness is because of the moon," thought Raskolnikov. "It must be posing a riddle now." He stood there and waited, waited a long time; the quieter the moon, the louder his heart pounded, even beginning to hurt. Stillness prevailed. All of a sudden he heard a momentary dry crackling, as if a twig had broken, and then everything became silent again. An awakened fly suddenly bumped into the windowpane and began buzzing plaintively. At that very moment in the corner, between the small wardrobe and the window, he noticed what seemed to be a cloak hanging on the wall. "Why's there a cloak here?" he wondered. "It wasn't there before . . ." He approached it quietly and guessed that someone might be hiding behind it. He cautiously drew back the cloak with his hand and saw a chair on which the old woman sat, all huddled over, holding her head in such a way that he couldn't see her face—but it was she. He stood over her. "She's afraid," he thought and quietly freed the axe from its loop and struck the old woman on the crown of her head once and then again. But it was strange: she didn't even stir under the blows, as if she were made of wood. He grew fearful, bent over, and began looking at her more closely; she bent her head even lower. Then he crouched all the way down to the floor and glanced up at her face; he took one look and froze in horror: the old woman was sitting there, laughing— she was overcome with quiet, inaudible laughter, trying with all her might to make sure he didn't hear her. Suddenly it seemed that the door to her bedroom was opening slightly and there, too, someone was laughing and whispering. Rage overcame him: he began striking the old woman on the head with all his strength, but with each blow of the axe the laughter and whispering from the bedroom sounded stronger and louder, and the old woman shook with mirth. He tried to flee, but the entire entryway was filled with people, the door to the staircase was open, and on the landing, the staircase, and below—stood a crowd of people, side by side, everyone looking, but everyone quiet, all waiting, all silent! His heart skipped a beat, his feet wouldn't budge, and he felt rooted to the spot. . . . He wanted to cry out and—woke up.

He took a deep breath—but, strangely, his dream seemed to continue: his door was wide open and a complete stranger stood on the threshold, staring at him fixedly.

Raskolnikov had not quite opened his eyes completely when he shut them again. He lay on his back and didn't stir. "Is this still my dream or not?" he wondered and opened his eyelids ever so slightly to take a look: the stranger stood on the same spot and was still staring at him. All at once he carefully stepped over the threshold, closed the door behind himself thoughtfully, walked over to the table, waited a minute—all this time not taking his eyes off Raskolnikov—and quietly, without a sound, sat down on a chair next to the sofa. He placed his hat to one side, on the floor, and rested both of his hands on his cane, lowering his chin to his hands. It was apparent that he was prepared to wait a long time. As much as Raskolnikov could see through his eyelashes, this man was no longer young; he was solidly built and had a thick, light-colored, almost white beard . . .

About ten minutes passed. It was still light, but evening was already setting in. It was absolutely still in the room. Not a sound was drifting in, even from the staircase. Only a large fly kept buzzing and beating against the windowpane. At last this became unbearable; Raskolnikov suddenly raised himself and sat up on the sofa.

"Well, say something. What do you want?"

"I knew that you weren't asleep, but merely pretending," the stranger replied peculiarly, grinning serenely. "Allow me to introduce myself: Arkady Ivanovich Svidrigaylov . . ."

PART IV

I

"Can this really be the continuation of my dream?" Raskolnikov wondered again. He stared cautiously and distrustfully at the unexpected guest.

"Svidrigaylov? What nonsense! It couldn't be!" he uttered aloud at last, in perplexity.

The visitor did not seem surprised at all by this exclamation.

"I've come to see you for two reasons: first, for some time I've heard extremely interesting and favorable reports of you, and I wanted to make your acquaintance; second, I hope that perhaps you won't refuse to assist me in an undertaking that directly concerns the interests of your sister, Avdotya Romanovna. As a result of prejudice, she might not agree to see me alone without a recommendation; on the other hand, with your help, I can count on . . ."

"You count badly," Raskolnikov interrupted him.

"May I ask if they just arrived yesterday?"

Raskolnikov made no reply.

"Yesterday, I know. I myself arrived only two days ago. Well, sir, this is what I have to say to you on that score, Rodion Romanovich; I consider it unnecessary to justify myself, but allow me to inquire: in this entire affair, was there, as a matter of fact, anything criminal on my part, that is, judging sensibly and without prejudice?"

Raskolnikov continued examining him in silence.

"The fact that in my own home I pursued a defenseless young

woman and 'insulted her with my vile proposals'—is that it? (I'm jumping ahead!) But you must assume that I'm merely a human being, *et nihil humanum** . . . in a word, that I'm capable of being attracted and falling in love (which, of course, doesn't depend on our own will); then everything can be explained in the most natural manner. Here the whole question is: am I a monster or a victim myself? Well, how can I be a victim? When I proposed to the object of my affections that she run away with me to America or Switzerland, perhaps I nourished the most honorable feelings in myself and even thought I was making arrangements for our mutual happiness! One's reason serves one's passions; perhaps I did more harm to myself than to anyone else!"

"That's not the point," Raskolnikov interrupted with disgust. "You're simply repulsive, whether you're right or not. They don't even want to know you, and they want you to leave. So go away!"

Svidrigaylov suddenly burst out laughing.

"However . . . however, there's no way of knocking you off track!" he said, laughing in a most sincere manner. "I thought I could outwit you, but no, right away you put your finger exactly on the main point!"

"You continue trying to outwit me even now."

"What if I do? What if I do?" repeated Svidrigaylov, laughing aloud. "It's what's called *bonne guerre*,† and the most permissible deceit! But you interrupted me all the same. One way or another, I can state once more: there would've been no unpleasantness if it hadn't been for the incident in the garden. Marfa Petrovna . . ."

"They say you also hastened Marfa Petrovna's end," Raskolnikov interrupted rudely.

"You've heard about that, too? But how could you not have heard? Well, as far as that question of yours is concerned, I really don't know what to say, although my own conscience is absolutely clear on that score. That is, don't think I'm afraid of anything related to that matter. It was all conducted in accord with absolute order and complete accuracy; the medical investigation determined that it was apoplexy

---

* Part of a common misquotation from a comedy by the Roman playwright Terence: "I am a man: nothing human is alien to me" (Latin).

† "Fair enough" (French). Literally, "a good war."

resulting from bathing too soon after consuming a heavy meal, including almost a full bottle of wine; they couldn't come to any other conclusion. . . . No, sir, here's what I've been thinking to myself for some time, especially on the way here, while sitting on the train: didn't I contribute in some way to this entire unfortunate episode, through some moral disturbance or something of that sort? But I concluded that it couldn't possibly be the case."

Raskolnikov started laughing.

"Why should you worry about that?"

"What are you laughing at? Just think: I struck her only twice with a riding switch; it didn't even leave any marks. . . . Please, don't think I'm a cynic; I certainly know how vile it was on my part, and so forth; but I also know for sure that Marfa Petrovna might even have been pleased by my display of passion, so to speak. The business concerning your sister had been wrung out to the last drop. Marfa Petrovna had been forced to stay at home for two days; there was no reason for her to go into town; everyone was fed up with that letter of hers. (Did you hear about the reading of that letter?) Suddenly these two blows of the switch came down upon her like a bolt out of the blue. The first thing she did was order the carriage to be harnessed! I'm not even referring to the fact that women sometimes find it very, very pleasant when they're insulted, in spite of their apparent indignation. They all have these moments; have you noticed that, in general, people like being insulted very, very much? But it's particularly true for women. One can even say that it's the only thing they subsist on."

For a while Raskolnikov thought about getting up and leaving to end the meeting. But a certain curiosity and even some calculation restrained him for a moment.

"Do you like to fight?" he asked absentmindedly.

"No, not much," Svidrigaylov replied calmly. "I almost never fought with Marfa Petrovna. We lived very amicably, and she was always content with me. I used a riding switch only twice during all our seven years together (if you don't count a third time that was, however, extremely ambiguous): the first time—two months after our marriage, right after our arrival in the country, and now this latest incident. Did you think I was some sort of monster, a reactionary, or a taskmaster? Ha, ha. . . .

By the way, don't you recall, Rodion Romanovich, how several years ago, during the time of beneficial openness, a certain landowner—I forgot his name!—was slandered for having beaten a German woman in a railway car, don't you remember? At that time, in that same year, it seems that 'the Disgraceful Act of the Century' occurred. (Well, do you recall the public reading of Pushkin's *Egyptian Nights*?* Those dark eyes? Oh, where is the golden age of our youth?) Well, sir, here's my opinion: I don't sympathize at all with the gentleman who struck that German woman, because, as a matter of fact, what's there to sympathize with? But at the same time, how can I not state that at times one comes across such provocative 'German women' that, it seems to me, not a single progressive person could manage to answer for himself. At the time nobody regarded the incident from this point of view, yet it's the genuinely humane one, it really is, sir."

After saying this, Svidrigaylov suddenly burst out laughing again. It was clear to Raskolnikov that this man was someone whose mind was firmly set on something and who was also very crafty.

"You must have spent several days without anyone to talk to," Raskolnikov said.

"Almost. Why do you ask? Are you surprised that I'm such an obliging fellow?"

"No, I'm surprised that you're too obliging."

"Because I haven't been offended by the rudeness of your questions? That's it, isn't it? Yes . . . why should I be offended? You've asked and I've answered," he added with an astonishing expression of open-heartedness. "I'm not particularly interested in anything at all, so help me God," he continued pensively. "Especially now, not busy with anything. . . . However, you may think I'm trying to ingratiate myself with you for some reason, all the more so since I have business with your sister, as I myself stated. But I'll tell you candidly: I'm very bored! Especially these last three days, so I'm even glad to see you. . . . Don't be angry, Rodion Romanovich, but for some reason you yourself seem terribly strange to me. As you wish, but there's something about you:

---

* A newspaper article published in 1861 attacked a woman in Perm who read Pushkin's unfinished short story "Egyptian Nights" "shamelessly and with provocative gestures."

precisely now—that is, not at this very minute, but now in general. . . . Well, well, I won't, I won't, don't be so overcast! I'm not such a boor as you think."

Raskolnikov regarded him gloomily.

"Perhaps you're not a boor at all," he said. "It even seems to me that you come from very good society or, at least, if need be, you know how to behave like a decent person."

"I'm not particularly interested in anyone's opinion," Svidrigaylov replied matter-of-factly, even with a hint of arrogance. "And therefore why not be a vulgarian for a while, when it's so appropriate to appear as such in our climate and . . . and especially if one's naturally inclined to be so," he added, laughing again.

"I've heard, however, that you have many acquaintances here. You're someone who's said to be 'not lacking in connections.' What use do you have for me, unless it's for some special purpose?"

"You're right that I have acquaintances," Svidrigaylov replied, bypassing the main point. "I've already met with them; I've been wasting time here for the last two days; I recognize them, and they seem to know me. The fact is, I'm well dressed and a person of considerable means; even the peasant reforms passed us by: my income, derived from forests and water meadows, remains undiminished. But . . . I won't go back there; I was already sick of all that. I've been wandering around here for three days, and I haven't seen anyone. . . . What a city this is! I mean, how did we create it, tell me please! A city of clerks and all sorts of seminarians! True, there's much that I didn't notice before, about eight years ago, when I was whiling away my time around here. . . . But now I'm counting only on anatomy, so help me God!"

"What kind of anatomy?"

"I mean those clubs, those Dussot's, and those spits of land,* perhaps, that's progress for you—well, that'll all be without me," he continued, once more taking no note of the question. "Besides, who wants to be a cardsharp?"

"Were you also a cardsharp?"

---

* Dussot's was a famous hotel and restaurant in St. Petersburg; the spit of land is probably a reference to the fashionable spot at the end of Yelagin Island.

"How could we have done without that? We made up a whole group, extremely respectable, some eight years ago; we spent time together; and, you know, we were people of refined manners, some poets, some capitalists. In general, in Russian society, those with the best manners are those who have been beaten—did you ever notice that? I only let myself go when I moved to the country. Nevertheless, they almost put me in jail then for my debts, and for some trouble with that Greek from Nezhin. That's when Marfa Petrovna happened to show up, bargained with him, and ransomed me for thirty thousand silver rubles. (I owed a total of seventy thousand.) We were legally married, and she carried me off at once to her estate in the country, as if I were her treasure. She was five years my senior. She loved me. I didn't leave the country for seven years. Note well: all her life she held that document for thirty thousand against me, made out in someone else's name, so if I ever took it into my head to rebel, I'd fall right into the trap! And she'd have done it! Women have no trouble reconciling such things."

"If it hadn't been for that document, would you have flown the coop?"

"I don't know what to say. I was hardly constrained by that document. I didn't want to travel anywhere; Marfa Petrovna invited me to go abroad several times, seeing that I was bored. So what? I had been abroad before and had always found it sickening. There was no particular reason: you look and the dawn comes up, there's the Bay of Naples, the sea, and somehow one feels sad. The worst part is that you really do feel sad about something! No, it's better to stay in one's own country: here, at least, you can blame other people for everything and manage to justify yourself. Now I might join an expedition to the North Pole, because *j'ai le vin mauvais;*[*] I hate drinking and, besides that, there's nothing else left to do. I've tried. They say that on Sunday Berg is going to attempt an ascent in an enormous hot-air balloon in the Yusupov Garden,[†] and that he's inviting passengers for a fee. Is that true?"

"Would you go up with him?"

---

[*] "Drinking makes me mean" (French).

[†] Wilhelm Berg was a showman and adventurer who organized hot-air balloon rides in Petersburg.

"Me? No . . . just so . . ." Svidrigaylov muttered, as if considering seriously it.

"Is he really serious?" wondered Raskolnikov.

"No, the document didn't constrain me," Svidrigaylov continued pensively. "It was my own decision to stay in the country. Soon it'll be a year since Marfa Petrovna returned that document to me on my name day and, in addition, presented me with a significant sum of money. She had her own capital. 'You see how I trust you, Arkady Ivanovich,' that's just how she put it. You don't believe that's what she said? Then know this: I became a respectable landowner in the country; I'm well known in the neighborhood. I also used to order some books by mail. At first Marfa Petrovna approved, but then she grew afraid that I'd overdo it."

"It seems you really miss Marfa Petrovna?"

"Me? Possibly. It really is possible. By the way, do you believe in ghosts?"

"What kind of ghosts?"

"Ordinary ghosts. What do you mean, what kind?"

"And do you believe in them?"

"Not really, *pour vous plaire.**. . . That is, I don't really disbelieve . . .'"

"Have you ever seen any?"

Svidrigaylov regarded him somehow oddly.

"Marfa Petrovna's kind enough to visit me," he said, curling his mouth into a strange smile.

"What do you mean, visit you?"

"She's come to see me three times already. I saw her first on the very day of her funeral, an hour after we were at the cemetery. It was on the eve of my departure to come here. The second time was two days ago, en route, at dawn, at the Malaya Vishera Station; and the third time was two hours ago, at the apartment where I'm staying, in my room. I was alone."

"Were you awake?"

---

* "To please you" (French).

"Absolutely. I was awake all three times. She comes, chats for a minute or two, and then leaves by the door, always by the door. It's even as if I can hear the door open and close."

"Why was it that I thought something like that might happen to you?" Raskolnikov remarked suddenly and was astonished at the same time that he had said it. He was very agitated.

"So-o-o. You really thought that?" Svidrigaylov asked in amazement. "Really? Well, didn't I say that there was a common bond between us, eh?"

"You never said that!" Raskolnikov replied abruptly and heatedly.

"Didn't I?"

"No!"

"It seemed to me that I did. Just before, when I came in and saw that you were lying there with your eyes closed, pretending to sleep—right then I said to myself, 'He's the one!'"

"What do you mean, 'the one'? What are you talking about?" cried Raskolnikov.

"What am I talking about? I really don't know," Svidrigaylov mumbled frankly and seemed somehow confused.

They were silent for a minute. They both stared at each other with rapt attention.

"It's all nonsense!" Raskolnikov cried with irritation. "What does she say to you when she comes to visit?"

"She? Just imagine, she talks about the most trivial things; you have to marvel at her: that's just what makes me so angry. The first time she came (you know, I was tired: the funeral service, the hymns, then the litany, and the meal—at last I remained alone in my study; I lit up a cigar and was lost in thought), she entered in through the door. 'And you,' she says, 'Arkady Ivanovich, in the midst of all your bustle today, you forgot to wind the clock in the dining room.' As a matter of fact, all seven years I myself used to wind the clock once a week, and if I forgot—she'd always remind me. The next day I was already on my way here. I arrived at the station at daybreak—I'd dozed off during the night, exhausted, barely able to keep my eyes open—to get some coffee; I look—and Marfa Petrovna suddenly sits down next to me, holding a deck of cards. 'Shall I tell your fortune for the trip with these cards, Arkady Ivanovich?' She was a master at fortune-telling. I won't ever forgive myself for not letting her do it! Frightened, I ran away, and just then I heard the bell announce the train. Today I was sitting with a full stomach after a terrible dinner from an eating house—I was sitting there and smoking—all of a sudden Marfa Petrovna shows up again, all dressed up, in her new green silk dress with a very long train. 'How do you do, Arkady Ivanovich! How do you like my dress? Aniska doesn't make them like this.' (Aniska's the seamstress in the country, a former serf, who learned to sew in Moscow—she's a pretty girl.) She stood there and turned around in front of me. I examined the dress, then looked carefully into her face: 'Why, Marfa Petrovna, do you come to see me and trouble me with such trivial matters?' 'Ah, good Lord, my dear, it's impossible to trouble you with anything!' I say to tease her: 'Marfa Petrovna, I want to get married.' 'That's just like you, Arkady Ivanovich; it's not very honorable: you've hardly managed to bury your wife, and you want to go off and get married. If you could only choose well, but I know that nothing will come of it either for her or for you, and you'll only make good people laugh.' She said this and then up and left; her train seemed to rustle as she went out. What nonsense, isn't it?"

"Perhaps you're just telling lies," replied Raskolnikov.

"I rarely tell lies," answered Svidrigaylov pensively, as if not noticing the rudeness of the question.

"And before this, did you ever see any ghosts?"

"N . . . no, well, I did, only once, six years ago. I had a house serf, Filka; we'd just buried him. I forgot that and shouted, 'Filka, bring me my pipe!' and he came in and went right to the cabinet where I keep my pipes. I sat there thinking, 'He's taking revenge on me' because we'd had a bad quarrel just before his death. 'How dare you,' I said, 'appear before me with a torn shirt? Get out, you scoundrel!' He turned and left and never came again. At the time, I didn't tell Marfa Petrovna. I was about to have a memorial service said for him, but then I felt ashamed."

"You should see a doctor."

"I'm aware without your help that I'm not well, but I really don't know what's the matter with me; in my opinion, I'm five times healthier than you are. I didn't ask whether you believe that people see ghosts. I asked whether you believe that ghosts exist."

"No, nothing could make me believe that!" Raskolnikov cried, even with some malice.

"What do people usually say?" muttered Svidrigaylov, as if to himself, looking to one side and tilting his head slightly. "They say, 'You must be ill; what you see is merely the result of unreal delirium.' But there's no strict logic to that. I agree that ghosts appear only to sick people, but that merely proves that they can appear only to sick people, and not that they don't exist at all."

"Of course they don't," Raskolnikov insisted irritably.

"They don't? Is that what you think?" continued Svidrigaylov, regarding him steadily. "Well, let's say we reason like this (help me out here!): 'Ghosts, so to speak, are shreds and fragments of other worlds, their beginning. A healthy person, naturally, has no need to see them because he's primarily a being of this earth; therefore, he must live only his earthly life, for fullness' sake and for orderliness. But if he falls slightly ill, if the normal earthly order of the organism is destroyed, then the possibility of another world begins to open up; the sicker the person, the more contact with the other world, so that when this person dies, he passes immediately into the other world.' I started to think about this a long time ago. If you believe in a future life, then you can believe in this line of reasoning."

"I don't believe in a future life," said Raskolnikov.

Svidrigaylov sat there, deep in thought.

"What if there are only spiders there or something of that sort?" he said suddenly.

"He's insane," thought Raskolnikov.

"Eternity is always presented to us as an idea that we can't grasp, as something enormous, enormous! Why does it have to be enormous? All of a sudden, instead of all that, imagine there'll be a little room, something like a country bathhouse, sooty, with spiders in all the corners, and that's the whole of eternity. You know, I sometimes imagine it like that."

"But surely, surely you can imagine something more consoling and more just than that?" Raskolnikov cried, feeling pained.

"More just? How can we know? Perhaps that is just, and, you know, I'd arrange it exactly like that!" replied Svidrigaylov, smiling vaguely.

A chill seized Raskolnikov at this hideous answer. Svidrigaylov raised his head, stared at him intently, and burst out laughing.

"No, just think about this," he cried. "A half hour ago, we'd never seen each other, we considered ourselves enemies, with some unfinished business between us; we left that matter behind, and now look at how far we've come! Well, wasn't I telling the truth when I said that we were both cut from the same cloth?"

"Do me a favor," Raskolnikov continued with irritation. "Allow me to ask you to explain yourself immediately and inform me as to why you've bestowed the honor of a visit on me . . . and . . . and . . . I'm in a hurry, I have no time, and I have to leave soon . . ."

"Certainly, certainly. Your sister, Avdotya Romanovna, is planning to marry Petr Petrovich Luzhin, right?"

"Might it be possible somehow to sidestep any questions about my sister and not mention her name? I don't even understand how you dare utter her name in my presence, if you really are Svidrigaylov."

"But I came precisely to talk about her; how can I help mentioning her name?"

"All right; speak, but quickly!"

"I'm sure that you have already formed an opinion about this Mr. Luzhin, a relative of mine through marriage, even if you spent only a half hour with him or heard something about him reported faithfully and accurately. He's no match for Avdotya Romanovna. In my opinion, Avdotya Romanovna is sacrificing herself in an extremely generous and improvident manner for . . . for her family. It seemed to me, as a result of all I've heard about you, that you, on your part, would be very pleased if this marriage could be broken off without harming her interests. Now, having met you personally, I'm even sure of this."

"This is all very innocent, coming from you; excuse me, I wanted to say 'impudent,'" said Raskolnikov.

"That is, you wish to say that I'm concerned only for my own interests. Don't worry, Rodion Romanovich. If I were concerned only for my own advantage, I wouldn't have spoken so openly; I'm not such a fool after all. On this score I'll reveal a psychological oddity to you.

A little while ago, justifying my own love for Avdotya Romanovna, I said that I myself was a victim. Well, you should know that I feel no love for her now, none at all; I even think it strange that I experienced something before . . ."

"Due to your idleness and depravity," Raskolnikov interrupted.

"I really am a depraved and idle person. Besides, your sister has so many fine qualities that how could I not be somewhat enthralled by them? But this is all nonsense, as I see now."

"Have you known this for long?"

"I began noticing it even before; I was convinced of it for sure two days ago, almost at the very moment when I arrived in Petersburg. Besides, while still in Moscow I imagined that I was coming here to seek Avdotya Romanovna's hand and become Mr. Luzhin's rival."

"Excuse me for interrupting you. Do me a favor: is it possible to curtail your account and get right to the purpose of your visit? I'm in a hurry and have to leave . . ."

"With the greatest pleasure. Having arrived here and now having decided to undertake a certain . . . voyage, I'd like to carry out all the necessary preliminary arrangements. My children have remained with their aunt; they're well off, and they don't need me at all. And besides, what sort of father am I? I've retained only the money that Marfa Petrovna gave me a year ago. That will suffice for me. Excuse me, now I'll move on to the matter at hand. Before this trip that I may undertake, I wish to conclude my business with Mr. Luzhin. It's not that I can't stand him, but he was the cause of my quarrel with Marfa Petrovna, when I found out that she had concocted this wedding. Now I wish to arrange a meeting with Avdotya Romanovna through your good offices, and perhaps, in your presence, explain to her, in the first place, that not only will she receive not the least gain from Mr. Luzhin, but also that it will certainly entail even a significant loss. Then, begging her forgiveness for all the recent unpleasantness, I would ask her permission to present her with ten thousand rubles, thus enabling a break with Mr. Luzhin, which I am sure she would not oppose if it were possible."

"You're insane, really, insane!" cried Raskolnikov, not so much angry as astonished. "How dare you speak like this?"

"I knew that you'd holler; but, in the first place, even though I'm not wealthy, I have ten thousand rubles to spare, that is, I have absolutely, absolutely no need for them. If Avdotya Romanovna doesn't accept them, I'll probably spend them even more foolishly. That's the first thing. Secondly: my conscience is completely clear; I have no ulterior motives in making this offer. Believe it or not, but later both you and Avdotya Romanovna will find that out. The thing is that I really did cause significant trouble and unpleasantness to your sister, whom I greatly respect; therefore, feeling genuine remorse, I sincerely desire—not to redeem myself financially or pay her for the unpleasantness, but simply to do something advantageous for her, on the grounds that I have not reserved the right for myself to perform only evil acts. If in my proposal there was even a one-millionth part of calculation, I wouldn't have made it so openly; and I wouldn't be offering her only ten thousand, when only five weeks ago I was offering her more. Besides, very, very soon I may be marrying a young woman, and consequently, that fact alone should eliminate any suspicion that I still have designs on Avdotya Romanovna. In conclusion, I will say that in marrying Mr. Luzhin, Avdotya Romanovna will be accepting the same money, only from a different source. . . . Don't be angry, Rodion Romanovich; consider this calmly and coolly."

While saying this, Svidrigaylov himself was extremely calm and cool.

"I ask you to finish," said Raskolnikov. "In any case, it's unforgivably insolent."

"Not at all. If that were the case, a person could only do evil to another person in this world, and wouldn't have the right to do even a tiny bit of good, because of empty conventional formalities. That's absurd. If, for example, I were to die and leave this sum of money to your sister in my will, would she really refuse to accept it?"

"Very possibly."

"I doubt that, sir. However, if so, then let it be so. But ten thousand—is a fine thing on occasion. In any case, I ask you to convey my offer to Avdotya Romanovna."

"No, I won't."

"In that case, Rodion Romanovich, I myself will be forced to seek a private meeting with her, which would mean upsetting her."

"And if I convey the message, you won't seek a private meeting?"

"I really don't know what to say. I'd very much like to see her once."

"Don't count on it."

"I'm sorry. However, you don't know me. Perhaps we'll become closer."

"You think we'll become closer?"

"Why not?" Svidrigaylov said with a smile, standing and picking up his hat. "I really didn't come here wishing to trouble you for long; I wasn't even expecting very much, although this morning your physiognomy impressed me . . ."

"Where did you see me this morning?" Raskolnikov asked uneasily.

"By chance, sir. . . . It seems to me that in some way you're very similar to me. . . . Don't be upset; I'm not a bore; I got on with cardsharps, I didn't bore Prince Svirbey, my distant relative and grandee, I was able to write in Mrs. Prilukova's album about Raphael's painting of the Madonna, I spent seven years with Marfa Petrovna without leaving the country, I spent nights in Vyazemsky's lodging house on Haymarket Square in the old days, and perhaps I'll go up in Berg's hot-air balloon."

"Well, all right, sir. Allow me to ask, will you leave on your travels soon?"

"What travels?"

"That is, on your 'voyage'? You said it yourself."

"On my voyage? Ah, yes! As a matter of fact, I did mention a voyage. . . . Well, that's a very big question. . . . If you only knew what you were asking!" he added suddenly in a loud voice and gave a brief laugh. "Perhaps, instead of a voyage, I'll get married; they're trying to find me a bride."

"Here?"

"Yes."

"When did you find time for that?"

"I'd very much like to meet with Avdotya Romanovna once. I'm making a serious request. Well, good-bye. . . . Ah, yes! Here's what I forgot! Tell your sister, Rodion Romanovich, that she was left three thousand rubles in Marfa Petrovna's will. That's definitely the case. Marfa Petrovna made the arrangement a week before she died, and it was in my presence. Avdotya Romanovna can receive the money in about two or three weeks' time."

"Are you telling the truth?"

"Yes. Tell her. Well, sir, I'm at your service. I'm staying not far from here."

As he was leaving, Svidrigaylov met Razumikhin in the doorway.

II

It was already almost eight o'clock; they both were hurrying to Bakaleev's house, hoping to arrive before Luzhin did.

"Well, who was that?" asked Razumikhin as soon as they got out to the street.

"It was Svidrigaylov, that same landowner in whose house my sister was insulted when she was working there as a governess. She left as a result of his amorous advances, driven away by his wife, Marfa Petrovna. Afterward this same Marfa Petrovna asked Dunya's forgiveness, and now she's suddenly died. We were talking about her a while ago. I don't know why, but I'm afraid of that man. He arrived here right after his wife's funeral. He's very strange and has resolved to do something. . . . It's as if he knows something. . . . Dunya must be protected from him . . . that's what I wanted to tell you, you hear?"

"Protected! What can he do to Avdotya Romanovna? Well, thank you, Rodya, for telling me this. . . . We'll, we'll protect her! Where does he live?"

"I don't know."

"Why didn't you ask? Hey, it's a pity! But I'll find out!"

"Did you see him?" asked Raskolnikov after a silence.

"Yes, I did; I got a good look at him."

"Did you really see him? Clearly?" insisted Raskolnikov.

"Yes, I clearly remember him; I could pick him out of a thousand. I have a good memory for faces."

They were both silent again for a while.

"Hmm . . . all right," muttered Raskolnikov. "Otherwise, you know . . . I wondered . . . it seemed to me . . . that it might have been an apparition."

"What are you talking about? I don't understand you very well."

"All of you keep insisting," Raskolnikov continued, twisting his mouth into a smile, "that I'm mad; it seemed to me now that perhaps I really am mad and that I just saw an apparition!"

"What are you saying?"

"But who knows? Perhaps I really am mad, and everything that's happened these last few days, everything, perhaps has only been in my imagination . . ."

"Hey, Rodya! They've upset you again! What did he say? Why did he come?"

Raskolnikov made no reply. Razumikhin thought for a moment.

"Well, listen to my report," he began. "I dropped in on you and you were asleep. Then I had dinner and went to see Porfiry. Zametov was still with him. I tried to speak, but nothing came of it. I couldn't find the right way to say it. It's as if they really don't understand and won't be able to, but they're not ashamed of it. I drew Porfiry over to the window and began talking to him, but once again nothing came of it: he looked away and I did, too. Finally, I raised my fist to his mug and said that I'd smash him, in a familial sort of way. He merely looked at me. I spat and left, and that was that. It was very foolish. I didn't exchange a word with Zametov. Only you see: I thought that I'd ruined things, but then, as I was going down the stairs, I had an idea, it dawned on me: what are we worrying about? If there was any danger to you, or anything of the sort, then of course. But what's it to you? You're not involved in it, so the hell with them; we'll laugh at them later; and if I were in your place, I'd still try to mystify them further. They'll be so ashamed afterward! The hell with them; later we can beat them up, but for now, we'll just laugh!"

"Of course, that's true," replied Raskolnikov. "What will you say tomorrow?" he wondered to himself. Strange to say, but up until this moment it never occurred to him to wonder, "What will Razumikhin think when he finds out?" With this thought, Raskolnikov stared at him intently. He was not much interested in Razumikhin's account of his visit to Porfiry: so much had been lost and gained since then!

In the corridor they bumped into Luzhin: he showed up precisely at eight o'clock and was searching for the number of the room, so all three of them entered together, but without looking at or greeting each other. The young men went in first; for propriety's sake, Petr Petrovich hesitated a while in the entryway, taking off his coat. Pulkheriya Aleksandrovna came out promptly to meet him on the threshold. Dunya greeted her brother.

Petr Petrovich came in and rather politely, although with redoubled solemnity, exchanged bows with the ladies. However, he looked as if he was a bit confused and had yet to recover. Pulkheriya Aleksandrovna also seemed a bit embarrassed and immediately hastened to seat them all at a round table where a samovar was boiling. Dunya and Luzhin were seated diametrically across from each other. Razumikhin and Raskolnikov were facing Pulkheriya Aleksandrovna—Razumikhin was closer to Luzhin, Raskolnikov next to his sister.

There was a moment of silence. Without hurrying, Petr Petrovich took out a cambric handkerchief that smelled of cologne and blew his nose with the look of a virtuous man, but one whose dignity was still somewhat offended, and who had firmly resolved to demand an explanation. Back in the entryway, a thought occurred to him: to keep his coat on and leave, thus severely and impressively punishing the two women, and making them feel the entire situation at once. But he'd been unable to make that decision. In addition, this man didn't appreciate uncertainty, and it was necessary to clarify the situation: if his instructions had been so blatantly ignored, that meant there was some reason for it; therefore, it was better to find out right now. There would always be time to punish them, and the power to do so was in his hands.

"I hope your journey was agreeable?" he said, addressing Pulkheriya Aleksandrovna formally.

"Yes, thank God, Petr Petrovich."

"I'm extremely glad, ma'am. And Avdotya Romanovna's not too tired, either?"

"I'm young and strong; I don't tire easily, but Mama had a very difficult trip," replied Dunechka.

"What's to be done, ma'am; our national roads are extremely long. So-called Mother Russia is vast. . . . In spite of all my desires, I was unable to meet you yesterday. I hope, however, that everything went without any particular difficulties."

"Alas, no, Petr Petrovich. We felt very disheartened," Pulkheriya Aleksandrovna hastened to declare, with a special intonation. "And if God Himself hadn't sent us Dmitry Prokofich yesterday, we'd have been completely at a loss. Here he is, Dmitry Prokofich Razumikhin," she added, introducing him to Luzhin.

"Why, I've already had the pleasure . . . yesterday," muttered Luzhin, with an unfriendly sidelong glance at Razumikhin; then he frowned and fell silent. In general, Petr Petrovich belonged to that category of people who appear to be extremely cordial in society and, especially, affect politeness but who, once something is not to their liking, immediately lose all their good qualities and begin to resemble sacks of flour more than relaxed and animated society gentlemen. Everyone fell silent once again: Raskolnikov was stubbornly silent, Avdotya Romanovna didn't want to interrupt the silence prematurely, Razumikhin had nothing to say, and so Pulkheriya Aleksandrovna felt anxious again.

"Have you heard that Marfa Petrovna died?" she began, resorting to her main topic of conversation.

"Why yes, I did hear that, ma'am. I was one of the first to learn, and I even came to tell you that Arkady Ivanovich Svidrigaylov, not long after his spouse's funeral, set off at once for Petersburg. That, at least, is the latest news I received."

"Petersburg? Here?" Dunechka asked anxiously, exchanging glances with her mother.

"Precisely so, ma'am; of course, not without some purpose, taking into account the hastiness of his departure and, in general, the previous circumstances."

"Good Lord! Will he really not leave Dunechka in peace even here?" cried Pulkheriya Aleksandrovna.

"It seems to me there's no particular reason for you or Avdotya Romanovna to be alarmed, of course, if you don't wish to have anything to do with him. As for me, I'm making inquiries and will discover where he's staying . . ."

"Ah, Petr Petrovich, you won't believe how you frightened me just now!" continued Pulkheriya Aleksandrovna. "I've seen him only twice, but he seemed horrible to me, horrible! I'm sure that he was the cause of Marfa Petrovna's death."

"It's impossible to arrive at a definite conclusion about that. I have accurate information. I can't argue that perhaps he contributed to hastening the course of events, so to speak, by the moral impact of his insult; but as far as his conduct is concerned and, in general, the moral character of the person himself, I'm in agreement with you. I don't know if he's rich now, or how much precisely Marfa Petrovna left him; I'll find that out in a very short time; but, of course, here in Petersburg, even having any financial resources at hand, he'll resume his former course of action. Of all people of that kind, he's the most depraved man and entirely devoted to vice! I have substantial grounds to assume that Marfa Petrovna, who had the misfortune of loving him and redeeming him from his debts eight years ago, was of service to him in another respect: it was only her efforts and her sacrifice that resulted in suppressing at the outset a criminal matter with an element of beastly and, so to speak, fantastical murder, for which he might very well have been sent packing to Siberia. That's the sort of man he is, if you want to know."

"Ah, Lord!" cried Pulkheriya Aleksandrovna. Raskolnikov was listening carefully.

"Are you telling the truth when you say you have accurate knowledge of this?" asked Dunya, sternly and imposingly.

"I'm only saying what I myself heard in secret from the late Marfa Petrovna. I must observe that from a legal standpoint, this matter is extremely obscure. A certain woman by the name of Resslikh was living here, and it seems, still does; she's a foreigner and, furthermore, a petty moneylender who also engaged in other sorts of business. Mr. Svidrigaylov was recently involved with this Resslikh in some extremely close and mysterious relations. A distant relative was living with her, a niece, it seems, a deaf-mute, a girl of about fifteen or even fourteen, whom this Resslikh despised intensely, reproaching her for every crumb she ate; she even used to beat her mercilessly. One day she was found hanging in the attic. It was ruled a suicide. After the usual procedures, the matter was even concluded, but subsequently it was alleged that the child had been . . . cruelly abused by Svidrigaylov. True, all this is obscure; the testimony came from another German lady, an inveterate liar whose word had no credibility; finally, in the end, no formal charge was brought, thanks to Marfa Petrovna's efforts and money; it was all limited to rumors. However, these rumors were very significant. Of course, Avdotya Romanovna, you've also heard, while at their house, the story of the servant Filipp, who died from being tormented some six years ago, still during the time of serfdom."

"On the contrary, I heard that this Filipp hanged himself."

"Exactly so, ma'am, but Mr. Svidrigaylov's continual regime of persecutions and punishments compelled him or, more accurately, inclined him to his violent end."

"I don't know that for certain," Dunya replied drily. "I've heard only a very strange tale that this Filipp was some sort of hypochondriac, a kind of homespun philosopher; people said that he 'read himself silly,' and that he hanged himself more as a result of taunts, and not as a result of Mr. Svidrigaylov's beatings. In my presence, he treated other people well; the serfs even loved him, although they also accused him of Filipp's death."

"I see, Avdotya Romanovna, that you're suddenly inclined to defend him," observed Luzhin, twisting his mouth into an ambiguous grin. "He's really a devious man and very captivating with ladies; Marfa Petrovna, who died so strangely, stands as a pitiful example of this. I merely hoped my advice would serve you and your mama, in light of his new, undoubtedly imminent attempts. As far as I'm concerned, I'm absolutely convinced that this man will certainly vanish again into debtors' prison. Marfa Petrovna never really had the intention of providing him with any security, considering her own children, and if she left him anything, then it must have been only the most necessary, insignificant, temporary sum, which wouldn't suffice a man with his habits for even a year."

"Petr Petrovich, I beg you," said Dunya, "let's not talk about Svidrigaylov. The subject bores me."

"He just came to see me," Raskolnikov said suddenly, breaking his silence for the first time.

Exclamations arose on all sides, and everyone turned to him. Even Petr Petrovich was agitated.

"He came into my room about an hour and a half ago, while I was asleep; he woke me and introduced himself," continued Raskolnikov. "He was rather relaxed and cheerful, and is absolutely certain that he and I will become close. Meanwhile, he'd very much like and is hoping to arrange a meeting with you, Dunya, and he's asked me to serve as an intermediary. He has a proposal to make to you; he told me what it is. Besides that, he informed me unequivocally that a week before her death, Marfa Petrovna, in her will, arranged to leave you, Dunya, the sum of three thousand rubles, and that you'll be able to receive that money very soon."

"Thank God!" cried Pulkheriya Aleksandrovna, crossing herself. "Pray for her, Dunya, pray for her!"

"It's absolutely true," Luzhin blurted out.

"Well, what else is there?" Dunechka hastened to ask.

"Then he said that he himself was not wealthy and that his entire estate would pass to his children, who are now living with their aunt. Then he said that he was staying not far from me, but where—I don't know and didn't ask . . ."

"But what is it, what on earth is he proposing to Dunechka?" asked the frightened Pulkheriya Aleksandrovna. "Did he tell you?"

"He did."

"What then?"

"I'll tell you later." Raskolnikov fell silent and turned to his tea.

Petr Petrovich took out his watch and looked at it.

"I have to attend to some business and, thus, will not interfere," he added with a somewhat offended look and began to rise from his place.

"Stay here, Petr Petrovich," said Dunya. "You intended to spend the evening here. Besides, you yourself wrote that you wished to discuss some matter with my mother."

"Precisely so, Avdotya Romanovna," Petr Petrovich said imposingly, sitting down in his chair again, but keeping his hat in his hands. "I really did wish to have a discussion with you and your much-esteemed mother, even about some very important matters. But just as your brother can't discuss certain proposals made by Mr. Svidrigaylov in my presence, I also don't wish and can't converse . . . in the presence of others . . . about certain extremely, extremely important matters. Besides, my principal and most pressing request was not fulfilled . . ."

Luzhin made a sour face and fell into a dignified silence.

"Your request that my brother not be present during our meeting was not honored only as a result of my insistence," said Dunya. "You wrote that you'd been insulted by my brother; I think that the matter should be discussed immediately and that you should make peace. If Rodya really did insult you, then he *must* and *will* beg your forgiveness."

Petr Petrovich immediately took heart.

"There are some insults, Avdotya Romanovna, that, in spite of all goodwill, cannot be forgotten, ma'am. There's a line in everything that's dangerous to cross; once having done so, it's impossible to go back."

"That's not exactly what I was talking about, Petr Petrovich," Dunya interrupted with some impatience. "Remember that our entire future depends on whether you can clear all this up and be reconciled as quickly as possible, or not. I can say honestly, from the outset, that I cannot regard this matter otherwise, and that if you value me even slightly, then, even though it's difficult, this whole episode must be concluded today. I repeat, if my brother is to blame, he will ask your forgiveness."

"I'm surprised that you state the problem like that, Avdotya Romanovna," Luzhin said, getting more and more irritated. "While valuing and, so to speak, adoring you, it's possible that, at the same time, I may very much dislike a member of your family. Seeking the happiness of your hand in marriage, at the same time I cannot assume any obligations incompatible with . . ."

"Ah, drop all this touchiness, Petr Petrovich," Dunya interrupted with feeling, "and be the clever and noble man I've always considered you and still want to consider you to be. I made a big promise to you: I'm your fiancée. Trust me in this matter and believe that I can reach an unbiased conclusion. The fact that I take upon myself the role of judge is as much a surprise to my brother as it is to you. When, after receiving your letter, I invited him to come without fail to our meeting today, I didn't communicate to him any of my intentions. You must understand that if you don't make peace, I'll be forced to choose between you: either you or him. That's how the question stands both for him and for you. I don't wish to be mistaken in my choice, nor should I. For you, I'd have to break off with my brother; for my brother, I'd have to break off with you. I want to find out and will be able to learn, for certain, whether he's a brother to me or not. And as for you: am I dear to you, do you value me: are you a husband to me or not?"

"Avdotya Romanovna," Luzhin said, unpleasantly surprised. "Your words are too loaded with meaning for me, too, I might even say, offensive in view of the position I have the honor to hold in relation to you. Without saying a word about the insulting and strange juxtaposition, on one level, between me and . . . an arrogant young man, by your words you're admitting the possibility of breaking the promise you made to me. You say, 'It's me or him.' Therefore, you're demonstrating how little I mean to you. . . . I can't allow this in the relations and . . . obligations existing between us."

"What?" cried Dunya. "I place your interest alongside everything that has been precious in my life up to this point, that which comprised my *entire* life up to now, and suddenly you're offended by the fact that I place too *little* value on you?"

Raskolnikov smiled silently and sarcastically; Razumikhin winced deeply. But Petr Petrovich didn't accept the reproach; on the contrary, he became more and more annoyed and irritated with every word, as if he were starting to enjoy it.

"Love for one's future partner in life, for one's husband, must exceed the love for one's brother," he announced sententiously. "In any case, I can't stand on the same level. . . . Although I insisted a while ago that in your brother's presence I don't wish to declare, and cannot, everything about why I came, nevertheless, I now intend to address your much-esteemed mother regarding a necessary explanation of one principal matter, one that I find offensive. Yesterday your son," he said, turning to Pulkheriya Aleksandrovna, "in the presence of Mr. Rassudkin* (or . . . is that right? Excuse me, I can't remember your surname," he said, bowing politely to Razumikhin), "insulted me by distorting an idea that I conveyed to you in a private conversation, over coffee, namely, that marriage to a poor young woman, one who had already experienced hardship in life, in my opinion, was more advantageous for conjugal relations than marriage to someone who's known prosperity, since it's more propitious for moral development. Your son deliberately exaggerated the meaning of my words to the point of absurdity, accusing me of evil intentions and, in my view, basing his allegations on your correspondence. I'd consider myself fortunate if you, Pulkheriya Aleksandrovna, could convince me of the opposite view and thus set my mind at ease considerably. Please tell me in what terms you conveyed my words in your letter to Rodion Romanovich."

"I don't recall," said Pulkheriya Aleksandrovna in some confusion. "I conveyed them as I myself understood them. I don't know what I wrote to you, Rodya. . . . Perhaps he even did exaggerate something."

"Without your suggestion, he couldn't have exaggerated them."

"Petr Petrovich," Pulkheriya Aleksandrovna proclaimed in a dignified manner. "Proof of the fact that Dunya and I didn't take your words amiss is that we are *here*."

"Well said, Mama!" Dunya replied approvingly.

"So that's my fault as well?" Luzhin said, offended.

"There you go, Petr Petrovich, always blaming Rodion, yet you yourself told an untruth about him in your letter," Pulkheriya Aleksandrovna added, gathering her courage.

"I don't recall that I wrote any untruth, ma'am."

"You wrote," Raskolnikov began abruptly, without turning to Luzhin, "that yesterday I gave some money not to the downtrodden widow, as I really did, but to her daughter (whom I'd never met before yesterday). You wrote this to cause a quarrel between my family and me, and you added something in vile terms about the conduct of this

---

* A garbling of Razumikhin's surname resulting from the confusion of *rassudok* (reason, intellect) and *razum* (reason, mind).

young woman, whom you don't even know. All of that is gossip and baseness."

"Excuse me, sir," replied Luzhin, trembling with rage. "In my letter I enlarged on your qualities and actions solely in fulfillment of your mother's and sister's request to describe to them the condition in which I found you and what sort of impression you made on me. As far as the matter mentioned in my letter is concerned, try to find even a single line that's unjust—that is, that you didn't squander your money and that, in that family, though unfortunate, there were no unworthy people."

"It's my opinion that with all your merits, you aren't worth the little finger of that unfortunate young woman at whom you're casting stones."

"That means you'd be willing to introduce her into the company of your mother and sister?"

"I've already done just that, if you want to know. Today I sat her down right next to my mother and Dunya."

"Rodya!" cried Pulkheriya Aleksandrovna.

Dunechka flushed; Razumikhin knitted his brows. Luzhin smiled caustically and haughtily.

"You may see for yourself, Avdotya Romanovna," he said, "whether any agreement is possible. I hope that now this matter is closed and cleared up once and for all. I shall leave so as not to interfere with the further pleasantness of a family meeting and in the relaying of secrets." (He stood and picked up his hat.) "But, while leaving, I dare request that in future I hope to be spared any similar meetings and, so to speak, compromises. I want to make this request of you in particular, much-esteemed Pulkheriya Aleksandrovna, since my letter was addressed to you and to no one else."

Pulkheriya Aleksandrovna was slightly offended.

"You seem to think that you already have complete power over us, Petr Petrovich. Dunya's told you the reason why your request was not honored: she had good intentions. Besides, you were writing to me as if you were giving me orders. Must we really consider your every wish our command? On the contrary, I say that now you should be particularly tactful and indulgent, because we gave up everything and, trusting you, came here; therefore, we're almost in your power as it is."

"That's not quite fair, Pulkheriya Aleksandrovna, especially at the present moment, when Marfa Petrovna's bequest of three thousand rubles has just been announced, which, it seems, is very opportune, judging from the new tone you've adopted with me," he added caustically.

"Judging from that remark, one can really suppose that you were counting on our helplessness," Dunya observed irritably.

"But now, at least, I can no longer count on it and, in particular, I don't wish to interfere with the communication of Arkady Ivanovich Svidrigaylov's secret proposals, which he authorized your brother to convey and which, as I see, have an important, perhaps even extremely pleasant significance for you."

"Ah, my God!" cried Pulkheriya Aleksandrovna.

Razumikhin could scarcely remain in his chair.

"Aren't you ashamed now, Dunya?" asked Raskolnikov.

"I am, Rodya," she replied. "Petr Petrovich, get out of here!" She turned to him, pale with rage.

Petr Petrovich seemed not to have expected such an ending. He was relying too heavily on himself, on his power, and on the helplessness of his victims. He couldn't believe it even now. He turned pale, and his lips began to tremble.

"Avdotya Romanovna, if I walk out the door now, in the face of such parting words, then—consider this well—I will never come back. Think it over carefully! This is my last word."

"What impudence!" cried Dunya, quickly standing up from her place. "I don't want you ever to come back!"

"What? So that's how it is!" cried Luzhin, unable to believe up until the last moment in such an outcome and, therefore, having lost the thread completely. "That's how it is! But do you know, Avdotya Romanovna, that I could even lodge a complaint, ma'am."

"What right do you have to talk to her like that?" Pulkheriya Aleksandrovna intervened angrily. "What do you have to complain about? What right do you have? Do you think I'll give my Dunya away to a man such as you? Go away; leave us altogether! We're to blame for embarking on this unseemly course of action; I'm most at fault . . ."

"Nevertheless, Pulkheriya Aleksandrovna," Luzhin cried in angry fury. "You bound me by your word, and now you're going back on it . . . and finally, finally, I was drawn in, so to speak, and have incurred expenses . . ."

This last claim was so much in keeping with Petr Petrovich's character that Raskolnikov, growing pale from rage and his efforts to control it, suddenly could no longer restrain himself and . . . burst out laughing. But Pulkheriya Aleksandrovna was beside herself.

"Expenses? What sort of expenses? Surely you don't mean shipping our trunk? The conductor conveyed it without any charge to you. Good Lord, we bound you! Just come to your senses, Petr Petrovich; it's you who bound our hands and feet, and not we who bound you!"

"Enough, Mama, please, that's enough!" begged Avdotya Romanovna. "Petr Petrovich, do us a favor, get out!"

"I'm going, ma'am, but only one final word!" he said, having now almost lost control of himself. "Your mother, it seems, has entirely forgotten that I decided to accept you, so to speak, after the gossip in town concerning your reputation had spread throughout the entire district. Disregarding public opinion for your sake and restoring your reputation, of course I could very well have counted on some requital and even have claimed your gratitude. . . . But only now have my eyes been opened! I myself see that perhaps I behaved in an exceedingly rash fashion, disregarding public opinion as I did . . ."

"Does he think he has nine lives, or what?" cried Razumikhin, jumping up from the chair and getting ready to finish him off.

"You're a vile, evil man!" said Dunya.

"Not a word! Don't make a move!" cried Raskolnikov, restraining Razumikhin. Then he advanced point-blank on Luzhin.

"Be so good as to get out!" he said softly and distinctly. "Not one word more, or else . . ."

Petr Petrovich regarded him for several seconds, his pale face distorted by malice, then turned and walked out; of course, rarely had anyone carried away such vicious hatred in his heart as this man felt toward Raskolnikov. He blamed him, and him alone, for everything. It is remarkable that even as he went down the stairs, he kept imagining that the matter, perhaps, was not entirely lost, and that even, as far as the ladies were concerned, it was even "very, very" reparable.

III

The main point was that up to the very last moment, he had in no way expected such an outcome. He kept trying to embolden himself as best he could, not even admitting the possibility that two poor and defenseless women could escape his power. His conviction was fortified by his vanity and a level of self-confidence that could best be described as self-infatuation. Petr Petrovich, who had fought his own way out of poverty, had become accustomed to admiring himself to an extreme degree; he valued his own intelligence and abilities highly, and even sometimes, while alone, admired his face in a mirror. But more than anything else on earth, he loved and treasured his own money, earned by his hard work and other means: it made him the equal of everything above him.

Now, reminding Dunya with bitterness that he had decided to take her despite those nasty rumors about her, Petr Petrovich was speaking in complete sincerity and even feeling deep disgust toward such "black ingratitude." Meanwhile, at the time he'd proposed to Dunya, he'd been completely convinced of the absurdity of all the rumors, which had been publicly refuted by Marfa Petrovna herself and long since discarded by the entire town, which had vindicated Dunya. And he himself would not now deny the fact that he'd known it all at the time. Nevertheless, he still highly valued his resolve to elevate Dunya to his own level and considered it a valiant feat. When he'd spoken about it to Dunya just now, he'd been expressing his secret, cherished thought, which he himself had admired more than once, and he couldn't understand how other people could fail to admire his feat. When he'd paid his visit to Raskolnikov, he had entered with the feeling of a benefactor preparing to reap the fruits and hear extremely gratifying compliments. Now, of course, on his way down the stairs, he felt offended and unappreciated to the highest degree.

Dunya was simply indispensable to him; it was unthinkable that he might have to lose her. For some time—for several years, in fact—he had been having sweet sensual dreams about marriage, but he'd kept saving up money and biding his time. With rapture he contemplated in deep secrecy a virtuous young woman who was poor (she had to be poor), very young, very pretty, of honorable birth, well educated, and very timid, one who had experienced very many misfortunes and who would humble herself before him to such an extent that all her life she would consider him as her savior; she would venerate him, submit to him, and idolize him and only him. He devised so many scenes, so many delightful episodes in his imagination on this seductive and playful theme as he rested after a long day tending to his business affairs! And this dream of so many years had almost been realized: he was impressed by Avdotya Romanovna's beauty and education; her helpless position excited him in the extreme. There was even somewhat more than he had hoped for here: a proud young woman had appeared, strong of character, virtuous, more highly educated and developed than he was (he felt this), and such a creature would be slavishly grateful to him for his valiant feat her whole life and would efface herself reverently before him, and he would lord it over her completely and without limit! It was as if on purpose, not that long before this, after considerable thought and waiting, he had decided at last to change his career definitively and enter a wider circle of activity, at the same time, little by little, moving into higher social circles, a move that he had been contemplating voluptuously for some time. . . . In a word, he had resolved to try Petersburg. He knew that with a woman's help it was possible to gain "a very great" deal. The fascination of a charming, virtuous, and educated woman could embellish his path to an astonishing degree, could attract others to him, create an aura . . . and all of this was about to fall through! This sudden, awful rupture now struck him like a clap of thunder. It was like a hideous joke, an absurdity! He had blustered only a little; he hadn't even managed to say everything; he'd simply been joking, had gotten carried away, but it had all ended so seriously! In the end, he was already in love with Dunya in his own way; he was already lording it over her in his dreams—and all of a sudden—no! Tomorrow, yes, tomorrow it could all be restored, cured, corrected, and the main thing—he would destroy that insolent youth, that little boy, who was the cause of it all. With a painful feeling he recalled, also somehow unintentionally, Razumikhin. . . . But on that score he soon felt at ease: "As if he could be placed on the same level with me!" But the person he really feared was Svidrigaylov. . . . In a word, there were many problems ahead.

■   ■   ■

"No, it's me, I'm the one most at fault," said Dunechka, embracing and kissing her mother. "I was tempted by his money, but I swear to you, brother—I never imagined that he was such an unworthy human being. If I'd seen through him before, I never would have been tempted. Don't blame me, brother!"

"God spared us, He spared us!" muttered Pulkheriya Aleksandrovna, but somehow unconsciously, as if still not taking in everything that had just happened.

Everyone rejoiced, and within five minutes they were all laughing. At times it was only Dunya who turned pale and frowned, recalling recent events. Pulkheriya Aleksandrovna had never been able to imagine that she, too, would be so glad; even that morning, a break with Luzhin had seemed to be a terrible misfortune. But Razumikhin was in ecstasy. He was not yet able to express it all, but he was trembling as if in a fever, as if a great weight had been lifted from his chest. Now he had the right to devote his whole life to them, to serve them. . . . Almost anything could happen now! However, he drove away any future thoughts more apprehensively and feared his own imagination. Only Raskolnikov sat in the same place, almost gloomy, even distracted. He, who had insisted more than anyone on Luzhin's dismissal, now seemed to be the least interested in what had occurred. Dunya couldn't help feeling that he was still very angry with her; Pulkheriya Aleksandrovna kept examining him timidly.

"What did Svidrigaylov say to you?" Dunya asked, approaching him.

"Ah, yes, yes!" cried Pulkheriya Aleksandrovna.

Raskolnikov raised his head.

"He very much wants to present you with ten thousand rubles and wishes to see you once in my presence."

"To see her! Not for anything on earth!" cried Pulkheriya Aleksandrovna. "How dare he offer her money?"

Then Raskolnikov conveyed (rather drily) his conversation with Svidrigaylov, omitting mention of Marfa Petrovna's ghost so as not to go into pointless material and feeling an aversion to engaging in any conversation except the most necessary.

"What answer did you give him?" asked Dunya.

"First I said that I wouldn't convey anything to you. Then he declared that he himself would seek a meeting with you, by any means possible. He maintained that his passion for you was just a whim and that now he doesn't feel anything. . . . He doesn't want you to marry Luzhin. . . . In general, he was full of contradictions."

"How do you explain his behavior to yourself, Rodya? How did he seem to you?"

"I confess that I don't understand him very well. He offers you ten thousand, and he himself says that he's not rich. He declares that he wants to depart for somewhere, and ten minutes later forgets that he mentioned it. Suddenly he says that he also wants to get married and that a bride's being sought for him. . . . Of course, he has his own aims, and most likely they're bad ones. But once again, it's somehow strange to assume that if he had evil intentions concerning you, he'd go about it in such a foolish way. . . . Naturally, I refused the money on your behalf, once and for all. In general he seemed very strange, and . . . even . . . to show signs of madness. But I could be mistaken; it might simply be some sort of trickery. It seems that Marfa Petrovna's death made quite an impression on him . . ."

"Lord rest her soul!" cried Pulkheriya Aleksandrovna. "I'll pray to God for her forever and ever! What would've happened to us now,

Dunya, without those three thousand rubles? Lord, it's like a bolt from the blue! Ah, Rodya, this morning we had only three rubles to our name; Dunechka and I were wondering if we could pawn her watch somewhere so we wouldn't have to take any money from that man until he figured it out for himself."

Dunya was too overwhelmed by Svidrigaylov's proposal. She stood there deep in thought.

"He's conceived something horrible!" she muttered to herself almost in a whisper, almost shuddering.

Raskolnikov observed this extreme fright.

"It seems that I'll have to see him again more than once," he said to Dunya.

"We'll follow him! I'll track him down!" Razumikhin shouted enthusiastically. "I won't let him out of my sight! Rodya's given me permission. He himself said to me a while ago: 'Take care of my sister.' Will you allow me, Avdotya Romanovna?"

Dunya smiled and extended her hand to him, but the worried look didn't leave her face. Pulkheriya Aleksandrovna glanced at her timidly; however, apparently the thought of three thousand rubles was comforting her.

In a quarter of an hour, they were all engaged in the most animated conversation. Even Raskolnikov, though he wasn't speaking, was listening attentively for some time. Razumikhin was holding forth.

"Why, why should you leave?" The words flowed out of him with ecstatic feeling. "What are you going to do in that little town? The main thing is that here you're all together and you need each other, very much so—if you understand me! Well, even for just a while. . . . Take me as your friend, a companion, and I assure you that we'll devise an excellent enterprise. Listen, I'll explain the whole thing to you in detail—the whole project! This morning, before anything happened, an idea came to me. . . . Here's what it is: I have an uncle (I'll introduce you to him; he's an agreeable, respectable old fellow!), and this uncle has a sum of one thousand rubles; he lives on his pension and is not in need. For two years he's been nagging me, telling me to take this thousand and pay him six percent interest. I see the point of it: he simply wants to help me; but last year I didn't need it, and this year while I'd been waiting for him to arrive, I'd decided to take it. Then, if you contribute another thousand from your three thousand, we'll have enough in the first instance; we'll form a partnership. And what will we do?"

Razumikhin started to develop his plan; he went on at length about how all the booksellers and publishers knew very little about their own merchandise, and therefore were usually bad publishers; meanwhile, good editions generally did well and produced a profit, sometimes a considerable one. Razumikhin had been dreaming about the publishing business, having worked for two years at various places; he had a decent knowledge of three European languages, in spite of the fact that some six days ago he had told Raskolnikov that his German was "feeble," since his aim had been to convince him to take half his translation job and three rubles in advance: he'd been lying at the time, and Raskolnikov had known that he was lying.

"Why, why should we allow this opportunity to get away when one of the most important resources has turned up—our own money?" said Razumikhin heatedly. "Of course, it'll take a great deal of work, but we will work, you, Avdotya Romanovna, me, Rodion. . . . Some editions now produce a handsome profit! The mainstay of our enterprise consists in our knowing precisely what to translate. We'll translate, publish, and study, all together. I can be useful now because I have experience. For almost two years I've been poking around publishers, and I know all the ins and outs: it's not as hard as it seems, believe me! Why, why should we miss this chance? I myself know, and I've kept it to myself, of two or three such works; the mere idea of translating and publishing them might yield one hundred rubles for each book, and for one of them I would refuse even five hundred rubles just for the idea. And what do you think, if I told someone, he might have real doubts, the blockhead! As far as the actual details, printing, paper, and sales, you can leave all that to me! I know all the ins and outs! We'll start small, grow larger, and at least we'll be able to feed ourselves; in any case, we'll break even."

Dunya's eyes shone.

"I really like what you're saying, Dmitry Prokofich," she said.

"Of course, I don't know anything about this," Pulkheriya Aleksandrovna put in. "Perhaps it's a good idea, but then again, God only knows. It's somehow new and unknown. Of course, we have to stay here, at least for some time . . ."

She looked at Rodya.

"What do you think, brother?" asked Dunya.

"I think he has a very good idea," he replied. "Naturally, it's too early to dream about a publishing house, but one could publish five or six books with indisputable success. I myself know of one work that will definitely suit. As to whether he knows how to conduct the business, there's no doubt about that either. . . . However, there's still time for you to reach an agreement . . ."

"Hurrah!" cried Razumikhin. "Now, wait: there's an apartment here, in this building, from the same landlords. It's separate, on its own, and doesn't connect with any other rooms; it's three small furnished rooms, and the rent is modest. Take it for the time being. I'll pawn the watch for you tomorrow and bring you the money; the rest will all be arranged later. The main thing is, all three of you can live here together, both of you and Rodya. . . . But where are you going, Rodya?"

"What, Rodya, are you leaving already?" Pulkheriya Aleksandrovna asked with some alarm.

"At a time like this?" cried Razumikhin.

Dunya looked at her brother with distrustful astonishment. He was holding his cap, preparing to leave.

"It seems as if you're burying me or saying farewell forever," he said in a somewhat strange manner.

He seemed to smile, but it wasn't quite a real smile.

"Who knows, perhaps we really are seeing each other for the last time," he added unexpectedly.

He thought he was muttering to himself, but somehow it was uttered aloud.

"What's the matter with you?" cried his mother.

"Where are you going, Rodya?" Dunya asked somehow peculiarly.

"Just so, I have to," he replied vaguely, as if hesitating in what he really wanted to say. But his pale face showed a kind of firm resolution.

"I wanted to say . . . as I was coming here . . . I wanted to tell you, Mama . . . and you, Dunya, that it would be better for us to separate for some time. I don't feel well; I'm not at peace. . . . I'll come later, on my own, when . . . it'll be possible. I remember you and love you. . . . Let me be! Leave me alone! I decided this a while ago. . . . I've decided this for certain. . . . Whatever happens to me, whether I perish or not, I want to be alone. Forget all about me. . . . It's better that way. . . . Don't inquire about me. When necessary, I'll come myself or . . . I'll summon you. Perhaps everything will resurrect! But now, while you love me, give me up. . . . Or else, I feel that I'll get to hate you. . . . Farewell!"

"Good Lord!" cried Pulkheriya Aleksandrovna.

Both his mother and his sister were terribly frightened; Razumikhin, too.

"Rodya, Rodya! Make peace with us and let's go back to how we were before!" cried his poor mother.

He turned slowly to the door and slowly started to leave the room. Dunya caught up with him.

"Brother! What are you doing to our mother?" she whispered, her eyes burning with indignation.

He looked at her gravely.

"It's all right, I'll come, I will!" he muttered in a low voice, as if not fully aware of what he was saying, and walked out of the room.

"What an insensitive, spiteful egoist!" cried Dunya.

"He's in-sane, not in-sensitive! He's mad! Don't you see that? You're the insensitive one," Razumikhin whispered heatedly into her ear while keeping a tight hold on her hand.

"I'll be back right away!" he cried, turning to Pulkheriya Aleksandrovna, who was mortified, and ran out of the room.

Raskolnikov was waiting for him at the end of the corridor.

"I knew that you'd come running out," he said. "Go back to them and stay with them. . . . Stay with them tomorrow and . . . always. I . . . perhaps, I'll come . . . if possible. Farewell!"

And, without extending his hand, he left him.

"Where are you going? What is it? What's the matter? How can you do this?" Razumikhin muttered, completely at a loss.

Raskolnikov paused once again.

"Once and for all: don't ever ask me about anything. There's nothing I can tell you. . . . Don't come to see me. Perhaps I'll come here. . . . Leave me, but *don't . . . leave them*. Do you understand?"

It was dark in the corridor; they were standing near a light. For a minute they stared at each other in silence. Razumikhin would remember this moment for the rest of his life. Raskolnikov's intense and burning gaze seemed to grow stronger with every moment, penetrating his soul and his consciousness. All of a sudden, Razumikhin shuddered. It was as if something strange passed between them. . . . An idea crept in, something like a hint; something horrible, hideous, and immediately understood on both sides. . . . Razumikhin turned as pale as a corpse.

"Do you understand now?" Raskolnikov said suddenly, his face painfully distorted. "Go back, be with them," he added abruptly; turning swiftly, he left the building.

I won't describe now what happened that evening with Pulkheriya Aleksandrovna, how Razumikhin went back to them, how he tried to calm them down, how he swore that it was necessary to allow Rodya to rest from his illness, swore that Rodya would certainly come to see them, how he would come every day, that Rodya was very, very upset, and that it was important not to irritate him; how he, Razumikhin, would look after him, find him a good doctor, the best, arrange for a consultation. . . . In a word, from that evening on, Razumikhin became like a son and a brother to them.

IV

Raskolnikov proceeded directly to the house on the canal where Sonya lived. It was an old, three-story green house. He looked for the caretaker and received vague directions for where to find the tailor Kapernaumov. After locating the entrance to a narrow, dark staircase in a corner of the courtyard, he finally climbed up to the second floor and emerged into a large hall surrounding it from the side of the courtyard. While he wandered in the darkness and confusion, trying to find the entrance to the Kapernaumovs', suddenly, three steps away from him, a door opened; he grabbed it automatically.

"Who's there?" a woman's voice asked in alarm.

"It's me . . . coming to see you," replied Raskolnikov, and he entered a tiny hall. There, on a broken chair, in a twisted copper candlestick, stood a candle.

"It's you! Good Lord!" cried Sonya weakly, standing there as if rooted to the spot.

"Which way to your room? This way?"

Trying not to look at her, Raskolnikov proceeded quickly into her room.

A minute later Sonya entered with a candle, put it down, and stood in front of him, completely at a loss, in inexpressible agitation, apparently frightened by his unexpected visit. All of a sudden her pale face became flushed and tears even appeared in her eyes. . . . She felt sick and ashamed and pleased all at once. . . . Raskolnikov turned around quickly and sat down on the chair next to the table. In one fleeting glance he managed to take in the entire room.

It was a large room, but with an extremely low ceiling, the only room rented out by the Kapernaumovs, whose apartment was located behind the wall to the left behind a locked door. On the opposite side, in the wall to the right, there was another door, always locked tight. It led to a neighboring apartment with a different number. Sonya's room seemed to resemble a barn; it had an irregular quadrilateral shape that suggested something deformed. A wall with three windows facing out on the canal cut through the room at a slant; as a result, one corner, terribly acute, trailed off into the distance so that in dim light it was impossible to make out anything very well; the other corner was too hideously obtuse. There was almost no furniture at all in this large room. In a corner on the right was a bed; near the door leading into the other apartment stood a simple wooden table covered in a blue tablecloth; two cane chairs were next to the table. Then, on the opposite wall, closest to the narrow corner, stood a small, simple wooden chest of drawers, as if lost in empty space. That was everything in the room. Yellowish, dirty, worn wallpaper was blackened in all the corners; it must have been damp and smoky during the winter. The inhabitant's poverty was obvious; there weren't even any curtains in front of the bed.

Sonya silently regarded her guest, who was so carefully and unceremoniously examining her room; ultimately she even began trembling in fear, as if she were standing in front of a judge and the ruler of her fate.

"I've come late. . . . Is it eleven o'clock yet?" he asked, still not raising his eyes to her face.

"It is," she muttered. "It is, yes!" she hastened to add suddenly, as if it was some sort of escape for her. "The landlord's clock just chimed . . . and I heard it myself. . . . It is."

"I've come to see you for the last time," Raskolnikov continued gloomily, even though this was only his first visit. "I may not see you again . . ."

"Are you . . . going away?"

"I don't know. . . . Tomorrow it'll all . . ."

"So you won't be at Katerina Ivanovna's tomorrow?" Sonya asked, her voice trembling.

"I don't know. Tomorrow morning it'll all be. . . . That's not the point: I came to tell you one thing . . ."

He raised his brooding glance to her face and suddenly noticed that he was sitting, while she was still standing in front of him.

"Why are you standing there? Sit down," he said suddenly, but in an altered, soft, and polite voice.

She sat down. He looked at her warmly, almost with compassion.

"You're so thin! Just look at your hand! It's completely transparent. Your fingers are like a dead person's." He took her hand. Sonya smiled weakly.

"I've always been like that," she said.

"Even when you were living at home?"

"Yes."

"Well, of course!" he uttered abruptly, and both the expression on his face and the sound of his voice suddenly changed again. He glanced around the room again.

"You rent this from the Kapernaumovs?"

"Yes, sir . . ."

"Do they live there, behind that door?"

"Yes. . . . They have a room just like this."

"All together in one room?"

"Yes, sir."

"I'd be afraid to be in your room at night," he observed glumly.

"The landlords are very kind, very polite," replied Sonya, seeming not yet to have come to her senses or to be understanding properly. "All the furniture and everything else . . . all belongs to the landlords. They're very nice people, and the children often come to see me . . ."

"Do they stutter?"

"Yes, sir. He does and he's also lame. His wife, too. . . . It's not that she stutters, but she can't pronounce her words clearly. She's a good woman, very kind. He's a former house serf. They have seven children . . . and only the eldest stutters; the others are simply unwell . . .

but they don't stutter. . . . How do you know about them?" she added in some surprise.

"Your father told me all about them. He told me all about you. . . . How you left at six o'clock and came back at nine, and how Katerina Ivanovna fell to her knees next to your bed."

Sonya was embarrassed.

"It's as if I saw him today," she whispered hesitantly.

"Who?"

"My father. I was walking along the street, just nearby here, on the corner, after nine o'clock, and it was as if he was ahead of me. It looked just like him. I wanted to call on Katerina Ivanovna . . ."

"You were out walking the streets?"

"Yes," Sonya whispered abruptly, once again embarrassed and dropping her eyes.

"Did Katerina Ivanovna ever beat you when you were at your father's place?"

"Oh, no, what are you saying? Why do you say that? No!" Sonya said, looking at him, even in fear.

"So, do you love her?"

"Her? Of course, I do!" Sonya wailed pitifully, suddenly crossing her arms in suffering. "Ah! You don't. . . . If you only knew. She's just like a child. . . . She's almost lost her mind . . . from grief. She used to be so clever . . . so generous . . . so kind! You don't know anything, not a thing . . . ah!"

Sonya said all this as if she were in despair, agitated and suffering, wringing her hands. Her pale cheeks flushed once more, and her eyes expressed her torment. It was apparent that she was deeply moved, that she very much wanted to express something, to say something, to defend Katerina. Some kind of *insatiable* compassion, if it's possible to express it like that, was suddenly reflected in all the features of her face.

"Beat me! What on earth are you saying? Good Lord, beat me! Even if she had beaten me, what of it? So, what of it? You don't know anything, not a thing. . . . She's such an unhappy woman, ah, so unhappy! And sickly. . . . She's looking for justice. . . . She's pure. She believes steadfastly that justice must exist, and she demands it. . . . Even if you tormented her, she'd never do anything unjust. She herself doesn't realize that it's impossible to find justice among people, and she gets irritated. . . . She's like a child, a child! She's just, very just!"

"What will happen to you?"

Sonya regarded him questioningly.

"They're on your hands, you know. True, they depended on you before, and your late father would ask you for money so he could drink to cure his hangover. Well, what will happen now?"

"I don't know," Sonya said glumly.

"Will they stay there?"

"I don't know. They're in debt for that apartment; I hear that the landlady just served them notice, but Katerina Ivanovna says that she herself doesn't want to stay there a moment longer."

"Why's she being so brave? Is she relying on you?"

"Oh, no, don't talk like that! We live in complete harmony," Sonya said, suddenly agitated again and even irritated, just as if a canary or some other little bird had gotten angry. "What on earth can she do? What else can she do?" she asked, growing heated and upset. "She wept and wept so much today! She's going mad, didn't you notice that? She's so muddled; she's either agitated like a little girl, hoping that tomorrow everything will be right, the refreshments, and everything else . . . or she wrings her hands, coughs up blood, weeps, and suddenly begins banging her head against the wall, as if in despair. Then she calms down again; she's relying entirely on you: she says that now you're her helpmate. She'll borrow some money from somewhere and go back to her town with me, and she'll open a boarding school for noble young women; she'll take me on as a supervisor and we'll start a splendid new life; she kisses me, hugs me, comforts me, and believes all this! She believes in these fantasies! Well, do I dare contradict her? Meanwhile, she herself washes, cleans, mends, and with her feeble strength drags the washtub into the room, panting, and then has to fall into bed; this morning she and I went to the market stalls to buy some shoes for Polechka and Lenya, because theirs were all worn out, but we didn't have enough money to pay for them, not nearly enough, and she'd chosen such sweet little shoes, because she has good taste, you just don't know. . . . She started crying right there in the shop in front of the merchants, because we didn't have enough money. . . . Ah, it was pitiful to see."

"Well, after that one can understand how you . . . live like this," Raskolnikov said with a bitter smile.

"Don't you feel sorry for her? Don't you?" Sonya grew angry again. "I know that you gave her your last kopecks before you'd seen anything. If you'd seen it all, oh, good Lord! I've driven her to tears so often, so very often! Even as recently as last week! Oh, yes, me! Just one week before his death. I acted cruelly! I've done that so many times, so many. Ah, it's so painful to remember this now all day long."

Sonya even wrung her hands as she spoke, recalling the pain.

"You mean to say you're cruel?"

"Yes, me, me! I went there," she continued, weeping, "and my late father said, 'Read to me, Sonya,' he says, 'my head aches. Read to me . . . here's the book.' It was some book he had; he'd gotten it from Andrey Semyonych Lebezyatnikov, who lives there; he used to get such funny books. And I said, 'I have to leave,' because I didn't want to read; I'd stopped by mainly to show some collars to Katerina Ivanovna. Lizaveta, the market woman, had sold me some collars and cuffs cheaply, very nice ones, new, with a pattern. Katerina Ivanovna liked them very much; she put one on and looked at herself in the mirror. She really, really liked them. 'Give them to me as a present, Sonya,' she says, 'please.' She said 'please,' she wanted them so much. But where would she wear them? They just reminded her of the good old days! She looked at herself in the mirror, admired them, but she had no dresses, none at all, no pretty things for so many years! She never asked anyone for anything; she's proud; she'd sooner give away her last coin, and here she was asking for something—she liked them so much! But I didn't want to give them to her. 'What do you need them for, Katerina Ivanovna?' I said. 'What for?' That's what I said. I shouldn't have said that to her! She looked at me and was so very sad that I'd refused; it was pitiful to see. . . . She wasn't sad about the collars, I realized, but because I'd refused her. Ah, if I could change it all, do it all again, all those words I said. . . . Oh, me . . . but what am I saying? It doesn't make any difference!"

"Did you know Lizaveta, the market woman?"

"Yes. . . . Did you know her, too?" asked Sonya with some surprise.

"Katerina Ivanovna has consumption, a bad case; she'll die soon," said Raskolnikov, falling silent and not answering Sonya's question.

"Oh, no, no, no!" Sonya unconsciously seized both his hands, as if begging him not to let it happen.

"After all, it'll be better if she does."

"No, not better, not at all, not better at all!" she repeated anxiously and unconsciously.

"And the children? What will you do with them, if you don't take them in yourself?"

"Oh, I don't know!" cried Sonya almost in despair, and she clutched her head. It was apparent that this thought had already occurred to her many times before and that he had reminded her of it once again.

"Well, what if, while still living with Katerina Ivanovna, you fall ill now and they take you to a hospital, then what will happen?" he insisted pitilessly.

"Ah, what are you saying, why say that? That can't possibly happen!" Sonya's face was distorted with horrible fear.

"Why can't it happen?" continued Raskolnikov with a cruel smirk. "You're not insured, are you? Then what will happen to them? The whole bunch will be driven out into the street; she'll cough and beg, bang her head against the wall somewhere, just like she did today, and the children will cry. . . . She'll fall down, be taken to the police, to the hospital, and she'll die, while the children . . ."

"Oh, no! God won't allow that!" The words burst forth at last from Sonya's constricted chest. She was listening, looking at him imploringly and folding her hands in mute supplication, as if everything depended on him.

Raskolnikov stood up and began walking around the room. About a minute passed. Sonya stood there, her hands and head lowered, in terrible distress.

"Can't you save up? Put some money away for a rainy day?" he asked, stopping suddenly in front of her.

"No," whispered Sonya.

"Of course not! But have you tried?" he added, almost with derision.

"I have."

"And it fell through! Well, of course, it did. Why even ask?"

He walked around the room again. Another minute passed.

"Don't you earn some money every day?"

Sonya was more embarrassed than before; her face flushed with color once again.

"No," she whispered with tormented effort.

"Polechka will probably wind up the same way," he said suddenly.

"No! No! It can't be, no!" Sonya cried loudly, as if in despair, as if someone had stabbed her with a knife. "God, God won't allow such a terrible thing!"

"He lets it happen to other people."

"No, no! God will protect her, He will!" she repeated, beside herself.

"Perhaps there's no such thing as God," Raskolnikov replied, even with some malicious delight. He began laughing and glanced at her.

Sonya's face suddenly changed terribly: a shudder ran across it. She glanced at him with inexpressible reproach, wanted to say something, but couldn't utter a word. All of a sudden, she just started weeping bitterly, covering her face with her hands.

"You say that Katerina Ivanovna's mind is muddled; your mind is muddled, too," he said after some silence.

About five minutes passed. He kept pacing the room in silence, without glancing at her. At last he went up to her; his eyes were shining. He put his hands on her shoulders and looked into her weeping face. His gaze was dry, inflamed, and sharp; his lips were trembling violently. . . . All at once, he bowed down quickly and, falling to the floor, kissed her foot. Sonya took a step back from him in fear, as if from a madman. And, in fact, he looked completely mad.

"What's this? What are you doing? To me?" she muttered, turning pale; her heart suddenly ached in agony.

"I didn't bow down to you; I bowed down to all human suffering," he uttered madly and went over to the window. "Listen," he added, returning to her a minute later. "A little while ago, I said to an offensive fellow that he wasn't worth even your little finger . . . and that I did my sister an honor today when I sat her next to you."

"Ah, why did you tell them that? In her presence?" cried Sonya in alarm. "To sit with me? An honor? But I have no honor. . . . I'm a great, great sinner! Ah, why did you say that?"

"I said it about you not because of your dishonor and your sin, but because of your great suffering. As for your being a great sinner, that's true," he added almost enthusiastically. "Worst of all is that you're a sinner who's destroyed and betrayed herself *in vain*. Isn't it really terrible! Isn't it terrible that you live in this filth that you despise and, at the same time, you yourself know (all you have to do is open your eyes) that you're not helping anyone and not saving anyone from anything! Tell me once and for all," he said, almost in a frenzy, "how this disgrace and this baseness can be combined in you together with other contradictory and sacred feelings? Why, it would be more just, a thousand times more just and more reasonable to plunge your head into the water and end it all at once!"

"And what will become of them?" Sonya asked weakly, glancing at him full of suffering, but at the same time not at all surprised by his suggestion. Raskolnikov regarded her strangely.

He was able to understand everything in that one look. Apparently, this idea must have occurred to her already. Perhaps she had even seriously considered many times in her despair how to end it all, so seriously that his suggestion almost didn't surprise her. She didn't even notice the cruelty of his words (of course, she also didn't notice the meaning of his reproaches and of his peculiar view of her disgrace, and this was obvious to him). But he understood completely how monstrously she was tormented, and had been for some time, by the thought of her dishonorable and shameful predicament. What, what on earth could possibly, he wondered, have impeded her resolve up to this point to end it all at once? And only then did he completely understand the meaning these poor little orphan children had for her, and the pitiful half-mad Katerina Ivanovna, with her consumption and her banging her head against the wall.

Yet it was clear to him once again that Sonya, with her character and the upbringing she had nonetheless received, could in no way stay as she was. Still the question remained for him: how could she have stayed in her present situation for so long and not lost her mind, if she wasn't strong enough to throw herself into the water? Of course, he understood that Sonya's position in society was accidental, although, unfortunately, not singular and not exceptional. But this very chance, this smattering of education, and all her previous life could have destroyed her at her very first step on this abominable path. What had supported her? It wasn't the depravity. Why, this disgrace, obviously, had affected her only mechanically; not one drop of genuine disgrace had yet penetrated into her heart: he saw this; she stood before him in reality . . .

"She has three ways she can go," he thought. "She can throw herself into the canal, wind up in a madhouse, or . . . or, in the end, immerse herself in depravity, stupefying her mind and hardening her heart." This last thought was the most repulsive of all; but he was already skeptical; he was young, philosophical, and therefore cruel. As a result, he couldn't help believing that the last escape, that is, depravity, was the most probable of all.

"But is that really the truth?" he cried to himself. "Is it really possible that this creature, who still preserves her purity of spirit, will consciously be drawn in the end into that filthy, stinking pit? Hasn't that process already begun, and isn't it only because she's managed to resist up to now that vice no longer seems so repulsive to her? No, no, that can't possibly be!" he cried, as Sonya had before. "No, up to this point the thought of sin kept her from the canal, and the thought of *them, the children*. . . . And if she hasn't lost her mind up to now? But who's to say that she hasn't already lost her mind? Is she really in her right mind? Can one really talk the way she does? Can one reason the way she does in one's right mind? Can she stand over her own ruin, directly above that stinking pit into which she's being drawn, and can she wave her arms and block her ears when she's being told about the danger? Is it that she's waiting for a miracle? She must be. Aren't these all signs of madness?"

He paused stubbornly on this thought. He even liked this way out more than any other. He began staring at her more intensely.

"So, do you pray to God a great deal, Sonya?" he asked her.

Sonya was silent; he stood next to her and waited for an answer.

"What would I be without God?" she whispered rapidly, energetically, quickly glancing at him with her sparkling eyes and firmly grasping his hand in her own.

"Just as I thought!" he said to himself.

"And what does God do for you in return?" he asked, inquiring further.

Sonya was silent for a long time, as if she could make no reply. Her weak chest heaved in agitation.

"Be quiet! Don't ask! You're not worthy!" she cried suddenly, looking at him sternly and angrily.

"Just as I thought! Just as I thought!" he repeated persistently to himself.

"He does everything!" she whispered hurriedly, dropping her eyes again.

"That's a way out! That's the explanation of her way out!" he decided, regarding her with greedy curiosity.

With a strange, new, almost painful feeling, he looked into her pale, thin, irregular, angular little face, her meek blue eyes, which could shine with such fire, such severe strong emotion, at her small body, still trembling from indignation and rage, and all of this seemed stranger and stranger to him, almost impossible. "A holy fool! She's a holy fool!" he repeated to himself.*

A book lay on her dresser. He had noticed it each time he'd walked past it; now he picked it up and looked at it. It was a Russian translation of the New Testament. It was an old book, worn, bound in leather.

"Where's this from?" he shouted to her from across the room. She stood in the same place, three paces away from the table.

"It was given to me," she replied, as if reluctantly and without looking at him.

"By whom?"

"Lizaveta gave it to me; I asked her for it."

"Lizaveta! Strange!" he thought. Everything about Sonya seemed somehow stranger and more astounding with each passing minute. He brought the book nearer to the candle and began thumbing through its pages.

---

* A *yurodivy*, or holy fool, was a saintly person or ascetic in the early Christian tradition; later, in common usage, the term came to mean a crazy person or a simpleton.

"Where does it talk about Lazarus?" he asked suddenly.

Sonya stared stubbornly at the floor and made no reply. She stood with her side facing the table.

"Where's the raising of Lazarus?* Find it for me, Sonya."

She cast a sidelong glance at him.

"It's not where you're looking. . . . It's in the Fourth Gospel," she whispered sternly, not approaching him.

"Find it and read it to me," he said. He sat down, placed his elbows on the table, rested his head on one hand, and stared gloomily to one side, preparing to listen.

"In a few weeks they'll be welcoming her to a madhouse! I may wind up there, too, if something worse doesn't happen," he muttered to himself.

Upon hearing Raskolnikov's strange request with distrust, Sonya moved hesitantly to the table. But she picked up the book.

"Haven't you read it before?" she asked, looking at him distrustfully across the table. Her voice was becoming more and more severe.

"A long time ago. . . . When I was at school. Read it!"

"Haven't you heard it in church?"

"I . . . don't go to church. Do you go often?"

"N-no," Sonya whispered.

Raskolnikov smirked.

"I see. . . . And, of course, tomorrow you won't go to your father's funeral?"

"I will. I was at church last week, too . . . to have a requiem sung."

"For whom?"

"For Lizaveta. She was killed with an axe."

His nerves grew more and more irritated. His head began spinning.

"Were you friendly with Lizaveta?"

"She . . . she was very fair. . . . She came here . . . not often. . . . It wasn't possible. We used to read together . . . and chat. She will see God."

---

* Sonya reads from and recites verses from the Gospel of John 11:1–45.

These bookish words sounded strange to him, and once again it was something new: some sort of mysterious meetings with Lizaveta, both of them—holy fools.

"I myself will become one here! It's contagious!" he thought. "Read!" he cried insistently and irritably all of a sudden.

Sonya was still hesitating. Her heart was pounding. For some reason, she didn't dare read to him. He looked at this "unhappy deranged woman" almost with torment.

"Why should I read to you? You don't even believe," she whispered quietly, almost gasping for breath.

"Read! I want you to!" he insisted. "You used to read to Lizaveta!"

Sonya turned the pages of the book and searched for the place. Her hands were trembling, and her voice failed. Twice she tried to read but was unable to utter even the first word.

" 'Now a certain man was sick, named Lazarus, of Bethany . . .' " she said at last, with effort, but all of a sudden, from the third word her voice began to vibrate and break off, like a string stretched too tight. Her breath failed her, and her chest tightened.

Raskolnikov understood in part why Sonya had refused to read to him, and the more he understood that, the more abusively and irritably he insisted on her reading. He understood all too well how painful it was for her to expose and betray all that was *her own*. He realized that these feelings seemed perhaps to constitute her genuine and cherished secret, perhaps from her own girlhood, when she was living with her family, with her unfortunate father and her stepmother, demented by grief, among hungry children, hideous cries, and reproaches. But at the same time, he now knew, and knew for certain, that even though she grieved and feared something terrible as she now set about reading, she also felt a tormenting desire to read, in spite of her grief and all the dangers, and to read just *to him*, so that he heard, and precisely *now*—"whatever happened afterward!" He could read this in her eyes, he could understand it in her emotional distress. . . . She gained control of herself, suppressed the throat spasms that had broken her voice at the beginning of the verse; then she continued reading the eleventh chapter of the Gospel of John. Thus she reached the nineteenth verse:

" 'And many of the Jews came to Martha and Mary, to comfort

them concerning their brother. Then Martha, as soon as she heard that Jesus was coming, went and met him: But Mary sat still in the house. Then said Martha unto Jesus, Lord, if thou hadst been here, my brother had not died. But I know, that even now, whatsoever thou wilt ask of God, God will give it thee.'"

Here she paused again, sensing shamefully that her voice would falter and break off once more . . .

"'Jesus saith unto her, Thy brother shall rise again. Martha saith unto him, I know that he shall rise again in the resurrection at the last day. Jesus saith unto her, I am the resurrection and the life: he that believeth in me, though he were dead, yet shall he live. And whosoever liveth and believeth in me shall never die. Believest thou this? She saith unto him—'"

(And, seeming to draw her breath with pain, Sonya read clearly and compellingly, as if she herself was confessing for all to hear:)

"'Yea, Lord: I believe that thou art the Christ, the Son of God, which should come into the world.'"

She was about to pause and glance quickly up at him, but soon gained control of herself and began reading again. Raskolnikov sat and listened without moving, without turning, his elbows on the table, looking to one side. They read up to verse thirty-two.

"'Then when Mary was come where Jesus was, and saw him, she fell down at his feet, and saying unto him, Lord if thou hadst been here, my brother had not died. When Jesus therefore saw her weeping, the Jews also weeping which came with her, he groaned in the spirit, and was troubled, And said, Where have ye laid him? They say unto him, Lord, come and see. Jesus wept. Then said the Jews, Behold how he loved him! And some of them said, Could not this man, which opened the eyes of the blind, have caused that even this man should not have died?'"

Raskolnikov turned to her and looked at her with agitation: yes, that was it! She was already trembling in real, genuine fever. He had been expecting this. She was nearing the words of the greatest and most unprecedented miracle, and a feeling of immense triumph took hold of her. Her voice became as clear as a bell; triumph and joy resounded in it and strengthened it. The lines became confused in front of her because things darkened in her eyes, but she knew the passage by heart. At the last verse, "Could not this man, which opened the eyes of the blind," she lowered her voice, conveying passionately and heatedly the doubt, reproach, and censure of the unbelieving, unseeing Jews, who very soon, a moment later, as if struck by thunder, would fall down, begin weeping, and believe. . . . "And *he, he*—also unseeing and unbelieving—he, too, would hear at once, and he, too, would believe. Yes, yes! Right now, immediately," she dreamed and trembled in ecstatic expectation.

" 'Jesus therefore again groaning in himself cometh to the grave. It was a cave and a stone lay upon it. Jesus said, Take ye away the stone. Martha, the sister of him that was dead, saith unto him, Lord, by this time he stinketh: for he has been dead *four* days.' "

She energetically emphasized the word: *four*.

" 'Jesus saith unto her, Said I not unto thee, that if thou wouldst believe, then thou shouldst see the glory of God? Then they took away the stone from that place where the dead was laid. And Jesus lifted up his eyes, and said, Father, I thank thee that thou hast heard me. And I knew that thou hearest me always: but because of the people which stand by I said it, that they may believe that thou hast sent me. And when he thus had spoken, he cried with a loud voice, Lazarus, come forth. *And he that was dead came forth—*' "

(She read in a loud and ecstatic voice, trembling and growing cold, as if she had seen it with her own eyes:)

" '—bound hand and foot with graveclothes; and his face was bound about with a napkin. Jesus saith unto them, Loose him and let him go.

" '*Then many of the Jews which came to Mary, and had seen the things which Jesus did, believed on him.*' "

She didn't read any further, nor could she; she closed the book and stood up quickly from her chair.

"That's all there is about the resurrection of Lazarus," she whispered abruptly and sternly; she remained motionless, turned to one side, not daring, as if ashamed, to raise her eyes and look at him. Her feverish trembling continued. The candle stub had long since burned down in the twisted candleholder, dimly illuminating in this impoverished room the murderer and the prostitute, strangely united for the reading of the eternal book. Five or more minutes passed.

"I came to tell you something," Raskolnikov said all of sudden in a loud voice and with a frown; he stood up and went over to Sonya. She silently raised her eyes and looked at him. His glance was especially stern, expressing some fierce resoluteness.

"Today I deserted my family," he said, "my mother and my sister. I won't go to see them now. I have broken off with them completely."

"Why?" asked Sonya in astonishment. The recent meeting with his mother and sister had made an extraordinary impression on her, although it was still unclear to her why. She heard this news of the rupture almost in horror.

"Now I have only you," he added. "We'll go together. . . . I've come to you. We're both damned. We'll go together!"

His eyes were shining. "He seems half mad!" Sonya thought in her turn.

"Go where?" she asked in fear, unintentionally taking a step back.

"How should I know? I know only that it's along one road; that I know for certain—and only that. One goal!"

She looked at him, not understanding a thing. She understood only that he was terribly, infinitely unhappy.

"Not one of them will understand anything, if you tell them," he continued, "but I understood. I need you; that's why I came to see you."

"I don't understand," whispered Sonya.

"You'll understand later. Haven't you done the same thing? You've also stepped over . . . you were able to do it. You laid hands on yourself, you destroyed your *own* life. (It's all the same!) You could have lived by reason and spirit, but you'll end up on the Haymarket. . . . But you can't endure it, and if you remain alone, you'll lose your mind, just as I will. Even now you're like someone deranged; therefore, we'll go together, along the same road! Let's go!"

"Why? Why are you saying this?" said Sonya, strangely and passionately agitated by his words.

"Why? Because you can't remain like this—that's why! You must finally judge things seriously and directly, and not weep and yell like a child that God won't allow it! What will happen if you get taken away to a hospital tomorrow? Katerina Ivanovna's not in her right mind and she has consumption; she'll die soon; then what will happen to the children? Won't Polechka be ruined? Haven't you seen children here, on street corners, whose mothers send them out to beg for charity? I've found out where these mothers live and in what circumstances. There it's impossible for children to stay children. A seven-year-old child is depraved and a thief. But children are the image of Christ: 'for of such is the kingdom of heaven.' He commanded us to cherish them and to love them; they're the future of humanity . . ."

"What, then, what must we do?" Sonya repeated, crying hysterically and wringing her hands.

"What must we do? Destroy what's necessary, once and for all, that's all: and take the suffering upon us! What? You don't understand? You will later. . . . Freedom and power, and power's the main thing! Over all trembling creatures and over the entire anthill! . . . That's the goal! Remember this! Those are my parting words to you! This may be the last time I speak with you. If I don't come tomorrow, you will hear about it all yourself and then remember these words I'm saying to you now. And sometime, afterward, in a few years, after you've lived a while, perhaps you'll come to understand what they meant. But if I come tomorrow, I'll tell you who killed Lizaveta. Farewell!"

Sonya began trembling in fright.

"Do you really know who killed her?" she asked, turning cold in horror and regarding him wildly.

"I know and I'll tell. . . . You, and you alone! I've chosen you. I won't come to ask your forgiveness, I'll simply tell you. A while ago I chose you to tell; back when your father spoke about you and when Lizaveta was alive, I thought of this. Farewell. Don't give me your hand. Tomorrow!"

He left. Sonya looked at him, as he walked away, as if he were mad; but she herself was like a madwoman, and she realized it. Her head was spinning. "Lord! How does he know who killed Lizaveta? What did those words mean? This is terrible!" But at the same time the *thought* did not occur to her. By no means! Not at all! "Oh, he must be terribly unhappy! He deserted his mother and sister. Why? What happened? And what does he intend to do?" What had he said to her? He had kissed her foot and said . . . said (yes, he'd said it clearly) that he couldn't live without her any longer. . . . "Oh, good Lord!"

Sonya spent the whole night in a fever and delirium. At times she would jump up, weep, wring her hands, and then fall back into a feverish sleep; she dreamt of Polechka, Katerina Ivanovna, Lizaveta, reading the Gospel, and of him . . . him, with his pale face and shining eyes. . . . He would kiss her feet and cry. . . . "Oh, Lord!"

Behind the door on the right, the door that separated Sonya's apartment from Gertruda Karlovna Resslikh's, there was an intervening room, long since empty, belonging to Madame Resslikh's apartment, and rented out by her; notices to that effect had been placed on gates and announcements stuck to windows overlooking the canal. For a long time, Sonya had grown accustomed to thinking the room was uninhabited. Meanwhile, all this time, Mr. Svidrigaylov had been standing hidden behind the door in the empty room, and eavesdropping. When Raskolnikov left, he stood there, thought for a while, returned on tiptoe to his own room, which was next to the empty room, got a chair, and silently brought it up to the door leading into Sonya's room. The conversation struck him as interesting and significant, and he'd enjoyed it very, very much—so much so that he had brought a chair in order that in the future, even tomorrow, for example, he wouldn't have to subject himself again to the unpleasantness of standing on his feet for a whole hour, but he could make himself more comfortable, so that he could derive pure enjoyment in all regards.

V

The next morning, at precisely eleven o'clock, when Raskolnikov entered the department of criminal investigations in the building housing the district police station and asked to be announced to Porfiry Petrovich, he was somewhat surprised by how long it took for him to be admitted: at least ten minutes passed before he was called. According to his calculations, it seemed, they should have seized upon him at once. Meanwhile, he stood in the reception room while people who had no interest in him at all came and went. In the next room, resembling an office, several clerks were busy writing; it was obvious that not one of them had any idea who or what this Raskolnikov was. He looked around with a restless, suspicious glance, observing closely: was there a prison guard anywhere near him, or a mysterious gaze from someone designated to keep an eye on him so he wouldn't leave? But there was nothing of the kind: he saw only office workers engaged in trivial matters, as well as several other people, but nobody there had any need for him, as if he were free to leave and go wherever he wished. Raskolnikov became more and more convinced of the idea that if the enigmatic man from yesterday, that apparition who had appeared from out of nowhere, had really seen everything and known everything—would they ever have allowed him to stand there now and wait patiently? And would they have waited for him here until eleven o'clock when he'd decided to come all on his own? It must be either that the man still hadn't reported anything or . . . or else he, too, simply didn't know anything and hadn't seen anything with his own eyes (and how could he have seen anything?); therefore, all that had occurred to him, Raskolnikov, yesterday was an apparition, exaggerated by his aggravated and sick imagination. This guess, even as early as yesterday, during his severe anxieties and despair, had begun to strengthen in him. Having thought it all through, while preparing for a new struggle, he suddenly felt that he was trembling—indignation even began to seethe in him at the thought that he was trembling in fear before the hated Porfiry Petrovich. The most terrible thing of all was to have to meet this man once again: he hated him beyond all measure, without limit, and he was even afraid that this hatred would cause him to betray himself. His indignation was so intense that it immediately curtailed his trembling; he prepared to enter with a cold, insolent appearance and promised himself to maintain his silence for as long as he could, to watch carefully and listen attentively, so that this time, at least, no matter what happened, he would conquer his own morbidly agitated nature. At that very moment, he was summoned to see Porfiry Petrovich.

It turned out that this time Porfiry Petrovich was alone. His office was neither large nor small; a large desk stood in front of a sofa covered with an oilcloth; there was also a bureau, a bookcase in one corner, and several chairs—all official furniture, made of polished yellow wood. In one corner, in the rear wall—or, that is, the partition—there was a closed door: farther on, behind the partition, must have therefore been some other rooms. At Raskolnikov's entrance, Porfiry Petrovich quickly and quietly closed the door through which he had entered, so that they remained alone. He met his guest, apparently, with the most cheerful and welcoming look; it was only a few minutes later that Raskolnikov, by certain indications, noticed his embarrassment, as if he was suddenly unsettled or had been discovered doing something very private and secret.

"Ah, my dear fellow! Here you are . . . in our territory," began Porfiry, extending both hands to him. "Well, have a seat, old boy! But perhaps you don't like to be called 'dear fellow' or . . . 'old boy' like that *tout court?** Please don't consider it too familiar. . . . Sit here, sir, on the sofa."

Raskolnikov sat down without taking his eyes off him.

"In our territory," excuses for the familiarity, the French phrase *"tout court,"* and so on and so forth—all characteristic indications. "He extended both his hands to me, yet didn't give me even one; he withdrew his hand in time," flashed through his mind suspiciously. They both watched each other, but as soon as their eyes met, they turned away from one another instantly.

"I brought you this paper . . . about that watch . . . here it is. Is it all right or shall I recopy it?"

"What? A paper? Yes, yes . . . don't worry, that's fine," said Porfiry Petrovich, as if hurrying to go somewhere, and only after saying this did he take the paper and glance at it. "Yes, it's fine as is. Nothing more's needed," he confirmed with the same speed and placed the paper on the table. Then, a minute later, already talking about something else, he picked it up from the table and placed it on the bureau.

"I believe that yesterday you said you wished to question me . . . officially . . . about my acquaintanceship with . . . the murdered woman?" Raskolnikov began again. "Why did I insert the word 'believe'?" flashed through his mind like lightning. "Well, and why am I so worried that I inserted that word 'believe'?" Another thought occurred to him immediately, also like lightning.

Suddenly he felt that his suspiciousness, as a result of one encounter with Porfiry, from only a few words, a few glances, had in one moment already grown into something of monstrous proportions . . . and that this was very dangerous: his nerves were irritated, and his anxiety was increasing. "This is dreadful, simply dreadful! I'll say too much again."

"Yes, yes, yes! Don't worry! There's no hurry, no hurry at all, sir," muttered Porfiry Petrovich, pacing back and forth around the table, but seemingly without any objective, as if hastening first to the window, then to the bureau, then back to the table, first avoiding Raskol-

---

* "Simply" (French).

nikov's suspicious glance, then suddenly stopping in one place and staring directly at him. His small, plump, round figure, like a ball rolling in various directions and bouncing off all the walls, seemed very strange indeed.

"We'll have plenty of time, plenty of time, sir! Do you smoke? Do you have any cigarettes? Here's one, sir," he continued, offering his guest a cigarette. "You know, I'm receiving you here, but my apartment's over there, behind the partition . . . the official one. Right now I'm staying in a private apartment for some time. It was necessary to complete some repairs here. It's almost ready now. . . . You know, an official apartment is a wonderful thing, eh? What do you think?"

"Yes, a wonderful thing," replied Raskolnikov, regarding him almost with a smirk.

"A wonderful thing, a wonderful thing," repeated Porfiry Petrovich, as if suddenly beginning to think about something altogether different. "Yes, a wonderful thing!" he said, almost shouting at last, suddenly looking directly at Raskolnikov and pausing two steps away from him. This foolish incessant repetition that an official apartment is a wonderful thing, its vulgar triviality, was in marked contrast to the earnest, thoughtful, and enigmatic glance he now aimed at his guest.

But this inflamed Raskolnikov's spite even further, and he could scarcely refrain from issuing a sarcastic and somewhat careless challenge.

"Do you know," he asked abruptly, looking at him almost insolently and, as it were, enjoying his own insolence, "it seems there's a legal procedure, a legal device—for all possible investigators—to begin at first from afar, with trivialities, or even with something serious, but completely irrelevant, in order to, so to speak, encourage or, to put it more directly, to distract the person being interrogated, to lull his sense of caution, and then, all of a sudden, to hit him over the head in the most unexpected manner with the most fatal and dangerous question—isn't that so? Isn't this still described reverently in all the textbooks of rules and instructions?"

"Yes, yes . . . so, you think I went on about the official apartment . . . eh?" While saying this Porfiry Petrovich squinted, winked;

something cheerful and sly crossed his face quickly; the wrinkles on his forehead were smoothed out, his little eyes narrowed, his features slackened, and suddenly he burst into nervous, prolonged laughter, his whole body quaking and quivering, while staring directly at Raskolnikov. He, too, began to laugh, forcing himself somewhat; but when Porfiry, seeing that he was also laughing, collapsed into such peals of laughter that he almost turned bright red, Raskolnikov's repulsion suddenly overtook his caution: he stopped laughing, frowned, and for a long time stared maliciously at Porfiry without taking his eyes off him, all during the time of his long and, as it were, intentionally prolonged fit of laughter. Carelessness was, however, obvious on both sides: it turned out that Porfiry Petrovich seemed to be laughing right in the face of his guest, who was taking this laughter maliciously, and Porfiry wasn't the least bit ashamed of this circumstance. This last fact was very significant for Raskolnikov: he realized that a little while ago Porfiry Petrovich had probably not been ashamed; on the contrary, perhaps he himself, Raskolnikov, had fallen into a trap; there was something here that he didn't know about, some sort of goal; perhaps everything had already been prepared, and now, at any moment, it would be revealed and would ensnare him . . .

At once he came straight to the point; he stood up and picked up his cap.

"Porfiry Petrovich," he began decisively, but with rather clear irritation. "Yesterday you declared that you wished me to come here for some sort of interrogation." (He especially emphasized the word "interrogation.") "I have come; if you need anything, ask me; if not, then let me go. I have no time; I have things to do. . . . I must attend the funeral of that same civil servant who was trampled by horses, about whom you . . . you also know," he added, immediately growing angry at his addition and, therefore, feeling even more irritated than before. "I'm fed up with all of this, sir, do you hear, and have been for some time. . . . I became ill partly as a result. . . . In a word"—he was almost shouting, aware that the words about his illness were even more inappropriate—"in a word: please either ask me whatever you want to, or let me go, right now. . . . And if you do question me, then only in the proper form, sir! Otherwise, I won't allow it; therefore, farewell for the time being, since there's nothing now left for the two of us to talk about."

"Good Lord! What are you saying? What's there for me to ask?" clucked Porfiry Petrovich suddenly, at once altering his tone and his look; he stopped laughing immediately. "Please don't be concerned," he added, once again racing around the room, suddenly urging Raskolnikov to sit down again. "There's no hurry, there's plenty of time, sir, and all this is mere nonsense, sir! Just the opposite: I'm so glad you finally decided to visit us. . . . I want to receive you as a guest. As for that blasted laughter, Rodion Romanovich, old boy, will you forgive me? That is your patronymic, isn't it? I'm a nervous man, sir, and you really did amuse me with your witty remark; sometimes, I must admit, I start shaking like a piece of rubber, and keep it up for half an hour. . . . I'm easily moved to laughter, sir. With my constitution, I even fear that I might suffer a stroke. Won't you have a seat? Please, old boy, or else I'll think you're angry . . ."

Raskolnikov was silent; he listened and observed, still frowning angrily. He did sit down, but he didn't let go of his cap.

"I'll tell you one thing, Rodion Romanovich, old boy, about myself, to explain my character, so to speak," Porfiry Petrovich continued, still bustling about the room and, as before, avoiding meeting his guest's eyes. "You know, I'm not married, not sophisticated, and not well known; in addition, I'm all washed up, finished, sir, gone to seed and . . . and . . . and have you noticed, Rodion Romanovich, that here among us, that is, in Russia, sir, especially in our Petersburg circles, if two clever men, not yet acquainted with each other but, so to speak, who mutually respect one another, the way you and I do now, sir, if they come together, they spend half an hour without ever finding anything to talk about—they freeze up in front of each other, they sit there and they're both embarrassed. Everyone has something to talk about, ladies, for example . . . or fashionable people, for example, people in high society, there's always something to talk about, *c'est de rigueur*, but people in the middle, like us—that is, those who think—we're always embarrassed and not talkative. . . . Why do you think that's so, old boy? Do you think it's because we have no interest in social matters, or is it that we're very honest and don't wish to deceive one another? I don't know, sir. Eh? What do you think? Put your cap down, sir, it looks as if you plan to leave at once; really, it's uncomfortable to see it. . . . On the other hand, I'm so glad, sir . . ."

Raskolnikov put his cap down, maintained his silence, and listened seriously, with a scowl, to Porfiry's empty, disjointed chatter. "Is he really trying to distract me with his foolish chatter?"

"I won't offer you coffee, sir, it's not the place; but why not sit here with a friend for five minutes or so for some amusement," Porfiry chattered on without stopping, "and you know, sir, all these official obligations . . . don't be offended, old boy, if I keep pacing back and forth, sir; forgive me, old boy, I'm most afraid to offend you, but exercise is simply essential to me, sir. I sit all the time, and I'm so glad to spend five minutes moving . . . it's hemorrhoids, sir. . . . I keep meaning to try gymnastics to treat them; they say that state councillors, active state councillors, and even privy councillors, like to jump rope, sir; that's science for you, in our day and age, sir. . . . Yes, sir. . . . And as far as my obligations here, interrogations and all that formality . . . you yourself, old boy, were good enough to mention interrogations, sir . . . well, you know, really, Rodion Romanovich, old boy, these interrogations sometimes confound the interrogator more than they do the person being interrogated. . . . You just remarked on this, old boy, with complete fairness and wittiness." (Raskolnikov had made no such remark.) "You get mixed up, sir! Really, mixed up! And it's always one and the same thing, one and the same, like beating a drum! So the reform* will take place and at least they'll call us something different, ha-ha-ha! And as for our legal procedures—as you so wittily expressed it—I'm in complete agreement with you, sir. Who, tell me, who out of all the people accused of crimes, even if they're absolute muzhiks,† who doesn't know, for example, that at first they begin to lull you with irrelevant questions (in your own fortuitous expression) and then all of a sudden hit you over the head, with an axe, sir, ha-ha-ha, over your head, in your fortuitous phrase, ha-ha! So you really thought I wanted to use

---

* A reference to the judicial reforms of 1864.

† Russian peasants; in common usage, also means louts or bumpkins.

the matter of this apartment with you . . . ha-ha! You're an ironic fellow. No, I won't do it! Ah, by the way, one little word calls up another; one idea summons another. You were good enough to mention form just a little while ago, you know, the forms of the interrogator, sir. . . . Why bother with the proper forms? The forms, you know, in many cases, are just nonsense, sir. Sometimes, you just chat like friends, and it's more useful. Formality leads nowhere, allow me to reassure you, sir; and what is there in the forms, I ask you? Forms mustn't hamper the interrogator at every step. The business of the interrogator is, so to speak, a kind of freewheeling art, or something of the sort . . . ha-ha-ha!"

Porfiry Petrovich caught his breath for a moment. He had been spurting these empty, meaningless phrases without stop, suddenly dropping in some enigmatic words, then wandering off into nonsense again. He was now almost running around the room, moving his stout little legs faster and faster, looking down at the floor, his right hand thrust behind his back, his left constantly waving about, executing various gestures, each time astonishingly ill-suited to his words. Raskolnikov suddenly noticed that, as he ran about the room, he paused a few times, as it were, next to the door for a moment, and seemed to be listening. . . . "Is he expecting something?"

"But you were really quite correct, sir," Porfiry resumed again, cheerfully, regarding Raskolnikov with unusual sincerity (as a result of which Raskolnikov even shuddered and promptly prepared himself), "really correct, sir, when you were so witty at the expense of our legal forms, ha-ha! These profoundly psychological devices of ours (certain of them, of course) are extremely amusing, sir, perhaps even useless, sir, if one is confined by these formalities, sir. Yes, sir . . . I'm talking about forms again: well, if I recognize—or, more correctly, suspect—that someone or other has committed a crime, sir, in a case I've been assigned. . . . Why, you're studying law, aren't you, Rodion Romanovich?"

"Yes, I was . . ."

"Well, then here's a little example for the future—that is, don't think I'd dare to instruct you: why, just look at those articles on crime you publish! No, sir, it's just as a fact that I dare present you with a little example—so then, if I, for instance, consider someone guilty of committing a crime, why, I ask you, would I want to alarm him prematurely, even if I had definite evidence against him, sir? For example, I'm obliged to arrest one person sooner, but someone else has a different character, sir; so why shouldn't I let him gallivant around town, sir, ha-ha! No, I can see you don't quite understand, so I'll explain it to you more clearly: for instance, if I were to put him in jail too soon, then I'd be giving him moral support, so to speak, ha-ha! You're laughing?" (Raskolnikov wasn't even tempted to laugh: he sat there, his teeth clenched, without taking his angry gaze from Porfiry Petrovich's eyes). "Meanwhile, that's how it is, especially with some subjects, because people are different, sir, yet there's only one procedure for all of them, sir. Now you'll say, what about the evidence? Well, let's suppose there is evidence, sir, but evidence, old boy, cuts two ways, for the most part, sir. I'm an investigator and, as a result, I confess that I'm an imperfect man: I'd like to present an investigation that is, so to speak, mathematically clear; I'd like to have evidence that is the equivalent of two times two makes four! It would be direct and incontrovertible proof! But if you lock someone up before it's time—even if I were convinced that it was *him*—I might be depriving myself of the means of further exposure, and why? Because I'd be giving him a definite position, so to speak, defining him psychologically and reassuring him, and he'd retreat from me into his shell: he'd understand at last that he was being accused of the crime. They say that in Sevastopol, right after the Battle of the Alma,* clever people were terrified that at any moment the enemy would attack with all its might and would soon capture the town; but when they saw that the enemy preferred to stage a regular siege and was digging the first row of trenches, they say that these same clever people rejoiced and felt reassured, sir: if they were going to mount a regular siege, then the affair would drag on for at least two months! You're laughing again. You don't believe me? Well, of course, you're right. You're right, sir, quite right! These are special cases, I agree with you; the example I presented is really a special case,

---

* In 1854, during the Crimean War, Russian armies were defeated at the Alma River and retreated to Sevastopol.

sir! But here's what you need to keep in mind, my dear Rodion Romanovich: the average case, sir, the one for which all these legal forms and procedures are devised, and with which they're intended to cope and are recorded in books, doesn't really exist at all, for the simple reason that every case, every crime, for example, as soon as it occurs in reality, immediately becomes a completely special case, sir; in fact, it's like nothing that's ever happened before, sir. Very amusing cases of this kind sometimes occur, sir. If I leave a particular gentleman all alone: if I don't arrest him and don't disturb him, but if he knows at every hour and every minute, or at least if he suspects, that I know everything, all there is to know, and that I'm following him day and night, watching him constantly, and if he feels the weight of my conscious suspicion and fear, well then, he's absolutely certain to lose his head. He himself will come forward of his own accord, sir, and might perhaps do something that, just like two times two makes four, will provide, so to speak, mathematical clarity—that would be very nice, sir. This can happen even with a coarse peasant, all the more so with people of our ilk, a clever contemporary man who's developed in a certain direction. For this reason, my dear boy, it's very important to understand the direction of a person's development. And the nerves, sir, the nerves, you've forgotten all about them, sir! These days everyone's so sick, and frayed, and irritable! And they're all so full of bile, so very full! And this, in its own way, I can tell you, sir, can be a mine of information! Why should I be upset if a person wanders around town unhindered? Let him, let him go wherever he pleases for now; I know that he's my prey and won't get away from me! Where could he run to, ha-ha! Abroad, or what? A Pole would go abroad, but not *him*, the more so since I'm following him and have taken precautions. Would he run into the depths of the countryside? But peasants live there, genuine, homespun Russian peasants; so our contemporary, a developed person, would sooner prefer prison than life with such strangers as our peasants are, ha-ha! But this is all nonsense and beside the point. What does it mean to run away? It's a formality; it's not the main thing. This isn't why he doesn't run away from me: it's that he has nowhere to run; he won't run away *psychologically*, ha-ha! What a fine little expression that is! He won't escape from me by the law of nature, even if there was somewhere to run to. Have you seen a moth near a candle? Well, just like that he'll circle, circle around me, like a moth around a flame; his freedom will no longer satisfy him; he'll start thinking, become confused, leading himself all around; he'll get tangled up in a net and worry himself to death! Even more than that, he'll present me with some sort of mathematical proof, like two times two—if only I allow him enough time between the acts. . . . And he'll keep on, keep circling around me, constantly narrowing the radius of his circle—and then—plop! He'll fly right into my mouth; I'll swallow him up, sir, and that will be very nice, sir, ha-ha-ha! You don't believe me?"

Raskolnikov made no reply; he sat there pale and immobile, staring at Porfiry's face with the same strained attention.

"It's a fine lesson!" he thought, growing cold. "By now it's not even a game of cat and mouse, as it was yesterday. After all, it isn't that he's showing off his strength and prompting me for nothing: he's much too clever for that! There must be some other motive, but what is it? Hey, brother, you're frightening me with this nonsense and trying to trick me! You don't have any evidence, and the man I saw yesterday doesn't really exist! You're simply trying to confuse me, to annoy me prematurely, and pounce on me when I'm in such a condition, but you're wrong, you'll slip and fall! But why, why is he prompting me this way? Is he counting on my frayed nerves? No, brother, you're mistaken, you'll slip and fall, even if you've prepared some surprise. . . . Well, now, we'll see what you've come up with."

He braced himself with all his might, preparing for some terrible and unknown catastrophe. At times he felt like hurling himself at Porfiry and strangling him on the spot. When he'd first come in, he had been afraid of his own rage. He felt that his mouth was dry, his heart was pounding, and foam was forming on his lips. But he still resolved to remain silent and not utter one word until it was time. He realized that this was the best tactic in his situation because then he wouldn't say anything he'd regret later; on the contrary, he'd irritate his foe with his silence and perhaps Porfiry might even say something he'd come to regret later. At least, that was what he was hoping.

"No, I see you don't believe me, sir; you think I'm playing innocent pranks on you," Porfiry resumed, becoming more and more cheerful, giggling constantly with enjoyment, and beginning to move around the room once again. "And, of course, you're right, sir. God created me in such a way that I arouse only comic thoughts in other people; I'm a buffoon, sir; but here's what I can tell you, sir, and I can repeat it again, sir, that you, old boy, Rodion Romanovich, you should excuse me, just an old man, while you're still so young, sir, so to speak, in your first youth, and therefore you value human intelligence above all else, according to the custom of all young people. Playful wit and abstract conclusions of reason merely tempt you, sir. It's precisely like the former Austrian Hofkriegsrath,* for example, as much as I can judge military matters: on paper they defeated Napoleon and took him prisoner; they had calculated and figured it all out in their study, but then, you see, General Mack went and surrendered with his entire army, hee-hee-hee! I see, old boy, I see, Rodion Romanovich, that you're laughing at me, a civilian, for taking my examples from military history. But what's to be done? It's a weakness. I love military affairs, and I love reading about all these military communications. . . . Clearly I missed my true calling. I really should have served in the military, sir. I might not have become a Napoleon, but I might have become a major, sir, hee-hee-hee! Well, sir, now, my dear, I'll tell you the whole truth about this *special case*, that is: reality and nature, my dear sir, are very important, and they sometimes undercut the most farsighted calculation! Hey, listen to an old man, I'm speaking in earnest, Rodion Romanovich." (Saying this, Porfiry Petrovich, who was barely thirty-five, suddenly seemed to grow older; even his voice changed, and he seemed more hunched over.) "Besides, I'm a very candid man, sir. . . . Am I candid or not? What's your opinion? It seems to me that I'm completely candid: I'm telling you all these things for nothing, and I'm not even asking any reward, hee-hee! Well, then, sir, I'll continue, sir: wit, in my opinion, is a majestic thing, sir; it is, so to speak, the glory of nature and a consolation for life, and what tricks it can sometimes play, so that at times, it seems, it can bewilder even some poor little investigator, who's distracted by his own fantasy, as always happens, because

---

* "Court Council of War" (German). In 1805, the Austrian army, commanded by General Mack, surrendered to Napoleon during the War of the Third Coalition.

he's also only human, sir! Human nature comes to the aid of the poor investigator, that's the point. A young person, carried away by his own wit, 'overstepping all obstacles' (as you were pleased to express it in the wittiest and cleverest fashion), never even thinks about this. Let's suppose that he, that is, this man, our *special case*, sir, this *incognito*, sir, will lie brilliantly, in the cleverest way; this might seem to be a triumph, and he could enjoy the fruits of his wit, but, all of a sudden, bang, he falls into a faint in the most interesting and scandalous place. Let's suppose it's an illness, rooms can sometimes be very stuffy, but all the same, sir! Nevertheless, it suggests an idea! He lied incomparably well, but he couldn't rely on his own nature. There it is, the perfidy, sir! Another time, distracted by the playfulness of his wit, he'll begin to make fun of the man who suspects him; he'll grow pale, as if on purpose, as if playing a game, but he grows pale in *too natural a way*, too much like it was the truth, and once again he's suggested an idea! Even if his trick succeeds at first, the investigator will think it over at night, if he's nobody's fool. And it's like that every step of the way, sir! Why? He'll begin to run ahead, butting in where he's not asked for, he'll begin talking incessantly about those things he really should keep silent about, he'll use sly allegories, hee-hee! He himself will come and begin asking questions: why hasn't he still been arrested? Hee-hee-hee! And this can happen with the cleverest fellow, with a psychologist or a writer, sir! Human nature's a mirror, a mirror, sir, the most transparent, sir! Look into it and admire, that's what, sir! Why have you turned so pale, Rodion Romanovich? Is it too stuffy in here? Shall I open a window?"

"Please don't trouble yourself," cried Raskolnikov and suddenly burst out laughing. "Please don't trouble yourself!"

Porfiry paused opposite him, waited a bit, and then suddenly started laughing himself. Raskolnikov stood up from the sofa and abruptly cut short his spasmodic laughter.

"Porfiry Petrovich!" he said in a loud and distinct voice, even though he could barely stand on his trembling legs. "At last I can see clearly that you positively suspect me of the murder of the old woman and her sister Lizaveta. I must tell you that, on my part, I'm sick and tired of this matter. If you find that you have the legal right to prosecute me, then do so; if you have the right to arrest me, than do so. But I won't allow you to laugh in my face and torment me."

All of a sudden his lips began trembling, his eyes shone with rage, and his voice, which had been restrained up to this point, began to rise.

"I won't allow it, sir!" he cried suddenly, banging his fist on the table with all his might. "Do you hear me, Porfiry Petrovich? I won't allow it!"

"Good Lord! Not again!" Porfiry Petrovich cried, apparently in a real fright. "Old boy, Rodion Romanovich! My dear fellow! Friend! What's the matter with you?"

"I won't allow it!" Raskolnikov started shouting again.

"Quiet down, old boy! They'll hear you and come in! Just think, what will we tell them?" Porfiry Petrovich whispered in horror, bringing his face right up to Raskolnikov's.

"I won't allow it, I won't!" Raskolnikov repeated automatically, but also suddenly in a low whisper.

Porfiry quickly turned around and ran to open a window.

"I'll let in some fresh air. You should drink some water, my dear boy, this is an attack, sir!" He rushed to the door to ask for some water, but there in the corner, fortunately, was a carafe.

"Here, old boy, drink some," he whispered, rushing to him with the carafe. "It might help . . ." Porfiry Petrovich's fright and sympathy seemed so natural that Raskolnikov quieted down and began examining him with intense curiosity. He didn't, however, accept the glass of water.

"Rodion Romanovich! My dear boy! You'll drive yourself mad this way, I can assure you. Ah! Have a drink of water! Drink at least a little bit!"

He managed to force him to take the glass of water in his hand. Raskolnikov was automatically about to raise the glass to his lips, but, after coming to his senses, placed the glass on the table with repulsion.

"Yes, sir, you had a little attack, sir! That way you'll bring your illness back, my dear boy," cooed Porfiry Petrovich with friendly sympathy, although he still looked rather disconcerted. "Good Lord! How can you take such bad care of yourself? Dmitry Prokofich came to see me just yesterday—I agree, I agree, I have a nasty, caustic character, but the conclusions he drew from it! Good Lord! He came yesterday after you did; we had dinner, chatted for a long time, and I merely threw my hands up in astonishment; well, I think . . . ah, you, good Lord! Did you send him here? But sit down, old boy, take a seat, for Christ's sake!"

"No, I didn't send him! But I knew he came to see you, and I know why he came," Raskolnikov replied sharply.

"You knew?"

"I did. So what of it?"

"It's just that, Rodion Romanovich, old boy, I know about your other exploits, too; I know everything, sir! I know that you went to *rent an apartment*, toward nighttime, when it was growing dark; you began ringing the bell, asking about the blood, and got the workmen and the caretakers all upset. Why, I understand your spiritual state, that is, at that time. . . . Nevertheless, you'll simply drive yourself mad like that, so help me God, sir! You'll make yourself crazy! Indignation is seething too violently inside you, sir, noble indignation, sir, from the insults you've suffered, first from fate, and then from the police, so you rush around, here and there, to force everyone to speak out, and that way to finish with everything all at once, because you're fed up with all this nonsense and all these suspicions. Isn't that so? Have I guessed your state? But that way you're upsetting not only yourself but also Razumikhin; he's too good a person for this, as you yourself know. You have your illness, but he has his virtue; your illness can also infect him. . . . I can tell you, old boy, when you calm down. . . . But sit down, old boy, for Christ's sake! Please, have a rest; you look terrible; do sit down."

Raskolnikov sat down; his trembling was ending, and his entire body felt hot. In deep amazement, he listened intently to the frightened Porfiry Petrovich, who seemed affably solicitous of him. But he didn't trust even one of his words, although he felt some strange inclination to believe him. Porfiry's unexpected words about the apartment completely stunned him. "How can it be that he apparently knows about the apartment?" he suddenly wondered to himself. "And he himself even tells me about it?"

"Yes, sir, we had a case that was almost the same in our legal practice, sir, a psychological case, a morbid one, sir," Porfiry rattled on, speaking very quickly. "That fellow also tried to cast aspersions on himself as a murderer, sir, and this is how he did it: he invented an extensive hallucination, presented facts, explained circumstances, became muddled, and wound up confusing everyone and everything. And what for? He himself, absolutely unintentionally, was partly the cause of the murder, but only in part, and as soon as he learned that he had given the murderers a pretext for the crime, he became miserable, lost the ability to think clearly, began seeing visions, went completely mad, and even persuaded himself that he was the murderer! Finally, the Governing Senate heard the case, and the unfortunate man was acquitted and provided with care. Thanks to the Governing Senate! Oh dear, ay yi yi! So what then, old boy? You can end up with a fever if such impulses happen to irritate your nerves and you go around at night ringing doorbells and asking about blood! I've learned all this psychology in my legal practice, sir. In this way a man can sometimes feel inclined to throw himself out a window or jump from a bell tower; the emotion can be very seductive. Same for ringing doorbells. . . . It's an illness, Rodion Romanovich, an illness! You've begun to neglect your illness too much, sir. You ought to consult an experienced doctor, and not that chubby fellow you see! You're delirious! You're doing all these things in your delirium!"

For a moment, everything seemed to be spinning around Raskolnikov.

"Could he, could he," flashed through his head, "be lying even now? It's not possible, not possible!" He kept pushing this thought away, foreseeing to what degree of rage and fury could it drive him, and feeling that he might lose his mind from that rage.

"That wasn't in a delirium; I was completely conscious!" he cried, gathering all the powers of his reason to discern the point of Porfiry's game. "I was conscious, conscious! Do you hear?"

"Yes, I understand you, and I hear you, sir! You also said yesterday that you weren't delirious, you even insisted on that! I understand, sir, everything you can say! Hey! Listen to me, Rodion Romanovich, my good fellow, there's this circumstance at least. If, as a matter of fact, you really were guilty, or in some way involved with this accursed business, would you be insisting that you weren't delirious when you did it all and, on the contrary, were in full command of your faculties? And so very insistent, with such obstinacy, especially insistent—could this possibly be so, could it? In my opinion, it is just the opposite. If you really felt something was wrong, then surely it would make sense for you to insist that you were definitely delirious! Isn't that so? Well, isn't it?"

There was something crafty contained in this question. Raskolnikov recoiled all the way to the back of the sofa, away from Porfiry, who was leaning over him, and he stared directly at him in silent perplexity.

"And then about Mr. Razumikhin, that is, whether it was his own idea to come here yesterday to speak on your behalf or was it at your instigation? But you don't even hide it! You insist that it was at your instigation!"

Raskolnikov had never insisted on that. A chill ran up and down his spine.

"You're still lying," he said slowly and weakly, his lips distorted into a sickly smile. "You want to show me once again that you know my whole game, you know all my answers in advance," he said, feeling that he wasn't weighing his words as he should. "You want to frighten me . . . or you're simply laughing at me . . ."

He continued staring at him intently while saying this, and once again boundless rage flashed suddenly in his eyes.

"You keep lying!" he cried. "You yourself know well that the criminal's best dodge is to reveal anything that doesn't have to be hidden insofar as possible. I don't believe you!"

"What a slippery fish you are!" Porfiry said with a giggle. "There's no way to deal with you; you're suffering from some sort of monomania. So, you don't believe me? I say that you do believe, you believe me one inch of the way, but I'll make you believe me the whole way, because I truly like you and sincerely wish you well."

Raskolnikov's lips trembled.

"Yes, sir, I do wish, sir, and I will tell you definitively, sir," he continued, gently, amicably, taking Raskolnikov by the arm, just above his elbow. "I'll tell you definitively, sir: take care of your illness. In addition, your family has now come to see you; you should think about them. You should attend to them and cherish them, but all you do is frighten them . . ."

"What business is that of yours? How do you know that? Why are you so interested? Is it that you're following me and therefore you want me to know that?"

"My dear fellow! Why, it was from you, from you that I found all this out! You don't notice that, in your agitated state, you yourself blurt everything out to me and to others. I also found out many interesting details yesterday from Mr. Razumikhin, Dmitry Prokofich. No, sir, you interrupted me, but I'll say that in spite of your suspiciousness, all your wit, you've managed to lose your sensible view of things. Take, for example, that theme of the doorbells once again: I, that is, the examining magistrate, wholeheartedly revealed that precious detail to you, that fact. (And it is a fact, sir!) And you don't see anything in that? Why, if I suspected you in the slightest, why would I proceed in that way? On the contrary, I'd first have lulled your suspicions, and not revealed that I already knew that fact; thus, to distract you to the opposite side and then, all of a sudden, to startle you with an axe over your head (borrowing your own expression): 'What were you doing, sir, in the murdered woman's apartment at ten in the evening, even closer to eleven? And why were you ringing the doorbell? And why were you asking about the blood? And why did you try to deceive the caretakers and urge them to go to the police lieutenant?' If I'd had even a drop of suspicion about you, that's how I should've behaved. I should've taken a proper statement from you, conducted a search, why perhaps I even should've arrested you. . . . If I've acted otherwise, then I'm not harboring any suspicions of you! You've lost your sensible view of things; I repeat, you don't see anything, sir!"

Raskolnikov's entire body jerked so violently that Porfiry Petrovich noticed it too well.

"You keep lying!" he cried. "I don't know your aims, but you keep lying. . . . A little while ago you weren't talking like that, and I can't be mistaken about that. . . . You're lying!"

"Me? Lying?" Porfiry took up the idea, obviously getting excited but maintaining his most cheerful and mocking look, and, it seems, not troubling himself at all about Mr. Raskolnikov's opinion of him. "Me?

Lying? Well, and how was I behaving toward you just a little while ago (that is, as the examining magistrate), when I prompted you and offered you all the means for your defense, providing all that psychology: 'Illness,' I said, 'delirium, insults; melancholy and policemen,' and all the rest? Eh? Hee-hee-hee! Although I'll say, by the way, that all of these psychological means for defense, these excuses and evasions, are extremely unsupported, and they cut both ways: 'Illness,' you said, 'delirium, daydreams, fantasies, I don't recall,' all that may be so, sir, but why is it, old boy, that you see precisely these daydreams in your illness or your delirium, and not others? After all, could there have been other ones, sir? Isn't that so? Hee-hee-hee-hee!"

Raskolnikov looked at him with pride and contempt.

"In a word," he said in a loud, insistent voice, standing up and pushing Porfiry away slightly as he stood, "in a word, I want to know: do you acknowledge that I'm completely free of suspicion or *not*? Tell me, Porfiry Petrovich, tell me once and for all, definitively and quickly, immediately!"

"What a task! What a task you're setting," cried Porfiry with an absolutely cheerful, crafty, and completely untroubled look. "Why do you want to know, why do you want to know so much if no one's even started pestering you yet? You're like a little child: asking to play with fire! Why are you so worried? Why do you thrust yourself upon us, for what reasons? Eh? Hee-hee-hee!"

"I repeat," cried Raskolnikov in a fury, "I can't tolerate this any longer . . ."

"What, sir? Is it the uncertainty?" Porfiry interrupted.

"Don't mock me! I won't have it! I tell you, I won't have it. I can't stand it, and I won't! Do you hear me? Do you?" he cried, banging his fist on the table again.

"Quiet down, quiet! They'll hear! I warn you in earnest: take care of yourself. I'm not joking!" Porfiry said in a whisper, but this time there was none of his previous womanly generosity and frightened expression; on the contrary, now he was plainly *ordering* him, sternly, knitting his brows and seeming to banish at once all secrets and ambiguities. But that lasted only a moment. Raskolnikov, now perplexed, suddenly flew into a complete fury; but, strange to say, once again he obeyed the order to speak more quietly, even though he was suffering a strong paroxysm of rage.

"I won't allow you to torment me!" he whispered suddenly, the same way he had before, instantly aware that he was unable to ignore the order; as a result of this thought, he felt even greater rage. "Arrest me, search me, but be so good as to act in accordance with the proper forms; don't play with me, sir! Don't you dare . . ."

"Don't trouble yourself about the proper forms," Porfiry interrupted with his previous crafty smile, even seeming to admire Raskolnikov with some enjoyment. "I've invited you here now, old boy, informally, in a completely friendly manner!"

"I don't want your friendship, and I spit at it! Do you hear? Now, look: I'm taking my cap and leaving. Well then, what do you say now, if you intend to arrest me?"

He grabbed his cap and headed for the door.

"Don't you want to see the little surprise I have?" Porfiry said with a giggle, once again grabbing him a little above his elbow and stopping him at the door. He was clearly becoming more and more cheerful and playful, and that positively caused Raskolnikov to lose control of himself.

"What sort of surprise? What is it?" he asked, suddenly pausing and regarding Porfiry with fright.

"A little surprise, sir, right here, waiting on the other side of my door, hee-hee-hee!" (He pointed to the closed door in the partition that led to his official living quarters.) "I locked it in, so it wouldn't run away."

"What is it? Where? What?" Raskolnikov approached the door and wanted to open it, but it was locked.

"It's locked, sir. Here's the key!"

And as a matter of fact, he took the key from his pocket and showed it to him.

"You're still lying!" howled Raskolnikov, no longer able to restrain himself. "You're lying, you clown, you damned Punchinello!"* he cried,

---

* A classical character of seventeenth-century commedia dell'arte that became a stock character in Neapolitan puppetry.

and rushed at Porfiry, who retreated toward the door but didn't flinch in the least.

"I understand everything, everything!" he said, leaping in his direction. "You're lying and teasing me, so I'll give myself away . . ."

"You can't give yourself away any more, old boy, Rodion Romanych. You're in a rage. Don't shout or I'll call the others in here, sir!"

"You're lying. Nothing will happen! Call them in! You knew I was ill, and you wanted to annoy me, drive me into a fury, so that I'd give myself away; that was your aim! No, present your facts! I've understood everything! You have no facts. You have only worthless, insignificant guesses, Zametov's guesses! You knew my character; you wanted to drive me into a fury and then suddenly startle me with priests and deputies. . . . You're waiting for them? Eh? What are you waiting for? Where are they? Present them!"

"What sort of deputies are you talking about, old boy? The things a person imagines! And to do as you say would not be according to the form; you don't know what the proper procedure is, my dear. . . . The form hasn't gone away, sir, you'll see for yourself!" muttered Porfiry, listening at the door.

And as a matter of fact, at that moment some noise could be heard in the other room, right behind the door.

"Ah, here they come!" cried Raskolnikov. "You sent for them! You've been waiting for them! You were counting on it. . . . Well, bring them all in here: deputies, witnesses, whatever you want . . . bring them in! I'm ready! I am!"

But then a strange thing happened, something so unexpected in the normal course of events that neither Raskolnikov nor Porfiry Petrovich could have counted on such a denouement.

VI

Afterward, remembering this moment, Raskolnikov recalled it as follows.

The noise coming from behind the door suddenly increased, and the door opened slightly.

"What's the matter?" cried Porfiry Petrovich with annoyance. "I warned you that . . ."

For a moment there was no reply, but it was clear that several people were standing behind the door and seemed to be pushing someone.

"What's going on?" Porfiry repeated in agitation.

"They've brought in the prisoner, Nikolai," someone's voice was heard saying.

"Not now! Go away! Wait a bit! How did he get here? What a lack of discipline!" Porfiry cried, rushing to the door.

"But he . . ." that voice was about to begin again but stopped short.

For a few seconds, not more, an actual struggle occurred; then it suddenly seemed that someone shoved someone else forcefully, after which a very pale man stepped into Porfiry Petrovich's office.

This man's appearance, at first glance, was very strange. He was staring straight ahead but seemed not to see anyone. Resolution shone in his eyes, but at the same time his face revealed a deathly pallor, as if he were being led to his execution. His lips, totally white, were trembling slightly.

He was still very young, dressed like a common worker, of medium height, gaunt, hair cropped around his head, and with fine, seemingly dry facial features. The person he had unexpectedly shoved aside came rushing into the room and managed to grab him by the shoulder: this was a guard, but Nikolai yanked his arm away and freed himself once again.

A few curious onlookers crowded into the doorway. Some of them tried to get into the room. Everything described here took place almost in a single moment.

"Go away, it's too early! Wait till you're called! Why did you bring him so soon?" Porfiry Petrovich muttered in extreme annoyance, as if completely confused. But Nikolai suddenly sank to his knees.

"What are you doing?" Porfiry cried in astonishment.

"I'm guilty! I'm a sinner! I'm the 'moiderer'!" Nikolai suddenly announced, as if gasping for breath somewhat, but in a rather loud voice.

The silence lasted about ten seconds, as if they were all stunned; even the guard took a step back and no longer tried to approach Nikolai; he retreated automatically to the door and stood there motionless.

"What's all this?" cried Porfiry Petrovich, emerging from his momentary stupor.

"I'm the . . . 'moiderer,'" repeated Nikolai, after a brief pause.

"What . . . you. . . . What. . . . Who did you kill?"

Porfiry Petrovich, apparently, was flustered.

Nikolai paused once again.

"Alyona Ivanovna and her sister Lizaveta Ivanovna . . . I killed them . . . with an axe. Everything went blank . . ." he added suddenly and fell silent again. He was still on his knees.

Porfiry Petrovich stood there for several moments, as if lost in thought, but suddenly came back to life and waved the uninvited witnesses away. They immediately disappeared, and the door was closed. Then he glanced at Raskolnikov, who was standing in the corner staring wildly at Nikolai. Porfiry was about to approach him, but stopped suddenly, looked at him, shifted his gaze at once to Nikolai, then back to Raskolnikov, then again to Nikolai, and at once, as if carried away, and then turned on Nikolai again.

"Why are you rushing ahead with your 'everything went blank'?"

he shouted at him, almost in a fury. "I haven't asked you yet whether everything went blank or not . . . tell me: did you kill them?"

"I'm the 'moiderer' . . . I'll testify . . ." declared Nikolai.

"E-eh! How did you kill them?"

"With an axe. I got one."

"Eh, he's in a hurry! Alone?"

Nikolai didn't understand the question.

"Did you kill them alone?"

"Alone. Mitka's innocent and had nothing to do with it."

"Don't be in such a hurry to talk about Mitka. E-eh! Why did you, well, why did you run down the stairs just then? The caretakers bumped into the two of you, didn't they?"

"I did it to hoodwink them . . . then . . . I ran with Mitka," replied Nikolai as if hurrying and having prepared his answer beforehand.

"Well, so that's it!" Porfiry cried angrily. "He's using someone else's words!" he muttered, as if to himself; then, all of a sudden, he noticed Raskolnikov once more.

Apparently, he was so distracted by Nikolai that for a moment he had even forgotten all about Raskolnikov. Now he suddenly came to his senses and was even embarrassed . . .

"Rodion Romanovich, old boy! Excuse me, sir!" he said, rushing over to him. "This isn't right, sir; please, sir. . . . You have no business here . . . and I myself. . . . You see what surprises we have! Would you mind, sir?"

Taking him by the arm, he showed him to the door.

"It seems you weren't expecting this?" said Raskolnikov, still not understanding anything very clearly, of course, though he had already managed to take heart.

"You didn't expect it either, old boy. Look at how your hand is trembling! He-he!"

"You're trembling, too, Porfiry Petrovich."

"I am trembling, sir; I didn't expect it, sir!"

They were standing in the doorway. Porfiry waited impatiently for Raskolnikov to leave.

"Aren't you going to show me your little surprise?" Raskolnikov said all of a sudden.

"He can say that even though his teeth are still chattering, he-he! What an ironic fellow you are! Well, sir, good-bye, sir."

"In my opinion, we might as well say *farewell*."

"As God wills it, sir, as God wills it!" muttered Porfiry with a twisted smile.

As he made his way through the office, Raskolnikov noticed that many people were staring at him intently. In the hallway, among the crowd, he noticed the two caretakers from *that* house, the same two he'd told to fetch the police that night. They were standing there waiting for something. But as soon as he reached the stairs, he suddenly heard Porfiry Petrovich's voice again. Turning around, he saw that he was running after him, panting for breath.

"One more word, sir, Rodion Romanovich, about all this; it's as God wills it, nevertheless, according to our procedure, there are still some things I want to ask you about, sir. . . . So we'll see each other again, we will, sir."

Porfiry stopped in front of him with a smile.

"We will, sir," he added once more.

One might suppose that he wanted to say something more, but somehow didn't manage it.

"And you must forgive me, Porfiry Petrovich, for what I said before. . . . I got angry," Raskolnikov began, now feeling completely encouraged, even experiencing a desire to swagger a bit.

"Never mind, sir, never mind," Porfiry replied almost joyfully. "I, too, sir. . . . I have a venomous character, I confess, I confess! We'll see each other again, sir. If God wills it, we'll see each other many times, sir!"

"And really get to know each other well?" observed Raskolnikov.

"And really get to know each other well," agreed Porfiry Petrovich. Squinting, he looked at him very seriously. "Are you going to a name-day party now, sir?"

"To a funeral, sir."

"Oh, yes, to a funeral! Take care of your health, your health, sir . . ."

"I don't know what to wish you in return," replied Raskolnikov, already heading down the stairs, but suddenly turning again to Porfiry. "I'd wish you great success, but you see how amusing your job is!"

"How is it amusing, sir?" asked Porfiry Petrovich, who had turned to go. He pricked up his ears.

"Well, what about that poor Mikolka, whom you must have tormented and tortured, psychologically, that is, in your own way, until he confessed. Day and night, you must have been trying to prove to him: 'You're the murderer, you're the murderer.' And now that he's confessed, you start to pick him to pieces again: 'You're lying,' you tell him, 'you're not the murderer! You couldn't be! You're repeating someone else's words!' Well, after all that, isn't it really an amusing job?"

"He-he-he! So you noticed that I told Nikolai just now that he was 'using someone else's words'?"

"How could one not notice?"

"He-he! Clever, sir, very clever. You notice everything! You've a genuinely playful mind, sir! You seize hold of the most comical aspects . . . he-he! It's Gogol, the writer, who's said to possess that trait to the highest degree, isn't it?"

"Yes, Gogol."

"Yes, sir. Gogol, sir. . . . Till our next most pleasant meeting, sir."

"Our next most pleasant meeting . . ."

Raskolnikov went straight home. He felt so confused and bewildered that when he got there he threw himself on the sofa; he sat for a quarter of an hour merely resting, trying somehow or other to collect his thoughts. He didn't even begin thinking about Nikolai: he felt dumbfounded; there was something inexpressible, incredible in Nikolai's confession, something he was completely unable to grasp now. But Nikolai's confession was a genuine fact. The consequences of it immediately became clear to him: the lie had to be uncovered, and then they would come after him again. But at least he was free until that time, and he absolutely had to do something for himself, because the danger was unavoidable.

But to what degree? The situation began to clarify. Recalling in rough form, in general, the entire recent scene with Porfiry, he couldn't keep from shuddering once again in terror. Of course, he still didn't know all of Porfiry's aims; he couldn't fathom all of his recent moves. But a part of his game had been revealed, and nobody, of course, could better understand than he how terrifying this last "move" was. A lit-

tle more, and he *might* have given himself away completely, in actual
fact. Knowing the morbidity of his character, having understood him
and grasped him from the first glance, Porfiry was acting almost with
certainty, although perhaps too decisively. There was no argument:
Raskolnikov had already managed to compromise himself too much,
but no *facts* had yet been established. It was all still only circumstantial.
But did he really, really understand it all now? Wasn't he perhaps making a mistake? What result had Porfiry been after today? Had he really
had something prepared for him today? What exactly was it? Had he
really been waiting for something or not? How would they have parted
today if the unexpected disaster with Nikolai hadn't occurred?

Porfiry had shown almost his entire game; of course, he took a risk,
but he showed it (so it all seemed to Raskolnikov), and if he'd really
had anything more, he would have revealed that, too. "What on earth
was that 'surprise'? Was it a joke? Did it mean anything, or not? Could
it have concealed anything resembling facts or a positive accusation?
The man from yesterday? Where had he gone? Where was he today? If
Porfiry really had anything positive, then of course it was in connection
with the man from yesterday . . ."

He sat on the sofa, his head hanging down, resting his elbows on
his knees and covering his face with his hands. A nervous tremor shook
his whole body. At last he stood up, took his cap, thought for a bit, and
headed for the door.

He had the strong feeling that, at least for today, he could almost
certainly consider himself out of danger. All of a sudden, he experienced a feeling like joy in his heart: he felt like hurrying to Katerina
Ivanovna's. Of course, he was late for the funeral, but he would get
there in time for the wake, and there, right now, he would see Sonya.

He stopped, thought for a while, and a sickly smile appeared on
his lips.

"Today! Today!" he repeated to himself. "Yes, today! It has to
be . . ."

He was just about to open the door when it suddenly began to
open on its own. He shuddered and jumped back. The door opened
slowly and quietly, and all of a sudden a figure appeared—it was yesterday's man from *out of nowhere*.

The man paused on the threshold, stared at Raskolnikov in silence, and took a step into the room. He looked exactly the same as he had yesterday: the same figure, dressed the same way, but a major change had taken place in his face and in his glance: he now looked somehow saddened; standing there for a little while, he sighed deeply. The only thing missing was for him to place his hand on his cheek and to lean his head to one side for him to resemble a peasant woman.

"What do you want?" asked the mortified Raskolnikov.

The man was silent and suddenly bowed deeply to him, almost down to the ground. At least, he touched the ground with one finger of his right hand.

"What are you doing?"

"I'm guilty," said the man quietly.

"Of what?"

"Of wicked thoughts."

They both stared at each other.

"I felt irritated. When you came there then, perhaps you were tipsy; you told the caretakers to summon the police, and you asked about the blood; I felt annoyed that they left you in vain and because they thought you were drunk. I was so annoyed that I lost sleep. But recalling your address, I came here yesterday and made inquiries . . ."

"Who came?" Raskolnikov interrupted, momentarily starting to remember.

"I did. I offended you."

"So you come from that same house?"

"I was there, standing with them in the gateway, or have you forgotten? I've had my own profession there, for many years. We're furriers, tradesmen, and work at home. . . . But most of all I was irritated . . ."

And suddenly Raskolnikov remembered clearly the whole scene from two days ago under the gateway; he recalled that in addition to the caretakers there had been several people standing there, including some women. He remembered one voice proposing that he should be taken right to the police. He couldn't recall the face of the speaker, and even now he didn't recognize him, but he did recall that he had turned toward him and had even made some reply at the time . . .

So this, therefore, was how all of yesterday's terror was resolved.

The most terrible thing of all was to think that he'd almost perished, that he'd nearly destroyed himself as a result of this *insignificant* circumstance. This meant that besides the question about renting the apartment and the discussion about blood, this man could say nothing further. Therefore, Porfiry also had nothing, nothing except for this *delirium*, no facts, just *psychology*, which cut two ways, nothing positive. Therefore, if no more facts were to appear (and they mustn't appear, they mustn't, they mustn't!), then . . . then what could they do to him? What could they prove definitively, even if they arrested him? Therefore, Porfiry had found out about the apartment only now, just now, and hadn't even known about it before.

"Did you tell Porfiry this today . . . the fact that I came?" he cried, struck by a sudden idea.

"What Porfiry?"

"The chief investigator."

"I did. The caretakers didn't go to the police, but I did."

"Today?"

"I was there a minute before you. I heard everything, how he tormented you."

"Where? What? When?"

"Right there; I was sitting there the whole time, behind his partition."

"What? So you were the surprise? How could that be? For heaven's sake!"

"After seeing," began the tradesman, "that the caretakers wouldn't listen to me and go to the police, because, they said, it was already too late, and perhaps he'd get angry that they hadn't come right away, I felt irritated and couldn't sleep, and I started to make inquiries. After finding out everything yesterday, I went today. At first when I came, he wasn't there. I went back an hour later, but they wouldn't admit me; the third time I came—they let me in. I began telling him everything that happened, and he began pacing around the room, beating his chest: 'What,' he says, 'what are you scoundrels doing to me? If I'd known this, I'd have sent a guard to bring him here!' Then he ran out, summoned someone, and began talking to him in the corner; then he came back to me—and began asking questions and abusing me. He scolded me a great deal; I informed him about everything and said that you didn't dare reply to what I'd said yesterday and that you hadn't recognized me. He began running around again and kept on beating his chest, getting angry, and dashing about, and, when they said that you'd come, 'Well,' he says, 'hide behind the partition, sit here a while and don't move, no matter what you hear.' Then he brought me a chair and locked the door: 'Perhaps,' he says, 'I'll ask you to come in.' When they brought in Nikolai, he sent me away after you left: 'I'll want you again,' he said, 'and will ask you more questions . . .'"

"Did they question Nikolai while you were still there?"

"When you were shown out, then I was also shown out, and they began to question Nikolai."

The tradesman paused and suddenly bowed once again, touching the floor with his finger.

"Forgive me for my slander and my malice."

"God will forgive you," replied Raskolnikov, and as soon as he said this, the tradesman bowed down to him, but this time not to the ground, only from his waist; he turned slowly and left the room. "Everything cuts two ways, now everything cuts two ways," repeated Raskolnikov to himself, and he left the room feeling bolder than ever before.

"Now we'll keep on fighting," he said with a spiteful smile as he went down the stairs. The spite was directed at himself: he recalled his "cowardice" with contempt and shame.

PART V

I

The morning that followed Petr Petrovich's fateful meeting with Dunechka and Pulkheriya Aleksandrovna produced a sobering effect on him as well. To his extreme displeasure, he was compelled little by little to accept as an accomplished and irrevocable fact what yesterday had seemed to him to be an almost fantastic occurrence, still inconceivable, even after it had actually occurred. The black serpent of wounded self-esteem had been sucking the blood out of his heart all night. The moment he got out of bed, Petr Petrovich looked at himself in the mirror. He was afraid that he might have had a bilious attack during the night. However, on that score, all was well for the time being; after seeing his pale, dignified face, which had grown fuller of late, Petr Petrovich even felt consoled for a moment in the full conviction that he could find another bride somewhere else, and she might even be a better one; but he immediately came to his senses and spat vigorously to one side, which caused his young friend and roommate, Andrey Semyonovich Lebezyatnikov to smile sarcastically. Petr Petrovich noticed this smile and immediately held it against his young friend. Lately he'd found many things to hold against him. His anger was redoubled when he suddenly realized that he shouldn't have told Andrey Semyonovich about the results of yesterday's interview. That was his second mistake yesterday, done in the heat of the moment, as a result of excessive expansiveness, in a moment of irritation. . . . Then, all that morning, as if intentionally, one unpleasantness followed another. Even in the Senate a setback awaited him in the case he was pursuing. He was especially annoyed by the landlord of the apartment he had rented in view of his imminent marriage and decorated at his own expense: this landlord, a German tradesman who had become rich, would under no circumstance agree to cancel the contract that had just been signed, and demanded all of the penalties specified therein, in spite of the fact that Petr Petrovich was returning the apartment to him almost completely redecorated. It was the same in the furniture shop, where they didn't want to refund even one ruble of his deposit for the furniture he had purchased, but which had still not been delivered to the apartment. "After all, I'm not going to get married just because I bought some furniture!" Petr Petrovich said to himself, grinding his teeth; and yet at the same time a desperate hope occurred to him once again: "Has this all really fallen through and is it over and done with once and for all? Is it really impossible to attempt it once more?" The thought of Dunechka was gnawing seductively at his heart. He experienced this moment with agony, and, of course, if he could have killed Raskolnikov just then by his wish alone, Petr Petrovich would have carried out that desire at once.

"Another mistake I made, besides that, was that I didn't give them any money," he thought glumly as he returned to Lebezyatnikov's little room. "Why the devil did I act like a stingy Jew? There wasn't even anything to be gained by it! I thought I could keep them on a short leash and make them see me as their good fortune, but look what happened! Damn it! No, if I'd handed them some fifteen hundred rubles for a dowry and for gifts, nice little boxes, toilet cases, jewelry, fabrics, and all sorts of trifles from Knop's and the English shop, then everything would have turned out better and . . . more certain! They couldn't have refused me so easily! They're the sort of people who certainly would have considered it their obligation to return both the gifts and the money in the case of a refusal; and it would have been difficult and painful for them to do so! Besides, their consciences would have bothered them: how, they'd say, can we suddenly drive away a man who's been so generous and sensitive up to now? Hmm! I let the chance slip by!" Grinding his teeth once again, Petr Petrovich called himself a fool—of course, only to himself.

After coming to that conclusion, he returned home feeling twice as spiteful and irritated as when he'd left. The preparations for the wake in Katerina Ivanovna's room aroused his curiosity somewhat. He had already heard something about it yesterday; he even recalled that he had been invited; but as a result of his own affairs, he let everything else slip from his attention. Hastening to be informed by Mrs. Lippevekhsel, who was bustling about the table in Katerina Ivanovna's absence (she was at the cemetery), he learned that the wake would be very festive, that almost all of the lodgers had been invited, even those unacquainted with the deceased, that even Andrey Semyonych Lebezyatnikov had been invited, in spite of his previous quarrel with Katerina Ivanovna, and, finally, that he, too, Petr Petrovich, had not only been invited, but his arrival was expected with great impatience, since he was almost the most important guest among all the lodgers. Amaliya Ivanovna herself had also been invited with great fanfare, in spite of all the previous unpleasantness, and therefore she was fussing and taking charge now, almost deriving enjoyment from it all; in addition, even though she was dressed for mourning, her apparel was all new and silk; she was in her finery and proud of it. All of these facts and information suggested an idea to Peter Petrovich; he returned to his room—that is, to Andrey Semyonych Lebezyatnikov's room—in deep thought. The point was that he'd also found out that among the invited guests would be Raskolnikov.

For some reason, Andrey Semyonych had remained at home all that morning. Petr Petrovich's relationship with this gentleman was rather strange, though also natural: Petr Petrovich despised and hated him beyond all measure, almost from the very first day when he had moved in, but at the same time he seemed to be somewhat afraid of him. Upon his arrival in Petersburg he had stayed with him not merely for reasons of tightfisted economy, although that was really the main reason, but also for another reason. While still in the provinces he had heard about Andrey Semyonych, his former ward, regarded as one of the most advanced young progressives, and even about the significant role he played in various intriguing and legendary circles. This surprised Petr Petrovich. These powerful, all-knowing circles, which despised and attacked everyone, had for a long time inspired Petr Petrovich with a particular kind of fear, one that was, however, completely undefined. Of course, he himself, while still in the provinces, couldn't possibly come to a precise understanding, even an approximate one, of something *of this kind*. Like everyone else, he heard that especially in Petersburg, there existed some progressives, nihilists, denouncers, and so on and so forth, but like many others, he exaggerated and distorted the meaning and importance of these names to the point of absurdity. Most of all, he was afraid, and had been for several years, of *denunciation*, and that was the principal basis of his constant, exaggerated uneasiness, especially when he considered his dreams of transferring his activity to Petersburg. In this regard he was *scared*, as they say, the way little children are often *scared*. Several years ago in the provinces, while still only beginning his career, he'd encountered two instances of cruel denunciation of rather important local personages to whom he had up to then attached himself and who served as his patrons. One instance ended for the exposed personage in a particularly scandalous way, and the other almost ended in an extremely troublesome manner. That was why on his arrival in Petersburg, Petr Petrovich decided to investigate as soon as possible what all this was about and, if necessary, to anticipate matters and ingratiate himself with "our younger generation." In this instance he was relying on Andrey Semyonych; during his visit with Raskolnikov, Petr Petrovich had somehow learned to repeat well-worn phrases blindly . . .

Of course, he had quickly managed to discern in Andrey Semyonych an extremely vulgar and simpleminded man. But this neither undermined nor encouraged Petr Petrovich's views. Even if he had been convinced that all progressives were such fools, even then his uneasiness would not have been alleviated. He himself had no particular interest in all these teachings, ideas, and systems (which Andrey Semyonych threw at him). He had his own aims. He merely wanted to discover as soon and as quickly as possible what had occurred *here* and how. Were *these people* influential or not? Did he personally have anything to fear or not? Would they denounce him if he embarked on some enterprise or not? And if they were to denounce him, then what for, exactly? And why were people being denounced these days? Moreover, could he not ingratiate himself somehow with them and deceive them, if they really were all that powerful? Was this necessary or not? Was it possible, for example, to advance his own career precisely through their intervention? In a word, there were hundreds of questions before him.

This Andrey Semyonych was a short, weedy, and scrofulous little man who had served in some post, and whose hair was strangely fair, with muttonchop side whiskers of which he was very proud. In addition, his eyes were almost always sore. He had a rather soft heart, but his speech was self-assured, and at times even extremely arrogant—which, when compared to his slight figure, almost always appeared comical. Amaliya Ivanovna, however, considered him among her most respected lodgers, that is, he didn't drink heavily and he paid his rent on time. In spite of all these qualities, Andrey Semyonovich really was a rather stupid man. He had attached himself to the idea of progress and to "our younger generation" out of eagerness. He was one of a countless and diverse legion of vulgar people, feeble retards, and uneducated morons who instantly and without fail latch onto the most fashionable current idea in order to vulgarize it and immediately caricature the cause they themselves sometimes serve in a most sincere manner.

However, Lebezyatnikov, in spite of the fact that he was a nice man, had also begun to have some difficulty tolerating his fellow lodger and former mentor Petr Petrovich. This had occurred on both sides somehow unexpectedly and mutually. No matter how simple-minded Andrey Semyonovich was, little by little he still began to see that Petr Petrovich was deceiving him, that he secretly despised him, and that he was "not the man he seemed to be." He tried to explain Fourier's system and Darwin's theory to him, but Petr Petrovich, especially as of late, had begun listening to him with excessive sarcasm, and most recently of all—had even begun to quarrel with him. The fact is, instinctually he was beginning to realize that Lebezyatnikov was not only a vulgar and stupid little man, but, perhaps, even a paltry liar, and that he had no more important connections whatsoever even in his own circle, and merely heard something thirdhand; furthermore, perhaps he didn't even know his own *propagandistic* business very well, because he would get all mixed up; so how could he possibly be a denouncer? By the way, we'll mention in passing that Petr Petrovich, during this last week and a half, willingly accepted (especially at first) Andrey Semyonych's even extremely strange words of praise, that is, he didn't object, for example, and even remained silent, if Andrey Semyonych ascribed to him a willingness to assist with the future and speedy organization of a new "commune" somewhere on Meshchan- skaya Street or, for example, not to interfere with Dunechka if, during the first month of their marriage, she were to decide to take a lover, or not to christen his future children, and so on and so forth—all in this same vein. Petr Petrovich, as was his usual custom, didn't object to such qualities attributed to him and even allowed himself to be praised for them—since he found any praise pleasant to hear.

Petr Petrovich, who that morning had for some reason exchanged several five percent government bonds, was sitting at a table counting packets of banknotes and bonds. Andrey Semyonovich, who almost never had any money, was pacing the room and pretending that he regarded all these packets with indifference and even with disdain. Petr Petrovich couldn't possibly believe, for example, that Andrey Semyo- novich could view such money with indifference; Andrey Semyonov- ich, on his part, thought bitterly that in fact Petr Petrovich was capable of thinking that about him, and perhaps he was even happy to annoy and tease his young friend with the packets of banknotes displayed, reminding him of his insignificance and the substantial difference between the two of them.

This time he found him unbelievably irritable and inattentive, in spite of the fact that he, Andrey Semyonovich, had begun to expati- ate on his favorite theme of establishing a new, special "commune." The brief objections and remarks that emerged from Petr Petrovich in the intervals between the rhythmic clicking of the abacus beads were steeped in the most obvious and intentionally impolite sarcasm. But the "humane" Andrey Semyonovich ascribed Petr Petrovich's disposi- tion to the lingering effects of yesterday's break with Dunechka; he was burning with a desire to speak about that subject. He had something to say on that account that was both progressive and propagandistic and could console his esteemed friend and "undoubtedly" promote his subsequent development.

"What sort of feast is being organized at that . . . widow's apartment?" Petr Petrovich asked suddenly, interrupting Andrey Semyo-novich at the most interesting point.

"As if you didn't know; I told you about it yesterday and expressed my thoughts about all these rituals. . . . I hear that she's also invited you to attend. You yourself spoke with her yesterday . . ."

"I never expected that this penniless fool of a woman would spend all the money she received from that other fool . . . Raskolnikov . . . on a funeral feast. . . . As I walked past, I was even quite astonished: such preparations are under way—wines! They've invited quite a few people—the devil knows what's happening!" continued Petr Petrovich, expanding on this conversation as if he had some purpose. "What? You say that they've even invited me?" he suddenly added, raising his head. "When was that? I don't recall, sir. But I won't go. What will I do there? I merely spoke with her yesterday, in passing, about the pos-sibility of her receiving a year's salary as one-time assistance since she's the destitute widow of a civil servant. Could that be why she's inviting me? He-he!"

"I'm not planning to go, either," said Lebezyatnikov.

"I should think not! You gave her quite a beating with your own hands. I can understand that you're ashamed, he-he-he!"

"Who gave a beating? To whom?" Lebezyatnikov suddenly became alarmed and even blushed.

"Why, it was you. You gave Katerina Ivanovna a beating a month ago, didn't you? I heard about it, sir, yesterday, sir. . . . So that's what your convictions are! So much for the woman question.* He-he-he!"

Petr Petrovich, as if satisfied, went back to clicking the beads on his abacus.

"That's all nonsense and slander!" Lebezyatnikov retorted, his temper flaring up. He constantly feared any reminders about this epi-sode. "It wasn't like that at all! It was completely different. . . . You didn't hear the truth; it's just gossip! I was merely defending myself at the time. She came at me first with her nails out. . . . She plucked out all my side whiskers. . . . Every man's entitled, I hope, to defend his

---

* Another reference to Chernyshevsky's novel *What Is to Be Done?* and its progressive ideas about the liberation of women.

own person. Besides that, I won't allow anyone to use violence against me. . . . On principle. Because that's already almost despotism. What was I supposed to do? Just stand there in front of her? I simply pushed her away."

"He-he-he!" Luzhin continued to mock him maliciously.

"You're provoking me because you're angry and in a bad temper. . . . This is nonsense and in no way, none at all, does it concern the woman question. You don't understand; I even thought that if a woman's equal to a man in all regards, even in physical strength (which, arguably, is possible), then, of course, there must be equality there, too. Of course, later I decided that such a question, in essence, shouldn't even arise because there shouldn't be any fights at all, and that such fights would be inconceivable in a future society . . . and that it was a strange thing, of course, to look for equality in a fight. I'm not that foolish . . . although fights do occur, that is, they won't in the future, but for now they still do. . . . Phew! Damn it all! It's hard to talk to you! The fact that there was this unpleasantness is not why I won't go to the wake. I won't go simply on principle, so as not to participate in this vile superstition, that's what! However, one could attend merely to make fun of it. . . . It's a pity there won't be any priests there. Or else I'd certainly go."

"That is, you'd enjoy someone's hospitality and then spit on it, the same as you would on those who invited you there. Is that it?"

"I wouldn't spit on it at all, but I would protest. I have a beneficial aim. I might indirectly serve the cause of their development and our propaganda. Every person is obligated to develop and propagandize, perhaps the tougher the better. I might be able to toss out an idea, a seed. . . . From this seed, facts could grow. How would I be offending them? At first they may take offense, but then they themselves will see that I've rendered them a service. Consider the case of Terebeva (who's in the commune now); she was criticized when she left her family and . . . gave herself to a man; she wrote to her mother and father that she didn't want to live among prejudices and was going to enter a common-law marriage; people thought this was being too rude to her parents, that it should have been possible to spare them, to express it more gently. In my opinion, that's all nonsense: it wasn't necessary to write more gently; on the contrary, on the contrary, it's necessary to protest. Consider that Varents spent seven years living with her husband, abandoned her two children, and in her letter she quipped to her husband, 'I realized that I couldn't be happy with you. I'll never forgive you for having deceived me, for hiding the fact that there exists another way of organizing society in the form of a commune. I found all this out recently from a very magnanimous man, to whom I gave myself; we'll establish a commune together. I'm telling you this in all honesty because I think it's dishonorable to deceive you. Do whatever you think is best. Don't try to make me come back; it's too late for that. I wish you happiness.' That's how such letters should be written!"

"Is that Terebeva the same one you told me about, the one who's entered her third common-law marriage?"

"Only the second, if you count properly! Even if it's the fourth, or the fifteenth, that's all nonsense! If I ever regretted that my father and mother died, I do now, of course. I've even dreamt more than once that if they were still alive, I'd wallop them with my protest! I'd let them down intentionally. . . . Another 'bird flown the coop'! I'd show them! I'd astound them! It's really a pity that there's no one left!"

"Astound them? He-he! Well, let it be," Petr Petrovich interrupted. "But tell me this: you seem to know the daughter of the deceased man, that very frail girl! Is what they say about her completely true, huh?"

"So, what of it? In my opinion, that is, according to my personal conviction, that's exactly the most normal condition of a woman. Why not? That is, *distinguons.** In today's society, of course, it's not altogether normal, because it's forced on her, but in the future it will be completely normal because it will be freely chosen. Why, even now she had a right: she was suffering, and that was her fund, so to speak, her capital, which she had the absolute right to expend. Naturally, in a future society, there'll be no need for such funds; but her role will have a different meaning, organized harmoniously and rationally. As far as Sofiya Semyonovna herself is concerned, at the present time I regard her actions as a vigorous and personal protest against the social order, and I respect her deeply for it; I even rejoice looking at her!"

---

* "Let's distinguish" (French).

"But I was told that you're the one who forced her out of this apartment house!"

Lebezyatnikov was absolutely furious.

"That's more slander!" he wailed. "That's not at all how it was, not how it was at all! That's just Katerina Ivanovna telling tales because she didn't understand a thing. I didn't make a play for Sofiya Semyonovna at all! I was simply trying to educate her, completely innocently, trying to incite her to protest. . . . It was only the protest I wanted, but Sofiya Semyonovna herself felt that she couldn't remain here in this apartment house!"

"Was she being invited to join the commune then?"

"You keep laughing; allow me to observe that it's not very appropriate. You don't understand a thing! There are no such roles in a commune. A commune is organized so that there won't be any roles like that. In a commune, her role will change its present meaning; that which is foolish here will become clever there; that which is unnatural here, under present circumstances, will become completely natural there. Everything depends on circumstance and environment. It all depends on the environment, and the person himself means nothing. I'm on good terms with Sofiya Semyonovna even now, and you can take it as proof that she never considered me her enemy or her offender. Yes! I'm trying to tempt her to join the commune now, but on a completely different basis! What's so funny? We want to organize our commune in a special way, but only on a broader foundation than previously. We've gone further in our convictions. We reject more things! If Dobrolyubov were to rise from the grave, I'd have a quarrel with him. As for Belinsky, I'd make mincemeat of him!* Meanwhile, I continue to educate Sofiya Semyonovna. She is a splendid, splendid individual!"

"Well, and you're taking advantage of this splendid individual, eh? He-he!"

"No, no! Oh, no! On the contrary!"

"Well, then, on the contrary! He-he-he! What a thing to say!"

---

* Both Nikolai Dobrolyubov (1836–1861) and Vissarion Belinksy (1811–1848) were important radical critics in the mid-nineteenth century.

"You must believe me! For what reason would I hide it from you, please tell me! On the contrary, this seems strange even to me: she's somehow intensely, timidly chaste and shy with me!"

"And, of course, you're educating her . . . he-he! You're proving to her that all this shyness is nonsense?"

"Not at all. Not at all! Oh, you're so rude, you even interpret—forgive me—the word 'development' in a stupid manner! You don't understand a thing, not a thing! Oh, Lord, you're still so . . . undeveloped! We're working for the emancipation of women, while you have only one thing on your mind. . . . Ignoring completely the question of chastity and women's shyness as useless things in and of themselves, and even prejudicial, I fully, absolutely support her chastity with me because that's a matter of her own free will, her own right. Of course, if she herself were to say, 'I want to have you,' then I'd consider myself very fortunate, because I really do like the young woman; but now, now at least, no one, of course, ever treated her more politely and courteously than I do, or with more respect for her dignity. . . . I wait and hope—and that's all!"

"It would be better if you gave her some sort of gift. I bet you haven't even thought of that."

"You don't understand a thing, I told you! Of course, that's the position she's in, but there's another question involved here! Completely different! You simply despise her. Seeing a fact that you mistakenly consider worthy of contempt, you refuse to regard a human being in a humane way. You still don't know what sort of person she is! I'm merely sorry that of late she seems to have stopped reading and no longer borrows any books from me. Previously she did. It's also a pity that with all her energy and resolve to protest—which she's demonstrated before—she still seems to have little self-reliance, so to speak, little independence, too little negation in her to free herself completely from various prejudices and . . . stupidities. This is in spite of the fact that she understands some of these questions perfectly. For example, she understood the matter of kissing a woman's hand perfectly—that is, that a man offends a woman by unequal treatment if he kisses her hand. This question was debated among us, and I told her about it immediately. She also listened very attentively when I told her about the workers' associations in France. Now I'm explaining to her the matter of a couple's free access to each other's rooms in a future society."*

"What's that about?"

"The question has been debated recently: does a member of the commune have the right to enter another member's room, a man's or a woman's, at any time. . . . Well, it was decided that they do . . ."

"What if he or she is occupied at the moment with a natural necessity, he-he!"

Andrey Semyonovich grew very angry.

"You go on about the same thing, these damned 'necessities'!" he cried with hatred. "Bah! I'm so angry and annoyed that in explaining the system I mentioned to you prematurely these natural necessities! Damn it all! It's a stumbling block for anyone like you, and worst of all—you ridicule it before finding out what it's all about! As if they were right! As if they had something to be proud of! Bah! I've insisted several times that this question can be explained to novices only at the very end, when a person's already committed to the system, when he's educated and politically progressive. Please tell me what you find so embarrassing and contemptible, even in cesspools? I myself would be the first to clean out any cesspools you like! There's no kind of self-sacrifice involved! It's simply work, a noble, useful activity to society, one worth as much as any other, and is a much higher activity, for example, than that of some Raphael or Pushkin, because it's more useful!"†

"And more noble, more noble, he-he-he!"

"What's 'more noble'? I don't understand such expressions when used to describe human activity. 'More noble,' 'more magnanimous'— that's all nonsense, foolishness, old prejudicial words that I reject! Everything that's *useful* to humanity, that's noble! I understand only one word: *useful*! Sneer as much as you like, but that's the truth!"

Petr Petrovich was laughing wholeheartedly. He had already finished counting his money and had hidden it away. However, for some

---

* Another reference to Chernyshevsky's novel.

† An allusion to the views of the radical critic Dmitry Pisarev (1840–1868).

reason, a certain amount of cash had been left on the table. This "question of cesspools," in spite of all its vulgarity, had served several times as the cause of a dispute and disagreement between Petr Petrovich and his young friend. The stupid thing was that Andrey Semyonych was really angry. Luzhin, on the other hand, had gotten a load off his chest by mentioning it and at the present time, particularly, felt like teasing Lebezyatnikov a little.

"It's because of your bad luck yesterday that you're so mean and you're pestering me," Lebezyatnikov burst out at last; generally speaking, in spite of all his "independence" and his "protests," he was somehow afraid to oppose Petr Petrovich; in general, he treated him with deference, as he had in previous years.

"It would be better for you to tell me," Petr Petrovich said, interrupting him arrogantly and with annoyance, "whether you can . . . or, to put it better, are you on good enough terms with the aforementioned young person to invite her in here for a minute, into this room? They seem to have returned from the cemetery. . . . I hear the sound of people moving around. . . . I'd like to have a word with her, sir, with that person, sir."

"What do you want her for?" Lebezyatnikov asked in surprise.

"Just so, sir, I'd like to, sir. I'll be leaving here today or tomorrow, and therefore would like to tell her that. . . . However, please stay here during my conversation with her. That would be even better. Or else, God knows what you might think."

"I won't think anything at all. . . . I merely asked you. If you have some business, there's nothing easier than inviting her here. I'll go at once. And you can be sure that I won't interfere with you."

As a matter of fact, about five minutes later, Lebezyatnikov returned with Sonechka. She entered in extreme surprise and, as was her usual state, very timidly. She was always timid in similar circumstances and was very afraid of new people and new acquaintances; she'd been afraid even before, from childhood, and was now all the more so. . . . Petr Petrovich greeted her "in a friendly and polite manner," however, with a certain hint of cheerful familiarity, which, in his opinion, was appropriate for such an esteemed and solid person as he was, in relation to such a young and *interesting* (in a certain sense) creature as Sonya. He hastened to "reassure" her and seated her at the table opposite himself. Sonya sat down, looked around—at Lebezyatnikov, at the money lying on the table, at Petr Petrovich again, and then didn't take her eyes off him, as if her gaze were riveted to him. Lebezyatnikov started to head for the door. Petr Petrovich stood up, indicated that Sonya should stay where she was, and stopped Lebezyatnikov in the doorway.

"Is that fellow Raskolnikov there? Has he come?" he asked in a whisper.

"Raskolnikov? He's there. What of it? Yes, he is. . . . He's just arrived, I saw him. . . . Why?"

"Well, I especially want you to stay here with us, and not leave me alone with this . . . girl. My business is inconsequential, but God knows what people might think. I don't want Raskolnikov talking about it *there*. . . . Do you understand what I'm saying?"

"Ah, I understand, I understand," Lebezyatnikov cried suddenly, realizing what was happening. "Yes, you have the right. . . . Of course, in my personal opinion, you're exaggerating the risks, but . . . still, you have the right. All right, I'll stay here. I'll stand by the window and won't interfere. . . . I think you have the right . . ."

Petr Petrovich returned to the sofa, sat down opposite Sonya, looked at her intently, and suddenly assumed an extremely imposing, even somewhat stern appearance: "Now, don't you get any ideas, young lady." Sonya was completely baffled.

"In the first place, please extend my apologies, Sofiya Semyonovna, to your esteemed mama. . . . That's right, isn't it? Katerina Ivanovna has taken the place of your mother, hasn't she?" Petr Petrovich began very imposingly, but rather tenderly. It was apparent that he had the friendliest intentions.

"Yes, sir, that's so, sir; the place of a mother, sir," Sonya replied hastily and timidly.

"Well, please apologize to her: due to certain unforeseeable circumstances, I'll be forced to miss the pancakes . . . that is, the funeral feast, in spite of your mama's kind invitation."

"Yes, sir; I'll tell her, sir; right away, sir." Sonechka hastened to jump up from her chair.

"That's *still* not everything," Petr Petrovich said, stopping her, smiling at her simplicity and her unfamiliarity with proper decorum. "And you know me too little, dearest Sofiya Semyonovna, if you thought I'd disturb you personally to summon a person such as you for such an unimportant reason concerning me alone. I have a different aim."

Sonya sat down hastily. The gray- and rainbow-colored banknotes, still left on the table, flashed in her eyes once again, but she quickly turned her face away and raised it to look at Petr Petrovich: all of a sudden it felt terribly inappropriate, especially for *her*, to stare at someone else's money. She suddenly began to fix her gaze on Petr Petrovich's golden lorgnette, which he held in his left hand, and on a large, massive, very beautiful ring with a yellow stone on the middle finger of that hand—but suddenly she averted her eyes from that, too, and not knowing where to look, wound up staring once again directly into Petr Petrovich's eyes. After an even more imposing silence than before, he continued:

"I happened to have had a brief chat with the unfortunate Katerina Ivanovna yesterday. A few words were enough to learn that she's in a very . . . unnatural condition, if I may express it that way . . ."

"Yes, sir . . . unnatural, sir," Sonya hastened to agree.

"Or, it's simpler and more understandable to say . . . she's ill."

"Yes, sir, it's simpler and understand— . . . yes, sir. She's ill, sir."

"Well then. So, out of a feeling of humaneness and, and, and, so to speak, compassion, I would like, on my part, to be useful in some way, foreseeing her inevitably unhappy fate. It seems that the entire destitute family now depends on you alone."

"Allow me to ask," Sonya said, suddenly standing up, "whether you spoke with her yesterday about the possibility of receiving a pension? Because she told me yesterday that you had taken on yourself the task of obtaining a pension for her. Is that true, sir?"

"No, not at all, it's even ridiculous in a certain sense. I merely hinted about temporary assistance to the widow of a civil servant who dies while still in service—if she happens to have some patronage—but it seems that your deceased father not only failed to serve out his time, but recently didn't even work at all. In a word, though there might be some hope, it's extremely slight, because in this case there's no right to assistance, even maybe the opposite. . . . And she was already thinking about a pension, he-he-he! What a daring lady!"

"Yes, sir, about a pension. . . . Because she's gullible and kind; she's so kind that she believes everything, and . . . and . . . and . . . she has that sort of mind. . . . Yes, sir . . . excuse her, sir," said Sonya, and she got up to leave once again.

"If you please, you still haven't heard me out."

"Yes, sir, I haven't heard you out, sir," muttered Sonya.

"Do sit down."

Sonya was terribly embarrassed and sat down again, for the third time.

"Seeing her situation, with the unfortunate young children, I would like—as I already indicated—to be useful in some way, as best I can, that is, as best I can, but no more. For example, it might be possible to organize a subscription for her, or a lottery, so to speak . . . or something of that sort—as is always done in similar cases by relatives or even by strangers, but in general by people wishing to assist. I had the intention of informing you about this. It might be possible."

"Yes, sir, very good, sir. . . . God will reward you, sir . . ." Sonya murmured, staring intently at Petr Petrovich.

"It might be possible . . . but we'll talk about it later . . . that is, we could start it even today. We'll see this evening; we'll discuss it and lay, so to speak, the foundation. Come to see me here this evening around seven o'clock. Andrey Semyonych, I hope, will also participate with us. . . . But . . . there's one circumstance involved that must be mentioned beforehand and in detail. That's why I have disturbed you, Sofiya Semyonovna, with my summons here. Namely, it's my opinion that money must not be given directly to Katerina Ivanovna: it's dangerous; the evidence for that is the funeral feast planned for today. Without having, so to speak, a crust of bread for tomorrow's meals and . . . well, any money for shoes or anything else, she's purchased Jamaican rum and even, it seems, Madeira, and—and—and coffee. I saw it as I came past. Tomorrow it will all fall upon you again, for the last piece of bread; this is absurd. Therefore, even the subscription, in my personal opinion, must be carried out so that the unfortunate widow, so to speak, doesn't know about the money, but that you, for example, are the only one who knows. Am I right?"

"I don't know, sir. She's only doing this today, sir . . . it's once in a lifetime . . . she very much wanted to remember him, to honor him, his memory. . . . But she's very smart, sir. But it's as you like, sir, and I'll be very, very, very . . . they'll all be . . . and God will, sir . . . and the orphans, sir . . ."

Sonya didn't finish and instead burst into tears.

"Well, then. So, keep this in mind; and now be so kind as to accept, in the interests of your relative, in the first instance, this modest sum from me personally. I very, very much hope that my name won't be mentioned in connection with this gift. Here you are . . . having, so to speak, my own concerns, I'm not in a position to . . ."

Petr Petrovich extended a carefully unfolded ten-ruble note to Sonya. Sonya accepted it, blushed, jumped up, muttered something, and hastily began to take her leave. Petr Petrovich ceremoniously escorted her to the door. At last she bolted from the room, all agitated and exhausted, and returned to Katerina Ivanovna in extreme confusion.

All during this scene, Andrey Semyonych stood next to the window or paced the room, not wishing to interrupt the conversation; after Sonya left, he suddenly approached Petr Petrovich and formally extended his hand.

"I heard everything and I *saw* everything," he said, placing special emphasis on the word "saw." "It's noble, that is, I wanted to say, humane! You wanted to avoid her gratitude, I saw! And although, I confess, I can't, in principle, sympathize with private charity, because it not only fails to eradicate radically the evil and even sustains it further, nevertheless, I can't help confessing that I looked upon your act with pleasure—yes, yes, I like it very much."

"Eh, it's all nonsense!" muttered Petr Petrovich, appearing somewhat agitated and looking somehow closely at Lebezyatnikov.

"No, it's not nonsense! A man who's been insulted and provoked as you were by yesterday's incident, and who is at the same time able to think about the misfortune of others—such a man, sir . . . although by his actions he is committing a social blunder—nevertheless . . . is worthy of respect! I certainly didn't expect it from you, Petr Petrovich, all the more so given your understanding of things—oh! How your understanding still hinders you! How, for example, your failure yesterday upsets you," exclaimed the tenderhearted Andrey Semyonych, once again feeling more strongly disposed to Petr Petrovich. "And why, why exactly do you want this marriage, this *legal* marriage, my dearest, most generous Petr Petrovich? Why precisely must you have this *legality* in marriage? Well, if you wish to, beat me, but I'm glad, very glad that it didn't succeed, that you're free, that you're still not altogether lost for humanity, glad. . . . You see: I've had my say!"

"Because, sir, in this common-law marriage of yours I don't want to wear a cuckold's horns and bring up someone else's children. That's why I want a legal marriage," said Luzhin, in order to have something to reply. He was particularly preoccupied and thoughtful.

"Children? You mentioned children?" Andrey Semyonych shuddered like a warhorse who'd heard the sound of the trumpet. "Children are a social question and one of primary importance, I agree; but the question of children will be resolved in another manner. Some people even reject the idea of children, like any other indication of family life. We'll talk about children later, but for now, we'll deal with a cuckold's horns! I confess that this is my weak point. It's a nasty, hussar-like, Pushkinian expression even unthinkable in a future lexicon. And what are those horns? Oh, what a delusion! What horns? Why horns? What nonsense! On the contrary, there won't be any horns in a common-law marriage! Horns are merely the consequence of any legal marriage, so to speak, its correction, a protest, so that in this sense they're not even humiliating in the least. . . . And if at some time—let's assume an absurdity—I were in a legal marriage, then I would even be glad of your accursed horns. Then I would say to my wife: 'My friend, up to now I merely loved you; now, however, I respect you because you were able to protest!'* Are you laughing? That's because you're not strong enough to free yourself from these prejudices! Damn it, but

---

* A parody of an idea expressed in Chernyshevsky's novel.

I understand where the unpleasantness resides when people deceive each other in a legal marriage; but that's merely the vile result of the vile fact in which both parties are humiliated. When the cuckold's horns are worn openly, as in a common-law marriage, then they no longer exist; they're inconceivable and even lose the designation as horns. On the contrary, your wife will merely prove to you that she respects you, considering you incapable of opposing her happiness, and so advanced in your thinking that you won't take revenge on her for her new husband. Damn it all, sometimes I dream that if I were ever given in marriage—bah! I mean if I ever chose to marry (by a common-law marriage or a legal one, it doesn't matter which), I might even personally bring my wife a lover, if she took too long to find one herself. 'My friend,' I'd say to her, 'I love you, but even more than that, I want you to respect me—so here!' Am I right in what I say? Am I?"

Petr Petrovich snickered as he listened, but without any special amusement. He didn't even listen very attentively. He was really thinking about something else, and even Lebezyatnikov finally noticed this. Petr Petrovich was even nervous, rubbing his hands, deep in thought. Andrey Semyonych thought about this and remembered it subsequently . . .

It would be difficult to specify precisely the reason why the idea of this ridiculous funeral feast was conceived in Katerina Ivanovna's distraught brain. As a matter of fact, almost ten rubles had been squandered on it out of the more than twenty rubles she had received from Raskolnikov for Marmeladov's funeral. Perhaps Katerina Ivanovna considered herself obligated to her deceased husband to honor his memory "as befitting," so that all the lodgers, including Amaliya Ivanovna, in particular, would know that "not only was he no worse than they, but perhaps, even much better," and that not one of them had the right to "look down his nose" at him. Perhaps the most powerful influence on her was that particular "pride of the poor," as a result of which many poor people, in observing those social rituals required of each and every person by our way of life, strive with all their strength and spend the last kopecks of their life savings in order to appear "no worse than others," and so that those same others won't "criticize them." It is also extremely likely that Katerina Ivanovna wanted, precisely in this case, precisely at this moment in time, when it seemed as if she'd been abandoned by everyone in the whole world, to show all these "worthless and nasty lodgers" that she not only "knew how to live and how to entertain guests," but had been brought up not for such a fate in life but in the "noble, one could even say, aristocratic home of a colonel," and that she had never been raised to sweep the floor or to wash the children's rags at night. These paroxysms of pride and vanity sometimes occur in the poorest and most downtrodden people and at times turn into irritating and irrepressible necessity. Moreover, Katerina Ivanovna was not downtrodden: circumstances might defeat her entirely, but they could not crush her morally, that is, they could not intimidate her or overpower her will. In addition, Sonechka had solid grounds for saying that her mind was deranged. True, it was still not possible to state this absolutely and definitively; lately, for the entire past year, her poor brain had been tormented too much to escape without some damage. The rapid course of consumption, as doctors say, also promotes the impairment of one's mental faculties.

There wasn't a great deal of *wine* or an array of different kinds, nor was there any *Madeira*: that was an exaggeration; but there was some wine. There was vodka, rum, and Lisbon wine, all of very poor quality, but all in sufficient quantity. As for the food, besides the traditional *kutya*,* there were three or four dishes (including pancakes, incidentally), all from Amaliya Ivanovna's kitchen; in addition, two samovars were brought in to provide tea and punch after the meal. Katerina Ivanovna had provided the purchases herself, with the help of one lodger, some pitiful Pole, who was living at Madame Lippevekhsel's for some reason or other, and who'd immediately volunteered to assist Katerina Ivanovna with her errands, and had run around all the day before, and had raced around all that morning with his tongue hanging out, apparently hoping that this activity would be noticed by everyone. He kept running constantly to Katerina Ivanovna herself for every little thing, even searching for her at the shopping arcade, persistently calling her "Madame Ensign." She finally grew so sick and tired of him, even though at first she would say that she would have been completely lost had it not been for this "obliging and generous" man. It was characteristic of Katerina Ivanovna to paint everybody and anybody she met in the best and brightest colors, to praise him such that others felt embarrassed, to conceive of various circumstances on their behalf that had never existed, to believe completely sincerely and wholeheartedly in their existence, and then all at once, suddenly, to be disillusioned,

---

* Boiled rice with raisins and honey, traditionally eaten at a funeral repast.

break off with them, humiliate them, and banish the person she had literally worshipped only a few hours ago. By nature she had a humorous, cheerful, and peace-loving character, but as a result of continual misfortunes and failures, she had begun *furiously* to desire and demand that everyone live in peace and joy and that they *dare not* live otherwise, that the least dissonance in life, the smallest failure, would drive her immediately into a frenzy, and in one moment, after the brightest aspirations and fantasies, she would begin to curse fate, tearing and smashing anything that came to hand and banging her head against the wall. Amaliya Ivanovna, for some reason, had also suddenly acquired unusual importance and unusual respect from Katerina Ivanovna, perhaps solely because the funeral feast was being prepared and Amaliya Ivanovna had resolved with all her heart to take part in all the work: she took it upon herself to set the table, procure the linen, crockery, and so forth, and to prepare the food in her kitchen. Katerina Ivanovna entrusted everything to her and left her alone, while she herself set off for the cemetery. As a matter of fact, everything had been wonderfully prepared: the table was set even rather elegantly; the dishes, forks, knives, goblets, glasses, cups—everything, of course, had been collected from various lodgers and didn't match in style or quality, but everything was in place by the appointed time. Amaliya Ivanovna, feeling that she had accomplished her task extremely well, even greeted those returning with a certain pride; she had changed her clothes and was wearing a black dress and a cap with new mourning ribbons. For some reason, Katerina Ivanovna didn't appreciate her pride, even though it was well deserved: "As if no one else knows how to set a table except for Amaliya Ivanovna!" And she also didn't like her cap with the new ribbons: "Isn't this stupid German woman taking pride in the fact that she's the landlady and has agreed to help some poor lodgers out of charity? Out of charity! I ask you, really! At the house of Katerina Ivanovna's papa, who was a colonel and had almost become a governor, the table was sometimes set for forty guests; someone like Amaliya Ivanovna—or, rather, Amaliya Lyudvigovna—wouldn't even be allowed in the kitchen . . ." However, Katerina Ivanovna decided not to vent her feelings for the time being, although she resolved in her heart to put her in her place and remind her of who she really was, or else

God knows what she might start thinking of herself; meanwhile, she merely treated her with coldness. Another unpleasant circumstance furthered Katerina Ivanovna's irritation: at the funeral, almost no one, not one of the lodgers who had been invited, showed up, except for the little Pole, who even managed to make it to the cemetery; but at the wake—that is, for the refreshments—the most insignificant and poorest of them appeared, many of them even already intoxicated, the wretched good-for-nothings. But the older and more respectable of them absented themselves, as if on purpose, as if they had agreed in advance to skip the event. Petr Petrovich Luzhin, for example, perhaps the most respectable of all the lodgers, did not attend; meanwhile, yesterday evening Katerina Ivanovna had managed to tell everyone on earth—that is, Amaliya Ivanovna, Polechka, Sonya, and the little Pole—that this most respectable and most generous man, with his vast number of connections and his wealth, her first husband's former friend, someone who had been received in her father's house and who had promised to use all possible means to procure a considerable pension for her, this same Luzhin did not appear. We'll observe here that if Katerina Ivanovna bragged about anyone's connections and wealth, it was without any self-interest, without any personal calculation, but was completely innocent, so to speak, out of the fullness of her heart, the sheer pleasure of bestowing praise and conferring more value to the person being praised. Like Luzhin and, probably, "following his example," "that nasty scoundrel Lebezyatnikov" had also failed to show up. "Just who does he think he is? He was invited only out of kindness, and only because he shares a room with Petr Petrovich and is his acquaintance, so that it would have been awkward not to include him." A fashionable lady with her "overripe spinster" of a daughter also failed to appear; they had resided at Amaliya Ivanovna's rooms for only about two weeks, but had several times complained about the noise and shouts coming from the Marmeladovs', especially when the recently deceased arrived home drunk, about which Katerina Ivanovna had been informed by Amaliya Ivanovna, when she was quarreling with her and threatening to throw the whole family out; she was screaming at the top of her lungs that they were disturbing her "respectable lodgers, whose shoelaces she was unfit to tie." Katerina Ivanovna made a point of intentionally inviting this lady and her daughter, whose "shoe-laces she was unfit to tie," all the more so since up to then in any incidental meeting, the lady would haughtily turn her face away—so that this lady would know that here "respectable people have thoughts and feelings, and invite others without holding a grudge," and so that she would see that Katerina Ivanovna was not used to living in such circumstances. She definitely intended to make this clear to them at the table, as well as making the point about her late papa's near governorship and, at the same time, hinting indirectly that there was no reason for her to turn away when meeting them and that such behavior was extremely foolish. The fat lieutenant colonel (in reality, a retired second lieutenant) also didn't attend, but it turned out that he had been "dead tired" since yesterday morning. In a word, the only people who came were: the little Pole, a shabby, silent pimply clerk in a soiled jacket who had a nasty smell; and also a deaf and almost blind little old man who at one time had served in a post office; he was a man someone had been supporting at Amaliya Ivanovna's for ages and for unknown reasons. There was also a retired drunken lieutenant, in fact a quartermaster, with the most unpleasant loud laugh and, "just imagine," who came without a vest! One of them sat right down at the table without even greeting Katerina Ivanovna. At length, one person was about to appear in his dressing gown because he didn't own a suit, but this was so inappropriate that the combined efforts of Amaliya Ivanovna and the little Pole succeeded in excluding him. The little Pole brought with him two other Poles who had never resided at Amaliya Ivanovna's, and whom no one had seen before in these rooms. All of this irritated Katerina Ivanovna in an extremely unpleasant manner. "After all, who were all these preparations made for?" Even the children, to save space, were not seated at the main table, which already occupied the entire room. Their places had been set on a trunk in the far corner; the two little ones were placed on a bench, and Polechka, as the biggest, was supposed to mind them, feed them, and wipe their noses "like respectable children." In a word, Katerina Ivanovna was obligated against her will to greet everyone with redoubled dignity, even with haughtiness. She regarded several of the guests with particular sternness and condescendingly invited them to sit down at the table.

Having decided for some reason that Amaliya Ivanovna was responsible for those who didn't appear, she suddenly began to address her with excessive rudeness, which Amaliya Ivanovna noticed immediately, becoming extremely piqued. Such a beginning did not bode well for a good ending. At last everyone was seated.

Raskolnikov entered almost exactly at the same time they were returning from the cemetery. Katerina Ivanovna was terribly glad to see him, in the first place because he was the only "educated guest" out of all those present and, "as is well known, he was preparing to occupy a professor's chair at the local university two years hence." In the second place, it was because he promptly and respectfully apologized to her that in spite of his strong desire, he had been unable to attend the funeral. She pounced on him at once and sat him down at the table on her left side (Amaliya Ivanovna was sitting on her right); in spite of her constant fussing and concern that the food would be served properly and that there be enough for everyone, and in spite of the tormenting cough that plagued her continually and choked her and, it seems, had worsened particularly in the last two days, she constantly turned to Raskolnikov and in a half whisper hastened to pour out to him all her pent-up feelings and all her righteous indignation over the unsuccessful funeral feast; this indignation alternated with fits of the most cheerful and most unrestrained laughter at the assembled guests, primarily directed at her landlady.

"That cuckoo is to blame for everything. You understand who I'm talking about: about her, her!" Katerina Ivanovna nodded at the landlady. "Just look at her: her eyes are popping out; she knows we're talking about her, but she can't understand, and her eyes are wide open. Phew, what an owl she is! Ha-ha-ha! *Cough-cough-cough!* And what's she trying to prove with that cap of hers? *Cough-cough-cough!* Have you noticed that she wants everyone to think she's patronizing me and doing me an honor by coming? I asked her, as a respectable woman, to invite a better class of people, especially acquaintances of the deceased, but just look at who she's brought: such clowns! Sluts! Look at that fellow with the dirty face: he's a snotnose on two legs! And those nasty little Poles . . . ha-ha-ha! *Cough-cough-cough!* No one, no one at all has ever seen them here before, and I've never seen them either; why did they come, I ask you? They're sitting properly, all in a row. Hey, sir!" she cried out suddenly to one of them, "have you had any pancakes? Have some more! Drink some beer, more beer! Wouldn't you like some vodka? Look: he's jumped up and is bowing. Look, look: they must be very hungry, the poor fellows! Never mind, let them eat. At least they're not making any noise, only . . . only, I'm afraid for the landlady's silver spoons! Amaliya Ivanovna!" she said almost audibly, suddenly turning in her direction, "if by any chance they pinch your spoons, I'm not responsible for them, I warn you in advance! Ha-ha-ha!" She roared with laughter. Turning back to Raskolnikov, she nodded again at the landlady and enjoyed her little attack. "She hasn't understood, once again she didn't understand! She's sitting there with her mouth open wide, just look: she's like an owl, a genuine screech owl in her cap with new ribbons, ha-ha-ha!"

Again her laughter turned into unbearable coughing that lasted five minutes. Some blood was left on her handkerchief, and beads of perspiration stood out on her forehead. She silently showed the blood to Raskolnikov and, with hardly a pause, whispered to him again with extreme animation and with red blotches on her cheeks:

"Just look: I gave her a most delicate commission, one could say, to invite that lady and her daughter. Do you understand whom I'm talking about? One must behave in the most delicate manner, act in the most skillful way, but she carried it out so that this newly arrived fool, this haughty creature, this insignificant provincial woman, simply because she's some sort of major's widow who's come to petition for a pension and is beating down office doors, and who, at the age of fifty-five, dyes her hair black and wears both powder and rouge (this is well known) . . . this creature not only didn't think it fitting to appear, but didn't even send a message of apology that she couldn't come, as considered correct by the most ordinary rules of politeness in such circumstances! I can't understand why Petr Petrovich didn't come, either! And where's Sonya? Where has she gone? Ah, here she is at last! Well, Sonya, where've you been? It's strange that you're late even for your father's funeral. Rodion Romanovich, allow her to sit next to you. There's your place Sonechka . . . take whatever you want. Have some of the jellied fish, that's the best. Soon there'll be pancakes. Have they fed the children? Polechka, do you have everything over there? *Cough-cough-cough!* Well, all right. Be a clever girl, Lenya, and you, Kolya, don't kick your feet; sit like a well-behaved child. What are you saying, Sonechka?"

Sonya hastened to convey Petr Petrovich's apology, trying to speak loud enough so that everyone could hear and using the most carefully chosen respectful expressions, purposely composed by Petr Petrovich and embellished by her. She added that Petr Petrovich had specially ordered her to say that as soon as it became possible, he would come very soon to talk privately *about business* and to agree on what could be done and what to undertake in the future, etc., etc.

Sonya knew that this would pacify and reassure Katerina Ivanovna, flatter her, and—the main thing—her pride would be satisfied. She sat down next to Raskolnikov, to whom she bowed hurriedly, and in passing cast an inquisitive glance at him. However, for the most part she avoided both looking at him and talking to him. She even seemed to be distracted, although she kept looking at Katerina Ivanovna's face and tried to please her. Neither she nor Katerina Ivanovna was dressed in mourning, because they lacked the clothes; Sonya was wearing some sort of dark brown dress, and Katerina Ivanovna had on her only dress, a drab cotton dress with stripes. The news about Petr Petrovich was well received. Katerina Ivanovna heard Sonya out pretentiously and, with the same pretentiousness, inquired about Petr Petrovich's health. Then, quickly and almost out loud, she *whispered* to Raskolnikov that it really would be strange if a respected and solid man like Petr Petrovich would find himself in such "unusual company," in spite of all his devotion to her family and his former friendship with her papa.

"That's why I'm especially grateful to you, Rodion Romanych, that you didn't disdain my hospitality, even in such circumstances," she added almost aloud. "However, I'm convinced that only your special friendship with my poor deceased husband inspired you to keep your word."

Then she surveyed her guests again with pride and dignity and suddenly, with special solicitude, inquired loudly across the table of the deaf old man whether he'd like some more roast and had he been served some Lisbon wine? The old man didn't reply and for a long time was unable to understand what he was being asked, even though his neighbors began shaking him to amuse themselves. He merely looked around with his mouth open wide, which aroused general merriment.

"What an oaf! Look, look! Why did they bring him? As far as Petr Petrovich is concerned, I was always certain of him," Katerina Ivanovna continued to Raskolnikov. "And, of course, he's not like . . ." she said loudly and harshly, turning to Amaliya Ivanovna with an extremely stern expression, which caused the latter to cringe, "not like those overdressed tail draggers of yours who wouldn't have been admitted as cooks into my papa's kitchen; and my late husband, of course, would've done them a great honor receiving them, even though it was only out of his inexhaustible kindness."

"Yes, ma'am. He loved to drink; he really loved it and he used to drink, ma'am!" the retired quartermaster cried suddenly, draining his twelfth glass of vodka.

"Indeed, my late husband did have that weakness, and everyone knew that," said Katerina Ivanovna, pouncing on him in a flash. "But he was a kind and generous man who loved and respected his family; his one fault was that out of kindness he used to trust all sorts of depraved creatures; God knows who he used to drink with, people who weren't even worth his shoe sole! Just imagine, Rodion Romanovich, they found a gingerbread rooster in his pocket: he was dead drunk, but he was thinking about his children."

"A roo-ooster? Did you say a roo-ooster?" cried the quartermaster.

Katerina Ivanovna didn't deign to reply to him. She was deep in thought and sighed.

"You probably think, like everyone else, that I was too strict with him," she continued, turning to Raskolnikov. "But that wasn't the case! He respected me, he respected me very, very much! He was a man with a kind soul! I would sometimes feel so sorry for him! He used to sit in the corner looking at me, and I would feel so sorry for him; I wanted to be nice to him, and then I thought to myself, 'I'll be nice to him and then he'll go out and get drunk again.' Only by being so strict was it possible to restrain him somewhat."

"Yes, ma'am, he had his hair pulled, ma'am, more than once,

ma'am," roared the quartermaster again and poured another glass of vodka down his gullet.

"Never mind the hair pulling, but it might even be useful to sweep out some of those fools. I'm not talking about my late husband now!" Katerina Ivanovna replied to the quartermaster.

The red blotches on her cheeks were growing brighter and brighter, and her chest was heaving more and more. Another minute or so, and she'd be ready to make a scene. Many people giggled; obviously, they found this pleasant. Some people began poking the quartermaster and whispering something to him. Clearly, they were eager to provoke the two of them.

"All-low me to inquire what you're referring to, ma'am," the quartermaster began, "that is, on whose . . . honorable name . . . you were good enough just now to. . . . However, there's no need! It's nothing! Widow! Hey, widow! I forgive you. . . . I pass!" he said, and he downed another vodka.

Raskolnikov sat there and listened in silence and with disgust. He ate a bit, only tasting out of politeness the morsels Katerina Ivanovna kept piling onto his plate, and that he did only to avoid offending her. He stared intently at Sonya. But she was becoming more and more agitated and anxious; she also foresaw that the feast would not end serenely; with apprehension she observed Katerina Ivanovna's growing irritation. Meanwhile, she knew that she herself was the main reason why both of the invited ladies had treated Katerina Ivanovna's invitation so disdainfully. She'd heard from Amaliya Ivanovna herself that the mother had been offended by the invitation and had posed a question: "How could she possibly seat her own daughter next to *that young woman?*" Sonya foresaw that Katerina Ivanovna already knew about this somehow, and an insult to Sonya meant more to Katerina Ivanovna than an insult to her personally, her children, or her papa—in a word, it was a mortal insult; Sonya knew that Katerina Ivanovna wouldn't calm down "until she had proved to these two tail draggers that they're both . . ." and so on and so forth. As if on purpose, someone at the other end of the table sent Sonya a plate depicting two hearts pierced by an arrow, all carved out of black bread. Katerina Ivanovna flared up and immediately remarked in a loud voice, across the table, that the person who'd sent it was, of course, a "drunken ass." Amaliya Ivanovna, also foreseeing something unpleasant, while at the same time feeling offended to the depths of her soul by Katerina Ivanovna's arrogance, in an effort to deflect the nasty mood of the company in another direction and, by the way, to elevate her own standing in the general opinion, suddenly began, for no good reason, to relate a story about an acquaintance of hers, "Karl from ze pharmazist's shop," who was taking a cab one night and "ze driver vanted to kill him, und Karl begt und begt not to kill him, und he vept und clasped ze hands, and vas frightened, and from ze fear his heart vas vounded." Although Katerina Ivanovna smiled, she remarked at once that Amaliya Ivanovna shouldn't be trying to tell stories in Russian. At that, Amaliya Ivanovna was even more offended and objected, saying that her "*Vater* from Berlin vas a very, very important mann, and alvayz valked mit ze hends in ze pockets." Katerina Ivanovna was so amused that she couldn't refrain and burst into loud laughter, as a result of which Amaliya Ivanovna lost her last bit of patience and self-control.

"Look at that screech owl!" an almost cheerful Katerina Ivanovna whispered to Raskolnikov again. "She was trying to say that he walked around with his hands in his pockets, but it came out that he picked other people's pockets. *Cough, cough!* And did you notice, Rodion Romanovich, once and for all, that all these Petersburg foreigners— that is, mainly the Germans—who come to us from somewhere or other are all stupider than we are? Well, you have to agree that you can't just say, 'Karl from ze pharmazist's shop from ze fear his heart vas vounded,' and that he (the snotnose!), instead of tying up the cabdriver, 'he clasped ze hands, und vept, und begt.' Ah, what a nitwit! And she thinks it's a very touching story, and doesn't even suspect how stupid she is! In my opinion, this drunken quartermaster is much smarter than she is; at least it's apparent that the profligate drank away the last of his brains, but they're all so prim and proper. . . . Just look at her: her eyes are popping out. She's angry! Very angry! Ha-ha-ha! *Cough, cough!*"

Having cheered up, Katerina Ivanovna was immediately distracted by various details and suddenly began talking about how, with the assistance of an obtained pension, she would definitely open a boarding school for noble young ladies in her home town of T——. Raskolnikov had not heard of this plan before from Katerina Ivanovna, and she immediately delved into all the most alluring details. It was not at all clear how that "certificate of merit" had suddenly turned up in her hands, the one that the late Marmeladov had mentioned to Raskolnikov, explaining to him in the tavern that Katerina Ivanovna, his wife, had done the shawl dance "in the presence of the governor and other distinguished people" at the institute graduation ball. This certificate of merit, obviously, was now supposed to bear witness to Katerina Ivanovna's right to establish a school; but the main thing was, it was kept in reserve with the goal of finally putting those "two overdressed tail draggers" in their place, in case they came to the funeral feast, and to demonstrate clearly to them that Katerina Ivanovna was descended from a noble, "one could even say aristocratic, household and was a colonel's daughter, and that she was much better than certain adventure seekers who had become so very common as of late." The certificate of merit was immediately passed around by the drunken guests, which Katerina Ivanovna did not prevent, because it really did indicate *en toutes lettres* that she was the daughter of a decorated court councillor, and as a result, almost in fact a colonel's daughter. Now inspired, Katerina Ivanovna soon enlarged on all the details of her future splendid and serene way of life in T——; about the gymnasium teachers she would invite to give lectures at her school; about a respectable old Frenchman, M. Mangot, who had once taught Katerina Ivanovna French in school and who was living out his years in T—— and would certainly agree to teach in the school for a very reasonable fee. Finally the plan included even Sonya, "who would accompany Katerina Ivanovna to T—— and there would assist her in everything." But here someone at the other end of the table suddenly started chuckling. Although Katerina Ivanovna tried to pretend that she disregarded the laughter at the end of the table, she immediately raised her voice and began animatedly describing Sofiya Semyonovna's unquestionable abilities to serve as her assistant, "her gentleness, patience, self-sacrifice, nobility, and her education"; then she patted Sonya on the cheek and, standing up, kissed her warmly twice. Sonya blushed, but Katerina Ivanovna suddenly burst into tears, remarking that "she was a nervous fool and was too distraught, that it was high time she stopped, and since the meal was finished, it was now time to serve tea." At that very moment Amaliya Ivanovna, now absolutely offended that she had taken not the least part in the entire conversation, and that others weren't even listening to her at all, suddenly risked a last attempt and, with secret anguish, ventured to make one extremely practical and profound remark to Katerina Ivanovna, about how in her future school it would be important to pay particular attention to the girls' clean undergarments (*die Wäsche*) and that "she must haff one such good voman"—"*die Dame*"—"who the linen lookt after," and, second, "that all ze girls must at night secretly no novels read." Katerina Ivanovna, who was really distraught and very tired and already fed up with the funeral feast, immediately snapped at Amaliya Ivanovna and said that she was "talking nonsense" and didn't understand a thing; that *die Wäsche* was the concern of the woman in charge of the linen, and not the director of a boarding school for noble young women; and as far as reading novels was concerned, that was simply indecent, and she asked her to keep quiet. Amaliya Ivanovna flushed; now angered, she remarked that "she visht ze best," and that "she visht only ze very best," and that Katerina "for ze apartment had yet to pay ze rent." Katerina Ivanovna immediately "put her in her place," saying that she was lying when she said that "she visht ze best," because as recently as yesterday, when the deceased was still lying on the table, she had pestered her about the rent for the apartment. To this Amaliya Ivanovna replied extremely logically that "she invited zose ladies, but zose ladies didn't come because zose ladies were respectable ladies und couldn't disreputable ladies visit." Katerina Ivanovna immediately "emphasized" to her that since she was a slut, she couldn't judge what genuine nobility really was. Amaliya Ivanovna wouldn't accept this and declared at once that her "*Vater* from Berlin vas a very, very important *Mann* and valked mit ze hends in ze pockets and always said, 'Poof! Poof!'" and in order to represent her *Vater* more accurately, Amaliya Ivanovna jumped up from the chair, shoved both her hands into her pockets, puffed out her cheeks, and began making some sort of vague sounds with her mouth similar to puff, puff, to the accompaniment of loud guffaws from all the other lodgers, who intentionally encouraged Amaliya Ivanovna with their approval, expecting a fight. But Katerina Ivanovna could no longer stand it and rapidly, for all to hear, "blurted out" that perhaps Amaliya Ivanovna never even had a *Vater*, that Amaliya Ivanovna was simply a drunken Petersburg Finn, and that most likely she had worked somewhere as a cook before, perhaps even worse than that. Amaliya Ivanovna turned red as a lobster and shrieked that perhaps Katerina Ivanovna "had no *Vater* at all; that her *Vater* vas from Berlin, and he vore ze long frock coat und kept mit ze puff, puff, puff!" Katerina Ivanovna remarked with contempt that her own background was known to everyone and that the same certificate of merit indicated in print that her father was a colonel; while Amaliya Ivanovna's father (if she even had one) was probably some poor Petersburg Finn who peddled milk; that most likely she didn't have a father at all, because even up to now Amaliya Ivanovna's patronymic was still unknown: Ivanovna or Lyudvigovna. Then Amaliya Ivanovna, furious at last, banging her fist on the table, took to shouting that she was Amal-Ivan, and not Lyudvigovna, that her *Vater* "vas called Johann und he vas ze *Burgmeister*,"* and that Katerina Ivanovna's *Vater* "vas never ze *Burgmeister*." Katerina Ivanovna stood up from her place and sternly, in an apparently calm voice (although she was completely pale and her chest was heaving deeply), remarked to her that if she dared "to compare for one moment her worthless *Vater*" with her own papa, that she, Katerina Ivanovna, "would tear off Amaliya's cap and trample it underfoot." After hearing this, Amaliya Ivanovna ran around the room, shouting with all her might that she was the landlady and that Katerina Ivanovna "must zis very minute vacate the apartment." Then for some reason she rushed to collect her silver spoons from the table. An uproar and commotion ensued; the children began crying. Sonya hastened to restrain Katerina

* "Mayor" (German).

Ivanovna; but when Amaliya Ivanovna suddenly yelled something about a yellow ticket, Katerina Ivanovna pushed Sonya away and went after Amaliya Ivanovna to carry out her threat about the cap immediately. At that very moment the door opened and Petr Petrovich Luzhin suddenly appeared on the threshold of the room. He stood regarding the entire company with a severe and attentive glance. Katerina Ivanovna rushed to him.

"Petr Petrovich!" she cried, "at least you will protect us! Make this stupid creature understand that she has no right to treat a respectable lady in distress that way. There are laws about such things. . . . I'll go to the governor-general himself. . . . She'll have to answer for it. In memory of my father's hospitality, protect his orphans."

"Excuse me, madam. . . . Excuse me, excuse me, madam," Petr Petrovich said, waving her away. "As even you must know, I didn't have the honor of knowing your papa at all . . . excuse me, madam!" Someone guffawed loudly. "And I'm not inclined to get involved in your endless quarrels with Amaliya Ivanovna, ma'am. . . . I came here on necessary business . . . and I wish to speak at once with your stepdaughter, Sofiya . . . Ivanovna. . . . That's it, isn't it? Allow me to pass, ma'am . . ."

Petr Petrovich, sidling past Katerina Ivanovna, headed to the opposite corner, where Sonya stood.

Katerina Ivanovna remained standing in the same place as if thunderstruck. She couldn't understand how Petr Petrovich could disavow her papa's hospitality. Having once imagined this hospitality, she had come to believe in it as a sacred thing. She was also struck by Petr Petrovich's dry, businesslike tone, even full of some contemptuous menace. Everyone gradually fell somehow silent at his appearance. Besides, this "businesslike and earnest" man seemed in such disharmony with the entire gathering; in addition, it was clear that he had come for something important, probably only some unusual reason could bring him into such company; therefore something was about to happen, something would occur. Raskolnikov, standing next to Sonya, stepped aside to let him approach; Petr Petrovich, it seemed, didn't even notice him. A moment later, Lebezyatnikov appeared on the threshold; he didn't enter the room, but paused, also with some particular curiosity, almost in astonishment; he listened, though for a long time seemed not to understand anything.

"Excuse me if I'm interrupting, but I've come on rather important business, ma'am," Petr Petrovich remarked to everyone in general, not addressing anyone in particular. "I'm even glad other people are here. Amaliya Ivanovna, I humbly request that you, in your capacity as landlady of this apartment, pay special attention to the conversation I'm about to have with Sofiya Ivanovna. Sofiya Ivanovna," he continued, turning directly to an extremely surprised and already frightened Sonya, "immediately after your visit to my friend Andrey Semyonovich Lebezyatnikov, a government banknote belonging to me worth one hundred rubles disappeared from my table. If there is any way you know about it and can show us where it is now, then I give you my word of honor, which everyone here can witness, that will be the end of the matter. In the opposite case, I will be forced to take very serious measures, and then . . . you will have only yourself to blame, ma'am!"

Complete silence reigned in the room. Even the crying children quieted down. Sonya stood there, deathly pale, regarding Luzhin, unable to utter any reply. It was as if she still didn't understand. Several seconds passed.

"Well, ma'am, how about it?" asked Luzhin, staring at her intently.

"I don't know. . . . I don't know anything . . ." Sonya finally uttered in a weak voice.

"No? You don't?" Luzhin repeated his question and was silent for several seconds. "Think, mademoiselle," he began sternly, as it were, still exhorting her, "consider carefully. I'm willing to give you more time to reflect. Please understand, ma'am: if I were not so certain, with my experience, of course, I wouldn't risk accusing you so openly; for such a direct and open, but false, even erroneous accusation, I would, in a certain sense, be held responsible. I know this, ma'am.

This morning I exchanged, for some necessary expenses, several five percent bills with the nominal value of three thousand rubles. I have a receipt to that effect in my wallet. Upon returning home, I—Andrey Semyonovich is my witness—began counting the money; after counting two thousand and three hundred rubles, I placed that sum in my wallet and then put my wallet in the side pocket of my jacket. About five hundred rubles in banknotes were left on the table; among them were three notes of one hundred rubles each. At that moment you arrived (at my request); all the while you were extremely agitated, so that three times in the middle of our conversation you even stood up and prepared to leave for some reason, even though the conversation had not yet ended. Andrey Semyonych can bear witness to all this. Most likely, you yourself, mademoiselle, won't refuse to confirm and declare that I asked you to come, through Andrey Semyonych, solely in order to talk about the orphaned and desperate situation of your relative Katerina Ivanovna (whose funeral dinner I was unable to attend), and about how it might be useful to organize something like a subscription, a lottery, or something similar, for her benefit. You thanked me and even shed some tears (I'm relating everything as it happened in order, first, to remind you and, second, to show you that not the smallest detail has been erased from my memory). I took a ten-ruble note from the table and gave it to you, on my own behalf, as a contribution for your relative and as the first form of assistance. Andrey Semyonovich saw all this. Then I escorted you to the door—while you were still agitated—after which, left alone with Andrey Semyonovich, and conversing with him for almost ten minutes, he left and I turned back to the table where the money was lying, with the aim of finishing my counting and then putting it aside, as I had planned to do previously. To my surprise, a one-hundred-ruble note was not to be found among all the others. Please think carefully: I can't suspect Andrey Semyonovich, ma'am; I'm even ashamed of the suggestion. I can't be making a mistake in the amount, because just before your arrival, I'd finished my counting and found the total correct. You'll agree that recalling your agitation, your haste to leave, and the fact that for a while you had your hands on the table, and, finally, taking into account your social position and its associated habits, I was compelled, so to speak, against my will and with horror, to reach a conclusion—a cruel one, of course, but justified, ma'am! I will add, and I repeat, that in spite of all my *evident* certainty, I understand that there is still some risk for me in making this accusation now. But as you see, I haven't left the matter unattended; I have risen up and will tell you why: solely, madam, solely because of your blackest ingratitude! What? I invited you to stop by in the interests of your poor relative; I gave you ten rubles as a contribution within my powers; and you, right here, are repaying me for everything with such an action! No, ma'am, this is not very nice, ma'am! A lesson is needed, ma'am. Consider carefully; moreover, as your true friend, I ask you (since at this moment you don't have a better friend than I) to reconsider! Otherwise, I will be merciless! Well, ma'am, how about it?"

"I didn't take anything from you," Sonya whispered in horror. "You gave me ten rubles; here, take them back." She drew her handkerchief from her pocket, untied the knot, pulled out a ten-ruble note, and extended her hand to Luzhin.

"So you deny knowledge of the other hundred rubles?" he said reproachfully and insistently, not taking the note.

Sonya looked around. Everyone was staring at her with such horrified, severe, mocking, hateful faces. She glanced at Raskolnikov . . . he was standing near the wall, arms folded across his chest, regarding her with a fiery gaze.

"Oh, Lord!" Sonya burst forth.

"Amaliya Ivanovna, we'll have to inform the police; therefore I humbly request that you send for the caretaker," Luzhin remarked quietly, even politely.

"*Gott der barmherzige!** I knew she vas a thief!" Amaliya exclaimed, clasping her hands.

"You knew?" Luzhin repeated. "That means you already had some reason for coming to that conclusion. I beg you, most respected Amaliya Ivanovna, remember the words you just spoke here in the presence of witnesses."

---

* "Merciful Lord!" (German).

Loud conversation suddenly arose on all sides. Everyone began stirring.

"Wha-a-at?" Katerina Ivanovna cried suddenly, coming to her senses—and, as if breaking loose, she rushed at Luzhin. "What? You're accusing her of theft? Sonya? Ah, what scoundrels, scoundrels!" Rushing to Sonya, she clutched her tightly in her wasted arms.

"Sonya! How dare you take ten rubles from him! Oh, you stupid girl! Give it to me! Give me the ten rubles—here!"

After snatching the banknote from Sonya, Katerina Ivanovna crumpled it in her hand and hurled it straight at Luzhin's face. The ball of paper hit him in the eye and bounced onto the floor. Amaliya Ivanovna rushed to pick up the money. Petr Petrovich grew angry.

"Restrain this madwoman!" he shouted.

Just at that moment, several people appeared in the doorway together with Lebezyatnikov, among whom were the two recently arrived ladies.

"What? Madwoman? I'm a madwoman, am I? You fool, you!" Katerina Ivanovna shrieked. "You're a fool, a shyster, a vile creature! Sonya, Sonya steal his money? Sonya, a thief? Why, she'd even give you money, you fool!" Katerina Ivanovna began laughing hysterically. "Have you ever seen such a fool?" She rushed around the room, pointing out Luzhin to everyone. "What? And you, too?" she said, catching sight of the landlady. "You, too, you German sausage-maker, you state that she 'stole,' you revolting Prussian chicken leg dressed up in crinoline! Oh, you! You! She hasn't left this room; as soon as she returned, you scoundrel, she sat down right next to Rodion Romanovich! Search her! If she didn't leave the room, the money must still be on her! Search her, go on, search her! But if you don't find it, then, excuse me, my dear, you'll have to answer for it! To the tsar, the tsar, I'll go to the tsar himself, the merciful tsar; I'll throw myself at his feet at once, today! I'm an orphan! They'll admit me! You think they won't? You lie! I'll get to him! I will! You were counting on the fact that she's timid, right? You were relying on that, were you? But, my friend, I'm fearless! You'll pay for it! Search her! Search her, go on, search her!!"

In her fury, Katerina Ivanovna grabbed Luzhin and dragged him over to Sonya.

"I'm ready, ma'am, and will answer for it . . . but calm down, madam, calm down! I see all too well that you're fearless! This . . . this . . . how to proceed, ma'am?" muttered Luzhin. "The police should be present, ma'am . . . although, as it is, there are more than enough witnesses. . . . I'm ready, ma'am. . . . But in any case, it's difficult for me as a man . . . because of my sex. . . . If, with Amaliya Ivanovna's help . . . although, this isn't the way it's done. . . . How to proceed?"

"Anyone you like. Let anyone you like search her!" cried Katerina Ivanovna. "Sonya, empty your pockets! There, there! Look, you monster, it's empty; there was a handkerchief and now the pocket's empty, you see! Now the other pocket, there, there! You see? You see?"

And Katerina didn't merely empty Sonya's pockets so much as grab both of them, one after the other, and turn them inside out. But from the second pocket, the one on the right, a piece of paper came flying out; describing a parabola in the air, it fell at Luzhin's feet. Everyone saw it; many people cried out. Petr Petrovich bent over, picked up the paper from the floor with his two fingers, unfolded it, and lifted it up for all to see. It was a one-hundred-ruble banknote, folded in eighths. Petr Petrovich moved his arm around in a circle, displaying the banknote to everyone.

"Thief! Get *auss* of zis apartment! Police! Police!" howled Amaliya Ivanovna. "Zey muss to Siberia be sent! Get *auss*!"

Exclamations flew from all sides. Raskolnikov kept silent and didn't take his eyes off Sonya; from time to time he glanced quickly at Luzhin. Sonya stood in the same place, as if unconscious: she didn't even seem very surprised. Suddenly her entire face turned red: she cried out and covered her face with her hands.

"I didn't do it! I didn't take it! I don't know anything about it!" she cried in a heart-rending wail and rushed to Katerina Ivanovna. She embraced Sonya and held her close, as if shielding her with her chest from everyone else.

"Sonya! Sonya! I don't believe it! You see, I don't believe it!" cried Katerina Ivanovna (in spite of the clear evidence); she shook Sonya in her arms like a child, kissing her repeatedly, catching hold of her hands and kissing them, too, almost devouring them. "Even the idea of your taking it! What stupid people they are! Oh, Lord! You're stupid,

CRIME AND PUNISHMENT   437

stupid," she shouted, turning to face everyone. "You still don't know, you don't know, what sort of girl she is, what a heart she has! Steal it? Sonya? She would take off her last dress, sell it, go barefoot, and give it to you, if you needed it; that's the sort of person she is! She got a yellow card because my children were dying of hunger; she sold herself for us! Ah, her poor deceased father! Her poor father! Do you see? Do you? So much for your funeral feast! Good Lord! Protect her! Why are you all standing there? Rodion Romanovich! Why won't you intervene? Do you believe it, too? You're not worth her little finger, all of you, all, all, all of you! Good Lord! Defend her at last!"

The lament of poor, consumptive, bereaved Katerina Ivanovna seemed to produce a strong effect on the public. There was so much pathos, so much suffering in her wasted, consumptive face distorted by pain, in her dried-out lips caked with blood, in her voice's hoarse shrieking, in her sobs resembling a child's complaint, in her trusting, childish, and, at the same time, desperate prayer for help that everyone seemed to pity the poor unfortunate woman. At least Petr Petrovich immediately *pitied* her.

"Madam! Madam!" he cried in an imposing voice. "This matter doesn't involve you! No one will accuse you of having the intention or of complicity, especially since it was you who discovered the banknote by turning her pockets inside out, which means you had no idea of it beforehand. I'm absolutely prepared to sympathize, if, so to speak, it was poverty that incited Sofiya Semyonovna. But why, mademoiselle, didn't you want to confess? Were you afraid of the disgrace? Was it your first time? Did you become flustered, perhaps? It's understandable, ma'am, completely understandable, ma'am. . . . But why did you embark on such a course? Ladies and gentlemen!" He turned to everyone present. "Ladies and gentlemen! Sympathizing and, so to speak, pitying, I may be ready to forgive, even now, in spite of the personal insults I've received. And let your present shame, mademoiselle, be a lesson to you for the future," he said, turning to Sonya, "and I shall leave the matter here; so be it, I'll stop. Enough!"

Petr Petrovich cast a sidelong glance at Raskolnikov. Their eyes met. Raskolnikov's fiery look was ready to incinerate him. Meanwhile, Katerina Ivanovna seemed not to hear anything more; like a madwoman she was embracing and kissing Sonya. The children also embraced Sonya from all sides with their little arms, while Polechka— who didn't quite understand what it was all about—seemed to be drowning in tears, shaking with sobs, burying her pretty little face, now swollen from her crying, into Sonya's shoulder.

"How despicable!" a loud voice suddenly boomed from the doorway. Petr Petrovich glanced around quickly.

"What baseness!" repeated Lebezyatnikov, staring directly at him.

Petr Petrovich actually seemed to shudder. Everyone noticed this. (They recalled it later.) Lebezyatnikov took a step into the room.

"And you dared call me as a witness?" he said, approaching Petr Petrovich.

"What does this mean, Andrey Semyonych? What are you talking about?" muttered Luzhin.

"It means you're a slanderer, that's what I'm saying!" Lebezyatnikov cried passionately, regarding him severely with his shortsighted little eyes. He was terribly irate. Raskolnikov fixed his eyes on him, as if seizing on and weighing every word. Silence prevailed once again. Petr Petrovich seemed almost at a loss, especially at first.

"If you're accusing me . . ." he began, stuttering. "What's wrong with you? Are you in your right mind?"

"I am in my right mind, sir, and you . . . are a scoundrel! Oh, this is so vile! I heard everything; I waited intentionally to understand it all, because, I confess, even up to this moment it hasn't been quite logical. . . . But I don't understand why you did all this."

"But what have I done? Will you stop uttering your nonsensical riddles? Perhaps you've been drinking?"

"It's you, you vile man, who may have been drinking, not me! I never touch vodka, because it's against my principles! Just think, it was he, he himself, who gave Sofiya Semyonovna that one-hundred-ruble note with his own hands—I saw it, I'm a witness, I'll swear an oath! It was him, him!" repeated Lebezyatnikov, turning to each and every person present.

"Have you gone mad or what, you pipsqueak?" cried Luzhin. "Right here in front of you—right here, just now, she confirmed to everyone that she received nothing from me but the ten rubles. How could I have possibly given her anything more?"

"I saw it, I saw it!" shouted and affirmed Lebezyatnikov. "Although it's against my principles, I'm prepared to swear any sort of oath in court this very minute, because I saw how you secretly slipped it into her pocket! But, fool that I am, I thought you gave it to her out of generosity! In the doorway, as you were saying good-bye, when she turned away and you were shaking her hand with your right hand, you secretly slipped the banknote into her pocket with your left. I saw it! I saw it!"

Luzhin blanched.

"What lies you're telling!" he cried valiantly. "And how could you, standing over by the window, tell that it was a banknote? You just imagined it . . . in your shortsighted way. You're delirious!"

"No, I didn't imagine it! Even though I was standing far away, I saw everything, everything, and even though from the window it was hard to make out a banknote—you're right about that—by a special circumstance I know for certain that it was indeed a hundred-ruble banknote, because when you were just about to give Sofiya Semyonovna a tenruble note—I myself saw it—at the same time you took from the table a hundred-ruble note. (I saw it because I was standing nearby and the thought occurred to me just then; therefore, I didn't forget that you had a banknote in your hand.) You folded it and held it tight in your hand all the while. Then I almost forgot again, but when you went to stand up, you transferred it from your right hand to your left and almost dropped it; then I remembered the banknote once more because that same thought occurred to me again, namely, that you wanted to do something generous for her without my knowing. You can imagine how I began to follow things—and I saw how you managed to slip it into her pocket. I saw it, I saw it, and I'll swear to it!"

Lebezyatnikov was almost gasping for breath. Exclamations of various kinds rang out from all sides, most of them expressing astonishment; but there were also some exclamations that took on a more menacing tone. Everyone crowded toward Petr Petrovich. Katerina Ivanovna rushed to Lebezyatnikov.

"Andrey Semyonych! I've been mistaken about you! Protect her!

You're the only one who stands up for her! She's an orphan; God has sent you! Andrey Semyonych, my dear friend, you kind man!"

Katerina Ivanovna, almost unaware of what she was doing, threw herself on her knees before him.

"Nonsense!" wailed Luzhin, enraged to a fury. "You're talking nonsense, sir. 'You forgot, you remembered, you forgot'—what's all that about? So I planted it on her? Why? For what reason? What do I have in common with this . . ."

"What for? That's just what I don't understand myself; but what's for sure is that I'm stating the facts! I'm so certain, you disgusting, wicked man, that I can recall precisely how that same question occurred to me just as I was thanking you, shaking your hand. Why indeed did you slip it secretly into her pocket? That is, why secretly? Was it really simply because you wished to conceal it from me, knowing that I hold opposite principles and reject private charity, which achieves no radical solutions? Well, I decided that you were embarrassed to give away such a large sum in front of me. Besides that, perhaps, I thought, you wanted to surprise her, astonish her when she found one hundred rubles hidden in her pocket. (Because some benefactors very much like to show off their charity; I know this.) Then it also occurred to me that you wanted to test her; that is, after finding it, would she come back to thank you? Then, that you wanted to avoid her gratitude. What does it say there: so the right hand, isn't it, doesn't know . . . in a word, something like that. . . . Well, a lot of different ideas occurred to me at that time, so I decided to consider it all later, but still I thought it indelicate to reveal that I knew your secret. However, one question occurred to me at the time: that Sofiya Semyonovna might lose the money before she noticed your good deed; therefore, I decided to come here, call her over, and inform her that one hundred rubles had been slipped into her pocket. On the way here, I dropped into the Kobylyatnikovs' to take them *A General Deduction from the Positive Method** and, in particular, to recommend an article by Piderit (as well as one by Wagner); then I came here, and what a scene I found

---

* A collection of articles translated from French and German and published in Petersburg in 1866.

in progress! Well, how could I have had all these thoughts and ideas if I really hadn't seen that you put one hundred rubles into her pocket?"

When Andrey Semyonych finished his lengthy explanation, with such a logical conclusion at the end of his speech, he was terribly tired; sweat was even dripping from his face. Alas, he didn't really know how to express himself properly in Russian (not knowing, however, any other language), so now he was suddenly utterly exhausted, as if he had even wasted away following his lawyerly feat. Nevertheless, his speech produced an extraordinary effect. He'd spoken with such fervor, such conviction, that everyone apparently believed him. Petr Petrovich felt that things were not good.

"What do I care if such foolish questions occurred to you?" he cried. "That's no proof, sir! You could have dreamt all this raving in your sleep, and that's all there is to it, sir! I tell you, sir, you're lying! You're lying and slandering me out of some malice toward me, out of anger that I don't agree with your freethinking, godless social propositions, that's what, sir!"

But this latest turn didn't work to Petr Petrovich's advantage. On the contrary, grumbling resounded on all sides.

"Ah, so that's where you've got to!" cried Lebezyatnikov. "You're lying! Call the police, and I'll swear an oath! There's only one thing I don't understand: why did you risk your reputation on such a vile act? Oh, you pitiful, base man!"

"I can explain why he took a risk on that act, and if necessary, I myself will take an oath!" Raskolnikov spoke at last in a steady voice and stepped forward.

He was apparently steady and serene. It somehow was clear to everyone, merely by glancing at him, that he really knew what it was all about and that the matter had reached its denouement.

"Now I've clarified it all to myself," continued Raskolnikov, turning directly to Lebezyatnikov. "From the very beginning of this story, I'd already begun to suspect that there was some dirty trick involved, as a result of several special circumstances known only to me, which I'll now explain to everyone: they embrace the whole point! It was you, Andrey Semyonych, with your valuable evidence, who clarified everything for me once and for all. I ask you all, all of you, to listen: this gentleman"—he pointed to Luzhin—"was recently engaged to a young woman, namely, to my sister, Avdotya Romanovna Raskolnikova. But upon arrival in Petersburg two days ago, he quarreled with me at our first meeting and I drove him away, to which event there are two witnesses. This man was very angry. . . . The day before yesterday, I didn't know he was renting a room here, from you, Andrey Semyonych; therefore, the same day we quarreled—that is, two days ago—he was a witness to how I, as an acquaintance of the late Mr. Marmeladov's, presented his wife, Katerina Ivanovna, with some money for funeral expenses. He immediately wrote a note to my mother and informed her that I'd given the money not to Katerina Ivanovna, but to Sofiya Semyonovna; in addition, he made reference in the vilest language to her . . . her character, that is, he hinted at the nature of my relations with Sofiya Semyonovna. He did all this, you understand, with the goal of causing a rift between me and my mother and sister, convincing them that I was squandering their last kopecks, with which they were supporting me, for unworthy purposes. Yesterday evening, in the presence of my mother and my sister, and in his presence, I established the truth after proving that I had given the money to Katerina Ivanovna for the funeral, and not to Sofiya Semyonovna, and that two days ago I was still unacquainted with her and had not even once seen her face-to-face. Furthermore, I added that he, Petr Petrovich Luzhin, with all his merits, wasn't worth Sofiya Semyonovna's little finger, about whom he'd expressed himself so offensively. To his question, 'Would I seat Sofiya Semyonovna next to my sister?' I replied that I'd done so already, that very day. He grew angry that my mother and my sister, in spite of his slander, didn't want to quarrel with me; word for word, he began to utter unforgivably impudent things to them. A definitive break occurred, and we drove him from the room. All of this occurred last evening. Now I beg your particular attention: imagine if he were now able to demonstrate that Sofiya Semyonovna is a thief. First he would prove to my sister and my mother that he was almost right in his suspicions; that he had been justified in getting angry at me for having placed my sister on a level with Sofiya Semyonovna; that by attacking me, he was therefore defending and preserving the honor of my sister and his fiancée. In a word, through it all he could even provoke a rift between my family and me, and, of course, he hoped once more to restore himself to their good favor. I'm not even mentioning the fact that he'd get his personal revenge against me, because he would have the grounds to suppose that Sofiya Semyonovna's honor and happiness were important to me. Those were all his calculations! That's how I understand this affair! That's the whole reason; there can't be any other!"

Raskolnikov finished his speech this way, or almost this way; he was frequently interrupted by exclamations from the listeners, who were, of course, paying great attention. But, in spite of all the interruptions, he spoke briskly, calmly, precisely, clearly, and decisively. His sharp voice, his persuasive tone, and his stern face produced an extraordinary effect on everyone.

"Yes, yes, that's true!" Lebezyatnikov affirmed in ecstasy. "It must be so, because as soon as Sofiya Semyonovna entered the room, Petr Petrovich asked me, 'Were you here? Hadn't I seen you among Katerina Ivanovna's guests?' He called me over to the window so he could question me in secret. Therefore it was essential to him that you be here! It's true, it's all true!"

Luzhin remained silent and smiled contemptuously. However, he looked very pale. He seemed to be thinking about how he could extricate himself. Perhaps he would have dropped the entire matter with pleasure and walked out, but at the present moment that was almost impossible; that would mean admitting the accuracy of the accusations against him—namely, that he really was slandering Sofiya Semyonovna. In addition, the people here, many of whom had already drunk a fair amount, were too agitated. The quartermaster, although he didn't understand everything, was shouting more than anyone and proposed some very unpleasant measures against Luzhin. But there were also some people who were not drunk; they came in from the other rooms and gathered together. All three of the little Poles were terribly angry and were shouting constantly: *'Pan jest łajdak!'** In addition, they were muttering still other threats in Polish. Sonya listened with effort, but

---

* "The man is a scoundrel!" (Polish).

also seemed not to understand everything, as if she were recovering from a fainting spell. But she didn't take her eyes off Raskolnikov, feeling that he was her best defense. Katerina Ivanovna was breathing with difficulty and wheezing; she seemed to be terribly exhausted. Amaliya Ivanovna stood there, looking the most foolish of all, her mouth open wide and without a thought in her head. She merely saw that Petr Petrovich had somehow been exposed. Raskolnikov was about to speak again but wasn't allowed to do so: everyone was shouting and crowding around Luzhin with curses and threats. But Petr Petrovich didn't cringe. Seeing that his attempt to accuse Sonya had failed completely, he resorted directly to effrontery.

"Allow me, ladies and gentlemen, allow me; don't crowd me. Allow me to pass!" he said, making his way through the crowd. "And be so kind as to stop your threats; I can assure that nothing will come of them; you won't do anything. I'm not easily scared, sirs. On the contrary, ladies and gentlemen, you will be responsible for concealing a criminal act. The thief has been unmasked, and I intend to prosecute, sirs. The court will not be as blind . . . nor drunk, sirs, and they will not believe two acknowledged atheists, troublemakers, and freethinkers who are accusing me out of personal revenge, which, in their own stupidity, they even admit. . . . Yes, sirs, allow me to pass!"

"I want you out of my room at once; be so good as to leave, and everything between us is over! Just think, I did my utmost, I've been explaining to him . . . for two whole weeks!"

"I myself told you recently that I was leaving, Andrey Semyonovich, while you were still trying to detain me; now I'll add simply that you're a fool, sir. I hope you'll be cured of your mental illness and your shortsightedness. Allow me to pass, ladies and gentlemen!"

He pushed his way through; but the quartermaster didn't want to let him go so easily, with only verbal abuse: he grabbed a glass from the table, swung his arm, and hurled it at Petr Petrovich; but the glass flew directly at Amaliya Ivanovna. She screamed, but the quartermaster, who had lost his balance from the swing, fell clumsily under the table. Petr Petrovich passed into his room, and a half hour later was no longer in the building. Sonya, who was timid by nature, had known beforehand that it was easier to demolish her than anyone else and that anyone could insult her almost with impunity. Nevertheless, up to this very moment, it had seemed to her that she could somehow avoid misfortune—by her caution, meekness, and humility before each and every person. Her disappointment was too painful. Of course, she could tolerate everything with patience and almost without complaint—even this. But at first all this was too painful. In spite of her triumph and vindication—after the first fright and the passing of her stupor, when she had grasped and understood everything clearly—a feeling of helplessness and insult weighed painfully on her heart. She became hysterical. Finally, unable to refrain, she rushed out of the room and ran home. This was almost immediately following Luzhin's departure. Amaliya Ivanovna, when the glass had hit her amidst sounds of loud laughter from those present, had also been unable to stand being made a scapegoat. With the shriek of a madwoman, she rushed at Katerina Ivanovna, holding her to blame for everything.

"Get *auss* of my apartment. Right now. *Marsch!*" With these words she began grabbing hold of all of Katerina Ivanovna's things she could lay her hands on and flinging them onto the floor. Already almost completely exhausted, practically in a faint, pale and gasping for breath, Katerina Ivanovna jumped off the bed (where she had collapsed in exhaustion) and threw herself at Amaliya Ivanovna. But the struggle was too uneven; Amaliya Ivanovna pushed her away like a feather.

"What? It's not enough they've slandered me godlessly—now this creature's attacking me! What? To be driven out of the apartment onto the street the day of my husband's funeral, after all my hospitality, driven out with orphans! Where will I go?" the poor woman howled, sobbing and panting. "Good Lord!" she cried suddenly, her eyes flashing. "Is there really no justice? Who's supposed to defend us, poor widows and orphans? But we'll see! There's justice and truth on earth, there is, and I'll find it! Just you wait now, you godless creature! Polechka, stay here with the children; I'll come back. Wait for me, even out on the street! We'll see if there's truth to be had on this earth."

Throwing over her head the same lightweight green shawl the late Marmeladov had mentioned in his account, Katerina Ivanovna squeezed through the disorderly drunken crowd of lodgers, who were still pushing into the room. She ran out onto the street with a tearful wail—and with the vague intention of finding justice somewhere, this very moment, no matter what. Polechka, terrified, cowered with the children on a trunk in the corner, where, embracing the two little ones and trembling, she began waiting for her mother's return. Amaliya Ivanovna rushed around the room, screaming, moaning, brawling, and flinging everything she could lay her hands on onto the floor. The lodgers were bawling, each doing his own thing—some were discussing, as best they could, what had just occurred; others were quarreling and cursing; still others struck up a song.

"Now it's time for me to leave, too!" thought Raskolnikov. "Well, then, Sofiya Semyonovna, we'll see what you have to say for yourself now!"

And he set off toward Sonya's apartment.

IV

Raskolnikov was an active and bold advocate for Sonya against Luzhin, in spite of the fact that he carried so much of his own distress and suffering in his soul. But having endured so much that morning, he was glad for the chance to alter his focus, which had become so intolerable, not to mention the sincere and personal emotions in his desire to intervene for Sonya. In addition, he had in view and at times felt terribly agitated about his forthcoming meeting with Sonya: he felt *obligated* to tell her who'd killed Lizaveta; he foresaw terrible suffering for himself, which he tried to push away. Therefore, upon leaving Katerina Ivanovna's, when he exclaimed, "Well, then, Sofiya Semyonovna, we'll see what you have to say for yourself now!" he was obviously still in an externally excited state of elation, occasioned by the challenge and recent victory over Luzhin. But something strange happened to him. When he arrived at the Kapernaumovs' apartment, he felt a sudden weakness and fear. He stood in front of the door, deep in thought, with a strange question: "Do I have to say who killed Lizaveta?" The question was strange because he suddenly, just at that moment, felt not only that it was impossible not to say, but that it was impossible to put off this moment for even a little while. He still didn't know why it was impossible; he merely *felt* it, and this tormenting awareness of his frailty before this necessity almost overpowered him. In order to cease his deliberations and to end his suffering, he opened the door quickly and looked at Sonya from the threshold. She was sitting there, resting her elbows on the little table, covering her face with her hands; upon seeing Raskolnikov, she stood up hastily and went to meet him, as if she were expecting him.

"What would have happened to me without you?" she said rapidly, greeting him in the middle of the room. Apparently she wanted to say this one thing to him as quickly as possible. That was why she'd waited for him.

Raskolnikov went to the table and sat down on the chair from which she had just stood up. She stopped a few steps away from him, just as she had yesterday.

"Well, Sonya?" he said; suddenly he felt his voice trembling. "The whole matter depended on your 'social position and its associated habits.' Did you understand that just now?"

Her face expressed suffering.

"Just don't talk to me as you did yesterday!" she interrupted him. "Please, don't start. There's enough suffering as it is . . ."

She smiled quickly, afraid that he wouldn't like the reproach.

"It was foolish of me to leave. What's happening there now? I wanted to go back at once, but I kept thinking that you'd . . . you'd come here."

He told her that Amaliya Ivanovna was driving them out of the apartment and that Katerina Ivanovna was rushing off "to look for justice."

"Ah, my God!" Sonya cried. "Let's go right now . . ."

And she grabbed hold of her cape.

"It's always the same!" cried Raskolnikov irritably. "They're all you ever think about. Stay here awhile with me!"

"But what about . . . Katerina Ivanovna?"

"Ah, Katerina Ivanovna, of course, you can't miss her. If she's gone out of the house, she'll come to see you herself," he added peevishly. "If she doesn't find you here, then it'll be your fault . . ."

Sonya sat down on a chair in tormenting indecision. Raskolnikov was silent, staring at the floor, thinking about something.

"Let's assume that Luzhin didn't want to do it right now," he began, without looking at Sonya. "But what if he had wanted to or it had been part of his plans? He could have had you put in jail if Lebezyatnikov and I hadn't happened to be there! Right?"

"Yes," she said in a weak voice. "Yes!" she repeated, distracted and alarmed.

"And I really might not have been there! And Lebezyatnikov? He turned up completely by chance."

Sonya was silent.

"And if you were taken to jail, what then? Do you remember what I was saying yesterday?"

Once more she made no reply. He waited.

"I thought you'd cry out again, 'Ah! Don't say it! Stop!'" Raskolnikov said with a laugh, but his laugh was somehow forced. "Why this silence again?" he asked a moment later. "We have to talk about something, don't we? I'd be interested in knowing how you would now resolve one 'question,' as Lebezyatnikov says. (He seemed to get a bit muddled.) No, really, I'm being serious. Imagine, Sonya, that you knew all of Luzhin's intentions beforehand, you knew (that is, for certain) that as a result Katerina Ivanovna would come to grief, and the children; and you, too, in the bargain (since you consider yourself worthless, let's say *in the bargain*). Polechka as well . . . because she'll take the same road. Well, then: suppose that suddenly all this depended on your decision: whether this person is to live, that is, should Luzhin live and do nasty things, or should Katerina Ivanovna die? How would you decide: which of them has to die? I ask you."

Sonya looked at him with anxiety: she heard something peculiar in his unsteady voice, which seemed to come from far away.

"I had a feeling you'd ask me something like that," she said, regarding him inquisitively.

"All right, so be it; but how would you decide?"

"Why do you ask something so impossible?" Sonya said with distaste.

"That means it might be better for Luzhin to live and do nasty things! Surely you wouldn't dare to decide that?"

"But I can't know God's plan. . . . Why are you asking something that's so impossible? Why pose such empty questions? How could it happen that it would depend on my decision? Who made me a judge to decide who gets to live and who doesn't?"

"If God's plan is mixed up in this matter, there's nothing we can do about it," Raskolnikov grumbled sullenly.

"Tell me plainly what it is you want!" Sonya cried, clearly suffering. "You're leading up to something again. . . . Did you really come here just to torment me?"

She couldn't restrain herself and suddenly burst into bitter tears. He looked at her in gloomy anguish. Some five minutes passed.

"But you're right, Sonya," he said softly at last. He had in that moment been transformed; his artificially arrogant and weakly challenging tone had disappeared. Even his voice suddenly slackened. "Yesterday I told you that I'd come not to ask forgiveness, yet I almost began by asking for it. . . . What I said about Luzhin and about God was for myself. . . . I asked forgiveness, Sonya . . ."

He began to smile, but there was something feeble and incomplete in his pale smile. He bent his head down and covered his face with his hands.

At once a strange, unexpected sensation of some scathing hatred for Sonya passed through his heart. As if surprised by this sensation and frightened by it, he suddenly raised his head and stared directly at her; he met her anxious and painfully solicitous glance directed at him; there was love reflected in it; his hatred vanished like a shadow. That was not it; he had mistaken one feeling for another. It only meant that *the moment* had come.

Once more he covered his face with his hands and bent his head down. Suddenly he grew pale, stood up from his chair, looked at Sonya, and, without uttering a word, sat down automatically on her bed.

This moment in his feeling was terribly similar to the one when he'd stood over the old woman, after he had freed the axe from its loop and felt that "he had not a moment to lose."

"What's the matter with you?" Sonya asked, feeling extremely frightened.

He couldn't utter a word. This was not at all the way he had planned to *announce* it; he himself didn't understand what was happening to him. She approached him gently, sat down on the bed next to him, and waited, without taking her eyes off him. Her heart was pounding and skipping beats. It became unbearable: he turned his deathly pale face toward her; his lips twisted helplessly, trying to utter something. Terror passed through Sonya's heart.

"What's the matter with you?" she repeated, withdrawing slightly from him.

"Nothing, Sonya. Don't be afraid. . . . It's all rubbish. Really, if you think about it—it is rubbish," he muttered with the look of a person unaware of himself and in delirium. "Why in the world did I come to torment you with this?" he added suddenly, looking at her. "Really. Why? I keep posing that question to myself, Sonya . . ."

Perhaps he had even posed this question to himself a quarter of an hour ago, but now he uttered it in complete helplessness, hardly aware of himself and feeling constant tremors throughout his whole body.

"Oh, how you torment yourself!" she uttered, with feeling, looking intently at him.

"It's all rubbish! . . . That's what, Sonya." Suddenly he smiled for some reason, a pale and feeble smile, for a few seconds. "Do you remember what I wanted to tell you yesterday?"

Sonya waited anxiously.

"As I was leaving, I said that I might be saying good-bye to you forever; but if I came today I would tell you . . . who killed Lizaveta."

All at once her whole body shuddered.

"Well, then, I've come to tell you."

"So yesterday you were really . . ." she whispered with effort. "How do you know?" she asked quickly, as if coming to her senses suddenly.

Sonya's breathing became labored. Her face grew paler and paler.

"I know."

She was silent for a minute.

"Did they find *him*?" she asked timidly.

"No, they didn't."

"So how do you know about it?" she asked, barely audibly, once again after almost a minute's silence.

He turned toward her and stared at her very, very intensely.

"Guess," he said with his previous twisted, feeble smile.

Convulsions seemed to pass through her whole body.

"You're . . . I . . . why are you . . . scaring me?" she asked, smiling like a child.

"It must mean that I'm *his* close friend . . . if I know," Raskolnikov continued, staring steadfastly at her face as if he lacked the power to look away. "He didn't want to . . . kill Lizaveta. . . . He killed her . . . accidentally. . . . He only wanted to kill the old woman . . . when she was alone . . . and he came. . . . Then Lizaveta walked in . . . He was there . . . and he killed her."

Another terrible minute passed. They both continued staring at each other.

"So you can't guess?" he asked abruptly, with the feeling that he was throwing himself down from a bell tower.

"N-no," Sonya whispered, barely audibly.

"Take a good look."

As soon as he said this, once again a prior, familiar feeling all at once turned his soul to ice: he glanced at her and all of a sudden he seemed to see Lizaveta's face in hers. He clearly recalled Lizaveta's expression as he approached her with his axe and she retreated from him toward the wall, holding up her hand, childlike fear in her face. It was just like little children when they suddenly get frightened of something: they stare motionlessly and anxiously at what's scaring them, they retreat and, stretching out their little hands, they get ready to burst into tears. Almost the same thing was happening now with Sonya: just as weakly, with the same fright, she looked at him for a while, and all of a sudden, stretching out her left hand, she gently pushed her fingers against his chest and slowly began standing up from the bed, moving farther and farther away from him, fixing her intense stare on him all the while. Her horror was suddenly communicated to him: it was as if the same fright showed in his face; he began staring at her the same way, almost even with the same *childlike* smile.

"Have you guessed?" he whispered at last.

"Good Lord!" burst forth from her breast with a terrible wail. She fell helplessly onto the bed and buried her face in the pillow. But a moment later she quickly raised herself up, moved swiftly toward him, seized his two hands, squeezing them tightly with her slender fingers, as if in a vise, and once more fixed her unmoving gaze on his face as if it were glued to it. With this last, despairing look she wanted to search for and find some last vestige of hope. But there was no hope; no doubt remained whatsoever; it was all *true*! Even afterward, subsequently, when she recalled this moment, she felt strange and full of wonder: why was it that she realized *immediately* at that time that there was no doubt? She couldn't say, for example, that she foresaw something of this sort. Meanwhile, now, as soon as he had said it, it suddenly seemed to her that it was just as if she had foreseen exactly *that*.

"Enough, Sonya, enough! Don't torture me!" he begged her pitifully.

This wasn't at all the way he had planned to reveal it to her, but this was how it turned out.

As if she were unaware of what she was doing, she jumped up; wringing her hands, she reached the middle of the room, but quickly returned and sat down next to him once again, her shoulder almost touching his. All of a sudden, as if pierced, she shuddered, cried out, and threw herself on her knees before him, not really knowing why she did so.

"What have you done, what have you done to yourself?" she said desperately. Jumping up from her knees, she threw herself around his neck, embraced him, and squeezed him tightly in her arms.

Raskolnikov recoiled and regarded her with a sad smile.

"You're so strange, Sonya—you hug me and kiss me when I just told you about that. You don't know what you're doing."

"No, there's no one more miserable than you in the whole world!"* she cried as if in a frenzy, without hearing his last remark; she burst into sobs as if hysterical.

A long-unfamiliar feeling poured like a wave into his soul and instantly softened it. He didn't resist it; two tears formed in his eyes and clung to his eyelashes.

"So you won't desert me, Sonya?" he asked, regarding her almost with hope.

"No, no; never and nowhere!" Sonya cried. "I'll follow you, I'll fol-

---

* The Russian indicates a significant change in Sonya's speech from the formal *vy* ("you") to the informal *ty*.

low you everywhere! Oh, Lord! . . . Oh, I'm so unhappy! . . . Why, oh, why didn't I know you before? Why didn't you come sooner? Oh, Lord!"

"I've come now."

"Now! Oh, what can be done now? . . . Together, together!" she repeated as if distracted and embraced him again. "I'll go with you to prison!" All of a sudden, he felt a convulsion and his previous, hateful, almost haughty smile appeared on his lips.

"Sonya, perhaps I don't want to go to prison yet," he said.

Sonya looked at him quickly.

After her initial, passionate, tormenting sympathy for the unfortunate man, the terrible thought of the murder struck her once again. In his altered tone of voice she suddenly heard a murderer. She looked at him in amazement. She still didn't know anything about it, neither why, nor how, nor what for. Now all of these questions flooded into her mind. Once again she didn't believe it: "He's, he's a murderer! Could that be possible?"

"What's this? Where am I standing?" she asked, deeply perplexed, as if unable to come to her senses. "But how did you, you, *a man like you* . . . how did you decide to do this? . . . What is this?"

"Well, yes. To rob her. Stop, Sonya!" he replied wearily, almost even irritated.

Sonya stood as if thunderstruck, but cried out:

"You were hungry! You did it . . . to help your mother? Is that so?"

"No, Sonya, no," he muttered, turning aside and hanging his head. "I wasn't that hungry. . . . I really did want to help my mother, but . . . that's not completely true. . . . Don't torment me, Sonya!"

She clasped her hands.

"Is this really, really all true? Good Lord, what sort of truth is it? Who can believe this? . . . How then, how could you give away your last kopecks, but you killed to rob her! Oh!" she cried suddenly. "The money you gave Katerina Ivanovna . . . that money. . . . Good Lord, could it have been that money . . . ?"

"No, Sonya," he interrupted hastily. "It wasn't that money, calm down! My mother sent me that money through a certain merchant; I received it when I was ill, the same day I gave it away. . . . Razumikhin saw it . . . he took the money for me. . . . That was my money, my own, really mine."

Sonya listened to him in bewilderment and tried with all her might to understand something.

"As for *that* money . . . I don't even know if there was any money there," he added quietly, as if in deep thought. "I took the purse from her neck, a leather one . . . full, tightly packed. . . . I didn't look in it; I must not have had time. . . . As for the items, some cuff links and chains—I buried those things and the purse the next morning in a courtyard on Voznesensky Prospect under a stone. Everything's still there."

Sonya listened attentively.

"Well, then why . . . how did you say: to rob her, but you didn't take anything?" she asked quickly, grasping at straws.

"I don't know. . . . I still hadn't decided whether I would take the money or not," he said, once more as if in deep thought; then, coming to his senses suddenly, he smiled quickly and briefly. "What nonsense I just blurted out, eh?"

A thought flashed through Sonya's mind: "Is he mad?" But she repressed it at once: no, it's something else. She didn't understand a thing, not one thing!

"You know, Sonya," he said suddenly with inspiration. "Do you know what I can tell you: if I'd merely killed because I was hungry," he continued, emphasizing every word and regarding her enigmatically but sincerely, "then I would be . . . *happy* now! You should know that!

"What do you care, what do you care," he cried with actual desperation after a moment, "what do you care if I even confess now that I did something wrong? What do you care about this stupid triumph over me? Ah, Sonya, is that why I came to see you now?"

Sonya wanted to say something, but she kept silent.

"That's why I wanted you to come with me yesterday, because you're all I have left."

"Go where?" Sonya asked timidly.

"Not to rob or murder, don't be alarmed, not for that." He smiled sarcastically. "We're very different. . . . You know, Sonya, only now, just this moment, did I understand: *where* I was asking you to go yesterday. Yesterday, when I asked you to come with me, I didn't know where myself. I asked you for one reason; I came for one reason: so you wouldn't leave me. You won't leave me, will you, Sonya?"

She squeezed his hand.

"Why, why did I tell her? Why did I reveal it to her?" he cried in despair a moment later, regarding her with endless suffering. "You expect some explanation from me, Sonya; you're sitting there waiting, I see that; but what can I tell you? You won't understand anything; you'll merely be worn out with suffering . . . all because of me! Just look, you're crying and embracing me again—why are you embracing me? Because I myself couldn't endure it and came to unburden myself on someone else: 'you'll suffer, too, and it'll be easier for me!' Can you possibly love such a scoundrel?"

"Can it be that you're not suffering as well?" cried Sonya.

Once again the same feeling, like a wave, flooded into his soul and softened him in a moment.

"Sonya, I have a wicked heart, take note of that: that can explain a great deal. I came to see you precisely because I'm wicked. There are others who wouldn't have come. But I'm a coward . . . and a scoundrel! But . . . let that be! All this isn't the point. . . . I must speak now, but I don't know how to begin . . ."

He paused and became thoughtful.

"Oh, we're not like each other," he cried again, "we don't match. Why, why did I come? I'll never forgive myself for it!"

"No, no, it's good that you came!" Sonya exclaimed. "It's better for me to know! Much better!"

He looked at her with agony.

"What if it really was that?" he said, as if he'd made up his mind. "That's how it really was! Here's the thing: I wanted to become Napoleon, that's why I killed. . . . Well, do you understand now?"

"N-no," Sonya whispered innocently and timidly. "But . . . speak, go on! I'll understand, I'll understand everything *in my own way*!" she begged him.

"You'll understand? Well, all right, we'll see!"

He fell silent and thought for a long time.

"The thing is—I once posed this question to myself: what would happen, for example, if Napoleon were in my place, and if, to begin his career, there was no Toulon, no Egypt, and no crossing Mont Blanc;* instead of all these beautiful and monumental things, there was merely some ridiculous old woman, a civil servant's widow, who, moreover, must be killed so he could steal money from her trunk (for his career, do you understand?); well, would he dare to do it if there was no other way out? Would he have been repulsed by the fact that it was too colossal and . . . and sinful? Well, I'm telling you that I spent a terribly long time suffering over this 'question,' as a result of which I became extremely ashamed when at last I guessed (somehow all of a sudden) that not only wouldn't he be repulsed, but it wouldn't even have entered his head that this wasn't colossal at all . . . and he wouldn't even have understood one bit: what was there to be repulsed by? And if he had no other way open to him, he would have strangled her without letting her utter a sound, without even stopping to think! And so I . . . stopped thinking . . . and strangled her . . . according to the example of my authority. . . . That's precisely how it was! Do you find it amusing? Yes, Sonya, the most amusing thing of all may be that this was exactly how it was . . ."

Sonya didn't find it amusing in the least.

"It would be better if you told me directly . . . without examples," she said even more timidly and barely audibly.

He turned toward her, looked at her glumly, and took her hands.

"You're right again, Sonya. This is all nonsense, almost all idle talk! You see: you know that my mother has almost nothing. My sister received an education by chance and is condemned to seek positions as a governess. All their hopes were placed on me alone. I was a student, but was unable to support myself at the university and was forced to leave it for a while. Even if things would've dragged on like that, in ten or twelve years or so (if circumstances proved favorable), I could hope to become some sort of teacher or civil servant, with a salary of a thousand rubles. . . ." (He was speaking as if he had memo-

---

* References to Napoleon's significant military victories and audacious crossing of Mont Blanc, the highest mountain in the Swiss Alps.

rized these words.) "By that time, my mother would have withered away from worry and grief, and I still wouldn't have had the chance to comfort her, and my sister . . . well, something even worse could have happened to her! Who would want to spend his whole life passing things by, turning away from everything, forgetting his mother, and, for example, politely enduring insults to his sister? For what? Merely to bury them and then acquire new responsibilities—a wife and children, and then leave them also without a kopeck or a crust of bread? Well, well, so I decided, once I got the old woman's money, to use it for my early years, so as not to torment my mother, to support myself at the university and for my first steps afterward—and to do all that broadly, radically, to start a whole new career and set out on a new, independent way of life. . . . Well, well, that's all there is to it. . . . Of course, the fact that I killed the old woman—that was a bad thing. . . . Well, that's enough!"

He had dragged himself in some sort of exhaustion to the end of his story and now hung his head.

"Oh, that's not it, not it," Sonya exclaimed in anguish. "How could you. . . . No, that's not right, not right."

"You yourself can see that it's not right! But I told you sincerely, the whole truth!"

"What sort of truth is that? Oh, good Lord!"

"I merely killed a louse, Sonya, a useless, vile, pernicious louse!"

"That louse was a human being!"

"Even I know she wasn't a louse," he replied, looking at her strangely. "But I'm lying, Sonya," he added. "I've been lying for a long time. . . . This isn't right at all; you're telling the truth. There are other reasons, completely different reasons! . . . I haven't talked to anyone for a long time, Sonya. . . . My head aches very badly now."

His eyes burned with a feverish fire. He was almost beginning to rave; an anxious smile wandered across his lips. A terrible weakness showed through his agitated state of mind. Sonya understood that he was tormented. Her head also began spinning. And he was speaking so strangely: as if it were coherent, "but how? How could it be? Oh, Lord!" She wrung her hands in despair.

"No, Sonya, that's not it!" he began again, suddenly raising his head as if struck and aroused again by an unexpected turn of thought. "That's not it! It would be better . . . to suppose (yes! that would really be better!), to suppose that I'm proud, envious, wicked, loathsome, vengeful, well . . . and, perhaps, even disposed to madness. (Let it all come out in one clean sweep! People mentioned madness before, I noticed!) I told you previously that I wasn't able to support myself at the university. But do you know that I might even have been able to do so? My mother would've sent money for the required fees, and I could've earned enough for boots, clothes, and bread—most likely! There were lessons to give; I was offered half a ruble for each. Razumikhin's working! But I turned spiteful and didn't want to do it. *Turned spiteful*, precisely. (That's a good phrase!) Then, like a spider, I took refuge in my corner. You were in my lair, you saw it. . . . Do you know, Sonya, that low ceilings and cramped rooms oppress the soul and the mind! Oh, how I hated that lair! And yet I didn't want to leave it. I stayed there intentionally! I didn't go out for days; I didn't want to work, and didn't even want to eat; I just lay there. If Nastasya came and brought me food—I'd eat; if she didn't bring anything—the day would pass; I didn't ask for anything deliberately, from spite! There was no light at night; I lay there in the darkness because I didn't want to earn money to buy candles. I was supposed to study, but I sold all my books; now there's a thick layer of dust on the table covering my papers and notebooks. I much preferred to lie there thinking. I thought all the time. . . . I had such dreams, strange, diverse dreams; there's no point in trying to tell you about them! But it was only when I started to imagine that. . . . No, that's not right! Once again I'm not telling the truth! You see, at the time I kept asking myself: why am I so stupid, what if other people are stupid and I know for sure that they are? Don't I want to be smarter than they are? Then I found out, Sonya, that if I waited for everyone to become smart, it would take much too long. . . . I discovered this would never happen, that people wouldn't change, there's no one to remake them, and it's not worth the effort! Yes, that's true! That's their law. . . . A law, Sonya! It's true! . . . And now I know, Sonya, that he who's strong of mind and spirit, he is their master! He who dares much is right in their eyes! He who can spit on most things is considered their lawgiver, and he who dares more than anyone, he's the one most in the right! This is how things have always been and this is how they always will be! Only a blind man can't see this!"

Saying all this, even though Raskolnikov was looking at Sonya, he no longer worried about whether she would understand him or not. A fever had seized him completely. He was in a state of gloomy ecstasy. (It really was a long time since he'd had anyone to talk to!) Sonya understood that this gloomy catechism had become his faith and his law.

"That's when I guessed, Sonya," he continued with enthusiasm, "that power is given only to the one who dares to bend down and pick it up. There's only one thing that matters, only one: to be able to dare! It was then I conceived an idea, for the first time in my life, one that nobody had ever thought up before me! Nobody! It suddenly became clear as day: how could it be that up to now not one person had dared or dares, while bypassing all this absurdity, simply to seize it by the tail and heave it to the devil? I . . . I wanted to *dare* and so I killed. . . . I only wanted to dare, Sonya, and that's the whole reason!"

"Oh, stop it, be quiet!" Sonya cried, clasping her hands. "You've strayed from God, and God has struck you and given you over to the devil!"

"By the way, Sonya, when I was lying there in the darkness and imagining all these things, was that the devil who was misleading me? Huh?"

"Stop it! Don't make fun, you blasphemer; you don't understand a thing, not one thing! Oh, Lord! He won't understand anything, not one thing!"

"Be quiet, Sonya, I'm not making fun at all. I myself know that the devil was leading me astray. Be quiet, Sonya, be quiet!" he repeated gloomily and insistently. "I know it all. I've thought this through many times already and whispered it all to myself while I lay there in the darkness. . . . I argued it through with myself many times, to the very last detail: I know it all, everything! Then I became so fed up with all this chatter, so very fed up! I wanted to forget everything and start all over again, Sonya, and to stop chattering! Do you really think that I went like a fool, without thinking? I went like a clever man, and that's just what destroyed me! Do you really think I didn't know, for example, that if I started to ask and examine whether I had the right to take power, that meant of course that I didn't have that right. Or that if I posed the question, is a person a louse, then of course that person is not a louse *for me*, but is a louse for someone to whom that question never occurs and who acts without asking questions. . . . If I agonized for so long about whether Napoleon would've advanced or not, then clearly I felt I was not a Napoleon. . . . I endured all the torment of this chatter, Sonya, and wanted to shake it all off my shoulders: I wanted, Sonya, to kill without casuistry, to kill for myself, for myself alone! I didn't want to lie about it, even to myself! I didn't kill to help my mother—that's nonsense! I didn't kill to acquire the means and power to become a benefactor of humanity. That's nonsense! I simply killed: I killed for myself, for myself alone. Whether I became someone's benefactor or else, like a spider, caught everyone in my web and sucked out all their vital juices—at that time it didn't matter to me! . . . The main thing, Sonya, was that I didn't need the money when I killed; it wasn't the money, so much as it was something else. . . . I know all this now. . . . Understand me: perhaps proceeding along the same path, I might never commit another murder. I had to find out something else; something else was urging me along. I had to find out then, and find out quickly, whether I was a louse like everyone else or a human being? Could I overstep or not? Dare I stoop and take power or not? Am I a quivering creature or do I have the *right* . . ."

"To kill? Have the right to kill?" Sonya clasped her hands.

"Oh, Sonya!" he cried irritably. He was about to protest but remained contemptuously silent. "Don't interrupt me, Sonya! I wanted to prove only one thing to you: that yes, it was the devil who led me astray then, but he later showed me that I didn't have the right to act like that because I'm the same kind of louse as everyone else! He made a fool of me; that's why I've come to you now! Receive your guest! If I weren't a louse, would I have come to see you? Listen: when I went to the old woman then, it was only a test. . . . You should know that!"

"And you killed! You killed!"

"But how did I kill? Is that how people kill? Do people go to kill the way I did then? I'll tell you sometime how I acted. . . . Did I even kill the old woman? I killed myself, not the old woman! Right then and there I did myself in, forever! . . . But it was the devil that killed the old woman, not me. . . . Enough, enough, Sonya, enough! Leave me," he cried suddenly in a feverish agony. "Leave me!"

He rested his elbows on his knees and squeezed his head tight in his palms.

"What suffering!" burst forth from Sonya in a tormented wail.

"Well, tell me what to do now!" he asked, lifting his head suddenly and looking at her, his face hideously distorted by despair.

"What to do?" she cried, jumping up from her place; her eyes, previously full of tears, suddenly began to flash. "Stand up!" (She grabbed him by the shoulder; he got up, looking at her almost in bewilderment.) "Go at once, this very minute, and stand at the crossroads, bow down, and begin by kissing the ground that you've fouled; then bow down to the entire world, all four sides, and say aloud to everyone: 'I killed!' Then God will send you life once more. Will you go? Will you?" she asked him, trembling in her whole body, as if in a convulsion; she had grabbed his hands and was holding them tightly in hers, directing her fiery gaze at him.

He was amazed and even struck by her sudden enthusiasm.

"Are you talking about prison, Sonya? Do you mean that I have to denounce myself?" he asked glumly.

"You must accept suffering and atone that way."

"No! I won't go to them, Sonya."

"But how will you live? What will you live with?" she cried. "Is that possible now? How will you speak with your mother? (Oh, what will happen to them now, what?) What am I saying? You've already forsaken your mother and sister. You've forsaken them, abandoned them. Oh, Lord!" she cried. "But he knows this all himself! How on earth, how can you live without anyone? What will become of you?"

"Don't be a child, Sonya," he said softly. "What am I guilty of before them? Why should I go? What will I say? All this is merely a phantom. . . . They themselves destroy millions of people and consider it a virtue. They're liars and scoundrels, Sonya! . . . I won't go. What would I say: that I killed but didn't dare take the money and hid it under a stone?" he added with a bitter smile. "They themselves will laugh at me; they'll say I'm a fool for not taking it. A coward and a fool! They won't understand a thing, not a thing, Sonya, and they're not worthy of understanding. Why should I go? I won't. Don't be a child, Sonya . . ."

"You'll suffer and die suffering," she repeated, stretching her arms toward him in desperate entreaty.

"Perhaps I'm *still* slandering myself," he remarked glumly, as if in deep thought. "Perhaps I'm *still* a human being, not a louse, and I rushed to condemn myself. . . . I'll *still* fight a while longer."

A haughty grin appeared on his lips.

"What a torment to bear! And for your entire life, your entire life . . . !"

"I'll get used to it . . ." he said grimly and thoughtfully. "Listen," he began a moment later, "enough crying; it's time for action. I came to tell you that they're looking for me now, they're trying to catch me . . ."

"Ah!" screamed Sonya, terrified.

"Why did you scream? You yourself said you wanted me to go to prison, but now you're frightened? Here's the thing: I won't give myself up. I'll still struggle with them, and they won't do a thing. They have no real evidence. Yesterday I was in great danger and thought all was lost; today things have improved. All their evidence cuts two ways—that is, I can turn their accusations to my own advantage, do you understand? And I'll do so because now I've learned how. . . . But they'll certainly send me to prison. If it hadn't been for one accidental occurrence, then perhaps they'd have sent me to prison today; perhaps they may *still* send me to prison today. . . . But that doesn't mean anything, Sonya: I'll be there a little while and then they'll release me . . . because they have no real proof and they won't have, I give you my word. And it's impossible to drag a man off with what they have. Well, enough. . . . I'm saying this so you know. . . . I'll try to reassure my mother and sister so they won't be frightened. . . . Now my sister seems to be provided for . . . so is my mother, too. . . . Well, that's everything. But be careful. Will you come to see me in prison when I have to spend time there?"

"Oh, I will! I will!"

They sat side by side, miserable and dazed, as if they had been cast upon a deserted shore after a storm at sea. He looked at Sonya and felt how much love was directed at him; strange to say, he suddenly felt oppressed and pained at being so loved. Yes, it was a strange and horrible sensation! Coming to see Sonya, he felt that she was his only hope and his only way out; he thought he could divest at least a part of his torments. Now, all of a sudden, when her entire heart was turned toward him, he felt and was aware that he had become immeasurably unhappier than before.

"Sonya," he said, "it'd be better not to come see me when I'm in prison."

Sonya made no reply; she wept. Several minutes passed.

"Do you have a cross?" she asked suddenly and unexpectedly, as if she had just remembered.

At first he didn't understand the question.

"No, probably not. Here, take this one, it's cypress wood. I have another one, a copper one; it was Lizaveta's. She and I exchanged crosses; she gave me hers, and I gave her my little icon. Now I'll wear Lizaveta's cross, and this one is for you. Take it . . . it's mine! It's mine!" she urged him. "We'll go suffer together, we'll bear our crosses together!"

"Give it to me!" said Raskolnikov. He didn't want to distress her. But at once he withdrew the hand he had extended to take the cross.

"Not now, Sonya. It'd be better later," he added, to appease her.

"Yes, yes, that would be better, much better," she responded with feeling. "When you accept your suffering, then you'll wear it. Come to see me and I'll put it on you; we'll pray and go together."

At that moment, someone knocked on the door three times.

"Sofiya Semyonovna, may I come in?" a very familiar voice asked politely.

Sonya rushed to the door in a fright. Lebezyatnikov's blond head glanced into the room.

V

Lebezyatnikov looked uneasy.

"I've come to see you, Sofiya Semyonovna. Excuse me. . . . I thought I might find you here," he said, turning suddenly to Raskolnikov. "That is, I didn't think anything . . . like that . . . but I did think. . . . Katerina Ivanovna's lost her mind," he blurted out suddenly to Sonya, turning away from Raskolnikov.

Sonya screamed.

"That is, it seems to be the case. However. . . . We don't know what to do, that's what! She came back—it seems she was driven away from somewhere, and perhaps she was even beaten . . . it seems that way, at least. . . . She ran to Semyon Zakharych's superior, but he wasn't home; he was having dinner with another general. . . . Just imagine, she rushed to where they were eating . . . to the other general, and imagine—she insisted on calling Semyon Zakharych's superior, yes, it seems, calling him away from the table. You can imagine what occurred there. Of course, they chased her away; but she herself says she abused him and threw something at him. One can even imagine the scene. . . . I don't understand why they didn't arrest her! Now she's telling this to everyone, including Amaliya Ivanovna, but it's hard to understand her; she's shouting and thrashing about. . . . Oh, yes: she's talking and shouting that since everyone's deserted her now, she'll take the children and go out onto the street with a barrel organ; the children will sing and dance, and she will, too; they'll collect money and go to the general's window to play every day. . . . 'Let him,' she says, 'let him see how the well-born children of their father who was a civil servant now go begging in the streets!' She's beating the children and they're crying. She's teaching Lyonya to sing 'The Little Hut,' and teaching her little boy to dance, Polina Mikhailovna, too, and she's tearing their clothes; she's making them little caps like the ones actors wear; she herself wants to carry a washbasin and beat time instead of making music. . . . She won't listen to anything. . . . Just imagine what it's like! It's simply impossible!"

Lebezyatnikov would have gone on, but Sonya, who had been listening to him, hardly daring to breathe, suddenly grabbed her cloak and hat and ran out of the room, dressing as she went. Raskolnikov ran out after her, and Lebezyatnikov followed.

"She's surely gone mad!" he kept telling Raskolnikov as they emerged onto the street. "I merely didn't want to frighten Sofiya Semyonovna, so I said 'it seems,' but there's no doubt. They say that in consumption there are little tubercles that invade the brain; it's a pity that I don't know anything about medicine. I tried, however, to dissuade her, but she won't listen to a thing."

"Did you talk to her about tubercles?"

"That is, not exactly about tubercles. Besides she wouldn't have understood anything. What I mean is this: if you convince someone logically that in essence they have nothing to cry about, they'll stop crying. That's clear. Is it your belief that they won't stop?"

"It would be too easy to live like that," replied Raskolnikov.

"As you please, just as you please; of course, Katerina Ivanovna would find it rather difficult to understand; but are you aware that in Paris they've already conducted serious experiments regarding the possibility of treating the insane, using only logical persuasion? One professor there, who died not long ago, a very serious scholar, formulated that it was possible to cure people. His main idea is that the insane have no particular derangement of their organism, but that insanity is, so to speak, a logical error, an error in judgment, an incorrect view of things. He gradually contradicted his patient and, just imagine, they say he achieved results! But since he was also using cold showers while doing this, the results of this treatment can naturally be subject to question. . . . At least, that's the way it seems . . ."

Raskolnikov had long since stopped listening. Having drawn even with his building, he nodded to Lebezyatnikov and turned into the courtyard. Lebezyatnikov came to, looked around, and ran on ahead.

Raskolnikov entered his little room and stood in the middle of it. "Why had he come back here?" He looked around at the worn yellowish wallpaper, at the dust, his couch. . . . Some sort of sharp, continuous knocking sound could be heard in the courtyard; something some-where was being hammered, some sort of nail. . . . He went over to the window, stood on his tiptoes, and for a long time surveyed the court-yard with extraordinary attention. But the courtyard was deserted, and no one could be seen knocking. On the left, in the building's wing, there were a few open windows; pots of straggly geraniums stood on the windowsills. Laundry was hanging outside the windows. . . . He knew all this by heart. He turned away and sat down on the couch.

Never, never before had he felt himself so terribly alone.

Yes, once again he felt that he might really come to hate Sonya, precisely now, when he had made her even unhappier. Why had he gone to seek her tears? Why was it so necessary for him to ruin her life? "Oh, how vile!"

"I'll stay alone!" he said suddenly and decisively; and she won't visit me in prison!"

About five minutes later, he raised his head and smiled strangely. A strange thought occurred to him suddenly: "Perhaps it would really be better in prison."

He didn't remember how long he sat there, his head swarming with vague ideas. All of a sudden the door opened and Avdotya Romanovna walked in. At first she stopped and regarded him from the threshold, as he had looked at Sonya before; then she came in and sat opposite him on a chair, the same place she had been sitting yesterday. He looked at her in silence and without any particular thoughts.

"Don't be angry, brother; I've come for only a few minutes," Dunya said. Her expression was thoughtful, but not stern. Her gaze was clear and calm. He saw that this woman had also come to him in love.

"Brother, now I know everything, *everything*. Dmitry Prokofich told me and explained everything. You're being pursued and tormented on a stupid, foul suspicion. . . . Dmitry Prokofich told me that there's no danger and that you shouldn't be so dismayed by it. I don't agree with him; I *understand completely* how outraged you are at everything and how this indignation might leave its traces on you forever. That's what I'm afraid of. I don't judge you, nor dare I, for having deserted us; forgive me for having reproached you previously. I myself feel that if I had such deep unhappiness, I too would want to get away from everyone. I won't say a word to our mother *about this*, but I'll talk about you constantly and tell her you'll come to see her very soon. Don't worry about her; *I'll* calm her down; but don't torment her—come just once; remember, she's your mother! And now I've come merely to say"—Dunya began to stand up—"that if, by any chance, you need me or will need me for anything . . . my whole life, or anything . . . just call me and I'll come. Good-bye!"

She turned abruptly and headed for the door.

"Dunya!" Raskolnikov stopped her, stood up, and went to her. "This Razumikhin, Dmitry Prokofich, is a very fine man."

Dunya blushed slightly.

"Well!" she asked, after waiting a minute.

"He's a practical man, hardworking, honest, and capable of loving deeply. . . . Good-bye, Dunya."

Dunya blushed fully, then suddenly became anxious:

"What's this, brother, are we parting forever that you're . . . giving me such instructions?"

"It doesn't matter. Good-bye."

He turned and moved away from her, over to the window. She stood there, looking at him uneasily, and then left in alarm.

No, he was not being cold to her. There was one moment (the very last one) when he'd desperately wanted to embrace her tightly and *say good-bye* to her, even to *tell* her, but he couldn't resolve even to take hold of her hand:

"Afterward she might shudder when she recalls that I embraced her now, and she'd say I stole her kiss."

"Will *this one* endure it or not?" he wondered to himself after a few minutes. "No, she won't endure it; such people are unable to endure *something like this*! People like her never endure it . . ."

Then he thought about Sonya.

Fresh air wafted in through the window. The light was no longer so bright in the courtyard. He suddenly took his cap and left.

Of course, he was unable and didn't even want to worry about his unhealthy condition. But all of this constant anxiety and mental anguish couldn't pass without consequences. If he weren't still lying there in a real fever, then perhaps it was precisely because this constant inner anxiety was keeping him on his feet for the time being and aware, at least artificially.

He wandered without any goal. The sun was setting. Some sort of peculiar sadness had begun to manifest itself in him lately. There was nothing particularly caustic or burning about it; but from it there arose something constant, eternal; he had a premonition of endless years of this cold, deadening sadness, a premonition of some eternity in "one *arshin* of space."* This sensation usually began to torment him more during the evening hours.

"With such a very stupid, purely physical sickness that depends on something like a sunset, just try not to do something stupid! Not only to Sonya, but next you'll go to Dunya!" he muttered hatefully.

Someone called him. He turned around; Lebezyatnikov came running toward him.

"Imagine, I went to your room; I've been looking for you. Imagine, she made good on her promise and took the children! Sofiya Semyonovna and I have finally found them. She's banging a frying pan and making the children sing and dance. The children are crying. They stop at crossroads and in front of shops. Stupid people are running after them. Let's go."

"And Sonya?" asked Raskolnikov anxiously, hastening after Lebezyatnikov.

"She's simply in a frenzy—that is, not Sofiya Semyonovna, but Katerina Ivanovna is in a frenzy; but so is Sofiya Semyonovna. How-

---

* A Russian measure equivalent to twenty-eight inches.

ever, Katerina Ivanovna's in a complete frenzy. I tell you, she's completely insane. They'll be carted off to the police. You can imagine how that'll affect her. . . . They're at the canal now, by the Voznesensky Bridge, not far from where Sofiya Semyonovna lives. It's close."

At the canal, not far from the bridge, and not two houses away from where Sonya lived, a crowd of people had gathered. Mostly they were street urchins, boys and girls. Katerina Ivanovna's hoarse, strained voice could be heard as far away as the bridge. It really was a strange spectacle, capable of arousing the interest of a street crowd. Katerina Ivanovna was in her old dress, her green shawl, and her tattered straw hat with its brim bent awkwardly to one side; she really was in a genuine frenzy. She was weary and gasping for breath. Her exhausted and consumptive face looked more martyr-like than ever before (besides which, outside in the sunlight, a consumptive always seems sicker and more unattractive than at home); but her agitated state had not abated, and with each passing minute she became more irritated. She threw herself on her children, shouted at them, urged them on, instructed them in front of everyone how to dance and what to sing, began explaining to them why this was necessary, despaired at their lack of understanding, and beat them. . . . Then, without even finishing, she threw herself at the public; if she noticed someone who was decently dressed, she stopped to look and immediately began explaining to him, in her words, that this is what children "from a respectable, one might even say aristocratic, home" were reduced to. If she heard any laughter from the crowd or some provocative remark, she would immediately hurl herself at the impertinent fellow and begin arguing with him. As a matter of fact, some people really were laughing, while others were shaking their heads; in general, everyone was curious to see this madwoman and her terrified children. The frying pan Lebezyatnikov had mentioned was nowhere to be seen; but instead of that, Katerina Ivanovna began to clap out the time with her hands as she forced Polya to sing and Lyonya and Kolya to dance; then she herself even began to join in the singing; but, as a result of her tormenting cough, she broke off each time on the second note and collapsed into despair again, cursed her own cough, and even wept. Worst of all, she was infuriated by Kolya and Lyonya's crying and fear. She really had made an effort to dress the children like street singers. The little boy wore a turban made of some red-and-white material, so that he resembled a Turk. Lyonya didn't have a costume; she wore only the late Semyon Zakharych's red knitted worsted cap (or, rather, nightcap), into which a broken piece of white ostrich feather had been inserted: it had belonged to Katerina Ivanovna's grandmother and had been kept in a trunk up to now as a family treasure. Polechka was wearing her usual dress. She regarded her mother timidly; flustered, she didn't leave her mother's side; she hid her own tears, guessed at her mother's madness, and glanced around uneasily. The street and the crowd frightened her terribly. Sonya followed Katerina Ivanovna closely, weeping and constantly imploring her to return home. But Katerina Ivanovna was implacable.

"Stop it, Sonya, stop it!" she cried rapidly, hurrying, gasping for breath, and coughing. "You don't know what you're asking; you're just like a child! I've already told you that I won't go back to that drunken German woman. Let everyone see, all Petersburg, how the children of a respectable father beg for charity, a father who served the truth and in good faith all his life, and who, one might say, died in the service." (Katerina Ivanovna had already managed to create this fantasy, and she believed in it blindly.) "Let that worthless general see. You're being foolish, too, Sonya: what do we have to eat now, tell me! We've tormented you enough; I don't want to do so anymore! Ah, Rodion Romanych, it's you!" she cried, catching sight of Raskolnikov and rushing up to him. "Please explain to this little fool that there's nothing better we can do! Even organ grinders can scrape money together; now everyone will pay special attention to us and will realize that we're a poor, respectable family of orphans, reduced to poverty. That worthless general will lose his job, you'll see! We'll stand by his window every day, and when the tsar drives by, I'll go down on my knees. I'll push these little ones forward and point to them: 'Protect them, Father!' He's the father of orphans; he's merciful; he'll defend them, you'll see, while that worthless general. . . . Lyonya! *Tenez-vous droite!** You, Kolya, start dancing again. Why are you whining? Whining again!

---

* "Stand up straight!" (French).

Well, what are you afraid of, you little fool! Good Lord! What will I do with them, Rodion Romanych! If you only knew how stupid they are! What can one do with children like this?"

Almost crying herself (which didn't hinder her incessant and uninterrupted rapid speech), Katerina Ivanovna pointed at her sniveling children. Raskolnikov tried to persuade her to go home, and even said, hoping to appeal to her pride, that it was indecent for her to be out on the street like an organ grinder, because she was planning to become the director of a boarding school for respectable young ladies . . .

"Boarding school, ha-ha-ha! The grass is always greener!" cried Katerina Ivanovna, overcome by a coughing fit immediately after her laughter. "No, Rodion Romanych, that dream is gone! Everyone's abandoned us! As for that wretched general. . . . You know, Rodion Romanych, I threw an inkwell at him. There in the servants' quarters; it was on the table, next to the book where you sign in; so I signed in, threw the inkwell, and ran off. Oh, the vile scoundrels. But I don't care; now I'll feed them myself; I won't bow down to anyone! We've tormented her enough!" She indicated Sonya. "Polechka, how much did we collect? Show me. What? Only two kopecks? Oh, what dreadful people! They don't give us anything, merely chase after us with their tongues hanging out! Why is this blockhead laughing?" She pointed at someone in the crowd. "It's all because this wretched Kolya's so stupid, he's such a bother! What's the matter, Polechka? Speak French with me, *parlez-moi français.** I taught you after all, and you know some phrases! How else can they tell you're from a respectable family, you're well-brought-up children, and not at all like all those organ grinders; we're not presenting some Punch and Judy show on the streets; we'll sing a few respectable romances. . . . Ah, yes! What shall we sing? You keep interrupting me, and we . . . you see, we stopped here, Rodion Romanych, to choose what to sing—so Kolya could dance . . . because all this, as you can imagine, is without any preparation; we must agree so we can rehearse it all thoroughly, and then we'll head for Nevsky Prospect, where there'll be far more people of high society and they'll notice us at once; Lyonya knows

---

* "Speak French to me" (French).

'The Little Hut.' That's the only song she knows, and everyone sings it! We have to sing something much more respectable. . . . Well, what have you come up with Polya? You could help your mother! I have no memory, none at all, or I'd remember! Let's not sing 'A Hussar Leaned on His Sword,'* for heaven's sake. Ah, let's sing 'Cinq sous' in French!†
I taught it to you, I did. And the main thing, it's in French, so people will see that you're respectable children, and that'll be much more poignant. . . . We could even sing 'Marlborough s'en va-t-en guerre,'‡ since it's a genuine children's song and is sung in all aristocratic homes when they're putting the children to sleep:

> *Marlborough s'en va-t-en guerre,*
> *Ne sait quand reviendra . . ."*§

She began singing. . . . "But no, it's better to sing 'Cinq sous'! Well, Kolya, hands at your sides, quickly, and you, Lyonya, turn around in the opposite direction; Polechka and I will sing and clap our hands in time!

> *Cinq sous, cinq sous,*
> *Pour monter notre ménage . . ."*¶

She erupted in a spell of coughing. "Fix your dress, Polechka, the shoulders have slipped down," she remarked through her cough as she caught her breath. "Now you really have to be prim and proper, so that everyone will see that you're respectable children. I said before that the bodice should be made longer and sewn in two pieces. But at the time, Sonya, you chimed in with your advice: 'Shorter, much shorter,' and now it's made the child look awful. . . . Well, you're all

---

* A song to words by the poet Konstantin Batyushkov (1787–1855).

† "Five pennies" (French). A beggar's song from a French melodrama.

‡ A popular French song about the Duke of Marlborough.

§ "Marlborough is leaving for the war, / He doesn't know when he'll return" (French).

¶ "Five pennies, five pennies, / To start our household" (French).

crying again! What's the matter, you silly children? Well, Kolya, begin quickly, quickly, quickly. Oh, what an unbearable child he is . . .

> Cinq sous, cinq sous . . .

Another policeman! Well, what do you want?"

As a matter of fact, a policeman was making his way through the crowd. But at the same time, a gentleman in a civil servant's uniform and an overcoat, a respectable man of about fifty with a medal around his neck (this was especially pleasant for Katerina Ivanovna and had an effect on the policeman), drew near and silently presented Katerina Ivanovna with a green three-ruble note. His face expressed sincere compassion. Katerina Ivanovna received it and bowed to him politely, even ceremoniously.

"I thank you, kind sir," she began from on high. "The reasons that have prompted us . . . here, take the money, Polechka. You see, there are respectable and generous people prepared to help a poor noble-woman in distress. You see, kind sir, respectable orphans, one could even say with aristocratic connections. . . . And that wretched general just sat there and ate his grouse . . . stamping his feet because I disturbed him. . . . 'Your Excellency,' I said, 'protect these orphans, because you knew,' I said, 'the late Semyon Zakharych so well, and since the meanest of scoundrels slandered his own daughter the day he died . . .' There's that policeman again! Defend us!" she cried to the civil servant. "Why's this policeman coming after me? We've already run away from one on Meshchanskaya Street. . . . Well, what do you want, you fool?"

"This is not allowed on the streets, ma'am. Please don't create a disturbance."

"You're the one making a disturbance! It's just as if I were playing a barrel organ. What business is it of yours?"

"You have to have permission to play a barrel organ; but you're doing this on your own and gathering a crowd of people. Where do you live, may I ask?"

"What? Permission?" cried Katerina Ivanovna. "I buried my husband today. What sort of permission do I need?"

"Madam, madam, calm yourself," began the civil servant. "Let's go. I'll escort you . . . It's indecent here with this crowd. . . . You're not well . . ."

"Kind sir, kind sir, you don't know a thing!" shouted Katerina Ivanovna. "We're heading for Nevsky Prospect. Sonya, Sonya! Where is she? Also weeping! What's wrong with all of you? Kolya, Lyonya, where are you going?" she shrieked suddenly in a fright. "Oh, you stupid children! Kolya, Lyonya, where are they going?"

It happened that Kolya and Lyonya, absolutely terrified by the crowd on the street and by the antics of their deranged mother, having at last noticed the policeman who wanted to arrest them and take them away, suddenly, as if having agreed in advance, grabbed each other's hand and set off running. Wailing and weeping, poor Katerina Ivanovna took off after them. It was a sorry and pitiful sight to see her running, crying, and gasping for breath. Sonya and Polechka ran after her.

"Bring them back, Sonya, bring them back! Oh, those stupid, ungrateful children! Polya! Catch them. . . . It was for you that I . . ."

Running at full speed, she stumbled and fell.

"She's hurt herself badly and is bleeding! Good Lord!" cried Sonya, bending over her.

Everyone came running, crowding all around. Raskolnikov and Lebezyatnikov rushed up first; the civil servant followed, and then the policeman, grumbling, "Oh, dear!" He waved his arm dismissively, foreseeing that this would turn out to be a bothersome affair.

"Get away! Get away!" he kept saying, trying to break up the assembled crowd.

"She's dying!" someone shouted.

"She's lost her mind!" said another.

"Lord preserve us!" said one woman, crossing herself. "Have they caught the little boy and girl? There they are, they're bringing them; the older one caught them. . . . Those crazy children!"

But when they had taken a good look at Katerina Ivanovna, they saw that she hadn't hurt herself on a rock, as Sonya had thought, but that the blood coloring the roadway was coming up from her chest and gushing out her throat.

"I know what this is, I've seen it before," mumbled the civil servant to Raskolnikov and Lebezyatnikov. "It's consumption, sir; the blood gushes and chokes the patient. I was a witness not long ago when this happened to one of my relatives; she lost a glass and a half of blood . . . all of a sudden, sir. . . . What can we do? She'll die soon."

"This way, this way, to my place!" Sonya implored. "I live right here! Over here, in this house, the second one. . . . Hurry, hurry, to my place!" She rushed from one person to the next. "Send for a doctor. . . . Oh, good Lord!"

This was organized with the civil servant's efforts; even the policeman helped carry Katerina Ivanovna. They brought her to Sonya's room almost dead and laid her on the bed. She kept losing blood but was beginning to regain consciousness. Besides Sonya, Raskolnikov and Lebezyatnikov, the civil servant, and the policeman who had dispersed the crowd, others entered the room; several people had accompanied them to the doorway. Polechka led the way, holding Kolya and Lyonya by the hand, both of whom were trembling and crying. People also gathered from the Kapernaumovs' apartment, including Kapernaumov himself, lame and blind in one eye, a strange-looking man with bristling hair and whiskers standing up straight; his wife, who always had a frightened look; and several of his children, their expressions fixed in constant astonishment and their mouths wide open. Suddenly Svidrigaylov appeared amidst this large crowd. Raskolnikov regarded him with surprise, not understanding where he had come from, and not recalling him in the crowd on the street.

They spoke about a doctor and a priest. Although the civil servant whispered to Raskolnikov that perhaps a doctor was unnecessary now, they sent for one all the same. Kapernaumov went to fetch one himself.

Meanwhile, Katerina Ivanovna had caught her breath and the bleeding had stopped for the time being. She cast her sickly but intense and penetrating glance at poor, trembling Sonya, who was wiping the perspiration from her forehead with her scarf; at last she asked to be raised up. They sat her up in bed, supporting her on both sides.

"Where are the children?" she asked in a weak voice. "Did you find them, Polya? Oh, you silly children! Why did you run away? Oh!"

Blood was still caked on her parched lips. She looked around the room, examining everything:

"So this is how you live, Sonya! I haven't been here before . . . now it's just happened . . ."

She looked at her with suffering:

"We've sucked you dry, Sonya. . . . Polya, Lyonya, Kolya, come here. . . . Well, here they are, Sonya, all of them. Take them . . . from my hands into yours. . . . I've had enough! The party's over!" *Cough!* "Lay me back down. Let me die in peace . . ."

They lowered her onto the pillow again.

"What? A priest? It's not necessary. . . . Where would we get the money to pay him? I have no sins! Even without that God should forgive me. . . . He knows how I've suffered! And if He doesn't forgive me, so be it!"

A restless delirium was taking hold of her more and more. At times she shuddered, cast her eyes around, recognized everyone for a moment; but then her consciousness was replaced by the delirium once again. She was breathing hoarsely and with difficulty, as if something were caught in her throat.

"I said to him, 'Your Excellency!'" she cried, resting after every word. "That Amaliya Lyudvigovna . . . ah! Lyonya, Kolya! Hands at your sides, quickly, quickly, *glissez-glissez, pas de Basque!** Stamp your feet. . . . Be graceful.

Du hast Diamanten und Perlen . . .†

How does it go? That's what we should sing . . .

Du hast die schönsten Augen,
Mädchen, was willst du mehr?‡

---

* "Slide, slide, the Basque step!" (French).

† "You have diamonds and pearls" (German). From a song by Franz Schubert (1797–1828) set to words by Heinrich Heine (1797–1856).

‡ "You have the most beautiful eyes, / Girl, what more do you want?" (German).

Well, yes, that's it! *Was willst du mehr*—the things he thinks of, the blockhead! Ah, yes, here's some more:

> *In the midday heat, in a valley of Dagestan . . .**

Ah, how I've loved it. . . . I used to adore that romance. Polechka! You know that your father . . . used to sing that song when he was courting me. . . . Oh, those days! That's what we ought to sing now! Well, how does it go? I've even forgotten. . . . Remind me, how does it go?" She was extremely agitated and tried to lift herself up. At last she began in a terrible, hoarse, broken voice, crying out and gasping on every word, with a look of growing terror:

> *In the noonday heat! . . . in a valley! . . . of Dagestan!*
> *With a bullet in my breast!*

"Your Excellency!" she suddenly wailed in a harrowing cry, overflowing with tears, "protect these orphans! Knowing the late Semyon Zakharych's hospitality! One could even say aristocratic!" *Cough!* She shuddered suddenly; she came to and looked around at everyone with horror, and recognized Sonya immediately. "Sonya, Sonya!" she said gently and affectionately, as if surprised to see her there. "Sonya, my dear, are you here, too?"

They lifted her up again.

"Enough! It's time! Farewell, you poor soul! They've ridden this poor nag to death! I'm all done in!" she cried with despair and hatred; her head fell back onto the pillow.

She lost consciousness again, but this oblivion lasted only a short while. Her pale yellow, emaciated face dropped back, her mouth opened, and her legs stretched out convulsively. She sighed very deeply and died.

Sonya fell upon her body, embraced her, and remained there motionless, her head pressed against the deceased's withered chest.

---

* A song by Mily Balakirev (1837–1910) set to the words of a poem by Mikhail Lermontov (1814–1841).

Polechka knelt at her mother's feet and kissed them, sobbing. Kolya and Lyonya, still not understanding what had happened, but sensing something very terrible, took hold of one another by the shoulders and, staring at each other, all of a sudden, together, at the same instant, opened their mouths and began howling. They were both still wearing their costumes: he in his turban and she in her nightcap with the ostrich feather.

How could that "certificate of merit" have turned up suddenly on the bed next to Katerina Ivanovna? It was lying there, beside the pillow; Raskolnikov saw it.

He walked over to the window. Lebezyatnikov rushed over to him.

"She's dead!" said Lebezyatnikov.

"Rodion Romanych, I have a few words I wish to say to you," said Svidrigaylov, approaching. Lebezyatnikov immediately yielded and withdrew politely. Svidrigaylov led the astonished Raskolnikov farther away, into a corner.

"I will take on myself all this bother, that is, the arrangements for the funeral and so forth. You know that it takes money, and I've told you that I have more than enough. I shall place these two little ones and Polechka in a good orphanage and will settle a stipend of fifteen hundred rubles on each of them for when they come of age. That way Sofiya Semyonovna can rest easy. I will also rescue her from the muck and mire, because she's a fine girl, isn't she? Well, sir, you can tell Avdotya Romanovna that this is how I used her ten thousand rubles."

"What prompts this fit of generosity?" asked Raskolnikov.

"Hey! You're a suspicious fellow!" Svidrigaylov said with a laugh. "I told you that I had more money than I need. Well, won't you allow me to act simply out of humanity? After all, she wasn't a 'louse' "—he pointed his finger to where the dead woman was lying—"like some old woman moneylender. You'll agree, won't you: 'Should Luzhin go on living and doing nasty things, or should she die?' And if I don't help, then 'Polechka, for example, will go down the same road . . .' "

He said this with a look of some twinkling, cheerful craftiness, without taking his eyes off Raskolnikov. Raskolnikov turned pale and grew cold, hearing his own words to Sonya. He took a quick step back and looked wildly at Svidrigaylov.

"How . . . how do you know?" he whispered, barely drawing a breath.

"Why, I'm living here, on the other side of the wall, at Madame Resslikh's. Kapernaumov lives here, and Madame Resslikh's over there; she's an old and devoted friend of mine. I'm a neighbor, sir."

"You?"

"Me," continued Svidrigaylov, shaking with laughter. "I can assure you on my honor, my dearest Rodion Romanych, that you've really aroused my curiosity. Why, I said that we'd become close; I predicted it—well, and now we have. And you'll see what an obliging fellow I am. You'll see that you can get along with me . . ."

PART
VI

I

A strange time began for Raskolnikov: it was as if a fog had suddenly descended in front of him and surrounded him in hopeless and painful isolation. Recalling this period later, after a very long time, he surmised that his awareness had seemed to grow dim, and that this state continued, with certain interruptions, right up to the definitive catastrophe. He was absolutely convinced that at that time he had been wrong about many things, for example, the time and sequence of several events. At least remembering subsequently and trying to explain these recollections, he learned a great deal about himself, already being guided by information received from other people. For example, he confused one event with another; he would consider another a consequence of something that had happened only in his imagination. At times he was overcome with painfully tormenting anxiety, which even grew into panic. But he also recalled that there were moments, hours, and even, perhaps, days full of apathy that overwhelmed him, as if in opposition to his previous fear—apathy resembling the painfully indifferent condition of certain people on the edge of death. In general, in these last days he himself seemed to be trying to escape a clear and complete understanding of his predicament: he found especially oppressive certain urgent facts demanding immediate clarification; he would have been so glad to be free of them and escape certain worries, although to do so would have threatened him with total and inevitable ruin.

Svidrigaylov alarmed him particularly; one could even say that he seemed to be obsessed with him. From the moment of his extremely threatening and clearly articulated words in Sonya's apartment at the time of Katerina Ivanovna's death, it seemed that the normal course of Raskolnikov's thoughts had been interrupted. Although this new fact upset him a great deal, he seemed in no rush to clarify the matter. At times, finding himself somewhere in a remote and isolated part of town, in some pitiful tavern, alone, at a table, deep in thought, barely recalling how he'd gotten there, all of a sudden he would remember Svidrigaylov; he'd suddenly become all too clearly and alarmingly aware that he had to come to terms with this man and, as soon as possible, had to resolve this matter with him once and for all. Once, walking somewhere outside the city, he even imagined that Svidrigaylov was waiting for him there and that they had made an appointment to meet. Another time he awoke before dawn lying somewhere on the ground, in the midst of bushes, and he could hardly recall how he had wound up there. However, in those two or three days after Katerina Ivanovna's death, he did meet Svidrigaylov a few times, almost always at Sonya's apartment, where he would drop by without any reason, but always stay for only a minute. They always exchanged only a few words but not once did they mention the main point, as if they had an agreement between them to keep silent about it for the time being. Katerina Ivanovna's body was still lying there in its coffin. Svidrigaylov was busy making all the funeral arrangements. Sonya was also very preoccupied. At their last meeting, Svidrigaylov explained to Raskolnikov that he had made provisions for Katerina Ivanovna's children and had been successful; that he had, thanks to some connections, located certain people with whose help he had been able to place all three orphans, immediately, in an extremely respectable institution; that the money he had set aside for them helped a great deal, since it was much easier to place orphans who possessed some capital than impoverished children. He also said something about Sonya, promised to stop by to see Raskolnikov shortly, and reminded him that he "wished to confer with him, that he very much wanted to talk to him, that he had certain matters . . ." This conversation took place in the hallway, near the staircase. Svidrigaylov stared into Raskolnikov's eyes and all of a sudden, after a short pause, lowered his voice and asked:

"What's the matter with you, Rodion Romanych? You seem not to be yourself. Really! You look and listen, but it's as if you don't understand. You should pull yourself together. Let's have a talk; it's a pity that I have so many affairs to attend to, other people's and my own. . . . Hey, Rodion Romanych," he added suddenly, "everyone needs air, air, air, sir. . . . First and foremost."

He suddenly stepped aside to allow a priest and a deacon who were climbing the stairs to pass. They were coming to perform a funeral service. Svidrigaylov had arranged for a requiem to be sung punctually twice a day. Svidrigaylov went on his own way. Raskolnikov stood there, thought for a while, and followed the priest into Sonya's apartment.

He stood in the doorway. The service began, quietly, decorously, somberly. From his childhood he had always felt something heart-rending and mystically terrible in the awareness of death and in the feeling of its presence; and it had been a long time since he had heard a requiem. And there was something else involved, something too awful and upsetting. He looked at the children: they were all on their knees at the coffin; Polechka was crying. Behind them, weeping quietly, almost timidly, Sonya was praying. "These last few days she hasn't looked at me even once or said a single word to me," Raskolnikov thought suddenly. The bright sun illuminated the room; smoke from the censer rose in clouds; the priest read, "Oh, Lord, grant eternal rest." Raskolnikov stood there for the whole service. As he blessed those present and took his leave, the priest looked around somewhat strangely. After the service, Raskolnikov went up to Sonya. She suddenly took both his hands and rested her head on his shoulder. This brief gesture struck Raskolnikov with confusion; it was even strange. What? Not the slightest revulsion, not the slightest loathing for him, not the slightest shudder in her hand! This was some sort of infinite self-humiliation. At least, that was the way he understood it. Sonya didn't say a thing. Raskolnikov shook her hand and left. He felt terribly distressed. If it had been possible for him to go somewhere at that moment and remain completely alone, even for the rest of his life, he would have considered himself fortunate. But the thing was that as of late, even though he was almost always alone, he could in no way feel that he was alone. It sometimes happened that he would be outside the city and emerge onto the main road, and once had even made his way into some grove; but the more isolated the place, the more strongly was he aware of someone's close and alarming presence, not exactly frightening, but somehow very irritating, so that he would return to town as soon as possible, mingle with the crowd, enter a tavern or a bar, go to the flea market or the Haymarket. There he seemed to feel better and even more alone. In one eating place, toward evening, they were singing songs: he sat there for a whole hour listening and later recalled that he even felt very good. But toward the end, he suddenly felt very distressed again; it was as if pangs of conscience suddenly began to torment him: "Here I sit, listening to songs, as if this is what I should be doing!" he thought to himself. However, he guessed right away that this wasn't the only thing that was upsetting him; there was something demanding immediate resolution, but he was unable to figure out what it was or to put it into words. Everything was tangled up in one ball. "No, some sort of struggle would be better than this! Better to see Porfiry again . . . or Svidrigaylov. . . . If there were some sort of challenge again, someone's attack. . . . Yes, yes!" he thought. He left the eating place and set off almost at a run. The thought of Dunya and his mother for some reason suddenly plunged him into some sort of panic. Late that night, just before morning, he awoke in the bushes on Krestovsky Island, shivering and in a fever; he headed for home and got there early in the morning. After a few hours of sleep the fever passed, but it was late when he woke up: it was two o'clock in the afternoon.

He remembered that Katerina Ivanovna's funeral had been scheduled for that day and he felt glad that he was not there for it. Nastasya brought him something to eat; he ate and drank with a hearty appetite, almost greedily. His head was clearer, and he himself felt calmer than in the last three days. He was even surprised in passing at his previous bouts of panic. The door opened, and in walked Razumikhin.

"Ah! He's eating; therefore he's not ill!" said Razumikhin. He took a chair and sat down opposite Raskolnikov. He was agitated and didn't try to hide it. He spoke with visible annoyance, but without hurrying or raising his voice. One could conclude that some sort of special intention, even an exclusive one, had lodged in his mind. "Listen," he began decisively, "as far as I'm concerned, you can all go to the devil. But from what I know now, I clearly see that I can't understand a thing; please, don't think I came to interrogate you. I don't give a damn! I don't want to! If you were now to reveal all your secrets to me, I might not even listen; I might just spit and walk away. I've come merely to find out for myself once and for all: in the first place, is it true you're mad? You see, there's a belief about you (out there, somewhere) that you might be insane or close to it. I confess, I myself was strongly inclined to support that opinion, judging, in the first place, from your stupid and somewhat vile actions (completely inexplicable) and, in the second, from your recent conduct toward your mother and sister. Only a monster and a scoundrel, if not a madman, could behave with them the way you did; consequently, you are insane . . ."

"Have you seen them recently?"

"Just now. Haven't you seen them since then? Where have you been gallivanting, tell me, please? I've stopped by three times to see you. Your mother's been seriously ill since yesterday. She was planning to come see you; Avdotya Romanovna tried to restrain her, but she didn't want to listen. 'If he,' she said, 'is ill, if his mind's in a muddle, who'll help him if not his mother?' We all came here together, since we couldn't let her come alone. We kept urging her to calm down all the way to your doorstep. We came in, but you weren't here; she sat right here. She waited for ten minutes, and we stood over her in silence. She stood up and said, 'If he went out, then he must be well and he's forgotten his mother; that means it's improper and shameful for his mother to stand on his doorstep and beg for affection, as if for alms.' She went back home and took ill; now she's in a fever. 'I see,' she said, 'he has time for his *own girl*.' She supposes that Sofiya Semyonovna is your *own girl*, your fiancée or your lover, I don't know which. I went at once to Sofiya Semyonovna, because, my friend, I wanted to find out everything—I arrived and looked around: the coffin was standing there and the children were crying. Sofiya Semyonovna was trying their mourning clothes on them. You weren't there. I looked around, excused myself, and left; I went to tell Avdotya Romanovna. So all of that was just nonsense, and you don't have your *own girl*, and so, most likely, you must be insane! But here you sit and devour boiled beef as if you'd had nothing to eat for the last three days. Let's suppose that madmen also have to eat; but, even though you haven't said a single word to me, you're . . . not insane! I can swear to that. First and foremost, not insane. And so, to hell with all of you, because there's some sort of mystery here, some secret; I don't intend to rack my brains over your secrets. I came just to curse you," he concluded, getting up, "to relieve my soul, and I know what I have to do now!"

"What do you want to do now?"

"What do you care about that?"

"Be careful, you'll start drinking!"

"How . . . can you tell?"

"I know you well!"

Razumikhin was silent for a minute.

"You were always a very reasonable man and never, never were you insane," he remarked suddenly, with feeling. "It's true: I'm going to get drunk! Good-bye!" And he was about to leave.

"Two days ago I spoke with my sister about you, Razumikhin."

"About me? But . . . where did you see her the day before yesterday?" Razumikhin stopped suddenly, even growing a bit pale. One could guess that his heart was pounding slowly and intensely.

"She came here alone, sat down, and spoke with me."

"She did!"

"Yes, she did."

"What did you say . . . that is, what did you say about me?"

"I told her you were a fine, honest, hardworking man. I didn't tell her that you love her, because she knows that herself."

"She does?"

"I'll say she does! Wherever I go, no matter what happens to me—you must remain their divine caretaker. I'm entrusting them to you, so to speak, Razumikhin. I'm telling you this because I know for sure that you do love her, and I'm certain of the purity of your heart. I also know that she might come to love you; perhaps she even does already. Now you decide, the best way you know—whether you should get drunk or not."

"Rodka. . . . You see. . . . Well. . . . Oh, damnit all! And just where are you planning on going? You see: if this is all a secret, then so be it! But I . . . I'll find out your secret. . . . I'm certain it's absolutely some sort of nonsense and terrible rubbish, and that you made it all up your-self. But you're an excellent fellow! An excellent fellow!"

"And I also wanted to tell you, but you interrupted me, that you were right just now when you decided not to try to learn these myster-ies and secrets. Leave it alone for the time being and don't worry about it. You'll find out everything in its time, precisely when it'll be neces-sary. Yesterday someone said to me that a man needs air, air, air! I want to go see him right now and find out what he means by that."

Razumikhin stood there deep in thought and uneasiness, trying to ponder something.

"He's a political conspirator! No doubt! And he's on the verge of some decisive step—that's for sure! It can't be anything else and . . . and Dunya knows . . ." he thought to himself.

"So Avdotya Romanovna's come to see you," he said, enunciat-ing his words, "and you yourself want to go see a man who says you need more air, air, and . . . and therefore, and that letter . . . that's also related," he concluded, as if talking to himself.

"What letter?"

"She received a letter today that upset her very much. Very much. Even too much. I began speaking about you—and she asked me to stop. Then . . . then she said that perhaps we'd part very soon; she began thanking me warmly for something; afterward she went to her room and locked the door."

"She received a letter?" Raskolnikov inquired pensively.

"Yes, she did. You didn't know? Hmm."

They both remained silent for a while.

"Good-bye, Rodion. My friend, I . . . there was a time . . . how-ever, good-bye. You see, there was a time. . . . Well, good-bye! I must go, too. I won't drink. Now I don't have to . . . you were lying!"

He hurried to leave, but just as he was going, almost closing the door after him, he suddenly opened it again and said, glancing some-where off to the side:

"By the way! Do you recall that murder, well, the one where Por-firy was involved: the old woman? Well, you should know that the murderer's been found; he himself has confessed and presented all the evidence. It was one of those two workers, the painters; just imagine, you remember, I was defending them here? Would you believe that he intentionally staged that whole scene of a struggle with his friend and the laughter on the staircase, when those men were going upstairs, the caretaker and the two witnesses, precisely as a diversion. What guile, what presence of mind in such a young pup! It's hard to believe; he himself explained it and confessed to everything! And I fell for it! Well then, in my opinion, he's simply a genius of pretending and inventiveness, a genius of legal diversion—and therefore there's nothing to be particularly surprised about! Are there really people like that? And the fact that he didn't stand firm and he's confessed makes me believe him all the more. It's more credible. . . . But I really fell for it, I did! I got all worked up!"

"Tell me, please, where did you find this out, and why are you so interested in it?" Raskolnikov asked with obvious agitation.

"What do you mean? Why am I interested? You have to ask? I learned about it from Porfiry, among others. But I found out almost everything from him."

"From Porfiry?"

"Yes."

"What . . . what exactly did he say?" Raskolnikov asked fearfully.

"He explained it all to me very well. He explained it psychologically, in his own way."

"He explained it? He explained it to you himself?"

"Yes, he did; good-bye! I'll tell you more later, but for now I have my own affairs. There . . . there was a time when I thought. . . . Well, so what? Later! Why do I need to get drunk now? You've gotten me drunk even without drinking. I'm drunk, Rodka! Now I'm drunk without drinking. Well then, good-bye; I'll drop in on you, very soon."

He left.

"He's a political conspirator, that's for sure, absolutely!" Razumikhin resolved definitively to himself as he slowly descended the staircase. "And he's involved his sister; that's very, very possible, with Avdotya Romanovna's character. They've been meeting. . . . She also hinted as much to me. From many of her words . . . and hints . . . and allusions—it's all very clear. How else to explain this entire muddle? Hmm! And I would've thought. . . . Oh, Lord, what would I have thought? Yes, indeed, it was a mental imbalance that came upon me. Damn it! What a rude, vile, mean idea on my part! Good for Mikolka, that he's confessed. . . . This now explains everything that happened before! His illness then, all his strange actions, even before, when he was still at the university, when he was so morose and gloomy. . . . But what does this letter mean now? There may be something to it. Who sent the letter? I suspect. . . . Hmm. No, I'll find it all out."

He remembered and thought about Dunechka and his heart skipped a beat. He went running off.

As soon as Razumikhin left, Raskolnikov stood up, turned to the window, bumped into one corner and then another, as if he had forgotten how small his room was, and . . . sat down on the sofa again. He felt entirely refreshed; once again, a struggle—in other words, a way out had been found.

Yes, that meant a way out had been found! Otherwise everything had been too overbearing and confining, it had started to oppress him unbearably, as if he were in a stupor. From the moment of the scene with Mikolka at Porfiry's, he had begun to gasp for breath in the cramped space with no way out. After Mikolka, on that same day, came the scene at Sonya's; he had conducted it and concluded it not at all, not in the least as he had imagined it all before. . . . In other words, he had grown weak, instantly and radically! All at once! And he had agreed with Sonya at the time, agreed himself, agreed in his heart, that he could no longer go on living alone with this thing in his soul! But Svidrigaylov? Svidrigaylov was a riddle. . . . He was making him uneasy, that was true, but somehow not from that point of view. Perhaps there would still be a struggle with him, too. Svidrigaylov might also be another way out; but Porfiry was another matter.

So, Porfiry himself had explained it to Razumikhin, explained it to him *psychologically*! Once again he had begun to bring in his damned psychology! Porfiry? How could Porfiry believe, even for a moment, that Mikolka was guilty, after what had taken place between them then, after that scene, face-to-face, before Mikolka arrived? Surely it was impossible to arrive at any other correct interpretation except for *one*. (Several times during the last few days, Raskolnikov had recalled fleetingly, in snatches, that scene with Porfiry; he couldn't bear thinking about it as a whole.) The words exchanged between them at that time, the movements and gestures that occurred, the glances exchanged, the tone of voice employed had reached such a point that after this it wasn't for Mikolka (whom Porfiry had understood completely from his very first word and gesture), it wasn't for Mikolka to shake the basis of his convictions.

"How do you like that! Even Razumikhin had begun to suspect him! The scene in the hall, near the lamp, hadn't passed unnoticed. He had rushed off to see Porfiry. . . . But for what reason did Porfiry try to dupe him like that? Why was he trying to divert Razumikhin's eyes to Mikolka? He must have had something in mind; there must have been some intention, but what? True, since that morning a great deal of time had elapsed, too much, much too much, and there had been no news at all about Porfiry. And, of course, that made things worse . . ." Raskolnikov took his cap; still deep in thought, he left his room. This was the first day, in all this time, that he himself felt in his right mind at least. "I must settle matters with Svidrigaylov," he thought, "no matter what, as quickly as possible: he, too, seems to be waiting for me to come see him myself." At that moment, such hatred suddenly arose from his weary heart that perhaps he could have even murdered one of the two of them: Svidrigaylov or Porfiry. He felt, at least, that if not now, he would be capable of doing it later. "We'll see, we'll see," he repeated to himself.

But as soon as he had opened the door into the entryway, he suddenly bumped into Porfiry himself. He was coming to see him. Raskolnikov froze for an instant. Strange to say, he was not very surprised to see Porfiry and was almost unafraid. He merely shuddered, but quickly, and immediately prepared himself. "Perhaps this is the denouement! But how had he approached so quietly, like a cat, and why didn't I hear a thing? Could it be that he was eavesdropping?"

"You weren't expecting a guest, Roman Romanych," cried Porfiry Petrovich with a laugh. "I've been meaning to look in on you for some time; I was passing and thought—why not drop in for a visit for five minutes or so. Were you planning to go out? I won't detain you. Only one cigarette, if you'll allow me."

"Go ahead, take a seat, Porfiry Petrovich, do sit down," Raskol-

nikov said, seating his guest with such an apparently satisfied and amicable look that even he would have been surprised if he could have
seen himself. The leftovers and dregs were being scraped up! Sometimes a man endures half an hour of mortal fear with a robber and then
as soon as the knife is finally placed against his throat, even his fear
disappears. He sat down right in front of Porfiry and looked directly at
him, without batting an eyelash. Porfiry screwed up his eyes and began
lighting a cigarette.

"Well, go on, speak." These words seemed about to leap out of
Raskolnikov's heart. "Well, why, why, why aren't you saying anything?"

II

"Oh, these cigarettes!" Porfiry Petrovich began at last, having lit his cigarette and inhaled a few puffs. "Poison, pure poison, but I can't stop! I cough, sir, I have a tickle in my throat, and I'm short of breath. You know, I'm a coward, sir; a few days ago I went to see Dr. Botkin—he spends a minimum of half an hour examining each patient; he even started laughing when he saw me; he tapped my chest and listened—'Tobacco,' he says, 'is no good for you; your lungs are inflamed.' Well, how can I give it up? What will I replace it with? I don't drink, sir, that's the whole problem, hee-hee-hee, that I don't drink, sir, it is a problem! Everything's relative, Rodion Romanych, it's all relative!"

"What's all this about? Is he resorting to his previous practice, or what?" thought Raskolnikov with revulsion. He suddenly recalled the entire scene of their last meeting; the feelings he had experienced then flooded into his heart like a wave.

"I dropped in on you two days ago, in the evening; you didn't know that?" continued Porfiry Petrovich, examining his room. "I came right into this room. Just like today, I was passing by—and I thought, why not pay him a little visit? I stopped by and your room was wide open; I looked around, waited a bit, and didn't even tell your servant—then I left. Don't you lock your door?"

Raskolnikov's face grew darker and darker. It was as if Porfiry had guessed his thoughts.

"I came to have it out with you, my dear fellow, Rodion Romanych, to have it out with you, sir! I owe you an explanation and feel obligated to provide you with one, sir," he continued with a little smile and even tapped his hand on Raskolnikov's knee lightly. But at almost the same time his face suddenly assumed a serious and worried expression; it even seemed to be clouded with sadness, to Raskolnikov's surprise. He had never before seen such an expression or suspected it of him. "A strange scene occurred between us last time, Rodion Romanych. Perhaps a similar one also occurred between us at our first meeting; but at that time. . . . Well, now it's one thing on top of another! Here's the point: perhaps I'm very guilty before you; I feel this to be the case, sir. You remember, don't you, how we parted: your nerves were tingling and your knees were trembling, and my nerves were tingling and my knees were trembling. You know that at the time we even behaved in a dishonorable and ungentlemanly manner. After all, we're both still gentlemen; that is, in any case, gentlemen first of all; that must be understood, sir. You recall the point it reached . . . it was completely unbecoming, sir."

"What's he doing? Who does he take me for?" Raskolnikov asked himself in astonishment, lifting his head and staring intently at Porfiry.

"I've reached the conclusion that it's now best for us to be forthright with one another," continued Porfiry Petrovich, tilting his head back slightly and lowering his eyes, as if not wishing to embarrass his former victim with his gaze and disregarding his previous tricks and subterfuge. "Yes, sir, such suspicions and such scenes cannot go on for long. Mikolka resolved things then, or else I don't know what might have occurred between us. That damned tradesman was sitting behind the partition in my office—can you imagine that? Of course, you know that already; and I myself know that he came to see you afterward; but what you supposed then didn't really happen: I hadn't sent for anybody and hadn't made any arrangements at the time. You'll ask, why not? How can I say it? It was as if I myself was completely dumbfounded then. I could scarcely arrange to summon the caretakers. (You probably saw them as you went by.) An idea occurred to me at the time, quickly, like lightning; you see, Rodion Romanych, I was firmly convinced then. Even, I thought, even if I let this one go for a while, I can grab the other one by the tail—my own, my own, at least I won't let that one go. You're very irritable, Rodion Romanych, by nature, sir, even too much so, sir, in the face of all the other main qualities of your character and your heart, which I flatter myself with the hope that I have partially understood, sir. Well, of course, even then I couldn't conclude that it doesn't always happen that a man gets up and blurts out the whole truth to you. It does happen, especially when you wear out a man's last drop of patience, but, in any case, it's rare. I could've reached that conclusion. No, I thought, I have to find some shred, some tiny shred, only one, but one that I could grab hold of, so that it was a real thing and not merely some psychology. Therefore, I thought if the man's guilty, then of course one could, in any case, expect something substantial from him; one could even count on a most unexpected result. I was counting on your character at the time, Rodion Romanych, on your character most of all, sir! I was very much relying on you then."

"But you . . . why on earth are you talking like this now?" muttered Raskolnikov at last, not even comprehending the question very well. "What's he going on about?" he wondered to himself. "Does he really take me for an innocent man?"

"What am I talking about? I came, sir, to explain myself, so to speak; I consider it my sacred obligation. I want to lay it all out to you, how it all occurred, the whole story of that entire confusion, so to speak. I caused you a great deal of suffering, Rodion Romanych. I'm not a monster, sir. After all, I understand what it's like for a man to lug all this on his back, a man who's despondent but proud, strong, and impatient, especially impatient! In any case, I regard you as a most honorable man, sir, even possessing the rudiments of magnanimity, although I don't agree with all your convictions, which I consider it my obligation to inform you about in advance, directly, and in complete sincerity, primarily because I don't wish to deceive you. After making your acquaintance, I felt an attachment to you. Perhaps you'll laugh at such words? You have the right, sir. I know that you didn't like me from the first glance because, in essence, there was no reason to like me, sir. But think what you will; now, for my part, I wish to make amends for that first impression and to prove that I'm a man with a heart and a conscience. I'm speaking sincerely, sir."

Porfiry Petrovich paused with dignity. Raskolnikov felt a flood of some new fear. The idea that Porfiry considered him an innocent man began to frighten him.

"It's hardly necessary to relate the whole story in order, how it all suddenly began at that time," continued Porfiry Petrovich. "I think that's even superfluous. And I'd hardly be able to do so. Because how could it be explained properly? First of all there were the rumors. What sort of rumors and from whom and when . . . and why, precisely, did they involve you—I also think it superfluous to say. For me, personally, it all began by chance, with the most accidental chance, which in the highest degree could or could not have happened. What was it? Hmm, I think there's also no reason to say. All this, the rumors and the accident, combined to produce an idea at the time. I confess candidly— because, if I'm to confess, then it must be complete—it was then that I first seized upon you. The old woman's scribbles on the items, let's say, so on and so forth—all that's rubbish, sir. You can count hundreds of similar things. I also had the opportunity to learn in detail about the scene in the police office, also by chance, sir, not merely in passing but from a particular, reliable source, who, without knowing why himself, grasped the scene surprisingly well. You see, it was one thing on top of another, sir, one thing on top of another, Rodion Romanych, my dear fellow! Well, how could I help it if I focused on a specific direction? A hundred rabbits never make a horse, and a hundred suspicions never make a proof, as an English proverb has it, but that's merely good sense, sir. But just you try to deal with passions, sir, passions, because even an examining magistrate is a human being, sir. Then I recalled your little article in that journal, you remember, the one we talked about at length during your first visit. I derided it then, but that was in order to draw you out further. I repeat, you're very impatient and unwell, Rodion Romanych. The fact that you're daring, arrogant, serious and . . . that you've felt, felt a great deal—all that I've known for a long time, sir. I'm familiar with all those feelings, and as I read your article, its ideas seemed familiar to me. It was conceived on sleepless nights and in a state of ecstasy, with much racing and pounding of the heart, with suppressed enthusiasm. But this proud, suppressed enthusiasm is dangerous in youth! I derided it then, but now I'll say that in general I really do appreciate, that is, as an admirer, that first, ardent, youthful literary effort. Smoke, mist, and a string echoing in the mist. Your article is absurd and fantastic, but there's a flash of such sincerity; it contains a youthful, incorruptible pride, and the audacity of despair; it's a gloomy article, sir, but a good one, sir. I read your little article and put it aside . . . and after I put it aside, I thought: 'That's not the last from this person.' Well then, tell me now, after such a beginning, how could I not be carried away by what followed? Ah, good Lord! Was I saying something? Was I alleging something now? It's just what I noticed at the time. 'What is it?' I thought. There's nothing, that is, nothing at all, and perhaps absolutely nothing. And it's improper for me, an examining magistrate, to be carried away like that; I had Mikolka on my hands, and already had facts—say what you will, there were facts! And he brought in his psychology, too; I had to devote some time to him, because this was a matter of life and death. Why am I explaining all this to you now? So you know and so with your mind and heart you won't accuse me of behaving wickedly toward you then. It wasn't vindictive, sir, I tell you that sincerely, sir, hee-hee! What do you think: that I didn't come to conduct a search then? I was here, sir, I was, sir, hee-hee, I was here, sir, when you were lying sick in bed. Not officially and not me personally, but we were here, sir. Without losing any time your room was searched down to the smallest thread; but *umsonst!** I thought: now this man will come, he'll come on his own and very soon; if he's guilty, he'll definitely come. Another person wouldn't, but this fellow will come. Do you remember how Mr. Razumikhin began letting the cat out of the bag? We arranged all that to upset you, therefore we intentionally spread the rumor that he would leak to you. But Mr. Razumikhin is the sort of person who won't endure indignation. Most of all, Mr. Zametov was struck by your anger and your evident boldness: how someone in a tavern could suddenly blurt out, 'I killed her!' It was too bold, sir, too arrogant, sir, and if, I thought, he is guilty, then he's a terrifying fighter! It was at that time I thought, sir, I'll wait, sir! I'll wait for you with all my might, but you simply crushed Zametov

---

* "In vain!" (German).

then . . . the whole point is that all this damned psychology cuts two ways! Well, then I waited for you; I looked around and God delivered you—you came on your own! My heart started pounding. Hey! Why did you come then? That laughter, your laughter when you came in that time, do you recall? I guessed it as if seeing through a clear pane of glass; if I hadn't been waiting for you in that exact way, then I wouldn't have noticed anything about your laughter. That's what it means to be in a certain mood. And Mr. Razumikhin then—ah! That stone, that stone, you remember, the stone under which all those items are hidden? Well, I can almost see it somewhere in a garden—a garden, isn't that what you told Zametov, and then repeated to me a second time? And when we started scrutinizing your article then, when you began expounding on it—we understood each and every one of your words in two ways, as if there were another word implied by each! Well now, Rodion Romanych, that's how I reached the utmost limit, how I bumped my head against it, and then came to my senses. No, I said, what am I doing? If you like, all this, I said, could be explained in an entirely different way, and it even winds up being more natural. Agony, sir! 'No,' I thought, 'it'd be better if I had one small detail!' And then when I heard about those doorbells, I froze completely and even felt a shudder. 'Well,' I thought, 'there's a small detail at last! That's it!' I didn't even think about it at the time, I simply didn't want to. I'd have given a thousand rubles at that moment, of my own money, to have observed you *with my own eyes:* how you walked side by side with that tradesman for a hundred paces after he called you a 'murderer' to your face, while you didn't dare ask him anything all along the way! Well, and the chill that ran down your spine? Those doorbells, in that illness of yours, in your semi-delirium? And so, Rodion Romanych, why should you be surprised if I played a few tricks on you? And why did you come on your own at that very moment? It was, so help me God, as if someone had made you come, and if Mikolka hadn't distracted us, then . . . do you remember Mikolka? Do you remember him clearly? That was a thunderbolt, sir! It was a peal of thunder from a storm cloud, a thunderous bolt! Well, how did I meet it? I didn't believe in that thunderbolt even for a moment, as you could see! Quite the contrary! Later, after you'd left, when he began replying to various points in an extremely coherent way, I myself was surprised, and didn't believe him then, not in the least. . . . That's what it means to be hard as a rock. No, I thought, *Morgenfrüh!** What does Mikolka have to do with this?"

"Razumikhin just told me that even now you're accusing Nikolai and you assured him of that . . ."

Raskolnikov was out of breath and didn't finish what he was saying. He listened in inexpressible agitation as this man, who had seen right through him, disavowed his own words. He was afraid to believe him and did not. He greedily searched for and tried to catch something more precise and definitive in his ambiguous words.

"Mr. Razumikhin!" cried Porfiry Petrovich, as if overjoyed by the question from Raskolnikov, who up to then had maintained his silence. "Hee-hee-hee! Mr. Razumikhin had to be deflected: two's company, but three's a crowd. Mr. Razumikhin's not the one, sir; he's an outsider; he came running to me completely pale. . . . Well, never mind about him. Why involve him in this? As far as Mikolka's concerned, would you care to know what sort of fellow he is, in the sense that I understand him? First of all, he's still an immature child; not exactly a coward, but more like some artist. It's true, sir, don't laugh at the way I'm explaining him. He's innocent and very impressionable. He has a heart and a vivid imagination. He knows how to sing and dance, and, they say, he tells stories so well that people come from afar to listen. He goes to school, is too easy to make laugh, and drinks himself silly, not from debauchery, but in spurts, when someone plies him with drink, again just like a child. And at that time when he stole something, he himself didn't know what he was doing, because 'if he picked it up from the floor, what sort of theft was that?' Do you know that he's one of the schismatics,† not exactly a schismatic, but simply a sectarian; some people in his family were Runners.‡ Not long ago, he himself ran off and spent two whole years in the country under

---

* "Early morning!" (German).

† A reference to the *raskolniki*, schismatics, or Old Believers, who split from the Russian Orthodox Church in the mid-seventeenth century. Note the similarity with the hero's surname.

‡ A radical sect of Old Believers who fled from every sort of obedience to social institutions.

the spiritual guidance of an elderly monk. I found all this out from Mikolka and from his friends in Zaraysk. Imagine that! He wanted to run off into the wilderness! He was a zealot, prayed to God at night, studied the 'genuine' old books and read himself silly. Petersburg made a very strong impression on him, especially the female sex, and the vodka as well. He's very impressionable, sir, and he forgot all about his elder and about everything else. I know that a local artist took a liking to him: he started visiting Mikolka, and then this incident occurred! Well, he lost heart—and attempted to hang himself. He tried to run away! What can be done about this view of our judicial system widespread among the people? Some find the words 'he will be condemned' simply terrifying. Who's to blame? The new courts may change all that. Oh, God grant they will! Well, sir, now that he's in prison, he's apparently remembered his honest elder; his Bible's also reappeared. Do you know, Rodion Romanych, what the word 'suffering' means for some of these people? It's not exactly for anyone else, but it's simply 'necessary to suffer.' That means to accept suffering; if it's from the powers that be, so much the better. In my time, there was an extremely submissive convict who spent a whole year in prison; he read the Bible at night sitting on the stove bench, and read himself silly to such an extent that for no reason at all he grabbed hold of a brick and hurled it at the prison warden without any particular grievance. And how did he throw it? He intentionally threw it a yard wide so it wouldn't hurt anybody! Well, you know what happens to a prisoner who attacks a supervisor with a weapon: 'he accepted his suffering.' So I suspect that now Mikolka wants to 'accept his suffering' or something like that. I know this for certain, even from the facts, sir. Only he himself doesn't know that I know. What, don't you think that such wildly imaginative types can come from the common people? There are a lot of them! The elder's begun influencing him again, especially after Mikolka tried to hang himself. However, he'll come to me and tell me everything. You think he'll be able to hold out? Just wait, he'll deny it all! I'm waiting for him to come at any moment and recant his testimony. I've taken a liking to this Mikolka and am investigating him thoroughly. What do you think? Hee-hee! He replied to several points extremely coherently; obviously he'd received the necessary information and had prepared himself skillfully; but he simply doesn't know anything about certain other matters, and he waded in too deep; he knows nothing, and he himself doesn't even suspect that he doesn't know! No, my dear Rodion Romanych, Mikolka's not involved in this affair at all! This is a fantastic case, an ominous, contemporary case, and an instance of our time, sir, when the human heart has grown dark; when one can hear it said that blood 'refreshes'; when all of life is devoted to comfort. There are bookish dreams here, sir, a heart that's irritated by theories; one sees decisiveness at every step, but decisiveness of a special kind—he did resolve, but as if falling off a mountain or jumping from a bell tower, and he went out to commit the crime as if unwillingly. He forgot to lock the door behind him, and he killed, he killed two people in accordance with a theory. He killed, but he didn't know how to steal the money; and what he managed to grab, he hid under a stone. It wasn't enough for him to endure the torment as he stood behind the door, as they banged on it and rang the doorbell— no, later he goes back to this empty apartment in a semi-delirium to recall that doorbell; he needs to experience yet again that cold shiver running up and down his spine. . . . Well, that was probably his illness, but here's what else: he killed, but he considers himself an honest man; he despises people, he walks about like some pale angel—no, how can Mikolka be connected with this, my dear Rodion Romanych? Mikolka's not involved at all!"

These last words, after all that had been said before, which had seemed like a disavowal, were too unexpected. Raskolnikov started shuddering as if he had been stabbed:

"So then . . . who is . . . the murderer?" he asked, gasping for breath, unable to refrain. Porfiry Petrovich leaned back against his chair, as if astonished by the sudden question.

"Who's the murderer?" he repeated, as if unable to believe his own ears. "Why *you* are, Rodion Romanych! You're the murderer, sir . . ." he added with complete conviction, almost in a whisper.

Raskolnikov jumped up from the sofa, stood there a few seconds, and sat down again without saying one word. Slight convulsions passed suddenly across his entire face.

"Your lip is trembling again, as it did then," muttered Porfiry

Petrovich, as if sympathetically. "It seems, Rodion Romanych, that you didn't understand me, sir," he added after a brief silence, "and that's why you were so astounded. I came precisely to tell you everything and to bring this matter out into the open."

"I'm not the murderer," whispered Raskolnikov, the way frightened little children do when they're caught at the scene of a crime.

"No, it is you, sir, Rodion Romanych, you, sir, and no one else, sir," Porfiry whispered sternly and compellingly.

They both remained silent, and that silence lasted for a peculiarly long time, about ten minutes. Raskolnikov rested his elbows on the table and silently ran his fingers through his hair. Porfiry Petrovich sat there quietly and waited. Suddenly Raskolnikov glanced at Porfiry with contempt.

"You're up to your old tricks, Porfiry Petrovich! Still those same methods of yours: how is it you're really not fed up with them?"

"Oh, enough of that! What methods do I need now? It would be another matter if there were witnesses here; but we're all alone, whispering to each other. You yourself can see that I didn't come to chase you and catch you like a hare. Whether you confess or not—it makes no difference to me now. I'm completely certain of it even without you."

"If that's so, then why did you come?" Raskolnikov asked irritably. "I'll pose my previous question to you: if you consider me guilty, why don't you take me to prison?"

"Well now, that's the question! I'll answer you in order: in the first place, it's not advantageous for me to arrest you so soon."

"Not advantageous! If you're convinced, then you should . . ."

"Oh, so what of it if I'm convinced? For the time being, this is all my dream, sir. And why should I put you away there to live *in peace*? If you're asking for it, then you yourself know. For example, if I bring that tradesman here to testify against you, you'll say to him, 'Were you drunk or not? Who saw me with you? I merely took you for a drunk, but you really were drunk.' What would I reply to you then, all the more so since your version's more credible than his, because his testimony is pure psychology—which doesn't fit his mug at all—while you hit it right on the mark, because that scoundrel drinks heavily and that's even very well known. And I myself confessed to you candidly, several times already, that this psychology cuts both ways, and the second way is greater and more credible than the first; and, besides that, I have nothing more against you at this time. And even though I still intend to arrest you, and even came (not in the usual way) to tell you everything in advance, still I can say candidly (also not in the usual way), that this would not be advantageous for me. Well, sir, in the second place, I've come to see you . . ."

"Well then, in the second place?" (Raskolnikov was still gasping for breath.)

"Because as I stated to you before, I consider myself obligated to provide an explanation. I don't want you to think of me as a monster, all the more so because I'm sincerely well disposed toward you, believe it or not. As a result of which, in the third place, I've come to you with an open and honest proposal: that you should come forward and confess. That would be infinitely more advantageous for you, for me as well—because it would be a load off my mind. Well then, am I being open with you or not?"

Raskolnikov thought for a minute.

"Listen, Porfiry Petrovich. You yourself say it's mere psychology; meanwhile, you've veered off into mathematics. What if you yourself are making a mistake now?"

"No, Rodion Romanych, I'm not making a mistake. I have a certain piece of evidence. I found it even back at the time, sir; God sent it to me!"

"What kind of evidence?"

"I won't say, Rodion Romanych. Besides, in any case, I have no right to delay any further; I shall arrest you, sir. So you be the judge: it's all the same to me *now*; consequently, I'm doing this solely for you. So help me God, Rodion Romanych, it'll be better for you!"

Raskolnikov laughed spitefully.

"This is not merely amusing, it's even shameless. Even if I were guilty (which is not at all what I'm saying), for what reason should I come to you and confess, when you yourself say that if I'm arrested, I'll be *at peace*?"

"Oh, Rodion Romanych, don't believe everything I say; perhaps you won't be *at peace* at all! After all, it's only a theory and my theory at that, sir, and what sort of authority am I? Perhaps even now I'm hiding something from you, sir. I can't just up and reveal everything to you, hee-hee! Another thing: what do you mean, how could it be advantageous to you? Don't you know what sort of reduced sentence would follow from this? When would you appear, at what moment? Just use your own judgment! When someone else has already confessed to the crime and muddied the whole affair. As for me, I swear to God that I'll arrange matters and contrive things 'there' in such a way that your appearance will seem as if it were completely unexpected. We'll totally disprove all this psychology, I'll make all those suspicions against you disappear, so your crime will appear as the result of confusion, because, in all good conscience, that's just what it was. I'm an honest man, Rodion Romanych, and I'll keep my word."

Raskolnikov maintained a gloomy silence and lowered his head; he thought for a long time and smiled again at last, but his smile was meek and gloomy.

"Hey, that's unnecessary!" he said, as if no longer concealing anything from Porfiry. "It's not worth it! I don't need your sentence reduction at all!"

"Well, that's just what I was afraid of!" Porfiry exclaimed warmly and as if unwillingly. "That's just what I was afraid of, that you wouldn't need our reduction."

Raskolnikov regarded him gloomily and impressively.

"Hey, don't scorn your life!" continued Porfiry. "You still have a great deal of it ahead of you. What do you mean, you don't need the sentence reduction, how can that be? You're a hasty man!"

"A great deal of what ahead of me?"

"Life! Are you some sort of prophet? How much do you know? Seek and ye shall find. Perhaps God was waiting for this moment. You won't wear those fetters forever . . ."

"There'll be a reduction in the sentence . . ." Raskolnikov said with a laugh.

"Well then, are you afraid of the bourgeois shame? It may be that you fear it without even knowing it—because you're young! Nevertheless, you shouldn't be afraid or ashamed of making a confession."

"Hey! I don't give a damn!" Raskolnikov whispered with contempt and revulsion, as though not wishing to speak. He stood up again, as if wanting to go somewhere, but then he sat down again, in visible despondency.

"You don't give a damn! You've lost your faith and you think I'm flattering you crudely; but have you really lived much yet? Do you understand all that much? You conceived a theory and felt ashamed that it failed, that it proved to be not very original! It turned out poorly, that's true, but you're still not a hopeless scoundrel. You're not such a scoundrel at all! At least you didn't deceive yourself for long; you headed straight for the final posts. Do you know how I regard you? I consider you one of those people who, if their innards were being cut out, they'd stand there smiling at their tormentor—if only they've found faith or God. Well, find it and you'll go on living. In the first place, you've needed a change of air for some time. So, suffering's also a good thing. Go on, suffer. That Mikolka may even be right to want to suffer. I know you don't believe it—but don't philosophize too cleverly; give yourself up to life directly, without deliberating; don't worry—it'll carry you over to the other shore and stand you on your feet. Onto what shore? And how do I know? I merely believe that you still have a long life ahead of you. I know that now you hear my words as a long, boring prepared exhortation; but you may recall it afterward, it may be of use to you at some time; that's why I'm speaking. It's a good thing that you killed only an old woman. If you'd conceived of another theory, you might even have done something a hundred million times worse! Perhaps you should thank God; how do you know? Perhaps He's saving you for something. Have a great heart and be less afraid. Are you afraid of some great impending responsibility? No, that would be shameful. If you've taken such a step, then have courage. That's justice. You must fulfill what justice demands. I know that you don't believe it but, so help me God, life will carry you over. Afterward you'll even come to like it. For now you need only air, air, air!"

Raskolnikov shuddered suddenly.

"And just who are you?" he cried. "Some sort of prophet? From what heights of majestic serenity do you utter these philosophical prophecies?"

"Who am I? I'm a man who's finished with life, nothing more. A man who, perhaps, has feelings and sympathies, who may know a thing or two, but who's lived his life. But you—you're something altogether different: God has prepared a life for you (but who knows, perhaps it will only vanish like smoke and nothing will come of it). Well then, so what if you have to join a different category of men? With your heart, will you long for comfort? What will it matter if perhaps no one sees you for a very long time? It's not time that matters, but you yourself. Become a sun and everyone will see you. Most of all, the sun should be the sun. Why are you smiling again: because I sound like Schiller? I bet you suppose that I'm now trying to worm myself into your good graces! Well, perhaps that's just what I'm trying to do, hee-hee-hee! Perhaps, Rodion Romanych, you shouldn't believe what I say, and should never believe it completely—that's my disposition, I agree. However, here's what I'll add: you can judge for yourself how base or honest I am!"

"When do you plan to arrest me?"

"I can allow you to roam freely for another day and a half or two days. Think about it, my dear fellow, and pray to God. It'll be more advantageous, so help me God, more advantageous."

"And what if I run away?" Raskolnikov asked with a strange grin.

"No, you won't run away. A peasant runs away, or a modern sectarian—a lackey of someone else's ideas—because if you just show him the end of your finger, like Gogol's midshipman Dyrka,* he'll believe in anything you like for the rest of his life. But you no longer believe in your own theory—why should you run away? What good would it do you? Running away is vile and difficult; most of all you need life, a defined position, and suitable air; well, what sort of air would you have? If you ran away you'd return on your own. *You can't get along without us.* If I were to lock you up in a prison cell—well, and if you sat there a month or two, or three, and all of a sudden you recalled my words, you'd come forward on your own, perhaps not even expecting it yourself. You won't know it even an hour before that you'll come forward with a confession. I'm even sure that 'you'll decide

---

* A reference to a character in the play *The Marriage* (1842) by Nikolai Gogol.

to accept suffering'; you don't believe what I'm saying now, but you'll come to the same conclusion. Because suffering, Rodion Romanych, is a great thing; pay no attention to the fact that I've grown fat, there's no need; on the other hand, don't laugh at this, but I know that suffering contains an idea. Mikolka's right. No, you won't run away, Rodion Romanych."

Raskolnikov stood up and took his cap. Porfiry Petrovich also stood up.

"Are you planning to go for a stroll? The evening will be a fine one, if only there won't be a storm. However, it'd be better if it freshens the air . . ."

He also took his cap.

"And as for you, Porfiry Petrovich, please don't get it into your head," Raskolnikov stated with stern insistence, "that I've confessed to you today. You're a strange man, and I listened to you merely out of curiosity. I haven't confessed to anything. . . . Remember that."

"Yes, I know that, I'll remember—look, he's even trembling. Don't worry, my dear fellow; let it be just as you like. Go out for a stroll; but don't go too far. In any case, I have a small request to make of you," he added, lowering his voice. "It's a bit delicate but important: if, that is, in any case (but one that I don't think will happen and consider you completely incapable of), if by any chance—well, just in case—the idea occurs to you during these forty or fifty hours to conclude this affair in some other way, in some sort of fantastic manner—to raise your hand against yourself (an absurd supposition, forgive me for saying), then leave a short but detailed note. Just a few lines, only a few little lines, and mention the stone: it'll be more decent of you, sir. Well, sir, good-bye. . . . I wish you good thoughts and auspicious undertakings!"

Porfiry left, slouching a little and trying to avoid looking at Raskolnikov. Raskolnikov went to the window and with irritable impatience waited for the time when, by his calculation, Porfiry had emerged onto the street and gone some distance. Then he himself hurriedly left the room.

III

He hurried to Svidrigaylov's. He himself didn't know what he could hope for from this man. But concealed within Svidrigaylov was some sort of power over him. Once he was aware of this, Raskolnikov was unable to compose himself; besides, now the time had come.

Along the way, one question troubled him especially: had Svidrigaylov been to see Porfiry?

As far as he could tell, no, he hadn't, and he was prepared to swear to it! He kept thinking about it over and over, recalling Porfiry's entire visit, and he concluded: no, he hadn't been there, of course he hadn't!

But if Svidrigaylov still hadn't been there, would he or would he not go to see Porfiry?

Now, for the time being, it seemed to him that he wouldn't go. Why not? He was unable to explain it, but even if he could have, he wouldn't rack his brains over that right now. All of this tormented him; yet at the same time he felt that he couldn't be bothered with it. It was strange: perhaps no one would believe it, but he seemed to care only slightly, absentmindedly about his present, impending fate. He was tormented by something else, much more important, extraordinary— about himself and no one else, but something different, something major. In addition, he felt endless moral exhaustion, even though his reasoning was functioning better than it had for all these last few days.

And was it worth it now, after all that had happened, to try to overcome these paltry new difficulties? Was it worth it, for example, to attempt to conspire so that Svidrigaylov didn't go to see Porfiry? Or to study, investigate, and waste time over this fellow Svidrigaylov?

Oh, he was so sick and tired of it all!

Meanwhile, he still hurried to Svidrigaylov's; did he expect something *new* from him, a sign or a way out? Was he grasping at straws? Was it fate or some instinct that was bringing them together? Perhaps it was just his exhaustion, his desperation; perhaps he didn't need Svidrigaylov at all, but someone else; but Svidrigaylov had turned up for no particular reason. Sonya? And why would he go to see her now? To beg for her tears once again? He was afraid of Sonya. She represented an inexorable sentence, an irreversible decision. Here—it was either her road or his. Especially now, he was not in any state to see her. No, wouldn't it be better to try Svidrigaylov: to find out what that was all about? He couldn't help but admit to himself that for a long time he really had felt a need for him.

However, what could they have in common? Even their evil deeds could not be considered equivalent. Besides, this man was very unpleasant, obviously extremely depraved, absolutely devious and deceitful, perhaps even evil. Tales were circulating about him. True, he was making efforts on behalf of Katerina Ivanovna's children; but who knows why or what that meant? This man always had his own intentions and schemes.

During all these days, another thought had kept constantly running through Raskolnikov's head and upsetting him terribly, although he'd tried to drive it away because he found it so painful! He sometimes thought: Svidrigaylov was constantly skulking around him and was doing so now; Svidrigaylov knew his secret; he had harbored designs against Dunya. What if he still did now? One could say *yes*, he did, almost for certain. And what if now, knowing his secret and having thus acquired power over him, Svidrigaylov wanted to use that power as a weapon against Dunya?

Sometimes this idea tormented him even in his dreams; but now, as he made his way to Svidrigaylov's, it was the first time the idea had so clearly appeared in his consciousness. This idea alone drove him into a dark rage. In the first place, everything would be changed, even his own situation: he would have to reveal his secret to Dunechka immediately. He might have to give himself up to save her from taking some careless step. The letter? This morning Dunya had received some sort of letter! Who in Petersburg could she be receiving letters from? (Could it be from Luzhin?) True, Razumikhin was standing guard; but he didn't know anything. Perhaps he'd have to reveal himself to Razumikhin as well? Raskolnikov pondered all this with loathing.

"In any case, I must see Svidrigaylov as soon as possible," he decided definitively. "Thank goodness the details aren't necessary, as much as the heart of the matter; but if, if only he was capable, if Svidrigaylov was devising some intrigue against Dunya, then . . ."

Raskolnikov had been so exhausted during all this time, for the whole past month, that there was no way he could resolve similar questions except for one solution: "Then I'll kill him," he thought in cold desperation. A painful feeling gripped his heart; he stopped in the middle of the street and began looking around: what road was he on and how far had he come? He found himself on Obukhovsky Prospect, about thirty or forty paces from the Haymarket, which he had just crossed. The whole second floor of the house on the left was occupied by a tavern. All the windows were open wide; the tavern, judging by the movement of the figures in the windows, was packed full of people. From the large room came the sound of songs, the music of a clarinet, a violin, and the beat of a Turkish drum. He could hear women squawking. He was about to set off in the opposite direction, not understanding why he had turned onto Obukhovsky Prospect, when all of a sudden, in one of the farthest open windows of the tavern, he saw Svidrigaylov sitting there by the window at a tea table, a pipe in his mouth. This was terrifying and struck him with horror. Svidrigaylov was observing and scrutinizing him in silence, which also struck Raskolnikov at once; it seemed as if he wanted to get up and slip out of the tavern surreptitiously so that no one would notice him. Raskolnikov immediately pretended that he himself didn't recognize him; he looked to one side pensively, while he continued observing him out of the corner of his eye. His heart pounded in agitation. So it was: Svidrigaylov obviously didn't want to be seen. He took the pipe out of his mouth and started to get away; but, after he stood up and pushed his chair back, he suddenly noticed that Raskolnikov was looking at and observing him. Between them occurred something like the scene of their first meeting at Raskolnikov's room when he was asleep. A mischievous smile appeared on Svidrigaylov's face and began spreading across it. Both knew that each was looking at and observing the other. At last Svidrigaylov burst into loud laughter.

"Well, well! Come on in, if you like; I'm here!" he cried through the window.

Raskolnikov went upstairs to the tavern.

He found him in a very small back room, with one window, adjoining the bigger room where merchants, civil servants, and a large number of working people were drinking tea at twenty small tables amidst the shouting of a forlorn chorus of male peasants. From there the clattering of billiard balls could be heard. On the table in front of Svidrigaylov stood an open bottle of champagne and a glass half full of wine. In the room stood a young lad with a small hand organ and a healthy, ruddy girl wearing a striped skirt, tucked up, and a Tyrolean hat with ribbons; she was a singer, around eighteen years old, and, in spite of the songs from the chorus in the other room, she was singing some sentimental ditty in a rather hoarse contralto to the accompaniment of the organ . . .

"Well, that's enough!" Svidrigaylov said, interrupting her at Raskolnikov's entrance.

The girl immediately broke off and stood in respectful expectation. She had been singing her rhymed ditty with the same serious and respectful look on her face.

"Hey, Filipp, a glass!" cried Svidrigaylov.

"I won't have any wine," said Raskolnikov.

"As you like. That's not for you. Drink up, Katya! Nothing more's needed today. Go away!" He poured her a full glass of wine and put down a yellow banknote. Katya drank the glass at one go, the way women usually drink, that is, in twenty gulps, without pausing; she took the banknote, kissed Svidrigaylov's hand, which he had solemnly extended to her for that reason, and left the room; the boy with the hand organ trailed along after her. They had both been brought in from the street. Svidrigaylov hadn't been in Petersburg a week, but everything around him was already on a patriarchal footing. The waiter at the tavern, Filipp, was already an "acquaintance" and fawned over him. The door to the larger room could be locked; Svidrigaylov felt at home in this little room and may have spent entire days in it. The tavern was dirty, dilapidated, and not even of average quality.

"I was going to your apartment to look for you," began Raskolnikov, "but why did I suddenly turn into Obukhovsky Prospect from the Haymarket? I never turn there and I don't come here. I usually turn to the right from the Haymarket. Besides, this isn't the way to your place. I just turned and here you are! It's strange!"

"Why don't you just say it outright: it's a miracle!"

"Because it may be only an accident."

"What a cast of mind all these people have!" laughed Svidrigaylov. "You won't admit it even if you really believe that miracles occur. Why, you yourself say that 'it may be' it's only an accident. You can't imagine, Rodion Romanych, what cowards people are about having their own opinions! I'm not talking about you. You have your own opinions and aren't afraid to do so. That's why you've attracted my curiosity."

"Nothing else?"

"Why, that's sufficient."

Svidrigaylov was obviously in an excited state, but only slightly; he had drunk only half a glass of wine.

"It seems that you came to see me before you found out I was capable of having what you call my own opinion," observed Raskolnikov.

"Well, that was another matter. Each of us has our own steps to take. As for a miracle, I'll say that you seem to have slept through these last two or three days. I mentioned this tavern to you myself, and it's no miracle that you came here directly; I myself explained the way here, said where it was, and named the time when I could be found here. Don't you remember?"

"I forgot," Raskolnikov replied with astonishment.

"I believe it. I told you twice. The location must have registered in your memory automatically. You turned here automatically, and without even knowing it, you came right to this address. When I was speaking to you then, I wasn't at all sure that you understood me. You really give yourself away, Rodion Romanych. There's something else: I'm certain that in Petersburg there are many people who walk around talking to themselves. It's a city full of half-crazy people. If we had real science, then doctors, lawyers, and philosophers could conduct the most valuable research about Petersburg, each according to his own specialty. There are few places where you can find so many gloomy, harsh, and strange influences on man's soul as you can in Petersburg. Consider the impact of the climate alone! Meanwhile, it's the administrative center of all Russia and its character must be reflected in everything. But that's not the point now; the thing is, I've observed you from the side several times. You leave your house with your head held high. After twenty paces or so, you drop your head and clasp your hands behind your back. You look, but obviously you don't see anything either in front of you or to the side. At last you begin moving your lips and talking to yourself; moreover, you sometimes free one arm and start declaiming; finally you pause in the middle of the street for a long time. That's not good at all, sir. Someone may notice you beside me, and that won't be to your advantage. I really don't care; I'm not here to cure you, but, of course, you understand me."

"Do you know whether I'm being followed?" asked Raskolnikov, glancing at him inquisitively.

"No, I don't know anything," Svidrigaylov replied as if surprised.

"Then why not leave me in peace," Raskolnikov muttered with a frown.

"Fine; we'll leave you in peace."

"Tell me, rather, if you come here to drink and mentioned it to me twice so that I'd come to you, then why now, as I saw you through the window from the street, why did you hide and wish to leave? I observed that very well."

"Hee-hee! And why, when I was standing there on your threshold, and you were lying there on your sofa with your eyes closed, did you pretend you were asleep, when you really weren't asleep at all? I observed this plainly."

"I could have had my . . . reasons . . . you know that yourself."

"And I could have had my reasons, although you won't learn them."

Raskolnikov placed his right elbow on the table, rested his chin on the fingers of his right hand, and stared intently at Svidrigaylov. For about a minute he examined his face, which had always struck him, even previously. It was a somewhat strange face that seemed to resemble a mask: white, ruddy, with rosy, scarlet lips, a light blond beard, and a head of rather thick blond hair. His eyes were somehow too blue, and their gaze was too intense and unmoving. There was something terribly unpleasant in this handsome, extremely young-looking face, judging by his age. Svidrigaylov's clothes were fashionable, summery, and light; his linen was particularly elegant. He wore a huge ring on his finger with a valuable stone.

"Do I really have to trouble myself also with you?" Raskolnikov asked suddenly, coming straight to the point with feverish impatience. "Even though you might perhaps be a most dangerous person if you chose to harm me? But I don't want to burden myself anymore. I'll show you now that I don't regard myself as highly as you probably think. You should know that I came to see you to tell you outright that if you persevere with your previous intentions concerning my sister, and if you're thinking of making use of what's been revealed lately, then I will kill you before you can send me to prison. My word is good: you know that I can keep it. In the second place, if you wish to tell me anything—because it's seemed to me all the while that you've wanted to say something to me—then tell me quickly what it is, because time is valuable and perhaps it'll soon be too late."

"Where are you going in such a hurry?" asked Svidrigaylov, glancing at him inquisitively.

"Each of us has our own steps to take," Raskolnikov replied darkly and impatiently.

"You yourself were just demanding candor, yet you refuse to answer my first question," remarked Svidrigaylov with a smile. "You seem to think I have some special aims; therefore you regard me with suspicion. Well then, that's completely understandable in your situation. But, however much I wish to become closer to you, I won't take it upon myself to convince you of the opposite. So help me God, the game isn't worth the candle, and I wasn't intending to talk to you about anything very special."

"Then why did you need me? Why were you hanging around?"

"Simply as an interesting subject for observation. The fantastic nature of your position appealed to me—that's what! Besides, you're the brother of a person who's interested me a great deal; lastly, at the time I heard a considerable amount about you from that person, from which I concluded that you have great influence on her. Isn't that enough? Hee-hee-hee! Besides, I confess, your question is extremely complicated for me, and I find it difficult to answer. Well then, for example, have you come to see me now not only about that matter but about something new? That's so, isn't it?" insisted Svidrigaylov with a mischievous smile. "Well, just imagine that as I was on the train on my way here, I was counting on you to tell me something *new* and on the fact that I might be able to borrow something from you! That's how rich we are!"

"Borrow what?"

"What can I tell you? How do I know what? You see the sort of tavern I spend my time in; it gives me pleasure—that is, not exactly pleasure, but I must have somewhere to sit. Take that poor Katya— did you see her? Well, if I were a glutton, for example, or a clubhouse gourmet, but you see what sort of food I eat!" (He pointed his finger to the corner where the remains of an awful beefsteak with potatoes sat on a small tin plate.) "By the way, have you had dinner? I've eaten a little and don't want any more. Wine, for example, I don't drink at all. Except for champagne, nothing at all, and only one glass of champagne for the whole evening, and even then my head aches. I ordered it now to fortify myself because I plan to go somewhere, and you see me in a peculiar frame of mind. That was why I was hiding before, like a schoolboy, because I thought you might disturb me; but it seems"—he took out his watch—"that I can spend an hour with you; it's now half past four. Believe me, I wish I were something; well, a landowner, a father, a lancer, a photographer, a journalist . . . but, nothing, I have no specialty! Sometimes it's even boring. True, I thought you might tell me something new."

"Who are you, and why did you come here?"

"Who am I? You know: a member of the gentry who served two years in the cavalry, then wandered around here in Petersburg, married Marfa Petrovna, and lived in the country. That's my biography!"

"It seems you're a gambler?"

"No, what sort of gambler am I? A cardsharp's not a gambler."

"You were a cardsharp?"

"Yes, I was."

"Were you ever beaten for it?"

"I was. So what?"

"Well, therefore you could've challenged men to a duel . . . in general, it livens things up."

"I won't contradict you, and besides, I don't love philosophizing. I confess, I came here as soon as I could mostly because of the women."

"You've just buried Marfa Petrovna?"

"Well, yes." Svidrigaylov smiled with proud candor. "What of it? You seem to find it wrong that I talk about women in this way?"

"That is, do I see anything wrong in debauchery?"

"In debauchery! So that's what you're driving at! However, I'll reply in order and answer you about women in general; you know, I'm inclined to rattle on. Tell me, why should I restrain myself? Why should I give up women if I really like them? At least it's something to do."

"So you're here only counting on engaging in debauchery?"

"Well, what of it? So it's debauchery! People are obsessed with debauchery. But at least I like a direct question. In this debauchery, at least, there's something constant, even based on nature and not subject to fantasy, something always present in the blood like a burning coal, ready to ignite, which you might not be able to put out for a long time, for many years. You yourself will agree that it's something to do, isn't it?"

"What's there to celebrate? It's a disease, and a dangerous one."

"So that's what you're driving at! I agree that it's an illness, just like everything else that's in excess—and it's essential that it go to excess—but, in the first place, it's different for everyone, and in the second place, of course, one must maintain moderation, judiciousness, even if it's base, but what's to be done? If it weren't for this, one might have to shoot oneself. I agree that a decent man is obliged to be bored, but still . . ."

"And could you shoot yourself?"

"Well, really!" Svidrigaylov retorted with revulsion. "Do me a favor: don't speak of that," he added hurriedly, without the bragging that had accompanied all his previous words. Even his face seemed somehow to change. "I confess to unforgivable weakness, but what's to be done? I'm afraid of death and I don't like to talk about it. You know I'm part mystic?"

"Ah! Marfa Petrovna's ghost! Does it still haunt you?"

"Don't mention that; it hasn't happened in Petersburg; the devil take it!" he cried with an irritated expression. "No, let's talk about . . . however. . . . Hmm! Hey, time is short; I can't stay here with you for very long. It's a pity! I could tell you something."

"What is it, a woman?"

"Yes, a woman, an unexpected chance. . . . But, I'm not talking about that."

"Well, doesn't the squalor of this setting have some impact on you? Have you already lost the strength to stop?"

"And do you claim to have the strength? Hee-hee-hee! You just astonished me, Rodion Romanych, though I knew before that it would be the case. You're talking to me about debauchery and aesthetics! You're a Schiller, you're an idealist! All this, of course, had to be so, and one would be surprised if it were any different; however, it's still somehow strange in reality. . . . Ah, it's a pity there's so little time, because you're such an interesting subject! By the way, do you like Schiller? I like him very much."

"What a braggart you are!" Raskolnikov remarked with some revulsion.

"No, so help me God, I'm not!" Svidrigaylov replied with a loud laugh. "However, I won't argue. Perhaps I'm a braggart. But why shouldn't I brag if it's harmless? I lived in the country with Marfa Petrovna for seven years and therefore, now having come upon a clever man like you—clever and interesting in the highest degree—I'm simply glad to have a chat; besides that, I drank this half a glass of wine, and it's gone to my head a bit. The main thing is, there's something I'm very agitated about, but about which I . . . I will keep silent. Where are you going?" Svidrigaylov asked suddenly in alarm.

Raskolnikov had begun getting up. He felt oppressed, confined, and somehow awkward about having come here. He was convinced that Svidrigaylov was the most shallow and worthless villain in the world.

"Hey! Sit down; stay here," begged Svidrigaylov. "Order yourself some tea at least. Sit here awhile; I won't blather nonsense—about myself, that is. I'll tell you something. Well, if you like, I'll tell you how a woman tried to 'save' me, to use your language. It will even be an answer to your first question, because this person is your sister. May I tell you? It will kill some time."

"Go on, but I hope that you . . ."

"Oh, don't worry! Besides, Avdotya Romanovna can inspire only the deepest respect, even in such a despicable and shallow man like me."

IV

"You may know (however, I already told you myself)," began Svidrigaylov, "I served in debtors' prison here, with an enormous debt, and without any way to settle it. There's no need to go into detail about how Marfa Petrovna bought me out at that time: do you know to what degree of stupefaction love can sometimes transport a woman? She was an honest woman, quite smart (although completely uneducated). Imagine that this same jealous, honest woman, after much frenzy and terrible reproaches, resolved to stoop to forge some sort of contract with me that she upheld all during our marriage. The point is that she was much older than me; besides that, she constantly kept some sort of clove in her mouth. I was enough of a swine and sufficiently honest to declare openly that I couldn't be completely faithful to her. This confession drove her into a frenzy, but it seems that she somewhat appreciated my rude frankness: 'That means,' she said, 'if he announced it in advance, he doesn't want to deceive me.' Well, that's the most important thing for a jealous woman. After many tearful scenes, something like an oral contract was concluded between us: first, I would never leave Marfa Petrovna and would always be her husband; second, I would never absent myself without her permission; third, I would never take a permanent lover; fourth, in exchange, Marfa Petrovna would allow me to cast an eye at the servant girls from time to time, but not without her secret knowledge; fifth, God help me if I were to fall in love with a woman of our own social class; sixth, if by chance, God forbid, I were to conceive some sort of major, serious passion, I should disclose it to her. As for the last point, however, Marfa Petrovna was fairly calm all along; she was a clever woman and, therefore, couldn't regard me in any other way than as a depraved and dissolute man, incapable of genuine love. But a clever woman and a jealous woman—those are two different things, and that was the problem. However, to judge in an impartial way about certain people, it's necessary to discard some preconceived notions and one's habitual way of regarding the people and objects that usually surround us. I have the right to rely on your judgment more than on anyone else's. You may have already heard much about Marfa Petrovna that was amusing and absurd. In fact, she did possess some very amusing habits; but I'll tell you openly that I sincerely regret the numerous sorrows I caused her. Well, that seems enough for an extremely respectable *oraison funèbre** on the most loving wife of the most loving husband. On the occasion of our quarrels, I remained silent for the most part and didn't get irritated; this 'gentlemanization' almost always achieved my goal; it had an impact on her, and she even liked it; there were incidents when she was even proud of me. But she still couldn't stand your sister. How did it happen that she risked taking such a beauty into her house as a governess? I explain it by saying that Marfa Petrovna was a passionate and impressionable woman and that she simply fell in love, literally fell in love, with your sister. Yes, indeed, Avdotya Romanovna! I realized very well from the first that this was not good, and—what do you think?—I was even ready not to look at her. But Avdotya Romanovna herself took the first step—believe it or not! Would you believe that Marfa Petrovna went so far as even to be angry at me at first because of my constant silence about your sister, that I was so indifferent to her incessant and adoring tributes to Avdotya Romanovna? I myself don't understand what she wanted! Well, of course Marfa Petrovna told Avdotya Romanovna the whole truth about me. She had the unfortunate trait of telling all our family secrets and complaining continuously to absolutely everyone about me; how could she possibly miss the opportunity

---

* "Funeral oration" (French).

to talk about such a new and splendid friend? I suppose that all they talked about was me; without a doubt, Avdotya Romanovna heard all those dark, mysterious tales that are ascribed to me. . . . I bet you've heard something of that sort, too?"

"I have. Luzhin said you were even the cause of a young child's death. Is that true?"

"Do me a favor, leave all those vulgar tales alone," Svidrigaylov replied squeamishly and with revulsion. "If you absolutely wish to know about that nonsense, I'll tell you about it sometime, but for now . . ."

"They also mentioned some servant lad in the country, that you were also the cause of what became of him."

"Enough, please!" Svidrigaylov interrupted him again, with obvious impatience.

"Wasn't he the servant who came, after his death, to fill your pipe . . . that you told me about yourself?" Raskolnikov said, growing irritable.

Svidrigaylov glanced closely at Raskolnikov; and to Raskolnikov it seemed that a malicious smirk momentarily flashed like lightning in his glance, but Svidrigaylov restrained himself and replied with extreme politeness:

"The very same. I see that you also find all this intriguing, and I will consider it my duty to satisfy your curiosity on all matters at the first convenient opportunity. Damn it all! I see that to some people I can really seem to be a romantic figure. Judge for yourself to what degree I'm obligated to thank the late Marfa Petrovna for having told your sister so many mysterious and intriguing things about me. I can't judge the impression it made; but in any case, it was advantageous for me. In the face of all the natural revulsion Avdotya Romanovna felt toward me, and in spite of my gloomy and repulsive appearance—at last she began to feel pity for me, pity for a fallen man. And when the heart of a young woman experiences *pity* for someone, then, naturally, that's the most dangerous thing for her. She conceives at once a desire 'to save' him, to make him listen to reason, to restore him to life, to summon him to nobler aims, and to initiate him into a new life and new activity—it's well known what can be dreamt up in this vein. I realized at once that the bird was flying into the net on its own, and I prepared myself. You seem to be frowning, Rodion Romanych? There's no need for that, sir. As you know, the whole affair turned out to be nothing. (Devil take it! How much wine I'm drinking!) You know, I always felt sorry, from the very beginning, that fate hadn't allowed your sister to be born in the second or third century of our era, somewhere as the daughter of a ruling prince or some governor or proconsul in Asia Minor. Without doubt, she'd have been one of those who suffered martyrdom, and, of course, she would've smiled when they singed her breast with red-hot pincers. She'd have embraced this fate intentionally, and in the fourth or fifth century she'd have gone off to the desert in Egypt and lived there for thirty years, nourishing herself on roots, ecstasies, and visions. She's a person who hungers and demands to accept some sort of torment for someone else, and if she's denied this torment, then she might throw herself out a window. I've heard something about a Mr. Razumikhin. He's said to be a reasonable fellow (which his surname shows; he must be a seminarian); well, let him watch over your sister. In a word, it seems that I understood her; I consider that to my credit. But then—that is, in the beginning of an acquaintance—as you yourself know, you're always more superficial and foolish, you make mistakes and see what's not there. Damn it all, why is she so pretty? I'm not to blame! In a word, it all began with a fit of uncontrollable voluptuousness. Avdotya Romanovna's terribly chaste, to a degree never seen or heard before. (Notice that I'm telling you this about your sister as a fact. She may be chaste to a morbid degree, in spite of her broad intelligence, and this will harm her.) There happened to be a young girl in our house, Parasha, dark-eyed Parasha, who'd just been brought in from another village; she was a serf girl I'd never set eyes on before— very pretty but unbelievably stupid: she burst into tears, raised a loud howl, and created a scandal. Once, after dinner, Avdotya Romanovna intentionally sought me out alone on a path in the garden and, with flashing eyes, *demanded* that I leave poor Parasha in peace. This was almost the first time we talked one-on-one. Naturally, I considered it an honor to fulfill her request; I tried to pretend to be astounded and embarrassed; in a word, I played my part very well. Relations began between us, secret conversations, moral instructions, sermons, entreaties, implorations, even tears—do you believe it, tears! That's the degree to which some young women feel a passion for propaganda! Of course, I blamed it all on my fate, pretended to hunger and thirst for light, and finally set in motion the greatest and most certain means of conquering a woman's heart, a means that never deceives anyone and that acts decisively on every woman, without exception. That means is well known— it's flattery. There's nothing more difficult in the world than straightforwardness, and there's nothing easier than flattery. If in straightforwardness there's only a one-hundredth part of a false note, then dissonance results at once, followed by a scandal. If in flattery everything up to the last note is false, it's received and heard not without enjoyment; even though it's crude, it's enjoyment nonetheless. And, however crude the flattery, at least half of it will certainly seem to be true. That's true for all stages of development and every social class. Even a vestal virgin could be seduced by flattery. There's no need even to speak about ordinary people. I can't recall without laughing how I was trying to seduce a noble lady who was devoted to her husband, her children, and her virtue. It was so enjoyable and required so little effort! The lady really was virtuous, at least in her own way. My entire strategy consisted of being crushed all the time and groveling before her chastity. I flattered her shamelessly; no sooner had I received a squeeze of the hand or even a glance than I reproached myself for having obtained it by force, for the fact that she'd resisted me, resisted me so that I'd never have achieved a thing if I myself hadn't been so depraved; that she, in her innocence, hadn't foreseen any treachery and submitted unintentionally, without knowing or suspecting, and so on and so forth. In a word, I attained everything, and my lady remained certain in the utmost degree that she was innocent and chaste, that she was fulfilling all her duties and obligations, and that she'd fallen completely by accident. How angry she was at me when I finally declared that it was my sincere conviction that she was merely in search of pleasure, just as I was. Poor Marfa Petrovna was also terribly susceptible to flattery, and if I'd only wanted to, then, of course I could've appropriated her whole estate while she was still alive. (But I'm drinking a great deal of wine and prattling on.) I hope you won't get angry if I mention that this same effect began to show on Avdotya Romanovna. But I myself was foolish and impatient and spoiled the whole affair. Avdotya Romanovna had several times before (and once in particular) taken a dislike to the expression of my eyes. Do you believe it? In a word, a certain fire flared up in them more brightly and more carelessly, and that fire frightened her, and she found it hateful in the end. There's no need to go into detail, but we parted. Then I acted stupidly again. In the crudest manner, I mocked all her propaganda and her attitude; Parasha stepped onto the scene again, and not just her—in a word, it was a real Sodom. Oh, if only you'd seen, Rodion Romanych, even once in your life, how your sister's eyes can sometimes flash! It doesn't matter that I'm drunk now and have consumed an entire glass of wine: I'm telling the truth. I assure you that I saw this look in my dreams; in the end I was unable to bear the rustle of her dress. Really, I thought I would have some sort of fit; I never imagined that I could reach such a state of frenzy. In a word, it was necessary to make peace; but that was no longer possible. And just imagine what I did then! To what degree of stupefaction rage can drive a man! Never undertake anything in a frenzy, Rodion Romanych. Considering that Avdotya Romanovna, in essence, was impoverished (ah, excuse me, I didn't want to . . . but does it matter how that idea's expressed?), in a word, she lived by the work of her hands, she helped support both her mother and you (oh, damn it, you're scowling again . . .); I decided to offer her all my money (I could raise around thirty thousand rubles at that time) if she'd run away with me, even here to Petersburg. Naturally, I would have pledged my eternal love, happiness, and so on and so forth. Do you believe that I'd fallen in love to such an extent that had she said to me: cut Marfa Petrovna's throat or poison her and marry me—it would've been done at once! But it all ended in catastrophe, which you already know, and you yourself can judge what a pitch of rage I reached when I learned that Marfa Petrovna had found that vile official Luzhin and practically arranged a marriage— one that, in fact, was just like the one I was offering. Isn't that so? Well? Isn't it? I notice that you've begun listening very attentively. . . . Such an interesting young man . . ."

Svidrigaylov struck his fist on the table with impatience. His face had turned red. Raskolnikov clearly saw that the glass or glass and a half of wine he'd consumed, drinking it gradually, in small sips, had affected him adversely—he decided to make use of the opportunity. He was very suspicious of Svidrigaylov.

"Well, after this I'm completely convinced that you came here also with my sister in mind," he said frankly to Svidrigaylov, without concealing it, in order to irritate him even more.

"Hey, enough of that," said Svidrigaylov, suddenly recovering, "I've told you . . . and besides, your sister can't stand me."

"I'm certain about that, too, but that's not the point."

"Are you certain that she can't stand me?" Svidrigaylov squinted and smiled mockingly. "You're right, she doesn't like me; but you mustn't vouch for what happens between a husband and his wife, or between a man and his mistress. There's always one little corner that remains a secret to the whole world and that's known only to the two of them. Can you vouch for the fact that Avdotya Romanovna regards me with loathing?"

"From several words and hints during your account, I see that even now you have your own views and the most pressing designs against Dunya—vile ones, of course."

"What? Did I let slip such words and hints?" Svidrigaylov was suddenly naïvely alarmed, without paying the least attention to the epithet characterizing his intentions.

"Yes, and they continue to slip out. Well, what are you so afraid of? Why are you suddenly scared?"

"I'm afraid and scared? Scared of you? You ought to be afraid of me, *cher ami*.* In any case, what nonsense that is. . . . However, I see that I'm drunk; I almost let the cat out of the bag again. To hell with the wine! Hey, bring me some water!"

He grabbed the bottle of wine and hurled it offhandedly out the window. Filipp brought him some water.

"It's all nonsense," said Svidrigaylov, wetting a towel and applying it to his head. "I can put you in your place with one word and demolish all your suspicions. Do you know, for example, that I'm getting married?"

---

* "Dear friend" (French).

"You told me that before."

"I did? I'd forgotten. But at the time I couldn't be positive because I hadn't even seen my future wife; I merely intended to marry. Well, now I have a fiancée, it's all arranged, and if it weren't for some pressing matters, I'd definitely take you to meet her right away—because I want to ask your advice. Hey, devil take it! There's only ten minutes left. Look at my watch; but I'll tell you about it because it's an interesting little matter, my marriage, that is, in its own way. Where are you going? Are you leaving again?"

"No, I'm not going away now."

"You're not? We'll see! I'll take you there, it's true, and I'll show you my fiancée, but not now; you'll have to leave soon. You go to the right, while I turn to the left. Do you know this Resslikh? The one in whose house I'm living? Well? Do you hear? No, what do you think, the same one about whom it's said that this girl . . . was pulled from the water . . . last winter—well, are you listening? Are you? Well, she was the one who arranged all this for me. 'You,' she says, 'seem bored. Amuse yourself for a while.' But I'm a gloomy, dreary person. You think I'm cheerful? No, I'm gloomy: I don't do any harm, just sit in a corner; sometimes they can't make me talk for three days in a row. But that Resslikh woman is a rascal, I tell you, and here's what she had in mind: I'll get bored, desert my wife, and leave; she'll get control of my wife and put her into circulation, in our social class, that is, and higher. 'There is,' she says, 'an invalid father, a retired civil servant, who sits in a wheelchair and hasn't been able to move his legs for three years. There is,' she says, 'a mother, a very reasonable lady, this mama. Their son works somewhere in the provinces, but he doesn't help out. The daughter got married but doesn't visit; she has two small nephews on her hands (as if her own children weren't enough); they took their youngest daughter out of school before she finished her course; she'll turn sixteen in a month, which means that then she can be married off. That's where I come in. We went to see them; what an amusing situation it was. I introduced myself: landowner, widower, from a well-known family, with certain connections, and with some capital—so what if I'm fifty and she's only sixteen years old? Who'll pay any attention to that? Well, it's tempting, isn't it? It is tempting, ha-ha! You should have seen how I chatted with her papa and mama! It would have been worth paying just to see me then. She comes out, curtsies, just imagine, still wearing a short skirt, like an unopened bud; she blushes and flares up like the dawn (they'd told her, of course). I don't know what you think of women's faces, but in my opinion, these sixteen years, those still childish eyes, that shyness, and her little tears of embarrassment—in my opinion, all that's even better than beauty; in addition, she's quite a picture. Fair hair in little ringlets like lamb's wool, full, rosy lips, little feet—charming! Well, we got acquainted; I declared that I was in a hurry because of some family matters; the next day—that is, the day before yesterday—we were betrothed. Since then, whenever I go there, I take her on my knee and won't let her go. . . . Well, she flares up like the dawn, but I keep on kissing her; her mother, naturally, reassures her that 'he is your future husband: this is what you have to do'; in a word, it's a piece of cake! And this present state, that is, being betrothed, might even be better than being married. It's what's called *la nature et la vérité*!* Ha, ha! I've exchanged a few words with her—she's not at all stupid; sometimes she steals a glance at me—it burns right through me! You know, she has a face like Raphael's Madonna. Has it ever occurred to you that the Sistine Madonna has a fantastic face, the face of a sad holy fool? Well, something like that. The day after we'd received her parents' blessing, I brought her about fifteen hundred rubles' worth of things: a set of diamonds, one of pearls, and a lady's silver dressing case—about so big, with all sorts of items in it, so that even this little Madonna's face flushed deeply. I sat her on my knees yesterday, and it must have been very unceremoniously—she flared up and little tears formed in her eyes, but she didn't want to show me how excited she was. Everyone else had gone away for a minute; she and I remained completely alone; then she suddenly threw herself around my neck (for the first time herself), embraced me with her little arms, kissed me, and swore that she'd be an obedient, faithful, good wife; that she'd make me happy and would use her entire life, every minute of it, sacrificing everything, absolutely everything, and for all this she wished

---

* "Nature and truth!" (French). An ironic reference to the ideas of philosopher Jean-Jacques Rousseau (1712–1778).

merely to have *only my respect*. Beyond that, she said, 'I need nothing at all, no more gifts!' You'll agree that to hear such a confession privately from such a sixteen-year-old little angel, wearing a tulle dress, with lovely ringlets, blushing with a maiden's shame, and with little tears of enthusiasm in her eyes—you'll have to agree that it's rather seductive. Isn't it? It's worth something, right? Well, isn't it? Well . . . well, listen . . . well, let's go visit my fiancée . . . but not right now!"

"In a word," said Raskolnikov, "this monstrous difference in years and development arouses your voluptuousness! Will you really be married like that?"

"What of it? Absolutely. Every man must fend for himself, and the one who deceives himself the best winds up the happiest of all. Ha-ha! Why have you embraced virtue so wholeheartedly? Have mercy, kind sir, I'm a sinful man. Hee-hee-hee!"

"Yet you've made arrangements for Katerina Ivanovna's children. However . . . however, you had your own reasons for that . . . I understand everything now."

"I'm fond of children in general, very fond of them," Svidrigaylov said with a laugh. "On that score, I can even tell you about a most interesting incident, one that continues up to now. On the first day after my arrival, I visited a number of foul places—well, after seven years, I threw myself into it. You've probably noticed that I haven't hurried to rejoin my old pals, my former friends and acquaintances. I intend to go on without them as long as possible. You know, living in the country with Marfa Petrovna, I was tormented to death by memories of all these mysterious nooks and crannies where one can find so many things. Damn it all! Common people get drunk, educated young people having nothing to do but burn with unrealizable dreams and fantasies and deform themselves with theories; Yids have flocked here from somewhere, they hoard all the money, while all the rest lead debauched lives. That's how this town's affected me from the very beginning, with its familiar stench. Once I happened to find myself at a so-called dance evening—a horrible cesspool (but I do love cesspools, with all their filth); well, naturally, they performed a cancan, a dance such as there never was in my own time. Yes, sir, that's real progress. Suddenly I look and see a girl of about thirteen, well dressed, dancing with a professional; there was another one in front of her, vis-à-vis. Her mother was sitting on a chair near the wall. Well, you can imagine what sort of cancan it was! The girl's embarrassed, blushes, finally takes offense, and begins to cry. The expert grabs hold of her and begins to twirl her around and show off in front of her; around them everyone was laughing—I love our public at such times, even though it was our cancan public—they were laughing and shouting, 'That's it, that's the way! Don't bring children in here!' It was all the same to me; it wasn't any of my business: was it logical or not for them to console themselves like that! I made a decision, sat down next to her mother, and began telling her that I was a recent arrival, and saying what boors these people were, that they didn't know how to distinguish genuine worth or to show due respect. I let her know that I had a fair amount of money; I offered to take them home in my carriage; I escorted them home and became acquainted with them (they'd just come to Petersburg and lived in some small room rented from tenants). She told me that both she and her daughter regarded my acquaintance only as an honor; I learned that they have neither house nor home, and they came here to plead for something or other from some civil servant; I offered my services and some money; I discovered that they came that evening by mistake, thinking that it was a place where they give dancing lessons. I offered to assist as best I could with the young girl's education, arranging French and dancing lessons. They accepted my offer with enthusiasm and considered it an honor; since then we've been acquainted. . . . If you like, we'll go see them—but not now."

"Enough, that's enough of your vile, base stories, you debauched, base, voluptuous man!"

"A Schiller, a Russian Schiller, an absolute Schiller! *Où va-t-elle la vertu se nicher?*[*] You know, I'll tell you such tales on purpose, just to hear your shrieks. What a pleasure!"

"I'll say. Don't you think I seem ridiculous to myself right now?" Raskolnikov muttered with malice.

---

[*] "Where is virtue going to build her nest?" (French). An almost exact quotation from French writer Voltaire's (1694–1778) life of the playwright Molière (1622–1673).

Svidrigaylov laughed raucously; he finally called to Filipp, paid his bill, and went to stand up.

"Well, I'm drunk, *assez causé*!"* he said. "What a pleasure!"

"Of course, you find it a pleasure," cried Raskolnikov, also standing up, "a worn-out lecher like you talking about your adventures—having in mind some monstrous intention—talking particularly to a person like me and in such circumstances. . . . It arouses you."

"Well, if that's so," replied Svidrigaylov with some surprise, scrutinizing Raskolnikov, "if that's so, then you yourself are a considerable cynic. At least you have enormous material for being one. You can recognize many things, a great many . . . and you can also do many things. Well, enough of this, however. I sincerely regret that I've conversed so little with you, but you won't get away from me. . . . Just wait a little . . ."

Svidrigaylov left the tavern. Raskolnikov followed him. Svidrigaylov was, however, not so drunk at all; it had affected his head just for a moment, but the effect was passing with every minute. He was very preoccupied by something, something very important, and he was frowning. Some expectation, apparently, was agitating and disturbing him. In the last few minutes he had suddenly altered his behavior with Raskolnikov; with each passing moment he was becoming ruder and more mocking. Raskolnikov noticed all this and was also alarmed. He found Svidrigaylov very suspicious; he decided to follow him.

They descended onto the sidewalk.

"You go to the right, while I turn to the left, or, perhaps, just the opposite, but—*adieu, mon plaisir*,† until our next joyful meeting!"

He turned right, toward the Haymarket.

---

* "Enough talk!" (French).

† "Good-bye, my pleasure" (French).

V

Raskolnikov followed him.

"What's this?" cried Svidrigaylov, turning around. "But didn't I tell you . . ."

"This means that from now on I won't let you out of my sight."

"Wha-a-at?"

They both stopped and stared at each other for a minute, as if sizing each other up.

"From all your half-drunken stories," Raskolnikov replied abruptly, "I've definitely concluded that not only have you failed to give up your vile intentions concerning my sister, but that you're even more preoccupied with them than you were before. I happen to know that my sister received some sort of letter this morning. And all this while, you haven't been able to sit still. . . . Let's suppose you've managed to come up with a wife along the way; that doesn't mean a thing. I wish to make certain personally that . . ."

Raskolnikov could hardly define for himself what it was that he wanted now and what precisely it was that he wanted to ascertain.

"So that's it! Do you want me to call the police right now?"

"Go ahead!"

Once again they stood facing each other for a minute. At last Svidrigaylov's face changed. Having become convinced that Raskolnikov was not frightened by any threats, he suddenly assumed the most cheerful and amicable look.

"What a fellow you are! I didn't mention that matter of yours intentionally, although, needless to say, I'm tormented by curiosity. It's a fantastic business. I nearly put off speaking about it until another time, but really, you're capable of frustrating a dead man. . . . All right, come along, but I warn you in advance: I'm going to my apartment only for a minute to grab some money; then I'll lock my door, take a cab, and spend the entire evening on the Islands. So why should you follow me?"

"I'll follow you to your apartment, but not to your rooms; I'll go to Sofiya Semyonovna to ask her forgiveness for not having been at the funeral."

"As you like, but Sofiya Semyonovna's not at home. She took all the children off to a certain lady, an elderly aristocrat, a former longtime acquaintance of mine, the director of several orphanages. I delighted this lady when I provided money for the upkeep of all three of Katerina Ivanovna's fledglings, in addition to contributing more money for the institutions; then I told her Sofiya Semyonovna's history in great detail, without concealing a thing. It had an indescribable effect on her. That's why Sofiya Semyonovna's been summoned to appear today at the hotel where the aristocratic lady is staying temporarily, having just arrived in town from her dacha."

"It doesn't matter; I'll call in anyway."

"As you like, but you're on your own; what's it to me? Here we are at my house. Tell me, I'm convinced that you regard me with suspicion because I've been so tactful with you and up to now haven't pestered you with any questions . . . do you understand? This seemed extraordinary to you; I bet that's the truth. That shows what I get for being tactful."

"And for eavesdropping behind the door!"

"So that's what you're on about!" Svidrigaylov said with a laugh. "Yes, I'd have been surprised if after all this you'd let that pass without some comment. Ha-ha! I managed to understand a little bit of what you were saying then . . . there . . . to Sofiya Semyonovna, the tricks you were playing. But what's all that about? Perhaps I'm old-fashioned and unable to understand a thing. Explain it, for heaven's sake, my dear fellow! Enlighten me with the latest principles."

"You couldn't hear a thing. It's all lies!"

"I'm not going on about that, not that (although, however, I did manage to hear something). No, I'm talking about the way you sigh all the time! The Schiller in you is always getting confused. And now it seems one isn't supposed to eavesdrop behind the door. If that's so, go on and tell the authorities that 'such and such an amazing thing happened to me: I discovered a small error in my theory.' If you're convinced that one shouldn't eavesdrop, but that you can crack open the skulls of old ladies with anything at hand for your own enjoyment, then you'd best be off to America as soon as possible! Run away, young man! Perhaps there's still time. I mean it sincerely. You don't have any money? I'll give you some for the journey."

"I'm not thinking about that at all," Raskolnikov said, trying to interrupt him disgustedly.

"I understand (however, don't trouble yourself: you don't have to say much, if you don't want to), I understand what sort of current questions you're thinking about: moral issues, right? Questions of a citizen and a human being? Let them alone; why worry about them now? Hee-hee! Because you're still a citizen and a human being? And if so, there was no need to get involved in this matter; there was no reason to poke your nose into other people's business. Well, go shoot yourself; or don't you feel like it?"

"You seem to be trying to infuriate me on purpose, so that I'll leave you alone . . ."

"What an eccentric you are. But we've already arrived; welcome to my staircase. You see, here's the entrance to Sofiya Semyonovna's; you see, no one's home! You don't believe me? Ask Kapernaumov; she leaves her key with them. Here's Madame de Kapernaumov herself. What? (She's a little deaf.) Did she go out? Where to? Well then, now did you hear? She's not here, and she might not be back until very late at night. Well, now come into my rooms. You wanted to see me? Well, here we are. Madame Resslikh isn't at home. That woman's always busy, but she's a good person, I can assure you. . . . She might be of use to you if you were a bit more sensible. Well now, please take a look: I'm taking this five percent note (I still have so many of them) from the writing desk, and I'll take it right to the moneychanger today. Well, did you see that? I can't lose any more time. The desk's locked up, the apartment's locked up, and we're back on the staircase. Well, if you like, we can hire a cab! I'm heading to the Islands. Wouldn't you like a drive? I'll take this carriage to Yelagin Island. You refuse? You can't bear it? Let's go for a ride, it doesn't matter. It seems that rain is moving in; never mind, we'll put the hood up."

Svidrigaylov was already sitting in the carriage. Raskolnikov decided that his suspicions, at least for now, were unfounded. Without saying a word, he turned and headed back in the direction of the Haymarket. If he had turned around even once along the way, he would have managed to see how Svidrigaylov, after driving no more than a hundred paces, paid for the carriage and set off on foot once again, walking along the sidewalk. But Raskolnikov couldn't see a thing and had already turned the corner. Profound revulsion drove him away from Svidrigaylov. "How could I have expected anything even for a moment from that crude villain, from that voluptuous debaucher and scoundrel?" he cried involuntarily. It was true that Raskolnikov pronounced his judgment too hastily and thoughtlessly. There was something in Svidrigaylov's manner, at least, that conveyed an air of originality, if not mysteriousness. As far as his sister was concerned, Raskolnikov still remained convinced that Svidrigaylov would not leave her in peace. But it was too painful and unbearable to think about and ponder all of this!

As was his habit when left alone, after twenty paces or so he slipped into deep thoughtfulness. Walking onto the bridge, he paused by the railing and began looking at the water. All the while Avdotya Romanovna was standing above him.

He encountered her at the entrance to the bridge but walked on by, without recognizing her. Dunechka had never met him before like this, out on the street, and she was struck by fear. She stopped and didn't know whether to call him or not. All of a sudden she noticed that Svidrigaylov was rapidly approaching from the direction of the Haymarket.

But Svidrigaylov seemed to be moving mysteriously and cautiously. He didn't step onto the bridge but paused alongside it, trying with all his might not to let Raskolnikov catch sight of him. He had noticed

Dunya some time ago and was signaling to her. It seemed to her that by his signals that he was summoning her and asking that she not call her brother and leave him in peace.

That's just what Dunya did. She walked quietly past her brother and approached Svidrigaylov.

"Let's walk faster," Svidrigaylov whispered to her, "I don't want Rodion Romanych to find out about our meeting. I should tell you that I was just sitting near here with him in a tavern, where he himself had come looking for me, and it was with difficulty that I managed to get away from him. For some reason he knows about my letter to you and suspects something. Of course, you didn't tell him about it, did you? But if it wasn't you, who could it have been?"

"We've already turned the corner," interrupted Dunya. "Now my brother won't see us. I won't go any farther with you. Tell me everything here; you can say everything you have to say out in the street."

"In the first place, it's impossible to say it here on the street; secondly, you must also hear what Sofiya Semyonovna has to say; in the third place, I have some documents to show you. . . . Well, and finally, if you won't agree to drop in on me, then I'll refuse to provide any explanations and will leave immediately. In addition, I ask you not to forget that your beloved brother's extremely curious secret lies completely in my hands."

Dunya paused indecisively and regarded Svidrigaylov with a penetrating glance.

"What are you afraid of?" he asked calmly. "The town is different from the country. Even in the country you did me more harm than I did you, while here . . ."

"Has Sofiya Semyonovna been informed?"

"No, I haven't said a word to her, and I'm not even sure she's home now. However, she probably is. She buried her stepmother today: it's not the sort of day to go visiting. Until the right time comes, I don't want to say anything to anyone; I'm even a little sorry that I told you. Here the least carelessness is equivalent to denunciation. I live close by, in this house we're approaching. Here's the caretaker of our building; he knows me very well; he's bowing to us; he sees that I'm coming with a lady, and, of course, he's managed to observe your face; that will serve you well if you're afraid of me and suspicious. Forgive me for speaking so crudely. I myself am renting a room from lodgers. Sofiya Semyonovna lives on the other side of the wall, where she's also renting from lodgers. All the rooms on the floor are being rented. Why are you frightened like a little child? Or am I really so frightening?"

Svidrigaylov's face was distorted into a condescending smile; but he no longer felt like smiling. His heart was pounding, and he could scarcely breathe. He was intentionally speaking in a loud voice to conceal his growing excitement; but Dunya hadn't managed to observe this peculiar excitement; she was too irritated by his remark about her childish fear and how terrible she thought he was.

"Even though I know that you're a man . . . without honor, I'm not afraid of you at all. Go on ahead," she said, with apparent serenity, though her face was very pale.

Svidrigaylov stopped in front of Sonya's apartment.

"With your permission, I'll ask if she's home. No. No luck. But I know she may come back very soon. If she went out, it must be to see a particular lady on account of her orphans. Their mother died. I also got involved in this and made arrangements. If Sofiya Semyonovna doesn't return in ten minutes, I'll send her to see you, if you like, even later today. Well, here's my apartment. Here are my two rooms. My landlady, Mrs. Resslikh, lives behind this door. Now look in here; I'll show you the principal documents: from my bedroom this door leads into two completely empty rooms, which are for rent. Here they are . . . you must look in here more carefully . . .

Svidrigaylov occupied two rather spacious furnished rooms. Dunechka looked around distrustfully but didn't notice anything particular in the furnishings or in the arrangement of the rooms, although there was something to observe; for example, Svidrigaylov's apartment was located in between two almost uninhabited apartments. The entrance to his rooms was not straight from the corridor but through two of the landlady's almost empty rooms. From his bedroom, unlocking a door with a key, Svidrigaylov showed Dunechka another empty apartment, also for rent. Dunechka paused on the threshold, not understanding why she was being invited to look, but Svidrigaylov hastened to provide an explanation:

"Here, look here, at this second large room. See that door? It's locked with a key. Near it stands a chair, only one chair in both of these rooms. I brought it in from my apartment so that I could listen more comfortably. Just behind this door is Sofiya Semyonovna's table; she was sitting there, conversing with Rodion Romanych. And I was eavesdropping here, sitting on this chair, two evenings in a row, for about two hours each time—and, of course, I was able to find out a thing or two, don't you think?"

"You were eavesdropping?"

"Yes, I was; now come into my rooms; there's nowhere to sit here."

He led Avdotya Romanovna back into the first room, which served as his sitting room, and invited her to take a chair. He himself sat at the other end of the table, at least two yards away from her; however, most likely the same flame that had frightened Dunechka before was now gleaming in his eyes. She shuddered and looked around again distrustfully. This was an involuntary action. Apparently she didn't want to show her distrust. But the isolated situation of Svidrigaylov's apartment finally struck her. She wanted to ask if at least his landlady was home, but she didn't say anything . . . out of pride. Besides, another source of agony, one incomparably greater than fear for herself, was growing in her heart. She was suffering unbearably.

"Here's your letter," she began, placing it on the table. "Is what you wrote really possible? You hint at a crime supposedly committed by my brother. You hint too openly; you don't dare retract it now. You should know that even before this I'd heard this absurd tale and don't believe one word of it. It's a vile and ridiculous suspicion. I know the story—how and why it was conceived. You can't have any proof. You promised to prove it: well, speak! But you should know in advance that I don't believe you! I don't!"

Dunechka said all this very rapidly, and for a moment she blushed deeply.

"If you didn't believe that this could have happened, why have you taken the risk of coming to see me alone? Why have you come? Only out of curiosity?"

"Don't torment me; say what you have to say!"

"It's certainly true that you're a brave young woman. So help me

God, I thought you might ask Mr. Razumikhin to accompany you. But he was neither with you nor near you, that much I could see: that was courageous of you. It means you wanted to protect Rodion Romanych. However, everything about you is divine. . . . As far as your brother's concerned, what can I tell you? You yourself just saw him. What was he like?"

"Is that all you have to base your case on?"

"No, not on that, but on his own words. He came here to see Sofiya Semyonovna two evenings in a row; I showed you where they sat. He made a complete confession to her. He's a murderer. He killed an old woman, a civil servant's widow, a moneylender with whom he himself had pawned several things; he also killed her sister, a trader named Lizaveta, who came in accidentally when he was killing the pawn-broker. He murdered them both with an axe he'd brought with him. He killed to rob them, and he did so; he took the money and several items. . . . He told Sofiya Semyonovna all of this word for word; she's the only one who knows his secret, but she didn't participate in the murder, neither in word nor in deed; on the contrary, she was horrified, just as you are now. Rest assured, she won't give him away."

"This can't be true!" muttered Dunechka through her deathly pale lips; she was gasping for breath. "It can't be. There's no reason, not the least, no cause. . . . It's a lie! A lie!"

"He robbed them, that was the only reason. He took money and some items. True, according to his own confession, he hasn't made use of the money or the items; he hid them somewhere under a stone, where they still are. But that's because he hasn't dared to use them."

"But is it likely that he could murder and rob? That he could even conceive of such a thing?" cried Dunya, jumping up from her seat. "You know him, you've seen him. Could he really be a thief?"

She was almost entreating Svidrigaylov; she had forgotten all her fear.

"There are thousands and millions of combinations and possibili-ties, Avdotya Romanovna. A thief steals, but knows he's a scoundrel; on the other hand, I heard about a well-born fellow who robbed the mail; who knows, perhaps he thought he was doing a decent thing! Needless to say, I myself wouldn't have believed it, just like you, if I'd heard about it indirectly. But I believe my own ears. He explained all the reasons to Sofiya Semyonovna; at first even she didn't believe what she heard, but at last she believed her own eyes, her very own eyes. He himself reported it all to her."

"What kind of . . . reasons?"

"It's a long story, Avdotya Romanovna. How can I explain it to you? There's a kind of theory involved, according to which one finds, for example, that a single crime is permissible if the main goal is a good one. A single evil act and a hundred good deeds! Besides, it's infuriating for a young man of merit and inordinate pride to know that if only he had some three thousand rubles, his entire career, the future course of his life would be different; meanwhile he lacks the three thousand rubles. Add to this irascibility from hunger, from cramped quarters, from ragged clothes, from the clear consciousness of the beauty of his social position, together with that of his sister and his mother. Worst of all, vanity, pride and vanity; however, God only knows there might also be some good proclivities. . . . Don't think I blame him; it's none of my business. There was also this particular little theory of his—an ordinary one—according to which people are divided, don't you see, into raw material and special people, that is, people for whom, by means of their high position, the law has not been written; on the contrary, these people themselves create the law for others, for the raw material, the rabble. Well, it's not bad as a little theory; *une théorie comme une autre.** Napoleon enthralled him immensely, that is to say, he was fascinated that so very many men of genius didn't pay any attention to a single evil act, but advanced over them, without even thinking. Apparently, he also imagined himself to be a man of genius—that is, he was convinced of it for some time. He suffered a great deal and even now suffers from the thought that he was able to devise a theory but was incapable of stepping over obstacles without thinking; therefore, he was not a man of genius. Well, and for a young man with such self-esteem, this was humiliating, especially in our day . . ."

---

* "A theory like any other" (French).

"And pangs of conscience? Are you therefore denying him any moral feeling? Could he really be like that?"

"Ah, Avdotya Romanovna, these days everything's all mixed up; however, it was never in especially good order. Russians in general are broad-minded people, Avdotya Romanovna, broad as their land, and particularly disposed to the fantastic and the chaotic; but it's a misfortune to be broad without being a special genius. Do you recall how you and I spoke privately on this subject, sitting in the evenings on the terrace in the garden, each time after supper? You were constantly reproaching me precisely for this broadness. Who knows, perhaps we were talking at the very same moment he was lying here, devising his own plan. In our educated Russian society there are no sacred traditions, Avdotya Romanovna: someone may compile them from books for himself . . . or make some conclusions from the chronicles. But that's more the scholars, and you know, they're all simpletons; a man of the world would find them indecent. However, you know my opinions in general; I don't blame anyone definitively. I myself am a shirker, and I'm keeping to that. We talked about this many times. I even had the pleasure of interesting you in my opinions. . . . But you've turned very pale, Avdotya Romanovna!"

"I know his theory. I read his journal article about people to whom everything is permitted. . . . Razumikhin brought it to me . . ."

"Mr. Razumikhin? Your brother's article? In a journal? Is there such an article? I didn't know. It must be interesting! But where are you going, Avdotya Romanovna?"

"I want to see Sofiya Semyonovna," Dunechka said in a weak voice. "How do I get there? Perhaps she's returned; I definitely want to see her now. Let her . . ."

Avdotya Romanovna couldn't finish what she was saying; her breath literally failed her.

"Sofiya Semyonovna won't be back until nighttime. That's what I suppose. She should have been here by now; if not, she won't return until very late . . ."

"Ah, so you're lying! I see . . . you lied . . . you were lying all the time! I don't believe you! I don't! I don't believe you!" cried Dunechka in a genuine frenzy, completely losing her head.

Almost fainting, she fell into a chair that Svidrigaylov hastened to provide.

"Avdotya Romanovna, what's the matter? Come to your senses! Here's some water. Take a sip . . ."

He sprinkled her with water. Dunechka shuddered and came to herself.

"That had a powerful effect on her!" Svidrigaylov muttered to himself, frowning. "Avdotya Romanovna, calm yourself! You should know that he has friends. We'll save him, we'll rescue him. If you like, I'll take him abroad. I have money; I can get a ticket in three days. And as for the fact that he committed murder, he can still perform many good deeds, so that all that will be wiped away; calm yourself. He can still become a great man. Well, what's the matter? How do you feel now?"

"You evil man! You're still mocking me. Let me go . . ."

"Where to? Where are you going?"

"To him. Where is he? Do you know? Why is that door locked? We entered through that door, and now it's locked with a key. When did you manage to lock it?"

"We didn't want to shout what we were talking about for everyone to hear. I'm not mocking you; I was simply fed up with talking like that. Where will you go in such a state? Do you want to give him away? You'll drive him to madness and he'll betray himself. You should know they're following him; they're on his trail. You'll betray him. Wait a bit: I just saw him and spoke to him; he can still be saved. Wait a bit, sit down; we'll think together. That's why I invited you, so we could speak privately and consider it carefully. Sit down!"

"How can you save him? Is it really possible?"

Dunya sat down. Svidrigaylov sat next to her.

"It all depends on you, on you, on you alone," he began with flashing eyes, almost in a whisper, losing the thread, even failing to utter some words because of his excitement.

Dunya recoiled from him in fear. He was also trembling all over.

"You . . . one word from you and he's saved! I'll . . . I'll save him. I have money and friends. I'll send him away immediately and I'll get a passport, two of them. One for him and the other for me. I have friends; I know useful people. . . . Would you like that? I can get you a passport, too . . . and one for your mother . . . what do you need Razu-mikhin for? I love you, too. I love you without limit. Let me kiss the hem of your dress, let me, please! I can't bear listening to it rustle. Just tell me: do this and I'll do it! I'll do everything. I'll do the impossible. Whatever you believe, I'll believe in, too. I'll do everything, every-thing! Don't look, don't look at me like that! You know that you're killing me . . ."

He was even beginning to rave. Something suddenly happened to him, as though some thought had struck him. Dunya jumped up and rushed toward the door.

"Open it! Open it!" she cried through the door, calling to anyone who could hear; she shook the door with her hands. "Open up! Isn't anyone there?"

Svidrigaylov stood up and recovered his senses. A malicious and mocking smile slowly formed on his still trembling lips.

"No one's home out there," he said softly and unhurriedly. "The landlady's gone out, and it's no use shouting like that: you're merely upsetting yourself in vain."

"Where's the key? Open the door at once, right now, you vile man!"

"I lost the key and can't find it."

"Ah! So you're going to use force, are you?" cried Dunya; she turned deathly pale and rushed to the corner of the room, where she quickly shielded herself with the little table that was there. She wasn't shout-ing; but she stared at her tormentor and followed his every move care-fully. Svidrigaylov didn't budge from his place, either, and stood facing her at the other end of the room. He even managed to gain control of himself, at least outwardly. But his face was as pale as before. A mock-ing smile still played on his lips.

"You just said the word 'force,' Avdotya Romanovna. If there's to be force, you know yourself that I've taken appropriate measures. Sofiya Semyonovna's not home; it's a very long way to the Kapernaumovs, five locked rooms. Last of all, I'm at least twice as strong as you are. Besides, I have nothing to fear because it's impossible for you to make a complaint afterward: you really won't want to give your brother away, will you? In addition, no one will believe you: for what reason would a young woman visit a single man in his apartment all alone? So, even if you sacrifice your brother, you won't be able to prove a thing; force is very hard to prove, Avdotya Romanovna."

"You scoundrel!" whispered Dunya irately.

"As you like, but note that I was speaking only in the form of a proposal. In my personal opinion, you're absolutely correct: force is an abomination. I was saying only that your conscience would be completely clear if you even . . . if you even wished to save your brother voluntarily, as I'm suggesting to you. It means that you simply submitted to circumstances, well, even to force, if in the last analysis we can't avoid that word. Think about it; the fates of your brother and your mother are in your hands. I'll be your slave . . . all my life. . . . I'll sit and wait right here . . ."

Svidrigaylov sat down on the sofa, about eight paces away from Dunya. She had not the least doubt about his unshakable determination. Besides, she knew him . . .

All of a sudden she pulled a revolver from her pocket, cocked it, and rested her hand with the gun on the little table. Svidrigaylov jumped up from his place.

"Aha! So that's how it is!" he cried in astonishment, but he kept smiling maliciously. "Well, that changes things completely! You're making things much easier for me, Avdotya Romanovna! Where did you get that revolver? Was it from Mr. Razumikhin? Bah! But it's my own gun! An old friend! I was looking for it at the time! I see that our shooting lessons in the country, which I had the honor of giving you, were not wasted."

"It's not your revolver, but Marfa Petrovna's, whom you killed, you villain! You didn't have any possessions of your own in her house. I took it when I started to suspect what you were capable of. If you dare take even one step forward, I swear, I'll kill you!"

Dunya was in a frenzy. She held the gun ready.

"Well, and your brother? I'm asking out of interest," said Svidrigaylov, remaining where he stood.

"Denounce him, if you like! Don't move! Don't budge! I'll shoot! You poisoned your wife, I know, you're a murderer yourself!"

"Are you so firmly convinced that I poisoned Marfa Petrovna?"

"It was you! You yourself hinted at it to me; you talked about poison . . . I know, you went to fetch some . . . you had it prepared. . . . It was definitely you . . . you scoundrel!"

"Even if that were true, it would have been because of you . . . you still would have been the reason for it."

"You're lying! I've always hated you, always . . ."

"Hey, Avdotya Romanovna! You seem to have forgotten how in the heat of the moment you softened toward me and became excited. . . . I saw it in your lovely eyes; don't you remember the evening, the moonlight, the nightingale's singing?"

"You're lying!" Dunya's eyes shone with fury. "You're lying, you slanderer!"

"I'm lying? Well, perhaps I am. I lied. It's not a good idea to remind women about such little things." He grinned. "I know you'll shoot, you lovely little beast. Well, go on, shoot!"

Dunya raised the revolver and, looking deathly pale, her lower lip blanched and trembling, regarded him with her large black eyes flashing like fire; she was determined, measuring the distance between them, and awaiting the first move on his part. He'd never before seen her look so magnificent. The fire flashing in her eyes as she raised the gun seemed to set him on fire, and his heart contracted in pain. He took a step forward, and a shot rang out. The bullet grazed his head and hit the wall behind him. He paused and laughed softly:

"The wasp has stung! She's aiming right for the head. . . . What's this? Blood!" He took out his handkerchief to wipe away the blood that was flowing in a thin stream along his right temple; most likely, the bullet had grazed the skin of his skull. Dunya lowered the revolver and looked at Svidrigaylov not exactly in fear, but in some sort of wild bewilderment. She herself seemed not to understand what she had done and what was happening.

"Well then, you missed! Shoot again, I'm waiting," Svidrigaylov said quietly, still grinning, but somehow glumly. "Otherwise I shall manage to grab you before you can cock the gun!"

Dunechka shuddered, quickly cocked the revolver, and raised it once again.

"Leave me alone!" she cried in despair. "I swear, I'll shoot again. . . . I'll . . . kill you!"

"Well then . . . it's impossible not to kill me at three paces. But if you don't kill me . . . then . . ." His eyes were gleaming, and he took two more steps forward.

Dunechka pulled the trigger, but the gun misfired.

"You didn't load it properly. Never mind! You still have another percussion cap. Fix it; I'll wait."

He stood there in front of her, some two paces away, waiting and regarding her with a wild determination reflected in his passionately inflamed, painful gaze. Dunya realized that he would sooner die than let her go. And . . . and, she would certainly kill him now, at a distance of two paces!

All of a sudden, she threw the revolver aside.

"She's given up!" Svidrigaylov said in surprise and took a deep breath. Some burden seemed to have been lifted at once from his heart; perhaps it wasn't merely the fear of death; it's doubtful he felt it at that moment. This was relief from another, more somber and gloomy feeling, one he himself was unable to define in all its force.

He went up to Dunya and quietly put his arm around her waist. She did not resist; trembling like a leaf, she looked at him with imploring eyes. He was about to say something, but his lips merely curled and he was unable to speak.

"Let me go!" Dunya said, entreating him. Svidrigaylov shuddered: her words were spoken in a much more intimate way than previously.

"So, you don't love me?" he asked softly.

Dunya shook her head no.

"And . . . you can't? Not ever?" he whispered in despair.

"Never!" Dunya whispered.

A moment of terrible, mute struggle transpired in Svidrigaylov's soul. He looked at her with an indescribable expression. Suddenly he removed his arm, turned away, walked rapidly to the window, and stood in front of it.

A moment of silence passed.

"Here's the key!" He took it out of the left pocket of his coat and placed it behind himself on the table, without turning around to look at Dunya. "Take it; leave immediately!"

He stared steadfastly at the window.

Dunya went up to the table to take the key.

"Hurry! Hurry!" repeated Svidrigaylov, still without moving or turning around. But that word clearly contained some sort of terrible sound.

Dunya understood it, grabbed the key, rushed to the door, unlocked it swiftly, and dashed out of the room. A minute later, beside herself, like a madwoman, she ran toward the canal and headed in the direction of the Voznesensky Bridge.

Svidrigaylov stood at the window for another few minutes; at last he turned slowly, looked around, and quietly passed his palm over his forehead. A strange smile distorted his face, a pitiful, sad, weak smile, one of desperation. The blood, which was almost dry, was smeared on his hand; he looked at it sullenly; then he soaked a towel in water and wiped his temple. The revolver Dunya had thrown away, hurling at the door, suddenly caught his eye. He picked it up and examined it. It was a small, old-fashioned pocket revolver with three chambers; there were still two charges and one percussion cap left. It could be fired once more. He thought a bit, stuffed the gun in his pocket, took his hat, and left.

VI

All that evening he spent wandering among various taverns and foul places, moving from one to another. Katya even turned up again somewhere, and she sang another of her servants' songs about someone who was "a scoundrel and a tyrant" and "began to kiss Katya."

Svidrigaylov provided drinks for her, for the organ grinder, the singers, and two clerks. He associated with these clerks precisely because they both had crooked noses: one's nose turned sharply to the right, while the other's turned to the left. This circumstance struck Svidrigaylov as significant. They finally lured him into some sort of pleasure garden, where he paid for their drinks and their entrance fees. One thin three-year-old fir tree and three bushes stood in this garden. In addition, a "Vauxhall"* had been built, in reality a tavern, but there one could also order tea; moreover, there were several green tables and chairs. A chorus of some poor singers and some drunken Munich German clown with a red nose, who was extremely morose, entertained the public. The two clerks quarreled with some other clerks and almost came to blows. Svidrigaylov was chosen by them to be the judge. He tried to resolve the dispute for a quarter of an hour, but they were shouting so loudly that there was no possibility of understanding anything. The most likely explanation was that one of them had

* Named for a famous London entertainment garden.

stolen something and had even managed to sell it to some Yid who'd happened to turn up; but, having sold it, he didn't want to share the proceeds with his fellow clerks. It turned out, at last, that the item he'd sold was a teaspoon belonging to the Vauxhall. The item was missed in the Vauxhall, and the affair began to take on a troublesome aspect. Svidrigaylov paid for the spoon, stood up, and left the garden. It was around ten o'clock. He himself had not had even one drop to drink all this time and had merely ordered tea in the Vauxhall, and that he'd done more for the sake of appearances. Meanwhile, the evening was stuffy and gloomy. By ten o'clock heavy clouds had amassed on all sides; there was thunder, and rain pelted down like a waterfall. Water cascaded onto the ground not in drops, but in entire streams. Lightning flashed continually; once he could count to five while the flashes lasted. Drenched to the skin, Svidrigaylov made his way back home, where he locked the door, opened his bureau, took out all of his cash, and tore up several papers. Then, after stashing the money in his pocket, he wanted to change his clothes, but, glancing at the window and hearing the storm and the rain, he waved his arm dismissively, took his hat, and left, without locking his apartment. He went right to Sonya's room. She was at home.

She was not alone but was surrounded by Kapernaumov's four little children. Sofiya Semyonovna was serving them tea. She greeted Svidrigaylov silently and politely, glanced at his soaking wet clothes with astonishment, but didn't say a word. The children all ran away in indescribable fear.

Svidrigaylov sat down at the table and asked Sonya to take a seat next to him. She timidly prepared herself to listen to him.

"Sofiya Semyonovna," he said, "I may be going away to America, and therefore we're most likely seeing each other for the last time, so I've come to make some arrangements. Well, did you see that lady today? I know what she said to you, so there's no need to retell it." (Sonya was about to make some movement and began blushing.) "These people have a certain way of thinking. As far as your sisters and your brother are concerned, they really are provided for, and I have transferred the money due for each of them into reliable hands and have receipts for it. Here, take them. Well, now that's done. Here are three five percent notes, worth three thousand rubles in all. Take this for yourself, strictly for yourself, and let this remain between the two of us, so that no one else knows, no matter what you hear later. You'll have need for them because, Sofiya Semyonovna, to live as you were before is unseemly; now you'll have no need to do so."

"I'm so grateful to you, sir, and these orphans, sir, and my late mother," Sonya said hurriedly. "If I haven't thanked you properly before, then . . . don't think that . . ."

"Enough. That's enough."

"I'm very grateful for this money, Arkady Ivanovich, but I have no need for it now. I have only myself to feed; don't think me ungrateful: if you're so generous, sir, then take this money and . . ."

"It's for you, for you, Sofiya Semyonovna, and please, without further conversation, because I have no time for it. And you'll need it. Rodion Romanovich has two paths open to him: either a bullet in his brain or Siberia." Sonya looked at him wildly and began trembling. "Don't be upset. I know everything, from him, and I'm not a blabbermouth; I won't tell a soul. You gave him good advice before, when you told him to go to the police and confess. That would be much more beneficial for him. Well, if it's Siberia—he'll go and I suppose that you'll follow him. Is that the case? Is it? Well, if so, that means you'll have need of money. You'll need it for him, do you understand? Giving it to you is the same as giving it to him. Besides which, you just promised to pay your debt to Amaliya Ivanovna; I heard you. Why do you, Sofiya Semyonovna, assume all these contracts and debts so thoughtlessly? It was Katerina Ivanovna who owed money to that German woman, not you; you ought not to give a damn about her. That's not the way to go on living in this world. Well then, if someone should ever ask you—say, tomorrow or the day after—about me or concerning me (and they will ask), don't mention the fact that I've come to see you now and don't say anything to anyone or show anyone the money I've given you. Well, now it's good-bye." He stood up from the chair. "My regards to Rodion Romanych. By the way: keep the money with Mr. Razumikhin until it's time. Do you know Mr. Razumikhin? Of course you do. He's not a bad fellow. Take it to him tomorrow or . . . when the time comes. And until then, stash it away."

Sonya also jumped up from her chair and regarded him with fear. She very much wanted to say something, but at first she didn't dare and didn't even know how to begin.

"How can you . . . how can you go out now in such heavy rain?"

"Well, I plan to go to America, so how can I be afraid of a little rain? Hee, hee! Farewell, my dear, Sofiya Semyonovna! May you live a long, long time; you'll be needed by others. By the way . . . tell Mr. Razumikhin that I send him my regards. Tell him just like that: say that Arkady Ivanovich sends him regards. Don't forget."

He went out, leaving Sonya in astonishment, in fear, and in a state of vague and painful suspicion.

It turned out that around twelve o'clock that same evening he made one more extremely eccentric and unexpected visit. The rain still hadn't ended. Soaked to the skin, at twenty minutes past eleven he called at the crowded apartment of his fiancée's parents on Vasilievsky Island, at the corner of Malyi Prospect and the Third Line. He knocked at the door for a long time, until they opened it, and at first created a great deal of commotion; but Arkady Ivanovich, when he wanted to be, was a man of extremely charming manners, so that the sensible surmise of his fiancée's parents—namely, that Arkady Ivanovich, most likely, had gotten so drunk somewhere that he didn't even know what he was doing—was easily dispelled. The tenderhearted and sensible mother of Arkady Ivanovich's fiancée pushed her husband's wheelchair out to him, and, as was her custom, immediately began with some remote questions. (This woman never asked direct questions, but always began first with smiles and hand rubbing, and then, if she needed to find out something for sure—for example, when might it suit Arkady Ivanovich to set the date for the wedding—she would begin with the most peculiar and almost excited questions about Paris and local court life, and only then would she get to the Third Line of Vasilievsky Island.) At any other time, of course, all of this would inspire much respect, but this time Arkady Ivanovich seemed to be particularly impatient and emphatically wanted to see his fiancée, even though they had informed him earlier that she had already gone to bed. Naturally, his fiancée appeared. Arkady Ivanovich told her directly that he was obliged to leave Petersburg for an extremely important reason, and therefore he had brought her fifteen thousand silver rubles, in bills of various denominations, asking her to accept them from him in the form of a gift, since he had long been planning to give her this trifling sum before their wedding. The particular logical connection of this gift with his imminent departure and the urgent necessity of coming at midnight in the rain, of course, was not at all apparent from this explanation; however, the whole affair proceeded extremely smoothly. Even the inevitable exclamations and sighs, interrogations and astonishment, suddenly were all unusually moderate and restrained; on the other hand, the most enthusiastic gratitude was expressed and even accompanied with tears by the fiancée's most sensible mother. Arkady Ivanovich stood up, began laughing, kissed his fiancée, patted her cheek, and assured her that he would return soon; having observed in her eyes some childish curiosity, combined with a very serious, unspoken question, he thought for a bit, kissed her a second time, and sincerely felt some annoyance in his soul that his gift would immediately be locked away for safekeeping by this most sensible of mothers. He went out, leaving everyone in an unusually excited state. But the tenderhearted mama immediately began in a low voice and rapid speech to resolve certain important quandaries, namely, that Arkady Ivanovich was an important man, a man of affairs and connections, a wealthy man—God knows what he had in mind; he might up and leave, might give away money, and, therefore, there was no reason to be surprised. Of course, it was strange that he was so wet, but Englishmen, for example, are even more eccentric, and all these smart types don't care what others say about them and don't stand on ceremony. Perhaps he'd even come like that on purpose, to show that he wasn't afraid of anyone. The main thing was, not to say a word about this to anyone, because God knows what would come of it, and to lock the money away at once, and, of course, the best thing of all was that Fedosya was still in the kitchen, and the primary thing was that nothing, nothing, not one thing should be communicated to that rascal Resslikh, and so on and so forth. They sat there and whispered until around two o'clock in the morning. The fiancée, however, had gone to bed much earlier, in a state of surprise and somewhat glum.

Meanwhile, at the stroke of midnight, Svidrigaylov crossed the

Tuchkov Bridge in the direction of the Petersburg Side. The rain had stopped, but the wind was still blowing. He began shivering and for a minute regarded the black water of the Little Neva with particular curiosity and even with a question in mind. But soon he felt very cold standing above the water; he turned and set off on Bolshoi Prospect. He walked along the endless prospect for a long time, almost half an hour, stumbling more than once in the darkness on the wooden sidewalk, but he didn't cease searching for something along the right side of the prospect. Somewhere there, almost at the end of the prospect, he noticed, recently having passed by, a large wooden hotel, the name of which, as best he recalled, was something like the Adrianople. He was not mistaken in his recollections: this out-of-the-way hotel was so conspicuous that it was impossible to miss even in the darkness. It was a long dark wooden building in which, in spite of the late hour, lights were still burning and there were certain signs of life. He went in and asked the ragged fellow who met him in the corridor for a room. This fellow looked Svidrigaylov over, roused himself, and at once showed him to a remote room, stuffy and cramped, somewhere at the far end of the corridor, in the corner under the staircase. But there was no other vacant room; all the others were occupied. The ragged fellow regarded him inquiringly.

"Would you have some tea?" asked Svidrigaylov.

"It's possible, sir."

"What else is there?"

"Veal, sir, vodka, sir, and hors d'oeuvres, sir."

"Bring me some veal and some tea."

"Do you need anything else?" the fellow asked in some bewilderment.

"Nothing, nothing."

The ragged fellow left, thoroughly disappointed.

"What a splendid place," thought Svidrigaylov. "How is it that I didn't know that? I, too, must have the look of someone returning from a *café chantant* who's had some adventures along the way. I'm curious, however, about who spends the night here."

He lit the candle and examined his room more carefully. It was a tiny room, so small that it was barely tall enough for Svidrigaylov; it had one window; the bed was very dirty; a simple painted table and chair occupied almost the entire space. The walls looked as if they had been roughly assembled from boards and were covered with worn-out wallpaper, so dusty and torn that although one could still guess its color (yellow), it was no longer possible to make out the pattern. One part of the wall and the ceiling was cut away at an oblique angle, as if in an attic, but a staircase was located above this slope. Svidrigaylov set down the candle, sat on the bed, and fell into thought. But a strange and uninterrupted whispering in the next room, sometimes rising almost to shouting, at last attracted his attention. This whispering hadn't ceased from the moment he had entered his room. He began listening: someone was cursing and imploring the other person in tears, but only one voice could be heard. Svidrigaylov stood up, shaded the candle with his hand, and saw that light was shining through a crack in the wall; he approached it and began to watch. In the next room, somewhat larger than his own, there were two guests. One of them was not wearing a jacket, had extremely curly hair, and a red, inflamed face; he was standing in an oratorical pose, his legs spread wide to maintain his balance; beating his chest, he reproached the other in emotional terms about the fact that he was poor and didn't possess any rank, that he had dragged him out of the gutter, that when he wanted to, he could drive him away, and that only the finger of God saw everything. The person being reproached was sitting on a chair and had the look of a man who very much wanted to sneeze but was unable to do so. From time to time, with a sheepish and vague look, he glanced at the speaker but, obviously, didn't have any idea what he was talking about, and it was doubtful that he even heard him. A candle was burning down on the table; there was an almost empty decanter of vodka, some goblets, bread, glasses, cucumbers, and dishes from tea that had been consumed a long time ago. Having examined the scene attentively, Svidrigaylov moved away from the crack apathetically and sat down on the bed.

The ragged fellow, who had returned with the veal and tea, couldn't refrain from asking once more, "Do you need anything else?" After receiving a negative reply, he finally departed. Svidrigaylov pounced on the tea to warm himself up; he drank a glass, but as a result of his loss of appetite, he couldn't eat even one bite of the veal. Apparently he was beginning to feel feverish. He took off his coat and jacket, wrapped himself up in a blanket, and lay down on the bed. He felt annoyed: "It would be better to be healthy at this time," he thought and smiled to himself. It was stuffy in the room, the candle was burning dimly, the wind was howling outside, and somewhere in the corner a mouse was scratching; in fact the whole room smelled of mice and some kind of leather. He lay there and seemed to be daydreaming: one idea was replaced by another; he would very much have liked to fix his imagination on something in particular. "Under this window there must be some sort of garden," he thought. "The trees are rustling; I really don't like the sound of trees at night, in a storm, in the darkness; what a nasty feeling!" He recalled how he had just passed Petrovsky Park, and even thought about it with revulsion. In the process, he also remembered the Tuchkov Bridge, the Little Neva, and he felt cold again, as he had before when he was standing above the water. "I've never in my life loved water, even in landscape paintings," he thought again and suddenly smiled at one strange thought: "I mean, all those questions of aesthetics and comfort shouldn't matter to me now, yet I'm as fussy as a wild animal choosing a place for himself . . . in a similar situation. I should have gone into Petrovsky Park! I guess I thought it seemed too dark or too cold, hee-hee! As if I needed pleasant sensations! By the way, why don't I snuff the candle?" He blew it out. "They've gone to bed next door," he thought, no longer seeing light through the crack. "Now, Marfa Petrovna, it would be a good time to pay me a visit; it's dark, the place is fitting, and the time would be original. But, of course, it's now that you won't come . . ."

Suddenly, for some reason he recalled, as he had earlier, an hour before he'd carried out his plan for Dunechka, that he had advised Raskolnikov to entrust her well-being to Razumikhin. "As a matter of fact, I probably said that more for my own zeal, as Raskolnikov had guessed. That Raskolnikov's a rascal! He's experienced a lot of trouble in his life. He may eventually become a proper rascal in time, when that nonsense has vanished, but now he's *too* eager to live! Concerning this point, such people are rascals. Well, the hell with him; let him do as he likes; what's it to me?"

He couldn't sleep. Gradually the previous image of Dunechka began to appear before him; all of a sudden a tremor passed through his whole body. "No, I have to cast that aside," he thought, coming back to his senses. "I must think about something else. It was strange and amusing: I've never felt great hatred for anybody, never even wished to take revenge, but that's a bad sign, a bad sign! I didn't like arguing and didn't lose my temper—another bad sign! And I promised her so much then—the hell with it! But she might have remade me somehow . . ." He fell silent again and clenched his teeth: once more the image of Dunechka appeared before him, exactly as she had been when, after she'd fired the gun for the first time, she'd been terribly frightened. She had lowered her revolver and, completely stunned, looked at him; he could have grabbed her twice over—she wouldn't have raised her arms in her defense if he hadn't reminded her himself. He recalled how at that moment he had begun to feel sorry for her, as if his heart had contracted. . . . "Hey! Damn it all! Those thoughts again; I have to cast all this aside, I do!"

He was starting to doze off; his feverish trembling had subsided; suddenly something seemed to be running underneath the blanket along his arm and his leg. He shuddered. "Damn it all! I bet it's a mouse!" he thought. "All because I left the veal on the table . . ." He had no desire to unwrap himself, get up, feel cold, but once again something unpleasant suddenly came and rubbed against his leg; he tore off his blanket and lit the candle. Trembling with a feverish chill, he bent over to examine the bed—there was nothing there. He shook out the blanket and suddenly a mouse scampered onto the sheet. He tried to catch it, but the mouse didn't jump off the bed; it darted back and forth in zigzags, slipped out of his fingers, ran across his hand, and suddenly plunged underneath the pillow; he threw the pillow down, but felt at once that something jumped onto his chest and was running across his body, down his back, under his shirt. He began trembling nervously and awoke. It was dark in the room; he lay on the bed, wrapped up in the blanket as before, and the wind howled outside the window. "What filth!" he thought with annoyance.

He got up and sat on the edge of the bed, his back to the window. "It's better not to sleep at all," he decided. However, the cold and the damp were coming in through the window; without moving from his place, he pulled the blanket over and wrapped himself in it. He didn't light the candle. He wasn't thinking about anything and didn't want to think; but images arose, one after another, disconnected fragments of thoughts flashed by without beginning or ending. It was as if he had fallen into a state of semi-drowsiness. The cold, the dark, the damp, the wind howling under the window and shaking the trees aroused in him some sort of stubborn fantastic inclination and desire—but he kept on seeing flowers. He imagined a charming landscape; it was a bright, warm, almost hot day, a holiday—Whitsunday. There was a rich, luxurious country cottage in the English style, completely over-grown with fragrant flowerbeds, surrounded by flowery borders cir-cling the house; the porch was entwined with climbing plants and surrounded by beds of roses; there was a light, cool staircase, covered with a luxurious carpet and banked with rare flowers in Chinese vases. He noticed particularly the bouquets of delicate white narcissis in vases filled with water on the windowsills; the flowers were leaning on their bright green, long, thick stems, emitting a strong aromatic fragrance. He didn't want to leave them, but he climbed the staircase and entered a large, high room, and once again there were flowers everywhere—on the windowsills, near the doors opening onto the terrace, and on the terrace itself. The floors were strewn with freshly cut grass, the win-dows were open, and a fresh, light, cool breeze was blowing into the room; the birds were chirping under the windows, and in the middle of the room, on tables covered with white satin shrouds, there stood a coffin. This coffin was lined with white silk and bordered with a thick white frill. Wreaths of flowers surrounded it on all sides. A young girl was lying amidst the flowers; she was wearing a white tulle dress; her hands were folded and pressed against her breast—as if they were chis-eled out of marble. But her loosened hair, her fair blond hair, was wet; a garland of roses was on her head. The stern and already fixed profile of her face also seemed to have been chiseled out of marble, but the smile on her pale lips was full of some unchildlike, infinite grief and great pain. Svidrigaylov knew this girl; there was no icon and no lit candle near the coffin, and no prayers could be heard. This girl was a suicide by drowning. She was only fourteen, but her heart had been broken and had destroyed itself, ashamed of the insult that had so horrified and amazed this young childish consciousness, had overwhelmed her angelic pure soul with undeserved shame, and had torn from her a last cry of despair, unregarded, but boldly shrieked into the dark night, into the blackness, the cold, damp thaw, when the wind was howling . . .

Svidrigaylov woke up, stood up from the bed, and strode over to the window. He found the bolt by feel and opened the window. The wind rushed violently into his cramped little room and clung to his face as if with cold hoarfrost, and to his chest, covered only by a shirt. Under the window there really was some kind of garden, a pleasure garden, it seemed; most likely during the daytime musicians sang there and tea was served on the little tables. Now splashes of rain flew in the window from the trees and bushes; it was dark as a cellar, so that one could barely make out objects as vague dark spots. Svidrigaylov, leaning out and resting his elbows on the windowsill, stared into this gloom for five minutes or so, without tearing himself away. Amidst the darkness and night there came the sound of a cannon shot, and then another.

"Ah, the signal! The water's rising," he thought. "By morning, in the low-lying parts of town, water will pour onto the streets, flooding basements and cellars; the sewer rats will emerge, and amidst the rain and wind, people, soaking wet and cursing, will begin hauling their stuff up to the higher floors. . . . But what time is it now?" And just as he wondered about this, somewhere nearby, the soft sound of a wall clock, seeming to rush ahead, struck the hour of three. "Hey, it'll start getting light in an hour! Why wait? I'll head out now, to Petrovsky Park: somewhere in there I'll choose a large bush, dripping with rain, such that if I touch it at all with my shoulder, millions of drops will splash down on my head . . ." He left the window, locked it, lit the candle, pulled on his jacket and coat, put on his hat, and walked out, carrying his candle, into the corridor to find the ragged fellow, asleep somewhere in a room among all sorts of trash and discarded candle ends, pay him for the room, and leave the hotel. "This is the best time; I couldn't pick a better one!"

He walked for a long time down the long, narrow corridor without finding anyone; he was about to shout when suddenly, in a dark corner, between an old wardrobe and the door, he discerned some strange object, something that seemed alive. He leaned over with his candle and noticed that it was a child—a little girl aged five, no more, in a soaking-wet dress, damp as a dishrag, shivering and crying. She seemed not to be afraid of Svidrigaylov, but looked at him with dull wonder from her large black eyes; from time to time she burst into sobs, like a child who has been crying for a long while but has already stopped and even been consoled, but not quite, and then suddenly bursts into sobs again. The little girl's face was pale and exhausted; she was numb from the cold. "But how did she get here? She must have hidden here and not slept the whole night." He began to question her; the girl came to life and very quickly began to babble something to him in her childish language. There was something about "Mommy" and "how Mommy will be angry," and about some cup that was broken. The little girl talked on without stopping; somehow he was able to figure out that she was an unloved child whose mother was a cook and was constantly drunk; she probably worked in that very hotel and was in the habit of frightening and beating the child; the girl had broken a cup belonging to her mother and was so scared that she had run away that very evening; she had probably hidden for a long time in the courtyard in the pouring rain; finally, she had crept in here, hidden behind the wardrobe, and sat there in the corner the whole night—crying, trembling from the damp, the darkness, and from the fear that she would receive a beating for all of this. He picked her up, carried her into his room, sat her on the bed, and began to undress her. The worn shoes on her bare feet were as wet as if she had sat in a puddle the whole night. After undressing her, he put her to bed, covered her, and wrapped her from head to foot in a blanket. She fell asleep immediately. When he finished all this, he relapsed into gloomy thoughts once again.

"Now I've gone and gotten myself all involved!" he thought suddenly with a painful, malicious feeling. "What nonsense!" He picked up his candle in annoyance to go out and find that ragged fellow, no matter what, and get out of there as soon as possible. "Oh, the little girl!" he thought swearing an oath; just as he was opening the door, he returned to take another look at her, to see whether or not she was asleep. He lifted the blanket carefully. The little girl was sleeping soundly and peacefully. She had gotten warm under the blanket, and the color had already returned to her pale cheeks. But a strange thing happened: this color seemed to be brighter and stronger than the ordinary rosiness of childhood. "It's a feverish blush," Svidrigaylov thought, but it was more like a flush from wine, as if she'd been given a whole glass to drink. Her scarlet lips were aglow, burning or what? It suddenly seemed to him that her long black eyelashes were fluttering and winking, as if they were about to open, and from under them looked a sly, sharp, somehow unchildlike eye, as if the little girl were not asleep, and only pretending. Yes, indeed, it was so: her lips were parting into a smile; the ends of her lips were quivering, as if still restrained. But now she stopped restraining herself; now it was laughter, palpable laughter; something impudent and inviting shone forth in her very unchildlike face; it was corruption, the face of a courtesan, the impudent face of a mercenary French harlot. Now she was no longer hiding; both her eyes were open wide: they enveloped him with a fiery and shameless look, they beckoned him, laughing. . . . There was something infinitely disgusting and offensive in that laughter, in those eyes, in all the nastiness in the child's face. "What! A five-year-old!" whispered Svidrigaylov in genuine horror. "This . . . what on earth is this?" But now she was turning her glowing face toward him, stretching out her arms. . . . "Ah, the accursed child!" Svidrigaylov shouted in horror, raising his hand as if to strike her. . . . But at that very moment he woke up.

He was on the same bed, wrapped up as before in the same blanket; the candle was not lit; full daylight was showing through the window.

"Nightmares all night!" He raised himself up in a bad temper, feeling that he had been pummeled; his bones ached. There was a thick fog outside, and it was impossible to see through it. It was nearing six o'clock; he had overslept! He got up and put on his jacket and coat, which were still wet. Feeling for the revolver in his pocket, he pulled it out and adjusted the percussion cap; then he sat down, took his notebook out of his pocket; on the front page, in the most noticeable place, he wrote a few lines in large letters. After reading them over, he fell into thought, resting one elbow on the table. The revolver and the notebook lay there in the same place, near his elbow. Some flies, disturbed from their sleep, clustered around the untouched portion of veal still sitting on the table. He regarded them for a long time and finally began trying to catch one fly with his free right hand. For a long time he tried to grasp one but he couldn't; he was growing tired of his efforts. At last, catching himself in this interesting pastime, he came to his senses, shuddered, stood up, and resolutely left the room. A moment later, he was out on the street.

A thick, milky fog enveloped the town. Svidrigaylov went along the slippery, muddy wooden sidewalk in the direction of the Little Neva. In his mind he saw the waters of the Little Neva, Petrovsky Island, the wet paths, the wet grass, the wet trees and bushes, and, at last, that very bush. . . . With annoyance he began surveying the houses to think about something else. He didn't meet any passersby or cabs along the prospect. The bright yellow wooden houses with their closed shutters looked glum and dirty. Cold and damp penetrated his whole body, and he began to shiver. From time to time he stumbled upon signs for little shops and greengrocers, and he read each one carefully. The wooden sidewalk had ended. He was drawing even with a large stone building. A dirty mutt, trembling from the cold, ran across the road in front of him. Some sort of dead-drunk fellow in an overcoat was sprawled face-down on the pavement. He looked at him and went farther on. A tall watchtower caught his eye on the left. "Bah!" he thought. "This place will do. Why go to Petrovsky Park? At least there'll be an official witness . . ." He almost laughed at this new idea and turned into Syezhinskaya Street. There was a large building with a watchtower. Near the big locked gates of the house stood a little man, leaning his shoulder against the building; he was wrapped in a soldier's gray overcoat and was wearing a copper Achilles-like helmet. He directed his sleepy gaze coldly at the approaching Svidrigaylov. On his face was written that age-old querulous grief so sourly imprinted on the faces of all members of the Jewish tribe, without exception. Both of them, Svidrigaylov and Achilles, stood looking at each other in silence for some time. Finally it seemed to Achilles that something was amiss; here was a sober man, standing only three paces away from him, looking him right in the eye, saying nothing. "Aaa, vot do you vant here?" he said, still immobile and not altering his position.

"Not a thing, brother; hello!" replied Svidrigaylov.

"Zis izn't ze place."

"I'm going off to distant parts, brother."

"To distant parts?"

"To America."

"To America?"

Svidrigaylov pulled out his revolver and cocked the hammer. Achilles raised his eyebrows.

"Aaa, vot's zis? Zis is no place for joking!"

"Why isn't this the place?"

"It just isn't."

"Well, brother, never mind. The place is right; if they come and ask you, tell them that I up and left for—oh, America."

He put the revolver to his right temple.

"Aaa—you mustn't here. Zis is not ze place!" Achilles said with a shudder, his pupils growing wider and wider.

Svidrigaylov pulled the trigger.

VII

That same day, but toward evening, at around seven o'clock, Raskolnikov was nearing the apartment of his mother and sister—the same one in Bakaleev's house where Razumikhin had settled them. The entrance to their staircase was from the street. Raskolnikov drew near, still slowing his steps and seeming to hesitate: should he go in or not? But he wouldn't turn back on any account; the decision had already been made. "Besides, it doesn't matter; they still don't know anything," he thought, "and they're already used to thinking of me as an eccentric . . ." His attire was awful: all dirty, torn, and wrinkled, because he'd spent the previous night in the rain. His face was almost disfigured from exhaustion, inclement weather, physical fatigue, and his daylong internal struggle. He had passed the whole night alone, God knows where. But at least he had made his decision.

He knocked on the door; his mother opened it. Dunechka wasn't at home. Even the servant happened to be out at that time. At first Pulkheriya Aleksandrovna was speechless with elated surprise; then she seized his hand and dragged him into the room.

"Well, here you are!" she began, stammering from joy. "Don't be angry with me, Rodya, for greeting you so foolishly, with tears: I'm laughing, not crying. You think I'm crying? No, I'm overjoyed, but I have a silly habit: my tears flow. It's been that way since your father's death; I cry for everything. Sit down, my dear; I see that you must be tired. Ah, you're so dirty."

"I was out in the rain yesterday, Mama . . ." Raskolnikov started to say.

"No, oh, no!" cried Pulkheriya Aleksandrovna, interrupting him. "You thought I was just about to interrogate you, like a foolish old woman, but don't worry. I understand, I understand everything; now I've learned how things work around here, and I myself see that it's more sensible. Once and for all I realize that it's not for me to try to understand or demand to know your reasons. God knows what sort of ideas and plans you have in mind or what sort of thoughts you're conceiving; is it for me to pester you and ask what you're thinking about? I'm just. . . . Oh, Lord! What am I doing racing about here and there like a madwoman? I'm reading your journal article for the third time; Dmitry Prokofich brought it to me. I was so surprised when I saw it: you fool, you, I thought to myself, here's what he's been doing, here's the answer to the riddle! Perhaps he has new ideas in his head just now; he's thinking about them, while I'm tormenting and disturbing him. I read it, my dear, and, of course, I didn't understand a great deal of it; but that's how it should be; how could I understand it?"

"Show it to me, Mama."

Raskolnikov took the paper and cast a fleeting glance at his article. No matter how it contradicted his position and state of mind, he still experienced a strange, sarcastic-sweet sensation, the sort an author feels upon seeing himself in print for the first time, besides which, he was all of twenty-three years old. This lasted for only a moment. After reading through a few lines, he frowned and a terrible anguish grasped his heart. His entire spiritual struggle of the last few months came to him at once. He tossed the article onto the table with disgust and annoyance.

"But, Rodya, however foolish I may be, I can still see that very soon you'll become one of our leading figures, if not the most leading figure among all our learned men. They dared think that you were mad. Ha-ha-ha! You don't know it—but that's what they thought! Ah, what vile worms—how could they possibly understand what true intellect is? Even Dunechka almost believed them, too—imagine that! Your late father submitted work to journals twice—the first was a poem (I've saved the notebook and will show it to you sometime), and then there was a whole story (I asked him if I could recopy it for him). How we prayed that they'd publish it—but they didn't! Rodya, six or seven days ago I was distraught looking at your clothes, how you live, what you eat, and what you wear. But now I see that I was foolish once again, because if you want to, you'll achieve anything you desire with your intellect and talent. It's just that in the meantime, you don't want to and you're busy with much more important matters . . ."

"Isn't Dunya home, Mama?"

"No, Rodya. I don't see her at home very often; she leaves me all alone. Dmitry Prokofich, thanks be to him, drops in to see me and talks all about you. He loves you and respects you, my friend. I'm not saying that your sister's very disrespectful to me. I'm not complaining. She has her character, and I have mine; she has some secrets of her own; but I have no secrets from the two of you. Of course, I'm firmly convinced that Dunya's too clever, and besides, she loves both you and me . . . but I don't know where all this is leading. You've made me very happy, Rodya, by dropping in, but she missed you by taking a walk; when she returns, I'll tell her: your brother was here while you were out. And just where have you been spending your time? Rodya, don't spoil me too much: stop by if you can; if not, then there's nothing to be done about it; I'll wait. Still I'll know that you love me, and for me even that's enough. I'll read your writings, I'll hear about you from everyone else, but every once in a while you'll come to see me. What could be better? Why, you just came now to console your mother, that I can see . . ."

Here Pulkheriya Aleksandrovna suddenly burst into tears.

"There I go again! Don't mind a foolish old woman! Oh, good Lord! Why am I sitting here?" she cried, jumping up from her place. "There's coffee. I don't even offer you anything! That's an old woman's selfishness. Right away! At once!"

"Mama, there's no need. I'm going soon. That's not why I came. Please, hear me out."

Pulkheriya Aleksandrovna approached him timidly.

"Mama, no matter what happens, no matter what you hear about me, no matter what people say about me, will you go on loving me as you do now?" he asked suddenly from the fullness of his heart, as if not thinking about his words or weighing them.

"Rodya, Rodya, what's the matter? How can you even ask about that? Who will say something about you? I won't believe anyone, no matter who comes to see me; I'll simply drive him away."

"I've come to assure you that I've always loved you, and now I'm glad that we're alone, even glad that Dunya's not here," he continued with the same burst of feeling. "I've come to tell you plainly that even though you'll be unhappy, you should still know that your son loves you now more than himself and that everything you thought about me, that I'm cruel and don't love you, all of that is false. I will never stop loving you. . . . That's all; it seemed to me that this is what I had to do and what I had to start with . . ."

Pulkheriya Aleksandrovna embraced him silently, pressing him to her chest and weeping softly.

"What's the matter, Rodya, I don't know," she said at last. "All this time I thought you were fed up with us, but now I see from everything that a great misfortune is in store for you, which is why you're so upset. I've known this for a long time, Rodya. Forgive me that I began speaking of it; I think about it all the time, and I can't sleep at night. All last night your sister was talking in her sleep and kept mentioning you. I heard something, but couldn't understand it. I walked around this morning as if before an execution, waiting for something, full of foreboding, and now it's come to pass. Rodya, Rodya, where are you off to? Are you going somewhere?"

"I am."

"I thought so! But I could go with you, if you need me to. And Dunya; she loves you, she loves you very much, and Sofiya Semyonovna, she could also go with us, if necessary; you see, I'm even willing to accept her as a daughter. Dmitry Prokofich will help us prepare for the journey . . . but . . . where . . . are you going?"

"Farewell, Mama."

"What? Today?" she cried, as if losing him forever.

"I can't stay; it's time; I must go . . ."

"Can't I go with you?"

"No. Kneel down and pray to God for me. Your prayer, perhaps, will be heard."

"Let me make the sign of the cross over you, let me give you my blessing! That's it, that's it. Oh, God, what are we doing?"

Yes, he was glad, he was very glad that no one was there, that he was all alone with his mother. It was as if during all this horrible time his heart had suddenly softened. He fell down before her, kissed her feet, and after embracing, both of them wept. She was not surprised and did not ask any more questions at this time. For some time she had understood that something horrible was happening to her son, and she saw that now some sort of terrible moment for him had arrived.

"Rodya, my dear, my firstborn," she said, sobbing, "now you're just the same as you were when you were little; you would come to me like this, embrace me and kiss me like this; when your father was still alive and we were living in poverty, you consoled us by being there with us; and when I buried your father—we cried at his grave so many times, embracing each other just as we are now. If I've been crying a long time, it's because my maternal heart has foreseen misfortune. As soon as I saw you the first time, back then, that evening, you recall, when we first arrived here, I guessed it from your look alone; my heart faltered then. Today, when I opened the door for you, I took one look and thought, 'Well, the fateful hour has come.' Rodya, Rodya, you're not going now, are you?"

"No."

"You'll come here again?"

"Yes . . . I will."

"Rodya, don't be angry, I won't dare to ask any more questions. I know that I won't; but say only a few words: are you going far away?"

"Very far."

"What is it? Some form of service? Is it a career for you?"

"Whatever God sends my way. . . . Only pray for me . . ."

Raskolnikov went to the door, but she grabbed hold of him and, with a desperate glance, looked him in the eye. Her face was distorted with horror.

"Enough, Mama," said Raskolnikov, regretting deeply that he had decided to come.

"It's not forever? Surely it's not forever. You'll come again. Will you come tomorrow?"

"I'll come, I will. Farewell."

At last he tore himself away.

The evening was fresh, warm, and clear; the weather had improved since morning. Raskolnikov hurried back to his apartment. He wanted to finish everything before sunset. Until then, he didn't want to meet anybody. As he climbed the stairs to his room, he noticed that Nastasya, having turned away from the samovar, was staring at him fixedly, following him with her eyes. "Is there someone in my room?" he wondered. He imagined with revulsion that it might be Porfiry. But, reaching his room and opening the door, he saw that it was Dunechka. She was sitting there all alone, in deep thought, and seemed to have been waiting for him a long time. He paused on the threshold. She got up from the sofa in alarm and stood straight before him. Her glance, fixed on his face, expressed horror and inconsolable sadness. By this gaze alone he realized at once that she knew everything.

"Well, should I come in or go away?" he asked warily.

"I've been with Sofiya Semyonovna all day; we were both waiting for you. We thought you'd definitely come."

Raskolnikov entered the room and sat down on a chair in exhaustion.

"I'm feeling somewhat weak, Dunya; I'm very tired; but now at least I'd like to regain control of myself."

He cast a guarded glance at her.

"Where were you all last night?"

"I don't remember very well; you see, sister, I wanted to decide once and for all. I walked along the Neva several times; that I recall. I wanted to end it all there, but . . . I couldn't work up the courage to do it . . ." he whispered, once again glancing warily at Dunya.

"Thank God! That's exactly what Sofiya Semyonovna and I were afraid of! That means you still believe in life; thank God, Rodya, thank God!"

Raskolnikov smiled bitterly.

"I didn't believe, yet just now I was embracing and kissing my mother; I am not a believer, yet I asked her to pray for me. God knows how that happens, Dunechka; I don't understand a thing about it."

"You went to see Mother? Did you tell her?" Dunya exclaimed in horror. "Did you really decide to tell her?"

"No, I didn't tell her . . . in words; but she understood a great deal. She heard you talking in your sleep last night. I'm certain that she already understands half of it. Perhaps I did the wrong thing by going to see her. I don't even know why I went there. I'm a vile creature, Dunya."

"A vile creature, but you're prepared to suffer! You are, aren't you?"

"I am. Right now. Yes, to avoid this shame I wanted to drown myself, Dunya; but then I thought, standing there over the water, that if I considered myself strong up to this time, let me not be afraid of the shame now," he said, hurrying on. "Is that pride, Dunya?"

"It is, Rodya."

It was as if fire had flared up in his lifeless eyes; it was as though he was pleased that he was still able to feel proud.

"Do you think, sister, that I was simply afraid of the water?" he asked with an ugly grin, glancing at her face.

"Oh, Rodya, stop it!" Dunya cried bitterly.

The silence lasted for about two minutes. He sat there with his eyes downcast, looking at the floor; Dunechka stood at the other end of the table and regarded him with suffering. All of a sudden he stood up.

"It's late; it's time. I'm going to turn myself in now. But I don't know why I'm going to do so."

Large tears were flowing down Dunya's cheeks.

"You're crying, sister, but are you able to give me your hand?"

"Did you really doubt that?"

She embraced him firmly.

"Aren't you washing away half your crime by going to accept your suffering?" she cried, squeezing him in her embrace and kissing him.

"Crime? What crime?" he exclaimed suddenly, in an abrupt fit of indignation. "That I killed a vile, malicious louse, an old moneylender, needed by no one; to murder her would pardon forty sins; she used to suck the lifeblood out of the poor, and you call that a crime? I don't think about it and don't seek to wipe it away. Everyone's pestering me on all sides, saying, 'It's a crime, a crime!' Only now do I see clearly the full absurdity of my faintheartedness, now that I have resolved to face this unnecessary shame! I'm deciding this simply on the basis of my vileness and ineptitude, and perhaps the idea of advantage to myself, as that . . . Porfiry proposed!"

"Brother, brother, what are you saying? But you shed blood!" Dunya cried in despair.

"Which everyone sheds," he replied almost frantically. "Which flows and has flowed on earth, like a waterfall, which has been poured out like champagne, and for which they crown people on the Roman Capitoline and designate them benefactors of mankind. Just look more carefully and you'll see! I myself wanted to do good for people and I'd have done hundreds, thousands of good deeds instead of this stupid thing, not even stupid, but simply clumsy, because this idea was not at all as stupid as it seems now, given my failure. . . . (Everything seems stupid in failure!) By this stupid act I merely wanted to place myself in an independent position, to take the first step, to acquire the means, and then the whole thing would have been wiped away by relatively immeasurable benefits. . . . But I, I didn't even succeed in taking the first step, because—I'm a pitiful wretch! That's all there is to it! All the same, I won't look at it through your eyes: if I had succeeded, I'd have been crowned, but now I've fallen into a trap!"

"But that's not true, not at all! Brother, what are you saying?"

"Ah! It's the form that's incorrect; it wasn't the correct aesthetic form! I definitely don't understand: why is hurling bombs at people in a proper siege more respectable? The fear of aesthetics is the first sign of weakness! Never, never did I realize this more clearly than I do now; and more than ever do I fail to understand the nature of my crime! Never, never have I been stronger and more convinced than I am now!"

His pale, exhausted face even flushed with color. But as he uttered his last exclamation, he unexpectedly met Dunya's glance; there was so much, so very much suffering in her eyes that he instinctively came to his senses. He felt that he had made these two poor women unhappy. Moreover, he was the cause of it . . .

"Dunya, my dear! If I'm to blame, forgive me (although it's impossible to forgive me if I am to blame). Farewell! Let's not argue! It's time I went, high time. Don't follow me, I implore you, I have to make a stop along the way. . . . But go now and stay with our mother. I beg you to do this! It's the last and largest request I make of you. Don't leave her for a minute; I left her in a state of alarm, which she may not be able to bear; she'll either die or lose her mind. Stay with her! Razumikhin will be with you; I told him. . . . Don't cry for me: I'll try to be both courageous and honest all my life, even though I'm a murderer. Perhaps you'll hear my name sometime. I won't disgrace you, you'll see; I'll still prove. . . . Meanwhile, good-bye," he hastened to conclude, once again having noticed a strange expression in Dunya's eyes at his last words and promises. "Why are you crying? Don't cry, don't; we're not parting forever! Ah, yes! Wait a moment; I forgot something!"

He went over to the table and picked up a thick, dusty book, opened it, and extracted a small portrait stored between its pages, a watercolor on ivory. It was a portrait of the landlady's daughter, his former fiancée who had died in a fever, that same strange young woman who had wanted to enter a nunnery. For a minute or so he stared at her expressive and sickly little face; then he kissed the portrait and handed it to Dunya.

"I talked to her a great deal *about that*, only with her," he said pensively. "I confided to her heart much of what later turned out so monstrously. Don't be upset," he said, turning to Dunya. "She didn't agree with me, just as you don't, and I'm glad that she's no longer with us. The main thing is that now everything will proceed in a new direction; everything will be split into two parts," he cried suddenly, sinking into melancholy once again. "Everything, everything; am I ready for that? Do I want that myself? They say it's necessary for my ordeal! Why, why all these meaningless ordeals? What's their purpose? Will I be better if I acknowledge then, crushed by suffering and idiocy, in old-age impotence after twenty years of exile, what I acknowledge now, and why should I continue to live? Why do I agree now to live like this? Oh, I knew that I was a wretch when I stood today above the Neva at daybreak!"

They both went out at last. It was difficult for Dunya, though she loved him! She walked away from him, but after proceeding some fifty paces, she turned around to glance at him once more. She could still see him. But when he reached the corner, he also turned around; their eyes met for the last time; after noticing that she was looking at him, he waved her away impatiently, even in annoyance, while he himself turned the corner hastily.

"I'm spiteful, I see that," he thought to himself, a moment later ashamed of his dismissive gesture to Dunya. "But why do they love me so much, if I'm not worthy of it? Oh, if I were alone and no one loved me, and if I myself never loved anyone? *None of this would have occurred!* I'm curious as to whether in the next fifteen or twenty years my soul will be resigned, whether I'll whimper reverently before people, calling myself a criminal with every word I utter. Yes, that's it, precisely! That's just why they're going to exile me now, that's what they need to do. . . . Look at all these people rushing back and forth on the street; every one of them is a scoundrel and a criminal by his very nature; even worse than that—they're idiots! And if there was an attempt to avoid exiling me, they'd all go mad from righteous indignation! Oh, how I hate them all!"

He fell to thinking deeply about how it might transpire that at last he'd humble himself before them all without any argument, humble himself by conviction! And why not? Of course, that's how it must be. Won't twenty years of uninterrupted oppression finish him off? Water wears away a stone. And why, why live after this? "Why am I going now, when I myself know that all of it will be just as it is in the books, and not any different?"

He had been posing this question to himself a hundred times since last night, and yet he kept going.

VIII

When he went to see Sonya, it was already twilight. Sonya had been waiting for him all day in horrible agitation. She and Dunya were waiting together. Dunya had come to her that morning, after recalling Svidrigaylov's words yesterday that Sonya "knows about this." We won't convey all the details of their conversation and the tears of these two women, or how close they had become. From this meeting Dunya took away at least one consolation: that her brother would not be alone. He had gone to her first, to Sonya, with his confession; in her he'd sought another person, when he'd needed to find one; she would follow after him wherever fate sent him. Dunya didn't have to ask, but she knew that this would be so. She even regarded Sonya with some sort of reverence, and at first almost embarrassed her with the reverent emotion with which she treated her. Sonya was about to burst into tears: on the other hand, she considered herself unworthy of even looking at her. Dunya's splendid image, when she had first bowed to her with such kindness and respect during their first meeting at Raskolnikov's, had remained in her soul since then as one of the most beautiful and unattainable visions of her life.

At last Dunechka couldn't endure it any longer and left Sonya to wait for her brother in his apartment; it seemed to her that he would go there first. Left alone, Sonya immediately began tormenting herself with fear at the thought that perhaps he really would commit suicide. Dunya was afraid of the same thing. But they spent the whole day trying to convince each other constantly that this couldn't possibly be; they were calmer when they were together. Now, having just parted, they both began thinking only about this possibility. Sonya recalled how Svidrigaylov had told her yesterday that Raskolnikov had only two roads before him—Siberia or. . . . In addition, she knew about his vanity, arrogance, self-esteem, and lack of faith. In despair she wondered to herself, at last, "Could it be that only his faintheartedness and fear of death could keep him alive?" Meanwhile, the sun was already setting. She stood glumly in front of the window and stared at it intently, but all she could see was one main, unwhitewashed wall of the building next door. At long last, when she had already become completely convinced of the unfortunate man's death, he entered the room.

A cry of joy burst forth from her. But, staring fixedly at his face, she suddenly blanched.

"Yes!" said Raskolnikov with a smile. "I've come for your crosses, Sonya. You yourself sent me to the crossroads; why now, when it's time for action, do you have cold feet?"

Sonya regarded him in astonishment. This tone of his seemed strange; a cold shiver ran through her body, but a moment later she guessed that his tone and these words were all put on. He was speaking to her but looking to one side, as if he wanted to avoid staring her straight in the eye.

"You see, Sonya, I decided that perhaps it'd be more advantageous this way. There's a certain circumstance. . . . Well, it'll take a long time to explain, but that doesn't matter. Do you know what really irritates me? I'm annoyed that all these stupid, boorish mugs will surround me now, stare and gape at me, ask me all their stupid questions, which I'll have to answer—they'll point at me. . . . Phew! You know, I won't go see Porfiry; I'm fed up with him. I would rather go to my friend Porokh: I'll really surprise him, produce quite the effect on him. But I must behave more calmly; lately I've become too full of bile. Do you believe it: I almost threatened my sister with my fist just now simply because she turned around to look at me for the last time. What a swine I am! That's the place I've come to! Well, so, where are the crosses?"

He seemed not to be himself. He couldn't even remain standing in the same place for a minute, couldn't focus his attention even on one object; his thoughts kept jumping ahead, one over the other; his speech was rambling; his hands trembled slightly.

Sonya quietly took two crosses out of a drawer, one cypress and the other copper; she crossed herself, made the sign of the cross over him, and hung the cypress cross on his chest.

"This, then, is a symbol that I'm taking up my cross, hee-hee! As if I've suffered very little up to now! The cypress cross, that is, represents the common people, the copper cross—that's Lizaveta's. You keep that one. Show it to me. So, was she wearing it . . . at that time? I also know two similar items, a silver cross and a little icon. At that time I tossed them back onto the old woman's chest. They're really the ones I ought to be wearing now. . . . However, I'm telling lies and forgetting about the business at hand; I'm so absentminded! You see, Sonya, I really came now to inform you, so that you know. . . . That's all there is to it. . . . That's really why I've come. (Hmm, and I thought I'd have more to say.) You yourself wanted me to go; now I'll be sitting in prison and your wish will be fulfilled; why are you crying? You, too? Stop it, enough of that; oh, how painful all of this is for me."

However, emotion had been awakened in him; looking at her, his heart contracted. "What's all this about?" he wondered. "What am I to her? Why is she crying, why is she preparing me for a journey like my mother or Dunya? She'll be like my nanny!"

"Cross yourself, pray at least once," Sonya begged in a trembling, timid voice.

"Oh, very well, if you wish it! And with a pure heart, Sonya, a pure heart . . ."

He wanted, however, to say something else.

He crossed himself several times. Sonya picked up her shawl and put it over her head. It was a green cotton shawl, probably the same one Marmeladov had mentioned back then, "the family shawl." Raskolnikov suddenly wondered about this, but didn't ask. As a matter of fact, he had already begun to feel terribly distracted and extremely agitated. This frightened him. He was suddenly struck by the fact that Sonya wanted to go with him.

"What are you doing? Where are you going? Stay here, stay here!

I'll go alone," he cried in nervous annoyance, almost with malice, and he headed for the door. "Why do I need a whole procession?" he muttered as he left.

Sonya remained in the room. He didn't even say good-bye to her; he had already forgotten her; one scathing and rebellious doubt flared up in his soul.

"Is this all right, is this the right thing to do?" he wondered once again as he descended the stairs. "Isn't it possible to stop and make it all right once again . . . and not go?"

But he proceeded nonetheless. He suddenly felt once and for all that there was no reason to pose further questions to himself. As he emerged onto the street, he recalled that he hadn't said good-bye to Sonya, and that she had remained alone, standing in the middle of the room, wearing her green shawl, not daring to move as a result of his shouting. He paused for a moment. In that moment, an idea suddenly dawned upon him—as if it had been waiting to strike him forcefully.

"Well, why and for what did I go see her now? I said: the business at hand. What business? There was absolutely no business at hand! To announce that *I'm going;* so what of it? What need was there for that? Do I love her? Surely not, no. I drove her away just like a dog. Did I really need to get the crosses from her? Oh, how low I've fallen! No—I needed her tears; I needed to see her fear, to see how her heart aches and how she suffers! I needed to have something to cling to, some reason to delay, to see another person! And I dared rely on myself, to dream about myself; how base I am, how worthless, what a scoundrel I am, what a wretch!"

He walked along the embankment of the canal, and didn't have much farther to go. But when he reached the bridge, he stopped, suddenly turned onto the bridge, and went toward the Haymarket.

He looked eagerly to the right and the left, examined every object with effort, and was unable to focus his attention on anything; everything slipped away from him. "In a week or a month they'll take me away in one of those prison wagons, across this same bridge; how will I glance at the canal then—will I remember it?" flashed through his mind. "This street sign, how will I read these same letters? It says

'Campany'; well, I should remember that *a*, that letter *a*, and look at it in one month's time, at that very same *a:* How will I see it then? What will I be thinking and feeling? Oh, God, how vile all this is, all these present . . . concerns of mine. Of course, all this must be interesting . . . in its own way . . . (Ha-ha-ha! The things I think about!) I'm becoming a child, I'm bragging to myself; well, why am I making myself feel ashamed? Phew, how people shove each other! That fat fellow—he must be a German—the one who just shoved me: well, does he have any idea who he's just pushed? That peasant woman with a child is begging for alms; it's curious that she considers me more fortunate than she is. I should give her something for fun. Bah, a five-kopeck piece is still left in my pocket. Where did it come from? Here, here . . . take it, Mother!"

"God bless you!" said the beggar woman in a mournful voice.

He entered the Haymarket. He found it unpleasant, very unpleasant to mingle with the common folk, but he went precisely where there was the biggest crowd. He would have given everything on earth in order to remain alone, but he felt that he wouldn't be alone even for a moment. In the crowd some drunk was making a spectacle of himself: he wanted to dance but kept toppling over. People surrounded him. Raskolnikov squeezed through the crowd and watched the drunk for several minutes; suddenly he started laughing, but it was brief and abrupt. A moment later he had already forgotten about him, didn't even see him, even though he was looking right at him. At last he walked away, not even remembering where he was; but when he reached the middle of the square, he suddenly experienced a tremor, a sensation overcame him at once, seized hold of him entirely—both his body and his mind.

He suddenly recalled Sonya's words: "Go to the crossroads, bow down before the people, kiss the earth because you've sinned before it, and say aloud to the whole world, 'I'm a murderer!'" Remembering this, he began shaking. He was so crushed by the weight of inescapable sadness and agitation all this time, especially the last several hours, that he eagerly embraced the possibility of this new, complete, and pure sensation. It had descended upon him like a fit: it started burning in his soul like a spark and suddenly enveloped him completely, like fire. Everything softened in him at once, and tears gushed from his eyes. He fell to the ground where he stood . . .

He was on his knees in the middle of the square; he bowed down to the earth and kissed the dirty ground with pleasure and joy. He stood up and bowed down a second time.

"He's drunk as a skunk!" said a young man who was next to him.

Laughter burst forth from the crowd.

"It's because he's going to Jerusalem, lads; he's saying good-bye to his children and his motherland; he's bowing down to the whole world, kissing the capital city of St. Petersburg and the ground it stands on," added a tradesman who was also a little drunk.

"He's still a young man!" put in a third.

"Gentry, too!" someone observed in a respectable voice.

"These days it's hard to tell who's gentry and who's not."

All these remarks and comments restrained Raskolnikov, and the words "I have killed," ready, perhaps, on the tip of his tongue, died within him. However, he endured all these shouts serenely and, without looking around, continued directly through the crossroads in the direction of the police station. One vision flashed before him along the way, but he was not surprised by it; he'd had a premonition that all this must be so. When he'd bowed to the earth a second time in the Haymarket, turning to the left he'd glimpsed Sonya some fifty paces away from him. She'd been hiding behind one of the wooden booths in the square; thus she was accompanying his entire sorrowful procession! Raskolnikov felt and realized at that moment, once and for all, that Sonya was with him now and forever; she would go with him to the ends of the earth, wherever fate might send him. His heart skipped a beat . . . but—he had already arrived at the fateful destination . . .

He entered the courtyard rather boldly. He had to climb up to the third floor. "It will take me a while to climb the stairs," he thought. It seemed that there was still plenty of time before the fateful moment, a great deal of time remaining, and he could think about many things.

Once again the rubbish, the same eggshells on the spiral staircase; once more the apartment doors left wide open, the same kitchens from which smoke and stench emanated. Raskolnikov hadn't been here since then. His legs were ready to give way beneath him, but he kept going. He paused for a moment to catch his breath, to collect himself, in order to enter *like a man.* "But what for? Why?" he wondered suddenly, when he realized what he was doing. "If I must drain this cup, what difference does it make? The worse it is, the better." At that moment in his imagination there flashed the figure of Ilya Petrovich, Lieutenant Porokh. "Am I really going to see him? Wouldn't it be possible to see someone else? Perhaps Nikodim Fomich? Should I turn around now and go right to the police superintendent's apartment? At least it would all occur in a domestic setting. . . . No, no! To Porokh, Porokh! If I must drain the cup, then I must do so all at once . . ."

Feeling cold and barely conscious, he opened the door to the office. This time there were very few people inside; some caretaker and a man of the common people were there. The doorman didn't even glance up from behind the partition. Raskolnikov passed through into the next room. "Perhaps I still don't need to say anything," flashed through his mind. One of the clerks wearing a frock coat was getting ready to write something at his desk. Another clerk was about to take a seat in the corner. Zametov wasn't there. And Nikodim Fomich, of course, was also missing.

"Is no one here?" asked Raskolnikov, turning to the person at the desk.

"Who are you looking for?"

"Ah! Long time no see, but the Russian spirit . . . how does it go in that tale . . . I forget! M-m-my com-pli-ments, sir!" cried a familiar voice all of a sudden.

Raskolnikov shuddered. Porokh was standing in front of him; he had suddenly emerged from a third room. "This is fate itself," thought Raskolnikov. "Why is he here?"

"Have you come to see us? On what business?" cried Ilya Petrovich. (He was, apparently, in an excellent mood and even a little bit overexcited.) "If it's on business, it's too early. I just happened to drop in here. . . . However, I'll do what I can. I confess . . . Mr. . . . . Mr. . . . . Forgive me . . ."

"Raskolnikov."

"Of course, Raskolnikov! Surely you didn't think I'd forgotten!

Please don't think I'm that sort of person. . . . Rodion Ro . . . Ro . . . Rodionych, isn't it?"

"Rodion Romanych."

"Yes, yes, yes! Rodion Romanych, Rodion Romanych! It was on the tip of my tongue. I've inquired about you many times. I confess that since that last time I've felt very sorry that we treated you the way we did. Later I was told, I found out, that you're a young writer and even a scholar . . . and, so to speak, you're taking your first steps. . . . Oh, Lord! Who among our writers and scholars has not begun with some bizarre first steps? My wife and I—we both respect literature, and my wife is passionate about it! Literature and art! If a man's a gentleman, he can acquire all the rest through talent, knowledge, intelligence, and genius! A hat—well, what does a hat signify? A hat's as plain as a pancake; I can buy one from Zimmerman's shop; but what's under the hat and what's covered by the hat, that I can't purchase, sir! I confess, I even wanted to call on you and have it all out, but I thought that perhaps you'd. . . . But I haven't even asked you: do you really need something? I hear that your family has arrived."

"Yes, my mother and my sister."

"I even had the honor of meeting your sister—she's an educated and charming person. I confess that I'm sorry we became so heated at that time. What an extraordinary incident! As a result of your fainting, I regarded you in a certain light—that was later clarified in the most brilliant manner! Bigotry and fanaticism! I understand your indignation. Perhaps you're registering a new address because your family has arrived?"

"N-no, I merely. . . . I came to ask. . . . I thought that I might find Zametov here."

"Ah, yes! You've become friends; I heard that, sir. Well, Zametov isn't here; you missed him. Yes, sir, we've lost Aleksandr Grigorevich! Since yesterday we've been deprived of his presence; he's been transferred . . . and as he left, he quarreled with everyone . . . even rather impolitely. . . . He's an unstable young fellow, nothing more; he might have seemed promising. Just look at what happens to them, to our brilliant young people! It seems that he wants to take some sort of exam, but only to talk and brag about it here, that's all there was to it. It's not at all like you, for example, or that Mr. Razumikhin, your friend! Your career is a scholarly one, and you won't be dislodged by failures! To you all the beauties of life, one can say—*nihil est,** you are an ascetic, a monk, a hermit! For you a book, a pen behind your ear, learned research—that's where your spirit soars! I myself am partly. . . . Have you by any chance read Livingstone's journal?"†

"No."

"Well, I have. However, there are so many nihilists around these days; it's easy to understand why that's so; what times we live in, I ask you. However, you and I. . . . Why, you, of course, aren't a nihilist, are you? Answer honestly, honestly!"

"N-no . . ."

"No, you can be honest with me; don't be shy; speak as if we were alone! Public service is a different matter, very different. . . . You thought I was going to say *friendship*; no, sir, you guessed wrong! Not friendship, but the feeling of a man and a citizen, the feeling of human-ity and love for the Almighty. I can be both a public official and in the service, but I'm always obligated to feel that I'm a citizen and a human being myself and to render account. . . . You just mentioned Zametov. He'll create some sort of scandal in the French manner in a disreputa-ble establishment over a glass of champagne or sparkling wine—that's who your Zametov is! While I, perhaps, so to speak, have burned with devotion and lofty feelings; in addition, I have importance, rank, and position! I'm married and have children. I fulfill my duty as a citizen and a human being; allow me to inquire, who is he? I treat you as a person ennobled by education. And the number of midwives is still increasing."

Raskolnikov raised his eyebrows inquiringly. These words spoken by Ilya Petrovich, who had obviously just finished eating a meal, rattled and scattered before him for the most part like empty sounds. But somehow he still understood some of them; he looked at him quizzi-cally and didn't know how it would end.

---

* "There is nothing" (Latin).

† David Livingstone's (1813–1873) account of his travels in central and southern Africa.

"I'm talking about those girls with short hair," continued the talkative Ilya Petrovich. "I called them midwives, and I consider that name completely appropriate. Hee-hee! They creep into the academy and study anatomy; well, tell me, let's say I'm feeling ill, would I summon a young woman to treat me? Hee-hee!"

Ilya Petrovich laughed, completely satisfied with his own witticisms.

"Let's suppose this thirst for enlightenment is excessive; a man's educated, and that's sufficient. Why abuse it? Why offend decent people, the way that scoundrel Zametov does? Why did he insult me, I ask you? There again, there have occurred so many of these suicides—you can't even imagine it. All these people spend their last few kopecks and then kill themselves. Young girls, boys, old men. . . . Just this morning we had news of a gentleman who'd recently arrived here. Nil Pavlych, hey, Nil Pavlych! That gentleman, what's his name? The one we heard about just before, who shot himself on the Petersburg Side?"

"Svidrigaylov," someone replied from the next room in a hoarse and indifferent voice.

Raskolnikov shuddered.

"Svidrigaylov! Svidrigaylov shot himself?" he cried.

"What? Do you know Svidrigaylov?"

"Yes . . . I do. . . . He recently arrived here."

"Yes, indeed, he arrived here recently; he'd lost his wife a while ago; he was a dissolute man and he suddenly shot himself, and in such a scandalous manner, you can't even imagine. . . . He left several words in his notebook to the effect that he was dying in his right mind and asking that no one be blamed for his death. They say he had money. How did you happen to know him?"

"I . . . was acquainted . . . my sister worked as a governess in his house. . . ."

"My, my, my. . . . So, perhaps you can tell us something about him. Did you ever suspect it?"

"I saw him yesterday . . . he . . . he was drinking. . . . I didn't know a thing."

Raskolnikov felt that some great weight had fallen upon him and was oppressing him.

"You seem to have turned pale again. It's so stuffy in here . . ."

"Yes, it's time for me to go," muttered Raskolnikov. "Excuse me for disturbing you . . ."

"Don't mention it. Whenever you like! It's been a pleasure, and I'm glad to say so . . ."

Ilya Petrovich even extended his hand.

"I merely wanted . . . I came to see Zametov . . ."

"I understand, I do, and it's been a pleasure."

"I'm . . . very glad. . . . Good-bye," Raskolnikov said with a smile.

He went out; he was staggering. His head was spinning. He couldn't feel whether he was standing on his own two legs. He started down the stairs, using his right hand to support himself against the wall. It seemed to him that he was shoved by some caretaker with a book in his hand, as he was climbing the stairs up to the office; that a dog burst out barking somewhere on a lower floor and that some woman hurled a rolling pin at it and shouted something. He continued his way down and walked out into the courtyard. There, not far from the way out, stood Sonya, deathly pale, regarding him with wild, wild eyes. He stopped in front of her. Something painful and exhausted was expressed in her face, something desperate. She clasped her hands together. A hideous, lost smile took shape on his lips. He stood there awhile, smiled again, turned around, and once again headed up to the office.

Ilya Petrovich had seated himself and was rifling through some papers. The same peasant who had just shoved Raskolnikov as he was climbing the stairs was now standing before him.

"Ah? It's you again! Did you forget something? But what's the matter with you?"

Raskolnikov, with pale lips and immobile eyes, quietly approached him, stepping up to the desk; he rested his hand on it, and tried to speak, but was unable to; only incoherent sounds emerged.

"You're feeling faint. A chair! Here, sit down on this chair; so sit down! Water!"

Raskolnikov lowered himself onto the chair but didn't lift his eyes from the face of Ilya Petrovich, who was unpleasantly surprised. For a minute or so they looked at each other and waited. The water was brought in.

"It was I . . ." Raskolnikov began to say.

"Drink some water."

Raskolnikov pushed the water away and quietly, speaking slowly and deliberately but clearly, said: *"It was I who killed the old civil servant's widow and her sister Lizaveta with an axe and robbed them."*

Ilya Petrovich opened his mouth wide. People came running from all sides.

Raskolnikov repeated his testimony.

EPILOGUE

I

Siberia. On the bank of a wide, remote river stands a town, one of the administrative centers of Russia; there's a fortress in the town and a prison in the fortress. In the prison Rodion Raskolnikov, a second-class convict, has been confined for nine months. Almost a year and a half has passed since the day of his crime.

The legal proceedings had been conducted without any great difficulties. The criminal firmly, precisely, and clearly reaffirmed his testimony, without confusing the circumstances, not mitigating them in his own interest, not distorting the facts, and not forgetting the slightest details. He described to the last detail the whole process of the murder: he explained the mystery of the *pledge* (the piece of wood with the metal strip), which had turned up in the dead woman's hands; he narrated in detail how he took the dead woman's keys; he described these keys, described the chest and its contents; he even enumerated several of the objects contained within it; he explained the riddle of Lizaveta's murder; he described how Kokh had arrived and knocked at the door, followed by the student, and conveyed everything said between them; then how he, the murderer, ran down the stairs afterward, heard the shrieks of Mikolka and Mitka; how he hid in the empty apartment, then arrived back home; and, in conclusion, he showed them the stone in the courtyard on Voznesensky Prospect, under the gates, where they found the pawnbroker's things and her purse. In a word, the whole affair became clear. As this unfolded, the investigators and the judges were very surprised that he had hidden the purse and the items beneath a stone and made no use of them and, most of all, that not only did he fail to recall in detail all the items he had stolen, but he was even mistaken about their number. That circumstance in particular, that he had never even opened the purse and didn't have any idea how much money was contained within it, seemed improbable. (There turned out to be three hundred and seventeen silver rubles and three twenty-kopeck pieces; because they had been under a stone for a long time, some of the largest banknotes at the top of the pile had deteriorated significantly.) They spent a long time trying to determine why the accused was lying about this one circumstance, when he was confessing about everything else so willingly and accurately. At last several of them (especially the psychologists) even allowed for the possibility that perhaps he had not looked into the purse and, therefore, hadn't known what was in it and, not knowing, had placed it under the stone; but from this they concluded that the crime itself must have occurred during a period of temporary derangement of his mind, so to speak, accompanied by a morbid monomania of murder and robbery, without further aims or calculations of advantage. Here, as it happened, came into play the latest theory about temporary insanity, which people nowadays so often try to apply to various crimes. In addition, Raskolnikov's long-standing hypochondria was precisely affirmed by many witnesses, including Dr. Zosimov, his former university colleagues, his landlady, and her servant. All of these factors strongly furthered the conclusion that Raskolnikov was not completely like an ordinary murderer, a robber, or a thief but something altogether different. To the great annoyance of those defending this opinion, the criminal hardly attempted to defend himself. In reply to the crucial questions "What could it have been that induced him to homicide?" and "What prompted him to commit robbery?" he said with utmost clarity, with the most offensive precision, that the reason for all of it was his miserable condition, his poverty and helplessness, his desire to provide for the first steps in his life's work with the help, at least, of the three thousand rubles he had counted on finding at the old woman's apartment. He'd decided on murder as a result of his thoughtless and fainthearted character, further irritated by deprivation and failures. In reply to the question of what had caused him to offer a confession, he answered frankly that it was his heartfelt repentance. All this was said almost offensively . . .

The sentence, however, turned out to be more lenient than could have been expected, judging by the nature of the crime, and perhaps precisely because the criminal not only didn't try to justify himself, but even seemed to manifest a desire to incriminate himself further. All of the strange and peculiar circumstances of the affair were taken into account. That the criminal had endured a morbid and impoverished condition before committing the crime did not arouse the slightest doubt. The fact that he hadn't made use of the stolen property was considered partly an indication of his awakened remorse, and partly a result of the flawed condition of his mental faculties at the time of the commission of the crime. The circumstance of the accidental killing of Lizaveta even served as an example supporting that latter assumption: a man commits two murders yet at the same time forgets that the door to the apartment is wide open! Finally, his appearance with a confession, at the very moment when the affair was becoming extraordinarily tangled as a result of the false testimony of the dejected fanatic (Nikolai) and, besides that, when there were no clear clues pointing to the real criminal, or even any suspicions (Porfiry Petrovich kept his word completely), all of this definitely facilitated the mitigation of the defendant's fate.

In addition, other circumstances that strongly favored the defendant came to light completely unexpectedly. The former student Razumikhin unearthed from somewhere information, which he presented as evidence, that the criminal Raskolnikov, during his time at the university, was, with his last resources, helping a poor and consumptive fellow student and that he'd continued to support him for almost half a year. When that student died, he sought out the surviving feeble old father of his deceased comrade (who had been supporting and feeding his father almost from the age of thirteen); he ultimately moved the old man to a hospital, and when the old man died, he buried him. All of these circumstances had a certain positive influence on Raskolnikov's fate. His former landlady, the mother of Raskolnikov's late fiancée, the widow Zarnitsyna, also testified that when they were still living in another building, at Five Corners, during a fire one night, Raskolnikov rescued two young children from an apartment that had already been enveloped in flames, and that he himself received burns in that fire. This fact was carefully investigated and rather well corroborated by many witnesses. In a word, the result was that the prisoner was sentenced to penal servitude in the second class for a period of only eight years, in recognition of his confession and some other extenuating circumstances.

At the very beginning of the trial, Raskolnikov's mother became ill. Dunya and Razumikhin used it as an opportunity to remove her from Petersburg during the trial. Razumikhin chose a town along the railway close to Petersburg in order to have the chance to follow regularly the entire course of the trial and at the same time to see Avdotya Romanovna as often as possible. Pulkheriya Aleksandrovna's illness was a strange nervous ailment and was accompanied by something like insanity, if not completely, then at least partially. Dunya, returning from her last meeting with her brother, found her mother very ill, in a fever and delirious. That evening she conferred with Razumikhin about how to reply to her mother's questions about her brother, and even conceived with him a whole account about Raskolnikov's departure to somewhere far away, at Russia's frontier, on a private mission that would eventually bring him both wealth and fame. But they were surprised that Pulkheriya Aleksandrovna didn't ask anything more about it, either then or later. On the contrary, she herself invented an entire story to explain the sudden disappearance of her son: she would tearfully narrate how he had come to say farewell to her; she hinted that only she knew the many extremely important and mysterious circumstances; she said that Rodya had a great deal of very powerful enemies and, therefore, had to keep himself hidden away. As far as his future career was concerned, it also seemed indisputable and brilliant, once certain hostile circumstances were removed; she convinced Razumikhin that her son would in time even become a man of state, which was demonstrated by his article and his brilliant literary talent. She read his article over and over, even read it aloud sometimes, practically slept with it; still, she hardly inquired as to where exactly Rodya was now, in spite of the fact they were obviously avoiding that subject with her—that fact alone should have aroused her suspicions. At last they began to fear Pulkheriya Aleksandrovna's strange silence on several points. For example, she didn't even complain that there were no letters from him, whereas previously, back in their little town, she'd lived only in hope and expectation of receiving a letter as soon as possible from her beloved Rodya. This last circumstance was too inexplicable and disturbed Dunya a great deal; it occurred to her that her mother, perhaps, had a foreboding of something terrible in her son's fate and that she was afraid to ask, so as not to find out something even more terrible. In any case, Dunya clearly saw that Pulkheriya Aleksandrovna was not in her right mind.

Several times, however, it happened that she herself began a conversation in which it became impossible, in answering her, not to mention where Rodya was at the present time; when the replies were, of necessity, unsatisfactory and suspect, she suddenly became extremely sad, gloomy, and taciturn, which condition continued for a very long time. Finally Dunya realized that it was difficult to lie and invent a story; she arrived at the definitive conclusion that it was better to remain completely silent about certain points; but it was becoming clearer and clearer, to the point of obvious, that their poor mother suspected something awful. Dunya recalled, moreover, her brother's words to the effect that her mother had overheard her nighttime raving on the eve of that last fateful day, after the scene with Svidrigaylov: had she perhaps found out something then? Often, sometimes after several days or even weeks of gloomy, morose silence and silent tears, the sick woman became hysterically agitated and suddenly began talking aloud, almost without pausing, about her son, her hopes for him, about his future. . . . Her fantasies were sometimes very strange. They would console her, humor her (she herself, perhaps, clearly saw that they were humoring her and merely consoling her), but still she talked . . .

Five months after the criminal's confession came his sentencing. Razumikhin had gone to see him in prison whenever it was possible to do so. Sonya, too. At last came the separation: Dunya swore to her brother that this separation was not forever; so did Razumikhin. In Razumikhin's youthful and fiery mind, there took root a plan to establish within the next three or four years, as possible, the foundation of his future income, to accumulate even a certain amount of money and to move to Siberia, where the soil was rich in all respects, and where there were few workers, few people, and little capital; he would settle in the town where Rodya would be and . . . they would all begin a new life together. They all wept as they parted. The last few days, Raskolnikov was very absorbed; he inquired frequently about his mother, and was constantly worried about her. He even felt very tormented on her behalf, which upset Dunya. When he learned in detail about his mother's sickly condition, he became very gloomy. All this time, for some reason, he maintained his silence with Sonya. She, with the help of some money left to her by Svidrigaylov, had long ago planned and been preparing herself to follow the band of convicts in which he would also be sent into exile. Not a word about this was ever exchanged between her and Raskolnikov; but both of them knew that it would be so. At the very last farewell, he smiled strangely at the passionate assurances of his sister and Razumikhin about their happy future when he would be released from prison, and he predicted that his mother's illness would soon end in calamity. At last he and Sonya departed.

Two months later, Dunechka married Razumikhin. The wedding was somber and quiet. Porfiry Petrovich and Zosimov were among those invited to the ceremony. Throughout this time, Razumikhin had the air of someone firmly resolved. Dunya believed blindly that he would fulfill all his intentions, and, in fact, she had to believe him: this man had an iron will. Meanwhile, he began attending university lectures, again in order to complete his course. They were both drawing up plans for the future; they were both counting firmly on settling in Siberia after five years. Until then, they were relying on Sonya there . . .

Pulkheriya Aleksandrovna gladly blessed her daughter's marriage to Razumikhin; but after the ceremony, she seemed to become sadder and more troubled. In order to afford her some pleasant moments, as it were, Razumikhin informed her of the facts about the student and his decrepit father, and about how Rodya received burns and even took ill after saving two children from the fire the previous year. Both pieces of news brought Pulkheriya Aleksandrovna's already disordered mind almost to a state of ecstasy. She talked about it constantly, and even entered into conversations on the street (although Dunya always accompanied her). In public carriages or in shops, seizing upon some listener, she would lead the conversation to her son, his article, how he helped a student, how he was burned in the fire, and so forth. Dunechka didn't even know how to restrain her. Besides the danger of such an ecstatic, morbid mood, there was always the chance that someone might recall Raskolnikov's name from the former legal process and begin talking about it. Pulkheriya Aleksandrovna even found out the address of the mother of the two children rescued from the fire and wanted desperately to go see her. At last her agitation grew to an extreme degree. Sometimes she would suddenly start weeping; she frequently fell ill and would begin raving in a fever. One morning she declared openly that according to her calculations, Rodya should be coming back soon; that she recalled how, at their parting, he himself had reminded her that she should expect him in nine months. She began tidying up the apartment and preparing for the reunion, began to arrange the room intended for him (her own), to polish the furniture, to wash and hang new curtains there, and so on. Dunya became alarmed, but she kept silent and even helped her prepare the room for welcoming her brother. After a fretful day spent in endless fantasies, in joyful daydreams and tears, that night she fell ill and in the morning was in a fever and delirium. A burning fever set in. Two weeks later, she died. In her delirium, words escaped her from which one could conclude that she suspected a great deal more about her son's terrible fate than they had supposed.

Raskolnikov didn't learn about his mother's death for a long time, although a correspondence with Petersburg was instituted at the very beginning of his exile in Siberia. It had been established by Sonya, who faithfully wrote letters each month to Petersburg, addressed to Razumikhin, and she faithfully received a reply back from Petersburg each month. Sonya's letters at first seemed somewhat dry and unsatisfactory to Dunya and Razumikhin; but in the end they both found that it was impossible to write better letters, because these letters resulted in the fullest and most accurate picture of their unfortunate brother's fate. Sonya's letters were filled with the most ordinary reality, the simplest and clearest description of the circumstances of Raskolnikov's life as a convict. They contained no statement of her own hopes, no guesses about the future, no descriptions of her own feelings. Instead of an attempt to clarify his spiritual state of mind and his internal life in general, there were only facts—that is, his own words, detailed news about his state of health, what he wished for at their meetings, what he asked her for, what commissions he entrusted her with, and so forth. All of this news was communicated in extraordinary detail. In the end, the image of their unfortunate brother stood out on its own, was drawn clearly and accurately; there couldn't be any mistakes, because all of it was based on true facts.

But Dunya and her husband could derive little joy from this news, especially at the beginning. Sonya regularly wrote that Raskolnikov was constantly gloomy, uncommunicative, and even almost lacking all interest in the news she conveyed to him from each letter she received; that sometimes he would ask about his mother; and when Sonya, seeing that he was already surmising the truth, relayed to him at last the news of his mother's death, to her astonishment, even that seemed not to have much effect on him; at least that was how it seemed from his outward appearance. She wrote, by the way, that in spite of the fact that he was so absorbed in himself and seemed remote from everyone else, he related to his new life very openly and simply; that he understood his position clearly, didn't expect anything better in the near future, didn't harbor any frivolous hopes (so characteristic of his situation), and was hardly surprised by anything in his new circumstances, so unlike anything he had ever known before. She told them that his health was satisfactory. He went to work, neither avoiding nor approaching it eagerly. He was indifferent to food, but it was so bad, except for Sundays and holidays, that at last he willingly accepted some money from Sonya to provide for his own tea every day; as for all the rest, he asked her not to trouble herself, assuring her that all her worries merely annoyed him. Further, Sonya wrote that he shared living quarters with all the others in the prison; she hadn't seen the inside of their barracks but had concluded that it was crowded, horrid, and unsanitary; that he slept on a plank-bed with a strip of felt underneath him; and that he didn't want to arrange anything better for himself. But she said that he was living so crudely and poorly not at all as a result of some prearranged plan or intention, but simply from inattention and external indifference to his fate. Sonya wrote openly that especially in the beginning, he didn't take any interest in her visits, and even became annoyed at her; that he was uncommunicative and even rude to her, but that later these meetings became a habit and almost a necessity, so that he even missed them very much when she was ill for a few days and was unable to visit him. On holidays she saw him at the prison gates or in the guardroom, where they would summon him to her for a few minutes; on weekdays she saw him at work when she went into the workshops, or the brick factory, or the sheds on the banks of the Irtysh. About herself, Sonya informed them that she had even been able to make several acquaintances and patrons in town; that she'd found work as a seamstress, and since there were hardly any dressmakers in town, she had become essential in many houses; but she didn't mention that through her Raskolnikov also received a certain amount of patronage from the authorities, that his workload was lightened, and so forth. At last news arrived (Dunya even noticed a certain agitation and alarm in her latest letters) that he was shunning everybody, and that the other convicts in the prison didn't really like him; that he was silent for days at a time and was becoming very pale. Suddenly, in her last letter, Sonya wrote that he had fallen very ill and was in the convicts' ward in the hospital . . .

II

He had been ill for a long time; but neither the horrors of life as a convict, nor the work, nor the food, nor his shaved head, nor his tattered clothing had broken him. Oh, what did he care about all this torment and suffering? On the contrary, he even was glad for the work: by exhausting himself with physical labor, at least he could afford himself several hours of peaceful sleep. And what did food mean to him? Meatless cabbage soup with cockroaches in it? During his earlier life as a student, he had often lacked even that. His clothes were warm and adapted to his way of life. He didn't even feel the shackles he wore. Was he to be ashamed of his shaven head and his gray-and-black convict's jacket? But before whom? Sonya? Sonya was afraid of him, and was he supposed to feel ashamed before her?

So what then? He did feel ashamed, even before Sonya, whom he tormented with his contemptuous and rude treatment. But he was not ashamed of his shaven head and his shackles: his pride was deeply wounded, and he fell ill as a result of his wounded pride. Oh, how happy he would have been if he could have blamed himself! He could have tolerated everything, even shame and disgrace! But he judged himself severely, and his embittered conscience could find no particularly terrible guilt in his past, aside from his simple *blunder*, which could have happened to anyone. He was ashamed of the fact that he, Raskolnikov, had come to grief so blindly, hopelessly, obscurely, and stupidly, by some decree of blind fate, and that he had to humble himself and submit to the "nonsense" of such a decree if he ever wanted to set his mind at rest.

An aimless and idle anxiety in the present, and endless sacrifice in the future, by means of which he would obtain nothing—that was what the world held in store for him. And so what if in eight years he would be only thirty-two and could start to live his life all over again? Why should he go on living? What would be in store for him? What would he have to look forward to? To go on living merely to exist? Even previously he'd been prepared to sacrifice his existence for an idea, for some hope, even for some fantasy. But existence alone had always been too little for him; he'd always wanted more. Perhaps, merely by the strength of his desires, he had considered himself a man to whom more was permitted than to other people.

And if only fate had sent him remorse—burning remorse, crushing the heart, banishing sleep, to escape from which men dream of the noose or the maelstrom! He would have been glad of it! Torments and tears—that, too, means life. But he did not feel remorse for his crime.

At least he could have been furious at his own stupidity, just as before he had been angry at the hideous and stupid actions that landed him in prison. But now, already imprisoned, and *at liberty*, he once again judged and considered all his earlier actions and didn't find them so stupid and hideous as they had seemed to him previously, at that fateful time.

"How," he thought, "how was my idea any more foolish than other ideas and theories that have been swarming and conflicting with one another on the earth since the world was created? One must merely regard the matter with a completely independent, broad point of view, freed from everyday influences, and then, of course, my idea appears not at all . . . strange. Oh, you negators and so-called wise men, why do you stop halfway there?

"Why does my action seem so hideous to them?" he asked himself. "The fact that it was . . . an evil deed? What do the words 'evil deed' mean? My conscience is clear. Of course, it was legally a crime; of course, the letter of the law was broken and blood was shed; well, take my head for violating the letter of the law . . . that's sufficient! Of course, in that case, many benefactors of humanity, those who didn't inherit their power but who seized it for themselves, should have been punished when they took their very first steps. But these people managed to carry out those steps, and therefore *they were right*; but I wasn't able to, and therefore I didn't have the right to allow myself to take that step."

That was the only way he acknowledged his crime: only that he had failed to see it through and had turned himself in.

He also suffered from another thought: Why hadn't he killed himself then? Why had he stood over the river and then chosen to turn himself in? Was it really that the desire for life was so strong and so difficult to overcome? Hadn't Svidrigaylov, who was afraid of death, overcome it?

He tormented himself with this question and was unable to understand why, when he'd stood above the river, he could already sense a profound lie in himself and in his convictions. He didn't understand that such a premonition could be a prediction of a future crisis in his life, of his future resurrection, of a future view of life itself.

He would sooner admit to only the heavy burden of instinct, which he was unable to breach and which he once more lacked the strength to surmount (due to his weakness and insignificance). He observed his fellow convicts and was surprised: how they all, too, loved life, and how they valued it! It even seemed to him that in prison they loved, valued, and cherished it even more than when they had been free. What terrible suffering and torments some of them had endured, the tramps, for example! Was it really true that a ray of sunlight could mean so much to them, a thick forest, a cold spring somewhere in the remote backwoods, observed some years before; the tramp dreamt of a rendezvous with the spring as if it were a meeting with a beloved; he beheld it in his dreams, surrounded by green grass, a bird singing in the bushes. When Raskolnikov looked around, he saw even more inexplicable examples.

In prison, in his surroundings, there was a great deal that he didn't see, of course, and that he didn't want to see. He lived, as it were, with his eyes downcast: he found it loathsome and unbearable to look. But in the end, a great deal began to surprise him, and he, as if unintentionally, began to notice things that he hadn't even suspected before. In

general and most of all, he was surprised by the terrible and insupera-
ble abyss that separated him from all these common people. It seemed
as if he and they belonged to different nations. He and they regarded
each other with distrust and hostility. He knew and understood the
general reasons for such a separation; but he had never realized before
that these reasons were in fact so profound and so powerful. Also
in the prison were some exiled Poles, political prisoners. They simply considered all these common people to be ignorant peasants and
despised them superciliously; but Raskolnikov couldn't regard them
that way; he clearly saw that these ignorant folk were in many ways
much smarter than the Poles. There were several Russians who also
scorned these common people—one former officer and two seminarians; Raskolnikov saw their error clearly, as well.

No one much liked Raskolnikov; everyone shunned him. Eventually they even grew to hate him. Why? He didn't know. They despised
him and mocked him; those whose crimes were far worse than his
made fun of his crime.

"You're a gentleman!" they kept saying. "What were you doing
with an axe? That's not a gentleman's business."

During the second week of Lent, it was his turn, with those in his
barracks, to fast before taking Communion. He went to church to pray
with the other men. One day there arose a quarrel, though he himself
didn't really know why. The other men all turned on him in a fury.

"You're an atheist!" they shouted at him. "You don't believe in
God! We should kill you."

He had never once talked with them about God or faith, but they
wanted to kill him for being an atheist; he kept silent and made no
reply. One of the convicts was about to attack him in a rabid frenzy;
Raskolnikov waited for him serenely and in silence: he didn't budge;
not a single feature of his face quivered. A guard managed to come
between him and his would-be murderer just in time—or else blood
would have been shed.

There was still one other question that he was unable to answer:
why did all the men come to love Sonya so much? She didn't try to
ingratiate herself with them; they met her infrequently, sometimes
only when they were at work and she would stop for a minute to see

Raskolnikov. Meanwhile, they all knew her, knew that she had followed *him*, knew how she lived and where she lived. She didn't give them any money and didn't offer any particular services. Just once, at Christmas, she'd brought gifts for the entire prison: pies and rolls. But gradually warmer relations arose between them and Sonya: she wrote letters for them to their families and sent them off from the post office. Their relatives who arrived in town, both men and women, left things with her for the men, even money, according to their wishes. Wives and sweethearts knew her and visited her. When she appeared at their work sites, going to see Raskolnikov, or when she happened to meet a group of convicts on their way to work, they all doffed their caps and bowed to her: "Little mother, Sofiya Semyonovna, you're our mother, dear and tender little mother!" these crude, hardened convicts would say to this small, frail creature. She would smile and bow to them; they all loved it when she smiled at them. They even loved her gait and would turn to look at her as she went by and would praise her; they even praised her for being so small; they didn't even know what else to praise her for. When they fell ill, they even went to her to be treated.

Raskolnikov lay in the hospital all during the end of Lent and the Holy Week of Easter. Once he began to recover, he recalled his dreams when he'd lain there in a fever and delirium. During his illness he'd dreamt that the whole world was condemned to fall victim to some terrible, previously unknown pestilence, which was moving toward Europe out of the depths of Asia. Everyone would perish except for a chosen few, very few. Some kind of new trichina had appeared, and the microscopic organisms settled in human bodies. But these organisms were creatures endowed with intelligence and will. People who were affected immediately became possessed and insane. But never, never did these people consider themselves so intelligent and so infallible about the truth as when they were infected. Never did they consider their pronouncements, their scientific conclusions, their moral convictions and beliefs so infallible. Whole populations, whole towns and nations became infected and went insane. Everyone was anxious, no one understood anyone else, each one thought that truth resided in him alone and, regarding all the others, suffered, beat his chest, wept, and wrung his hands. They didn't know whom to try and how to judge; they couldn't agree on what constituted good and evil. They didn't know whom to condemn and whom to acquit. People killed each other in senseless rage. They assembled whole armies against one another, but when these armies were on the march, the troops suddenly began to fight among themselves, the ranks disintegrated, the soldiers fell on one another, stabbed and slashed one another, bit and ate one another. In towns the alarm sounded all day long: they summoned everyone, but no one knew who had called or why they had been called, and everyone was anxious. They forsook the most ordinary trades because everyone proposed his own ideas and suggestions, and they were unable to agree; agriculture was abandoned. In some places people formed into groups, agreed on something together, and swore not to disband—but immediately they began to do something quite different from what they themselves had just proposed. They began to accuse one another, to fight and slaughter one another. Conflagrations arose, famine followed. Nearly everything and everyone perished. The pestilence grew and advanced further and further. Only a few people in the whole world could be saved; these were the pure and chosen, destined to found a new race of people and a new life, to renew and purify the earth; but no one had ever seen these people, no one had ever heard their words or their voices.

Raskolnikov was tormented by the fact that this senseless delirium lingered in his memory so sorrowfully and painfully, that the impact of these feverish fantasies was taking so long to fade. It was already the second week after Easter; the springlike days were warm and clear; the windows had been opened in the convicts' ward (windows that were barred and guarded by a sentry). Sonya, all during his illness, was able to visit him in the ward only twice; each time she had to receive permission, and that was hard to obtain. But often she came to the hospital and stood under the windows, especially in the evening; sometimes it was only to stand there in the courtyard for a minute and glance from a distance at the windows of the ward. One evening, Raskolnikov, who had almost completely recovered, dozed off; when he awoke, he happened to approach the window and suddenly caught sight of Sonya in the distance, standing near the hospital gates. She stood there as if she were waiting for something. At that moment, something seemed to pierce his heart; he shuddered and quickly moved away from the window. The next day Sonya didn't appear, nor did she the day after; he realized that he was waiting anxiously for her. At last they discharged him from the hospital. When he returned to the prison, he learned from the other convicts that Sofiya Semyonovna had fallen ill and was staying at home, unable to go anywhere.

He was very upset and sent to inquire about her. Soon he found out that her illness was not dangerous. Having learned, in turn, that he was depressed and concerned about her, Sonya sent him a note written in pencil, informing him that she was much better, that she had caught a simple, mild cold, and that she would come to see him where he worked soon, very soon. When he read this note, his heart started beating violently and painfully.

The day was once again clear and warm. Early in the morning, around six o'clock, he set off for work on the banks of the river, where a kiln for baking had been set up in a shed and where the alabaster was crushed. Only three men were sent to work there. One of the convicts, accompanied by a guard, went off to the fortress to fetch a certain tool; another began to split firewood and load the kiln. Raskolnikov walked out of the shed and over to the riverbank, sat down on a pile of logs nearby, and began gazing out at the wide, empty river. A broad landscape opened up from the high bank. From the distant opposite bank he could hear the sound of singing. There, in the immense steppe, flooded with sunlight, dark tents of some nomads were barely visible. Over there was freedom; over there lived other people, not at all like the ones on this side of the river; it was as if time had stood still there, as if the age of Abraham and his flocks had not yet passed. Raskolnikov sat there, watching without moving, and couldn't tear himself away; his thoughts wandered into daydreams, into contemplation; he wasn't thinking about anything, but some longing troubled and tormented him.

Suddenly Sonya turned up right next to him. She had approached almost silently and sat down alongside him. It was still very early; the morning chill had not yet passed. She was wearing her shabby old cape and her green shawl. Her face still showed traces of illness; it had grown thinner, paler, more pinched. She gave him a welcoming, joyful smile but extended her hand to him timidly, as usual.

She always extended her hand to him timidly; sometimes she didn't even offer her hand at all, as if afraid that he would push it away. He always seemed to take her hand with reluctance, always greeted her with a kind of annoyance, sometimes maintaining his stubborn silence all during their meeting. Sometimes it happened that she felt afraid in his presence and left in deep sorrow. But now their hands remained joined; he cast a swift glance at her, said nothing, and lowered his eyes to the ground. They were alone; no one saw them. The guard had turned away for a time.

How it happened, he himself didn't know, but all of a sudden something seemed to seize hold of him and, as it were, cast him down at her feet. He wept and embraced her knees. At first she was terribly frightened, and her face froze. She jumped up and, trembling, looked at him. But immediately, at that very moment, she understood everything. Infinite happiness shone in her eyes; she understood, and had no doubt, that he loved her, loved her infinitely, and that at last the moment had arrived . . .

They wanted to speak, but could not. Tears stood in their eyes. They were both pale and thin; but in their sickly, pale faces already glimmered the dawn of a renewed future, of perfect resurrection to a new life. Love had resurrected them; the heart of one contained infinite sources of life for the heart of the other.

They determined to wait and endure. Seven years remained before them; until then there stood so much unbearable torment and so much infinite happiness! But he was resurrected, and he knew it; he felt it completely with the entirety of his renewed being, and she—well, she lived only in his life!

The same evening, after the barracks had been locked, Raskolnikov lay on his bunk and thought about her. That day it had even seemed to him as if all the other convicts, formerly his enemies, had already begun regarding him differently. He himself had even started to converse with them, and they'd replied to him politely. He recalled that now, but after all, wasn't that how it should be: surely now everything would change?

He was thinking about her. He remembered how he had constantly tormented her and rent her heart; he recalled her little pale, thin face, but now these reminiscences had almost ceased torturing him: he knew how his infinite love would compensate for all her suffering.

And what were they all now, *all* the torments of the past! Everything, even his crime, even his sentence and exile, now seemed to him, on first impulse, as some sort of external, strange facts that hadn't even happened to him. However, that evening he was unable to think for long or continuously about anything, or to focus on some thought; in fact, now he was not deciding anything consciously; he was only feeling. Instead of the dialectic, life itself had arrived, and in his consciousness something altogether different had to be worked out.

A Gospel lay under his pillow. He took it out automatically. The book belonged to her; it was the same one from which she had read to him the resurrection of Lazarus. At the beginning of his prison term, he'd thought that she would torment him with religion, that she would talk about the Gospel, and pester him with books. But, to his great astonishment, she didn't mention it even once, and had never even offered him the Gospel. He himself had requested it from her not long before his illness, and she'd brought him the book without comment. Up to now, he hadn't even opened it.

He still didn't open it now, but one thought occurred to him: "Could her convictions really become my convictions? Her feelings, her sufferings, at least . . ."

She, too, felt agitated all that day, and that night she even felt sick again. But she was so happy that she almost feared her own happiness. Seven years, *only* seven years! At the start of their happiness, at certain moments, they were both ready to regard those seven years as seven days. He didn't even know that a new life would not be granted to him for nothing, that he still had to pay a great deal for it, to purchase it with some great future deed . . .

But that is the beginning of a new story, the story of the gradual renewal of a person, the story of his gradual rebirth, and gradual transition from one world to another, of his getting to know a new, hitherto completely unknown reality. This could become the theme of a new narrative—but our present one is ended.